COW COUNTRY

Cow Country

First published in the United States of America in 2015 by

COW EYE PRESS
1621 Central Avenue
Cheyenne, WY 82001
www.coweyepress.com

For information about special discounts for bulk purchases,
please contact editors@coweyepress.com.

Cover design by Liana Moisescu

Publisher's Cataloging-in-Publication data
Pearson, Adrian Jones.
Cow country / Adrian Jones Pearson.
p. cm.
ISBN 978-0-9909150-0-3 (pbk.)
ISBN 978-0-9909150-2-7 (Hardcover)
ISBN 978-0-9909150-1-0 (e-book: EPUB)
1. Community colleges --Fiction. 2. Community college teachers --Fiction.
3. Academics --Fiction. 4. College teachers --Fiction. I. Title.
PS3616.E2544 C69 2015
813.6–dc23
2014954369

COW COUNTRY

ADRIAN JONES PEARSON

COW EYE
—PRESS—

WWW.COWEYE.ORG

PART 1. EMANATION

RETURN TO COW EYE

*Located in the heart of the Diahwa Valley
Basin, Cow Eye Community College offers
a well-rounded liberal arts and technical
education to its students so that they may
lead fulfilling and productive lives. As
stewards of the local community, we also
believe that we have a special obligation to
perpetuate the unique culture of the area we
serve both for present and future generations.*

- From the revised CECC mission statement

I n truth, my first impression of Cow Eye Junction was less of fulfillment
or productivity than of desiccation and despair. I'd just been offered a
job with the area's local community college and after selling all my earthly
possessions and leaving no forwarding address for family or friends – but
vowing to inform the world of my whereabouts *someday* – had jumped on
an old bus that would take me halfway across the country and deposit me
along the highway just outside the town. It was late summer then and the
entire area – from Cow Eye Junction all along the breadth of the Diahwa
Valley Basin – was in the midst of its worst drought in quantitative history.
Ranchlands were scorched and the golden pasture grasses that in wetter
seasons had waved poetically in the summer breeze now lay low and brown
outside the windows of late August like barren prose. By then the cattle
industry that once dominated the landscape was in its death throes, the
local ranchers were getting by as best they could, and the cottage enterprises
that always seem to rise from the carcass of moribund industry – the
writer's colonies, the yoga studios, the guided nostalgia tours through the
abandoned meat-processing plants and slaughter houses – were already
popping up like so many mushrooms from the scabbed-over dung piles
of the countryside. The area was both dying and being reborn. And as
I stood over my luggage in the hot sun, sweat running in thick streams

down the back of my neck, I got the clear sense that the air of the place had lost its ability to move, as if the wind were trying to blow in too many directions at once but instead had ceased to blow at all. Watching my bus drive away, I ran my hand over the back of my neck and shook the sweat from the tips of my fingers. Then I sat down on my suitcases to wait for my ride into town.

≈

THE PRESIDENT OF the community college where I'd been hired was a man named William Arthur Felch, an ex-rancher and veterinarian who'd held the school's highest position for more than thirty years and had come to be recognized by everyone in town as the grandfatherly face of higher education. It had been Dr. Felch's recommendation to bring me to Cow Eye despite a bruising three-hour screening committee interview that left me bewildered and insulted and questioning whether I really wanted to work at such an out-of-sorts community college in the middle of nowhere. "You'll be facing a deep cultural divide," he'd warned me by phone a few hours before my interview. "So be prepared for the worst."

The "worst" turned out to be a raspy phone connection and six unseen committee members who grilled me on everything from my favorite U.S. Supreme Court justice to my views on the current political situation in Cow Eye Junction. The connection was bad and as I listened I found myself squinting to make out their words. Several questions concerned my relevant experience in highly divisive work environments and how I might resolve a series of hypothetical conflicts – for example, what I would do if one of my colleagues tried to sever the head of a key administrator. Another hypothetical question asked me how I would respond upon learning that a tenured faculty member had provoked an untenured peer by leaving a bloated calf's scrotum in her faculty mailbox on a Friday afternoon knowing very well that it would sit there until at least the following Monday morning and that by then the grisly mess would be covered in swarms of flies and maggots. There was a question about a burning building (I was given a list of instructional disciplines – math, chemistry, philosophy, eugenics – and asked to rank the order in which I would drag their respective department chairs out of a flaming, smoke-filled meeting room); and a battery of word-choice exercises (in one I was offered a pair of nouns – *tenderloin* and *arugula*, for example, or *rawhide* and *tantra* – and asked to choose which of them, in my opinion, was more indicative of an effective student-centered learning environment). As part of my interview I was made to extemporaneously recite my philosophy of education in blank verse; then to give a self-critique of my recitation; and finally to self-critique the structure and meter of my own self-critique. One question asked me to choose a country of the world that best characterized my temperament (I chose *Switzerland*); another to name my favorite branch of Christianity (*Anglicanism?*); and a third to compare two significant works of literature from different cultural contexts and to provide an example of how these works illustrate a common theme or principal (my comparison of the Vedic imagery in the Upanishads to Gatsby's green light at the end of the dock concluded with a plea for a literary reconsideration of Fitzgerald's obscure yet defining work.) During the interview there were trick questions and leading questions and open-ended questions that provided just enough rope for me to hang myself like an effigy from a tree. There were allusions to ancient geometricians and medieval poets and a lumbering digression on the rise and fall of the Roman numeral. At one point the committee reminded me that I had neglected to provide the requisite urine sample, whereupon I quickly excused myself; yet when I came back into my living room holding the steaming plastic cup in one hand and my cold telephone receiver in the other, and when I had described this grave dichotomy in effervescent detail, the committee seemed decidedly unmoved by the results:

"What is your greatest strength?" they asked.

"I am a lot of different things," I answered.

"And your greatest fault?"

"Although I am many things," I sighed, "I am none of them *entirely*."

Other questions seemed to want to probe my family's history in Cow Eye Junction as my grandfather had once lived in the area before moving his wife and kids first to another part of the state and then across country; by now desperate for a job of any kind, and seizing upon this rare coincidence, I'd made sure to mention this bit of trivia in my cover letter.

"So you're a *descendant* of Cow Eye then?" one of the voices asked over the phone line.

"Well, I've never actually been there myself. But I have heard many stories…" And here I volunteered a legend passed down through our family about my grandfather, who had once rescued a naked woman from drowning in the Cow Eye River. Our family was truly proud of his gallantry and for several generations the tale had been told with fervor.

"So!" a female voice interjected just as my grandfather was laying the woman's limp but still-breathing body on the bank of the river. "Would you allow for the possibility that women are equals to men? Or do you think it fair that a female surgeon performing late-term abortions should earn significantly less than her male counterpart in the neighboring clinic?"

"And if so," another voice interrupted, "would you, or would you not, support one of the many initiatives to allow more red communists and their homosexual allies into our schools through the proliferation of government-subsidized arts programs?"

"If I may….?" a third voice chimed in just as quickly. "You mentioned in your application that you have some experience working with colleagues of diverse ethnic backgrounds. So would you please tell us which of them, in your opinion, has the greater natural facility for learning and should therefore be more highly represented in educational settings? Which is to say, if recruiting for an important administrative post would you be more inclined to hire the mongoloid, the caucasoid, or the negroid….?"

Then a fourth voice asked:

"Not to beat this particular horse to death, but if you happened to see a horse being beaten to death, would you intervene? Or would you simply turn away as if it were an inevitable aspect of life? Like the coming and going of the seasons. Or like the emergence and disappearance of this or that civilization of the world, along with its language, its culture, and the institutions that it holds dear?"

For three tiring hours the committee prodded and poked with question after question about my previous experiences, my current proclivities, and my long-term plans for the future. If hired as Special Projects Coordinator, would I stay at Cow Eye? Or would I leave within the first year like so many other transplants who'd been hired sight unseen after a single impressive phone interview? Would I buy a house? Was I looking to get married? Did I have any domesticated animals that I would be bringing? Any allergies? Did I practice yoga? Enjoy fishing? Hunt? What kind of truck did I drive and how many cylinders did it have? Were there any children on its front seat?

In my rearview mirror? Had I ever had a particularly severe case of scabies? And if so would I be willing to volunteer the specifics of a non-invasive yet reliable and effective cure?

But the most perplexing question came toward the end of the interview just as it seemed that the three hours had mercifully run their course and that all my various skeletons had been disinterred and brought to air before the committee. A voice on the other end broke in suddenly, even urgently:

"Look," it said. "Let's get to the heart of the matter here. What each of us really wants to know is….do you eat bovine or don't you? And what role, if any, should vegetarianism play in the ongoing rumination of innovative ideas?"

I admittedly had not been prepared for this particular question. But here my conciliatory instincts took over:

"Of course there is a time and a place for *all* things," I said over the crackling distance of the phone. "If you want to make a really good stew you need both beef *and* vegetables!"

(I later learned that it was this flavorless response to the vegetarianism question – even more than my brilliant and memorable reply to the hypothetical bloated scrotum, even more than my tenuous ties to Cow Eye Junction – that got me the job.)

It would take more than two weeks for the committee to make its decision, and so, hanging up the phone, I was left to replay in my mind the answers I had given and to wonder how they would be taken. Still in a daze, I pondered how I had fallen so low, so quickly: from unbridled salutatorian of my high school class; to aspiring English major; to weary graduate student running on fumes but with just enough left in the tank to cross the academic finish line clutching my Master's degree in Educational Administration – with a special emphasis in struggling community colleges. Now, after two failed marriages in quick succession (the first entirely my fault; the second, only *primarily* my fault) and a host of lackluster jobs leading pretty much back to where they started…here I was. Here I was in my dingy living room groveling before faceless strangers, a cup of tepid urine in my hand, pleading for a job at a community college I had never even seen. By now my life had become nothing more than a disjointed collection of half-starts and near-misses. My marriages tended toward ignominy. My jobs turned toxic. ("May we contact the references you've listed?" the committee had asked over the phone. "I'd rather you didn't," I replied.) Friends came and went – or I came and went from *them*. It was clear that the hot potential of my youth was cooling off like the cup of forgotten urine in my hand. Suddenly there was something very enticing about an ill-advised move to a desolate and distant place in the middle of a story that wasn't mine. In the general direction of a new beginning. Toward the makings of a fresh start. Strangely and surprisingly, I found myself coveting the uncoveted position at Cow Eye Community College; intuitively I must have seen the legacy that I might finally be able to leave if given the chance. "Just don't squander it," I told myself. "Don't flush it down the toilet like you have all the other advisable things in your life. Your marriages. Your career. Your friendships." And as I dumped the cold urine into the bowl in my bathroom I promised myself that if given yet another chance at creating a meaningful legacy I really would be more diligent about it this time around. For life is not a bowl of water to be cast away lightly with a single finger. It is a long and free-flowing river that meanders and winds in its own strange way but that *always* reaches its destination. A river is made of water, and water gets its essence from moisture. My life, I realized, was that very river and it had been dammed for too long. Let it flow! I told myself. Let my river flow from its eternal source through time and space to the awaiting campus of Cow Eye Community College!

❧

DR. FELCH PHONED me personally to offer the position. "Nice job handling the bloated scrotum," he said. "That was an inspired answer on your part." I thanked him and told him that I thought I'd blown the whole thing – *especially* the bloated scrotum question. "I'm grateful you're hiring me," I said. "And a little surprised."

"Well, it definitely wasn't easy. Your references weren't exactly unequivocal. But after two weeks of bitter debate among the committee, you were the only one left standing. Congratulations."

Dr. Felch outlined the terms of employment at Cow Eye and promised that if I accepted the position he would take me under his wing and personally help me navigate the cultural divide on campus that had come to the surface during the committee's questioning. "We're at a crossroads," he explained. "Not just the college. But the community as a whole. We need someone who can walk softly along the path. Someone unburdened by the encumbrance of meaningful friendships or strong personal beliefs. A person who can inspire others to action while himself remaining aloof and non-committal and slightly above it all. Someone who can do all this while being safe and dull and blandly palatable. In short, we need an effective educational administrator. And that's why we have high hopes for you here." These were not flattering words necessarily but I took them to heart. For once, it seemed, my ambivalence was a virtue. And what was more – my penchant for eschewing commitment offered a promise of sorts; strangely, it inspired *hope*! What had always been my greatest curse now became a great blessing as well: *to be a lot of different things, but none of them entirely*! I called back the next day to accept the job.

That was a month ago, and now, as I sat on my luggage next to the makeshift bus shelter, I took in what would be my first real view of the edge of the town proper. Across the road, two covered wagons from the nineteenth-century stood collapsed and broken, a flaming arrow still sticking out of one of them. Next to it was a filling station where an old rusted Model-T was returning to the earth near a battered gas pump from another era. Wrinkled men sat on a bench discussing the events of the day. A cashier in the general store across the way leaned her elbows into the newspaper pages she was reading; in the background the soulful drone of a harmonica could be heard. Everything, it seemed, was slow and sad and dusty. Sitting there I gazed across the ominous red dirt stretching around me through the centuries. The arid shrubbery reaching all the way to the horizon. The dead wind that could lay low for what felt like eons, then suddenly swirl up out of nowhere to lift the dirt high into the air. Large flies buzzed in the glare around me – I waved them off with the back of my hand – and black ants scrambled over the tops of my shoes. Everywhere I turned, it seemed, was a remnant of a thing that had once been, but now no longer was. A section of old train track where the trains used to go. An abandoned cotton gin lying on its side. A rusting phone booth, its cord severed and its windows smashed out. The decaying remains of a buffalo carcass with coyotes still picking at the meat. To the left of me was a bucket of wampum and to my right, nailed to a telephone pole with a single ten-penny nail, a faded flyer for a concert that had happened more than a generation ago. All of this struck me as sad and meaningful and somehow mildly poignant. This was a strange future to have.

But it was *my* future, and at this moment I was more ready for it than I had ever been before.

After a few minutes an old pickup truck pulled over to where I was sitting and Dr. Felch stepped out. "Sorry I'm late, Charlie," he smiled. "Nice to finally meet you!" Dr. Felch was a graying man in worn cowboy boots and green John Deere hat and his grip was so strong it crushed my hand when he took it. "Hop in," he said and hoisted my two heavy suitcases into the back of his pickup bed, easily, with one hand each; then he leaned over the tailgate and shoved a large bale of hay to one side so my suitcases could lie flat. "Sorry. This ain't the cleanest truck in the world...." He motioned toward the front of the cab, and I climbed in.

"Thanks for picking me up," I said and pulled the heavy door shut. The inside of the cab was cluttered with litter, and the seat between us held a stack of manila folders with papers sticking out at different angles and a box of bullets resting on top. Dr. Felch did not use his lap belt and my side of the cab had none at all – just a thick layer of grime between the grooves of the cracked vinyl seat.

"It's the least I could do," he said. Dr. Felch explained that it was his personal tradition to pick up every arriving employee to Cow Eye Community College and that he'd been doing it religiously for the past twenty years now. "In *this* truck!" he laughed and started the engine back up with a roar of the big-block V8. The air was hot and each of us kept our windows down. Dr. Felch was hanging his elbow out the driver's side and as he drove – never threatening thirty miles an hour – he had to raise his voice to be heard over the sound of the eight cylinders coming in through the windows. "I've picked up more than two hundred employees in my time," he added. "From as far away as *California!*"

The college was on the opposite edge of town and driving along the dusty road leading from one end to the other, Dr. Felch pointed out the notable sites of Cow Eye Junction. Bleak as it all might have seemed, there was also a strange charm to the place: the rusting railroad depot; the beat-up post office with its soaring flag pole and twenty-three stars at full mast; the sprawling log headquarters of the Cow Eye Ranch – the original outfit that spawned the town of Cow Eye Junction and inspired its name. A mile or so from the bus stop we passed a sign welcoming us to Cow Eye Junction – "*Where Worlds Meet!*" it promised – and a few miles later the town's lone convenience store where a single pickup truck was parked next to a hitching post with two horses tethered to it. Then we drove along the lip of a dried-up river that took us past abandoned sheds and pastures with decaying field equipment and shriveled cattle hides stacked up in heaps. There was a closed bait-and-tackle stand and a boarded-up nail salon and then we took a left and were driving through the town center where the mayor's office stood shuttered – it was a Saturday – next to the county jail and across a sidewalk from the building that housed the local newspaper and a one-room museum dedicated to the history of the cattle industry in Cow Eye Junction. All of this, I learned, was inextricably interconnected, and almost everything and everyone he pointed to would in very short time have something to do with my new role at the college:

"That's Mrs. Grisholm's place," he would say. "Our librarian. You'll meet her at convocation on Monday. And that house right there is where Merna Lee used to live before her kids came from the city to get her. She was our longtime data person but sorta lost her trinkets there toward the end..."

To each of these things I nodded.

At one point Dr. Felch pulled out a pack of Chesterfields from his shirt pocket.

"You smoke?" he said.

"No, sir, I don't."

"Your loss," he said and tapped out a cigarette on his steering wheel, then plucked a book of matches from his shirt pocket. As he drove he took both hands off the wheel to strike a match and cup it to his cigarette; immediately the truck began to veer into the oncoming lane and I couldn't help reaching out for the wheel. But Dr. Felch just laughed. "Relax, Charlie...I've been driving since I was eight!" Then he threw the match out the window and calmly took the wheel again.

Dr. Felch's manner was friendly and direct and you couldn't help liking him; yet there was also a detectable uneasiness in his movements – as if he were trying to have two conversations at once. We rode for a while without talking, and to kill the silence I asked him about my job; I had been so quick to accept the position of Special Projects Coordinator over the phone that I'd forgotten to ask what my new role would actually involve.

"I mean, I probably should have asked you *before* jumping on that bus."

Dr. Felch laughed.

"You must've been pretty eager to leave where you were coming from, Charlie?"

"Yes, I suppose I was. I suppose you could put it that way..."

"Well, whatever the case, I'm glad you're here. A Special Projects Coordinator doesn't have set duties. Or at least ours don't. You'll be my right-hand man, so to speak. Which means that from time to time I'll be asking you to put out some conflagrations on campus. As well as starting a few controlled burns of our own..."

I looked over at him for an elaboration. But none came.

"Sounds intriguing," I said, finally. "I hope I'm up to the task."

"Oh, don't worry – you'll be fine. I'm asking Bessie to show you the ropes ...." Here Dr. Felch informed me that Bessie was his assistant and she was "a Rottweiler" – but that I would love working with her because she was one of the few people in the world who had seen both day and night, and who wasn't afraid to articulate in blunt terms the difference between the two. In fact, he said, on an honesty scale of one to ten – with *ten* being an old nun testifying in a courtroom and *one* being what the college wrote in its most recent accreditation self-study – she was about a *twelve*. "Just be sure to keep your dick in your pants. Or she'll snap it off and hand it to you."

"The nun?"

"No. Bessie."

"I'll do my best, sir," I said.

Dr. Felch talked for some time about my position at the college – his manner optimistic and expansive, if seemingly cryptic at times – but then suddenly changed tone. "I don't want to discourage you, Charlie, but you're the third Special Projects Coordinator we've hired in the last two years. The first didn't even make it past his first bloated scrotum. And the one after him – well, she turned out to be an unmitigated disaster. So let's just say you won't exactly be wading into a sea of high expectations."

At the mention of my predecessor's failings my ears perked up. "What happened with your last coordinator?" I asked. "Why was she such a disaster?"

Dr. Felch paused to take a drag of his cigarette and it seemed that he might change the subject. "Well, it's kind of a long story...." But then, with no further invitation, he launched into the tale of how his most recent Special Projects Coordinator proved to be an unmitigated disaster.

"It's ultimately *my* fault," he began. "You see, we needed someone who could work with our divided campus and so we hired this gal after just a phone interview. She'd come to us with all the bells and whistles. Degrees from two Ivy League colleges. A sparkling curriculum vitae. Experience up the ying-yang. Countless awards and commendations. References from the Queen of England and Archduke of Canterbury. You know the type...."

I laughed.

"....So she gets in to Cow Eye and I pick her up at the bus stop. In this truck. And she refuses to get in. It's dusty, she says, and there's no passenger belt. You've got to be kidding me, I'm thinking to myself – *dusty*?! – but I give her the benefit of the doubt and call our art history teacher on a Sunday and she drives out here in her Saab and picks this lady up with all kinds of luggage and her Shih Tzu and takes her back to campus. The next day the two of us meet in my office and I start to lay out the job expectations with all the usual caveats: that she's facing a divided campus and that she'd better be prepared because these divisions run deep and if she's not careful they'll eat her up. Look, she says, I've got degrees from two Ivy League colleges, mediation experience up the ying-yang, personal references from the Israeli Knesset and the Shah of Iran...."

Here Dr. Felch stopped in mid-thought. Up ahead was an old house where a man in denim overalls was washing his truck in his driveway. Soapy water rushed down the pavement and spilled out into the street. "That's Rusty Stokes," he said. "Our animal science instructor. He runs the museum. And he's chair of our College Senate. A good person to know. He'll be at convocation on Monday too...." Dr. Felch gave a double-honk and a friendly wave to Rusty, who looked up, gestured back at our truck, and then went right back to his washing. Dr. Felch waited a few moments and then continued:

"So anyway I was just trying to warn this gal about some of the ins-and-outs of our college. How there are deep divisions. How the faculty is polarized. How there are two factions on campus that are as different as night and day and that these two factions despise each other and will do anything to keep the other from getting an upper hand. You know, in the way that vegetarians despise meat and meat-eaters despise.... vegetarians. So I'm telling her that she's got to find a way to work with them both. And here she holds up her hand and tells me I'm wasting my breath, that she's worked with diverse faculty in the past and they've all been happy omnivores and she doubts that Cow Eye will be any different. Well, of course it's different, I say. *All* places are different! But there's no shaking her. She's got it under control, she says. She's had training courses and she's an expert in finding win-win solutions. When she's done with everyone, she says, there will be no need for nocturnal or diurnal divisions, because our entire campus will be adamantly and happily crepuscular. Just trust her, she tells me. And so I step aside..."

"This sounds a bit ominous..."

"...Just wait. So I step aside and she starts her first day with guns a-blazing and I figure just to get her feet wet I'll put her in charge of the Christmas party because, well, what could be simpler than that? We've had a Christmas party every year for as long as we've been a college. It's a highlight for everyone. In fact it's the only time when all faculty and staff put aside their differences to come together in a display of harmony and good will. Of course having free alcohol doesn't hurt the cause! So it's a given, right? It's straight-forward and non-controversial! Well, to make a long story short: within a couple weeks the Christmas Committee was at each other's throats too. They were refusing to meet without their lawyers in the room. There was at least one physical altercation involving thrown chairs and hurt feelings. I tried to jump in to help, but it was too late. The Christmas party never happened. Just like that – POOF! – gone. A long-standing tradition wiped away. Charlie, last year was the first time in the history of Cow Eye Community College that we didn't even have a goddamn Christmas party!"

Dr. Felch had finished one cigarette and was using its butt to light another one. Angrily, he tossed the first butt out the window.

"So is that why she left?" I asked. "Because she failed to pull off the Christmas party?"

"As if...!" Dr. Felch shook his head. "Oh no, she still believed she was doing a great job. She felt that she was a great asset to the college. It wasn't her fault, of course. Nothing was ever her fault! Besides, we didn't have time to dwell on it too much because we had the accreditors breathing down our neck."

"Accreditors?"

"Yeah, we're on thin ice with our accreditation and so that was another thing she was working on. Every couple years the accreditors come for an inspection visit and this was our year. And she was coordinating the process – compiling the self-study report, organizing their accommodations and such.

So the day they're supposed to arrive I get a call from our chemistry instructor who just happened to be passing the bus shelter on the other side of town – where I picked you up – and he says they're all standing around waiting for a ride to campus. All twelve of them. In coats and dresses and holding clipboards. They've been waiting for two hours under the sun and by now they're hot and thirsty and pretty much acutely pissed off at the world in its entirety and at Cow Eye Community College and its aspirations for reaffirmation of its accreditation in particular. She'd mixed up the times! So I drop everything and rush out to pick them up before they get heat stroke from being in the sun much longer …"

"You picked them up… in *this* truck?"

"Right, in this truck. And I get there and only two of them can fit in my cab and so, out of respect for organizational hierarchy, I give the team chairman the seat next to the window – where you're sitting right now – and the vice chair gets the middle seat with one leg on my side of the stick shift and the other leg on *your* side…." Dr. Felch pointed to where the vice chair's two legs had once been splayed. "He's a President of his college – PhD in Applied Linguistics or some such – and I have to reach between his legs to go from second to third gear. And I'm driving about as slow as I can so I don't have to use the *fourth* gear because – well, no advanced degree is going to prepare you for that! And meanwhile the rest of the accreditation team is hanging out the back of my truck with their clipboards. All ten of them crammed into the back. If I'd a known they might end up there I would've hosed it down…."

I laughed:

"That's unfortunate, Mr. Felch. But I'm sure they took it all in stride. They probably saw it as one of those exotic small-town adventures that city people seek out. You know, like digging a hole with a shovel. They're probably still telling the story fondly to their friends…."

"I doubt that!"

"…Although in their telling it was probably even *hotter* and you drove even slower! But aside from that first impression, how did their visit go?"

"Not well. The college got knocked down to warning status. Now we're a report or two away from losing our accreditation. Sure, it wasn't entirely her fault – our college has some glaring shortcomings we need to work on. But that first incident just sort of set the tone for their visit. I mean, geez, at least we could have picked them up at the damn bus shelter!"

While Dr. Felch was saying this, an oncoming truck approached and he gave a familiar wave as it passed.

"One of my ex-wives. She runs our fiscal office."

I watched the truck retreating in the mirror.

"You said *one* of your ex-wives. How many ex-wives do you have?"

"Four. And that's not including my current wife...."

"You've been married five times?"

"That's right."

"To five separate wives?"

"Well, yes. And they all live in Cow Eye. Which means I get to see them on a daily basis. One's a career counselor at the college. Another just retired from the Ranch. One runs our fiscal office. And the other one, well, I'd rather not talk about *that* one."

"Sure, I understand completely. I have a couple ex-wives myself...."

Between us passed a tender moment of shared male remembrance. And when it had subsided I decided to divert the conversation:

"So, Mr. Felch, any children from your marriages?"

He laughed.

"Of course. I'm intact, you know. I've got three sons and a daughter. But they're all grown and moved away...."

Here Dr. Felch took his time telling me the name, age, and special talent of each of his children – along with their favorite cut of meat, what they drove, and at least one cute story from their respective childhoods. Proudly, he told me the names of his children's spouses, what *they* drove, and the different places around the country where they now lived with their own families.

"I keep inviting them to visit," he said, "you know, to see all the changes in Cow Eye. But they haven't made it back. I guess there's not much to see here once you've seen it. And it's quite a damn long bus ride for the pleasure...."

"It sure is," I said. Then I added, "You know, Mr. Felch, I give you a ton of credit. I can't help but have immense respect for any man who's been married five times...."

Between us passed another wistful moment, and when *it* had passed I continued:

"So it sounds like that last Special Projects Coordinator didn't exactly endear herself to the campus?"

"To put it mildly. And yet somehow she did. You see, there are some people who loved her, and still love her. But I haven't even gotten to the funny part yet. So now, if you remember, we've sunburned our accreditors and compromised our accreditation. We've got a dozen cases of Christmas liquor gathering dust in a storeroom somewhere because there's no party to drink it at. And to top it off, our divided faculty are starting to climb even further down each other's throats. If the cultural divide seemed bad *before* – and it was; in fact it's been escalating for years – now it's just totally out of hand. And would you believe, at the height of all that, this person comes into my office to ask me for a raise?"

"In salary?"

"She says she's tired of being everybody's bitch and wants a cost-of-living adjustment to accommodate her for the hardship of living in such a rural, godforsaken place. Keep in mind we'd already paid to ship her car here from halfway across the country, not to mention giving her a one-time allowance to relocate her dog and her eclectic collection of Siamese cats. We'd sent her to tantric conferences for professional development. We even gave her a couple months of free housing while she looked for a permanent place more to her liking."

"She didn't want to live in the faculty housing on campus?"

"Oh, no. That wouldn't work – not enough yard for the Shih Tzu. So it took her six months to find a place. All the while, she's canceling Christmas Committee meetings to check out places. Realtors are leaving notes on her door. And amid the rubble, she asks me for a *raise*. A raise! She probably believed she deserved one, too."

"Did you give it to her?"

"Oh, hell no! And I told her as much. Though I didn't use those exact words. And that's when she hit me with the lawsuit...."

As he was recounting this saga, Dr. Felch seemed to be getting even more animated. And as he got further into the telling of his story his smoking became more insistent. He had already gone through a second cigarette and used it to light a third, then held up the glowing end of the third to light a fourth. Clearly his lungs were now paying the price for his decision to hire my predecessor sight unseen after a single phone interview.

"...I mean, you figure you've done your due diligence by hiring an award-winning administrator with personal references from the president of Rhodesia. She should know what she's doing, right? Charlie, dammit, she had *two* Ivy League educations....!"

I shook my head sympathetically. Dr. Felch continued:

"So anyway, this is what you're stepping into as Special Projects Coordinator. You've got to do better, Charlie. I can't afford for this position to fail again. Too much is at stake. I can't afford for all these phone hires to keep turning out like this..."

"Well, it sounds like I've got my work cut out for me."

"Mildly speaking. I'll be asking you to help me shepherd the Christmas party this year. And I'll be trusting you to lead the accreditation process on your own. Our next report's due in November and the accreditation team will be visiting next March. And we really need to get that right. I mean, do you have any idea what it'll do to us if we lose our accreditation as a college?"

"Well, if Cow Eye isn't accredited, it'll mean your students can't get valid degrees. Their degrees won't be accredited."

"Right. Which means they'll have to go to other places for their education. And they *will*. All of our best and brightest will leave. And not come back. Just like my own kids went away and won't ever come back...."

Here Dr. Felch explained the recent demographic shift in the community: how families who'd lived in Cow Eye Junction for generations were moving away in search of jobs – and how a slew of newcomers were moving in. A few years back some rare healing minerals had been discovered in mines on the northern side of town – a part of the town called the Outskirts – and the makings of a new boutique industry were growing up around it: vendors sold magic mineral crystals to weekend visitors and mingled with a new throng of healers, hippies, prophets, and priests. "Freaking *weirdos*," Dr. Felch concluded. "Only half the people in Cow Eye were actually born here. The other half just moved to the area from some other place. Either in search of magic minerals. Or escaping their own histories. Or both. Did you notice that your screening committee had exactly six people?"

"That's what I heard...."

"Well three of them were from Cow Eye proper and three were from other places. That's how we get things done here. Nowadays each group makes sure it's never outnumbered...."

Dr. Felch had stopped at a cattle crossing and a line of cows was being herded in front of us by three men on horseback. Cattle dogs were trotting alongside to keep the herd in line.

"…I mean, don't get me wrong – it's great that we have faculty from exotic far-off places. Hell, we once had a tenure-track instructor from *California*…!"

Dr. Felch beamed. He seemed especially proud of this fact.

"…But it's getting tougher and tougher," he continued. "At some point you've got to hire your local folks too. And nowadays it's getting impossible to do that. Nowadays they have to go away to get their degrees – and once they leave they never come back. They say they will but they just don't. Would you?"

I shook my head:

"No," I said. "I guess not. Cow Eye has a certain allure for a stranger like me. But I could see why a local person might want something more."

But here Dr. Felch laughed.

"Actually," he said, "you're one of the few who's come back!"

"But I'm not from here! I'd never even been to Cow Eye before arriving at the makeshift bus shelter. I'm not from here at all."

"In a way, you aren't. And yet you are. Remember, your grandfather lived here. Hell, he even rescued that naked woman from drowning in the river – I'm sure there are descendents of that woman still living here in Cow Eye. And I'm sure her descendents have their own stories to tell. So you're about as close as we've had to anybody coming back. I think that's what the committee saw in you and why I was able to get all six to sign off on your hiring. Half of them liked the fact that you were from here. And the other half liked that you *weren't.*"

"That tends to be my story," I said. "Being a lot of different things, but none of them *entirely.*…"

We had moved on from the cattle intersection and were now passing an old meat processing plant whose long fence seemed to run ahead of us into infinity. The fence was weathered but imposing, and so extensive that it seemed it might never end.

"That's the world-famous Cow Eye Ranch. In its heyday it fed half the country. Now it's just barely hanging on.…"

The fence was old and made of wood about eight feet tall, faded white, and with red painted slogans every so often: "EAT MEAT", one would say and then, a few hundred yards later: "BEEF IS BETTER!"

Another oncoming horn sounded and Dr. Felch gave a slight wave. "Ex-wife," he said. "The career counselor." As he drove it seemed as if every second or third car coming in the opposite direction warranted a wave or a double-honk or a shout out the window. And of these, every fourth or fifth was an ex-wife of Cow Eye Community College's beleaguered president. To my right we were now passing a section of the long fence that proudly proclaimed, "COW COUNTRY."

"Ok," I said after a few moments. "So it sounds like I'm going to be helping with those two things? Accreditation and the Christmas party?"

"That's right..."

Dr. Felch was now pulling off the main road into a gravel parking lot where a sign outside read *Champs d'Elysees Bar and Grill*. In the lot were several parked trucks – though not a single car. "There are some other things you'll have to know before you start. But we'll get to that a bit later. First I want to introduce you to some of the guys...."

Dr. Felch shut off the engine and threw the key on the seat and without rolling up his window headed toward the entrance below the pink neon outline of a busty Frenchwoman riding a bronco. I followed him inside.

The bar was dark and cool and, once inside, it seemed as if we'd descended into a parallel realm of time and space. A fifty-year-old juke box spewed out a song from my grandparents' time. College football played on a single black-and-white television mounted above the bar, long rabbit ears jutting out of its back. We took our seats at a table in the corner and an old man in a cowboy hat clenching a cigar between his teeth came up and set two cans of Falstaff on our table.

"You drink beer?" Dr. Felch said.

"You could say that," I answered and opened the pull-tab on my can.

"Glad to hear it," he nodded. "You never can tell with educated men nowadays...." Dr. Felch opened his own can and set the curled ring in the metal ashtray. I took a long drink from my can and did the same. Then I said, "Thanks for bringing me to Cow Eye, Mr. Felch. I really appreciate it."

"Well, no need to thank me just yet. Save it for when you've made it through your first semester. Hell, thank me at our Christmas party!" And here he gave a sly wink.

"Right," I nodded. "I'll be sure to sing you a yuletide carol or two."

We drank and talked and a few minutes later two of Dr. Felch's friends came into the bar and pulled up chairs at our table.

"This is Charlie," Dr. Felch said when the two had joined us. The men opened their own cans and set their pull rings into the metal ashtray with the others: there were now four. As he spoke Dr. Felch lit a fifth cigarette with the butt of his fourth, then crushed out the dying ember just like he had with the three before. "Charlie's going to be our new Special Projects Coordinator," he said.

"Special Projects Coordinator?"

"I'll be Dr. Felch's right-hand man..."

The men nodded.

"...I'll be leading the college's accreditation process...."

The men nodded again.

"...And helping with the annual Christmas party."

Here they laughed.

"Good luck with *that*!" they said.

Dr. Felch continued:

"Guys, Charlie's the one I told you about....you know, with the unexpected answer to the bloated scrotum question."

"That's *you*?!" they said and slapped me on the shoulder congratulatorily.

We drank and when we were done, another round of beers was brought out by the third man and we drank again. As we sat, the conversation went where it might; here and there the men would look up at the game on the old television and a shout would ring out after a long run from scrimmage or an important defensive stop.

"I hope you brought the rain, Charlie!" one of them said after a discussion of the drought in the area – a drought for the ages, they called it – and I told them that I had in fact brought a little bit:

"It's outside in my suitcases."

The men laughed and the conversation meandered further along. With small-town curiosity they asked about my previous jobs and my marriages and what brought me back to Cow Eye after all these years – and I answered their questions as best I could. But mostly I listened as the three discussed the goings-on around town and other timely chatter that, in its very evanescence, is also infinitely timeless. Passionately they talked about the most pressing political issues of Cow Eye Junction and the ways the town had changed over the years from the one they used to know as young men. In tones of weary resignation they spoke about the new people and their strange ways and about the old-timers of the area that they hadn't seen for a while – those who had died, or moved away, and those who would soon be moving or dying away.

"Did you hear Merna's sister finally sold her house?" one of them would ask.

"Really?" another would answer. "The one who drives the Dodge?"

"No, that's her other sister. This is the one with the Ford."

"The six-cylinder?"

"That's right."

"With the wood paneling on the side?"

"Right."

"And the pipe rack?"

"Yes."

"That's a nice pipe rack she has….!"

And the men would nod in appreciation. "She will be missed," they would say and take a drink in Merna's memory. Again the conversation would meander and again it would come back to the important topics of the day: the changing politics of Cow Eye Junction, the various impositions caused by the new people, and the latest hardships and challenges of the many townsfolk they knew and had grown up with.

"I hear Merna's other sister is still trying to sell her truck…."

"The sister who drives the Dodge?"

"Right."

"And which of Merna's trucks is she selling? The Jeep?"

"No, the Ford. She already sold the Jeep."

"Really? Who bought *that* piece of junk?"

"Rusty."

"What does Rusty need with a Jeep? He's already got the two trucks!"

"No, he don't. His daughter wrecked his Chevy last month."

"You don't say?"

"Yeah, the girl pulled off into a ditch coming home from the river one night."

"Alone?"

"With her boyfriend."

"That's not good."

"No, it most certainly ain't."

"So Rusty only had the one truck left?"

"Right. Then he bought Merna's old Jeep. And now he's got the two."

"Gee....just goes to show you how behind the times *I* am...!"

"Yeah, man, you really ought to get out more!"

The four of us drank and at some point the two men went to play darts by the bar next to the bartender and Dr. Felch lit up another cigarette, his sixth. "One for the road...." he said and held up his can in my direction; by now there were seventeen rings in the metal ashtray. I added the eighteenth. Dr. Felch nodded approvingly and then said, "You'll do fine here, Charlie." I was holding my can in my hand as if it were the fragile fate of an entire community. "But just do me one favor...."

"Of course," I said.

"Don't forget to take us seriously."

"I'm sorry, Mr. Felch?"

"We've brought you here for a reason, Charlie. And we'll give you the benefit of the doubt in the beginning – that's our style. But don't take us for granted. That's one thing local people will never forgive you for."

(Suddenly I was hearing the words of my wife spoken to me so many times during our marriage. "You're taking me for granted," she would say in one set of words or another. But as usual I would just laugh it away: "That's exactly what my *last* wife used to say!" And then: "You women are all the same...!")

Dr. Felch was waiting with his beer, not drinking.

"I hear you, Mr. Felch," I told him. "Believe me, it's something I'm trying to get better at. Appreciating people while they are still around to understand my appreciation...."

"Just remember, Charlie, it's easy to love the *beautiful* things in this world. But if you're going to make it here at Cow Eye, you're going to need to love the other kind of things. You're going to have to love the things that are *unloved*."

"Unloved?"

"Yes. The substantial things. The things that defy easy admiration."

"I'll do my best, sir," I said.

And here we drank.

After a few moments of background noise – a bantering cigarette commercial over the television, the sound of a vinyl record skipping in the juke box, then the sound of another can of beer being popped open at the bar – Dr. Felch turned somber. For the first time since I'd met him his voice fell to almost nothing:

"But there's one thing I just don't understand. And maybe you can help me figure it out, Charlie…." I leaned in to hear his words over the ambient noise. "….Maybe you can explain how it is that a person can leave the place that's been their home and never come back? Maybe you can help me understand how a person can just…*leave?*"

I started to construct an answer but couldn't finish it. My experience was a different one, I knew, and wouldn't make much sense to him. And so the best I could do at that moment was to shrug my shoulders. Dr. Felch looked at me for a few moments, then shook his head and swallowed the last of his beer. Then he collected all of the rings from the ashtray and dumped them into his shirt pocket – for his granddaughter's collection, he explained. In the corner of the bar another roar went up around the television after a touchdown by the "home" team – which I recognized as a four-year college more than a thousand miles away. When I had finished my beer Dr. Felch slapped me on the shoulder.

"Alright, Charlie, it's about time we got you to campus. Plan on being in my office first thing Monday morning for convocation. There won't be any students around next week – only faculty and staff – so it'll be a good chance for you to meet your peers and get acclimated to the personalities. And like I said, Bessie will be helping you get up and running…."

Dr. Felch picked up the tab, and as we left we gave a nod to the three men at the bar and they shouted back from their darts:

"Take care, Charlie!" they said and: "Good luck!"

I thanked them and we headed out into the light of day.

꧁

BACK IN THE car, Dr. Felch drove the rest of the way amid a mixture of small talk and slightly inebriated silence.

"We're almost at the campus," he said when we'd driven for another ten minutes past dried-up trees and old houses with busted-out windows and yet another irrigation canal that had no water flowing through it. "The entrance is over there on the other side of the railroad tracks." We hopped over the tracks and made our way along the dusty road. Just as it had been since I'd arrived, the scenery around me was dry and desolate, bleak and unapologetic. Dr. Felch took a left onto a small road and then another left and drove straight ahead in the direction of a sign in the distance that said "WELCOME TO COW EYE COMMUNITY COLLEGE" and underneath it, in smaller letters: "*Where Minds Meet.*" A guard shack was set up in front of the campus and a wooden arm stretched across the road to bar our entrance.

"Good afternoon, Mr. Felch," the guard said, stepping out of his booth.

"Hey there, Timmy."

The guard handed Dr. Felch a clipboard with some forms to sign; he signed them without reading and then pointed back at me. "This is Charlie," he said. "He's going to be our new Special Projects Coordinator."

I leaned over to introduce myself.

"Nice to meet you," I said through the open trapezoid of Dr. Finch's window.

"Likewise, Charlie!" he said. "Welcome to Cow Eye!"

Dr. Felch had started to light an eighth cigarette with his seventh – or was it a ninth with his eighth? – but then reconsidered. Instead he stubbed it out in the dashboard ashtray.

"I almost forgot. New policy….we're a non-smoking campus starting this year." Dr. Felch shook his head and sighed. "Dammit…."

And with that the arm lifted and our truck made its way through the gate and onto the campus of Cow Eye Community College.

THE OPPOSITE SIDE OF THE GATE

Leading from the darkness of ignorance
To the light of higher learning,
There is a simple gate that stands
Old with age and somewhat heavy.
And I, the educational administrator,
Am its faithful gatekeeper,
Whose trained yet trembling hands
Must somehow dispel the latch.

To say the campus of Cow Eye Community College differed from the town surrounding it and from which it got its name is to note that a daughter is often unrecognizable from the mother whose house she shares and whose surname she can no longer return to – or that an island tends to differ in color and content from the moister things around it. As I stared in wonder at the scene unfolding before me, Dr. Felch drove through the gate separating the college from the dusty world outside – and into an emerald oasis of vast lawns and rich green grass where every blade was brilliant, and sprinklers sputtered and hissed. The distinct metaphorical threshold that one crosses when entering a campus of even the most humble institution of higher education – the sudden break in scenery meant to reinforce the divide between the barren world of ignorance on the other side of the gate and the realm of manicured enlightenment on *this* side – seemed more pronounced here at Cow Eye than at any other college I'd been to. And as Dr. Felch turned onto the main road bisecting the campus, I gawked at this inviting world of fresh grass and green hope and well-trimmed optimism. Tall pine trees rose up from a series of lakes and manmade lagoons where swans paddled and fish splashed and pelicans loafed on the banks. Hedges of rose and lavender grew along the paths to buildings, flowers of every imaginable

type and color sprang up in carefully ordained patterns, and it seemed
that all of it – every last petunia and tulip and daffodil, every orchid and
dandelion – was in full and fragrant bloom. Everything as far as the eye
could see was redolent and lush and the sudden emergence of this much
verdure and color and freshness out of the cracked heat and glare of my
long bus ride to Cow Eye Junction – out of the choking dust of the slow
road through town – was so abrupt and unexpected that I literally and
audibly gasped at the sight of it. In place of the stagnant heat of the last
few hours a cool breeze was now blowing from what seemed like both
ends of the campus. Birds were chirping and singing. Ducks quacked.
Jasmine bloomed under the late-afternoon sun. Surely there could be no
finer portrait of college life where undergraduates in school colors lounge
on opened textbooks while laughing gaily at the irrepressibility of their
own futures. Even the air of the place seemed cooler and more autumnal
– more collegiate – than it had just minutes before. Taking it all in I felt my
lungs filling up with the chill pregnant air that was so much more alive
than the heat and exhaust we had just left behind at the gate, as if all the
life and fertility had been sucked out of the town of Cow Eye Junction
and the surrounding Diahwa valley basin and concentrated here in this
fertile cradle of learning and productivity and fulfillment.

Dr. Felch's truck was the only one making its way through the campus
on a late Saturday afternoon, and driving slowly we passed the diverse flora
that bequeathed all this emerging life to the college. In the central mall, still
vacant of students toward the end of the summer break, a huge sycamore
tree cast its shade over a quaint eating area. By the administrative building
giant poplars mixed with birch trees and date palms to form an eclectic
vegetative canopy. A long esplanade lined with alternating saplings of fig
and elm led down the main thoroughfare. And in the distance I could
see a banyan tree, an old cedar, and a Dahurian larch, all planted within
several feet of each other yet none encroaching on the others' shade and all
managing to live side by side in ecosystemic harmony. Pomegranates grew
next to peaches. Grapefruit and apricot comingled. Love vines wrapped
their way around boughs of billowing cherry in a fond and nurturing
embrace. The campus was built around three manmade lagoons and as
our truck lumbered toward the faculty housing complex, we passed the
three thematic fountains – one in each lagoon – that shot water high into
the air out of imposing bronze statuary celebrating the richness of Cow

Eye's history: in the first fountain, by the library, an Appaloosa had risen up on its hind legs with water shooting out of its mouth; in the second, near the natural sciences building, a cowboy looked up at a lariat with water shooting out of his mouth; and in the third lagoon – the one that fronted the animal science complex and that served as the face of the campus – a huge bull was preparing to mount a heifer, with an impressive stream of water gushing out of him as well.

"This is a beautiful campus!" I exclaimed.

"Yes, unfortunately it is..." said Dr. Felch with a world-weary sigh.

At last we reached a two-story brick building covered in faux Ivy: the Francis K. Dimwiddle Center for Faculty and Transitional Housing. Dr. Felch pulled up to a curb and turned off the engine. The sound died away just as suddenly, and in the new quiet the ambient sounds of the birds and the breeze and the pelicans became even more striking.

"Well, this is the faculty housing complex," he said. "You're on the second floor."

Dr. Felch grabbed my suitcases and carried them up the stairs to the apartment door.

"Sorry, but you'll be staying next to the math faculty. I hope that's okay..."

"Why wouldn't it be?" I had begun to ask, but Dr. Felch had already unlocked the door and pushed it inward. Without stepping into the apartment he handed me the key and wished me a restful remainder of the weekend.

"See you first thing Monday morning," he reminded me and shook my hand. Then he clapped me on the shoulder again and said, "You'll do great, Charlie....the future is yours for the taking."

I thanked him and he left.

It took several minutes for the sound of Dr. Felch's engine to trail off into the distance, and not until the sound had disappeared entirely did I begin to unpack my suitcases and arrange my things: the requisite toothbrushes and medications and shaving supplies and notes that had to be prepared for my first day of work on Monday. Happily, I found the historical novel I'd been reading during my long bus ride and placed it on my pillow; the work of fiction still had its bookmark in the exact spot where I'd inserted it before arriving into Cow Eye Junction. When this was done I opened the living room window overlooking the cowboy with a lariat. The water shooting out of his mouth was being scattered by the wind and as it came down in a traveling mist the sun reflected off the water crystals and made shifting rainbows through the spray.

"My future!" I said and grabbing my apartment key, I set out for a closer inspection of the three fountains where the rainbows danced.

❧

THE CAMPUS WAS surprisingly spread out for such a small college with fewer than a thousand enrolled students and walking along the main sidewalk leading from one fountain to the next, I noted the Samuel Dimwiddle Memorial Gymnasium and, adjacent to it, Dimwiddle Field which bordered the Dorothy Dimwiddle Botanical Gardens and Nature Walk on one side and the Dimwiddle Gun and Archery Complex on the other. Building after building bore the Dimwiddle name and it was evident that all these Dimwiddles – whoever they were – nurtured a strong affection for the school and had left it a significant legacy.

At last I reached the large fountain at the entrance to the school. The campus was deserted and in the silent lull that is so strange yet so familiar before the beginning of a new semester I imagined myself the last straggler in a post-apocalyptic world devoid of living souls. If there is anything more lonely than a solitary bus ride across time and space, it can only be the quiet angst of a school that is missing its young people. The joy of living that comes from youthful laughter and spontaneity gives a campus its soul; take it away and you're left with an eerie void – the empty silence of grass growing and paperwork getting done. With no purpose to fulfill, the creaking swing sets, the vacant classrooms, the bicycle racks with no bicycles – all of it hints at the fleeting nature of life itself: the buoyant young people that have outgrown this most vivid time of their lives and moved on to the dull quietude of mature adulthood. Where earlier I'd felt the excitement of a new beginning while riding through campus in the cab of Dr. Felch's truck, now I experienced its opposite: the forlorn silence that is left behind when the newness of hope has faded – when all that remains is a school without its purpose, or a town that's foregone its soul, or a college that is at risk of losing its way, its history, and its accreditation all at the same time.

Against the fading light I sat on a cement bench in front of the largest lagoon; the hard seat was soaked with mist blown from the fountain. The bull in the center of the lagoon was just as virile and his heifer just as compliant as when I'd driven by them earlier in the day; but now the sun was low and the mist had turned cold. Sitting there I thought about the tortuous path that had brought me to Cow Eye Junction – the countless random coincidences that must occur to lead a man halfway across his country to a fountain in the chill where rainbows gather and a bull is forever mounting a heifer. One by one, I recalled the links in the chain, the random kindnesses of random people along the way that led me to where I was. Faces I had not seen or even thought of in many years – the second-grade teacher with auburn hair and a beautiful smile; the girl from high school who, unbeknownst to her, had inspired my most restless dreams during those burning years; the kind college counselor; the friendly cashier; the man with the cane; the nurse; the acquaintance from college who had let me escort her from innocence into womanhood; the three passersby who picked me up from the bloody asphalt – now these faces came before me in their clarity: the people who touched my life for a time, only to continue on in the relentless trajectory of their own lives, like arrows being shot past each other. How clear and straightforward it all seemed in retrospect. How perfectly meaningful the many meaningless encounters along the way that nudged me ever so slightly toward my fate as Special Projects Coordinator at Cow Eye Community College. And at that very moment how it all seemed so *right* – so relentlessly and purposefully organized to bring me to the only place in the world where a fountain like this could embody such hope and promise.

By now it was almost dark and the air was very cold. I had not brought a jacket and my jaw was shivering from the cold and the spray. But before I could turn back, there was one more thing I had to do. Pulling an old coin out of my pocket I looked up at the majestic bull and his heifer silhouetted in perpetuity against the dimming sky. In the near-darkness it seemed that the water streaming from this massive bull really would flow through eternal time and space all the way back to its ultimate source. With all my might I threw the coin at the center of the fountain and watched as it sailed away from me forever.

Back in my apartment I took a warm shower and lay quietly into bed. On the television the local news gave helpful tips on surviving the drought that was paralyzing the region; a sports anchor reported on the crushing loss by the football team the three men had been cheering at the bar; and the weather person followed it all by offering a five-day prognosis for an urban center so far away from Cow Eye Junction as to be irrelevant, even exotic. Wearily I turned the knob off and grabbed my historical novel. Within minutes I was tending toward sleep, and despite my best efforts I could feel the book slipping out of my hands. I had thought I might read another chapter at least – a few more pages to conclude this eventful day – but before I could even finish the next paragraph, a thick sleep overcame me and I drifted off with my bed lamp still on, my covers unturned, and the half-read paperback resting like a plate of armor on my chest.

〜

MY FINAL SUNDAY before my first day of work passed uneventfully in quiet contemplation in my apartment. I read a fresh chapter of the novel I'd started on the bus. I watched some old variety shows on the television in my room. Ambitiously, I made a list of three personal goals for my first year at Cow Eye Community College: 1) To find the moisture in all things; 2) To love the unloved; 3) To experience both day and night.

In the quiet of my apartment I looked at these goals and was happy at the sound of them. A person can never have too many goals in life, I thought, and *three* is as good a number as any. And yet something was incomplete. After a few minutes I took up the paper again and wrote a fourth, and final, goal for myself during my stay at Cow Eye. And this last goal – not to be forgotten – was surely the most ambitious of all:

4) To become something *entirely*.

〜

THE NEXT MORNING I made my way to the administration building to meet Dr. Felch, whose office was on the second floor offering a prime view of the fountain with the Appaloosa. I knocked lightly on the door and when there was no response I knocked again, this time louder.

"He's not in!" a voice said. I whirled around to see a woman about my age with thick hair tied up in a strict bun and wearing a dark blue polyester business suit and skirt. "He's not in yet. Did you need something? Or did you want to just keep on knocking like that?"

"Sorry," I said. "It's already after eight and I was supposed to meet Mr. Felch at exactly eight o'clock. I'm new here..."

"You're the new Special Projects Coordinator?"

"That's right! Nice to meet you....I'm Charlie...."

I extended my hand and the woman took it, crushing the bones in my fingers even more painfully than Dr. Felch had two days earlier at the makeshift bus shelter.

"Nice grip!" I said.

The woman did not smile:

"You don't *look* like a Special Projects Coordinator," she explained. The woman was appraising me curiously, almost suspiciously. "In any case, you can have a seat in that hard plastic chair and wait for President Felch. He should be in any minute now."

I took a seat and grabbed a magazine. The woman settled behind the paperwork at her desk and although she might have engaged me in some welcoming conversation, she did not apparently consider it a necessity. In the silence the clock on the wall ticked and the sounds of the pelicans could be heard outside the windows. And in the unprecedented juxtaposition of sound – clock and pelican and lawn mowers groaning in the distance – I was left to wonder, among countless other things, what exactly a Special Projects Coordinator *is* supposed to look like.

Sitting on the cold plastic chair I studied the mannerisms of this tightly wound woman. The deep v-neck in her blouse. The way her eyelashes fluttered when she squinted to read a letter. Furtively I stole glances at the supple contours of her shoulders beneath the polyester suit, and the way her bangs fell across her face as she arranged her pens and dusted off her typewriter. And then how her soft hands trembled ever so slightly as she paused to lovingly polish the two picture frames of what I assumed must be her young children.

I opened my magazine and began to flip through the articles. One story summarized the current conflict of the day; another gave a portrait of a recently disgraced politician; yet another talked about the withdrawal of ground troops from the world's latest hot spot. Listlessly I turned the pages and was halfway through an article about the demise of a once-great superpower when Dr. Felch walked into the office's waiting area.

"Morning, Bessie," he said and then, "Good morning, Charlie. Sorry I'm late. I see the two of you've met?" Dr. Felch motioned to me and I followed him into his office where he offered me a stick of chewing gum that I politely refused. "They say it helps kick the smoking urge," he explained. "But it sure as hell ain't helping *me!*"

I laughed.

Dr. Felch shuffled through some papers on his desk. His office was covered in dark-wood paneling with black leather chairs on either side of his desk. Above him a lacquered cow's head was bolted to the wall. Behind his chair was a large brass spittoon that gave the room a pungency of expectorated wintergreen chewing tobacco. Maroon-colored drapes fell from ceiling to floor around the window looking out onto the fountain with its Appaloosa. On his desk were various framed pictures of his children and their families: a young couple smiling red-faced in the middle of a snowy ski resort; several tanned bodies standing on a tropical beach; studio shots of smiling mom, dad, and children.

"So how'd you like Bessie?" he asked.

"That was Bessie?" I said. "She seems fine. Although I don't think she cares too much for *me.*"

Dr. Felch laughed.

"Yeah, she's like that with everyone. Don't take it personally though. Like I said, she's a bulldog. But with some time you'll grow on her."

"I hope so."

"Just be patient. And don't try to get under her skirt. That almost never works out well...."

Dr. Felch handed me a paper that he'd written some notes on.

"These are your primary assignments for the semester," he said. The list was enumerated and contained two imperatives and a circled tautology:

1. lead accreditation process
2. facilitate christmas party
3. DIVIDED FACULTY ⟵

"That last one's gonna be a bitch," he said. "I'm not even sure what verb to put before it. *Reconcile? Unite?* Anyway, you get the idea. Whatever verb you come up with, just make sure it's a good one. The future of our college depends on it."

Dr. Felch paused. Then he said, "Classes don't start until next Monday, but all faculty should be on campus this week. We'll be having our opening convocation this morning. I've told Bessie to give you all the back story you need. Try to remember the names and pay special attention to the personalities and the dynamics. Take note of the automobiles and try to keep straight the various points of origin that have led us all to this segment of time and space. It'll be a lot of information for you of course, but feel free to ask her any questions that you have. She'll also give you the key to your office. It's right down the hall from here, next to the institutional researcher's, so expect that the four of us will be seeing a lot of each other from now on."

Dr. Felch said that he would also provide me a copy of the college's most recent accreditation self-study along with the visiting team's disappointed response. ("We'll need to address all their recommendations and rebukes," he said.) And Bessie would get me a copy of the minutes from last year's Christmas Committee meetings so I could see where things had fallen apart and how we might start reassembling all the pieces.

"Other than that," he continued, "this week is just a chance to get ready for the upcoming semester. Use the time wisely. Trust me, things may seem slow right *now*, but once the semester starts, everything will start to move at a different pace: it'll take on a life of its own. For now just make sure you keep your eyes open to the different alignments and affiliations on campus. You'll be expected to navigate it all soon enough."

Dr. Felch checked his watch: it was almost eight-thirty.

"Bessie!" he shouted into the other room. Bessie entered and Dr. Felch pointed at me: "Bess, take Charlie here and walk him over to the cafeteria, will you? I need to prepare my notes for convocation."

The two of us left Dr. Felch's office and after collecting her things from her desk she gathered up a box of papers into a bear hug and, leaning back into the doorframe, flicked off the light to the reception area with her elbow.

"Ok, *Charlie*. Let's go...."

"Do you need some help with that box there? Here let me take something...."

"I'm fine. Just grab the door if you don't mind."

I did and we went down the stairs and out onto the esplanade.

As I quickly learned, Bessie was not an eager conversationalist. But on the long walk from the administration building to the cafeteria she acted as a faithful guide, dutifully explaining the things we were passing: the campus laundry facility, the college book store, the shooting range for faculty and staff, the stables where the animal science students conduct their special insemination projects. That is where you drop off your dry cleaning on Tuesdays, she would say. And *over there* is where you can buy a razor for that half-hearted collection of stubble on your upper lip.

"You mean my *mustache?*"

"If that's what you prefer to call it...."

Bessie had a forceful gait and as we walked I couldn't help noticing the rustling sounds that her skirt made with each shuffling step. She wore high heels and her legs were panty-hosed – and she was still grappling with the heavy box of papers – yet her pace was so brisk that it was all I could do to keep up.

"You walk so fast!" I said, and she grunted in response.

Soon we had passed the Dimwiddle Observatory and, a few minutes later, the Simon and Catherine Dimwiddle Concert Hall. When we were approaching the Dimwiddle Center for Animal Husbandry my curiosity finally gave in.

"Who are all these Dimwiddles?" I asked. "They're on every building!" Without slowing her pace Bessie explained that the Dimwiddle patriarch had made his fortune in the military industry and left a large stake in his company to Cow Eye. It was said that one out of every seven bullets fired in the world was made at the Dimwiddle Arsenal – and so each time an armed conflict flared up somewhere in the world, the college received a direct influx of cash from the Dimwiddle Estate.

"It's what you would call a mixed blessing," she said.

Eventually we reached the cafeteria where the convocation was being held – the Arthur and Mabel Dimwiddle Memorial Cafeteria – and after leaving the box of papers with the secretaries at the entrance Bessie made her way to a seat in the very back corner of the cafeteria where we would be able to observe the full panorama of faculty and staff as they filed in through the front door, received their materials for convocation, and then took their own seats around the room.

"You'd better get a note pad," she advised. "There's going to be a lot of facts and figures." Diligently I took out a yellow legal pad from my briefcase and dabbed a pen against my tongue.

"I'm ready!" I said.

As the first faculty and staff entered the room, smiling and greeting each other after the long summer break, the secretaries at the front desk checked them in and Bessie read off their names, ranks and distinguishing accolades, not unlike the auctioneer at a high-stakes livestock auction:

"Rusty Stokes. Animal science instructor and chain smoker," she would say and I would scribble furiously in my notebook. "Chair of the College Senate and one of the most feared people on campus. Has two trucks including the Jeep he just bought from Merna Lee's sister. Doesn't eat vegetables. Doesn't like communists. Doesn't believe in viable alternatives to heterosexuality. Loves guns."

After him came a middle-aged woman in flowing sari with dangling crystal earrings and an elegant red dot on her forehead:

"Marsha Greenbaum. Second-year nursing instructor. Moved here last fall from Delaware. Strict vegetarian. Prefers classical music. Runs a holistic medicine practice on the newer side of town commonly referred to as the Outskirts. Teaches yoga in her free time. Ardently pursuing nirvana and is about *this* close to achieving it." Bessie used her thumb and forefinger to indicate just how close Marsha was. "Unfortunately, she's also got a bad case of scabies...."

I scribbled it all down.

A minute later a small elderly man entered wearing a gray suit and red bow tie with a fedora. Bessie said:

"That's Will Smithcoate. The longest-serving faculty member here at the college. Teaches Early U.S. History and still reads from the same lecture notes he used when he started thirty years ago. Served as chair of the Christmas Committee last fall – the first and only time in the existence of our college that we didn't manage to have a party. Used to be a force on campus but these days he's just biding his time to retirement. Bourbon and tonic are helping him through that process...."

A line was beginning to form outside the cafeteria and the energy in the room was building with the impending start of the convocation, which would launch the college into the new academic year. The secretaries were scurrying to get everyone through the line and into the cafeteria, and it was all I could do to take down the mass of biographical and historical information that Bessie was throwing out at me in rapid singsong. There was the tall woman from Pennsylvania who taught art history and drove a Saab. And the short man on crutches who drove a Ford F-1 and taught botany. Behind him were Harold and Winona Schlockstein, the college's only *formally recognized* couple; to their left was Sam Middleton, medieval poetry expert and card-carrying institutional anarchist; and behind *him* was Alan Long River, a public speaking teacher and Native American descendent from the original tribe of the area, who hadn't spoken a word to anybody at the college – his students included – for more than twelve years.

"That's highly ironic," I said. "I mean, how does one teach public speaking without..."

"...*speaking?* Your guess is as good as mine, Charlie!"

One by one, my observant guide introduced me to the many personalities of Cow Eye Community College – not just to what my new colleagues did in their professional capacities but also to what they aspired to be in the shadows of their personal lives. In this way I learned about the forty-six-year-old anthropology professor and mother of six who had once been a cabaret dancer in New Jersey and who still harbored dreams of a career in interpretative dance. And the portly physical education teacher whose acquaintance with his toes was now limited to second-hand rumor and vague childhood remembrances – but who spent his summers entering bare-knuckle boxing tournaments back in his home state of Georgia. And the mesmerizing creative writing instructor with nary a publication to his credit but whose sexual exploits with his female students were the stuff of local legend. ("We might as well write him into New Student Orientation!" Bessie groused.) There was the psychology instructor who played guitar at the Champs d'Elysees on Wednesday nights; and the longtime head of the horticulture department who'd spent his most recent sabbatical traveling throughout the country researching the annals of American puppetry; and the recently promoted associate professor of astronomy who never once cracked a smile during his entire tenure at the college but who, Bessie swore, would drive six hundred miles on alternate weekends to do stand-up comedy in the nightclubs of the nearest city. Indeed, across the campus of Cow Eye Community College, talent blossomed in the off-hours like the many bushes of night-blooming jasmine on campus. And so it was in this way, and with the help of Bessie's useful prompts, that I came to see how a community college can be a haven of opportunity not only for its students but also for its faculty as well: for each of my peers had a vivid talent of some sort – a passion, a burning aspiration, a secret calling lodged very deep within the crevices of a creative soul – that was being supported by the teaching of undergraduates at Cow Eye Community College.

"Well, speak of the devil...!"

Bessie was now pointing to the front door where the English faculty had arrived as a group and were busily checking in with the secretaries. Among faculty of the college, Bessie explained, the English instructors were by far the most far-flung, with each engaged in a particular project of literary merit: a sci-fi novel set in futuristic Connecticut, a collection of impossibly short stories, an epic poem detailing the rise and fall of the cattle industry in Cow Eye Junction. Of the five tenured English faculty at Cow Eye, exactly three were working on first novels; two were active playwrights; three had self-published at least one chapbook of non-rhyming poems; one had a movie script on option; and *all five* were in continuous and desperate search for a reliable literary agent.

In fact, the only person in the room who did not seem to have a secret aspiration of any sort was Rusty Stokes. This struck me as odd and when I asked Bessie whether this had been an oversight on her part, she laughed and said that Rusty was exactly where he belonged – that he might just be the only person in the world (or at least the only one working anywhere at a *community college*) – whose ambitions and talents were perfectly aligned.

"And who are *those* people?" I motioned to a dark table in the farthest corner of the room where a gloomy collection of half-lit faces sat staring blankly ahead. Each of them was wearing a black armband.

"The adjuncts," she explained. "We're not allowed to refer to them by name."

Now more and more of the surging crowd was entering the cafeteria and in short order I was introduced to the school's recently hired eugenics instructor; its business department chair; the dean of instruction; Carmelita the diversity officer; the full-time grant writer; the head librarian and her staff; Gladys from personnel; the mayor of Cow Eye Junction (who also happened to be our part-time welding instructor); and the Saab-driving, Shih-Tzu-transporting art history professor whose house was not far from the makeshift bus shelter. One by one the surnames came at me like night through a windshield: Jumpston and Drumright and Manders and Poovey and Drisdell and Runkle and Toth. Crotwell and Voyles. Kilgus and Spratlin and Yaxley and Jowers. Quealy and Tutt. Prunty and Pristash. Clardy and Yerkes and Hotmire and Spritch. Breedlove and Tilly. Barnes and Weaver and Redfield and Tuley and Crootch and Slocum and Lineberry and Tibbs and....

At one point Bessie nudged me with her elbow and whispered, "Take special note of this one coming in now...."

An unassuming woman about forty-five years old had entered wearing simple jeans, a simple t-shirt, and wire-framed glasses that were also very simple. With a nondescript countenance and a look of internal calm she seemed to bask in the fact that there was nothing overtly notable about her, which made it all the more puzzling that Bessie had chosen to single this woman out from all the others.

"That's Gwendolyn Dupuis," she said. "Talisman of the new people. She's from Massachusetts originally but has been here for about fifteen years. Loves numbers. Teaches logic. Gwen's well known around campus for being Rusty's mortal enemy. If Rusty resides on one side of the fence, you can be sure she'll be parked on the exact opposite side. If Rusty wants this or that thing to happen in earnest, Gwen will no doubt be advocating just as earnestly for its antidote. If he were to represent our collective past, she would be more emblematic of our disunited present. If he be Maryland by light of day, she will most certainly be South Carolina in the darkest of nights...." Intrigued, I watched the woman walk into the room, carefully make her way to the exact opposite corner of the cafeteria from where Rusty had positioned himself under a flickering fluorescent light, and then take her seat at a less illuminated table next to Marsha Greenbaum.

"Any latent aspirations for her?" I asked.

"If there are, she's been able to keep them tucked well inside her blouse." And here I understood Bessie's words to mean that in this regard, these two polar opposites were really quite similar: like Rusty Stokes, Gwen Dupuis was at perfect peace with her place in this world – a place that was no greater and no smaller than her position as logic teacher and talisman for the newly arrived at Cow Eye Community College.

By now faculty and staff of every conceivable ilk were pouring into the room, and Bessie's introductions came even faster. That financial aid counselor over there, she gravely informed me, is from central New Hampshire and drives a Volkswagen. But the biology instructor sitting to her right drives a Dodge Dynasty and hails from Virginia.

"This is really overwhelming," I said at last. "There's no way I can remember all these names and faces. And automobile makes. Not to mention states of the Union. I mean, all at once like this?"

"Just soak up what you can. You'll have time to experience it for yourself soon enough...."

Around the cafeteria most faculty were now sitting with their respective departments and here and there I caught snippets of the competing conversations. Nearest to me, the English faculty were bemoaning the fickleness and corruption of the New York publishing industry and the hesitance of literary agents to take on writers from Cow Eye Junction. A table away, Rusty Stokes was presiding over the faculty from the animal science department, who occupied an entire table by themselves and were engaged in a lively discussion of a recent bovine insemination. From one table to the next I saw the nursing department, the automotive teachers, the financial aid counselors, maintenance and security, the history department. The humanities sat mostly on one side of the room and the sciences on the other. Liberal Arts occupied the tables closest to the front while the Trades took those furthest toward the back. For a college as small as this one all the academic disciplines appeared to be well-represented, though there was surprisingly little interaction among them.

"And that's not even the worst of it," Bessie agreed. "Take a closer look at the tables. A *better* look ...."

And when I looked even more closely I saw that among the broad divisions there were subdivisions and within these subdivisions there were subdivisions of the subdivisions. For even at the individual tables there were noticeable separations and stratifications and limitless groupings and affiliations. With Bessie's help I came to see how even among the humanities, things were not as harmonious as they outwardly appeared: that instructors from rural backgrounds sat together; as did those owning four-cylinder imports; those whose parents had been instrumental in repudiating majority rule; and those who, if pressed for an answer, would more readily identify themselves as *spiritual* rather than *religious*. PhDs huddled together quite apart from their less-decorated counterparts. Republicans sat to the left, Federalists to the right. Caucasoids kept largely to themselves leaving the college's mongaloids to fill in where they could – while off to the side, sitting quietly by himself and occupying three-fifths of a very small chair, was a single tenured negroid. In the bustling cafeteria it all came together to make a strange, chaotic, swirling sort of sense – such as the harmony found in a pointillist electoral map observed from afar. Yet despite the chaos, there was something vaguely reassuring about the scene until, amid the pulsating crowd, I noticed a curious absence.

Something important was missing. Something vital and essential. An oversight of incalculable proportions: Where were the math instructors?

"Ah yes, our illustrious mathematics department," Bessie sighed when I pointed out the subtrahend. "Something tells me they're still in North Carolina...."

"Why North Carolina? What does *that* mean?"

"Just wait. You'll see in a bit...."

At last the room was almost full. In one corner a small crowd of women had formed a semi-circle around an item of particular interest; shrieks of female delight rang out every so often.

"What's happening over there?" I asked.

"That's our new data analyst," Bessie explained. "Our *institutional researcher*, I think they're calling it now. He just moved to Cow Eye to take Merna Lee's position. And apparently he's *gorgeous*."

Finally when all of the faculty and staff of the college had taken their seats, Dr. Felch made his way to the lectern at the front of the room. Standing behind the microphone he raised his hand above his shoulder as if taking a pledge of fealty and there he held it for several moments. Slowly, very slowly, the dull roar began to die down. Dr. Felch tapped the microphone a few times so that the sound reverberated around the cafeteria. "Does this thing work?" he said. And then: "Can you hear me?"

"We hear you!" somebody shouted from the back of the room. And a few people laughed.

Dr. Felch adjusted his reading glasses.

"Ok, then," he said. "Let us begin..."

❧

"FIRST OF ALL," Dr. Felch said, "let me start by welcoming you all back to Cow Eye. Those of you who left for the summer, I hope you had a great respite and are ready to roll up your sleeves and get back to work. Those of you who stayed, I hope you folks didn't choke too much on all that dust over the summer."

A few light laughs went up around the room.

"But before going any further, there's one important announcement I've been asked to make...."

Dr. Felch reached into his pocket and pulled out a small piece of paper. Holding it at arm's length he let his glasses fall to the end of his nose as he read:

"...Will the owner of the lime green hybrid-electric vehicle with the highly individuated license plates please remove it from the handicapped stall where it is currently parked....?"

A murmur went up around the room; at the front table an embarrassed lecturer from the economics department stood up and made her way quickly outside.

"Thank you," said Dr. Felch. And then: "Yet another triumph for the better angels of our nature, wouldn't you say?"

Throughout the audience there was a sprinkle of laughter as well as some general eye-rolling directed at the economics department in particular and the study of economics as a whole.

"Okay," Dr. Felch continued. "Now that *that*'s done, I want to begin my welcoming address to you today with a message of unity. My dear friends and fellow citizens, I want to kick off this new academic year by reiterating the importance of what we all do – what *each* of you does – here at the college. Every single person at Cow Eye is vital to our organization and to the learning and success of our students. It doesn't matter whether you are the humble president of the institution as I happen to be. Or the tenured faculty member teaching our students to be more logical like Gwen Dupuis does in her classes. Or whether you contribute to the world by inseminating cows using extracted bull semen – thank you very much, Rusty Stokes! Whatever your role may be – from the dean of student services to our fantastic staff in the financial aid office....to the hardworking folks who cut our lawns so that every blade of grass is the exact length as the one next to it – *each* of you is vital to our mission and you should be proud of the contribution that you make here at Cow Eye Community College. Please know that your work is valued and that it has an incredible impact on the learning and success of our students." Here Dr. Felch flipped through his papers. "And as each of you should know by now, it is our mission statement that drives the workings of our institution. Let's see a show of hands....how many of you have committed our college's mission to memory?"

Dr. Felch waited for hands to go up but only a few did. Among the raised hands, the hand of Rusty Stokes was easily the largest, and the *highest*; proudly he was affirming his absolute knowledge and mastery of Cow Eye's institutional mission statement.

"Well, good for you!" Dr. Felch said. "Now for the *rest* of us, I want to do an exercise to remind everyone why we're here. I'm going to read our mission statement and I want each of you to repeat after me. Please stand...."

Chairs scraped on the cafeteria floor as everyone stood up from their tables. Amid the commotion there were some ironic asides and mild laughter and creaking bones, and when enough of it had died down to be heard, Dr. Felch began to read the mission statement of the college. In a somber voice he read each word ponderously and significantly. And as he did the crowd obediently repeated after him:

"The mission of Cow Eye Community College is...."
   (*The mission of Cow Eye Community College is!*)

"...to provide a nurturing and time-tested education...."
   (*To provide a nurturing and time-tested education!*)

"....grounded in American values and the proliferation of...."
   (*Grounded in American values and the proliferation of!*)

"....the American Way...."
   (*The American Way!*)

"....so that our students may become...."
   (*So that our students may become!*)

"....mindful, God-fearing, tax-paying citizens...."
   (*Mindful, God-fearing, tax-paying citizens!*)

"...of the United States of America."
   (*Of the United States of America!*)

"Thank you. You may be seated."

Everybody sat back down at their tables, chairs scraping and sliding in reverse.

"Now as faculty and staff please think about this mission statement in light of everything you do. This is no abstract document without practical relevance – it is a living, breathing, perspiring document. Yes, it may have halitosis at times. But that's because it is *alive*. So in your work, ask yourself: How does the mission of Cow Eye Community College apply to what I do? In my botany classes how do I ensure that my students pay their taxes? As I teach my culinary students to bake French croissants, how do I make sure that they are baking their French croissants *the American Way*? Math people – are there any math people here? Not yet? – math people…. as you teach your remedial students to convert a fraction to a decimal, ask yourself this: how does it ensure that they will become God-fearing citizens of the United States of America?"

A smattering of applause rose up around the room; aside from this, there was little reaction beyond respectful silence. Bessie nudged my arm:

"He's losing control of the ship," she whispered. "He's a great man and I love him dearly. But he's lost this ship…."

Unabashed, Dr. Felch continued:

"As you know, for some time now we have been on very thin ice with our accreditors. And so this year as part of our accreditation process we will be redoubling our efforts to demonstrate that we truly are committed to the success of our students. This will involve reviewing our mission statement and revising it as necessary, and each of you will be a part of that. So please think seriously about what you like within our current mission statement and what you don't appreciate and would want to change. How can we make it better? More efficient? More *effective*? What would make the statement more reflective of who we are as faculty and staff of Cow Eye Community College and of the learning that we want for our students…."

Dr. Felch looked up from his notes.

"Are there any questions about this?"

Rusty Stokes had stood up from his chair and was standing with a thumb tucked under each of his suspender straps. Dr. Felch looked over at him.

"Yes, Rusty?"

"I do have a question."

"Yes, Rusty?"

"Why?"

"Why *what*, Rusty?"

"Why should we change our mission statement? We spent a lot of time on the current one, and I think it's perfect enough as it is!"

"That's a very good point, Rusty. And I'm glad you raised it. Nobody's saying we have to change the mission statement. But we do need to *review* it and, if necessary, update it to reflect current realities. To make it *more perfect*, if you will. The last time we revised our mission statement was eleven long years ago. And do you know how much has changed since then? Compared to what our college was like eleven years ago?"

"Of course I do. I've been here longer than that."

"Right. And so you'll remember that eleven years ago we only had six tenured faculty on staff, and all of them were from Cow Eye Junction. There was no concert hall or observatory or nature walk. There were no pelicans. Among our faculty members we did not even have a single negroid – and that seemed perfectly fine with us. There was no such thing as the data analyst position – much less an institutional researcher – because Merna was still teaching math to freshmen. (Yes, we called them fresh*men* back then!) Our student enrollment was a quarter of what it is now and – can you believe it? – predominantly *male*! Outside the college, the Ranch was thriving and the railroad still ran and steam power seemed like the wave of the future. Things were more inalienable back then. But it's a different world now, Rusty, and Cow Eye needs to change with it. And we all need to be a part of that change. Including *you*...."

"So you're advocating change for its own sake then? I mean, do you even believe that, Bill? Do you yourself believe what you're telling us right now?"

"That's beside the point. As president I speak for the institution. And no, I'm not advocating change for its own sake...I'm advocating change so we don't lose our accredititation and get our asses shut down."

"I see. So what you're saying is..."

But here Dr. Felch spoke directly into the microphone:

"Let's move on, please...."

Watching the gray-haired ex-veterinarian clumsily trying to unify his troops behind the accreditation effort – observing him fumble through his handwritten notes in search of the next agenda item – I felt even more profoundly how important my role as Special Projects Coordinator would be for him. During his thirty years at the college, Cow Eye had clearly changed beyond recognition, which was no doubt due in large part to him. But it was also becoming clear – sadly clear – that the world as he knew it really was changing and that it would not remain handwritten for very much longer.

When Rusty had reluctantly retaken his seat Dr. Felch thanked him for his comments, then continued:

"Now at this time we'd like to introduce our new faculty and staff who have come to us from all corners of the world this semester. As I call out your name please stand up where you're sitting so we can recognize you...."

Dr. Felch turned over a page in his notes and began reading.

"Our first employee is Nan Stallings. Nan, can you stand, please....?"

Across the room from me a woman stood up from her seat.

"Nan comes to us from the great state of Rhode Island, where she was a private attorney and award-winning legal scholar and advisor to such prominent legal teams as the plaintiff in *West v. Barnes* and, more recently, the attorneys for *Brown vs. the Board of Education*. She also has extensive experience representing victims of ethnic genocide and has extracted settlements from pharmaceutical companies who have unethically placed faulty products on the market. She comes with enthusiastic references from a junior senator, a federal representative, and a retired Supreme Court justice. She will be teaching political science and we are glad to have her. Welcome, Nan."

Applause followed and Nan smiled and sat back down in her chair.

"Our next new employee is Luke Quittles. Luke, where are you....?"

Luke stood up and waved.

"Luke will be working in our culinary department. He comes to us from Paris, France, where he was the head chef in a quaint three-star restaurant on the Rue de Passy. Luke is an award-winning cuisinier who specializes in Tex-Mex and has served his unique delicacies to several former and current heads-of-state including the Sultan of Brunei and the Duchess of York. He will be living in faculty housing until he finds a place of his own, so if any of you happen to know of some reasonably priced accommodations near campus, please let him know. Thank you, Luke!"

Again everyone applauded and Luke sat back down.

"Next we have Raul Torres. Raul?"

Raul stood up and gave an elegant wave amid shrieks from the women in the audience.

"Raul will be our new data analyst. Or, I should say, our *institutional researcher.* Of course he will have large shoes to fill as our beloved Merna was in the position for more than ten years before leaving abruptly last semester – and we'll miss her. But please welcome him to his new position with open arms. Raul comes to us from….*California!*" Here Dr. Felch stepped back from the lectern to give his own personal applause at this joyous fact; then he stepped back up. "A little bit about Raul…. He earned his Master's degree in Statistical Methods and his PhD in Intercultural Statistics. He is an award-winning statistician and has been nominated for several humanitarian prizes for his contributions to world peace and cultural harmony through the proliferation of recursive algorithms. Raul also wanted you ladies to know that he plays flamenco guitar, sings ballads with a throaty vocal inflexion, and loves long romantic strolls along the timeless canals of Venice, the beaches of Rio de Janeiro, and the sultry banks of our very own Cow Eye River. He hails from Barcelona originally but claims that Cow Eye Junction is just as beautiful – if not *more* beautiful – than his hometown and is very happy to be here. Let's all welcome Raul to the college….!"

A loud applause followed and several women even rose to give a standing ovation. One by one, they sat back down.

Here Dr. Felch grew serious.

"You know – and this is not in my notes, folks, but I feel that I need to bring it up. We often talk about Merna. I talk about Merna. You talk about Merna. Everyone talks about Merna. We all talk about Merna because, well, she worked here for thirty-five years, and we all loved her. And of course you probably remember what happened to her last year. Or, if you happen to be new to the college, you may have *heard* what happened to her. There are a lot of things that have been said about her and some of them, of course, are true. But others are not true at all. And that's exactly my point. My point, you see, is this: whatever it is that you remember, or have heard, just forget it. Let it go. She was an amazing lady and an incredible human being who made a huge contribution to Cow Eye in her time. So when we think of her, let's just please think of her for the great years she had here and not for anything else that you may have heard or remembered, or that may have been said or done. Okay?"

Dr. Felch paused to collect his thoughts.

Seeing this, I leaned over to Bessie:

"What's all that about?" I whispered. "What happened to Merna?"

But Bessie just waved my question away.

"I'll tell you later…" she said.

When Dr. Felch had composed himself, he continued:

"Where was I? Oh yes, Stan and Ethel Newtown. Are Stan and Ethel here?"

The husband and wife stood up. They were holding hands in an adorable way and waving to their new peers.

"As you have probably guessed, Stan and Ethel are married and will therefore be rightly considered our college's *second* formally recognized couple. Ethel teaches journalism and comes to us from the Midwest where she was an award-winning investigative reporter. Her feature articles have been nominated for many prizes and her recent series exposing the American economic system as the tallest pyramid in the history of the world – and the controversial prediction of its impending downfall (the economic system, that is, not *the world*) – won her many awards…as well as many enemies. We've been eager to bring her to Cow Eye and are happy she will be joining us. Standing next to her is her husband Stan, who is just as impressive though somewhat shorter. He is an award-winning archaeologist who has discovered the remains of several lost civilizations and his work in East Africa has led to a radical shift in previously held notions of evolution. Stan is an ardent tennis player and conspiracy theorist and believes that under the town of Cow Eye Junction is a lost world of very little people that is waiting to be unearthed. Needless to say, Stan will be teaching *archaeology*…."

Dr. Felch waited for the Newtowns to sit back down amid the resounding applause from the audience. Then he said:

"….Okay, who's next? Oh *yes*, now we have our final new employee for this academic year. He comes to us from an undisclosed location halfway across the country. He just got in two days ago fresh off the bus. Charlie? Charlie, my boy, where are you?"

Hearing my name, I stood up.

Dr. Felch pointed at me and smiled:

"Charlie here will be our new Special Projects Coordinator. He'll be leading our all-important accreditation process in preparation for the team's visit next spring – which seems light years away, I know, but will arrive faster than you think. Charlie does not come with any successful employment history. He has achieved no awards or distinctions, and his personal life is also somewhat shambolic as he has been divorced *twice* while still at a relatively young age...."

A concerned murmur went up around the room.

"...Hey Charlie, how's the single life treating you...?"

I gave an unenthusiastic thumbs-up.

"...Enjoy it while you can, my friend! Anyway, Charlie has two ex-wives and a history of failed jobs and other half-starts and near-misses around the country. You see, Charlie has always been a lot of different things but none of them *entirely*...."

Here I could feel the concerned murmur of the crowd growing even louder around me.

"... But we have a lot of hope for him here. In fact, some of you may remember from his interview that Charlie's family used to live in Cow Eye Junction. His grandfather rescued a woman from certain death in the Cow Eye River. And he likes beef stew with lots and lots of *vegetables*! Charlie will be the third person in this position in less than two years, but we have every faith that he will overcome the daunting challenge and be a valuable long-term employee of our college. Welcome to Cow Eye, Charlie. And, most importantly, welcome *back*...!"

I waved again and sat down. Instead of applause, there was only the confused rumble of half-voices and whispers and fingers being pointed in my general direction.

"So..." Bessie whispered to me amid the rumble, "You're divorced too?" And in her voice I sensed the slightest beginnings of an iceberg that was melting.

Dr. Felch checked his notes again and then continued:

"Okay, so those are our new faculty and staff for the upcoming academic year. Let's have a round of applause for all of them...!"

Everyone applauded earnestly and I was thankful that my introduction to the faculty and staff of Cow Eye Community College was now behind me.

⬄

AFTER HIS INTRODUCTIONS, Dr. Felch moved to the next item in his agenda which happened to be updates and reminders for the upcoming semester.

"Before we get to our new initiatives on campus, I first want to remind everyone of some things that should be *old* information...." Dr. Felch stopped to take a deep breath, then he began:

"....Please remember to turn off the light when you leave a room for any length of time and, of course, to flush the toilet after every use. Don't park in the handicapped stalls unless you are truly handicapped. Use black ink for all important documents. Don't throw coins in the fountains. Don't rollerskate on the sidewalks. Try not to walk on the grass as it causes the individual blades to look uneven. Don't feed the pelicans. If you want to pick any of the colorful flowers on campus, please submit a notarized request to your department chair by the first of the month. Don't forget that in all spoken and written communication you will now be required to use gender-neutral language instead of the kind that has come down from our forefathers. Semi-colons should be used judiciously; passive tense should be avoided if at all possible. Never meet with a student alone in your office with the door closed – especially if she's litigious. Never touch a co-worker in a way that makes her fidget from discomfort – but if you absolutely *must*, please make sure that you have her signed written consent first. When providing feedback to a student, be constructive and positive and write neatly. Always be courteous to Timmy who works at the guard shack – after all, it's not *his* fault you left your house late even though you have an important exam to give in exactly three minutes. Support your colleagues. Respect your peers. Always honor the diversity of your students. (This goes doubly for those that happen to be negroids.) Try to show empathy to people who may not drive the same car or truck as you do. Go to church on Sunday. Tip your waitress. Believe in America and the sanctity of her institutions – especially marriage. Pay taxes religiously. Love your wife – which is hard enough – but also, and this is key, folks: love your *ex*-wives. When completing evaluations of campus activities don't forget to fill out both sides of the form. And most importantly....in everything you do here at the college always base your decision-making on hard, cold, objective *data* and don't neglect to document your every action using statistics or other verifiable evidence. Remember, when it comes to our accreditors, any decision made without the benefit of numerical justification is a *bad* decision.....and a thing that has no valid and measurable confirmation of its existence – no matter how beautiful that thing may be to observe or how heavy it might be to lift – is not really a thing at all...."

Dr. Felch paused and shook his head.

"Oh, and one more thing….and I'm surprised I still have to remind you all of this…. Out of respect and courtesy to your fellow employees at Cow Eye Community College, please do *not* leave any bloated scrotums in the faculty mailboxes to turn into a grisly mess over the weekend…."

Here I stared into the resulting silence. Dr. Felch was turning the pages of his notes and it gave me time to reflect upon my own personal goals, the benchmarks and objectives that would guide me through the upcoming semester and, if I could only make it that far, my first full year at the college: *To find the moisture in all things. To love the unloved. To experience both day and night.* And, of course: *To become something entirely.*

"Any questions on this?" Dr. Felch asked.

"Yes, I have one…." A woman's voice came from the side of the room. Gwendolyn Dupuis had stood up and was pointing at Dr. Felch. She did not look pleased. "You mentioned two things that don't make a lot of sense to me…."

"Yes, Gwen? What were they?"

"Of course I agree with the bloated scrotum thing – that simply has to stop. But somewhere along the way you stated that if we want to pick flowers we need a notarized request that has to be submitted at the beginning of the month. Then, later, you mentioned that if a faculty member desires to cause a female co-worker to fidget, he should get written permission first…."

"He or *she*…."

"Right. He or she should get permission to make that co-worker fidget. So, don't you think it should be a requirement for that request to be notarized as well? I mean, where's the consistency here? Or do you mean to imply that the picking of flowers is worthy of a higher standard of consent than the unsolicited touching of our female employees?"

"No, that's not what I'm trying to say, Gwen. But rather than delve into the details right now, let's just say that we've had a lot of discussion about this in College Senate. And in a few minutes we'll be talking about our upcoming professional development series for the new academic year. In fact, I've been told we will be devoting at least one of the planned sessions to the proper and ethical fondling of co-workers. I encourage you all to attend…."

Gwen sat down.

"So on to our next order of business….Some new initiatives on campus…."

As Dr. Felch listed the many changes on campus, I looked around the cafeteria to see that the majority of faculty and staff in attendance were listening diligently but with perfunctory expressions on their faces. Like developmental math students on the first day of class. Or like a herd of hungry cattle waiting for the hay to be kicked off the truck.

"As you know," Dr. Felch was now saying, "beginning this semester Cow Eye Community College will be a *smoke-free* campus...."

At this, half the room erupted in wild cheers and clapping; the other half loudly booed and whistled.

"Okay, settle down. I know this was – this still *is* – a divisive issue. But the decision has been made and we need to move on from it. We've decided to go cold turkey with this, which means that there will be absolutely *no* smoking anywhere on the campus of Cow Eye Community College...."

Again a loud mixture of boos and applause rained down on Dr. Felch.

"...As of today there will be a designated smoking area outside the entrance to the college right next to the guard shack, and you'll be perfectly within your rights to smoke there. But please know that Timmy has been instructed to make sure nobody brings any cigarettes onto campus. Violators will be written up and all tobacco products will be confiscated."

Again a torrent of derisive boos descended onto Dr. Felch and, in their wake, an equally thunderous storm of enthusiastic applause.

Dr. Felch waited for the tumult to subside and when it did he said: "...On a happier note... we are pleased to introduce our new professional development series that I mentioned earlier. The first weekly session will be devoted to assessing the immediate measurable impact of the lifelong learning that's happening in your classroom. The next will be a primer on devising inspirational and galvanizing acronyms for the various academic phenomena around you...."

More mumbling went up around the room.

"....After those two professional development sessions, there will be countless others, including: *Content and Context: The Use of Language for Effective Classroom Communication*; and *She Loves Me, She Loves Me Not: Do's and Dont's of Effective Workplace Interactions*; and then *Putting your Finger on the Colon: Devising Evocative Titles and Subtitles to Professional Development Sessions*."

"Finally, I want to remind all of our *new* faculty – that is to say, those of you who were introduced earlier this morning – that there will be a special day of welcoming activities planned for you tomorrow. We will be conducting a team-building event, along with some obligatory bonding exercises. And we've got a fantastic agenda that includes a long bus ride and a very special surprise that was lovingly developed by our diligent and hard-working New Faculty Orientation committee led by Professor Smithcoate. The guiding theme for this year is 'Loving the Culture of Cow Eye.' So be sure to come with covered shoes...."

"Covered shoes?" I turned to Bessie.

"Yes," she answered. "And an open mind."

"But why the bus? Are we going somewhere?"

"You might say that...."

After Dr. Felch's address, several other campus representatives came up to the lectern to give their own updates on the goings-on around campus. The chair of the aquaculture department gave a briefing on his initiative to introduce carp into the college's three fountains; the head of the fiscal office, Dr. Felch's ex-wife, gave an update on the Dimwiddle endowment, including a report on the fortuitous escalation of several ethnic conflicts around the world; the head of the IT department spoke about the college's attempts to implement its controversial technology plan by infusing electric typewriters and calculators into the work processes of Cow Eye Community College; finally, Carmelita the Diversity Officer reported on the campus's recent successes ensuring equity on campus as evidenced by Cow Eye's six faculty members of mongoloid persuasion, the astronomy professor from Bangladesh, and the recent hiring of a negroid.

At about eleven-thirty, Dr. Felch came back up to the lectern to give his final remarks and bring the convocation to a close.

"Before you all leave for your semesters," he said, "I want to remind you of a very important event. Please get out your notebooks and mark your calendars for December eleventh...."

Everyone looked at each other inquisitively as they took out their notebooks.

"As you know," he said, "that is the last day of the semester. It's a Friday. And the reason why that will be an important date in all of your lives is that it is on this very day that we will be having our annual *Christmas party.*"

A murmur of whispers went up around the room.

"Yes, that's right, folks, Christmas happens *annually*. And so on December eleventh of this most glorious year of our Lord – *anno domini* as the historians say – we *will* be having a Christmas party. This date falls well within your respective duty periods. And so you are all encouraged to attend. Which is to say, *strongly* encouraged."

Even more clamor arose.

Dr. Felch looked around the room, taking his time to make unhurried eye contact with each person in the crowd. "I am also declaring that as of today the Christmas Committee is officially disbanded. I have made this executive decision on the grounds that representative democracy has clearly not served us well. From this point forward the planning process will be led by a small group of trusted individuals – including myself and our new Special Projects Coordinator – who have the college's long-term interests in mind...." Dr. Felch again looked out at the crowd. Then he said slowly, gritting his teeth as if it were a challenge: "Any *questions?*"

Gwen Dupuis had seemed to want to raise her hand but sensing the determination in Dr. Felch's voice, reconsidered.

"No questions," Dr. Felch said after the tense pause had provided ample opportunity to speak up. "That's probably for the best. **But** if any do happen to come up, please feel free to direct them to me. Or to Charlie, our new Special Projects Coordinator. Otherwise, I'll expect to see you all on December eleventh at our annual Christmas party. Have a great semester, everyone, and please don't forget to turn in your evaluations of today's event to the secretaries on your way out...."

And with that the convocation was over.

❧

EXCEPT THAT IT wasn't. Just as Dr. Felch had uttered his final words and had shut off the microphone for the afternoon, the doors of the cafeteria burst open and into the room stumbled a whooping mass of wildly dressed clowns and mermaids and zombies in chains and shackles. There were six of them total, and they were all hoots and shouts and boisterous laughter.

"Are we late?!" one of them said and frantically pedaled a child's tricycle around the room wearing a conical party hat and blowing a loud kazoo while honking the tricycle's horn.

Another had jumped onto a long table and was proceeding to do somersaults from the end of the table where the marketing and outreach specialists were sitting to the end where the student debt counselor awaited; faculty and staff on both sides of the table jumped back to avoid the woman's flailing legs. Meanwhile, a man in a mermaid costume and a woman dressed as a zombie flapped and slinked their way around the room, respectively. Two others, a younger couple with their shirts off – the man bare-chested, the woman in a silk brassiere – were standing with their hands in each other's back pockets and locked in a passionate kiss so deep and penetrating – so statistically improbable – that it seemed it might defy probability itself.

The pandemonium continued for several minutes.

Even Bessie, who had always been quick to explain the college's quirks, simply rolled her eyes and pronounced the tersest of explanations:

"Our math faculty," she said. "Just back from their conference in North Carolina."

Dr. Felch watched this unfold for a while, then shrugged his shoulders at the scene and turned the microphone back on. A loud thump reverberated around the room.

"And a big Cow Eye welcome to you *too*, math faculty!" he said, and then: "I'm glad to see you're enjoying your tenure...!"

At this, the audience laughed and Dr. Felch switched off the microphone for good. Now the crowd knew that the convocation really was over. Gratefully, they stirred from their seats and made their way back to their offices to prepare for the upcoming semester, each of them leaving an evaluation with the secretaries on the way out.

"Follow me," Bessie said when the crowd had filed out of the cafeteria and we'd turned in our evaluations. "We need to get back to the administration building so I can show you where your office is. It'll be right across from the institutional researcher. Which is good because you're going to have some serious planning to do."

I looked at Bessie and smiled. Somehow, after everything I'd just heard and seen, she seemed to offer the clearest reassurance that I'd made the right decision in traveling halfway across my country to take the position of Special Projects Coordinator at Cow Eye Community College. And as she spoke I couldn't help paying even closer attention to the red of her lipstick and the way she had highlighted her eyes to smooth out the wrinkles of time and failed matrimony. In the fluorescent cafeteria lighting it was hard to imagine that someone like her might ever be unloved.

"Let's go, Bessie," I said and held the door open for her. And then: "After you....!"

LOVE AND THE COMMUNITY COLLEGE

If the opposite of learning is knowing,
And the opposite of love is efficiency,
What then is the opposite
of a community college?

- Will Smithcoate

"And there it is," Bessie said when we had made our way back to the administration building and she'd handed me the key to my office. "Enjoy." I turned the key and opened the door expecting to find a tidy and inviting work space only to stumble into the catacombs of my predecessor's cluttered inner sanctum. The woman had not cleaned out her office before leaving, and her belongings, all of them, were still there in the exact state she'd left them, as if she had been forced to flee ahead of an impending natural disaster – a great flood perhaps, or a typhoon of recriminations. Cautiously I stepped into the musty office as if into a crime scene. Old shoes were scattered around the room. Strewn papers crinkled under my feet. A pair of swimming goggles dangled from a screw that had been nailed into the drywall. Two slices of petrified goat cheese rested on a paper plate on the desk. Personal photographs were taped to the walls – at last I could put a black-and-white face to the colorful stories I'd heard – and dangling from the ceiling, so low that a person of medium height would need to duck to avoid it, was an enormous hand-crafted sign with words that had apparently inspired my predecessor in her duties:

LOVE IS LIKE A RIVER
THAT IS NEVER THE SAME
IN TWO PLACES

"Well, it looks like she decided to leave you a small legacy," Bessie said.
"*Legacy*'s a good word for it!" I laughed. "Can I get a dust pan and some garbage bags?"

"We'll have the maintenance people clean it up."

"No, that's fine. This won't take long...."

The room was filled with trinkets and artifacts from the woman's stopover at the college and as I surveyed the miscellany I was surprised at just how much paper and dust, how many personal mementos, could be accumulated in less than a year's time. Buttons and hairpins. A bottle of flea medication. Business cards from realtors. A Buffalo nickel. A half-empty box of birth control pills. A shaker of salt. Refrigerator magnets from a far-flung Volkswagen dealership. A cow figurine and laminated bookmark with Cow Eye's mission printed on it – the same statement we'd just recited at the convocation that morning.

"I feel like we should call in that archaeologist guy. What's his name.... Newton?"

"Newtown," Bessie corrected.

"Right. Maybe if Stan digs around in here he can find those mythical little people he believes in."

Bessie brought me some cleaning supplies and trash bags and then went back to her own work, leaving me to wade through the clutter in the office. Among the personal items that had been left behind, many had a clear reason for being in this world and could therefore be discarded with moral certainty: a dirty yoga mat and barbell set, a zodiac chart, a full-colored doggie calendar for the previous year. But there were also those that had no identity of their own: a necklace with a small crystal energy pendant, three tarot cards stapled to each other to form an isosceles triangle, a stainless steel Peace sign the approximate circumference of a very large bullet. On the desk was a desktop pendulum set – five stainless steel orbs at perfect rest – that I couldn't resist setting into motion; lifting the one at the furthest end of the pendulum I let it drop back down against the other four: as the orbs struck with a firm clack, the one at the opposite end rose up. This repeated in reverse: back and forth, up and down, one orb rising and falling while the others huddled together in expectation of the next collision. In time it would be this rhythmic sound – the clacking of stainless steel on stainless steel – that would become the soundtrack to my life here at Cow Eye. Friction be damned, the sound seemed to want to continue for as long as history itself.

When the desk was finally cleared off, I turned to the book shelf which was still packed with literature and would need to be denuded. Among the dross was an old atlas with a gilded cover; a photo album called *Cute Cats of the World*; a softbound copy of the *Bhagavad Gita* translated into Esperanto; a Quote-of-the-Day calendar still stuck on June 21st ("Love is the journey, not the destination"); and a series of self-help books with titles like *How to Write a Winning Resume*, *The Power of the Tantric Mind*, and *The Anyman's Guide to Swimming Without Sinking*. Volumes of inspirational literature and spiritual compendia covered the shelves. Women's romances were everywhere. A middle shelf featured a series of reference works including a rhyming thesaurus, a twenty-volume encyclopedia set missing volume K, and a dictionary of Catholic saints. On the very bottom shelf, its price tag still prominent, stood a single book of literary fiction – a sleek two hundred pages of contemporary insight told in efficient prose – and next to it a six-hundred page hardback called *The Anyman's Guide to Writing the Perfect Novel*. The writing guide was well-worn with handwritten margin notes and countless highlighted passages. (On page 61, my predecessor had drawn three exclamation marks next to an underlined apothegm that noted: "Writing is the pursuit of personal liberation – the ultimate act of unrequited love.")

Judging by the literary tastes of my predecessor – or at least by the books she left *behind* – it was clear how very little there was, aside from this office itself, that she and I would likely have had the occasion to share. In fact, of the hundreds of books littering the office, only one struck me deeply; intrigued by its title, I set aside *The Anyman's Guide to Love and the Community College*. The book was glossy and attractively bound with a front cover featuring two associate professors in full regalia locked in a romantic embrace: "Required reading," one blurb gushed, "for anyone trying to find true love at a regionally accredited community college!" After two divorces in restless turn – one entirely my fault, the other only primarily my fault – and with my new position at Cow Eye now secured, this guidebook offered a glimmer of hope. I would devour it before any other. And learn from it. And internalize it. And when I had found the love it promised, I would place it into a cardboard box to be donated to the library so that my fellow unloved colleagues might do the same. Gently, I set the book aside.

By now the cleaning was going well and in no time the three trash bags were bursting with discarded items. I'd left my office door open for ventilation and was so consumed with wiping down the dusty desk that

I hadn't noticed a nondescript figure standing in the doorway. A light knock on my door caused me to look up from the dust and when I did I saw that it was Gwen Dupuis standing in the doorway.

"Hi there," she said. "You're Charlie, right?"

"That's right."

"I'm Gwen. I teach logic. And I wouldn't change my life for any amount of romance or adventure."

Gwen offered her hand and I took it in a firm handshake, inadvertently crushing the bones of her fingers into each other. She winced in pain and withdrew her hand.

"That hurt me," she said.

"I'm sorry."

"Look, I know you've had some difficulties in your personal life. And I'm sorry about your failed marriages. These things happen, I'm sure. But that is no reason to take it out on *me*."

Gwen was standing and shaking the pain out of her hand. And again I apologized. But she just shook her head.

"Charlie," she explained, "I am a woman, not a steer. My heart is real. My soul is eternal. My body is flesh, not bronze."

"I'm sure they are. Look, I *said* I was sorry!"

"Well, at least you put vegetables in your beef stew." Here Gwen gave a hint of a smile. Then she said, "Gosh, Charlie, your office is a *mess*."

"The stuff's not mine." With a wide sweep of my arm to indicate the room's disorder I explained that I was cleaning up after my predecessor and that the trash bags and boxes actually held the remnants of *her* legacy at the college.

"Yeah, poor thing," Gwen said. "She didn't have a lot of time to get out before the lawsuit." And here Gwendolyn Dupuis informed me that the former Special Projects Coordinator had been a really sweet person and had done a great job for the college while she was here and was a real asset to the world in general, and to Cow Eye Community College in particular, and would be sorely missed. "It's a shame our college can't keep good people like her," she concluded.

I nodded.

"Charlie, if you are even one-tenth the Special Projects Coordinator she was, then you will be worthy of occupying this office!"

Gwen was still standing in my doorway.

"Please have a seat, Gwen. You can sit on this chair here. I just cleaned it...."

"I'll stand, thank you. The world is changing, you see. And we are tired of sitting."

"We?"

"Yes, *we*. I did not come to Cow Eye to sit, Charlie. Actually, I just stopped by today to invite you to our pre-semester get-together this Wednesday. There will be light snacks and watery music and we'll be talking about alternative paths to spirituality and enlightenment. Bring your own arugula if you want."

"Arugula?"

"Yes, feel free to bring as much as you like."

I thanked her for the invitation but respectfully declined:

"It's nice of you to think of me. But I'm not much of a socialite. I prefer to be on my own, actually. And I honestly have no idea what an arugula is or where I would even go to look for one."

"That may be true. But these are valuable lessons to be learned. And besides, some very good people will be there. So think of it as a chance to meet your fellow colleagues – you know, the personalities you'll be navigating this year."

And here it occurred to me that she might be right. I'd been so quick to politely decline her offer that I'd not considered how useful this occasion might be. Dr. Felch had entreated me to study the personalities on campus and this party would surely help that along.

"Well, since you put it that way...."

"Great. It'll be this Wednesday at five-thirty. In Marsha's studio at the Outskirts. Do you know the place?"

"Not really. I just got in from the makeshift bus shelter two days ago. I don't even have a car yet...."

"Then I'll pick you up. I hear you're staying at faculty housing next to the math teachers...?"

Gwen and I made the necessary arrangements for Wednesday evening, she turned and left, and I went back to cleaning out the drawers of the desk. A few minutes later I had taken out a fourth trash bag and was stuffing a large pile of newspapers into it when I heard another knock on the door. Again I looked up to see a figure in the doorway. But this time it was the imposing outline of Rusty Stokes standing in the exact place where Gwen Dupuis had stood just a few minutes before.

"Charlie!" he said and held out his hand. "Nice to finally meet you, Charlie! I'm Rusty Stokes!" Cautiously, I shook Rusty's hand and in response he shook mine vigorously, crushing the bones of my fingers yet again. Without waiting for an invitation, Rusty walked into the room and took a decisive look around, first swiping a finger of dust from a filing cabinet then sniffing the air as if detecting the scent of an unpleasant memory.

"Smells like *Shih Tzu* in here!" Rusty's face was contorted into a pained expression, as if he were remembering a lost civilization – or smelling the rotting carcass of a passenger pigeon. "You may want to try some air freshener, my boy...it works wonders."

"Thanks for the advice, Mr. Stokes. Every little bit counts."

"It's *Doctor* Stokes, actually. But I like you, Charlie. So please call me *Mister* Stokes."

Rusty pushed aside some papers from a chair and sat down onto it heavily:

"That's an interesting device you have there," he said, "that pendulum thing...."

"It is," I said. "It's called a Newton's Cradle and I set it in motion about ten minutes ago. And it's still ticking away. I guess it just goes to show how all-powerful the force of kinetic energy is over inertia ..."

Rusty grimaced.

"Yeah, well, we'll see about that. Anyway, I don't want to keep you from your cleaning, Charlie. I just wanted to stop by to tell you we're glad to have you here. We've all got high hopes for you at Cow Eye. I mean, I'm sure you can't be any worse than that last thing we hired!"

Rusty shook his head disapprovingly.

"...I mean what a waste of time *that* was!"

"You didn't like my predecessor?"

"Didn't like her? She's the reason our accreditors put us on warning. And why we didn't have a Christmas party last year. It's too bad we have to keep hiring people over the phone like that – you know, the award-winning professionals with the sparkling resumes and recommendations from key advisers to the Ottoman empire...."

Again Rusty shook his head.

"In any case, we're glad *you're* here, Charlie. Bill's told me a lot about you. He mentioned that your family used to live in the area. And how you recognize that the primary ingredient in beef stew is beef. He also related your response to the bloated scrotum question, which, I have to say, was pure genius...."

I thanked him.

Rusty gave a playful wink. Then, humbly, he told me of his many accomplishments in life. Of course he did not like to brag, he concluded, but he was also a preeminent authority on the history of the area and I should consider myself invited to visit him at the Cow Eye Museum where he was curator. It would be a good chance for me to explore my family's roots, and he might even be able to find the newspaper article about my grandfather's famous exploit. I thanked him again and promised that I would make it out to see him some day.

"In the meantime, Charlie, what are you doing this Wednesday? We're having a barbecue at the river and we're hoping you can come."

"We?"

"Yeah, *we*. Me and the others. It'll be nice for you to meet everyone informally before the semester starts. You know, since you'll be navigating all of us soon enough."

(Again I remembered Dr. Felch's entreaty. Perhaps meeting *both* groups – Gwen's *and* Rusty's – would give me a better idea of the nature of their disagreement and how they might be brought together?)

"We're also going to be having a little remembrance for Merna," Rusty continued. "You probably heard about what happened to her last year. So we'll be doing something in her memory. It'll be on Wednesday at five-thirty."

"Five-thirty?"

"That's right. After work. And no need to bring anything. We'll have more than enough carnage for everyone to eat."

"I'll see what I can do. I may be a little late though."

"Fine. Let me know if you need a ride. And don't worry about bringing any drinks either. We'll have plenty of Falstaff...."

Rusty left and I resumed my cleaning. A few minutes later Bessie stopped by to see if I needed more trash bags.

"The office looks transformed," she said. "I love the sudden re-emergence of original intent."

"I did my best. Interior design is not my strong suit."

"And that pendulum thing is pretty nifty."

"It sure is. I think I'll leave it here uninterrupted, to see how long it can continue its clacking!"

Bessie nodded. Then she said, "So I saw you talking to Gwen and Rusty. Separately of course. How'd *that* go?"

"I'm invited to two parties on Wednesday after work. And I'm committed to both."

"Congratulations."

"But I'm a little conflicted. They're at the same time."

Bessie laughed:

"Of course they are!"

"So what should I do?"

"Well, you should pick one of the parties and go to that one entirely."

"But that would entail not going to the *other* one…."

"Obviously."

"And that would imply an expressed preference, or dare I say, a *commitment*, on my part. No, that won't work – not yet anyway. I think I should go to *both*. I should go to both Rusty's barbecue and Gwen's watery get-together. But how?"

Bessie thought for a few moments. Then she said:

"Well, I'm planning to go to the barbecue – that is, assuming I can find a sitter. So if you really want to go to both, I should be able to pick you up from Gwen's get-together on my way to Rusty's. Just meet me outside on the curb at exactly seven-thirty. That should give you enough time to savor the arugula."

And with arrangements made for Wednesday, I thanked her and she turned to leave.

"Oh and one more thing…" Bessie said spinning back around to face me. Above the silence in the room only the pendulum could be heard; relentlessly, the orbs clacked against each other in perfect rhythm. "Don't forget your covered shoes for tomorrow morning. Our liability consultant is quite insistent about it…"

⌒

AT HOME AFTER my first day on the job I reflected on the day's achievements: I had successfully cleaned up my office and set an inert pendulum into relentless motion; I had begun to acquaint myself with school procedures;

I had survived my first convocation. And even though there were still many unresolved questions – *The root causes of disunion between Rusty and Gwen? The relative merits of loose constructionism? Bessie's ambiguous marital status?* – this was certainly an encouraging start.

Before going to bed I took out my shaving supplies and for the first time since stumbling across the finish line of graduate school I shaved off my mustache entirely. Newly liberated, I threw the whiskers in the trash and took up the unfinished historical novel I'd been reading since my bus ride to Cow Eye. Then, upon second thought, I set it aside in favor of the non-fiction work I'd just taken from my predecessor's office. *The Anyman's Guide to Love and the Community College* was dusty from its lengthy summer hiatus and when I opened it a silverfish crawled out and scurried across my pillow. In a few minutes I would fall asleep with the book on my chest. But for now I opened the front cover and carefully read the first page of this helpful guide to a love so true and simple that any man can find it. "The human desire for love," it explained, "is as old as the community college itself….."

~

{…}

In fact, love is even older – tracing its lineage back to the days, long before community colleges, when the heart was still an untamed beast like the many undomesticated cows that once roamed the world. These were the days of wandering and wonder, of vast unconquered lands that encouraged diaspora and discovery. For the history of humankind is the history of man's quelling of his own desires. Or, rather, of their pursuit. Across continents and through time. With a diligence that knows no parallel among other beasts of burden. More than any force of nature, it is love – of self, of family, of god and country, of great ideas – that has been the consistent catalyst in the making of the world as it is. Without love there would be no religion. No art. No philosophy. Without love we would not have saints or martyrs or prophets. And of course, without love, we would not have community colleges.

It is said that for a thing to exist it must live side by side with its opposite. Day cannot be day without night. Nor can the flow exist without the ebb. In this way, there can be no joy without despair. No enlightenment without ignorance. And no passage of time without the final resolution of death. But before there was a community college there could be none of this — nothing at all but a very dark void. And then came God and the universe that He created which in turn begat time and space, such that over the many billions of years and the many billions of miles, the lineage of learning came down from its timeless ancestors:

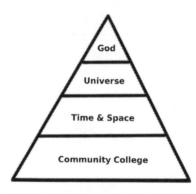

From God came the universe and from the universe came time and space. And from all of this came the community college where love itself is nurtured just as the sky nurtures the stars in her embrace. For surely there can be no truer love than the love of learning. The birth of an idea requires the transfer of knowledge from one mind to the next, just as the birth of a child requires the transfer of seed from one mammal to another. If a child is the offspring of the grown child's yearning for his childhood, then knowledge is just as surely the irrepressible offspring of learning's love for itself. This is why, among institutions of the world, the community college is the cradle of all that love aspires to be, and it is why, among lovers of the world, its faculty are a chosen people. And for this reason, the community college has always been,

and will always be, the breeding ground for love. Its eternal
source. The place it always returns to and whence it always
comes. For to know the world in its entirety is to know, in a
very small way, your local community college. And vice versa.

{...}

≈

THE NEXT MORNING I stood near the guard shack with my fellow new
hires waiting for the bus that would take us to our teambuilding activities.
"How're you doing, Mr. Charlie?" Timmy had asked when he saw me,
and I'd answered: "Fine, thanks, and you?" Now under the tall sky the
morning air was still cold and the six of us stood in a loose huddle, our
hands stuck straight into our pockets, bobbing from one leg to the other to
keep warm. Luke Quittles, the culinary instructor, was the most gregarious
of the bunch and seemed to be the best at leading the group into small
conversation. The Newtowns, Ethel and Stan, were also laughing and
joking with the others. Nan Stallings and Raul Torres stood slightly apart,
less outgoing but no less involved in the light conversation. As we spoke,
a trail of cold lingered in the air after our words.

"So what do you guys think of Cow Eye so far?" Luke asked.

"Stunning campus," Nan answered. "I just love the fountains."

"Yeah, they're really impressive," Ethel agreed. "Did you see the way
they make those rainbows against the light?"

"Not unlike the magic fountain of Montjuic," said Raul.

"Yeah but the cattle-themed statuary is better *here*," Luke added.
"Someone even told me the donors had an equal affection for bronze and
rainbows and that this was their way of bringing them together in a new
and surprising way."

Everyone nodded their agreement.

"Just watch out for those damn pelicans," Stan Newtown muttered.
"They can be vicious."

The conversation continued along these lines for some time, Nan
telling the group about a team of foundry workers she'd once helped to
unionize, Stan and Ethel detailing their search for a house close enough
to campus that the fountain with the bull and heifer could be easily
seen from their bedroom window. Luke shared an old family recipe for

pelican. Raul quickly calculated the calories in a romantic meal for two, to which Nan stated that she had never heard such a charming accent and that she'd always wanted to visit Barcelona. At a slight remove from all of this, I followed the conversation mostly in silence, though every now and then someone would pull me into the mix and I would reply dutifully, the conversation then moving just as dutifully past me and on to other, more interesting things.

Eventually a yellow school bus pulled up and its doors opened. Out stepped Dr. Felch in blue jeans and flannel shirt, a worn leather cowboy hat and work boots. "Good morning, everyone!" he said. "I'm glad to see you're all wearing covered shoes!"

While the bus idled in the background the group exchanged some friendly banter about the cold and a few jokes about the bus and then after Dr. Felch had collected all of our liability waivers he looked at us and said, "Colleagues. Today you're going to learn something extremely valuable. It's called working together as a team. Some people refer to it as *teamwork*, and it is critical in any institution – whether it be a sports team, an institution of higher education, or a working cattle ranch. Today you're going to see teamwork in action. Today you're going to *become* teamwork in action. Because today you're going to learn to work together.... Let's go!"

The six of us followed Dr. Felch into the large bus and made our way to our seats. It was a working school bus, complete with flashing red lights and octagonal stop sign that swung out into oncoming traffic when the door opened. The bus might have seated sixty elementary students comfortably so there was more than enough room for each of us to choose our own bench seat and to lounge comfortably on it – which we did. The Newtowns were in the middle of the bus across the aisle from each other; Raul was sitting halfway between their row and the front; Luke was in the very back and Nan was halfway between them. I too was sitting by myself.

Dr. Felch, standing arms-folded at the head of the aisle next to the driver, watched all of this with some amusement. When everyone had taken up their places throughout the bus, and had settled in comfortably for the ride, he uncrossed his arms and stepped forward.

"Well!" he announced. "You all just *failed* the first test! The first and most important step in teambuilding is to get to know the members of your team. So get up out of your seats and go sit next to somebody you don't know. Go on...!"

Surprised, we looked around at each other. Luke Quittles was first to move, getting up from his seat and going to sit next to Mrs. Newtown. Her husband followed suit and went to the back of the bus to occupy the spot next to Nan Stallings. That left Raul and me to ourselves and so I took the initiative to walk over to his seat and introduce myself.

"Well, Raul," I said. "It looks like you and I are going to be sitting rather closely together…."

Raul motioned gracefully for me to join him, shifting over as far as he could toward the window. The two of us were now sitting shoulder to shoulder on the narrow seat, which would have accommodated a pair of third graders perfectly but now felt suddenly undersized with two full-grown men in it. As Dr. Felch watched us all take our places, Raul and I peered back at him over the green vinyl upholstery in front of us.

Dr. Felch continued:

"Okay. Now that you're seated, I'd like to ask each of you get to know your seat mate. You've already learned a bit about each other yesterday at convocation. But now let's *really* get to know each other. To break the ice for good, I'd like to ask you all to share several important things about yourself. Be thorough with your answers because a bit later we're going to reconvene under a skimpy tree and share them with the group as a whole. So here's your assignment…."

Dr. Felch raised his fist and extended his thumb out to indicate that he was counting and that he would be beginning with the number *one.*

"….First," he said, "please tell your partner what your name is. And by this I don't just mean the simple name you go by. Give us your full name. And tell us its story. How were you given that particular name? Was it your mother's idea? Or your father's? How did they choose it? Does it have any cultural or historical meaning? Any symbolism or hidden significance? Be specific here because there really is no better clue to a person's inner being – to their deepest fears and hopes; to their presumed role in the world, not to mention the expectations that others have for them – than the name they've been given and that they use in their interactions with the world…."

Dr. Felch waited for all of us to write down his words. When everyone had looked back up from their notes he unfurled his forefinger along with his already extended thumb to indicate the number *two*:

"…Second….after you've told us about your name, tell us this: If you weren't at Cow Eye, where *would* you be and what would you be doing?

Would you be a stunt man? A prophet king? A deejay? Would you travel to the Parthenon? Run with the bulls in Pamplona? Visit the Taj Mahal on a weekday? Be creative here – after all, your personal talents are as diverse as your career aspirations. And the world itself is a very big place...."

Some of the faculty in the bus had already turned back to each other and were beginning to answer the questions, but Dr. Felch interrupted them:

"... Wait! That's not all! It's a long bus ride...." And here he extended his third finger, the middle one, along with the other two:

"Next, let's continue the discussion we started yesterday, by telling the world what brought you to Cow Eye Community College – how you came to be seated in this yellow school bus headed back into the heart of a drought for the ages – and how you see yourself contributing to the mission of our college when we get back. You've heard our mission statement first-hand. You've no doubt committed it to memory and have aligned your personal values accordingly. So now that you are embarking on your new life here at the college, tell us how you intend to contribute to our institutional mission ...?"

As Dr. Felch extended his fourth finger, his ring finger, I noticed for the first time that there was a thick wedding ring around it. The ring was both quaint and tight and seemed to suggest that it might never come off – that perhaps for no other reason than this it really might be the final ring he ever wore:

"...*Fourth*, please share at least one embarrassing personal secret that you would rather nobody ever find out about you...."

"Embarrassing secret?!" we objected.

"Yes. Something so personal and humiliating that you would never want anybody else – especially new colleagues you just met – to know about you."

Dr. Felch smiled and quickly extended his final finger, the smallest one, to make the number *five*:

"...And fifth – and take your time with this one, folks – please share an insight that you've learned from personal experience that will help your peers better understand the ins and outs of...."

At that very instant, as if to thwart his utterance, the engine roared up; the driver had put the bus in gear and it was accelerating forward with a loud groan. Dr. Felch tried to shout over the sudden sound but to no avail, and so, as the bus pulled out of the college and onto the dusty road, Dr. Felch grabbed the microphone next to the driver and switched it on.

"Can you hear me? Is this thing on...?"

"We hear you!" Luke shouted. "It's on!"

"....Well, it looks like we're on our way. So, *lastly*....please give us an insight that will help your seat mate better understand the ins and outs, the highs and lows, the unique peculiarities and idiosyncrasies, of...*love*."

Now the bus was rumbling over the railroad tracks and Dr. Felch, who was still standing in the aisle, had to reach out for the seat in front of him to keep from falling.

"Did you get it all?" he said. "I hope you were taking good notes because this is what you'll be expected to share with the larger group. So that by the time we reach our destination each of you will have learned all there is to know about your partner, and he – I'm sorry....he *or she* – will know everything there is to know about you. It's a thirty-five minute bus ride, so you should have plenty of time for the sharing. Ready? Set. GO...!"

Dr. Felch sat down.

Outside the window the scenery had changed again. The heat had returned and now we were moving over a desolate landscape with dead grass and white cattle skeletons and vultures circling overhead. In the aridity of unbridled sun, the air was newly barren, as if the waters that were so plentiful on campus had suddenly evaporated and the transplanted verdure had withered to dust as soon as we crossed the wooden barrier separating the college from the world outside. Raul was sitting closest to the window watching it all pass slowly and listlessly by, a lifeless continuum, like a string of numbers running ahead into infinity.

"It's quite beautiful, isn't it?" he said.

"I hadn't thought to notice," I answered. "But yes."

"There's nothing starker than drought. Or more timeless than the sun."

"Very nicely put, Raul."

"It makes me remember the times when I was a child and I would play outside for hours at a time, never concerned about the melodramas or the melanomas of the world. Life was so much simpler then..."

And here Raul launched into a wistful retelling of his life's story – of how he ended up at Cow Eye Community College – and as he did I listened for answers to the questions that Dr. Felch had assigned us. "When I was born," he said, "my mother named me Raul...."

≈

WHEN RAUL WAS born, he explained, his parents named him Raul. It wasn't his mother's first choice but his father had insisted on it as it was the name of his favorite uncle. In truth, Raul confessed, he hadn't been born within the city of Barcelona itself but in a small fishing village a few miles up the coast. His father had been a fisherman but had been swept away at sea one winter before Raul had even had a chance to know him. Raul's mother took to supporting her young son as a seamstress and one of Raul's earliest memories was of the men of the village stopping by his house to leave their pantaloons for his mother. Because she was so young and beautiful, the men would come with their hats in hand to request her services. Raul was only three or four at the time but he could still remember the smell of the ollada wafting through the house: the potatoes and legumes and salted pork cooking in the heavy pot in the kitchen. One day he came home from playing with his cousins to find a man he'd never seen before standing over his mother in their kitchen. The man claimed that his father owed him a large debt that was unsettled and that he had come to collect. Raul's mother was sobbing on the floor and begging the stranger for a pardon that he refused to give. A month later Raul and his mother were on a ship headed across the Atlantic for South America where they landed and then made their way northward by bus and foot and mule through Central America and Mexico and into California by way of Tenochtitlan, Tayasal and Cholula – but also Veracruz, Chapultepec, and Buena Vista. His mother's cousin had moved to Sonora with her husband a few years back and now in desperation she'd asked for her help in arranging the paperwork for her journey. The route was perilous and, along the way, they'd encountered armed pirates and assiduous missionaries and areas of jungle where malaria was still rampant so that when they finally arrived to the checkpoint at Tijuana and a Customs official waved them across the border into the U.S. it seemed to her that there would be no further destinations in her life. His mother found work cleaning houses and mending clothes in San Diego and Raul was put into the local school system. Astray from his native tongue Raul suffered initially when his English did not blossom as quickly as his teachers would have liked. But math was a different story: coming to him easily and fluently, it became his true passion. With numbers he could find the solitary reward of calculating a formula correctly, the joy of definitive truths in their blackest and whitest forms. Soon Raul was the best student in his class. Eventually, his English caught up to his math – his words even surpassing his numbers – and he was sent to a special magnet school in another part of the city where he studied relentlessly, living with cousins during the school week and returning home only on weekends. By now his mother was working three jobs and although older and more brittle with each passing school year, she continued to make every sacrifice for him. In fact it wasn't California that had been the ultimate destination of her dreams but the Texas she'd seen in movies with its wide open skies and vast expanses of land. She loved the romantic ideal of the cowboys on horses and the cattle roundups and the broad word spoken loud and strong. When she died during his senior year of high school Raul swore that he would visit Texas one day to fulfill her unfulfilled dream and to put her memory to peace.

And here Raul stopped his story.

Outside our bus, the long fence of the Cow Eye Ranch was passing by with its meat-loving propaganda recurring every few hundred yards. LIVE CARNIVOROUSLY, one sign would say and then, a ways down the road: BE BULLISH!

"So have you been there?" I asked. "Have you been to Texas?"

Raul looked out the window at the long fence with its fading slogans.

"Not yet," he said. "It just hasn't worked out for me. Though I did come close once...."

"Just once?"

"Yes, when I was younger."

And here Raul began his story of the time in his life when he'd come ever so close to visiting Texas and fulfilling his mother's dream posthumously.

"I even had the ticket...." he said.

It was while working on his master's degree, and he was being courted by a small private college outside Dallas. The college was recruiting promising statisticians for its new PhD program in Intercultural Statistics and Raul's academic and cultural background was compelling. They were even going to pay for him to visit the campus. It was the final year of his master's program and despite the good fortune of his striking looks, he had yet to fall in love with anything but numbers. In fact, he'd been so focused on his studies that the other things in life – everything from love to hygiene to the affections he might have had for the attentive young women around him – had always been set aside for later, like an irrational number multiplied by itself. This might have lasted forever, if not for the twist of random fortune that caused him to tutor an undergraduate who would show him what love could be. The girl was far from brilliant but had all the personality that he could ever want. "Why go so far away?" she asked. And so he canceled his trip, withdrew his application, turned down the scholarship in order to stay where he was. From that point on, he began to dress with a purpose, learned to play the guitar, spoke with a slightly inflected Catalan accent that suddenly caught the attentions of the opposite sex. And though it would be a life-changing decision for him, he never got over the moral choice he'd made or the opportunity he'd given up. "Love is a strange thing," he said. "My mother loved me for seventeen years. And I cast her memory aside for a girl I'd only known a few weeks."

"I'm sure your mother would understand…."

Raul shook his head.

"She probably would have. And that makes it so much *worse*…."

"What happened with the girl?" I asked.

"We broke up soon after. But not before she showed me what the consequences of love can be."

Here Raul grew pensive.

"You know, we're being asked to give our notions of love. And I've heard a lot of different opinions on the issue. Some say love is a process. Others argue that it's the result. But if you ask me, love is *neither* of these things. Because in fact it is not a thing at all, but its consequence. Without that consequence there can be no such thing as love. So to answer your question – or rather, Dr. Felch's question – love, I would say, is the very consequence of itself."

"And Texas, Raul? Do you have any plans to go there?"

"Of course. Though nothing specific at the moment."

"Why not? You seem very committed to it."

"It's just so far away…."

"From here?"

"Yes. From Cow Eye Junction."

"But, Raul, it would be really easy to do. I mean, when you think how far you've traveled to get *here*. Compared to the distance from Barcelona to this parched pasture, the distance from this pasture to Texas is almost nothing at all."

"I suppose that's true," he said. "And I'm sure I'll get there someday. But until then I'll just wait patiently. Until then I have no choice but to wait patiently."

And then an idea occurred to me. Like a sudden storm surge it washed through my mind and, without thinking, I let it out:

"What about next summer, Raul? We could go! I've always wanted to visit a place like Texas myself. And I have some money saved up. We'll take a road trip, you and me...!"

Raul laughed and offered me his hand. I shook it.

"You're very kind, my friend. I'll keep it in mind."

I blushed at my own enthusiasm. Then I said:

"And your embarrassing secret, Raul? Would you care to share that with me?"

"My secret?" he said. "Well, I do have a secret. But I would appreciate you not sharing it with the group."

"Sure," I said. "What is it?"

"I'm not really from Barcelona."

"You're not?"

"No, I'm not. And I never crossed the Atlantic. Truthfully, I've never been to Venice or Rio. The rest of my narrative is true, though. My mother did work three jobs to put me through college. And we did cross the border to get here. And she did die from her third job. And I do still regret never making it to Texas."

"But if you're not from Barcelona, then what culture *do* you come from?"

Raul paused to look out the window wistfully. Then he said:

"Nowadays mine is a culture of assessment."

"I see. So why the story then? Why the need for mythology?"

"Well, Charlie, I doubt that I'm the only one. You know what they say: in this world there are *lies*, *bald lies*, and *autobiography*."

"Not statistics?"

"Well, those too perhaps."

I laughed.

"You're probably right," I said. "Thanks for sharing. And in any case, don't worry – your secret is safe with me."

Now we were passing a scorched field with a beat-up pasture seeder lying abandoned on a hill. The sky was wide open and the heat in the bus was growing with each mile traveled. A few seats behind us Luke and Ethel were talking good-naturedly. And further behind them, on the other side of the aisle, Stan Newton and Nan Stallings looked to be exchanging important insights of their own. At the front of it all, Dr. Felch was sitting at the head of the aisle with a lit cigarette – his tenth – and laughing with the bus driver, an old friend from high school, seemingly secure in the knowledge that his ice-breaking activity was succeeding behind him.

"So what about you, Charlie?" Raul asked. "It seems I've told you both of my life stories. But what about yours? How did you get your name? And which place in the world would you most like to visit? What would you otherwise be doing if you weren't a Special Projects Coordinator at our struggling community college? And how did you end up here, in this very hot school bus, passing the fading fences of the Cow Eye Ranch?"

As I dutifully told the story of how I'd come so far, so quickly – from salutatorian of my high school class to down-on-his-luck habitual divorcee and father of nothing – Raul listened intently. "You know," I said, "if you had told me when I was younger that I'd end up working at a rural community college, I would have thought you were crazy. It would've been so far from what I'd ever imagined for myself. As if you'd told me that I would someday be a fisherman in Barcelona...."

"Why is that so surprising? What *did* you want to be?"

"Well, when I was in elementary school I wanted to be a fire fighter. And when I was in middle school I wanted to be an advertising executive. By high school my goals had changed and I wanted to be a poet, though that quickly changed in college when I realized that the money simply wasn't there and that I should be a philosopher instead. By graduate school, I was already leaning toward a career in educational administration. It's funny how we sort of ratchet down our expectations with the degrees we acquire...."

"So where would you be if you weren't *here*? And what would you be doing?"

"Well, I guess I would be someplace where I could stand slightly apart from a large crowd. A security guard perhaps. Or an usher at a theater.

But instead, here I am. You know, after the passing of so much time and space, here I am on this crowded seat with you, Raul. Not that I'm complaining, of course...."

"Of course...."

"....Actually, it all seems clear and straightforward and perfectly sensible to me now. In fact, just the other day I was remembering some of the people who, in small and unpredictable ways – and probably unbeknownst to them – have played a role in bringing me to where I am. The kindly elementary teacher. The friend from college who let me take her from innocence to womanhood. The three passersby who picked me up from the bloody asphalt...."

"Bloody asphalt?"

"Yes, bloody asphalt."

"Is that your most embarrassing secret?"

"No, but it's one of my most *painful*! And as I look back on all of these things I sometimes think to myself, wow, wouldn't it be great if I could retrace my steps. To go back to that asphalt. And to that classroom. To revisit those people along the way. To just connect with them for a few moments to let them know how they've impacted my life. To shake their hands and say, Hey, thank you for picking me up off the asphalt. And for steering me toward educational administration. And for letting me caress the contours of your innocence with my trembling hands. As fleeting as your presence in my life was – as trivial as it seemed at the time – it turned out to be pivotal and everlasting in the end...."

Raul nodded as if he understood. I continued:

"But I know it's impossible. Because they're traveling their own paths. Like a million different arrows all being shot at each other...."

Again Raul nodded.

"Crossing each other in flight?"

"Right. And continuing on their solitary way."

"It's a daring image."

"I am one of those arrows, Raul."

"And so am I," he said. Then he pulled his arm back into an imaginary bow aimed right at Texas.

"So, Charlie," he said after letting his arrow fly, "what more can you tell me about yourself...?"

Over the next few minutes Raul asked the questions we'd been assigned and I answered them one by one. When he asked about my reason for coming to Cow Eye I told him about my dingy apartment and the cup of tepid urine. And when he asked about my contributions to the college, I answered that Dr. Felch had made it very clear what my duties were to be: that I would be leading the accreditation process, helping organize the Christmas party, and doing my best to find a verb worthy of bringing our divided faculty together – and that if I could find a way to do these three things I would be saving the college from the precipice of institutional ruin. Then I told him that, on top of my professional assignments, I'd also developed my own personal objectives to guide me through the year.

At this Raul perked up.

"You have *personal* objectives?" he said. "That's admirable. Can I hear them?"

And so I told him that during the upcoming year I would be striving to find the moisture in all things, and to love the unloved, and to experience both day and night.

"And what about becoming something entirely?"

"Yes of course. That too."

"Well, those are noble aims," he said. "But are they achievable? Can you measure them?"

"Measure?"

"With numbers."

"I'm not sure. I've never thought about it that way."

"These sound like lofty goals. But what are the *outcomes* for them? For example, you say that you want to 'become something entirely.' But what does that mean exactly? Can you give me an example that shows a tangible outcome of that particular goal?"

I thought for a second or two over Raul's question. Then I said:

"Yes I can. Just yesterday I shaved my mustache. Before that I'd always let it grow out in fits and spurts, but it never really acquired the status of a respectable mustache. Bessie brought this to my attention yesterday before convocation and you know what – she's right! So I shaved it off completely. Yesterday I had a mustache but now I no longer do! So the outcome is a one hundred percent reduction in my mustache."

"Well, I suppose that's a start. But remember that your broad goals should have supporting objectives, and each of your supporting objectives should have tangible, measurable outcomes. And all of it should align with your overall reason for living, your purpose in this world, your own personal *mission statement,* if you will. In essence, people are no different from institutions because, if you get right down to it, Charlie, a human being is nothing more than a community college without the pelicans. In the case of a rural college like ours, the alignment looks something like this...." And here Raul took out a pen and a note pad from his shirt pocket and drew the following chart:

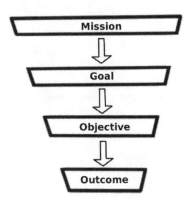

"Now, notice that it all comes down from the mission statement. And this means that everything the college does needs to trickle down from that statement. And I do mean *everything.* The developmental math class. The men cutting the grass. The indoor shooting range. The bull mounting the heifer. All of it!"

And here, again, he took to his diagram and filled it in with specifics from our college to demonstrate how even the simplest things we see on campus are a product of this alignment:

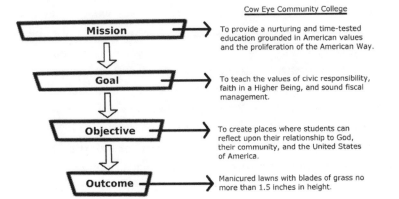

Cow Eye Community College

Mission → To provide a nurturing and time-tested education grounded in American values and the proliferation of the American Way.

Goal → To teach the values of civic responsibility, faith in a Higher Being, and sound fiscal management.

Objective → To create places where students can reflect upon their relationship to God, their community, and the United States of America.

Outcome → Manicured lawns with blades of grass no more than 1.5 inches in height.

"Or represented differently, it might look like this...."

"Of course you know better than me how this works, Charlie. After all, you're the one who'll be leading us through the accreditation process. But what you may not have considered is the value of this system for *individuals.* Each of us has our mission statement supported by broad goals, which are in turn supported by specific objectives and measurable outcomes. Of course, community colleges are on the cutting edge of this. But as human beings, we also have these statements buried very deep within us. And we tend to follow them intuitively, if haphazardly. But the problem is we almost never articulate them, which creates confusion and causes mission drift. So for example, in your case, it might look as follows...."

And here Raul took out a red pen and began writing alongside the original diagram of the College's mission that he'd already drawn. This took several minutes and while he scribbled I gazed past his profile out the window at the passing scenery. Beyond the window the sun was glaring and reflecting in heat waves off the black road. Tumbleweeds rested along the side of the highway waiting for a gust of wind, any wind, to blow them further along. An abandoned shack flashed by and then a lifeless windmill; strangely, not a single car or truck passed us going the opposite direction. Finally Raul tapped his diagram with his pen. "Okay, here it is, Charlie...." he said. "Here's a diagram of your purpose in life presented in a format that might help you see more clearly where there's room for continuous improvement...."

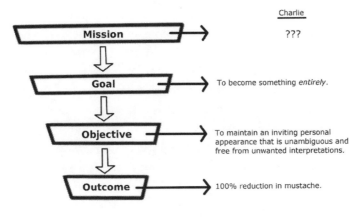

"Or, represented differently...."

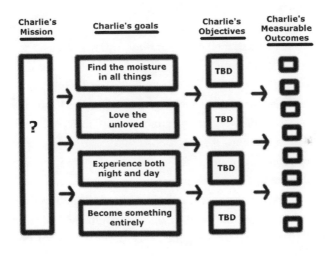

"Now as you look at these, you can see that you're strong in Goals but weak in Objectives and Outcomes. But most importantly, you really need to do some soul-searching to ask yourself: What is my Mission? Sure you have the goals, Charlie. And the objectives can come from there. But where is the overarching mission statement that gives meaning and unity to it all? What is the ultimate reason you want to find the moisture in things, to love the unloved, and to experience both day and night?"

"You mean, why do I want to become something *entirely*?"

"Right. Aside from the fact that these things sound nice and look good on paper? Until you find that ultimate mission statement, you're going to be simply floundering at the goals and objectives levels without ever knowing whether you're getting any closer to achieving your ultimate mission in life. And that, in turn, will keep you from moving efficiently toward specific measurable outcomes."

Raul ripped the page from his notebook.

"You can keep this...." He handed me the paper and I took it, folding the page into a small square and tucking it into my shirt pocket.

"Thanks," I said. "But I really don't know about all this, Raul. I mean, this seems awfully functional. Don't you think there's any room left in life for serendipity? Shouldn't we as human beings aspire toward *imperfection* rather than perfection? Inefficiency rather than efficiency? Flawed curricula vitae rather than the ones that are polished beyond recognition? I guess what I'm trying to say, Raul, is that it all seems purposeful and correct, yes....but also sort of *false*. For example, you say that a human being is nothing more than a community college without the pelicans. But doesn't this deny us the wonder that comes from being human? Isn't a community college a contrived place with aligned mission, goals, and objectives where the pelicans and diverse flora have been introduced according to plan.... whereas the human soul is the place with the overgrown weeds where the bystander still imagines Dahurian larch and dreams quixotically of pelicans?"

Raul thought a few moments. Then he said, "Perhaps. But you are clearly searching for something. So let me ask you this. You've lamented that you are a lot of different things but none of them entirely. So, what does that mean exactly? What are you really trying to get at?"

"It's hard to say, Raul. It's just. Well, take any two opposites, and I'll be something in the middle. I'm practical among idealistic people, but idealistic among pragmatic people. I'm masculine compared to feminine men but feminine compared to muscular ones. To the agnostics I seem religious, but to the religious I am merely spiritual. Culturally, I straddle. Philosophically, I meander. And professionally and personally, I lack the commitment to stay focused. I have no drive, no determination, no resolve. And that explains why I bounce from one thing to the next. Like a breeding bull in a pasture full of heifers."

"And this is bad?"

"Well, it's fine for the bull – and maybe even for the heifers. But it's bad too in a way. I guess, it's *both*."

"There you go again...."

"Exactly! You see, that's how it is with me. If I'm tall among short people and short among tall people, then what I really am is neither short nor tall. And in this way I'm neither practical nor idealistic. Neither authentic nor false. Neither an enemy nor a friend. To the West I am East, while to the East I am West. And all of this means that I am not really anything at all. I am not any*where* at all. And this is why I have such a longing to become something in its entirety. What I wouldn't give to be either tall *or* short! To be logical or intuitive. To be infinitely complex or infinitely simple. To be able to say, without hesitation, that I am this, or I am that. And that I am this or that *entirely*. Purity, Raul, that's what I'm seeking for myself! Purity!"

Raul nodded and moved to speak. But I was already consumed with the question at hand. And so I continued:

"For example, let's take yourself, Raul. There are things that you simply *are*, right? Things that you are without having to think too much about them. Nobody would argue that you're not tall, or that you're not logical, or elegant, or caucasoid, or attractive to members of the opposite sex..."

"I'm not a caucasoid!" he said.

"But you are attractive to members of the opposite sex?"

"I'm gorgeous, yes."

"Right. And these are good things, Raul. They allow you to move forward with purpose. Your life decisions are borne out by data. Your processes are replicable. You've been able to align your goals, objectives, and measurable outcomes to support your mission for being on this earth. It all works in harmony, like the ballads you sing. I guess what I'm saying, Raul, is that your life has purpose and efficiency. It is proper and data-driven. If you were aspiring to accreditation, you would no doubt receive glowing commendations from our accreditors along with a full six-year reaffirmation. But I am…well.….*different.*…."

Raul had moved to ask another question but we were already turning off the highway onto a dusty dirt road. The bus stopped in front of a large sign welcoming us to the Cow Eye Ranch (*"Where Cow's Meat"* it said) and sat idling while Dr. Felch stood up and grabbed the microphone. He flicked a switch. The speakers squeaked with feedback.

"Is this thing on?" he said. "Can you hear me?"

"We hear you!" we all yelled.

"Good. If you look out your windows you will see that we are now entering the Cow Eye Ranch. For those of you who are not familiar with the unique history of Cow Eye Junction, you will be interested to know that the Cow Eye Ranch was the original cattle ranch around which the town of Cow Eye Junction grew up. The ranch was created at the beginning of the last century and in its heyday it fed half the country. And by this, of course, we mean the half of the country that eats meat…."

The bus had now started to move forward and was crawling through the gate and into the vast territory of the ranch. On either side of our bus huge corrals and fences sprang up and within some of these there were collections of cattle and in others there were not. As we drove slowly past the orange and black herds, the cattle would lift their heads to regard us with vague bovine indifference, then return to the greater immediacy of their grazing.

At last our bus reached an area where a series of corrals and gates were arranged in a complex maze. It was an old part of the ranch that wasn't used so much anymore – Dr. Felch had made arrangements with his ex-wife to use it for the day – and it offered little in the way of accommodations: a single water faucet and a beat-up picnic table under a skimpy and shadeless tree. "Okay," Dr. Felch said. "We're here. Please watch your step as you exit the bus. It's a bit of a drop…" Dr. Felch thanked the driver, his friend from high school, and agreed on the time for lunch. The doors of the bus opened and we filed out.

⤳

AFTER THE LONG bus ride, our legs had cramped and it felt good to step outside – even though the sky was still cloudless and the sun shone down on us without relent. In the dead air, Luke Quittles was sweating profusely. Ethel Newtown was using her copy of the Cow Eye Express, the local classifieds section, to fan herself. Even Raul, who was usually a monument to physical grace and elegance, seemed slightly unnerved by the heat.

"Let's sit over here...." Dr. Felch said and led us to a picnic table under the skimpy tree whose sparse shade could not even hold back a tenth of the sun. The benches on either side of the table were weathered and splintered and they creaked as we took our turns positioning ourselves on them. "Let's wait a few more minutes," said Dr. Felch. "Professor Smithcoate should be here any time now."

As we waited for Will Smithcoate, chair of the New Faculty Orientation committee, the seven of us traded impressions of the bus ride and of the heat. Nan said that it was so hot she thought she would melt. And Luke joked that the seats of the bus were not meant for two adults but that he and Ethel had done their best under the circumstances and that if implicated in any subsequent paternity test he would do the right thing and pay for the abortion, though he would also forward it on to the college as a reimbursable work expense. Dr. Felch laughed at all this and said, "That's the price of teambuilding, my friends!" Then he said, "Well, it looks like Will's going to be later than I thought. Let's go ahead and get started."

Sitting on an overturned bucket at the head of the picnic table Dr. Felch repeated that we would each be presenting our partner's responses to the questions he'd assigned us on the bus. As he spoke, the sun continued to blaze down onto the tops of our heads, the breeze was nowhere to be found, and the six of us fidgeted and shifted in the heat.

"So remember the questions you need to answer," Dr. Felch reminded us. "Your partner's name; how they ended up at Cow Eye; what their contribution to our college will be; what they would be doing if they weren't here; their favorite humiliating secret; and, of course, something insightful about love. And to show you how this is done, and to underscore my democratic style of leadership, I will first give you my own answers to the questions....that is to say, I'll introduce *myself*...."

Dr. Felch took out a cigarette – his eleventh – and lit it.

"....So, my name is William Arthur Felch, a name chosen by my parents thirteen years before I was born. My parents never explained why they wanted this particular name so much, though my mother once told me that even if I'd been born a girl they would've given me the exact same name. Obviously, at Cow Eye I've played an important role in the college's emergence over the years, but now I see my immediate goal as leaving the college in good hands to the next person who comes in. I'm hoping it will be someone from Cow Eye, but I understand that it probably won't be. If I weren't here I would be visiting my children and their families in the many places around the country where they now live. My embarrassing personal secret is that I've been the subject of several personal lawsuits that, thankfully, have been settled out of court. And as to love…."

Dr. Felch took a long drag of his cigarette, then blew out the smoke.

"….As to love, well, at my age I think I'm more qualified to speak of what love *was* than what it *is*. You see, I've been married five times and each time the woman I married was thirty years old. A strange coincidence, I know, but it's also served as a control of sorts amid a host of otherwise complex variables. The first marriage, when I was twenty and she was thirty, was *amazing*! It was all flesh and hope and raw unadulterated nerves; much of what I know of life came from this amazing older woman. The second marriage, when I was thirty and she was also thirty, was democratic and realistic – a true partnership of equals. My third marriage, when I had just turned forty and she was barely thirty, was organic and relaxed and perfectly pragmatic; she and I were in our second and third marriages, respectively, and we didn't even need a ceremony – just a signing of prenuptials. The fourth, when I was fifty and she was thirty, was *reinvigorating*! Once again I felt the raw nerves of youthful desire and for the first time in many years I found myself using ellipses and exclamation marks rather than mundane commas and full stops! Unfortunately this one ended in exclamation marks for all the wrong reasons, and for that reason I would rather not talk about it. And then there was my fifth marriage, the current one, when I was already pushing sixty and she was only thirty, and it was – how should I put this? – a *victory over life*! All of these marriages were great in their own way. And so I can say that love was all I could have ever hoped it to be: amazing and comforting and democratic and reinvigorating and, ultimately, a victory over life. That's what love *was*. What it is nowadays I have no idea….."

Dr. Felch flicked the long ash that had accumulated on the tip of his cigarette.

"So anyway that's a little about me."

"Thank you for sharing, Dr. Felch."

"You're welcome. Now it's your turn. Who wants to go first...?"

"Well, I'll go first," said Luke and he pointed at Ethel Newtown whose pending paternity suit had so unsettled him. "This is Ethel Newtown. Ethel was named after a character in her mother's favorite television sitcom. She sees her role at the college as using her journalism classes to help students think and analyze the world critically. If she weren't here at Cow Eye she imagines that she would be living in upstate New York and working as a fashion designer. And her embarrassing personal secret is that....." Luke paused, looking over at Ethel as if seeking her approval to continue. Ethel giggled her consent to proceed. And so he said, "....Ethel's embarrassing personal secret is that she has never achieved orgasm with Stan."

"What!" said Stan. "That's not true! Ethel, tell them it's not true!"

Ethel giggled again. Stan shook his head.

Luke continued:

"....As to an insight into love, Ethel feels that love is a thing that has a beginning, a middle, and an end."

"Not with *Stan*, it doesn't!" said Nan. "With him it just has a beginning and a *middle*...!"

Everyone laughed.

"Very funny," said Stan, though he was laughing as well.

"...So Ethel believes that love should have all three of these things because without a beginning, love is not love; it is a fragment. Without a middle, it is not love either, just a byline. And without an end, even if it truly had been love at some point, it will no longer be love of the same kind but something else entirely. Without an end it will be a run-on sentence going on and on into oblivion...."

When Luke had finished introducing Ethel's notions of love, Dr. Felch thanked him and Ethel took her turn introducing Luke in return.

"Well, I'll be introducing Luke Quittles," said Ethel. "Luke's given name comes from biblical sources as both of his parents are ecumenical Baptists. Luke the Evangelist was chosen because he, the *biblical* Luke, was the patron saint of artists, butchers, and unmarried men – and Luke's parents were hopeful that he, the *culinary* Luke, would one day be all of these; unfortunately, when it became clear at an early age that Luke had other aspirations, they disowned him completely. Luke says that if he weren't at Cow Eye, he would be working as a celebrity chef somewhere, but that Fate and a well-concealed – and yes, *painfully embarrassing* – drinking habit have conspired to bring him here to the college during its time of drought and desolation. He's thankful for the second chance and sees his mission as helping students unlock their hidden potential not only in the kitchen but in every aspect of their existence. He believes that love is like an enchilada, with a simple veneer on the outside but with an infinite variety of intermingling flavors and textures at its core."

"And a personal secret?" we prompted.

"As if the drinking habit weren't enough," said Ethel, "Luke also has a weakness for violent pornography and under-aged hookers."

"Oh," said Dr. Felch. "Well, that definitely counts. Okay, who's next?"

"I'll go," said Nan, who cleared her throat and then continued: "As you all know, my partner is Stanley Isaac Newtown, or, as he himself noted, and not without pride, *SIN* for short. Stan got his first name because his parents were raised in a different social context and thought it sounded exotic. His *middle* name was chosen because they assumed the subtle reference to Isaac Newton would be a good thing. Stan says that if he weren't here at Cow Eye he would be living in Vermont and working as a consultant in survivalist bunker construction; but that as long as he's here, he might as well contribute to the college's mission by encouraging his students to explore the great diversity of the world's many cultures so that they may obtain a better appreciation of the virtues of doing things the American way. His embarrassing personal secret is that he once falsified research that was published by several academic journals and, ironically, it is this research that has since become the cornerstone on which his entire career is based. Being that it's all false, he worries that it will one day come to light and that he will be ruined as a scholar and as a man."

"Thank you, Nan," said Dr. Felch. "And Stan's insights on love? Did he reveal any of those?"

"Oh yes, I almost forgot. Stan believes that love is fleeting and deceptive but that it must be pursued at all cost. He maintains that it is not unlike a lost civilization that reveals itself only after years and years of blind faith in its existence and of course meticulous excavation efforts. He admits that although he has unearthed several lost civilizations in his time, he has never been able to reveal the secrets of true love. That is, he has never actually been in love."

A gasp went up around the table.

"You mean except for Ethel…?"

"Um, no.....*including* Ethel." Nan shrugged her shoulders as if to apologize for Stan's insensitivity.

Here a hush fell over the group. Amid the awkwardness, nobody around the table knew quite what to say. Finally it was Raul who put his arm around Mrs. Newtown and gave her a comforting squeeze.

"Don't worry, Ethel," he said. "There is no shortage of conspiracy theorists in this world."

"Alright!" said Dr. Felch trying to quickly redirect the discussion. "Who's up now? Nan just finished introducing Stan. So Stan, you heartless bastard, it looks like you're up next....."

At this, Stan checked his handwritten notes and pursed his lips to speak. But before he could begin his introduction, a low rumbling that had been growing in the distance became suddenly very loud and we all looked up to see a light blue Oldsmobile Starfire trailing a line of dust behind it. The car was huge and shiny and very polished and when it had pulled up next to the skimpy tree and come to a dead stop and the engine had been shut off, the door opened and out stepped Will Smithcoate, long-tenured history professor and recently appointed chair of the New Faculty Orientation committee. Will was dressed exactly as he had been at the opening convocation in a dapper gray suit and red bow tie and fedora hat. Only now he also sported a red rose pinned to his lapel and a cigar still in its wrapping which jutted out of his breast pocket.

"I'm very sorry to be late," he said when he had made his way over to the wooden picnic table. One by one he walked around the table to introduce himself to his new peers, calmly removing his fedora with his left hand and using the other to either shake the hands of the men around the table or to take the women's fingers and kiss their knuckles with a gracious and gentlemanly bow. As he passed from one person to the next, the strong smell of alcohol on his breath trailed after him like the cloud of dust behind his Oldsmobile. "I tried to get here sooner," he explained. "But the traffic was just terrible!"

Dr. Felch shook his head at Will's excuse. "Have a seat, Will. We're almost finished with our ice-breaker. We'll be ready for your teambuilding activity in a few minutes."

"Sure thing," said Will, brushing off his slacks before climbing over the bench to take his seat next to Raul, who offered his hand to help him into his place.

Meanwhile, Stan Newtown, who had been standing and waiting the entire time, continued to wait while Will took out his handkerchief to wipe the sweat from his temple and then, to everyone's surprise, remove a shiny metal flask from which he took a deep and committed swig. "I don't go anywhere without my *canteen!*" said Will and Dr. Felch again shook his head. And only when all the sweat had been wiped away and the cap to Will's flask had been twisted back into place did Stan begin his introduction of Nan. In a chipper voice he proclaimed: "Well, ladies and gentlemen, my seatmate was Nancy Stallings! But she prefers to be called Nan....."

Listening to Stan, I kept one eye loosely focused on him and the other intently on Will, who had put his "canteen" back into his coat pocket and was now peeling the wrapping from his cigar; the crinkling sound was almost as loud as Stan himself, who by now was saying:

"....And so *that*'s the long and amazing story of how Nan got her name....!"

People were smiling in obvious delight at Stan's story. Meanwhile, to the side of me, Will had taken his cigar out of its wrapping and was admiring it.

"....Now to answer Dr. Felch's other questions," Stan continued, "Nan believes that it is her mission at the college to ensure that every student has an understanding of the legal system that governs our existence. She feels that without that, we are no better than the cows being led from one stall to the other on a cruel and brutal march to slaughter. If not serving as the political science instructor at Cow Eye, she believes that she would be serving as a political science instructor at a different community college in an equally out-of-the-way setting some place in Kentucky or Tennessee. Her definition of love corresponds precisely to that found in Merriam-Webster, and when prodded repeatedly for an embarrassing secret – believe me, guys, I tried! – she finally stated that she would not reveal such personal information unless subpoenaed."

"Fair enough," said Dr. Felch. "Spoken as a true lawyer. So Charlie and Raul....you're up. Who wants to go first?"

"Shall I?" I asked.

"By all means," Raul answered.

And so I began.

"Wow," I said. "Where to begin? Raul and I just had a great talk on the bus and I feel like I've known him since, well, forever. Raul was named for his father's uncle. He came to Cow Eye by crossing the Atlantic Ocean in winter. He feels that love is not itself, but rather its own consequence, and he has implied that he would give up all of his prestigious awards if only he could travel to Texas for a day. Hey Raul, you know, I think I forgot to ask what your contribution to Cow Eye will be. But judging by our conversation I think it's safe to say that you will be helpful in aligning our Goals, Objectives, and overarching Mission – and ensuring that it all leads to measurable outcomes. These, of course, are worthy goals for our college – or are they *objectives?* – and I for one will be calling on you frequently as we make our way through accreditation. Finally, I would like to assure each of you individually – and all of you as a whole – that Raul does not have any embarrassing personal secrets. This is because he is absolutely transparent and accountable – what you see is what you get – and it is perhaps this feature more than any other – more even than his incredible good looks or his way of singing ballads with a throaty Barcelonan accent – that makes him such a favorite of the ladies and the envy of all intact men."

"Well thank you, Charlie," Dr. Felch said. "I'm glad the two of you will be working together on accreditation. Remember, the fate of our college is now in your hands. I have faith in you both. So Raul….can you introduce Charlie, please?"

Raul took out the notebook in which he had been taking notes during our discussion on the bus. Checking it carefully, he said:

"As you all know by now, this handsome young man sitting next to me is Charlie."

"Handsome?" Nan objected.

"Young?!" said Ethel.

"Well, young and handsome enough," Raul said. "Charlie received his first name because *Charles* would have seemed too formal and effeminate and *Chuck* would have given the impression that he is far more masculine than he actually is. You see, Charlie is somewhere in the middle. Professionally, he has stated that his contribution to Cow Eye will be to save us from institutional ruin, and that if he weren't here he would be back in his dingy apartment examining his cup of tepid urine for any traces of moisture. Charlie has many different views on love, many of them contradictory, and he has stated that he aims to love the things in this world that are not otherwise loved. For example, Ohio. He admits that his most embarrassing personal secret – the secret that he would not want any of us to learn under any circumstances – is that he has two competing phobia that he wrestles with on a daily basis: on the one hand, an inexplicable aversion to other human beings that borders on neurosis and, on the other hand, a corresponding fear of being alone. And that he has sought treatment for both though this has inevitably led to a bettering of one condition at the expense of the other."

Raul stopped. Then he said, "Did I leave anything out, Charlie?"

"No, Raul, you pretty much got it all...."

"So that's Charlie in a nutshell."

"Great. Thank you both for sharing," said Dr. Felch. Turning to the group, he added: "....And thanks to *all* of you for taking the time to share a little bit about yourselves with your peers. I think we're done with the first part of our day's activities. Anything you want to add, Will?"

"Not at the moment. Just that this is one hell of a cigar....!"

Everyone laughed. Then someone noted that since the traffic had caused him to come late, maybe Will should also introduce himself to the group:

"What about you, Mr. Smithcoate? We've all shared our innermost thoughts and secrets. But what about yours? Can you answer these ice-breaking questions so we can learn about you too?"

Will seemed surprised at the sudden attention being thrown his way but cleared his throat to answer. Then he said:

"Well, what is there to say? My name is about as American as you could ever want it to be. My father was William Smithcoate and my grandfather was Simon Smithcoate and if you trace the name back through the generations you will eventually end up at Jefferson Smithcoate who brought his family over on the Mayflower. In the Smithcoate family there are signatories to the Declaration of Independence and advisors to the Louisiana Purchase and generals on both sides of the Civil War. Smithcoates have been nation builders and pioneers and Indian killers and prohibitionists. One of my ancestors was instrumental in articulating the manifest destiny of our country and another, his own son, was active in championing the rights of our nation's indigenous people. A distant relative was a leading abolitionist of his time while another was the most ardent of slave owners. There have been Smithcoates in every state of the Union and on every side of every philosophical debate and political conflict. In short, the history of our county is a history of the Smithcoate family itself."

Will stopped to light his cigar. The smell was aromatic and sweet and even the non-smokers at the table – and we were now an evolving majority – appreciated the scent. Will took a long drag of the cigar, paused to savor the taste, then blew out the smoke. Then he continued:

"With all this as an inheritance you might assume that history would be a natural field of inquiry for me. However, you would be wrong. In truth I've always wanted to be a romantic poet. Now this is not to say that history does not have its perks. But how can you compare it to the freedom that comes from writing something that will exist forever? Wouldn't you all agree?"

"We would, Mr. Smithcoate, of course we would. But Mr. Smithcoate, doesn't history also last forever?"

Will laughed.

"Please call me Will."

"But *Will*, don't you think history also lasts forever?"

"You would think so. Except that there is probably nothing that bends more to the whim of the present than our past. Just think of all the reevaluations that have happened over the years. Slaves used to be thought of as unworthy of their own narratives and history. And now they're no longer slaves, but free men with a rich literature of their own. (Hell, I even have a negroid in one of my classes and I'll be damned if he doesn't sit in the *front* row!) And women! Women used to be daughters and sisters and wives and mothers. But now they're considered *individuals* just like you and me. Although, of course, my own wife would have preferred the former to the latter. She was an incredible lady...."

"*Was?*"

"She passed away two years ago. We were married for thirty-eight years."

"I'm sorry, Will."

"Oh don't be sorry. We had some amazing sex in our time!"

Everyone laughed.

"And it's not like I won't be seeing her again. But as I was saying there are things that last forever and things that merely come and go. History comes and goes. Poetry lasts forever. Technology comes and goes. Love lasts forever. Marriage comes and goes....hell, *life* itself comes and goes. But your wife's memory, well, that lasts forever..."

"And journalism?" Ethel asked. "Does journalism last forever?"

"No, Ethel, it merely comes and goes."

"And politics?" asked Nan.

"Comes and goes, of course."

"And archaeology? And data analysis? And special projects coordination?"

"It all comes and goes!" declared Will. "All of it! The only things that are worth a damn in this world are those that are timeless and eternal. The things that can't be taught but that come down through the generations as acquired wisdom and intuition. In other words, everything we do at the college is temporal. It's all fleeting and false. It's a waste of time and resources and institutional...."

"Moving on, Will!" said Dr. Felch.

"....Right. Anyway, I became a History teacher because, well, that was what we did back then. And I still use the same lecture notes I used when I first started thirty years ago. Everyone always tells me, Hey Will, why don't you do something different! Mix it up a bit? Adapt your lesson plans to your students. After all, the world has changed in the last thirty years and you should change with it! And my response is, Why the hell should I? Where's the eternity in that? After all, shouldn't we aspire to appreciate the things that last forever above the things that come and go? Shouldn't we aspire to leave at least one lasting legacy uncompromised by current fashion?"

Then Nan said:

"Mr. Smithcoate, tell us about love, please! Give us some insights into the nature of love itself. It is something we've all been thinking about over the last few hours but have not yet arrived at a conclusive definition. Can you help us?"

"Well," said Will, "love is a thing that is best left unspoken. For the more you try to explain it the more elusive it becomes. It is like the black scar on your retina that scurries away from you when you try to look at it directly. To see it you must look slightly away from it – for only then can it come into clearer focus. So too must love be approached indirectly. And so if you asked me what love is I would say that love is not what it is, but what it *would be*. Don't blather of love itself, the true philosopher will say, but tell me what love cannot be but would be if it weren't what it *is*. And so, I would tell you that if love were a bird it would be a pelican. If love were an ocean of the world it would be the Atlantic in winter. If love were a state of the Union it would be Indiana or Mississippi....or maybe even Illinois. (But never, ever, *ever* Alabama!) If love were a tree it would be a banyan. If love were a fish it would be a carp. And if love were an institution of higher learning – if its yearnings and heavenly bliss could be made into a campus of fir and sycamore – it would surely be a regionally accredited community college. For love requires open doors and open hearts. It demands hope and persistence. And of course self-sacrifice. It encourages dexterity in even the most rigid and logical among us as well as an ability to overcome the rugged terrain of life's unpredictable path. If love were an abstract math concept, it would be transcendental numbers. Or primality. If love were an animal it would be a ruminant. If love were an academic subject it would be philosophy. If love were the relic of a dying literary genre, it would be a rhyming poem. Or a very long novel. If love were a punctuation mark it would be ellipses. If love were a method of transportation. If love were a fountain. If love were a V-8 engine. If love were. If love. If...."

Will's voice trailed away and here we realized that he had dozed off, his head now resting like a baby's in the crook of his arm. He was snoring. Seeing this, Raul took the cigar from Will's fingers and crushed it out on the side of the table. Nan brushed a lock of gray hair from his face and Ethel gently placed his fedora over the brim of his nose to shield his eyes from the sun.

"Well," said Dr. Felch, "It looks like I'll be conducting the teambuilding exercise for you after all. This wasn't how we drew it up. But leadership requires resilience. Follow me...." Each of us stood up from the bench and followed Dr. Felch over to the edge of a corral. Behind us, Will Smithcoate was left to his snoring, his face still buried in the crook of his arm, on the picnic table. "Over here..." Dr. Felch said and led us to the aluminum fence that enclosed the large corral where a single black calf stood forlornly at the far end. The calf was picking at some hay that had been placed for him in a feeding trough in the corner. "And now it's time," he said, "for us to learn what teamwork *really* means..."

And with that he opened the aluminum gate for us to enter. Stepping into the corral we listened as a weak and woeful sound arose from the small calf on the other side.

{ }

The opposite of 'love' — now more than ever — is 'efficiency.'
Efficiency causes the ability to achieve a greater goal by
expending the same amount of effort, or to achieve the same
goal by investing less effort. Neither of these are worthy goals.
Because, in fact, the only things that are worthy are those that
cannot be streamlined. Love cannot be streamlined. Nor can
the learning of meaningful things be made more efficient; for
if it could it would no longer be truly meaningful. Love is
that which takes its own time, an eternal and unchanging
time. And if a thing has been made to happen more quickly
or efficiently, then that thing was not love to begin with.
Thankfully, the community college understands this…

{ }

WHEN DR. FELCH had closed the gate to the corral, he turned to us and
said:

"Now I know what you're thinking. Many of you have worked at other
community colleges around the world and you're thinking to yourself, Oh
no, here we go again. Not another *teambuilding* activity to make our work
processes more efficient! Be honest — that's what you're thinking, right?
Well, I don't blame you! Because if you're like the majority of faculty and
staff at your typical community college around the world you've no doubt
undergone so many teambuilding activities during your tenure that you
can't even name them all. At Cow Eye, we've tried every one: and this
includes the one with the yardstick and the one with the tennis balls
and the hula hoops and the one where you and a small team of fellow
faculty and staff carry an egg across great distances on a spatula. In fact
I bet you've done *all* of these too. And I also bet that at the end of the
day, when each of these activities was finished and the paid facilitator
had driven off with her check, you returned to your lonely office with no
clearer understanding of teamwork than you'd possessed before grabbing
the spatula. But why? Well that's because there's no practical or cultural
relevance to all that nonsense. What does a hula hoop have to do with

the specific community you serve? And who cares if you've succeeded in carrying an egg across a field? At the end of the day what have you really accomplished? Have you accomplished anything for the betterment of humanity and world civilization? Are you any closer to *Loving the Culture of Cow Eye*? Of course not! So why then do we spend so much time with these hula hoops and these tennis balls and these spatulas...?"

At the third mention of the word *spatula*, Raul leaned over to me and whispered, in exasperation, "Charlie, what the hell is he talking about? Do you have *any* idea?" "No clue, Raul," I answered. "I guess we'll find out soon...."

Dr. Felch had taken out another cigarette and was now lighting it. As he spoke, his lips twisted up around it and he squinted his eyes against the smoke:

"....As a person who is prone to metaphor I would like to suggest that we learn to see our world in metaphorical terms. Because the literal things that you are witnessing in front of you right now – this corral, this dirt, the small calf over there in the corner – all of this can be seen as a beautiful and complex metaphor for the community college itself. This corral, you see, is the educational realm that we occupy as an institution of higher learning – it is the vast intellectual space that we inhabit as scholars and shapers of youthful opinion. And surrounding it are these aluminum fences which represent the boundaries of our imagination, the traditional rules of time and space that confine us to thinking in the same ways and doing the same things in the exact ways we've always done them. And so, if we can see the world in this new light, if we can only learn to break out of our habit of viewing the phenomena around us in strictly literal terms and instead begin to view the things of the world *metaphorically*, then all of this...." – here Dr. Felch swept his arm to demonstrate the full breadth of the corral, the dirt, the small calf still slowly chewing his mouthful of hay – "....everything you see here, is not merely what it *appears* to be, but also something that exists on a higher rhetorical plane. Which in turn enriches our lives and makes it beautiful and interesting and worthy. Hey, Ethel...!"

Hearing her name suddenly jump out of the soliloquy, Ethel snapped to attention.

"Yes, Dr. Felch!"

"Ethel! Do you love metaphor?"

"Not really, Dr. Felch. I'm a journalist."

"Well, let's see if we can't expand your horizons a bit. Answer me this. Metaphorically speaking, if this corral is the educational realm that our college inhabits, and the fences are the limitations of our collective imagination….then what, in your dispassionate journalistic opinion, is the metaphorical significance of this dry dirt that we are standing on?"

"The dirt that we are standing on?" Ethel answered. "Well, the dirt that we are standing on would be the institutional foundation upon which our college rests. In other words it would be the college's mission statement that guides all that we do – especially the part about paying taxes."

"Nicely done, Ethel! Not bad for a journalist. Now, let's ask Luke…"

Hearing his name, Luke too straightened up in response.

"Luke! Tell us please…..if the corral is the realm of learning and the fences are limitations and the dirt that we are standing on is the mission statement that supports us in our work, then in this long and complicated – perhaps even convoluted – metaphor, what would you say is the *gate* that we just entered?"

"You mean this one right here? With the aluminum latch on it?"

"Yes. That one."

"Well, the gate that we just entered, Dr. Felch, might be the convocation that all of us attended yesterday. Just as you opened this aluminum gate to let us into the corral a few minutes ago, yesterday at convocation you flung open the gate welcoming us into the realm of higher education at Cow Eye Community College. The gate therefore is the threshold that takes us from the barren world of ignorance to the arena of manicured enlightenment."

"Right you are! That's exactly what it is, Luke. All of you are doing great – I knew I shouldn't have been so concerned about hiring you all sight unseen after a single phone interview! Stan!"

"Huh?" said Stan, who had been standing with his hands behind his back and trying not to make eye contact with Dr. Felch. "Who? Me…?"

"Stan! Tell us please…..if the dirt is the mission statement, and the corral is the realm of learning, and the gate is the convocation welcoming new faculty to Cow Eye, then what would you say is the metaphorical meaning of the hot bus ride that we all just stepped off of?"

Stan's face gave off a sheepish expression.

"The bus ride?"

"Yes, Stan, the bus ride from the misty verdure of our campus to this dry and dusty corral of higher learning?"

"Um, I'm not sure," he said and then, after a long pause: "I really don't know, Dr. Felch..."

"Stan! Come on, now! Use your god-given facility for higher thinking! What is the bus ride?"

"Is it....the...Cow Eye River?"

"The Cow Eye River?! How could it be the Cow Eye River?"

"Well....I was just thinking that the road and the river are both kind of long. And the river is mostly dry. But the road is dry too because of the drought. They're both.... I mean.... Aw hell, I don't know! I've never been good at this kind of thing...!"

Dr. Felch shook his head.

"No, Stan. The road is not the Cow Eye River. Anyone else want to take a stab at this?"

Here Ethel Newtown, recently hired journalism instructor, spoke up – whether in support of her husband, or in defiance of him – at this point nothing seemed as clear as it once did.

"Could it be," said Ethel, "that the bus ride symbolizes the shared path that we all must travel in our pursuit of teaching excellence and student success? Each of us came to Cow Eye via a different path. Yet, in the end, there we all were, sitting in that hot bus, being taken across a drought for the ages to this hot dusty corral. The bus ride, then, would surely represent our shared destiny. And, following from this, the bus itself represents the universe. Which means the driver of the bus, your friend from high school, Dr. Felch, is God. The green vinyl seats are the many different religions of the world....or perhaps the many churches in Cow Eye Junction. And this means that the waiver form we signed before being allowed to travel on the bus this morning is our silent assent to the hegemony of a higher power."

"Exactly, Ethel! And the tree that gave up its life for that waiver?"

"Well, the tree, of course, symbolizes His undying love for us."

"Excellent! So to summarize. The corral is our college. The dirt is its mission statement. The fences are rules and conventions. The bus is our destiny. My friend from high school is the Almighty. And because each of us was diligent in signing and turning in the written waiver form this morning we can rest assured that, on one level, our college has been indemnified and that, on *another* level, we have come to accept with quiet acquiescence the fact that it is not for any of us to determine the ultimate fate of our soul. And so, as we approach the matter even more closely, that is, even more *metaphorically*, the dusty turn-off from the highway to the Ranch becomes..."

"....our application to graduate school!"

"And the sign welcoming us to the place 'where cow's meat'...."

"....is the acceptance packet!"

"And the skimpy tree is...."

"....our financial aid office!"

"And Will's flask of bourbon...."

"....is Temptation!"

"And his cigar is...."

"....a dream unfulfilled!"

"And the story of the Smithcoate family...."

"....is a cautionary tale, told backwards rather than forwards!"

As Dr. Felch vigorously stress-tested our facility for metaphor, we responded eagerly and with a growing hunger for the non-literal. This continued for some time, until just when it seemed that we had established a great rhythm and would be able to move past this hurdle with flying colors, Dr. Felch threw an emasculator into the mechanics of our universe – or more specifically, into *mine*. Looking squarely at me, he said:

"So, Charlie...."

"Yes, Dr. Felch?"

"So, Charlie, now that all of this has been sorted out, tell me this. What about the calf....?"

"The calf?"

"Yes, Charlie....what is this lonely calf doing here....?"

"Well, he's raising his tail at the moment...."

"I mean *metaphorically*, Charlie...!"

I looked over at the calf, who was lifting his tail and beginning to do what calves do immediately after they lift their tails.

"I don't know, Dr. Felch. I hadn't thought too much about the calf. Can you give me a prompt of some sort?"

"No, Charlie, I cannot. But we will return to this question a bit later, so hold that thought...."

Dr. Felch lit up another cigarette using the butt of his previous one and took a long drag of it. Then clearing his voice, he began in a grave tone:

"Over there in the corner, my friends, is a three-month-old calf that has yet to be weaned. It is a male...."

On cue, we all looked over at the calf, who was staring at us from the hay that he was chewing. The calf was looking at us with slow, sad eyes, the long straws hanging out both sides of his mouth, yet didn't stop his slow, methodical chewing.

"This calf," said Dr. Felch, "is what we call *intact*. Can anyone tell me what it means to be intact? Stan?"

"Oh, how would *he* know?!" said Ethel. "He's from Maine! *Intact* means he still has testicles, Dr. Felch."

"Good, Ethel. And thank you for such an unequivocal response. You are absolutely correct. An intact calf is one that is still in possession of its testicles. As all of you can well imagine, for a male of any species there are certain very specific benefits to having testicles; these are well-documented so no need for us to spend a lot of time on that. However, from a point of view of animal husbandry, there are also practical, historical, economic, culinary, and humanitarian reasons to separate a calf from his testicles before he is weaned from his mother. The process is called *gelding* for equines and *cutting* for bovines, and it is a rite of passage, so to speak, that almost all male calves must go through. For the majority of calves, you see, castration is a normal and important part of a life lived within the aluminum fences...."

(Upon hearing the word *castration* I suddenly awoke from my daze. With all this talk of metaphor I had lost sight of the fact that we were standing in a *real* corral with *real* dirt and a *real* calf staring back at us with hay dangling out of the sides of his mouth and a sad helpless look on his face. Slowly, things were starting to take shape in my mind, and as they did I felt a growing uneasiness welling up in my groin.)

"This tool right here is what is referred to in the ranching industry as an *emasculator*...."

Dr. Felch held up a device that looked like a heavy-duty metal nut cracker only longer and more unsettling and with a sharp crimping edge. Seeing this device, the women in the group moved in tightly for a better look; the men took a collective step backward.

"Since the beginning of time, cattlemen have used castration as a tool for the management of their herds. In ancient times Babylonians introduced the practice using flint knives to manage their domesticated animals. Pigs, sheep, and goats could now be domesticated and made to coexist peacefully in newly formed human settlements. In eastern Europe recent evidence suggests that early Caucasoids were using castration to tame the beasts of burden that so diligently pulled their plows and their transports, and that this was taking place as far back as four thousand years.....before *Christ*! (If you thought it was *intact* bulls that were so diligently tilling these primitive soils in readiness for the seeds of European civilization and culture... you have another think coming!) In all agrarian societies, castrated males are more pliable, more reliable, and less likely to run away or challenge their masters or to physically abuse themselves or their peers. They are more inclined to be satisfied with the dull monotony of repetitive tasks and tedious labor and are more likely to know and accept their role in the hierarchy of male bovinity. Without the benefits of castration, it is safe to say that the world as we know it would not be the world that we know but instead would be something unrecognizable. If the oxen had been intact it would not have ploughed our rows so evenly. Temperamental bulls would not have co-existed within the confines of early agrarian settlements. And the pre-historic cattleman would not have eaten as well, proliferated so extensively, or had as much disposable free time to innovate and invent because he would have been spending so much of it chasing after his intact ruminants and making amends for the wounds inflicted. History itself would have developed along an entirely different, less progressive and slower trajectory. And this would have set the development of humanity back many millennia. And so, this ancient practice became both a cause and a result of human development. You see, like irrigation and literacy and marriage... castration, my friends, is not just a hallmark, but a catalyst, of civilized society...."

Dr. Felch threw his cigarette butt into the dirt of the corral and ground it out.

"...Over the years we've somewhat lost sight of that fact. And we've started to lose our way. But now, as newly hired faculty and staff of Cow Eye Community College, you will be participating in this proud tradition, a tradition that is recumbent in historical, economic, culinary, humanitarian, and, yes, *metaphorical* significance. Your goal today is to catch that calf and bring him to his destiny. Catch him, subdue him, put him onto his side, and hold him there in the dirt in a safe and secure position. I'll do the rest...."

Dr. Felch paused to let his words sink in. The silence lasted at least half a minute before anyone could articulate a cogent thought.

Ultimately it was Nan who broke the silence.

"Dr. Felch....? If I may? When you say 'the rest'..... are you suggesting that our teambuilding exercise today is to castrate that calf? Is that what I'm understanding when I hear you say that we will catch and subdue him and that you will do 'the rest'?"

"Correct. That is your assignment. Now I know that not all of you will have done something like this before and that you may be uncertain about your castrating abilities. But remember, in the act of castrating, as in the act of teaching, there can be no room for fear. If you are having doubts about your wrangling skills, please remember that the weight of this calf right now is only two hundred fifty pounds; collectively, the six of you in this corral weigh at least five times that. So you have the advantage of brute weight on your side. Not to mention the luxury of time. And human intelligence. And the entire burden of man's relationship with the world around him. But most importantly – and never forget this, my friends – you have....*each other*...."

Dr. Felch took another cigarette from his pack, but held it between his fingers without lighting it.

"...Teamwork, my friends, is what will make your time at Cow Eye Community College either an amazing success....or an unmitigated disaster. Working together is what connects the rainbows between fountains. It is the esplanade linking all of the different chambers of the human heart in a cogent and easily accessible network. And so, as you work together to accomplish this important and useful goal, I'd like you to keep in mind the deeper metaphorical significance of what you will be doing. For you are not merely castrating a calf, dear colleagues – oh no! – but paying homage to the glory of the learning process itself. So strategize with your peers. Formulate your plan. Communicate. Act boldly. Remember that it is not easy to subdue a male calf, even one that is only three-months old and that weighs barely two hundred fifty pounds. A calf who is still intact will have a strong preference to remain that way, and a single faculty member – especially a novice in such things – will not be able to disabuse him of this preference working alone. As you are about to find out, this will take a *coordinated* effort. It will require communication and the participation of every last one of you. It will demand....*teamwork!* So get together as a group and decide how you're going to get that bitch. I'll be watching you from outside the gate over there. And when I see that you've worked as a team to accomplish your mission, I'll come over to guide you through *the rest....*"

Dr. Felch put his emasculator into the back pocket of his jeans and exited the corral, closing the aluminum gate behind him and leaving the six of us to stand in the corral with the suddenly restless calf who had ceased to eat his hay and was already starting to move slowly but noticeably away from us.

LOVE AND THE COMMUNITY COLLEGE. PART 2

"...Blessed are the barren...."

- Luke 23:29

"So, Bessie, what do *you* think love is?" I asked.

"Huh?" Bessie answered. "Where did *that* come from? And why are you asking *me*? Why *now*?"

"Just curious," I said. "The question came up yesterday during our teambuilding exercise. And I was just wondering what *your* take on the issue was."

Bessie looked at me sternly.

"First of all, Charlie, that is not a question one poses to a woman over her typewriter. Secondly, if I had a nickel for every man who tried to get in my pants using an overt pickup line like that I would probably be able to buy a decent place for myself and my two young children instead of the extension off my mother's place where we're all living now."

"It's not a pickup line, Bessie. I really do want to know. Perhaps you could tell me over lunch today at the cafeteria?"

"Lunch?" she said. "Well, okay. But just know that I'll be paying for myself."

After my talk with Bessie, the slow Wednesday morning dragged on with the reassuring monotony of office work. Dr. Felch had provided me with a copy of the college's most recent accreditation self-study and I was slogging through the two-hundred-plus pages as best I could. While reading, I'd left my office door open and from time to time a new colleague would stop by to welcome me to Cow Eye and to crush the bones in my fingers – or to have the bones of her fingers crushed by *me*. All took the opportunity to introduce themselves genially and to comment on the worth of my predecessor (exactly half thought she was great, the others were glad to see her go) and to ask whether I would be attending this or that party after work. "Are you going to Rusty's barbecue tonight?" they would ask, or "Are you going to Gwen's watery get-together?" And to both questions, as was my inclination, I answered emphatically and affirmatively that I would. Standing in my door way, my new colleagues complimented me on the luster of the recently cleaned room. In reverential tones several even lauded the framed diploma I'd proudly mounted on my wall – my Master's degree in Educational Administration with an emphasis in struggling community colleges – and *all* expressed amazement at the vigorous pendulum that was still clacking away on my desk.

"How long has that thing been going back and forth like that?" they'd ask.

"Since Monday afternoon," I'd answer. "It hasn't stopped since then. And I'm curious to see how long it can go."

Later that morning, when the clock struck noon and I closed my office door to go to lunch, the metal orbs were still going strong.

"Can you believe it?" I said to Bessie as we were making our way down the esplanade from the administration building to the cafeteria. "All I did was lift the one orb and let it drop. Just once. A simple release of potential energy. And it's been tick-tocking back and forth for almost two days!" Bessie nodded. Without a heavy box to carry, she was walking even faster than she had on the way to convocation two days ago, and the pace of her gait did not make it very easy to keep up a conversation of any kind, let alone one about a person's faith in eternity.

"Can you believe it?" I said again. "It's like it's never going to stop."

"Of course I believe it," she said. "What's not to believe?"

"Well, that the pendulum has been going strong for two days. I mean, that's hard to believe, isn't it?"

"No, that's not hard to believe. What's hard to believe is that someone with your education can't walk a little faster...."

By the time we reached the cafeteria it was already ten past twelve and the line to the food was several instructors deep. At the head of the throng was Marsha Greenbaum and right behind her was Alan Long River, the Native American speech teacher who had not spoken to anybody for twelve years. Bessie grabbed her tray and napkin and silverware and I followed her lead.

"So, Bessie," I said. "*Now* can you tell me what you think love is? Now that you have your silverware in your hand and your tray tucked under your arm, can you tell me what you believe love to be?"

Bessie looked at me reproachfully yet again. But then, as if sensing my sincerity, she appeared to give in. All this talk of love had left me both hungry and with important philosophical reservations. And if I couldn't satisfy this hunger with *her*, my guide to the complexities of Cow Eye Community College, well then who *could* I expect to satiate it with?

"Love?" said Bessie. "You want to know what I think love is? Well, Charlie, you're asking the wrong person. I have not lived the sort of life that would allow me to tell anyone what love *is*. But I am impressed with your persistence. So let me tell you something else. Rather than tell you what love *is*, let me tell you, instead, what it *could have been….*"

(At the front of the line Marsha Greenbaum was standing with a heaping plate of salad. But she was sorting through the individual pieces of lettuce one by one and this had brought the line to a standstill. "We'll be here all day!" one of the economics instructors was complaining in back of us, and her friend agreed: "Yeah, she's lucky it's Long River behind her. Anyone else would be giving her hell…!")

Bessie took her napkin and wrapped it around her silverware. Then she said:

"Charlie, I don't know how to break this to you. But I've been married and divorced three times. Three separate times, Charlie. Now what does it say about a woman who has been divorced that many times? What does this say to any eligible man who might otherwise want to take her into a serious relationship? What do you think it says, Charlie? What does this say to *you*?"

"To me it says you're passionate and idealistic but also impetuous. You're prone to being hurt. And to making mistakes. These are not bad things, Bessie. The habitual divorcees of the world are not the ones to castigate….it's the promiscuously single we should be suspicious of – the ones who never love their world enough to marry it."

"Well, that may be *your* interpretation, as someone just off the bus from another place. And it is quaint, I suppose, in an urbane sort of way. But now let me tell you what it all means to *me* as someone who was born and raised in Cow Eye Junction. Do you see that lady behind the counter serving the hamburger steak?"

"The one with the hair net? And the pretty eyes?"

"Yes, her. Well she's my classmate from high school. I used to pierce her ears after church. And she used to do my nails. And you see that man carrying out the trash from the cafeteria? The one with the gloves on and greasy apron around his waist? Well, that's my son's football coach and an old friend of my family...."

"Really?"

"Yes. And do you know who my first flame was? The first man I ever gave myself to, mind, soul and body? In the back of a Chevy El Camino? Wearing a tight-fitting miniskirt and pink blouse? In the heat of the moment like a fifteen-month-old heifer? Charlie, do you know who my first *man* was?"

Bessie's question was an intriguing one and I thought about it for a few moments. But of course there was no way for me to know this.

"No, Bessie, I don't. Is it even someone I know?"

"Yes it is. You've seen him each time on your way into and out of the college. My first lover, Charlie, was Timmy."

"At the guard shack?"

"Yes. Timmy at the guard shack. And the three men you met at the bar on your way into campus? The three men watching the football game on television – you know, the ones whose names you didn't even take the time to learn....well, let me tell you who *they* are...."

(The food line had finally begun to inch forward, only to stop in its tracks after only a half-step; Marsha Greenbaum had moved on from the lettuce but was now picking through the baby carrots, holding each up to the light and then either putting it onto her plate or placing it back into the bowl to examine another.)

"....So those three men at the bar, Charlie? You want to know who they are? Well, one of them is my brother. The second is my dentist. And the third, well, let's just say that he has a more intimate knowledge of me than either of the other two will ever have."

"Your tax advisor?"

"My ex-husband. Charlie, after your stop at the *Champs d'Elysees*, I knew you were on your way to campus before you even showed up for work on the first day. My brother recited me your answer to the bloated scrotum question. My dentist told me that you didn't seem like much of a football fan and that you didn't look *anything* like a Special Projects Coordinator. And Buck, that's my ex-husband, even called to tell me that not only did you have some rain outside in your suitcases but that Merna's sister was selling her Ford. Charlie, I just bought that Ford. And *that*'s what it means to be divorced three times and still live in Cow Eye Junction…."

"Wow, I can't believe the man at the bar was your ex-husband. What a strange coincidence. Was he your first husband?"

"My second. My first husband was the bus driver. You know, the one who drove you to the teambuilding exercise."

"I guess this town really is small. And your third husband? I suppose I know him too?"

"My third husband? Sorry, but I really don't want to talk about that one. And yes, you know him…."

By now my head was spinning from all these unnamed husbands and previous lovers. And so as we stood in line waiting for Marsha Greenbaum to choose her cherry tomatoes, Bessie told me of the many men in Cow Eye Junction that had been her former loves. The clerk in the bookstore. The man who cuts the lawn outside our building. The technology specialist. The bus driver and his cousin. Even the man playing the harmonica out back of the makeshift bus shelter.

"Him too?"

"Him too. And so, Charlie, to answer your question, no I will not tell you what love is. But let me tell you instead what love could have been for me. What it could have been if life had turned out a little differently. You see, if life had turned out a bit differently for me, love *could have been* the beautiful color of freshly mowed grass or green vinyl. A soft touch on my arm before surgery. Or a soulful harmonica playing in the dark. It could have been football on Saturday afternoons with good friends at the bar; or a shared love for gardening; or weekly trips together to a Christian church of our favorite denomination. Hell, there was a time when it could have even been a romantic joy ride in an old truck missing its safety belt. Charlie, love could have been *any* of those things if it had all gone a bit differently. Of course I understand that love can't be all of these things *at once*, but even now I feel that it could have been any one of them individually. If only life had turned out differently…."

"Marsha!" somebody was shouting behind us. "Dammit, Marsha, let's get it going!" And at last Marsha put down the green olive she was examining and moved on from the salad section, right past the meats and gravies, straight to the cashier to pay.

"It's about time...!" Bessie said. "I thought we'd have to talk about love *forever*...!"

～

AFTER WE'D PAID for our food and taken our seats, I asked Bessie about the so-called Mentor Lunch that was mandatory for all new faculty the next day. Bessie explained that each new faculty member was assigned an older peer who would help with the adaptation to life at Cow Eye: things like where to pick up the laundry, how to request permission to pick flowers, and how not to receive an unwanted bloated scrotum in your mailbox on a Monday morning. Mentor duty, she explained, was not voluntary but was an expectation for older tenured faculty and the assignments were given out on a rotating basis. You did not pick your mentor and your mentor could not pick you.

"So do you know who's been assigned to us?" I asked. "You seem to know everything else that goes on around here."

Bessie explained that the assignments hadn't been posted yet.

"But whoever it is, just pray you don't get *him*...." Bessie motioned over at a cafeteria table that was empty except for a single faculty member sitting by himself and calmly reading a newspaper. It was Will Smithcoate and as he sat with his paper he was smoking a cigar and drinking from his flask of bourbon, unabashed, in full view of the rest of the cafeteria.

"That's Will Smithcoate!" I said. "He was with us yesterday for our team building exercise."

"You mean he showed up?"

"Well, he was late. But he came. And he shared his thoughts on love, which we appreciated. He seems like a nice guy, Bessie. Why do you say I should hope he's not my mentor?"

"Don't get me wrong – I've known Will Smithcoate for many years and I love the guy as a person. But he should not be let anywhere near a new faculty member. The man is jaded and cynical. All he does is sit at that table with his newspaper and his bourbon. He barely teaches anymore. And when he does he still uses the same notes he used when he first started thirty years ago."

"If he's that bad, why is he the chair of the New Faculty Orientation committee? Isn't that a strange responsibility to give someone who shouldn't be let near new faculty?"

"He only got that committee assignment because they're trying to keep him away from all the *real* committees. Last year they gave him the Christmas Committee, remember? That was supposed to be a mere formality, a bullet point for his curriculum vitae, but he ran that into the ground too. This year they figured they'd give him New Faculty Orientation since, in theory, that's a committee that should be even harder to screw up."

"Makes sense, I guess."

Bessie sprinkled some salt onto her hamburger steak.

"So how'd it go anyway?"

"How'd what go?"

"New faculty orientation?"

"You mean our bus ride to enlightenment?"

"Yeah, the teambuilding exercise. That was Will's brainchild. So I'm curious how it all turned out."

"It was fine...."

And here I told Bessie about the day I'd spent with my fellow new hires. About the six of us standing in the cold talking about fountains and how her ex-husband picked us up and drove us to the Cow Eye Ranch where we shared embarrassing secrets and then were taken into a corral and asked to castrate a calf. When I got to the part about Dr. Felch putting the emasculator in his back pocket and closing the corral gate behind him, Bessie knifed a slab of butter and spread it on her dinner roll.

"So what did you do?" Bessie asked, dipping the roll in the section of her tray that contained the hamburger gravy, then biting off a piece. "After Dr. Felch took his emasculator with him and left the six of you alone in the corral to castrate the calf, what did you guys do then?"

"Well, what *could* we do? We got together and started strategizing...."

"In the corral?"

"Yes. We stood in a circle and began to come together as a team. It was really very poignant."

"Tell me about it, Charlie. Tell me about your teambuilding exercise...."

"Are you sure, Bessie? I mean, we just started our meal. And I wouldn't want to spoil your appetite with the details...."

"I'm from Cow Eye Junction, Charlie – nothing can spoil my appetite. Take me there….!"

And so I resumed the story where I'd left off.

"Well, okay," I said, "so Raul got us into a circle to strategize on how best to castrate the little calf who had already started to back away from us…."

❧

"I think he knows," said Nan looking over at the calf. "I think he knows what we're planning to do to him."

"How could he know?" said Stan. "He's just a calf! Calves don't know anything!"

"That's what *you* think…." said Ethel. "Calves are like any other animal. They can sense and feel what's going on in a person's soul. Despite sixteen years of marriage, Stanley, I know that's still a difficult concept for you to grasp…."

"But even if he does," said Luke. "What difference does it make whether he knows or not?"

"Well, I'm just saying," said Nan, "because I'm not sure I want to go through with this. I mean did you see his eyes….how sad they looked? I don't think I can go through with this, knowing that he knows…."

"He doesn't know!" said Stan. "He doesn't know because he's a cow and cows are animals and animals don't know a fucking thing about anything in this world. That's why they're animals! That's what separates us from them! That's why he's inside these fences and we're…."

"Well technically, Stan, we're also inside the fences…."

"Look," said Raul. "Can we stay focused on the mission here? We've been given a specific assignment to accomplish. And I don't know about *you* guys, but I'm hot and thirsty and my black pressed slacks and carefully polished shoes are all dusty from this corral. I'd like to get this done and move on with my life. So can we do this, please?"

We all nodded our agreement.

"Great. Now I've been thinking about this and here's how we can do it. Let me represent it to you all visually…."

The six of us had been standing in a circle but as Raul kneeled down to the dirt, the rest of us followed his lead. Now we were all kneeling on one knee in a perfect huddle, like a grade-school football team around its quarterback. Raul rolled up the sleeve of his white collared shirt and began to draw with his finger in the dirt of the corral. He did this busily and while he did, the rest of us maintained an expectant silence. In the background the sounds of pre-castration could be heard: the bleating of the calf and the plaintive moans of the calf's mother calling out for him from a distant section of the corral. Meanwhile Dr. Felch was standing outside the aluminum gate with one foot resting on its lowest rail. He had grabbed a bullhorn and as he leaned forward with his elbows against the railing, the bullhorn dangled from his hand over the gate. Raul continued to furiously sketch in the dirt and when he was finished he pointed at what he had drawn:

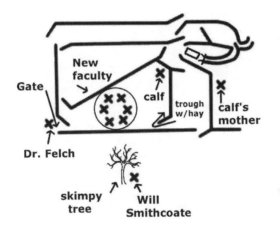

"Okay," he said, "this is our corral. I've drawn it quickly, but don't worry, it's to scale. On this end is the gate and on that end is the trough where the calf is. There are six of us and only one of him. Which means that it shouldn't be hard to force him into the corner. From there each of us will grab onto him and hold." And here Raul drew another diagram, this one showing our assignments:

"Once we've all got him, we'll tip him over and hold him there so Dr. Felch can do the rest. Just be careful when you grab the legs because he may kick. Any questions?"

"Yeah," said Stan. "What makes you think he'll kick?"

"Wouldn't *you*?! Anyway, I think this is how we'll need to do it."

Raul extended his hand into the middle of our human circle and looked around at each of us. Seeing his prompt, I put my hand on top of his, Ethel put her hand on mine, Luke put his on hers, Nan on his, and then Stan.

"Go TEAM!" we shouted and then stood up from our crouch.

At this, Dr. Felch's voice came over the bullhorn from where he was standing:

"Can you hear me?" he asked. "Is this thing on?"

"We hear you!" we yelled. "It's on!"

"Okay. I just want to remind you that the longer you take, the more nervous your calf is going to get. And the more nervous he is, the more blood he'll lose when we cut him. This is not foreplay, folks, where the longer the buildup the better the result. Get in there and get going...!"

Dr. Felch switched off the bullhorn.

"Okay," said Raul. "Are we ready? Charlie, are you ready?"

"I'm ready."

"Luke, are you ready?"

"Ready."

"Ethel. Ready?"

"As ready as I can be."

"Nan?"

"I still think he knows...."

"Nan? Are you ready or not?"

"Well, I guess I'm ready. I mean, yes, I'm ready."

"Great. Stan? Stan, are you ready? Stan....?"

And here we looked up just in time to see Stan's body collapse onto the ground of the corral with a thud. He was convulsing in the dirt, his eyes turned up into his skull and his mouth foaming.

"Get him some water!" said Raul.

Luke ran out of the gate and filled a bucket with water, but when he came back it was so hot that we couldn't use it.

Dr. Felch's bullhorn again switched on.

"Luke!" said Dr. Felch over the bullhorn. "Luke, you have to let the hot water run out of the hose before filling the bucket up!"

Again Luke ran over and back with the bucket and this time the water was cool enough to pour on Stan's head safely. Ethel had placed his head on her lap and was running her fingers through the wet hair on his scalp. Stan's eyes fluttered and flickered and then, to everyone's relief, popped open. Ethel dabbed more water on him.

"Let's take him under the skimpy tree," Nan said.

Luke, Raul and I lifted Stan up and carried him over to the tree. Under the sudden weight, the picnic table creaked and shuddered and as it did, Will Smithcoate began to stir from his deep sleep, groggy and confused, a string of glistening saliva dangling from his mouth:

"...If love were a fountain," he was muttering, "....it would be an Oldsmobile...."

As the five of us stood around, Stan looked up from the table where we'd laid him.

"What just happened?" he said.

"You passed out," we said.

"You're kidding me...."

"No."

"No, really? I passed out?"

"Yes."

"As in totally motionless?"

"Yes."

"So did you take advantage of me?"

"No," we said. "We didn't."

"Shucks!" he said. "Why not?"

And here we knew that Stan's wits had returned and that with a little rest and a lot more water and a little more shade he would be the Stan we'd come to love.

At this Will too seemed to regain his whereabouts.

"What'd I miss?" he asked. "Did you do it? Did you bring that calf to his destiny? And where's my cigar? Where's my damn cigar?!"

"It's in your pocket, Will."

"It damn well better be. So is the calf a steer yet?"

"No, Will. We tried but we failed. Nan expressed compassion and doubt, and Stan passed out under the hot sun. It seems that we are not up to this particular challenge. At least not right now."

"Really? So is that decided then? Are you done for the day? Are you giving up on the assignment? Packing it in? Raising the white flag?

Or are you going to get back in there and show that calf how the seeds of civilization are sown? Hell, if the American colonists had that same limp-dick attitude, we'd still be drinking tea with milk and watching snooker on Saturday afternoons. Come on, get back out there..."

"But, Will," we protested, "Stan is dehydrated and weak. Surely, if there is any excuse not to castrate a calf, it is this? Surely if there is any valid justification to let a scrotum remain intact, it is the severe heat stroke and dehydration that Stan is currently suffering from?"

Will took another swig from his flask. Then he sniffed his cigar.

"Look," he said, "If you think teambuilding with colleagues is hard, try living with another human being, in the same house, for thirty-eight years. Do you know how many times I wanted to give up? To pack up my emasculator and get the hell out? But I didn't.....I stuck with it another thirty-seven years. Another twenty-nine years. Another seventeen years...... And that's how I grew as a person and as an educator. If love were a *woman*, you see, it would be the one you wake up next to every morning for thirty-eight years. And not the beauty from the supermarket who came and went oh-so-long ago and whose distant memory still arouses you, even now....."

I stopped.

Bessie was taking a final bite of her hamburger.

"And so?" she said as she dabbed a forkful of hamburger in her gravy. "And so what happened then?"

"Well, then we all realized that Will was right. We realized that, like teaching, love required an unwavering commitment to the result, not just the process."

"And then?"

"And so then we went back into the corral and cornered the calf. It wasn't easy. As soon as he saw us closing in on him the calf spun around and threw himself into a gap in the fence, his head lodging and his legs kicking, but the six of us grabbed him and pulled him back through the boards and each of us took the leg we were supposed to grab and held onto it for dear life. Raul twisted the neck and brought the calf flailing onto his side, right on top of Stan, who made the mistake of grabbing the front legs from the wrong side. The calf was kicking and grunting and his tongue was sticking out from the twisting headlock Raul had him in, but we held him there on the ground. Seeing this, Dr. Felch jogged over with his emasculator and began giving us instructions. 'Nan, pull his tail through his legs.... Luke, use his top leg to hold his bottom leg.....Ethel, put your knee on his thigh and lean into it a bit....not too much!....Charlie, watch your face, boy, he can kick you from that angle....' Then he took out his pocket knife and cut off the tip of the calf's scrotum with a single slice. The calf jerked and struggled but we held him in place and here Dr. Felch forced out the testicles, pressing the white ovals out of their sac as effortlessly as if he were squeezing moist prunes out of a package. 'Where's my emasculator?' he said. 'Dammit, it must have fell out of my pocket...!' And so, with no emasculator, he took his simple pocket knife and using the sharp edge of its blade, began to shave the sac, grazing the sharp blade back and forth like a woodcarver whittling wood, until the ovals came off in his hands and the sac snapped back into the scrotum. Then he grabbed a spray can from his pocket and sprayed the cut where the blood was spurting out. 'Okay' he said, 'on *three* we let him up....just watch the back legs so he doesn't kick.... ready?.... one.... Two..... THREE!' On the count of three we all jumped up from the calf and he scrambled up and darted away from us. He was still stumbling to regain his balance and as he trotted off a thin stream of blood trailed after him in the dirt. Dr. Felch took the severed tip of the scrotum, with all the bristly black hairs covered in blood, and placed it in his flannel shirt pocket. Then he took the testicles and put them in a Ziploc bag....."

"And then?" Bessie asked.

"Well, and then all hell broke loose. Bessie, you wouldn't believe it. We were jumping and screaming and hugging each other! Ethel had jumped into Stan's arms and he was twirling her around like a figure skater. Raul and I were exchanging high-fives and everyone was shouting and clapping each other on the back. Dr. Felch just stood there watching all this and smiling like a proud father. 'My friends,' he said. 'Now you know the degree of teamwork that is expected of you during your tenure at Cow Eye Community College!' The bus drove up with our lunches, we hosed the blood off and the sweaty calf hair and as much of the green calf shit from our clothes as we could, and sitting on the bench under the skimpy tree, we had an enjoyable lunch....."

"So it all came out well in the end?"

"Yeah. It did. Of course, Stan had some bruised ribs. And Luke got kicked in the shin while trying to wrestle the calf. Ethel gashed her chin on the calf's muzzle and Nan hurt her shoulder and so that's why you see her wearing a sling today. And all of us were bathed in shit from trying to wrestle and hold the calf on the ground by the trough. But overall it was fine."

"And you?"

"I was fine too. In fact I'd come out relatively unscathed and was quietly enjoying my lunch with the others when, to my surprise, Dr. Felch looked over at me across his sandwich and said, 'So, Charlie, are you ready to answer the question now?' I didn't know what he was talking about. 'What question?' I answered. And everyone looked at me and laughed."

"He probably meant the unanswered question he'd posed. About the metaphorical significance of the calf."

"Exactly. So here he looks at me and says, 'If the corral is our college, the dirt is our mission, the fences are the accreditation standards, the bus is our destiny, the driver is Him (or Her), and the waiver form is our submission to a higher presence.….if all of this is true, then what, Charlie, is the *calf* whose testicles are now in this Ziploc bag…?'"

"And he held up the Ziploc?"

"Right. At a slight tilt so the blood pooled in one of its corners."

"And you said?"

"I didn't say anything. I didn't answer at all. I told him I needed more time to think about it. That I'd get back to him."

"And that was that?"

"For now. I promised to give him a definitieve answer by the end of the semester. He said he would hold me to it and that it will be a key component of my first annual performance evaluation."

Bessie laughed.

"Well good luck with that.…!" Bessie took a final drink of her iced tea. Then she checked her watch.

"It's been fun," she said. "But some of us need to get back to work. I'll see you tonight, though…"

"Absolutely. Seven-thirty at Marsha's studio. And thanks again for offering to pick me up. I'm glad I won't have to choose one of these parties over the other.…"

Bessie and I dumped the scraps of food from our trays into the trash cans and headed back toward the administration building to finish out our work day. As we left the cafeteria I could see the man in the greasy apron, whose name I would never learn, lifting the bag out of the can and tying its corners into a knot.

A FACULTY DIVIDED

"At the center of any good story is a conflict. It is the moisture that brings life to the parched, arid soil of the most barren imagination."

- The Anyman's Guide to Writing the Perfect Novel, p. 36

The College's most recent self-study document was not a fun read. In fact, as I diligently ploughed my way through the two hundred ambling pages – row after row of typewritten text – I was aghast at what I was reading. Amid the college's statements of its own condition I found factual errors and discrepancies and misrepresentations. There were numerous statements of fact that did not make logical sense and even more that seemed to be exaggerated or vague or even intentionally ambiguous or false. The mission statement was worded incorrectly. Goals were incorrectly aligned. Some sentences had no conclusion, meandering off into oblivion as if the writer had been interrupted in mid-thought or the editor had chopped off the sentence but forgot to complete it later on. On page 34, it was stated that Cow Eye Community College had a full-time enrollment of 987 students and a faculty count of 361, while a few pages later the two figures were reversed. Charts and tables were haphazardly labeled. Mispellings abounded. Some sections were written in first person, others in third. Information that could have been bulleted was written out in long-paragraph form, while information that should have been spelled out in paragraphs was compacted into terse, ineffective bullets. Amid the chaos there were maps with no legends and legends with no heroes and a bizarre passage about recent improvements to the English department that appeared to be written....in *verse*. One entire chapter seemed to be lifted from a later chapter about an unrelated topic. And another section included what appeared to be an aside – perhaps dictated by accident – that was not meant for actual inclusion in the document: ("This represents everything that is inherently wrong with the world.") Worst of all, there was virtually no evidence to support even those assertions that may have been given in earnest and that might have actually been true. Wild claims of success were made on almost every page, yet nothing had been presented to support them. On page 173, the writer – or writers – had stated that, "With the introduction of the shooting range and archery complex, there has been a huge increase in student satisfaction and faculty retention"; however there were no data in support of this claim, no chart or diagram, no helpful appendix – nothing to suggest that satisfaction or retention had actually increased as a result of the new shooting range and archery complex.

"Well," I said to Dr. Felch when I'd come into his office after reading the entire bewildering report. "I just finished the self-study."

"And?"

"It was brutal. I can't believe you submitted this to your accreditors. No wonder they shot us down."

"That's nothing. Wait 'til you see this…." Dr. Felch pulled out a stapled packet of papers and plopped it on the desk. "Their response….."

I cringed.

"I'm afraid to even look…."

Back in my office, my worst fears were confirmed. In their response to the self-study, the accreditors had flagged every single discrepancy and misstatement and flat-out lie that I'd just come across in my own reading. They had noted a "failure of leadership" and "gross misrepresentation of facts" and "mismanagement of resources" and "grave concerns" regarding the future of the college. In the very first paragraph, after highlighting the beauty of the campus and extolling its "fresh rows of lilac and grand sycamore tree," – seemingly the only nice thing they had to say about their visit – the accreditors stated that the aesthetic charm of the campus "belies the ability of the institution to provide a quality education to its students." What followed was a twenty-page institutional beat-down, an accreditational emasculation the kind of which I had never before experienced. And as I read the scalding comments – the acidic rebukes and recommendations, the caustic insinuations and searing criticism – I could almost smell the putrid scent of burning hair and pale unprotected flesh sizzling under the sun.

"So what do you think, Charlie?" Dr. Felch's voice was asking. Now he was standing in my doorway, waiting expectantly for my answer. "Do you think there's any hope for us?"

"I don't know, Mr. Felch. This is about as bad as it gets…"

"I warned you…."

"You did. But I guess I didn't realize it was that far gone. Who put this report together anyway?"

"Your predecessor. She was supposed to take all the rough drafts from the individual standard chairs and compile them into a single document. But she waited until the last minute. And by the time it came to me for signature, it was too late to do anything." Dr. Felch took out a third document, this one only six pages. "Here," he said. "This is our plan to respond to the comments of the accreditors…."

I opened it up and saw a table on the first page listing the accreditors' findings and the college's proposed response to address the findings. This too was not happy reading:

	Accreditor Findings	Response of Cow Eye Community College
1	The college is grossly behind in technology (ex: still using manual typewriters). As a result, faculty and staff are hampered in their work operations; even more depressingly, students are not being given the opportunity to develop skills necessary to compete in an increasingly technology-based world.	A Technology Committee has been formed and has developed a plan to introduce technology onto the campus. The three-year plan is currently being implemented and has included the purchase of an electric typewriter for our natural sciences division and one for the math department. We are also exploring the feasibility of acquiring one for the humanities division; initial discussions with the division chair have been conducted and despite significant resistance, there is reason to believe that this will be finalized by year 3 of the plan.

2	There is lack of cooperation and poor morale among faculty. Some faculty have mentioned receiving bloated scrota in their mailboxes, a bizarre practice that is shockingly widespread at this college.	Lack of cooperation is admittedly a problem on campus. However, a plan is in place to correct this. The plan includes the following elements: 1) A more robust process for New Faculty orientation incorporating team-building and culture-bridging activities grounded in the unique history of Cow Eye Junction. 2) An institution-wide focus on unity and cultural harmony, including social and other morale-building events (ex: Christmas party); 3) An awareness campaign to deter the leaving of bloated scrotums in faculty mailboxes.
3	The mission statement is a) outdated; and b) not understood by faculty and staff.	The current mission statement was developed during a period of relative isolation and unbounded optimism regarding the college's perceived manifest destiny. However, we recognize the need to reevaluate and update the statement and will be reviewing and revising it beginning next year. In the meantime, more emphasis will be placed on educating faculty and staff on the college's current mission, including at all-college assemblies and during Fall and Spring convocations.

4	The college has very few ADA-accessible pathways and ramps – and those that it *does* have it insists on referring to as being "for handicaps."	CECC's lack of handicapped facilities is not a reflection of the college's lack of sympathy for such individuals but rather a consequence of having so few of them on campus. Previously, the perception was, Hey, If we don't have any handicaps, why do we have to do anything for them? However, this perception has been corrected and a plan has been developed to introduce more accommodations into the campus, including: handicapped parking stalls, ramps and railings, etc. The use of the term "handicapped" will also be phased out in line with the college's recently adopted Policy on Inclusive and Non-Hurtful Language. According to the policy, language that shows any sort of bias or tendency to exclude will be replaced with words that are all-inclusive and that promote harmony and good will to the extent possible.
5	The college has an autocratic leadership structure. All hiring decisions are made by the college president with no input from faculty or staff.	Hiring procedures have been revised to include a hiring committee recommendation. Hiring committees will consist of six members. The recommendation of the committee will be a key consideration in all hiring decisions.
6	Faculty and Staff of the college (including the Dean of Instruction) did not know the difference between *Goals* and *Objectives*. No one could say what an *Outcome* is.	A Professional Development plan will be instituted to educate all faculty and staff of the college on the difference between Goals, Objectives, and Outcomes. The Dean of Instruction will be encouraged to attend.

7	Faculty do not assess the effectiveness of their instruction.	In addition to current departmental evaluations, the college's Special Projects Coordinator will be recruited to conduct in-class evaluations of key instructional faculty. The results of these independent non-departmental evaluations will provide subjective and objective feedback to instructors so they may better assess the effectiveness of their teaching methodologies and make appropriate improvements as necessary.

After reading this first page carefully, I flipped through the rest of the table in a funk. In all, there were thirty-six significant findings that the college had promised to address before the team's visit next March and as I read through them, cringing at each, I circled those that impacted me directly: the Christmas party for all faculty and staff that I would be organizing in the name of campus morale; the in-class evaluations that I had apparently been committed to conduct in the hope of increasing key faculty's ability to assess their own effectiveness; and the revision of the mission statement that would ensure that our goals were aligned and that we were achieving tangible, measurable outcomes. It was all too much to digest in one sitting, and on my way out of the building that afternoon I dropped by Dr. Felch's office to say goodbye for the day.

"You're not going to any parties tonight, Charlie?"

"I wasn't planning on it, honestly. But then Gwen stopped by. And then Rusty stopped by. So I guess I acquiesced to both. And you?"

"I'll be at Rusty's. We're doing a thing for Merna there and I can't miss it. Plus, I wasn't exactly invited to the other one." Dr. Felch laughed.

"I'll be there a little later," I said. "Bessie's picking me up at seven-thirty."

"Bessie? Oh! Well then, I guess we'll be seeing the two of you about the time you get there...!"

At my apartment I showered and waited for Gwen Dupuis to arrive. On the other side of the wall, loud thumping music was playing and I could hear the frequent sounds of banging and shrieking and crashing glass, as if plates were being broken. I'd been warned about our math faculty and now I was experiencing it first-hand. The last two nights they'd kept me up till the late hours with the constant sounds of partying and screaming and the guttural shrieks and moaning of what sounded like the sexual caterwauls of fertile felines. Struggling to fall asleep I'd put my pillow over my head and stuffed my ears with tissue paper. But nothing worked. If this kept up – if the noise lasted into the weekend or, especially, if it dragged into the upcoming semester – I would need to confront them about the inconsideration. The very thought of having to do this made me shudder: I had never been one to enjoy conflict, did not have a successful history with it, and as a rule tried to avoid it whenever possible. But that would be a thought for another time: Gwen's car had just pulled up and she was already honking her horn as a signal for me to come down.

~

LOOKING UP I saw three faces standing over me. Behind them was a powerful light that cut into my eyes. My head hurt and the taste of blood filled my mouth. The three were asking me something but when I tried to speak I could only gurgle the blood. "What happened to you?" they were saying. "Are you alright?" Beneath me the asphalt was rough and red. Cars were driving by, swerving to avoid me, their horns blaring as they passed. Dazed and confused I tried to raise myself off the road but the dizziness and the overwhelming nausea brought me back down. My head whirling, I tried to get up from the street but could not. The cars were passing. My head was throbbing and spinning. Horns were sounding in both directions. The three faces were looking down at me. To the sound of cars swerving around me and horns blaring. And then I blacked out. Right there on the asphalt. Again.

~

{ }

If love were an easy thing, it would surely be unworthy of
the pursuit. For only those things that come from the pains
of severe effort are truly worthwhile. Like the difficulties of
a woman's labor that bring children into the world, so too
do the pains of one's love of life bring even more love into the
world. And just as the seeds of the celery stalk are the only

ones that can cause more celery to be born, so too are the
seeds of love the only ones that will bring about the sowing
of even more love. Within the great garden of the community
college, love is the celery plant that awaits its seeding, the
cucumber flourishing on the vine, the fragile arugula plant,
still unfurled, waiting in quiet solitude for the spreading
water of life.

{ }

❧

GWEN DUPUIS'S CAR was a yellow two-seater and I immediately recognized that it must be hers when the small coupe pulled up below my apartment window a little after five. Hearing the horn, I headed downstairs, where Gwen leaned over to unlock the door and let me in. The bucket seat was soft and inviting and I was so captivated by the comfort of it all that I didn't realize at once how light her car door was compared to all the others I'd been closing lately; to my surprise, the door slammed shut with a violent, bone-jarring crash.

"Charlie," Gwen said, calmly and immediately. "This automobile you are sitting in is a refined work of human engineering. It is not a corral gate. Please put on your seat belt and be more careful next time...."

The interior of Gwen's car was immaculate and as she pulled out of the parking lot the scent of evergreen and cinnamon filled my senses. Outside her windows, the birds of the campus were chirping and the pelicans were loafing on the banks of the lagoons as if they had not moved since the last time I saw them. The campus was shutting down for the day and the administrative workers were already beginning to file out of their offices toward their cars. The two of us drove a minute or so in silence and then Gwen looked over at me with a quizzical expression on her face:

"So tell me, Charlie," she said – we had just turned onto the main thoroughfare bisecting the campus and were now passing a large swimming pool on one side and the Dimwiddle Institute on the other – "How do you like Cow Eye so far?"

"It's fine," I said.

"Really?"

"You sound surprised."

"I am. I mean, what exactly is it about our college that makes it *fine?*"

"Well, I love the campus. And the lagoons are great. Everyone I've met has been really helpful and friendly, either stopping by my office to introduce themselves and to share widely divergent impressions of my predecessor's worth to the world….or taking the time to point me toward the library where the remnants of her eclectic book collection will one day be left for posterity."

"You haven't dropped off her books yet?"

"No, but I *will.* In the meantime, a few colleagues have complimented me on my newly cleaned office. Others have expressed their deepest condolences over my failed marriages. And in three short days I feel like I've learned more about the political situation here in Cow Eye Junction than most historians will have the pleasure of learning in a lifetime…."

"Congratulations."

"Thank you."

"And how's your reading coming? Have you made any headway with the books you set aside to read?"

"Well, I've started a couple more. And so far I've gotten a few pages into several. And several pages into a few. In all, I'm reading about eight books at the moment…" – here I mentioned my unfinished historical novel; *The Anyman's Guide to Love and the Community College*; and the *Cute Cats of the World* – "….Of course, it's a lot to read, but I hope to get through them all in the near future."

"So things are going well for you then?"

"Swimmingly! Though I have to admit I'm still trying to make sense of the things I'm seeing. You know, the shifting rainbows and rippled reflections and all the complex personalities with their various alignments and aspirations. It's still a little overwhelming, honestly."

"You do look a little tired."

"Well, yeah, and I haven't been sleeping very much since the math faculty got back from North Carolina…."

"You shouldn't feel bad about that. I've been here for fifteen years. And I'm still grappling to understand the things I'm seeing. And as for the math faculty, well, you'll get used to them soon enough."

"Are they always so boisterous?"

"They're playful, yes. That goes with the territory. There's something about the rational mind that makes it cry out for the irrational. The two go together. I firmly believe that."

"As a logic teacher yourself?"

"Yes. I suppose you could say it's from personal experience. And personal observation. Obviously, there's a difference between logic and reason. But logical people require reason. And reasonable people require a great deal of rationality in their lives. And the greater the need for logic and reason and rationality....the greater the need for their opposites. That's true at any community college. It's just that *our* math faculty tend to take it to the extreme..."

As she drove, Gwen told me of the legendary antics of our math department. Of the late-night "Math Bashes" where students and faculty would dress in drag and get stoned and try to solve unprecedented algebraic formulae. And how, each year on March fourteenth, the entire department would come to campus with wagonloads of dried-up cow pies gathered from the countryside; and how they would distribute them to students in their classes; and how they would agree to meet at the sycamore tree a few minutes after three; and how when the large clock on the administration building hit exactly three-fourteen *and fifteen seconds*, the entire math community would run screaming to the sycamore tree to engage in an all-out cow pie fight. In tones of admiration Gwen described how the mathematics teachers had come to forcibly occupy an entire section of the faculty housing complex, claiming squatter's rights and turning the common area into a "math mausoleum" complete with charts and graphs and a life-size cut-out of Leibniz and Newton sharing a bong. And how these younger teachers were loved by students for their passionate devotion to mathematical inquiry. How they were hated by administration for their reckless indifference to rules and their unwavering devotion to the purity of their principles and priorities. And how they were famous for traveling to various professional development conferences where things always seemed to begin professionally and developmentally enough – a few workshops dutifully attended on the first morning perhaps, and then some obligatory note-taking during an afternoon session – only to devolve into yet another haze of all-night drinking and mathematics-infused orgies.

"They practice a severe form of math-love," Gwen explained.

"Yeah, well, that's all fine and good. But I just wish they'd keep their love fests to respectable hours. I haven't slept in two days!"

"Don't worry. It'll die down a bit once the semester starts."

"The math-love?"

"Oh no, that never goes away! I meant the partying."

"I hope so. I need my sleep. Those accreditation documents are hard enough to read as it is!"

Gwen laughed.

"I'm sure you'll get some sleep tonight. You might still be adjusting to the time zone change. Plus, I heard you got back from your teambuilding activity late last night. Ethel told me how your bus broke down on the way back and how you had to wait an extra hour along the side of the road. She was saying the activity was, um, *interesting*, if that's the best word to use….?"

"You could definitely call it that."

"She said you sowed some seeds of civilization."

"We sure did."

"And that you shared embarrassing and even humiliating secrets."

"We did that too."

"She said yours was especially illogical because, on the one hand you don't much like being around people, yet, on the other, you are also afraid of being alone. She says you're a lot of different things, but none of them entirely."

"She would be right."

"And she told me how Felch chain-smoked the entire time. And Smithcoate passed out on a table with a cigar in his mouth, drunk on the past, as usual!"

"Ethel told you all these things? So what else did she have to say?"

"Well, she also said that she and Stan are heading in opposite directions – and not just because of the orgasm thing. She was ready to forgive and forget. But I reminded her that relationships are fleeting and that orgasms are a husband's duty – and that this is simply non-negotiable. So I guess you could say it was an equally enlightening mentor meeting for us both!"

"Mentor meeting? Have the assignments been posted?"

"Of course. You got Long River."

"The speech teacher who doesn't *speak*? He's my mentor?!"

"Correct. That should be interesting, shouldn't it! But, hey, at least you didn't get *Smithcoate*….!" Gwen laughed again. Now she was passing the Harriet

Bowers Dimwiddle Health and Wellness Center. "So, Charlie, I'm curious to hear more about your teambuilding exercise yesterday. How *was* it? I have no doubts that it was *entertaining*. But was it truly *edifying*? I mean, as an educator you of course know the difference between the two, right?"

"I would hope so."

"So after that teambuilding exercise are the six of you ready to work together as a team?"

"Absolutely."

"Hand in hand for the success of our students?"

"I would say so."

"And the betterment of our community?"

"Ultimately, yes."

"And the proliferation of the American Way?"

"Pretty much."

"They're sick, Charlie."

"What? Who's sick?"

"They're *all* sick. Felch. Smithcoate. Stokes. I mean, name me another community college in the country – a community college from any historical period or culture of the *world* – where it would be acceptable to round up impressionable new faculty, herd them onto a school bus, drive them past abandoned buildings and a rotting buffalo carcass, and then force them all....all of them – even the women! – and then force them to....my god, the very thought makes me shudder....and then force them all to..."

"...It's okay, Gwen, you can say it...."

"....And then force them to talk about *love*! How demeaning!"

"But Gwen, it wasn't that bad. In fact, I think we all got what we were supposed to get out of the experience."

"Metaphorically, you mean? Or literally?"

"A little of each."

"I doubt that. But either way, love should not be a topic for mixed company."

"It shouldn't?"

"No, it shouldn't. And it's not something that should be spoken of in a hot school bus or under a skimpy tree. Love should not be a means of manipulation or subjugation. It should not be a vehicle with an ulterior destination. Or an instrument used for one's own purpose.

Love should never be wielded as a carrot or a stick. It should not be painful or laborious. Or *difficult*. And of course it should not be a means to achieve a greater goal, objective, or outcome. For obvious reasons it should never be seen as something rhetorical or metaphorical or allegorical. In fact, love should not be anything at all, except what it actually *is*. Whatever that may be...."

Gwen was slowing down to flash her badge to the guard at the shack. Timmy smiled and waved her through:

"Thanks, Ms. Dupuis!" he called out, but Gwen didn't seem to notice and drove past without acknowledging him.

"You know," Gwen said as we hopped over the railroad tracks yet again, "this sort of thing – that teambuilding fiasco, for example – begins at the very top. It all comes down from there. I mean, just look at who's leading our institution...."

"President Felch? He seems like a nice guy...."

"Felch? Are you kidding me? That man should be put to pasture already. After what he's done to our college! And what he's doing with our faculty. And especially after what he did to your predecessor last year...." Gwen was clenching her steering wheel tightly and shaking her head. "....After what he did to *her*, he's the one who should be gelded...!"

Here my ears perked up again. "Why? What happened with my predecessor? What did Dr. Felch do to her that was so bad?"

"It's an ugly story...." Gwen had come to a sudden stop to allow an armadillo to cross the road in front of her. The animal was in no hurry and as it took its time crossing the road, the two of us waited patiently. Unrushed, the armadillo moved from one side of the road toward the other but then, just as it had reached the opposite side, it stopped, turned around, and headed back toward where it had started, just as slowly and just as unrushed.

"I sense some hesitancy there," Gwen noted. "That kind of indecision will get you killed, Mr. Armadillo!"

When the indecisive armadillo reached the very spot from where it had originally set out on its journey, Gwen eased off the brake and the car edged forward, past the armadillo, past the boarded-up skeleton of the town's only printing press, and headlong into the complicated story of how Dr. Felch had inflicted a great injustice upon my predecessor during her abbreviated tenure as Special Projects Coordinator:

"Ultimately, it's all *Stokes's* fault," she began. "You see, he was the one who thought it would be a great idea to build a swimming pool on campus and that it should be in the exact shape of an American flag....."

Once again the scenery outside had changed from the foliage of our verdant campus to the hot desolation of the surrounding area. The wind had disappeared. The air was dead. The grass was brown and brittle under the fading sun of early evening. By now I had made the voyage in both directions and the shift between the two no longer surprised me in the same way.

"This was about ten years ago," Gwen continued as we drove past a stand of dried-up mesquite trees, "when our campus was only beginning to reap the benefits of the Dimwiddle contribution. We'd just built the Observatory and the Concert Hall and plans were in place for the Stadium and the Gun Range (which should have been completed earlier but had to be relocated farther away from the library due to noise concerns). This was an especially volatile time in the world and so things were going really well for us...."

(As she spoke I couldn't help noticing a certain idiosyncrasy of Gwen's driving. Her car was an automatic transmission and it seemed that at any given moment she was either stepping heavily on the gas or stepping heavily on the brake; there was no in-between with her – as if the two feet she was using for the pedals were conflicting tendencies buried deep within her heart and that she was wrestling with from moment to moment. As she drove, I felt my stomach lurching either forward or backward with the constant braking or accelerating.)

"...The college was flush with money for glamorous projects back then and at some point Stokes got it into his head that the campus really needed a swimming pool and that it should be in the shape of an American flag and so he proposed it to Felch and they pushed it through permitting – Felch is well-connected with local government, and the planners loved the idea of having the thirteen stripes and twenty-four stars painted on the bottom of the pool – and within a year or so the Olympic-sized venue was built and dedicated as the Albert Ross Dimwiddle Aquatics Complex. Stokes had gotten what he wanted and Cow Eye now had its pool...."

At this Gwen pressed firmly on the brake, then accelerated out of it even more firmly. In response, my stomach lunged forward and back, respectively. Already slightly seasick, I was doing my best to focus on this new story of emerging water:

"I'm not quite sure where you're headed with this, Gwen. Isn't it a *good* thing to have a pool? I mean, if there's going to be bloodshed in the world – and there is bound to be, of course – well then you might as well build yourself a pool from it, right? And besides, I'm not seeing how this has anything to do with Dr. Felch being gelded or my unfortunate predecessor whose pendulum is still ticking back in my office...."

"I'm getting to all that."

Now she was accelerating into her story again and as she did my stomach went with her.

"...Okay, so let's fast forward ten years to the hiring of our second Special Projects Coordinator. (You're the *third* hire. Remember, the first one had left after only a month?) Believe me, Charlie, this woman was no run-of-the-mill Special Projects Coordinator. She came to us with multiple Ivy League educations and previous administrative experience working at the League of Nations and the UN. She'd helped facilitate a peace accord between rival clans in Somalia and had once succeeded in getting a delegation of Israelis to sit side by side with a delegation of Palestinians at an impromptu Easter mass. Her qualifications were impeccable. Her sense of propriety was unimpeachable. She came with recommendations from the General Secretary and his top aide. And she'd won several awards for contributions to educational administration. So you could even say, without exaggerating in the least, that she was not just an administrator but an *award-winning* administrator...."

"She sounds great....But how does all this pertain to...."

"...The lawsuit? Right. So anyway, the pool was built from the blood of other countries' suffering and it was dedicated with a ribbon-cutting ceremony and the Dimwiddle family even flew all the way from Missouri to attend the ceremony and to dip their toes in the crystal-clear waters. Things were good for a while. Unfortunately, the cost of maintaining a pool in the middle of a place like Cow Eye Junction, well, as you might imagine, Charlie, it tends to be very steep. And so, over the years, a lot of resources have been redirected from our operating budget to pay for that stupid swimming pool. And this means that we've had to cut back on some salaries that could have otherwise gone to pay our instructors. All these expenditures on chlorine and pumps and lifeguards and liability insurance and everything else it takes to run a pool for the benefit of 987 students (of which maybe ten ever actually use the pool) and 361 faculty and staff (of which only *five* even know how to swim)....those are all resources that could have been used for other things. For example, to hire more Logic teachers....or to give a raise to a highly deserving Special Projects Coordinator in recognition of her outstanding contributions to our college...."

Gwen was now braking again. No, she was *accelerating*. My stomach couldn't figure out which way she was going and so it lurched in both directions at once.

"Are you saying my predecessor made real contributions to the college? Because I've heard otherwise."

"You've been talking to the wrong people, Charlie: the wrong half of campus opinion. In truth, she was amazing! You have to keep in mind that by the time she got here we'd basically hit rock bottom. The college was already on the verge of losing its accreditation. The mission statement hadn't been reviewed in years. There were two factions on campus divided along philosophical lines: one screaming for positive change, the other clinging desperately to a tired status quo. The campus was so polarized that some faculty had even begun to receive bloated scrota on *Wednesdays*. It couldn't have been any worse, Charlie. Trust me. And that's when she arrived at the makeshift bus shelter – you know, the same one you arrived at last Saturday...."

"Next to the general store. Where the man with the harmonica was playing."

"Well, yeah. Although that store's been closed for a while now...."

"How is that possible? I was just there four days ago!"

"Trust me, it's gone."

"And the woman reading the newspaper?"

"Gone. Both of them. Especially the newspaper...."

Outside, the front page of a printed newspaper blew across the front of our car. Gwen accelerated past it as she spoke:

"So as I was saying.....our college was already in a deep hole and we'd hired this amazing lady and she'd agreed to come to Cow Eye and when she gets into town from halfway across the country Felch drives out to pick her up from the makeshift bus shelter in... *that truck*...!" Gwen's face contorted as if she were recalling a severed calf's scrotum, or a bloody emasculator. "She's allergic to dust, poor thing, and so she has to drive in with the art history teacher, whose Saab is clean and features a passenger belt, and the next day Felch brings her into his office and says, 'Look, miss, I know you're a smart gal....'" – upon pronouncing the words *miss* and *gal*, Gwen's face contorted even more, as if she had been *handed* a severed calf's scrotum, or a bloody emasculator – "....'Now I know you're a smart *gal*,' he says, 'and there's nothing wrong with that, but you're also going to be up against a divided campus, and so you need to do *this*, and you shouldn't do *that*, and be careful not to step too heavily with either foot. Make sure you tread lightly so you don't tread heavily on either of the two factions on campus....' But here the woman reminded him that she had *two* Ivy League educations and rich experience in conflict mediation and that Cow Eye was no different from any other place and that women were no longer content to be merely the objects of male fantasy and that if she saw things that needed changing, by god, she was going to change them even if it meant stepping on some toes! Charlie, she could have simply sat around admiring the ticking of her pendulum and collecting her paycheck in quiet acquiescence. But she didn't. She really decided to grab the bull by the horns, so to speak, and to fight for meaningful change at the college. But where best to start? She thought long and hard and after a lot of careful and strategic thinking she decided to start with the Christmas Committee...."

"Why there?"

"Where better? Her rich theoretical experience told her that the whole concept of the party – its very premise – was antiquated and needed to be re-envisioned. So she talked to Will Smithcoate about making some slight improvements to it. Simple yet thoughtful innovations were proposed like changing the name of the gathering from a "Christmas Party" to a "Winter Extravaganza" and adding more vegetables to the menu and moving the stage to the opposite side of the room and prohibiting the consumption of alcoholic beverages at the event. She also suggested that it would be more highly attended if it were held on a weekend, that it should be non-denominational, that the napkins should be fuchsia and mauve instead of red and green, and that the music should be updated from the same old Christmas favorites sung year after year by our own faculty and staff to a more eclectic blend of recorded world music that would better reflect the changing demographics of the surrounding community as well as the ever-increasing diversity of our staff. She suggested an international theme and noted that the large flag on the wall with its thirteen stripes and twenty-five stars could be repositioned to better accommodate equally attractive flags from other countries of the world; there was plenty of room on the wall for other nations, she said, and there was no reason why a wall of that size could not be made more flag-friendly...."

"It sounds like an ambitious proposal...."

"It was. But Smithcoate was against every suggestion. And when she offered her suggestions he demurred. And when she insisted on them he resisted. And when she galvanized a progressive faction of the committee to support her, he galvanized the reactionary faction and they began stonewalling. Like Cleburne from Arkansas. If she thrust, he parried. If she prohibited, he repealed. In time neither side would meet without their lawyers in the room. And so, finally, she just gave up. All her good intentions were futile. It was too much for her. And besides, there was the impending accreditation team visit that she still needed to get ready for....."

"The accreditors were coming?"

"Yes. In fact, they'd already arrived and were waiting at the bus shelter for someone to pick them up."

"In the sun?"

"Right. With clipboards?"

"But I thought she was arranging all that? Wasn't she supposed to pick them up?"

"Oh, no! Why would that be the job of a Special Projects Coordinator? Especially one with her education and experience! No, that was a miscommunication between Felch and his counterpart on the visiting team, the one who was lucky enough to get the window seat...."

"You know, it's funny you mentioned accreditation because I just finished reading our self-study this afternoon. It was terrible!"

"Yeah, well, that's not *her* fault. She was compiling the report, but the chairs of the different standards were supposed to do the actual writing and should have gotten her the materials months earlier. But they couldn't do it. Or wouldn't do it. In fact, some of them refused to do anything at all. And those who did weren't conscientious. Stokes, as usual, inflated the number of cows he'd inseminated. The fiscal office couldn't explain how much it actually cost to run the Olympic-sized pool (which some faculty had already started referring to as the *Albatross* Aquatics Complex!) The Technology Committee was torn between introducing new electric typewriters and maintaining their loyalty to the manual ones. And then there was Sam Middleton, English instructor and specialist in medieval poetry, who balked at writing his section due to personal, professional, and *aesthetic* considerations. 'It's a perversion of language,' he told her one day, and months later when he finally did produce something, it wasn't a credible accreditation write-up but a treatise in verse that on one level appeared to celebrate the successes of the English department but, on a deeper (and much darker) level, bemoaned the compromising of academic freedoms and the corruption of poetic language. With no actual prose narrative to include, she had no choice but to use what he'd submitted. The final product wasn't insightful prose, Charlie, but it wasn't *her* fault either. What could she have done differently? In fact, she could only do the best with what she had been given to work with...."

"No, it definitely wasn't *insightful*. But I can see how this might not have been her doing completely...."

"...Meanwhile, all of this was happening while she was trying to overcome so much adversity in her own personal life. Poor thing. The college hadn't made allowances for her dogs or her allergies or her dilemma as an unmarried middle-aged female desperate to find a challenging and great partner in a rural place where most people tie their first knot by age twenty...."

"Look, Gwen.... I'm still waiting for the crux of this. How does this all relate to Dr. Felch? Why should he be gelded?"

"Because *he*'s the reason she filed the lawsuit."

"For what? I still don't understand? What lawsuit? And I still don't get what the pool has to do with anything... and why it's all Rusty Stokes's fault...!"

"Simple. When this highly deserving woman asked Felch for a raise, he said no. Actually, he said *Hell no*! And when she asked for a reason he refused to give one. And when she threatened to go above his head, he said that there was no head above his – as if he were some kind of godhead – and that, even if there were, there would not be enough money. And when she refused to accept those explanations ("You have to *show* me!" she said) he gave a specific example saying that the cost of the pool was too steep and was draining all the available resources and that there was no extra money for anything else – especially a newly hired Special Projects Coordinator who had yet to make any meaningful contribution to the college. Charlie, this probably would have been the end of it. Except that after all that, he did one more thing that was simply inexcusable...."

"This is all happening in his office?"

"Yes."

"Next to the spittoon?"

"No, the spittoon came later. You see, not only did he refuse her the raise she deserved by suggesting that she perform a sex act, but as she was leaving his office and he was holding open the door to show her out – and as she was going through the doorway he....he reached down and patted her on the butt. The butt, Charlie! Like a quarterback would do to one of his linemen after a successful bunt attempt. This is a woman with personal references from the Undersecretary of War and Commerce, mind you. And when she'd jumped in reaction – after all, nobody at the League of Nations had ever played a down of baseball! – he just laughed and reminded her that the pool was Olympic-sized and suggested that she might want to take a long swim in it. And then he laughed again and closed the door after her."

"And then?"

"Well and then she hit him with the lawsuit."

"That quickly?"

"Before the door closed."

"For harassment?"

"No."

"Gender bias?"

"No."

"Detrimental reliance?"

"No, but good guesses one and all...."

"What then?"

"Give up?"

"Yes."

"She sued him for workplace bullying and occupational stress."

"Huh?"

"You see, it wasn't the slap on the butt that pushed her over the edge – she'd grown up in a family of brothers. And it wasn't the low salary. Or the way she'd been lured to the fringes of academia with false promises. Or even the dust that was relentlessly accumulating in her office with each passing day. Actually it wasn't any of these things that caused her to react so negatively to her time at Cow Eye...."

"What was it then?"

"It was the comment about the pool! She couldn't swim...!"

"Oh!"

"So in that context the comment was clearly a hostile threat. And so she sued him for creating a stressful working environment that kept her from fulfilling her duties as Special Projects Coordinator. In retrospect, all of it together was too much for her to take. The swimming comment. The accreditation mess. The endless divisions and alignments. The duplicity of the Christmas Committee and its chair. Compared to working at Cow Eye, she once told me, getting the Israelis and Palestinians to attend a joint Easter mass was like convincing an American child to open presents on Christmas morning...."

"And this is somehow *Rusty*'s fault?"

"Right. If not for that damn pool in the shape of the American flag, we might still have our amazing Special Projects Coordinator here with us today...!"

"I see. This is all very logical. But Gwen, what about you? You've alluded to an inherent irrational streak. And I can see you're very passionate about your role here at the college. That's all great. But what else can you tell me about yourself? I mean aside from the many things that love *should not be*. What about your name? And how you came to be here at Cow Eye? And where you might otherwise be if you weren't so committed to perpetuating logical thinking? Oh and of course....an embarrassing personal secret of your own! Would you care to share any of those things with me in this cozy car that smells of evergreen and cinnamon?"

"Honestly, Charlie, you're asking a lot. But I like you and so I'll tell you a few things about myself."

"Thank you, Gwen."

"Sure, I'll tell you a few things. But please know that anything I tell you stays in this car. Like silverfish in a book of rhyming poetry, never to see the light of day. Do you understand?"

"Yes, of course, Gwen. I'll keep it between you and me and these cozy bucket seats that you and I have been sitting in for the past half hour as we make our way headlong into a drought for the ages."

"Good. So where should I begin?" Gwen had taken her foot off the accelerator and was beginning to apply the brake. Then she took her foot off the brake and began to apply the accelerator. Then she again applied the brake. Then the accelerator. "Well," she said, "I suppose I should probably begin unequivocally, which is to say, with my *past*...."

Outside our car, the sun had made its way beyond the horizon and the sky had turned a light shade of purple. This was the tail end of yet another vivid sunset; soon it would be dark. Gwen pressed firmly on the brake, then accelerated suddenly, then braked and accelerated yet again – so quickly each time that it seemed she might be doing both at once. And yet the car continued its forward progress toward the Outskirts where Gwen's watery get-together was already under way. "Yes," she was saying, "I suppose I should begin with my earliest childhood memories. You see, I was not always such a rational person. In fact, there was once a time in my life when I actually became something quite the opposite. Of course it seems so long ago. Yet when I look back at it now, it's still the thing that gives me the most joy to recall, and also the most embarrassment. But I'm getting ahead of myself. Let's begin in a logical fashion, shall we? At the *beginning* then...?"

And here she pressed her foot firmly against the accelerator and the car rolled on quietly and inexorably into the retreating sunlight.

"...EVEN WHEN I was little," Gwen began, "I always knew I wanted to be a teacher. While other children dreamt of being athletes or actresses or entrepreneurs, I knew that for me all roads led to teaching, and that of the many roads that might take me there the truest and straightest was also the most logical of them all. This did not come to me by chance but was nurtured within my inquisitive heart over the course of an entire childhood. From an early age I'd seen my peers grappling with the magnitude of the world's great questions and I'd seen how it inevitably led to ennui and angst and self-destruction. One of my friends from college, an aspiring philosopher, overdosed on his twenty-seventh birthday; another was lost to a life of drinking and aimlessness; yet another gave everything up under the weight of so many questions that could never be resolved; years later I discovered that he had become a successful investment broker. But why? Why did such terrible things have to happen to thoughtful people?

People with so much promise? Couldn't they see that all of it – or at least the things that we have some control over – can be categorized and isolated and reduced to definitive processes that would allow even the most complex phenomena of life to be explained in terms of their own inherent consistency, or, oppositely, to be dismissed? For me this was the beauty of logic, the reassurance it provided. Of course my views became more nuanced as I moved from middle school to high school, then from high school into college, and then on to graduate school...."

(At first as Gwen told her story I found myself actively nodding to reassure her that I was following her words. But as she settled into her narrative groove, I soon realized that all my nodding, all my listening – perhaps even my very presence in the car – was of little importance to her at that moment. As if in a trance, Gwen was immersed in the telling of her story and as she descended deeper and deeper into it I settled back in the cozy bucket seat to absorb her words. With no need for words of my own – the purest state of bliss – I gave myself to listening intently to her story while gazing through the window at the darkening countryside.)

"...For me life was a road," she was saying. "In fact life had always presented itself to me as a road and this road was broad and straight and though it was long it led in no uncertain terms from one point to another like the straightest line between two opposites. For me, life was a series of finite points, like coordinates on an axis. And if point A was my entry into this world (my parents named me after a cousin who had drowned when she was two); and point B was my accumulated experiences in their sum – my childhood tea parties, my educational exploits and accolades all rolled into one; and if C was my present milieu – the effortlessness of my graduate studies, the rigid predictability of my daily routine; well, then D and E and F were all my *future*. Along with G, H, I, and every other point along the straight line of life. For in this continuum D might be my tenure application, and E would be my promotion to Associate Professor, and F and G would surely be my full professorship and my chairing a department, respectively. And all of this would culminate somewhere later on this line of coordinates with my retirement as a respected academician from a prestigious ivy-walled college. Even then I allowed that there might be slight deviations along the way; and yet I knew with all the conviction in my logical mind that the path would be as straight as I could make it and that it would take me inevitably and efficiently to my destination...."

"…When I finally graduated I took my first teaching job at a commuter college in the heart of the city, an urban college, and on the very first day of class I was approached by a young man with an attractive face and an exotic accent. He looked to be from an Asian country – these were the days when students from such places were very rare and could still be categorized by continent – and in his eyes I could see that the world he was from, whatever country or community or continent it represented, was clearly a world of vast possibilities and boundless horizons with innumerable iterations of emanation and dissolution. There are some nations whose peoples have the eyes of all eternity housed in their sockets and his nation – whatever and wherever it may have been – was certainly one of them. I had just erased the blackboard after an awkward first lecture that had left me searching for my own answers, and as if sensing my inner turbulence and vulnerability, he had approached me after class just as I was gathering my things. The autumn sunlight filtered in through a window. A rotating fan blew. The other students were filing out and in my fingers I was still holding the chalk from my lecture. For several moments the boy – the man? – just stood there watching me in silence as if not knowing what to say, instead saying nothing, and just staring at me with those infinite eyes. Then suddenly, and in the clearest of voices, he spoke up: 'Professor,' he said, and here I was so startled at the firmness of his voice which sounded like the love cry of desire itself. 'Professor, I am very interested to learn what you have to teach us about the logic of our universe. For the universe is vast and daunting, and logic itself is a tool like all the others. I will come to every class of yours and sit right there in that front row seat where I sat today. And I will take copious notes. But before I do all that I would first like to address you with a few questions….?' This young man was not tall and as he spoke he looked up at me with dark black eyes not unlike wet anthracite or the extinguished stars in the sky that are as timeless as our collective soul and whose light we are now seeing though they themselves have long since died. 'Tell me this, Professor. If there are two neighbors living on opposite sides of a very thin wall – one neighbor who is boisterous and always chooses conflict over conciliation and another neighbor who is quiet and deferential and who always chooses conciliation over conflict – in such a living arrangement is it possible that these two neighbors living on opposite sides of the thin wall will *ever* be able to see eye to eye? And if so, may it ever happen that the two neighbors can maintain their respective preferences such that the deferential neighbor will be able to enjoy the benefits of peace and quiet without ever engaging in conflict?' It was a logical trap and so I said, 'Your premise is fuzzy. Or not fuzzy enough. For it is well known that sound comes not as an absolute but as a range, and so it is conceivable that on a scale of zero to one – with one being perfect sound and zero being perfect silence – that both neighbors will be able to agree upon a noise level that is neither one nor zero. This alone might be said to resolve the question of their respective preferences for noise – which would be sufficiently sufficient if not for the fact that, as you mention, one of the neighbors also prefers conflict to conciliation, while the other prefers conciliation to conflict. So, as to the strong desire for conflict (of one neighbor) and the equally strong desire to *avoid* conflict (of the other neighbor), well in this case you could argue that neither side will be able to find fulfillment in the end because the side that seeks out conflict will always impose conflict on the other, which means the one who desires to avoid conflict will never be at peace. But, at the same time, the neighbor who seeks out conflict will never be at peace himself because his soul will be in a constant state of conflict and no soul can be at peace when it is also in conflict. And so the answer to your question is *yes*. Which is to say, the answer to your question is just as likely *no*.'"

"...'I see,' the young man said and then: 'So let me ask you another. This is a true story that unfolds somewhere within the impossible cycle of time. You see, it is a very dark night – a night in late August perhaps – and a man and a woman are sitting in the front seat of the woman's recently purchased truck. The sky is clear and the moon is startling. Music plays softly on the AM car radio which is old and therefore very raspy. The rapturous sound of crickets can be heard in the distance. The two in the truck are mutually affectionate and mutually receptive. And yet as the man reaches out for the woman he suddenly comes to the logical realization that in order to reach all the way across the distance between them, he must first cross the distance between himself and the gear shift halfway in between....but that before he can cross this distance he must first cross the midpoint between himself and this midpoint and before he crosses *that* midpoint he must first cross yet another midpoint and so on and so forth *ad infinitum*.....So if this is true, and given that it is impossible to cross an infinite number of thresholds, will this man ever truly be able to reach across the infinite space between them to unfasten the buttons on her blouse?' At this question I laughed in recognition. It was an old dilemma that had been resolved numerous times over the centuries by the world's greatest lovers. And so I said, 'In this case, the moon too must be a woman because she is deceiving them both. You see, he will *never* be able to reach across that most intimate space. For the space that he must vanquish is not just the distance of the space itself, but also the ultimate space of time and feminine eternity. And such things can never be truly vanquished, no matter how close the buttons or how enticing the nipples under the blouse.' At this the young man smiled and then he looked at me once again with those dark black eyes and said, 'If that is so, then let me pose this final dilemma to you...'"

"The young man's eyes were as dark as darkness itself and here he said, 'My dilemma is this. Suppose it were the first day of class for an aspiring college student who disagrees in principle that the buttons of a loose-fitting blouse can never be undone, and suppose this same college student were to ask his Logic teacher, who happens to be wearing a pink skirt and white polyester blouse with the top two buttons unfastened ever so provocatively, to have dinner with him in a quaint restaurant around the corner. Given this supposition, dear Professor, what, in your expert opinion, would be her response?' Obviously, his question was surprising. But I'd made sure to choose my outfit carefully that day – the pink skirt and the white polyester blouse with the top two buttons opened ever so revealingly – and so, to quell his eagerness, I fastened one of the opened buttons and responded that his Logic teacher would not reply unequivocally to his invitation but instead would answer by saying this: that she would promise to have dinner with him if, and *only* if, he could predict the inevitable outcome of his own proposal, that is to say, whether she would have dinner with him that night or whether she would instead say no and dine by herself back in her lonely studio apartment; and if he could predict the correct outcome then she would in fact have dinner with him; but if his prediction were wrong, then she would not. To my response the young man thought for a moment and then said, without much additional need for reflection, 'Well then I will have to say that she will certainly have dinner with him.' 'Is that so?' I said. 'And what might be giving you grounds for such certainty?' And he said, 'It's simple. If this man answers that she *will* have dinner with him, then it will be her rightful choice whether to make his prediction come true by actually having dinner with him and in this case she will be free to make her choice openly, at her own discretion, and without fear of causing a deep conflict with the Professor's very logical approach to the world. But if, on the other hand, the student answers that she will *not* – in other words, if I say that she will *not* go to dinner with him – then not only would I be giving up the privilege of dining with you tonight but, logically speaking, I would be causing your system to come to a devastating impasse. And of course no student in search of his divine mother goddess would ever want to inflict that sort of intellectual violence upon a woman's system of beliefs. So yes, the teacher will go out to dinner with the young student at about seven o'clock tonight and the two of them will dine in mutual comfort, free of conflict, like the two great conversationalists that we call logic and paradox.'…"

"Of course I was taken aback at his response, because, well, he was *right*! In the true depths of my soul I was not just ready to say yes to his proposal but was singing it out to the accompaniment of lute and lyre and sitar – one of the few moments in my life where the logic of my mind happened to fall into perfect alignment with the logic of my heart. By now the class had long emptied out and the room was very still and perfectly quiet but for the sounds of our breathless intentions. Time no longer flowed. The two of us were alone, as if we had been there together in this state, forever and alone. Within a few passing minutes he had become the most beautiful student I would ever come to know: his shoulders were narrow and appropriate; his eyes shone as black as Christmas; and his name, I would soon learn, meant Devourer of the Universe in the language of his ancestors. In the hanging silence of the room it was clear I had succumbed to his proposal and that I would go to dinner with him that night. But I could not simply let things at that; in matters of logic I was, after all, the teacher and he merely the student. In the noble interests of classroom management one must always maintain this ancient hierarchy and never allow it to waver. And so coming to my pedagogical senses I said, 'You are right, young man! You are very right indeed. To keep things simple and respectful, your answer should be yes. And to avoid the paradox you mention, my answer can be either yes or no. Which is to say that it might in fact be *no*….but that it could just as well be *yes*. And so it *is* yes….' At this the man smiled. For a tantalizing second his smile spread across his

face and I paused to let him savor his triumph. Then I continued: 'But....'
– and here I saw the noble quiver of doubt flash in his eyes, that timeless
sliver of hesitation that is the consequence of a woman's most ancient
authority – '*But*,' I said, 'there is only one problem with all of this. You
see, women never tell the truth. Which means that because *I* am a woman
I too never tell the truth. Which means I always *lie*. And since I always
tell the truth when speaking, the sentence I have just spoken about never
telling the truth is true, which means that the sentence I just spoke – as
well as the sentence I am now speaking and the sentence that I might
have used to accept your invitation, *if* I did in fact appear to accept your
invitation on behalf of the hypothetical Logic teacher – is itself also a lie.
So when I said she would agree to eat dinner with you tonight it was not
true. In fact, she did not say this at all. And so it follows that she would
not. And I would not. And I *will* not. I'm very sorry to be the bearer of
bad inference, but tonight is also a moonlit night, it is getting late, and
my lonely studio apartment awaits....' Here I turned to leave. It was cruel,
yes, but logic is nothing if not cruel. I had turned quickly away and was
already on my way out of the classroom when I heard the boy call after
me: 'Professor...!'" And when I turned around I saw that he was smiling.
Smiling! 'Professor, if what you say is true – if your claims to untruth are
true, or if, as you say, your claims to truth are untrue – then surely your
logic is less than sound. For if you lie when you accept, then your denial is
also a lie. And if you tell the truth when you decline, then your acceptance
is also the truth! And so, far truer than this – than saying the two will not
dine – is to say that the young student with dark eyes will meet his Logic
teacher at a place not far from here at exactly seven o'clock tonight....'"

I shifted in my seat. Although I'd been listening in blissful wordlessness,
here I couldn't help interjecting:

"Sorry, Gwen," I said. "I was with you for a while. But you sort of
lost me there at the end. What actually happened? Did the two of them
go out to the restaurant or not?"

"...Of course we did!"

"You did?"

"....Of course. Like I said this was the time in my life when logic failed
me the most. Or I failed it. That night he met me outside the classroom and
we walked to an Asian restaurant around the corner where we talked about
the logic of illogic and the core of reason that is inherent in unreasonable

things. 'If the sentence I am now speaking is true,' he would say, 'then you are falling in love with me.' And I would respond with, 'Have you not regained your sense of reality?'" Over vegetables and rice we discussed the remotest beginnings of the universe and how, transcending eternal time, it has come down to us as fire and water and words and prayer. 'If the universe is infinite,' I would say, 'then it must also be timeless and unknowable and beyond our ability to call it infinite.' 'But if it is *finite*,' he would counter, 'then there must be a place where it ends and something else begins. And isn't that "something" *also* the universe?' And so, that night over dinner we came to an agreement that the universe is neither finite nor infinite but only as infinite as our ability to feel love for the infinite. Infinite love for god. Timeless love for the universe. Infinite and timeless love for all the regionally accredited community colleges that have come to us through the eras like radiating circles of energy....'"

"So things were good?"

"...Things were great. Every Tuesday and Thursday I would come to my afternoon lecture to see him sitting in his seat at the front of the room. And as I spoke to the class I saw only him. And when I listened to the world I heard only him, his voice spurring me to greater and greater levels of insight. I don't know about you, Charlie, but perhaps once in a lifetime there comes a person who galvanizes your ideas. Who stimulates your thoughts and spurs you to unbelievable creative accomplishments and frontiers. If you've ever had a person like this in your life, then you can consider yourself blessed. And I consider myself blessed that this young man came into my life and became my lover...."

At this, I awoke from my quiet gazing. The countryside was now almost black outside our window and the smell of evergreen and cinnamon had faded, as if chasing the sun beyond the horizon.

"Wait, Gwen. Did you just say that the two of you became *lovers*? As in actual *romantic* lovers? As opposed to the philosophical platonically intellectual community college kind?"

"That's right."

"Oh my! And is that an okay thing? I mean, given that you and he were on opposite ends of the learning curve. Ethically is it acceptable for a professor and her student to have a relationship like that?"

"Who cares? I mean, I definitely didn't care. Which is to say that, technically, no it probably wasn't acceptable. And accreditationally it wasn't acceptable. And of course rationally it made little sense. After all, here I was a newly hired faculty member with a clear track to tenure slinking away during breaks between lectures to have a secret affair with a student who was ten years my junior. In what educational institution would this have made sense? No, this would not have been a rational course of action at any institution of higher education – much less a community college! Looking back, it's clear that the two of us were from opposing worlds, different eras, competing social strata. Our life trajectories were incompatible: mine efficiently linear, his gracefully sinusoidal. Aside from a preemptory traffic sign, where else in the world would this have made any sense at all? But it made sense within the logical system of my own heart! And so I gave myself to it entirely."

"What do you mean, *entirely*?"

"Charlie, in the truest sense of that word. Entirely! That's how I gave myself to him. Over the next three and a half months, the two of us engaged in a meeting of the mind and body, a union of spirit and soul so vehement and all-encompassing that it could have easily been the subject of great literature – perhaps even rhyming poetry. Like a sudden monsoon he slaked my thirst. And like a love vine I wrapped myself around him as if he were my only source of nourishment. At first I was able to reconcile the two competing logics: the logic of my heart with the logic of my mind. Mondays, Wednesdays and Fridays, I told myself, were reserved for the logical mind; Tuesdays and Thursdays would be for the logical heart. In this way, I believed, the time continuum of the community college would serve as my own buffer of self-control. But gradually the heart began to take over the entire work week and then, like water spreading over dry ground, it began to infiltrate the days of the weekend as well. Charlie, I was hopeless. My teaching suffered. My relationships with my colleagues floundered. Despite my professional carelessness, and despite my failure to adequately teach them such things, my students came to make the correct inferential deductions. Whereas in the beginning we concealed our affections, in time my lover and I came to celebrate them in public. And to relish them in private. More than once I found myself canceling a Monday or Wednesday class to spend an extra morning in the passionate clutches of eternity. Once I asked a colleague to cover my Friday class three weeks in a row, and another time I sent my students home early under the guise of a take-home quiz. Charlie, this sacred man with the dark eyes was all I could think about. He was all that I could feel. Together we were travelers on a thrilling voyage to a world that was bright and new and beautiful. And it was pure and good and timeless. And then it all came to a screeching end. Our journey. My world. Not that my world *actually* came to an end – it never does, does it?; at least not until it actually does – but the world I'd known and come to love over the last three and a half months – this new bright world – was about to come to its logical resolution…."

⤳

"….IT WAS A Tuesday and he hadn't shown up at class. He'd been my most faithful student and my faithful lover and he'd lived up to every promise. Not just his commitments to me as his mother-goddess but also in his role as student-muse. Each Tuesday and Thursday he came to class where he sat in the front row and took prodigious notes. He was the rock in my gaseous universe. The pivot on an out-of-control axis. But now he was gone. Anxiously, I waited for him after class but he did not show. And when I phoned him he did not answer. And when, after he didn't come to my class on Thursday, I went to his apartment, I learned that he was gone for good: his roommate informed me that he had moved out but couldn't say where he'd gone. A week came and went in utter depression. I couldn't even find the strength to get out of bed. I wouldn't eat. I called the school to tell them I had pneumonia and couldn't teach my classes any time soon. They wished me well and reminded me to save my doctor's note; as soon as I hung up the phone I slept for another two days. Through nights of perilous dreaming and days of longing and remembrance, the season came and went. The semester came and went. And still there was no relief. In time I came to give up on my job at the college. I stayed in my apartment. I did not venture outside. This continued for several weeks and who knows how or when it would have ended. Then one day I received a letter from him. It was a lengthy letter but I could recite it to you by heart right now if I wanted, even twenty years later. 'Dear Professor,' he wrote. 'I am sorry that I had to go away. Such are the exigencies of life. Please know that I am now a better person for the logical universe that you have shared with me. This is knowable and forever. But since I began studying at your community college I have also come to realize that *some* time is not as eternal as we would like it to be and that some life does itself tend to come to an inglorious end. And now is the time that I must choose to move on to my new future…..' Charlie, I've read those lines a thousand times. And every time I see them, I see them differently. Standing with the letter in my hand, it occurred to me that everything was finished. That there would be no more dinners. That the sum of our discussions could now be archived in the great library of Time to be accessed only via the data retrieval tool called memory. And that our future would stay forever in the red-shifting realm of imagination like a siren whose pitch changes as it recedes into the distance. And then I stopped. Wait a minute! What was this? On the envelope he had written his return address. His address! It was a small town in Michigan. And it had the full street address. He put the address on the envelope, Charlie! With a new sense of purpose I jumped out of bed and for the first time in a month I brushed my hair and for the first time in a week I brushed my teeth and for the first time in three days I put on my clothes and left my apartment…."

"….An interesting turn of events…!"

"Just wait! So I pulled on my clothes and went to the bus station where I bought the first available ticket to Michigan and when I arrived I caught a taxi at the bus station and rode it to the address on the envelope; and when my taxi pulled up I paid the driver in full and told him he could leave and I made my way up the driveway toward the front door of the house. It was early winter by then and I hadn't been thinking about that enough when I'd boarded the bus and now as I stood in the open air I couldn't stop shivering on the steps of the house while trying to wrap my arms around myself to hold in my heat. I rang the doorbell and it echoed throughout the house: a dog barked. No one responded. By now the cold was grinding into my bones and my lips were chattering. I rang the doorbell again. Again the dog barked, a small dog. But again no answer. Now what would I do? If nobody answered, where would I go? It hadn't even occurred to me that I might ever have to come back from Michigan empty-hearted. And yet there I was standing in impossibly cold weather on a door step that had no connection to me other than a letter sent from a boy I'd met in one of my classes, a letter from a young man I'd known less than four months. Where would I go if nobody answered? What would I do? Charlie, this is where the heights of my irrationality – or was it the limitations of my rationality?! – had taken me: to the empty doorstep of a cold Michigan afternoon. With winter in my bones. A dog barking at me through the door. A single postmarked letter separating me from utter and complete desolation. At that moment I'd truly reached the lowest point of my life. And then the door opened...."

Gwen had ceased to use the brake a long time ago, and now as her story built from utter love to utter cold, she was pressing firmly on the accelerator, the small car screaming as it moved faster and faster through the growing night. For the first time since she'd picked me up I began to worry that her story might lead us into something calamitous. Another suicide. Or a ruthless break-up. Or even one of the waterless canals along the highway we were traveling. Somewhere between the icy door step and the hot drought of the night around us, there was something very eternal about the distance we were traveling.

"...The door opened, Charlie, and out stepped a dark-skinned man in a bath robe. 'Yes?' he asked in thickly accented English. And when I told him who I was and who I was looking for and when I showed him the letter, my hand shaking from the cold, he brought me inside the house, which was warm and moist and smelled of exotic foods and strange spices. The man at the door was my lover's father and he called out to his wife in their language and she made tea for the three of us. And while we ate biscuits and drank the tea at their kitchen table, my lover's parents explained that their son was not there anymore, that he had not lived with them since going away to community college earlier that year. And that he called from time to time, but had not called recently; he'd probably used the return address of his childhood home out of habit. Or maybe out of a sense of propriety. But he hadn't told them of his plans or where he would be and they weren't sure when he would be back. I thanked them and apologized for the inconvenience. They gave me some warm clothes to wear and some money for the bus ride back to the college and from there I returned across country to my lonely studio apartment and my job teaching Logic to promising undergraduates. I taught there for another four years before taking the job at Cow Eye. Of course there are a few missing pieces to the story. Like the disciplinary procedure I had to overcome to get my job back and how I fought the termination action and won on a technicality but only after being made to relive the entire humiliating episode in written form. Within six months I was able to pay back the couple for their kindness. And ever since this embarrassing adventure in passion and irrationality, I have been the most intentionally nondescript, consistently rational and stoically logical Logic teacher that you would ever want to hire. Charlie, since that day, I have not left a single button on my blouse unfastened."

"Wow, Gwen. So did you ever see this boy again?"

"No, I did not. And I never will. Even if I meet him again, it won't be him. That person is gone forever. He died when I got that letter. And I will never stop being human because of it...."

By now Gwen was pulling off the main road and entering a turnoff. As she took the turn, my stomach swerved and turned with it.

"I'm sorry, Gwen," I said. "I didn't realize you were a sexually sentient being prone to human vulnerabilities. I guess now I know."

"It's okay," she said. "It's an ancient history. One that I do tell from time to time. But not one that you should ever think about taking beyond the confines of these cozy bucket seats and these faint smells of evergreen and cinnamon."

"I understand," I said.

"Good," said Gwen. "And besides, we're here."

Looking up, I saw a large neon sign that said "WELCOME TO THE OUTSKIRTS OF COW EYE" – and below it in letters that were much smaller yet equally neon: "*Where Ideas Meet!*"

"So this is it?"

"Yes it is. The brighter side of town, as we like to call it...."

"We?"

"Yes, *we*."

⁓

AND GWEN WAS right. This new part of town really was brighter. In fact, the glamorous section of Cow Eye Junction known as the Outskirts had arisen astride a single narrow street lined with scenic wooden store fronts and charming hand-carved signs proclaiming "Carla's Massage" and "The Outskirts of Heaven Healing Salts." By now the sun was down and the night scene was already vibrant with bars and restaurants and theaters. Health food stores offered organic vegetables in crates propped outside, and shops sold handmade candles and incense and small packets of "magic salts" with Vedic prescriptions for longevity. Handwritten sandwich boards touted nostalgia tours through the abandoned meat-processing plants and slaughter houses, while women in seductive saris lured passersby into 45-minute tantric "discovery" sessions. Gwen explained that the local government looked the other way on the goings-on at the Outskirts. The town was in fact becoming a hotbed of activity for the weekend visitors from other places who mixed with a diverse collection of healers, hippies, prophets, and priests – the "weirdos" that Dr. Felch had referred to during my first ride into town, and the "we" that Gwen sometimes referenced in her own descriptions of the region's demographics. Tarot readers sold their fortunes in smoke-filled salons. Backroom abortions flourished. Bungee-jumping and ski jet rides were hawked alongside snorkeling trips and guided inner-tube expeditions down the Cow Eye River. One salon offered a freak show. Another promised spiritual enlightenment. Store after store peddled instant healing and secret elixirs to sickly expatriates while in the numerous opium dens white men with dreadlocks reclined on pillows smoking the latest blends of hashish. The street, while narrow, seemed to run into infinity itself, much longer even than the fence of the Cow Eye Ranch, and as interminable as man's longing for vice and adventure, his desire for simple remedies, his insatiable appetite for glamour and innovation and efficiency.

Gwen drove slowly along the street until she reached a sign that read "Marsha's Kundalini Yoga Studio" and there she decelerated one last stomach-rending time and took the first open parking spot next to a silver Saab.

"This is Marsha's studio," she explained. "And that's our art history teacher's Saab. We're a little late, but it's okay...."

Still queasy from the stop-and-go ride I exited the car and stumbled awkwardly on firm ground as I tried to regain my equilibrium. From there I followed Gwen to the entrance of the studio where she was already opening the front door. Through the door of the studio I could already feel the drifting aroma of marijuana and incense floating above the laughter of anonymous voices. Gwen motioned for me to follow her. Then, as if remembering something from her distant past, she turned around and aimed her key chain at her unlocked car. As she pressed the button, I saw the car's headlights flash and its horn sound in response.

"I used to leave my car door unlocked," she explained with a wistful smile. "But that was a long time ago. And I am much wiser now."

≈

{ }

Like any other muscle, the heart itself requires subtle and frequent tearing to become stronger. Only by this gradual tearing and rebuilding can it become bigger and stronger and more ready to suffer the vicissitudes of life's cruelties. For community college instructors, in particular, this rule is an important one. Like no other realm, the instructor must deal with the many instruments of heartbreak: the unapproved grant proposal, the fruitless committee meeting, the underappreciated tenure document, the negative student feedback and constant threat of academic grievance. These are all things that can lead to heartbreak. And so it is good to train the heart for such unavoidable trauma.

There are several things that an instructor can do to prepare the heart for trauma. Morning sessions spent with a newspaper can do wonders for increasing the heart's capacity for heartbreak. Afternoon walks through a quiet park are equally effective. And of course evening strolls, alone and unwanted, amid the bustling nightlife of your typical college town can reaffirm, in slow and less-traumatic ways, the accumulating realities of life. Seeing so many joyous couples in naïve embrace can help you recall the pangs of your own youthful exuberances when romance was still a birthright and love was something to be harvested, simply and without effort, like arugula on a planter's bed. And then of course there are the late evening activities that can train the heart and inure it to disillusionment: the platitudes of television, the sloppy comfort of romantic novels, the songs that sing of true love amid the unabashed comfort of rhyming couplets and three-part harmony. All of these things will enable the heart to become more pliant, more reliable, and more open to the trials of finding love at a regionally accredited community college.

Like any other muscle, though, the heart does not suffer severe trauma well. For such trauma may impair the ability of the heart to function as it was intended. Unlike many other muscles of the body, the tearing of the heart can be so traumatic that it can be permitted to happen only once. Like the eating of a delicious yet poisonous mushroom. Or like the professional suicide that happens when the emotions are allowed to intervene into the process of colleague-to-colleague romance. And so it is unfortunate that once this irreparable tearing has occurred, the heart will be ruined absolutely and, like a committee that has lost its chair, will be unable to serve its true master ever again.

{ }

THE MOISTURE IN ALL THINGS

> *"Mi eniros en ĉiu planedo, kaj por Mia energio*
> *ili resti en orbito. Mi fariĝis la luno kaj per tio*
> *provizi la suko de la vivo al ĉiuj legomoj."*
>
> - Bhagavad Gita

A s Gwen and I entered the dark studio, a small wind chime on the door announced our arrival. The chime was delicate and airy and seemed to suggest the sound of a soul passing wistfully from one spiritual state to another: from Michigan to Florida, perhaps, or from Iowa to Wisconsin. The studio was dimly lit – candles had been placed around the room – and out of the neon bustle of the street outside I felt the luxurious descent into a sweet and shadowy world of burning incense and melting wax. Exotic music played lightly in the background. The air was warm and dry and through the haze of smoke I could see the candles around the room arranged in the shape of a lotus blossom. On the walls colorful drawings had been hung showing oriental couples engaged in tasteful coitus. On the floor, bamboo mats were set up in a perfect ring so that the many representatives of Cow Eye Community College, each of them sitting cross-legged and serene, could form an eternal circle of life.

"Namaste!" Marsha called out at the sound of the door chime.

And Gwen responded: "Namaste, Marsha!"

The studio was a single room with a wooden floor – a former dance studio? – and thick saffron curtains that had been drawn tight to hold back the world outside: the bright light of an afternoon sun or the curious gaze of an unsuspecting passerby. The circle of bamboo mats was bedecked with teaching faculty and at various points in the circle, seated on their mats, I could make out those who had chosen to be at this particular get-together in lieu of the other one taking place at the river: Nan Stallings in her sling and Luke Quittles caressing a cup of wine next to the college's grant writer; and the ubiquitous art history instructor whose Saab was parked outside; and the economics professor whose article justifying the poll tax had recently been accepted for peer review; and the Schlocksteins, Harold and Winona, the college's first formally recognized couple, dressed in matching Roman togas. In the far corner was the gunsmithing instructor in a black silk scarf and next to him the college's Esperanto teacher wearing her hair down and a badge proclaiming "Mi amas Esperanton!" Seated throughout the circle were four out of five of the English faculty (only Sam Middleton was conspicuously absent), along with the embarrassed lecturer who'd parked in the handicapped stall during convocation and the mesmerizing creative writing instructor whose habit it was to enjoy the sexual favors of his female students. It was an eclectic bunch, to say the least, and in the small room now growing ever warmer from the incense and the fellowship and the smoke emanating from the marijuana that was being generously passed around, it was clear that so much intellectual and spiritual diversity had rarely if ever come together in such a small segment of time and space.

"Hey, Charlie!" a familiar voice called out. It was Ethel Newtown, who had been finger-picking some vegetables from the food table but now rushed over to greet me with an emphatic hug. "Glad you could make it, Charlie! Nan and I were just talking about you. We didn't think you'd come. But look…here you are!"

"Yeah, well, Gwen was nice enough to drive me. And I figured this would be a good way to get to know my peers a little more intimately. You know, the ones I'll be working with to save our college from the precipice of institutional ruin."

"By revising the outdated mission statement?"

"Right."

"And resurrecting the Christmas party?"

"Correct. I'm hoping this watery get-together will be helpful in that regard. Although I'm not sure why everyone keeps referring to it as 'watery.' After our long drive through ineffable drought, I don't see any *water* here…"

"Be patient, Charlie! It's on the way!"

Ethel laughed heartily and knocked back her cup of wine, and as she did I noticed the gash on her chin from yesterday's collision with the calf.

"How's your battle wound?" I asked. "It looks a lot better than it did yesterday."

"Oh, it's nothing. Just three stitches. A very small price to pay for sowing the seeds of civilized society. Wouldn't you agree?"

"I would. Absolutely, I would." I laughed. "Hey, Ethel, where's Stan? I assumed he would be here. But I don't see him...."

"No, you wouldn't. That's because Stan chose to be *elsewhere*. Which is fine with me. He's an adult. And being an adult, he is perfectly entitled to make his own decisions knowing full well what the consequences may be. He is capable of making that choice. And so are we."

"We?"

"Yes, *we*. I learned that today from Gwen at our first mentor meeting."

Here Ethel asked which mentor I'd been assigned and when I told her I'd gotten Alan Long River, the speech teacher who doesn't speak, she laughed and told me that it could have been much worse: poor Nan got Will Smithcoate and he'd already stood her up.

"They were supposed to meet in the cafeteria at his usual table. But when she got there he wasn't around. She waited for an hour but he never showed up."

"That's too bad. He seems like a nice guy. And what about you? How's your mentoring with Gwen working out? Are the two of you a good fit?"

"It's going great! Today she took me to lunch and we discussed the logic of the universe and the science of cosmic principles. Then we talked about how to format my tenure dossier and the best way to convince impressionable undergraduates that journalism is as timeless as anything else in this world – if not *more* so. Gwen also made a convincing argument that marriage, as a vehicle for male subjugation, is not unlike the plough that burdens the diligent bovine. I guess I always knew this, just never thought about it in such servile terms. Needless to say, I feel a lot more prepared for my first semester at Cow Eye. And for the rigors of my journey toward personal liberation and ultimate emancipation that shines with promise like a distant beacon on the horizon."

"Death?"

"Tenure!"

"That's good news then. Congratulations."

"Thanks. And you, Charlie? How's your own personal liberation coming along? Are you any closer to becoming something *entirely*? Or to finding the moisture in things?"

"Not really. To be honest, I'm not actually seeing a lot of moisture in *anything* at the moment. But who knows? The night is still young...."

"It certainly is!"

Across the room, Nan gave a friendly wave from where she was sitting. Excitedly she untwisted herself from her cross-legged stance and walked over to where Ethel and I were standing, and with her one arm in a sling, managed to give me a warm hug with the other arm.

"Nice to see you here, Charlie!"

"Thanks, Nan. How's the arm?"

"It's been better. My shoulder still hurts. But at least I can bend my wrist now. And you? Any progress on extending Dr. Felch's metaphor?"

"You mean the calf?"

"Yes. You know, the castrated calf's role within the corral of institutional learning. Any epiphanies on that front?"

"Not yet. But it's still early. The semester hasn't even started. I have until December. And the night is still young...."

"It is indeed!"

The two laughed.

"You know," said Nan, "Ethel and I were just arguing about whether you would even show up tonight. Ethel insisted you *wouldn't*. I also insisted that you wouldn't, so it looks like we both lost the argument!"

"Yeah," said Ethel, "Nan and I agreed that sometimes it seems like you consider yourself above it all. As if you can't be bothered by social interactions with your peers. As if the world inhabited by other human beings were a distraction, something distasteful to be scorned and avoided. And so we thought you might be more likely to choose the quiet solitude of your own apartment over tonight's sensual get-together."

"Me? Above it all? For one, there's not much quiet in my apartment with the math faculty next door. And as to being above it all, well, as far as I'm concerned I might as well still be lying back there on the bloody asphalt. Because metaphorically speaking, I never really got up from that asphalt. And may never get up. So obviously I'm in no position to consider myself *above* anything!"

"Does that mean you're here to stay then?"

"At Cow Eye?"

"No, at tonight's get-together?"

"Unfortunately, no. I need to leave at seven-thirty."

"Why so early? I thought you wanted to get to know us more intimately?"

"I do. But not to that extent. You see, I have another place I need to be at."

"In other words, you're consciously choosing to go to *both* places?"

"As best I can."

"Instead of going to just one?"

"Right."

"And instead of enjoying that one place *entirely* and to its fullest?"

"Well, yes."

"Too bad. You're going to miss the best part!"

"Yeah," Ethel added. "If only our institutional researcher were here...!"

The two giggled like schoolgirls.

Seeing this, Marsha Greenbaum, surprisingly resplendent in a loosely fitting sarong, came up to offer us some food. The white sarong was diaphanous and very revealing and, as she moved across the room with a single graceful fluidity, the fabric brushed lightly against her body in ways that left little to the imagination. "Help yourselves!" she said and led us over to the table where the finger foods had been placed: fish, wine, parched grain, and a bowl of M&Ms.

"It looks great!" said Nan.

"Yeah," I agreed. "That green stuff looks intriguing. What is it?"

"That, Charlie, is arugula."

"Arugula?"

"Yes, Charlie, arugula. I chose the individual leaflets myself."

Ethel made a small plate of arugula for me, and Nan sprinkled some M&Ms on top along with some parched grain. Marsha handed me a cup.

"Have some wine..." she said. "You do drink wine, don't you?"

I held up the cup affirmatively:

"You could say that....!"

Eventually, Nan and Ethel left to take their seats and Marsha moved on to greet others in the room. As I stood with my wine and my plate heaped with M&M's and arugula, I couldn't help noticing my colleagues' casual attire: by now each of them was wearing loose-fitting clothes; some were even wrapped in the same light sarong that Marsha was wearing.

Even Gwen, after the long drive from verdure to desiccation, had changed into a pair of shorts and a loose t-shirt and looked utterly reposed as she sat on a bamboo mat talking to the economics professor whose sarong was tied around his waist. (The professor was shirtless, well past middle-age, and flabby with an impossibly hairy back and chest that he displayed unapologetically.) Within a few minutes, Marsha had completed her circuit around the room and when she was back standing next to me she said:

"So, Charlie, will this be your first tantric experience?"

"My what?"

"Tantra, Charlie. Will this be your first brush with the ancient neo-Tantric rituals that have become so popular this side of the makeshift bus shelter? We're all surprised you decided to come. We thought you'd be above it. But we're glad to have you! There's nothing better than a great *sadhana* to raise your consciousness before the grind of a long semester. And as someone who's been divorced not just once but *twice*, you're no doubt ready to experience a life-affirming *chakra-puja?*"

"To be honest, Marsha, I have no clue what you're talking about. Hell, I didn't even know what arugula is. I'm just here to meet my peers. So I can get to know them on a more intimate level, you know, to navigate the personalities that I'll be dealing with as I try to find the moisture in all things."

"Well, in that case, Charlie, you're going to want to change clothes before we start. Those corduroys you're wearing are very restrictive and aren't going to allow your energy to flow where it needs to go. Come with me...."

Marsha led me into a small changing room and handed me a sheet of light floral fabric. "Here," she said. "This one looks about the right color for you ..." The sarong was very orange with hues ranging from Bengali tiger to sun rising in the Orient. "Orange is the color of the second *chakra.*"

"I'm sure it is," I said.

"And the second chakra is the one you need to work on most," she explained.

"Is that so?" Unconvinced, I stared at the dangling sarong which was still very orange. "Marsha, is this really necessary? You see, I'm not used to such revealing clothing. And orange has never been my color of choice. Now *beige* on the other hand....!"

"Look, Charlie, it's clear you're very uptight. You are an educational administrator. And that can't be helped. But tonight you're going to need to relax if you want to become one with the timeless universe....and with your new colleagues...."

"But...."

"...You'll need to relax if you want to absorb yourself into the mystic teachings of the tantra."

"Well, I'm not sure I do."

"You don't?"

"I'm not saying I *don't*. I'm just saying that I'm not *sure* that I do."

Marsha smiled and placed the flat of her hand on my heart.

"My goodness, Charlie, your heart is *racing!*"

"It is?"

"My god, yes! Wildly and uncontrollably! And that's not going to help you!" From here Marsha slid her hand down my chest to my abdomen, where her fingers settled just below my navel. "You're all in knots! Your energy can't flow. Look, don't worry about tonight – everything will be fine. Tantra isn't what everyone thinks it is. All that stuff about heightened sexual ecstasy and explosive orgasms....well, of course that's true. No doubt about that. But that's only a very small part of what tantra *really* is. That's only a part of what we'll be experiencing tonight...."

Here Marsha took my right hand and placed it on her own breast. With both hands she held it securely in place so that I could not move it. Then she looked into my eyes:

"What do you feel, Charlie?"

I looked at my hand on the flat of her breast.

"With my hand?"

"Yes, Charlie. What are you feeling now? Anything?"

"Well, your breast. But aside from that, not much."

"Your hand is on my breast, true. But it is also on my heart. Can you feel it?"

"No, I can't."

"You don't feel my heart quivering?"

"No."

"Its ancient trembling?"

"No."

"Nothing at all?"

"No. Sorry."

"My heart is quivering, Charlie. But you can't feel it because you are not yet ready to see the night that comes from day. And because I've trained my body to control its own shuddering. My flesh, you see, is like stone. My heart is calm. My soul is at peace. I've allowed myself to become soothed by the rhythms of the world, like the gentle passing of water over rocks, which is also very soothing. I am in a perpetual state of near-bliss. In fact, if not for the scabies, I would already be experiencing the cosmic orgasm that comes from ultimate oneness with the universe."

Marsha released my hand. Then, for a second time, she placed her own hand on my heart.

"Now *your* heart on the other hand....Yours, Charlie, is rampant. Clearly it has suffered severe trauma. And below the scar tissue, the gnarled residue of heartbreak and disappointment, your wounded heart is crying out for release. It is in anguish at its own suffering and now, more than anything, it needs its own form of soothing."

"It does?"

"Yes. It needs feminine soothing. And we will soothe it, Charlie. Tonight it will be soothed. Now please get changed...!"

Marsha left and I stripped to my boxers, then covered myself in the impossibly orange sarong, wrapping it around my waist and improvising an awkward knot at my hip, all the while wondering to myself how I had managed to fall so far, so quickly: from promising salutatorian of my high school class, to recently married educational administrator at an up-and-coming community college, to tantric divorcee standing alone in a dark changing room amid an extremely orange sarong. Hanging my clothes on the hanger I made my way back into the room where I poured myself another cup of wine. The wine was strong and good – was it even *wine*? – and when it was gone I poured another cup and downed it just as quickly. And when I had done the same with my third and fourth cups, I poured yet another and took a new look around the room at the peers that were surrounding me. By now these vibrant souls no longer appeared to me by their respective department affiliations but rather as the warm colors of the auras surrounding them. In the dark candlelit room Nan Stallings had become a most radiant pink and Ethel Newtown was effervescent yellow and the Esperanto teacher was lime and the English faculty – all four of them – were the slightly burnt hue of dried autumn leaves. Harold and Winona were cyan and olivine, respectively, and Luke was mauve and Gwen was fuchsia and the creative writing instructor was undulating hues of amber and violet and sienna. And as the wine flowed through my body toward my awaiting bladder and as the colors and the sounds of the room swirled around me like the relentless strains of sitar music, and as it all came like bold light into the enveloping warmth of my mind, I found myself easing comfortably into a state of graceful acceptance. In fascination I gazed at the moving art on the walls – the oriental men and women coupling and enjoying each other's bodies amid servant girls and elephants and flasks of wine being poured – each of them an act of creation and procreation; and as the wine I had been drinking came to flow like unfettered water down through my urinary tract I thought about this very new distance I had traveled: from the heat of hot asphalt to the cold moisture of wine. All these years I must have known that it would end up some place like this: before a table of arugula in a studio filled with copulating ancients and semi-nude community college faculty.

"Charlie!"

An insistent voice had jarred me from my reverie. It was Marsha and she was calling out to me from her place on the mats:

"Charlie, we're starting! Come sit by me! You can bring your wine….!"

Dutifully, I took a final long drink from my cup, then filled it back up again and found my seat on the mats between Marsha in her light sarong and Gwen in her shorts and t-shirt. Both smiled at me when I squeezed into the small space between them and as I looked back and forth at them – first to one side then the other – Marsha even stroked my knee encouragingly. "You look great in orange!" she whispered. Once again she placed her hand on my bare heart. But this time it was calm. Marsha smiled. "That's much better!" she said. "You're heart's settling down. That wine was good to you. Now you're relaxed and ready to begin!"

By now all the faculty and staff in the room were dressed in loose-fitting clothes – togas or sarongs or shorts or baggy sweat suits – and when everyone was seated on their mats, and when they had succeeded in crossing their stiff legs over each other so the soles of their feet pointed upwards, and when the watery music had been turned down in the background, Marsha picked up a candle and held it in front of her face. As she spoke the candlelight shone up under her chin casting sinister shadows across her face and darkening the red dot on her forehead.

"My friends," she said. "Dear colleagues, brothers and sisters, and fellow lovers of the universe. We are about to enter the place of our deepest origin where all matter and energy originates. It is the emanation phase in the cosmic cycle which in the ancient tantric tradition is referred to as *srsti*, and which in the modern tradition of the community college is referred to as...*a new semester*. As always, this is a time of great hope and rebirth and emerging consciousness as we leave behind the darkness of previous dissolutions and enter into the very early morning of new spirits and dreams...."

To my right, Gwen was tapping me on the shoulder and when I looked over at her she was offering me a stub of marijuana.

"Do you smoke this stuff, Charlie?" she whispered and held it out for me to take.

I accepted it:

"You could say that...."

As I took the hit I felt the warmth pass through my lungs and my mind began to exhale. Appreciatively, I passed the smoking stub back to her and watched it make its way back around the circle: from economics instructor to creative writing guru to Esperanto aficionado – or rather, from subdued pink to sedate lime and all the way through mauve and fuchsia via the burnt autumn brown of fallen leaves. By now my mind was losing its logical focus and my bladder was full of wine and as I struggled to reconcile these two realities it occurred to me that I should have made a trip to the bathroom before taking my place in the circle, but that this was now water under the bridge. And that I had left my watch in the pocket of my pants in the changing room. And that earlier today during our conversation at the cafeteria, I should have told Bessie what I really feel about love – what I truly believe it is, and how I find it so inconceivable that someone like her could ever be unloved. But it was too late now: all of this would have to wait; Marsha had already moved on in her narration:

"....And as we enter this new phase in the cosmic cycle, it is important that we remember the tantric principles that unite us with the universe. These are the principles of love and openness and spiritual insightfulness and sexual inquisitiveness. These are not masculine principles. Only in the feminine ideal of tantra can the desires of the heart be reconciled. Only in tantra can we move beyond the internal struggle that results from suppressing our deepest desires. For the conflict between what we have and what we *desire* to have takes place in each of us, and if we do not give it expression, it will undermine our quest for greater levels of awareness and a deeper spiritual understanding. No, for this very reason inner desire must be satiated! It must be celebrated and fulfilled so that the tension and conflict of our souls is released. Only through this can we find the enlightenment and deeper peace that we seek....!'"

Around the circle, my fellow faculty were listening and nodding. Those with notepads and pencils were taking notes. Others had folded their hands in their laps and were sitting with their eyes closed to more fully absorb the words. Marsha continued:

"....Now it is no secret that the universe works in cycles. The cycle of seasons, for example. And of the diurnal divisions of time. It can be seen in the eternal wheel of life that takes us from death to birth to life to death and then back around to birth. And it exists in the creative phases of emanation, incarnation, and dissolution. Just as the dissolution of night takes us into the emanation and incarnation of earliest morning, so too does the dissolution of morning take us into the emanation of brightest day, its incarnation, and then, ultimately, its dissolution. Thus, the countless cycles of the universe are everlasting and infinite, like spiraling circles radiating outward from a central point in time and space. And this central point, in all its vastness and timelessness....is *you!*"

Hauntingly, the candle under Marsha's chin flickered and sputtered as she spoke.

"....Now each of you comes to this circle with your own *kundalini* energy. It is the pulsating serpent coiled within your genital region just waiting to be directed through the different chakras of your body. As we begin to awaken these energies we will come to learn what these different chakras are, how they work, and how we can stimulate each of them to heightened levels of arousal in order to achieve the most earth-shattering, the most explosive, the most impossibly toe-curling and scream-inducing academic semester we've ever experienced...."

Here Marsha paused to scratch her thigh. Urgently and insistently, she dug into the skin as if it were a fire that could only be put out by scratching. When this was done, she cupped the candle she had been holding in her hands and placed it onto the floor in front of her.

"....Sorry about that. Now before we begin, please keep in mind that, to the tantric practitioner, conflict is neither a bad thing nor a good thing.

Among other philosophies of the world there may be much disagreement regarding the role of internal strife in our lives. Some glorify conflict; others demonize it. To the tantric mind, however, conflict is an *inevitable* thing, the rubbing of two sticks which brings fire. Or the friction between stone and windblown sand that shapes the hard earth around us. Conflict is as timeless as anything else. Yet inner conflict is also the antithesis of oneness. For the great secret of the universe comes not from the divisions that are inherent in conflict, but from the unity that comes from their resolution. And so tantra teaches us to transcend the opposites that reinforce conflict, whether they be male and female, emanation and dissolution, desire and attainment, climax and resolution, tenured and contingent, or even the stomach-churning tension between left-footed braking and right-footed acceleration. Under the enlightened guidance of an award-winning guru, all of the competing life forces will come together in a single moment of orgasmic clarity when the entire universe focuses upon a unified point of life-energy and bursts forward like the great explosion of semen, the resounding shudder of clitoral ecstasy, that only true union with god and the eternal universe can bring...."

At this, a hand went up. It was the Economics professor.

"Marsha," he was saying. "Some of us in this circle have been students of tantra for many years and have been through this cycle of knowing and unknowing many times before. We have experienced the flow of energy through the channels of our consciousness and the explosive orgasms and ecstatic enlightenment that result. But I'm sure there are at least a few new faculty here tonight who probably don't even know what *chakras* are. Maybe you could explain a bit before we move on?"

"Well, Max, I was getting to that. But since you brought it up...."

Marsha reached behind her and pulled up a poster board with a colorful representation of the human body and with different-colored circles drawn in. In the candlelight, it was hard to make out the numbers, and so as she spoke each of us leaned forward to better see the poster:

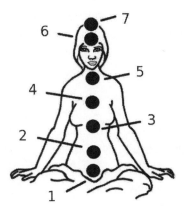

"These are the major chakras of the body," Marsha explained. "Chakras are the centers of consciousness. These are often numbered from bottom to top and correspond to the different parts of the body, the different colors of a shifting rainbow, and the different celestial bodies that govern them. You will also be interested to know that, in terms of accreditation, they do in fact correspond to the various life forces within the community college. So in tantric terms, the fourth chakra, commonly referred to as the Heart chakra, is green and governs our feelings of love and compassion. Above it is the fifth chakra, the Throat chakra, which is blue and is associated with communication. And below it is the third chakra, the Solar Plexus chakra that is yellow and is associated with will power. These chakras are historic and their functions well-documented; in the evolving tantra of the community college, meanwhile, these three energy centers correspond to the educational areas of Counseling, Informational Technology, and Upper Administration, respectively...."

(At the mention of the word *administration* I remembered my arrangement with Bessie. What time was it anyway? In the smoke of the room, the minutes had blended together like water in the endless river of time. And like any other river it was bound to flow slowly and relentlessly along its tortuous riverbed. But without a watch, how would I know when it was right to leave this circle? Could I trust my intuition to guide me? It was still early now; but it would not always be so. Without my watch, all I could do at this point was prostrate myself before the forces of the universe and hope for their mercy and guidance. And maybe in this way I would be able to find the soothing of my heart that had so far eluded me. And if all worked according to the divine will of the universe, might I not be able to do this in time to step out onto the bustling street at exactly seven-thirty to meet Bessie?)

I turned back to listen to Marsha, who was now pointing her finger at the chart:

"*This*," she was saying, "is the sixth chakra, where intuition resides; it is also called the 'third eye' and is associated with our Institutional Research Office. And here we have the first chakra which is also called the Root chakra; it is housed in the very base of the spine and provides grounding and stability and is associated with Facilities and Maintenance …."

Now Marsha took her finger and placed it in the middle of the second circle, the soft part of the abdomen near the navel where I'd felt the soft touch of her hand a few minutes before.

"And this," she said," is the *second* chakra. It is the chakra where the seeds of all sexual pleasure and procreation originate. It is governed by the moon, that most feminine of all celestial bodies. And its color is orange, like a female tiger on the prowl or like a low-hanging harvest moon. The second chakra, you see, is the wellspring of our deepest desires, the source of all creation, the womb of knowledge and enlightenment and spiritual connectedness. This, of course is the vaginal orifice of the learning process, the place where the idea is born and desire for knowledge originates and where the seed of all formal learning is planted. Of course it is connected with classroom instruction where student and teacher unite like sperm with egg in the eternal union of knowledge-insemination."

Marsha had started to move on to her next idea but seeing that the marijuana had made its way around the circle and was being offered to her by Harold Schlockstein, she stopped to accept the offering. Taking the hit, she passed it on to me and I took my own hit and passed it on to Gwen who again passed it on, and in this way it continued to make its journey around the unbroken circle of life until, once again, it came to Marsha, then to me – I took yet another drag – and then on to Gwen and all the way around the circle yet again. Marsha continued:

"…Where was I? Oh yes, about sperm and egg. And so, in terms of the community college, it looks like this…."

Here Marsha paused to adjust the front of her sarong which had come dangerously close to slipping below her nipples. Then she flipped over the chart to reveal the following diagram printed on the back:

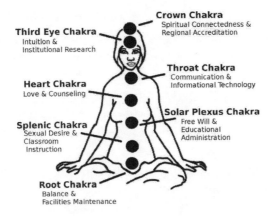

Crown Chakra
Spiritual Connectedness &
Regional Accreditation

Third Eye Chakra
Intuition &
Institutional Research

Throat Chakra
Communication &
Informational Technology

Heart Chakra
Love & Counseling

Solar Plexus Chakra
Free Will &
Educational
Administration

Splenic Chakra
Sexual Desire &
Classroom
Instruction

Root Chakra
Balance &
Facilities Maintenance

"So each of these lower six chakras," she explained, "serves to drive the energy upward from the lower regions up through the sternum and through the heart up past the throat and the third eye and eventually arriving at the seventh chakra at the top of the crown which is attainment of spiritual connectedness with the world, ultimate enlightenment, oneness with god, and a full six-year unconditional re-affirmation of our accreditation by the authorized accrediting body. Of course obtaining this goal is not easy. But it is this very path to final enlightenment that is the ultimate purpose for each of us as human beings aspiring to higher insights and for all of us as a community college aspiring to regional accreditation."

Marsha stopped.

"Are there any questions so far?"

"Yes, I have one...."

Luke Quittles was raising his hand. He and Ethel were sharing a mat and seemed to be sitting closer to each other than most others in the circle.

"My question is about cosmic orgasm."

"Yes, Luke. And what specifically?"

"Well, Ethel and I were just having a side discussion and we were wondering, you know, whether cosmic orgasms are as good as the earthly kind. We've heard a lot about them. And now Ethel and I.....well, we're wondering how likely it is that we'll experience one of those tonight...."

"Honestly, Luke, it is not likely. First of all, the cosmic orgasm is not like the intense physical orgasm that you and Ethel might feel as man and woman. Nor is it akin to the muted orgasm that she and Stan might feel as husband and wife. In fact, what we refer to as cosmic orgasm is not an orgasm at all, but a deep spiritual oneness with the world. It is the falling away of all earthly sensations, the transcendence of time, the shedding of your own awareness of self – in other words those very things that cause unhappiness and anguish for our souls. Such moments take an eternity to achieve. So no, Luke, you will not likely feel this tonight. But, at the very least, we can begin that process by exploring the *physical* orgasm that is the first, if lowest, step toward a closer relationship with god."

"I'm fine with that," said Luke.

"Me too," said Ethel.

Around the circle the faculty and staff nodded to affirm their general consensus with this sentiment.

Having answered Luke's question, Marsha continued:

"No further questions?" she said. "Well then now that we've introduced you to the key precepts of tantric philosophy, we're ready to start stimulating our different chakras to release the *kundalini* from its sleeping state within our genitals. To get this process started, let's partner up….."

Marsha looked around the circle and starting from where she was sitting at the head of the circle she proceeded to pair us up in male-female dichotomies, two at a time: Harold with Winnie; Luke with Ethel; Nan from political science with the mesmerizing creative writing instructor; the hirsute economics professor with the embarrassed lecturer; the gunsmithing instructor with the college's grant writer; developmental English with Esperanto; intermediate composition with art history; advanced composition with introductory eugenics; and British literature with logic. And when she had worked her way around the circle in this manner and when she had finished pairing Gwen with the shirtless Shakespeare aficionado sitting next to her, and when it was clear that I was the last one left in the circle and that I would not have a partner, Marsha looked at me and said, "Well, Charlie, it looks like you're the odd man out. No orgasms for you tonight! Just kidding….you can be *my* partner. Here, come sit across from me…."

Marsha motioned to the place in front of her where I should sit and I took my place there. The other couples followed suit – sitting across from each other in the circle, one facing inward and the other facing outward – and as I looked around at the pairs I saw the new and impressive color combinations that were resulting: mauve mixed with violet; fuchsia blended with pink; different shades of green merged; the autumn brown of dried leaves blended seamlessly into the dull gray of eternal winter.

More immediately, Marsha's Vedic white had come together with my own Bengali orange to from a striking combination of recessive albino orange, or bleached harvest moon. Marsha continued:

"In the tantric tradition, there are three ways to control energy: breath, posture, and sound. The first of these requires breathing, which stirs the energy and gets it ready to ascend to the higher chakras. Of course each of you already knows how to breathe; if not, you would not have made it through the rigorous hiring process at Cow Eye Community College. Like most mammals on the track to tenure, you know how to breathe. But do you know how to breathe *spiritually*? Breathing, you see, stimulates the third chakra, but only if it is breathing that is *spiritually purposeful....*"

And here Marsha demonstrated what spiritually purposeful breathing looks like, inhaling deeply and slowly and then exhaling it back out.

"Now as we inhale we should picture the entirety of our life experience poised just below our nostril. Every incident from our life. Every lost love. Every broken promise. Every American state we've visited. Every hangnail. Every joy and disappointment and heartache and fear. Every bad grade we've received, or given. Every good grade. All the women we've touched, even if only for an instant. All the men we've pleasured. The quivers we've felt. The colds we've caught. The guilt and pain and ecstasy. The asphalt. All of these should be right there in front of you. Picture them all. So that as we inhale we absorb all these experiences in through the left nostril passing it through our lungs and into the very depths of our soul. That's how profound our breathing should be. So that each breath becomes an affirmation of the entirety of our existence. For each breath contains the entire universe in a single moment. And this breath we hold in our soul for a count of three, and then we release it, expelling it through our *right* nostril. And with this we are consummating the act of dissolution in preparation for the upcoming emanation that will come with the new breath. And this continues and will continue forever. But remember, it is inhale through the left nostril, exhale through the right. The unbroken cycle of divine breath. Like this...."

Marsha took a series of impossibly deep breaths, in and out, just as she had instructed. One more time. Then again. And then once again. Then she looked up:

"Now *you* try...."

Carefully we took our turns breathing in and out. Slowly. And purposefully. While one partner would breathe out, the other sitting directly across would breathe in. And then this would take place in reverse, such that each partner's exhalation became the other's inhalation, and vice versa. It was not easy. With each breath I struggled to imagine the experiences in my life that had brought me to this tantric circle: the kind teacher with auburn hair; the man with the cane; the friend from college whose virginity will always be mine; the taste of the bloody asphalt; the smell of burnt wax. And as I breathed it all in through my left nostril I pictured my strange future just as vividly below me. The cowboy with the lariat. And the math faculty in drag. The calf's testicles in the Ziploc bag. And the supple nape of Bessie's neck with her hair tumbling forth. Now my breaths ceased to be short and irregular but instead became long and flowing like cirrus clouds over a dry pasture. Yet no matter how I tried, my breaths were not nearly as infinite as the universe. Nor was my soul as spiritual as it might be.

Marsha watched all of this calmly.

"You're doing fine," she would encourage us, and then, suddenly: "Luke! You've got it backward. It's inhale with the *left* nostril and exhale with the *right*....!"

"Oh, dammit!" Luke would answer.

For several minutes we exchanged breaths with our partners, and when this was done and when it had been done to her satisfaction, Marsha ushered us along:

"Okay," she said. "Now that we've opened up the passageways for the flow of energy, we can proceed to the stretching....."

Over the next several minutes Marsha led us through a series of stretches and poses that called to mind the amazing bronze statuary of our college's fountains: the pregnant crane; the dragon in flight; the corpse with a cause; the receptive heifer. And when we had performed these to her satisfaction she led us through a series of vocal exercises – mantras and chants and sacred syllables recited as incantations – that made the room vibrate with primordial sound. And when all of this was done she took another turn with the marijuana that had been passed to her yet again, then handed it to me (I did the same) and smiled:

"Very good!" she said. "Now we are ready to call up the *kundalini* from where it lies as a coiled serpent. Now to get the *kundalini* flowing let's all seek out the place where it resides. This can be found in the upper place on the inner part of the thigh. We do it like this...." And here Marsha placed her hand on my inner thigh tracing lightly over my skin with her finger nail. Involuntarily, a slight tingling welled up within me.

Marsha did this for a few seconds. And then she announced, loudly:

"What I'm doing is using my feminine energies to awaken Charlie's male serpent. That tingling that Charlie is now feeling is the very beginnings of the kundalini energy welling up from within his second chakra. This is the life force that courses through each of us and inspires us to new heights of awareness and consciousness. Do you feel the tingling, Charlie?"

I nodded.

"Do you feel the serpent rising up from within you?"

"Pretty much."

"Is it rising?"

"Yes, Marsha."

"Great. You see, this is the most primordial of energies. It has been sleeping over the long summer hiatus and needs to be awakened before we can begin our new semester. Now let's all find that spot...."

Around the circle, the pairs reached out to awaken each other's kundalini. Marsha rested her hand on my inner thigh. And in return I put my right hand on the inside of her left thigh and did the same.

"No, not quite like that," Marsha whispered and directed my hand even further. "Like this..." And she placed my hand squarely on her sacred triangle. I tried to withdraw my hand. But she held it there.

"Charlie, relax," she said. "Don't be intimidated by the literalness of this all. This is not you as a man touching me as a woman. This is your sacral male energy coming together with my sacral female energy and through this union the two of us becoming part of the larger energy of the universe. This is about me achieving cosmic orgasm and you achieving physical orgasm, and our college, despite its scabies, achieving a full six-year reaffirmation of our institutional accreditation...."

"Six years?" I asked. "Are you sure that's even possible at this point?"

"I'm positive."

"With no mid-term visit?"

"Yes!"

"Well, okay then." And I slid my other hand even further up her sarong to the inner part of her thigh where the moisture was already beginning to gather.

⚉

WHEN MARSHA WAS satisfied with the energy that had been awakened by the different couples in the room, she said:

"Great. Now each of you should be feeling the stirrings of the kundalini. We will stir it further in a few moments. But for now please remember that we are here to achieve *spiritual* bliss, not physical satiety. The physical ecstasy is just the bottom rung in the great staircase that will take us to the higher levels of understanding and awareness. Just as childhood is a necessary milestone toward adulthood, and death is a milestone toward birth, so too is the physical orgasm the first and most accessible milestone toward spiritual enlightenment. And like the lowest step in the spiraling staircase to eternity, it is the least difficult one to conquer. Yet it is only that: the lowest step. And while this lowest step will always be nothing more than what it is – the first and lowest – it is also true that you cannot climb higher without first transcending it. And so sexual ecstasy is like that first step: by itself it brings you not much higher than anything else; but without it you can never achieve the greater heights that are our ultimate destination…."

As Marsha spoke I felt the kundalini welling up like fire in my loins and mixing with the water that was churning like eddies in my bladder. The kundalini was rising through my chakras and the wine was settling into the depths of my soul. And somewhere in the middle the marijuana was trying to mediate the two. Sure, there was some kundalini going on – there could be no doubt about that. But sitting there with my bladder full and my imagination clouded and my skin tingling from the light tracing of Marsha's fingers, I could only wonder which of these powerful life forces was greatest. Was it the maintenance of my cosmic lawn? Or was it the will power of our upper administration? Surely it wasn't the Institutional Research Office? What could this all mean? And how, without a watch, would I ever come to find out what time it was?

"Marsha?" I said through the haze of my thoughts. "Hey, Marsha…?"

"Yes, Charlie?"

"Marsha, your hands are very experienced. And they are no doubt attuned to the energies of the universe. It is not something that I am indifferent to, as I'm sure you are quite aware. Kundalini is an amazing thing and I have learned to value it during this watery get-together. Thank you, Marsha, for teaching me these things. And please let Gwen know that I'm grateful to her as well for stopping by my office to invite me. And for bringing me here in her yellow two-seater. Please let her know that I am not above all this. But Marsha, there is also something very important that I need to ask you...."

"Yes, Charlie?"

"Marsha, there is a question that only you can answer."

"Yes, Charlie, what is it?"

"Marsha, can you tell me what time it is?"

"Time, Charlie?"

"Yes, Marsha. Can you tell me what the time is now? Because it seems that it is getting very late and I really need to know...."

"There is no time, Charlie. There is only eternity."

"Yes I understand that. But can you tell me the time anyway? I sort of need to know before it's too late. I don't want to miss my ride."

"There is no time. There is neither future nor past. There is only the eternity of the universe and the immediacy of the present physical moment. The moment that you and I are sharing. You see, Charlie, your search for moisture is a noble one and will not be in vain. Your hand is warm and inviting and it is approaching the wellspring of my creation. Compared to the cosmic ecstasy of our impending union, what else could you possibly need? Which is to say, what need could you possibly have for something as temporal as *time*?"

"But, Marsha, time is all around us. And if we're not careful it passes us by. Like a fast-flowing river. And so we need to pay it heed. That is to say, *I* need to pay it heed. Which is to say, Marsha, can you tell me what time it is? Please? Can you please tell me whether I need to leave this circle now even though it is too early for an orgasm of any sort and though I have not yet been fully prepared for the glories of the upcoming semester. Marsha, please, what time is it?"

Marsha took her hand from my thigh.

"If that is your true attitude toward time, Charlie – if you value the temporal more than the absolute, if you are more inclined to pay homage to the things that come and go above those that stay and stay forever – then it is probably best that you leave the circle *now*. Because time and eternity are opposites. Like love and efficiency. Or like paradox and itself. Once you enter the realm of one you can never go back to the other. Once you see eternity, Charlie, there can be no return. So you should probably leave now, before you are compelled to cross that eternal threshold *entirely*...."

Gratefully, I removed my hand from her upper thigh.

"Thank you, Marsha," I said.

"Namaste," she said.

And with my hand once again my own, I stood up from the perfect circle of life and made my way toward the door onto the bustling street. As I exited the dark studio, the delicate chime on the door sounded lightly behind me, announcing my premature departure, and back in the temporal world of bright lights and cold air I felt a great burden placed back onto my shoulders, as if my soul had passed heavily from one spiritual state to another: from Minnesota to Oregon perhaps, or from sienna to olivine.

≈

OUTSIDE, THE BRIGHTNESS of the neon stunned my eyes. The bustle along the main street of the Outskirts was loud and raucous and as I stumbled onto the creaking boardwalk I felt myself swept into a crowd making its procession in a joyous surging mass. Gaily we moved down the street further and further from the door I'd just come out of and as we passed the swelling crowds and the neon store fronts I felt myself caught up in an ecstasy I hadn't known before. Past smoky parlors and half-dressed salesgirls and sign after sign offering forbidden fruits organically grown I stumbled and stuttered against the oncoming crowd – losing sight of the people who had ushered me along – until I came to the very end of the universe: an empty alley with an empty bench where no other person was sitting and in that empty spot – the emptiest place in the world – I sat down. Sprawled on the bench I watched the throngs walking past me in spurts of exuberant revelry. It was very cold now and in the night air I felt suddenly underdressed – the warmth of the studio turning as it had to the cold of the open night air. And yet in the seclusion of my alley and in the solitary silence of my bench the crowds paid me no mind. The world had slowed down to a crawl. And in that moment it seemed that time had in fact come to its end. The colors of the world all blurred into one. The wafting aromas of hashish and chocolate and cinnamon and evergreen joined in perfect union. And sitting there, I felt a deep weariness coming over me. The throng had became one. The conflicting cacophony became a single solitary sound. Minutes melted into a single microcosm of silence. Light disappeared and sounds faded.

Blissfully, I closed my eyes.

~

{ }

The relationship between love and sex is as important at your local community college as it is anywhere else. And just as it is anywhere else, it is as ageless as the relationship between conflict and conciliation. Or sleep and wakefulness. Or knowledge-giving and knowledge-seeking. For it is rare that any of these opposites can exist in their purest forms together. When one is strong the other must surely be weak. And when the other takes ascendance it is inevitably at the expense of the first. And yet there is also a fine balance that can be achieved when neither is in ascendance. When pure love has become practical love and unfettered sex has become fettered sex, and it is under these conditions of perfect balance that these two can meet in the transcendent equilibrium of time and space. To the vast majority of tenured community college faculty, the competing loyalties to love and sex are incompatible — like those that the fireman harbors for both fire and water. But this does not need to be so. Sex and love are not opposites to be chosen at the expense of the other but rather opposite apexes of a swinging pendulum that are achieved, in measured turn, emphatically at first, then gradually less so over time, until the great pendulum of desire comes to rest at the exact middle point between the two. This moment of perfect rest is called many things in many different cultures: in Hinduism it is samdhi; in politics it is compromise; to the drunk who has been bounced from a bar it is unconsciousness; to atheists it is death; and to the teaching faculty of your local community college it is the dreaded yet inevitable descent into the ranks of educational administration.

*Balancing opposing realities is the key to living a full life
and to enjoying a rewarding academic career. For the place
where neither can exist is also the place where both can exist
in perpetuity. Like the bureaucracy that exists to preserve
itself and that achieves longevity through mediocrity, so too
can the state of achieving neither love nor sex exist until the
end of time. For it is the pursuit of these things individually
and to their logical and irrational conclusions that gives life
to life and brings everything ultimately to the swinging apex
that is the exact opposite of lifelessness and mortality.*

{ }

≈

WHEN I OPENED my eyes, Bessie was standing in front of me.

"Charlie!" she was saying. "What are you doing here? I thought we were supposed to meet at Marsha's? And what the hell are you *wearing...?!*"

"Hi Bessie," I said. "I just had a little bit to drink and some marijuana. And time just sort of, you know, stopped. It just sort of fell away against the imposing background of eternity."

Bessie spat on the ground to the side of her.

"Yeah, well, that's all fine and good. But for your information your pendulum is protruding through that light sarong of yours. And it's exactly eight twenty-two... *and fifteen seconds*, if you care to know. Which means I've been waiting on the curb for almost an hour. So get up off that damn bench and let's get going."

I stood up and followed Bessie back toward Marsha's studio, past the same storefronts and the same bustling crowds I'd just walked past. The same joyous faces. The same seductive salesgirls. Bessie's pace was brisk and as I followed her back over the boardwalk we weaved in and out of the oncoming crowd until she finally stopped. The noise of the street was great. The neon was bright. We were standing in front of Marsha's studio.

"Charlie, I'll wait here while you go in and get your clothes. I can't take you to the barbecue dressed like *that....*"

But here I protested.

"Bessie," I said. "If I go back in there, I may never return. You see, they're all in the midst of entering a higher level of consciousness. But I left early. I was the only one who didn't trust the universe entirely. I can't go back in after *that* ....I just can't!"

"Oh, alright!" she said and opened the door of the studio. By now my bones were raw with cold. The night was dark and deliberate. A few minutes later Bessie came back outside and handed me a pile of clothes. "I'm assuming these are yours?"

"How'd you know?"

"They're beige. Wait here. I'll go get my truck."

"Bessie...."

"Yes."

"Before you leave to get your truck can you tell me one thing?"

"What?"

"How was it in there? You know in the circle of life that I chose to leave prematurely?"

Bessie shook her head:

"You don't want to know...."

Bessie walked off and I stood waiting there in the cold night. And in the cold of the night I felt my senses slowly returning. Outlines became more distinct. The colors around me separated. People's faces came into focus. A few minutes later Bessie pulled up in an old Ford truck, the one she'd bought from Merna's sister after being informed of the sale by her ex-husband Buck.

"Climb in, Charlie," she said. I sat on the front seat and closed the heavy door behind me. The cab was warm and smelled of ash and old car heater. Bessie popped the clutch and the truck lurched into motion. We drove a few blocks in silence and when we'd come to the town's only stop light she looked over at me, very serious.

"Look, Charlie, just so you know – and I want to be very clear on this: I am *not* having sex with you tonight. So if that's what you're thinking, well now you know where that stands...."

There was nothing I could think to say to this; and so I said nothing. Bessie continued:

"I mean, I can see that you're definitely up for it and all...."

"What?"

"Charlie, you're clearly up for it."

"Up for what?"

"For sex."

"It's that obvious?"

"Yes it is. I'm a woman, Charlie. And I'm from Cow Eye. We know these things."

Embarrassed, I stammered to rectify myself:

"It's not that. It's just that, well, I don't smoke marijuana very often, and the wine was very strong – was it even *wine*? – and I'm just doing my best to understand the things that are happening around me. And inside me. You know, to see the darkness and the day. At the moment I just want to get to know my peers in new and interesting ways. Sex is the furthest thing from my mind. Trust me, Bessie. I mean, that's why I chose to work at a *community college*...!"

The light changed. Bessie nodded and put the truck into gear.

By now the road was dark and there wasn't much to see outside her windows. The backlit charm of the Outskirts gave way to sobering darkness and only when we were approaching the campsite along the river where Rusty's party was in full swing did another streetlamp appear. Pulling into a parking lot, Bessie pointed over at the camp grounds, which were dimly lit. "Everyone's down by the river...." she said. "You can change on the other side of Rusty's truck over there...."

I thanked her and in the darkness next to the old truck changed out of the sarong into my beige corduroys.

"Are you ready?" she asked when I'd returned with the orange fabric in my hands.

"Yes."

"How's your head? Is it clear?"

"I believe so. I really do need to get more sleep though...."

"Well, let's head over. They're probably wondering what happened to us."

≈

"CHARLIE!" RUSTY CALLED out when he saw me, and then: "Hey, Bess! Glad the two of you could come! Are you an item yet? Here, have a beer....!"

Rusty had reached into a cooler of ice, but stopped to look up at Bessie.

"He drinks beer, doesn't he?" he asked her.

"You could say that...." she answered.

Bessie and I took our beers from Rusty and sat down on one of the logs arranged in a circle around the camp area. A fire had been built in the middle, and in the glow of its periphery I could make out the silhouettes of the faculty and staff who had made a point to be at this get-together instead of the other one now reaching its cosmic climax in Marsha's studio: Dr. Felch and Rusty and Stan Newtown (minus Ethel) and Timmy from the guard shack and the business communications professor and the entire staff from the Maintenance department and the head of the fiscal office and the team of administrative secretaries and each of the tenured animal science instructors and, off to the side playing horse shoes in a barely illuminated stretch of river sand, two of the three men from the bar.

"Hey, isn't that....?"

"...My brother," said Bessie. "Yes it is. And my ex-husband. The ones you met at the bar on your way into town and whose names you still haven't bothered to learn. They happen to be very good friends of Merna's and so Rusty invited them tonight."

"It's funny how everything's so connected here. How every*one*'s so connected!"

"Yeah well my brother's a mechanic and he works for Merna's ex-husband who is on the planning commission and is currently married to Dr. Felch's second wife who's a higher-up at the Ranch and was able to secure the dusty corral for the teambuilding exercise. Meanwhile, Buck is a hunting buddy of Rusty's and the two of them fish on a part of the river that's owned by the family of Timmy who works at the guard shack and deflowered me when I was fifteen. Timmy is Merna's nephew and he's having an affair with one of the administrative secretaries – the one over there sitting next to Raul with her hand on his thigh – and Timmy's latest wife is my classmate who works at the cafeteria – you know, the one with the pretty eyes."

"Serving the hamburger steak in a hair net?"

"No. In a hair net serving hamburger steak. Anyway, you get the idea. She was supposed to be here tonight but my sitter got sick and so she volunteered to watch my kids for me."

"Wow, that's a lot of information, Bessie. Especially the part about your kids...."

"Well, you won't have to worry about this any time soon. My point is that it's all very predictable. And the fact that both men from the bar are here – my brother *and* my ex-husband – well, that shouldn't come as much of a surprise to you anymore."

"No, it doesn't. And I guess it shouldn't. But it is surprising that there's only two of them. You know, at the bar there were *three* men. But here there are two. Didn't they invite your dentist to come?"

"Oh, he knew Merna very well and surely would have been invited. He was a sweet man."

"Was?"

"He passed away recently."

"What? When did that happen?"

"He passed away in his sleep some time ago."

"Some time ago? How can that be? I mean, I just…. we just… you and I were just talking about him at lunch today …!"

"Things come and go, Charlie."

"Yes, but…."

"Time passes."

"I know, but…"

"It's finite."

"Sure, but…?"

"And such things have always been beyond our power to understand."

"But!"

"Drink, Charlie."

And I did.

And as I drank I took a closer look at the barbecue that was already in full swing. Sitting and standing round the campfire my peers were laughing and joking and nursing their beers over plates of beef and hamburgers from the grill and hot dogs that had been roasted on sticks over the open flames. Dr. Felch was tending a grill not far from the circle and the smell of sizzling steak made my mouth moist after so much arugula and parched grain – after so much marijuana. In the cold night air, small children without jackets were running and laughing and chasing after each other unattended while a group of older boys had climbed the dark trees along the river and were throwing sticks out into the water. "That's Rusty's daughter," Bessie explained pointing to an overly made-up teenager sitting in a corner of the circle with her boyfriend. "The one who wrecked his truck." I nodded. "And *that*," she said, "is the boy who got her pregnant. Try to stay off that subject, though, because Rusty's still coming to terms with it. And it's definitely a sore point for him."

On the other side of the fire a guitar was playing and a throaty singing voice could be heard above the general din: through the flickering light of the fire and the still-looming haze of my own mind I could see that it was Raul strumming his nylon-stringed guitar surrounded by a semicircle of enraptured clerical staff.

I shook my head in admiration:

"Just look at Raul!" I said to Bessie. "The man is amazing. Charming. Elegant. Logical. Everything in perfect alignment: physically, intellectually, accreditationally. His presence is commanding. His diction is good. His voice is superb. Even his leadership skills are exceptional. He was the one who managed to get us through the teambuilding exercise yesterday. If not for him we'd probably still be back in that corral debating the finer points of bovine sentience and formulating our plan to separate the little calf from his testicles."

"That may be a selling point for most women. But he's not *my* type."

"Really? I would think he would be any woman's type."

"Not mine. There's a certain kind of man that appeals to most women. And Raul falls into that category, no doubt. Smart. Handsome. Self-assured. Always with the right words to say. Unfailingly aware of a situation. I'm sure he's the type that's never left a sexual partner unpleasured. Most women would look high and low to find a man like that. But not me. Not anymore. Nowadays I have no patience for perfection. I long for a different kind of lover."

I looked at Bessie quizzically.

"Honestly, I prefer the ones like *you*, Charlie…."

"Me?"

"Yes, the imperfect ones. The ones with sizable teeth and awkward mannerisms. The man who stutters and stumbles and forgets to be careful in his appearance – or, even better, who doesn't even know enough about appearance to remember that he should care. The one whose pant legs are too short and whose sleeves are too long and whose fingers are double-jointed. You can keep the man with refined tastes and washboard stomach. Give me the potbellied oaf with the compromised past and crazy dreams. Give me the buck-tooth. The hunchback. The premature ejaculator. Give me the man with the misspelled resume. The dawdler with the incoherent value system and conflicting moral compass. You can have the highly paid department chair all to yourself. I'll take the underling who risks

the public obloquy of underemployment to pursue his truer passions."
Bessie took a long gulp from her can, then aspirated loudly. "You know,
Charlie, it's funny how a woman's tastes change over time. When I was
younger I would have been crazy for a man like Raul. His purity would
have melted me. His earnestness would have sent me reeling. But now
I just want somebody less...*aligned*. Someone imprecise and flawed. An
infinitely human being. A person with deep personal frailties. In other
words, Charlie, someone more like you...."

"That's sweet of you to say, Bessie. I appreciate it."

"You're welcome. But I am still not having sex with you tonight."

We drank and Dr. Felch came over with a plate of steak from the grill
that he had been tending. The pieces were sliced and juicy, expertly grilled,
and we picked the slices with our fingers. Dr. Felch smiled approvingly:

"So how are the two of you getting along? No plans for sex, I hope?"

"Nothing tangible," I said. "At least not tonight."

"That's good," said Dr. Felch. "Remember, Charlie, that's not going
to work out well for you in the end...!"

Bessie punched Dr. Felch's knee.

He laughed and sat down on the log next to her.

"Mind if I sit down?" he asked, though already seated.

"By all means."

Dr. Felch lit a cigarette and threw the match behind him.

"So, Bess, how's the new truck? I hear you bought the Ford from
Merna's sister?"

Bessie shrugged:

"It's okay. Except the carburetor's clogged and the muffler's rusted out."

"Sounds like your last marriage!"

Bessie laughed and punched Dr. Felch again, this time in the shoulder.

"No, my last marriage was definitely not *okay*...!"

Here the conversation inevitably slipped into institutional talk: Dr.
Felch mentioning some reports that Bessie would need to type before
the semester began; Bessie reminding Dr. Felch about some important
upcoming meetings that he shouldn't forget to attend. The two went back
and forth like this and then, after a lull, Dr. Felch turned to me:

"So, Charlie, how's Cow Eye been treating you? No regrets about
taking the job?"

"Not yet, Mr. Felch. Of course I've only been working three days.

And I've only been in Cow Eye Junction since Saturday. It seems like an eternity has passed since I arrived at the makeshift bus shelter. So much has seemed to change in that time. But I'm still excited to be here and can't wait for the semester to begin in earnest. I feel like I'm finally starting to get a handle on the different personalities. It hasn't been easy. But Bessie has been very helpful."

"I told you she would be. And I'm glad you're doing well. It's just too bad the two of you couldn't have been here a bit earlier. You missed a beautiful remembrance. You would've loved it. All of Merna's friends were here and we took turns sharing our favorite stories of our time with her. About her youthful escapades. And her midlife accomplishments. Even Raul talked about what it meant to be following in her footsteps. When we talked about what happened to her last year, about her unexpected demise, there wasn't a dry eye around the campfire. And it was all very touching when we scattered her ashes in the river. Too bad you missed it."

"Well that's completely my fault," I said. "And I feel terrible. You see, I drank too much wine at the watery get-together – was it even *wine*?! – and accepted too much marijuana and I didn't realize until it was too late that I'd left my watch in my pants…."

"Your pants?"

"Yes. They were restricting my kundalini so I had to take them off. And of course I couldn't go back into the studio to get them so Bessie had to fetch them for me. She's the one who found me on the bench at the very edge of the universe. But I wasn't passed out. I was just sleeping. You see, I've been really tired since the math faculty got back from their sojourn in North Carolina."

"I was afraid that might become a problem…."

"But it's okay. Bessie found me on the bench and I changed back into my beige corduroys. I missed out on a resounding orgasm, I'm sure. But at least I'm here."

"Well, Charlie, it sounds like you've had an eventful night. You're among friends now though. So just relax and enjoy the beautiful open air. And the crackling fire over there. And of course that amazing silver moon shining down on us like a mother's love for her children…. Here, have another piece of steak….!"

The meat was tender and lightly salted and still steaming from its time on the grill. I took a few more pieces and thanked him.

"And make sure you try one of these...."

Dr. Felch pointed at a small piece of charred meat on his plate. I took the morsel and put it into my mouth.

"This is great," I said. "So moist and succulent. Not like any other cut of meat I've ever tried before. What is it?"

"Those," said Dr. Felch, "are the seeds of civilized society."

"The what?"

"From yesterday. Why do you think I brought the Ziploc bag to the corral?"

Bessie chuckled.

"Welcome to Cow Eye!" she said, taking a piece for herself.

"Where civilizations meet!" Dr. Felch added.

The two laughed and Dr. Felch lit up another cigarette – his thirteenth. Bessie went to get another beer and when she came back Rusty Stokes was trailing behind her.

"Hey there!" Rusty said. "Looks like you've got your own little party going on over here. Mind if I join you?"

And without waiting for an answer he sat down next to me on the log.

By now the fire had died down a bit and the cold air seemed even colder. While the four of us sat together on the log – Rusty, me, Bessie, Dr. Felch – a stream of colleagues would pass by on their way to the open grill, or on their way back from it; and in this way I had a chance to meet the bulk of the animal science faculty and a good portion of the maintenance staff. A trio of administrative secretaries stopped by to congratulate me on my hiring and to express condolences over my failed marriages. One wished me luck resurrecting the Christmas party. Another complimented me on my lack of facial hair. ("You look a lot more like a Special Projects Coordinator *now*!") And a third gave me some suggestions on the metaphorical significance of the calf. ("The calf," she claimed, "represents the quest for a deeper knowledge, held captive within the confines of the corral." To which I said: "If so, then what are the succulent morsels I just consumed? What then is the seed that was prematurely severed?" "Those," she concluded – and not unconvincingly – "are the individual nuggets of wisdom that make up our larger body of knowledge!") At some point Raul walked over with his guitar in hand and I complimented him on his singing. And when Stan approached I congratulated him on his newfound independence from Ethel.

"If only she could see me now!" he preened.

("And if only you could see *her*!" I thought.)

In time the party seemed to coalesce around Rusty and Dr. Felch, and as we talked through our beers and drank through our sliced steak, the conversation settled into a comfortable groove. On the log next to ours Raul and Stan were recalling the previous day's triumph over the calf. And from the ends of our log Rusty and Dr. Felch were reminiscing about their high school trips to the river, while Bessie and I listened intently in the middle. Once approaching sobriety from the long ride in Bessie's truck, now I felt the beer coursing through me in the same way the wine had a few hours ago. I'd still not found a bathroom since leaving my apartment; yet the dark woods seemed hopelessly removed from the campground, and no sooner would I start out for their dark cover than a colleague would hand me another beer. "Hey, where you going, Charlie? Here have another...!" And I would sit back down. And as I drank the beer and ate the beef I found myself absorbing it all together: the food and the alcohol and the warmth of the fire and the conversation swirling around me. Slowly my bladder filled with each beer consumed and my stomach filled with each slice of steak and my heart filled with the warmth of the fire and of the gentle and soothing conversation enveloping me. On the log, Bessie had shifted over to make room for Dr. Felch and was now sitting so close to me that the entire length of her thigh pressed up against mine. From time to time she would lean to one side or the other and with each shift of her weight I could feel the press of her soft shoulder into mine – or its withdrawal. And this too kept me warm.

"So, Rusty," somebody finally said after the discussion had moved from sports to weather, then from cars to trucks, and then from foreign affairs to the current local politics of Cow Eye Junction: "So, Rusty, what do you think about that new Communist we hired last year for the philosophy department?"

"I don't like him," Rusty said.

"Really? Well how about the homosexual that teaches art?"

"I don't like him either."

"And the gun-control advocate in business?"

"Her either."

"And the recently promoted astronomy professor from Bangladesh?"

"Not funny."

"And the married lecturer with the hyphenated surname?"

"Nope."

"And the vegetarian? And the Hindu? And the negroid who just got tenure? What about the animal-rights activist? The environmentalist? The suffragette? And how about the proponent of government subsidies? The anti-war protester? The Whig? The economics lecturer with the fuel-efficient car?"

"I don't like none of them!"

"That's too bad. And what are your feelings about the new sign ordinance the County Council wants to pass? You know, the one that requires all signs to be backlit?"

"I'm opposed to it."

"And the opening of our borders? And the separation of prayer from school? And the delinking of our currency from the gold standard?"

"Opposed."

"And the banning of all smoking in public places?"

"Opposed."

"And the new electric typewriters for the science department?"

"Not in favor."

"And the emphasis on the use of data for institutional planning?"

"Vehemently opposed."

"You seem to be opposed to a lot of things, Rusty. So what exactly do you *favor*? Anything?"

"I favor what already is. If something exists, then by God there's got to be a reason for it! So just leave it alone. Let it *be* and stop meddling with it. There's enough damn change in the world as it is without aspiring to create more of it where it don't belong."

"But Rusty," Stan objected. "If we take your approach to its somewhat logical conclusion, then wouldn't that mean the end of all innovation? Wouldn't that imply that we should just accept things as they are? Rather than strive for progress?"

"Damn right!"

"But surely you can't be serious! As a scientist you can't really mean that! Just think of all the inadequacies that would remain unaddressed. I mean if we all just sat around accepting the status quo – if everyone believed like you – then we would never challenge our nation's great injustices. We never would have overturned Prohibition. Or protested the Stamp Act. Or abolished human slavery!"

"If everyone believed like me," Rusty said, "we wouldn't have had slavery in the first place! Or stamps...." Rusty held up his beer can. "... And God knows we wouldn't have needed Prohibition...!"

Dr. Felch laughed.

"I can vouch for him on that!"

"And yet," said Raul, "you are known throughout the region for artificially inseminating cows. This is not a natural process. It is a human contrivance. Is this not an inconsistency in your world view? A fatal contradiction? Is this not a paradox of sorts?"

"Nope. It is not a paradox. At least no more of a paradox than any other paradoxical thing in the world."

"But it is! And the proof is all around us. In fact, it's in your left hand at this very moment! Because if you get right down to it, Mr. Stokes, isn't beer itself a human construct? Without the very human yearning for innovation, wouldn't we all be reduced to drinking *water* right now?"

"Without innovation," Rusty explained, "we would all be free men drinking water. That's true. But given that we have become such slaves to innovation, well, we might as well make the most of it by drinking *beer*!"

Everyone laughed. Stan laughed too. Then he asked:

"So how many cows have you inseminated anyway?"

"What?"

"How many cows have you inseminated, Mr. Stokes?"

"Well, none *personally*. That's genetically impossible."

"Yes, but *artificially* how many have you inseminated?"

"Too many to name."

"And did you find it difficult at first?"

"It was messy, yes."

"But I assume it got easier with time?"

"Of course. Like anything else in this world."

"I imagine it takes a steady hand to inseminate a cow?"

"Yes, it does."

"And a steely resolve."

"That too."

"Anything else?"

"Well, and a shoulder-length glove."

"You've lived a good life, Mr. Stokes."

"I've been very fortunate."

We all nodded. Then someone said:

"Since you've touched upon the topic of insemination, is there anything that you would like to insert into our ongoing discussion of love?"

"Your what?"

"You know, our discussion of...*love*. Can you tell us what you think it is? You see, this topic also requires a firm hand. And it's been a point of contention for us recently. So we're trying to get some fresh insights into this very old topic. We're trying to heighten our awareness of the issue before the semester starts. So what can you say, Mr. Stokes?"

Rusty gave a guffaw.

"I don't know nothing about that," he said. "My field of expertise is narrow. Empiricism doesn't have much use for a thing like love."

"But Rusty, we're eager to learn from someone with so much experience!"

"Experience!"

"Yes, Dr. Stokes. After all, you've got a wife and three daughters and a grandchild on the way. So we're hopeful that you can be the one to shed some light on this topic. Because the night isn't as young as it once was. The moon is bold but evanescent. And our time to achieve some sort of deeper understanding seems to be running out."

"Yeah, well, I honestly can't tell you what love *is*. And I can't tell you what it *isn't*. But I can sure as hell tell you what it *ain't*...!"

"That'll be fine...."

Rusty took a swig of beer from his can. Then he said:

"You see, lots of people have misconceptions about love. They think it's some kind of romantic dinner for two at the Asian restaurant around the corner. Or a one-way bus ride to Michigan in winter. But actually love ain't anything of the sort. It ain't got nothing to do with ball gowns and candlelit dinners and romantic strolls down the beach. It ain't roses and Valentine's Day cards. It ain't candy hearts and sloppy-tongued kisses on a warm rainy night. It ain't unrequited blowjobs or a mouthful of moisture or an eleven-minute mistake to last the rest of your life. It ain't a starry night in mid-August down by the river. And it sure as hell ain't two horny fifteen-year-olds in the front seat of my Chevy last June!"

"We're sorry to hear about your truck, Rusty."

"It ain't the truck I'm pissed about. It's the principle."

"She's a beautiful girl, Rusty. I'm sure the baby will be a stunner."

Rusty finished off his beer and threw his can into the fire.

"Yeah, well, we'll see about that."

Bessie was nudging me in the ribs and when I looked over I could see that she was motioning for me to cease this line of discussion. And so I did. And, as always, it was Raul who gracefully rescued the moment:

"This is such a fantastic spot," said Raul pointing over at the river. "The darkness is striking. The smells are primordial. The sounds of the dark woods are so exotic. And I just love how the moonlight reflects off the water ever so gently. It's all very scenic. And calls to mind the Llobregat in early spring."

"I'm glad you like it," Rusty said. "This is my family's spot. We come here every summer."

"It's lovely," I added. "Is there a bathroom nearby?"

Rusty laughed.

"Sure. Which corner of the night would you prefer?"

Everybody else laughed.

"This is Cow Eye Junction, Charlie. You can just make yourself at home."

"Yeah, when you're in Cow Eye, do as the Cowesians do!"

Again everyone laughed. I laughed too but did not budge from the log.

"This place really does bring back so many memories," said Bessie. "I haven't been down to this stretch of the river for ages. My father used to go fishing not far from here. He had a special place around the bend where he always caught his limit. Even when no one else was catching, he always caught. He called it his Sanctuary. It was his secret spot."

"Your father was a helluva fisherman!" said Rusty. "I went with him a couple times. He could catch anything. The man was legendary! One of the best anglers I've ever known."

"That's what everyone tells me. I was small but I can remember him bringing his catch home and mom and me staying up late cleaning it. I used to hate that! He'd ice it in coolers and take it around to the neighbors the next day."

"In his old Dodge!"

"Right. Missing its windshield."

"With the tailgate down and the American flag sticking out the front grill."

"All fifteen stars waving proudly!" Bessie laughed. (With each remembrance her thigh seemed to press even more snugly against mine; as she talked, her body moved with her words and I felt the warmth of her hip – did she notice? – and the soft press of her shoulder.) "Sometimes he'd take me on his rounds to the neighbors. At each house we'd stop to visit with the person we were giving the fish to. Usually on the porch. Sometimes in their kitchen. It always felt like time standing still because they'd spend so long catching up on everything that happened since the last time they met. All the latest hunting stories. And each of the fish they'd caught. And the different people they knew. They always made sure to remember anyone who'd moved on or passed away since the last time. Oh, and their trucks. God, if I had to listen to any more talk about *trucks*! They'd go on for hours. And the whole time I'd just stand there taking it all in, child-bored, wishing we could move on to the next house so we could get back home, not realizing then that later in life I'd long for these very moments that I was now wishing away. The adults would talk and talk. I'd listen. And then before we left, the hosts would give us something to take back. A cut of beef. A comb of honey. Some leather work for my dad's saddles. It was like going shopping every time we went out to deliver his fish....!"

"It used to be like that in Cow Eye. But we've lost it somewhere along the way. Another casualty of progress."

"That's so true. In my family it died with him. I haven't been fishing since."

"You're not the only one. Fishing is what we did in those days. But your dad wouldn't recognize the river now. It's not the same river he knew. And the fishing itself ain't what it used to be. In your dad's days it was a different world. Back then the river ran different. The waters were cleaner. The flow was faster. The fish actually jumped out of the water. Those were the days when the railroad still ran and progress was still thought to be progressive and it still seemed like hydroelectric power would be the wave of the future. But now it's all different. And this poor river has really been abused over the years...."

"By progress?" Raul asked.

"Hell yeah," said Rusty. "This river has become everyone's bitch. The local whore. The retarded girl in the backroom. They've dredged her and redirected her. They pinched off her flow. Then they added chemicals upstream. Then algae to control the chemicals. Now they're looking for something – anything! – to manage the algae they brought in. They've pumped crude oil into her and expectorated their waste. And they've made huge messes from the boats that were dispatched to clean up the smaller messes. In my years along the river I've found tires in the shallows. Old televisions. Floating buffalo carcasses. Vacuum cleaner belts. One time I was fishing trout and I pulled in an entire vacuum cleaner. There's not a family in Cow Eye that hasn't come across washed up syringes and heroin needles and opium pipes. These are just a few of the things they've done to our river."

"*They?*"

"Yes, they."

"And who is that?"

"*They* are people with ideas. New people with new ideas. Foreign people with foreign ideas – some from right around the corner; others from as far away as California. No offense to the three of *you*...." Here Rusty swept his arm to indicate me and Raul and Stan. "But all these people from other places with their new ideas – all these healers, hippies, prophets, and engineers – they come to Cow Eye with their plans and their ideas. And while they're here they do their deeds and they have their parties and their orgies and then just throw their used rubbers in our river. It doesn't even occur to them that it's all washing down to the rest of us. Or that it's *our* kids that's gotta swim in it."

"Sorry, Rusty," we said.

"No need for apologies just *yet*. You're still new to Cow Eye – and maybe your ideas will be the ones that work...."

"We hope so!"

"...But I doubt it."

Stan and Raul and I looked at each other contritely.

Rusty continued:

"But the worst thing they ever did was build that dam. Once the dam got built and they flooded the old Indian village the river wasn't ever the same."

"Dam?" Raul asked.

"Indian village?" Stan asked.

Rusty shook his head.

"The dam's a well-known part of our history. But the flooding of the village, that's one of Cow Eye's dirty little secrets. I have a few article clippings at the museum about it. And I've got some before-and-after pictures. The village didn't have to get submerged like that. But that's what happens when you chase progress. When you strive for continuous improvement. When you worship *efficiency*. The river ran like it did for a thousand years. And it was good. But it wasn't good enough. It had to be better. More productive. To flow faster. And to travel to places where it wasn't meant to go. Places it otherwise wouldn't have gone of its own accord."

"Kind of like how the three of us ended up here? How our respective travels led us to Cow Eye – a place we wouldn't have otherwise gone!"

"Exactly. You see, a river is reactionary: it resists progress; it prefers the status quo. But human beings are slaves to innovation. For Americans, especially, it's a cruel master. And so the people with ideas came in and bent the river over a barrel. They slapped it on the ass and made it submit to their whims. They blocked it off and diverted it, and if that meant flooding the old Indian village, well, then so be it."

Here Bessie shifted on the log and the side of her body brushed lightly against me. Her thigh was soft and warm. Looking down I could see that she was wearing a mini-skirt that rose above her knees. Her white blouse was loose. Her full breasts grazed my upper arm when she turned toward me to get a better look at the words being spoken.

"The village," Rusty went on," was really nothing more than a settlement of old huts and a smokehouse and some fields where the people grew crops next to the river. The place was right on the river so the water could flow into their fields and replenish their wells. In the whole Diahwa Valley Basin there was probably no other piece of land as productive as this."

"It makes sense," said Stan. "They were the first ones here. So they had the first choice."

"I suppose so," said Rusty.

"They knew what they were doing when they chose that place!"

"Well, that's definitely true."

Dr. Felch nodded:

"You all might be interested to know that one of our faculty members used to live there. Alan Long River used to live in that village when he was small. In fact, he was named for the river."

"Long River?" Stan asked. "You mean the Speech teacher who doesn't speak?"

"That's right," said Dr. Felch. "Charlie's mentor."

"Yeah," said Rusty. "Long River was born in the village and lived there until the resettlement. Back when he was still talkative he told me the whole sad story about how the government showed up at the village one day to kick his people out."

"This was more than forty years ago...." Dr. Felch added.

"Forty-*two*, to be exact. A sheriff gathered them in the center of the village and said, 'You all have to leave because in one year the ground under your feet will be covered in water.' Long River's people shook their heads and said, 'It's impossible. The river has never come to this place before. So why would it gather here now?' And the sheriff pointed to the tallest tree in the village – an American pine – and said, 'Do you see that tree right there? In one year there's gonna be enough water where we're standing to cover the highest branches of that tree!' But the people still couldn't believe it. 'That's not possible,' they said. 'Water can't gather so suddenly!' And they refused to leave. A month later the government came in with bulldozers and sheriffs and eminent domain and evicted them. Long River was just learning to speak when all this was taking place. But he remembers it vividly and told me about it years later."

"My uncle was one of the sheriffs," said Dr. Felch. "For him it was one of the hardest things he ever had to do."

"But he did it?"

"He did it."

"What a tragedy!" Stan said. "An entire settlement wiped away! Under water! Where'd they all go? Where did the *people* go after they submerged the village?"

"They scattered. Some moved into town. Others left for the city. Long River's family stayed, but they were the exception."

"All of this for a dam? That's so wrong. Why didn't anyone stop this?"

"It wasn't a priority back then. And besides, it seemed like a good idea at the time."

"At the time. And now it's a tragedy!"

Rusty shook his head.

"No, it's not a tragedy. At least not anymore. It was a tragedy *then*. But now it's merely history. Take any contemporary *tragedy*, add *forty-two years* to it, and what do you get? You get...*history*."

"History?!" a loud voice rang out from behind us. All together we turned around to see that Will Smithcoate was walking up with a lawn chair tucked under his armpit. "Did I hear you call my name?!"

Everyone laughed.

"Come on over, Will." Dr. Felch motioned for him to have a seat next to our logs. "I see you came prepared....!"

"Yeah, well, sorry I got here a little late. The traffic was terrible. I got stuck behind a death march...."

Dr. Felch groaned.

Will plopped the folding aluminum chair next to our log and collapsed himself into it. He was holding his "canteen" in one hand and an unlit cigar dangled from his mouth.

"Why're you sneaking up on us like that?" Rusty said.

"I had a little matter to take care of over there in the woods."

"We don't need the details, Professor."

"Yeah," said Bessie. "You can keep that to yourself!"

"My wife used to tell me, Will, if someone gave me a dime every time you took a leak...I still wouldn't feel any better about it. My wife had a helluva wicked sense of humor like that!"

We laughed.

"So what've I been missing? What's all this talk about *history*?" Will had slumped into the chair and was brushing a piece of dust from his suit and straightening his bow tie. "And how can I be of assistance to my dear colleagues?"

"Oh, it's nothing, Will. We were just telling our new faculty here about the dam and how the Indian village got flooded. Rusty was just saying that the whole traumatic episode has passed into history."

"Exactly," said Rusty. "And now it's just accepted as an inevitable relic of progress and evolution. Like the extinction of the passenger pigeon. Or the emergence and disappearance of this or that civilization of the world, along with its language, its culture, and the institutions it holds dear."

"Of course the dam was a bad idea," Will said. "Most things are. But it's not without precedent. Water makes people do strange things, you know."

We all nodded somberly.

"In fact, it's one of the three *W*'s that cause men to lose their minds...."

Will paused for dramatic effect:

"The other two are women and words."

Will pulled his cigar from his coat pocket and twirled it in his fingers.

"And the main difference between these things is that *women* come and go. But *words* live forever. And as for *water*....well, that's something we haven't quite figured out one way or the other...."

We nodded.

"....Now the thing about history," Will continued, "is that it has quite a bit to do with *women* but even more to do with *words*. And if you examine the matter closely you'll see that history really is no different from *water*. It flows where it wants. It moves at its own pace and in its own time. We can observe it and remember it. We can try to quantify and explain it. And sometimes we can even be so lucky as to predict its eventual course. But it's only a fleeting achievement. You can't contain water any more than you can control history. Ninety-nine percent of all water in the world is too salty to consume. But what we call history is the one percent that remains. It's the tiny bit that we can drink. The rest just rises back into the clouds like a puddle off hot asphalt."

"Asphalt?

"Yes, asphalt."

Raul shook his head:

"For a history teacher, Mr. Smithcoate, you sure have a cynical view of history!"

"Yeah, well, it's like my wife used to say. She'd say the cobbler's kids go barefoot. The farmer's family goes hungry. And the historian and his wife, well, they are condemned to go heirless. No sons. No daughters. No lasting legacy of any kind. Of course it wasn't our choice. We had some amazing sex in our time – believe me, my wife could frigger like a doxy! – but *that* was one thing she never forgave me for ...!"

Shaking off the digression into Will's fruitless views on history, Rusty continued:

"Anyway, the original people from the village are having the last laugh. Long River told me that as they were leaving their village, the old people got together and put a blight on the area. 'You've done this thing to us because of water. So let water be *your* curse.' They pronounced this just before the bulldozers came in. And then they left. It was the last thing they ever spoke in their native tongue. And it was the last thing they ever said *as a people.*"

"Then what happened?"

"The rest is history. The dam opened the next year. The village got submerged. And the water hasn't been the same since. The dam was supposed to supply the whole area – from Cow Eye Junction all along the breadth of the Diahwa Valley Basin. But the rain stopped coming and now it barely feeds the town. The canals ran dry. Hell, the upper part of the river's got even less water now than it had before the dam was there. And the lower part has none at all. When I was little there were fishing stands all along this river. You could jump off the rock they call Big Rock and not worry about breaking your neck. Now the water's so low you'd be nuts to try that. Plus you might hit an old truck half-buried in the muck!"

"Or the roof of an abandoned house," said Dr. Felch.

"Or a discarded steam engine," said Bessie.

"Or the sunken remains of an eighteenth-century slave ship," said Will.

"Will?"

"Not literally, of course..."

(Here Will lit up his cigar and leaned back in his aluminum chair. Having injected himself into the conversation, he now seemed perfectly content to let it flow around him.)

"But why was the dam so necessary?" Raul asked. "It seems like a lot of trouble for everyone."

"It was," Rusty said. "But the region needed cheaper energy to run the Ranch. And they needed more power for the new settlements cropping up on the Outskirts. You know, to accommodate the future influx of hippies, healers, prophets and prostitutes. These were the times when steam power was in steep decline and hydroelectricity seemed like the wave of the future. And of course the area needed more water. Where do you think the college gets all its verdure from? Or the water for its lawns? The fountains? The bull mounting the heifer? Where do you think the campus gets all that virility?"

We nodded our complicity.

"I hate to say it....but where would our idyllic campus be without that dam?"

It was a rhetorical question, of course, and so Rusty did not wait for an answer; instead he reached into his cooler and pulled out another Falstaff.

"Stan? Care for another?"

"I'm good for now, thanks."

"Raul?"

"I don't touch the stuff."

"Oh, I almost forgot you're from *California*. You, Charlie?"

"Sure. I'll have another."

And Rusty handed me another beer.

❧

BY NOW THE playful sounds coming from the river had died down and in their place the snapping of the fire had grown louder. A few of the early attendees had left. Most of the secretaries had gone home. Gone were the majority of maintenance staff and the animal science faculty. Rusty's daughter and her boyfriend had left together in the boy's truck. And almost all of the children – the ones playing by the river and chasing each other unattended – were gone as well. The few of us still here – Will and Raul and Rusty and Stan and Dr. Felch – had settled around the warm fire, each of us lost in the impending darkness of this cloudless night. In the glow of the firelight Bessie and I still sat close together on the log; from time to time she would allow her hand to settle on my thigh for a moment – an accident? – and each time she did I felt the kundalini beginning to well up from within me.

"So does anyone know why Long River doesn't speak?" Stan asked when the latest round of beers had been passed around. "It seems strange that a person would just stop speaking like that. Especially a professional Speech teacher."

Rusty and Dr. Felch traded glances.

"It's a long story," Rusty said.

"It sure is," Dr. Felch agreed.

I laughed:

"They usually are around here...!"

"And a sad one," said Dr. Felch.

"Very sad," said Rusty.

"They always are," said Bessie lightly squeezing my knee.

"So what actually happened?" Stan persisted.

Both men seemed reluctant to tell the story. But when they saw that the grill had grown cold and the steak had been well eaten and that Raul's guitar had been set aside for the time being, and when they realized that a story of this sort might count as a form of professional development for accreditation purposes, they began to tell what they knew. Over the next half-hour we learned the sad story of how Alan Long River, my faculty mentor, became a Speech teacher who doesn't speak.

❧

"IN THE BEGINNING," Dr. Felch began, "Long River was the best hire we ever made here at Cow Eye. After high school he'd gone to a college up north where he graduated with all the degrees needed for the position. In one fell swoop we were able to hire a qualified faculty member with ties to the area, a Native American no less, who knew our local students on a deeper level and could connect with them in profound ways. Plus, there was something uplifting about a local boy coming up from tribal roots to get a higher education and then using that education to teach our students – others like him – how to express their ideas in beautiful, inspirational English. Long River himself was a poised speaker. He spoke rarely but when he did speak, you *listened*. His words were well-chosen and incisive and he made you actually want to hear him speak. And isn't that what you want from a speech instructor? From *any* instructor? Hell, isn't that what you want from any educated human being! And so we hired him and within a few months he had already started to make an impact on the college. He revamped all the Speech courses and made them more relevant for his students. He brought in new methodologies and fresh perspectives. He updated the textbooks and introduced a host of innovative ideas into his pedagogy...."

At the mention of the word *innovative*, we all looked over at Rusty. But he just shrugged his shoulders and took a drink from his beer. Dr. Felch continued:

"....Despite the ambitious innovations, Long River was humble and worked well with his co-workers and within five years had achieved his tenure. It seemed that the sky was the limit for him. He was popular among his students. Respected among his peers. He was the perfect example of how a person from Cow Eye could come back to Cow Eye and succeed. He could have been successful anywhere, but he chose to come back to Cow Eye and achieve his success *here*. All in all, Professor Long River was just about the best employee we could have imagined...."

"This sounds ominous," I said.

"...Right. And so it was about this time that he met one of the old people from his childhood village, the old site along the river that had been submerged many years before. The woman was living in a care home in the area and she was about to die. He'd heard from a friend that the woman's family had moved away after the resettlement but she'd refused to leave Cow Eye with them. They'd reluctantly left her behind with other family members who had died off one by one until she was by herself, and now that she was dying he visited her in the hospital while her family made the trip across country. He did this because for his people it was a great sin to let another person suffer in solitude. By then the woman was not well and by the time he got to the hospital she was in a delirium, sweating and shaking and speaking mysterious words. Long River recognized these words as the language he had heard in the village as a child and though he could no longer understand the words, they touched him in a deep way. How many others like her were out there somewhere in the world? Forgotten in a nursing home? Rotting on back porches? Scattered around the country like water spilling over a dam? The woman never knew that Long River was in the room with her – she passed away that night – and for him this was a gut-wrenching experience. Not just for the death of the old woman, who he'd never even known, but also because in her passing he sensed the final drifting away of his people and their language. In the hospital room he vowed to do something remarkable: to find the old people of his village and to collect their wisdom into a single volume of folk teachings. And so, over the next few years he devoted himself to this cause and it became his life's purpose...."

Dr. Felch stopped to take a smoke of his cigarette. Rusty used the break in the telling to pick up the narrative where Dr. Felch had left off:

"So, like Bill was saying, Long River really took this thing seriously. During this time he'd always come down to the museum where I was volunteering and he'd read the old newspapers looking for the names of the families that used to live in the old village where the dam now was. He was hellfire persistent and through the historical records and by interviewing local residents he found eight old-timers from the village who were still in the area. These were the elders who'd once spoken the native language as children and might still be able to speak it now – the last ones who might still be able to pass it down. Each of these elders was very old by then and when he traveled to visit them he came to see how tough his challenge really was. Of the eight elders he'd tracked down, one refused to talk to him at all: stubborn and still bitter, she preferred to take the language with her to the grave rather than to entrust it to him now. Another who was more willing died a few weeks before Long River could meet with him. That left six, and of these six, one was already suffering from irreversible memory loss and couldn't remember the names of her own children – much less the words of a language she hadn't spoken since her childhood. This meant only five of the original elders were left, and these five – four women and a man – were the only native speakers remaining, the tobacco-thin margin between the life of a language and its death. There was no time to waste. And so Long River stepped up his efforts. Immediately, he appealed for an early sabbatical, received it, and headed out into the field to conduct research with the five elders who carried the withering seeds of his people's language...."

Rusty stopped to take a drink of beer. Dr. Felch continued:

"....To what Rusty just said I should add that there was some consternation around the campus when Long River received his sabbatical early. One thing about tenured faculty is that they live in a shifting world of relative worth. And this can make them petty and myopic. Long River's early sabbatical wasn't standard practice and some feathers were definitely ruffled. Why had I let him go a year early when others had always waited the full term? Was this fair? Was this equitable? Wasn't this proof that I was showing favoritism? Well maybe! But, dammit, in my mind he'd proven the urgency. There was no guarantee that these old people would even be around a year from now. And this year could be used to document what he could before it was too late. And so I made the tough call, the sabbatical went through, and Long River took the year off to be with the five elders...."

Dr. Felch crushed out his cigarette and then continued:

"To say the year was life-changing for him would be an understatement. Long River spent all his waking hours with the elders, driving from one side of the Diahwa Valley Basin to the other, and from them he came to learn the silent words of the language his people used to speak. Day in and day out he meticulously documented their speech patterns, their ancient vernacular, the old words for the winds and the rains of the place – places that no longer were, winds that no longer blew, rains that no longer came – words that came from the earth of the place and that could not be in any other language; faithfully, he recorded the word play, the subtleties of humor, the double entendres and allusions and self-referential descriptions. In time he had catalogued the language to the extent that it could be passed on in written form, if only in that form alone. And though it was a triumph of sorts, there was also something bittersweet about the experience: during that year, two more of the elders – the ones he had spent so much time with – passed away, taking with them so many words and phrases and unique ways of seeing the world. Time was moving too fast. Now there were only three left. They were sick. They would soon be gone. And that's when he had an epiphany…."

Dr. Felch stopped. Rusty spoke up for him:

"The epiphany was…."

"Hold on, Rusty!" said Dr. Felch. "Let me finish this part….!"

"Sorry, Bill…."

Dr. Felch continued:

"The epiphany," he explained, "was that a language cannot continue to be a language if it is not spoken by young people. All his efforts over the last year had been to simply document the existence of the old language. To put it down so that it could be seen and studied and respected by future generations. And with this accomplished, it had gained a certain weight and could be placed into a museum to be admired alongside the other primitive artifacts of human evolution: the bone tools and arrow heads and shards of clay pottery – the steps in the evolutionary hierarchy that were only necessary in that they served to lead us to the apex of modern tools and advanced weaponry and non-breakable dishes and American Standard English. But without native speakers – without the voices of children – the language would be lost. It was not enough to document the existence of the language for posterity: it had to be perpetuated. And so it occurred to Long River that his mission was not just to preserve the language in written form but to create a population of native speakers. But for that to happen the language needed to be *taught*. Only through its teaching could the language be resurrected and preserved and, in so doing, perpetuated as a living language. The language needed to be taught *to young people*…!"

Dr. Felch paused.

"Okay, Rusty. Now you…"

And Rusty said:

"This was during the time when I'd just come to be chair of the College Council. I was new and green back then and one day Long River came to ask me about teaching the old language at the college. This was not long after the Dimwiddle contribution and there was new and enthusiastic money to spend. Our languages back then were the standard ones – the languages you might find in an airport or at an economic conference – and yet the Dimwiddle family, as eccentric as they are, wanted to make a different kind of impact: they wanted to support a different kind of language. 'It's perfect!' said Long River. And I agreed. We met in my office and I outlined the steps he'd have to follow – there were many steps, and even then there could be no guarantee that he would succeed. I honestly didn't think he'd be able to do it, but he followed all the steps to draft a proposal for the council to consider. In his vision the college could reach out to the community by establishing a place on campus where the language would be taught. This might eventually lead to a formal program of study – a certificate, perhaps, or maybe even a degree. And in this way our college would be supporting the language and the preservation of the indigenous culture. It was a beautiful idea and one that most of us supported. But…"

"*But*?!" we all said.

Dr. Felch continued:

"But," he said, "the world is not always as simple as our plans for it. Sometimes our beautiful ideas are too beautiful. You see, there are certain procedures and requirements and formalities that a proposal has to go through. And so Long River began the arduous process of pushing his proposal through. A feasibility study was required and he paid for it out of his own pocket. Countless forms needed to be filled out in triplicate. The Dimwiddles needed to be consulted. And along the way there were doubts and skeptics and questions. How many students would the program have? How much would it cost per student? Where would the classes be held? Why should we support this language instead of a more functional one? Representatives from other departments wanted to know what the impact would be on their own classes. The fiscal department wanted to know whether the program's enrollment could be increased by a fixed percentage every year. And of course the institutional research office demanded that he estimate the exact number of students who would actually be taking the classes, their demographic make-up, their postal addresses and ages and grade point averages. The impact his classes would have on our graduation rates. The likelihood that with this new knowledge they would be able to become god-fearing, tax-paying citizens of the United States of America. One by one, he provided every answer that was posed to him. I mean he really busted his butt. From morning to night he sat in his office detailing the plan. He was almost there! He just needed to get his proposal approved by the College Council! It was right there for the taking. The language was so close to being spoken that he could even taste the words on his lips...."

Rusty paused to savor this taste, then continued:

"....And then came the day for the College to consider his proposal. I remember it was late in the semester and the council was tired. We'd just gone over some rough issues – the budget for the new swimming pool was a big one – and when Long River began his presentation, well, it's just hard to say what happened. Even now I don't know where it went wrong. Because it started off so promisingly: 'Dear colleagues,' Long River began. 'I'm coming to you today because you are being given the opportunity to do the right thing. As human beings, there are very few times in our lives when we are given the chance to do a thing like this. And you now have that opportunity.' Of course everybody snapped out of their stupor. The intrigue in the room was palpable. Remember, now, that Long River was a Speech teacher. So he was well-versed in the rhetorical approaches and strategies to use. He used them all! And as he talked, we all hung on his every word. 'For more than a thousand years my people lived on the very lands that you see. They hunted buffalo. They fished in the waters that are now called the Cow Eye River. They lived off the land and coexisted peacefully with the world around them. This campus is built on the bones of my ancestors. Over the years many bad things happened to my people. They were displaced and dismembered. Our traditions were taken away. Our language was taken away. And gradually we lost it. There is nothing that any of us can do to bring it back to what it was. But there is something that can be done so that it can have its own place in this world once again. So that it can occupy that very small place under the sun that all languages used to have title to not so long ago.' And here, in a rhetorical flourish, he pulled out a tape recorder and hit play. In the room an old voice began speaking: it was a woman's voice, and she was very old, the voice crackling with age, and soon we understood that these were the words of the old language. The woman spoke effortlessly. Breathlessly. The recording played for a few minutes and then Long River hit stop. The voice died away. 'What you just heard was a legend of our people told by a woman who used to live in the village where I was born. The village is no more. The woman herself passed away last month. The legend she's telling is an old legend that was passed down through her family from one generation to the next. I'd never heard this story until I met this woman. It is a legend about a river that runs out of water, a legend that, if I had not been able to record it last year, might have been lost to the world forever. This is how fragile our language is right now. How tenuous is our place in this world. The legend, like all legends, is instructive. And like all world views it deserves to exist for the unique insights it imparts. The river that runs out of water is a story that we should all know. And so, in recognition of the great burden of our shared history, I will translate it for you into the language that *you* speak.' And here Long River told the legend that his people once told about the river that ran out of water....'"

～

IN THE OLD days before there even was a man on this earth, there was a river that ran from the top of the heavens all the way to the bottom of the sea. This was a wide river and in this river were all the elements of the world that would eventually come together to make our world what it is. There was mud in this river and there was sand. There was air and wind and sun. There was fire and fragrance. There were fish and stones and grasses. And of course there was water in the river – so much water that all the water of the world came from this very river and made its way through the many smaller rivers and streams of the world to the different places of the world. The river came from the heaven to the sea and in this river was everything that had ever been. And everything that would ever be. All the stars came from this river. And all the plants and animals came from this river. And it was from this river that the very first man came to be born from warm mud. From the seed of silence came the body of man and this man grew into a strong man who gave birth to other strong men until, through time, the earth was populated with this new ambitious animal that would come to be called man.

This new strange species possessed many qualities that made him well-suited to living in the world with all the other plants and animals.

For this man was slower than the fastest animals. And weaker than the strongest. He could not fly. He could not swim. He could not burrow. He could not climb. He was too large to be inconspicuous, yet too small to be imposing. He was quick to tire and quicker to fall sick. This species was weak and frail and entirely unremarkable. It was this that made him a good citizen of the world. And a faithful descendent of the river.

But there was also one thing that this new animal had that was not good for the river. And it was that the man was always very thirsty. Thirst was in everything this man did. It was his essence. More than hunger. More than desire. Thirst for moisture was what made him human. And it was the quenching of his thirst that allowed him to spread out across the earth and to find others like him. For when he drank he became strong and courageous and this gave him the strength to conquer new lands and to settle new territories and to make the many innovations that kept him from succumbing to the stronger and faster animals of the earth.

The day when the man began to drink from the river was the day that the river itself began to die. For he could not stop. From the earliest of morning he drank and he did not stop until the latest of night when, full from his drinking, he finally went to sleep. The next morning, as soon as the sun rose, the man would come to the river to drink from the river once again. Now the river was very long and it held much water. And through it all, the river gave its water so the man could prosper. Cold, clean, clear water that the man drank without hesitation. And without compunction. And without appreciation.

And if it could have spoken, the river would have told the man: Man, do not drink all of the water that is in me. For it must be for all animals and it must last forever. Do not take into yourself my water now flowing as if it will always be here to flow for you forever. Take what you need only. And let the rest be for the others. For there are consequences to everything you do. And there are consequences to your thirst. And to your drinking. And to the water that used to flow through you but is now dammed at that point where your greatest weakness protrudes.

But the river could not talk. And the man would not have listened. And so the man drank and drank. As he drank he became bigger. And as he became bigger he also became heavier and slower – so slow and heavy that he could barely move. And yet he continued to drink with even more thirst. With the thirst of a thousand generations. As if the water in the river were an endless stream of moisture stretching back from the very beginnings of time and flowing to the edge of the limitless universe.

And then one day the man went to the river only to find that there was no water there. He had drunk it all. The man by now was larger than the largest lake, as big as the ocean itself. For in his bladder he carried with him the water of all things. And without water to return to the heavens as evaporation there could not be water to return to the earth as rain. And without the eternal cycle of water there could be no more life and no more animals and no more anything over the earth.

The river had run out of water. And in time the river that had run out of water became the final resting place of the man who did not know the limits of his thirst. Or the consequences of his drinking. Unremarkably, the thirsty man lay down in the empty river bed and assumed the shape of the bed he lay in.

And as he lay in the bed he opened his ears for the very first time. And in his stupor he heard the sounds of the birds crying out for water, and the animals around him choking on the dust. For the first time he heard the words that the river had tried to impart. And as he lay there he began to cry. For the death of the river was also the death of the man. From the place where his greatest weakness protrudes, the man began to release the water over the land and through the straits of the channels and the water flowed in great streams from the place where he lay into the many lakes and streams and tributaries that make up the world's waters. And though these waters eventually came to nourish the fish, they were never the same again. For now they contained the jaundiced essence of death. And this death was universal. For the death of one man means the death of all men. Just as the death of one river means the death of all rivers. Just as the death of one idea means the inevitable death of all ideas.

∽

"AFTER HE'D TOLD his story, Long River looked up at the council members and said: 'That is the story that my people used to tell of the river that ran out of water.'"

Rusty stopped.

"I remember the looks on everyone's faces when Long River finished. Each was looking at him as if he were the final tongue speaking the dead language. But Long River did not waste any time. From there he went into the specifics of his proposal: Cow Eye would hire the remaining native speakers to team-teach the old language on campus. Classes would be held in the evenings to attract older students. Enrollment would be small at first but would increase by ten percent each year. As a direct result of our classes, the number of native speakers would increase over time from only four that day to more than twenty within a few years….to hundreds of young people speaking the language within a generation. The proposal would support the college's mission by furthering the American Way – because what could be more 'American' than a language that was here before any other? What could be more 'time-tested' than a culture that's been here since the earliest beginnings of time? Long River's presentation was skillfully crafted to appeal to logos and ethos and credos. And of course to pathos. 'Remember,' he said, 'what the river tells us. The death of one is the death of all. Please do not let my language die. Do not let it die alone and unattended.' When the formal presentation was finished – he ended exactly at the thirty-minute mark, just as he was allotted – I asked for a motion to approve the proposal, then for a second to the motion, and then called for discussion. Immediately, faculty began to speak up in favor of his proposal. Several praised him for such a moving presentation. A few spoke about their own ancestors and the many languages they'd lost along their tortuous journey to Cow Eye. Others lauded his conscientiousness. It looked like it was a done deal. The votes were locked up. I was just about to call for the question when I noticed a single hand go up. It was already late in the day and this was our last agenda item, so I'd hoped to move things along. But Robert's Rules are sacred. And so I looked over at the person raising the offending hand and I looked her directly in the eyes and politely asked her: 'Yes, Merna?' I said…."

"Merna!" we all exclaimed and looked around at each other. "The one whose ashes we scattered tonight?"

"Yes. She was our long-time math teacher at that point. Later she would take on the data analyst position. But when this was happening she was just a simple math teacher. She'd lived in Cow Eye all her life and was as local as they come. But she was also very logical. And she prided herself on being a numbers person. On her consistency. On objectivity. 'This sounds really good,' she said. 'But I just have one question. Would you be able to provide us with some evidence to *prove* what you've just said? Perhaps some objective data? Or mathematical justification? Or some statistical analyses? Some arithmetic calculations? Some cold hard numbers? Some unequivocal rationale. Some data-based reasoning? Some numerical computations. Some graphs? Some charts? A Venn diagram, perhaps? Believe me, Alan, I love your story of the river. And I feel for your people. I once considered going into the humanities myself. But when everything's said and done the numbers have to add up. Otherwise, it's all going to be futile. You see, it's numbers that will determine the ultimate fate of our world in the end and, in the short term, whether your proposal really holds water....'"

"The rest of the room was in shock. 'Merna,' said Long River. 'I can get you whatever numbers you need. But please pass this motion. The numbers can come later.' But Merna held her ground. 'No,' she said. 'The numbers have to come first. Justice without data — no matter how just it may seem, no matter how weighty it might appear to be — is not really justice at all.' A murmur went up around the room and after some discussion, the motion was withdrawn. It was the last council meeting of the year but Long River was given time to resubmit his proposal at the next meeting in September. I closed the meeting with his proposal still up in the air. I don't think any of us thought that his plan wouldn't be approved eventually. I don't think even Merna thought it wouldn't be passed. I really believe she just wanted to make sure all the numbers were in place. That all the *i*'s were dotted and the *t*'s crossed before moving forward with approval. But, unfortunately, that's not how things turned out."

"What happened?"

"Well," said Rusty, "over the summer a group of newer faculty got wind that the college might be looking to create a language program, and that Long River's proposal had been tabled, and they put together an alternate proposal for consideration by the council. The Dimwiddles could only fund one language program, not two. And so that next fall the council heard the other proposal, which was highly professional with colored charts and figures and statistics, and several of the newer council members fell in love with that proposal instead. The charts were more vivid. The numbers added up. When the time came for the vote, it was clear that Long River's proposal was no longer the one that would be supported. And sure enough: that's what happened."

"*What* happened?"

"The council voted down his proposal in favor of the other one. The newer faculty had won and two years later the college, with the support of the Dimwiddle endowment, launched its new Esperanto program to much international acclaim. The three elders Long River was working with have since passed on. A younger teacher died in an urban shooting a few years later. The language has since been put on the list of those headed for near-term extinction. It was devastating for Long River and he never forgave us. After the council meeting I pulled him aside. I'd been one of the few – the minority – who'd stuck with him and voted for his proposal. 'Look, Alan,' I said. 'We can do this another time. We'll come back next year. It's not over....' But he wouldn't even look at me. And he refused to answer. 'We'll get better numbers,' I repeated. 'More numbers! We'll get so much data that the correctness of the decision will be incontrovertible! We'll get colorful charts. It'll all add up. We'll....' But there was no response. He just walked away. He hasn't talked to me since. In fact, since that day at the council meeting, Long River hasn't said a single word to *anyone* at the college. Even his students."

"Does he talk to anyone outside the college?"

"Not that we know of. Though it's possible. We think it's his way of making a statement: since *his* language has been silenced forever, he refuses to use *ours*."

"Forever?"

"We don't know. It looks that way."

"Well, that does sort of make sense now," we said.

"And what about Merna? Didn't she regret what happened? Didn't she feel bad about derailing the proposal?"

"Maybe. I never talked to her about it. But the next year she took the data analyst position. So she must not have felt too bad about it. She held that position until last spring when she had to give it up."

"Why? What happened to *her*?"

"It's another long story...."

"*Another* one?!"

"Yes. And an even sadder one."

By now it was very late and the campfire had died down completely.

And in the near darkness, amid the smell of extinguished fire, they told this other story about the sad thing that happened to Merna Lee before she was taken by her kids to the city.

❦

AFTER THE LONG story of Long River, the speech teacher who doesn't speak
— and after they'd told the story of Merna's rise and fall — the discussion
grew somber. Rusty and Dr. Felch spoke about their friends from high
school who'd moved on or passed away. Stan told of a civilization that had
been wiped out by floods and famine. Raul sang a ballad of two lovers
separated forever by time and space.

"Look," said Rusty. "You all are depressing me. This is a remembrance,
not a funeral! I'm tired of dwelling on the whims of water. Let's talk about
things we can control."

And so they talked about their trucks. And their committees. And the
proposals they had prepared. Or rejected. And the simmering quarterback
controversy at the local high school.

And through it all, Bessie's thigh never left its resting place against mine.

"I'll be right back…." I finally said when the conversation had moved
on. Decisively, I started to get up.

"Don't be silly!" Rusty said and pulled me back down. Then with a
fatherly pat on the shoulder, he handed me another beer.

"But I….!"

"Drink, Charlie!"

And so I settled back down on the log.

In time the conversation moved on. Dr. Felch and Rusty were now
laughing about certain peers at the college who'd exhibited unexpected
talents. The creative writing teacher who could lick the back of his ear.
The horticulture professor with the surprising talent for ventriloquism.
The cleaning lady who could sing in two octaves at the same time. The
tenured automotive instructor who had once rescued a non-tenured
humanitarian from a burning, smoke-filled meeting room.

"Have you ever seen Gladys dance the Charleston?"

"Of course! And have you heard Belinda do her impression of a hapless
scalawag being tarred and feathered?"

"Many times! In fact she did it at our Christmas party a couple years
ago. It was almost as entertaining as the one Dexter does of a fifteen-
month-old heifer getting penetrated for the first time…!"

With each new beer I came to appreciate the impressiveness of this
new world that I had entered. The faculty with all their hidden talents and

ambitions. The campus with its groves of magnolia and sycamore. The Diahwa Valley Basin itself with its stark drought and disappearing tribes and myriad water pent up unjustly and in the most hopelessly artificial way. There is nothing more natural than the flow of water from a higher place to a lower one, and keeping this from happening – keeping so much moisture from being released – requires a huge amount of effort – a factor of human destiny that after so many beers was becoming increasingly clear to me at this late hour. And so I stood up again.

"Bessie!" I said. "I really need to head to the woods for a bit. Please wait for me right there on that log that we've been sitting on. It has been a pleasure to share such a small space with you tonight, to sit so tightly next to you. I feel like I know you a lot better than a few hours ago. I've enjoyed the firm press of your thigh against mine and the casual brushes of your body from time to time. My kundalini is rising, rest assured. So please wait for me and I'll be right back. I promise. I just need to reside in near darkness for a few minutes...."

I turned toward the woods.

"Charlie!" a voice called out. I ignored the voice but it was insistent: "Charlie!"

When I turned around I saw Stan Newtown heading toward me.

"Charlie!" he said. "Can I have a word with you?"

"Sure, Stan. But could it wait a minute. I was heading over there toward the dark woods...."

"Charlie, it's important."

"But...."

"Look, Charlie, I'm telling you this because I know I can trust you. I'm confiding in you because I know that you do not belong to either group entirely. You have no allegiances. No friends. No preconceptions. You do not fit in with anyone at all and so I know you can be trusted...."

"That's fine. But if you could just wait a few minutes...."

"It's Ethel, Charlie."

"Ethel?"

"Yes, I'm worried about her. She's not the same woman I married, Charlie. She's not the same woman I used to approach orgasm with. She's not even the same woman I ventured to Cow Eye with a few weeks ago. She's, well – how do I put this? – *different*. Ever since we castrated that calf, she hasn't been the same."

"That was only yesterday."

"Right. And things haven't been the same since."

"Well, people change, Stan. *Things* change. They come and go. And no one knows that better than….well, than that calf…."

"Yes, but, you see, she's not just different. She's so different it's like I don't even know her anymore."

"I'm sorry to hear that."

"Charlie, tell me the truth. Is there something I should know?"

"About Ethel?"

"Yes. Is there something you're seeing that I'm not? Something you think I should be aware of?"

At this I thought about the thin bamboo mat where Ethel and Luke had pondered the relative merits of cosmic orgasm. Surely they'd stopped somewhere along the way? Surely they'd remembered that there are many steps to enlightenment and that the lowest one is nothing more than precisely that: the lowest?

"Of course not, Stan."

"Really?"

"Of course. Ethel is the same woman you married. The same woman you ventured to Cow Eye Junction with. She still has dreams of working as a fashion designer. She still feels that the ending of love is just as important as its beginning. She is still very married. She is as journalistic as she's always been. So enough with the conspiracy theories, okay!"

"You're probably right."

"Of course I'm right. Life is short. So enjoy what you can from it. Did you try some of these sumptuous nuggets that Dr. Felch was offering? They're terrific. And while you're at it, here, have another beer…!"

And with that I led him over to Rusty's cooler where I pulled out another Falstaff on his behalf.

"Thanks, Charlie," he said.

"No problem. Now let me get back to the woods….!"

But just as I turned to leave, another voice called out:

"Charlie, my boy!"

It was Rusty.

"Charlie!"

"Yes, Mr. Stokes."

"Thanks for coming tonight."

"I wouldn't have missed it…"

"Charlie, I heard you spent some time talking to Gwen Dupuis earlier tonight. And I'm sure she had a lot to say. She is welcome to her opinions. But so are we."

"We?"

"Yes, we. Now let me tell you the *true* story of the swimming pool…!"

And he did. As well as the full truth about the Christmas Committee. And my predecessor's indiscretions. In meticulous detail he told me the opposite story of stripes and stars: Gwen's chronicle of braking and acceleration, only in reverse. And when he was done I thanked him for the information and said, "Mr. Stokes thank you for sharing all of that with me. It definitely adds to my understanding of the different issues on campus. Now if you'll excuse me, I was heading toward the woods over there…."

"No problem, Charlie. It's been a pleasure talking to you tonight. I'm glad you could make it to our get-together. And I hope you enjoy your time in the woods. Monday is fast approaching and it's going to be a very long semester. So just let me know if you need any help along the way."

"I'll do that, Mr. Stokes. I definitely will do that…."

I turned to leave and had taken two steps toward the darkness when I bumped right into a figure that must not have seen me on its own return to the campfire.

"Charlie?" a voice said.

"Raul?"

"Charlie, what are you doing over here on the edge of darkness?"

"Probably the same thing you're doing, Raul! Or rather what you just *did*….!"

"Oh, I doubt that. You see, I was just calculating the likelihood that two people from opposite sides of the world – Barcelona, say, and the unnamed locale you came from – can expect to meet each other in a place like Cow Eye at some point during their respective lifetimes. You know, the likelihood of two arrows actually striking each other at their very tips. The odds are really phenomenal, Charlie!"

"I'm sure they are."

"Here, let me show you how unlikely this is to happen. See, I've drawn an approximation here on this napkin…."

And here Raul took out a napkin that was dabbed in barbecue sauce. Under the stain was the following diagram:

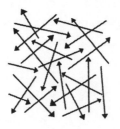

"See, Charlie? There's almost no likelihood. And yet it happens on a daily basis. It's one of the great paradoxes of life. Virtually everything that happens in a person's life is mathematically impossible. Or, rather, *everything* that happens is *virtually* impossible....! The odds are smaller than the likelihood of the most miraculous miracle. And yet that's not surprising because the odds of any single thing happening are infinitesimal. Life itself is a miracle: from its beginning to its end! And that's how the two of us could meet on that narrow school bus seat despite the impossible odds against it!"

Raul handed me the napkin.

"Here. You can have this...."

I folded the napkin and put it in my pocket.

"Raul, you are amazing. I don't care what Bessie says. We'll have to get together after the semester starts – you know when we're closer to sober – to talk more about this. And let's make sure we go to Texas next summer. Okay?"

"Of course!"

"Promise?"

"Sure."

"Great."

"But I'm sorry to have interrupted you, Charlie....where were you off to again?"

"I'm not sure. It seems I was headed over there towards the woods. So I'm fairly certain that's where I was going. But to be honest, Raul, I can't really remember *why* I was going there. Or what for. Perhaps it was to see if there was something to be seen on the other side of those trees right there. Or maybe it was to search for some broken arrow heads that may have been left by the displaced people who used to live here. Or then again, maybe I was just trying at last to do something – *anything*! – entirely.

In any case, I don't see much need for going to those woods anymore. Not without a clear sense of purpose. Not without an overriding mission. And especially when I can look back in the opposite direction past the smoldering coals of our campfire and see such a beautiful woman waiting for me next to the river. Bessie's really something, isn't she? And you're right, Raul. The odds of me meeting someone like that must be truly infinitesimal. The likelihood of two unloved people coming together in the middle of a night like tonight...in the middle of a drought for the ages....in a place like Cow Eye Junction. The odds that two people can come together to find love under a moon like this? Geez, Raul, that's something that must be absolutely beyond the realm of mathematical calculation. Just thinking about it has made me appreciate what I left behind. So let me head back to what I've given up. Let me return to that dark place by the river so that the two of us – she and I – can put an end to this lonely endeavor of being unloved...so that she and I can overcome that once and for all...."

And with that I headed back to the campground to look for Bessie.

⁓

"SO BESSIE," I said when I'd found her next to the river. The party had long broken up into individual conversations and she and I had taken seats by ourselves along the sand of the river bank. The children were gone. The river was flowing softly. In front of us the moon was shining over the moving water. "Bessie, I really am sorry I made you late for Merna's remembrance. I feel terrible about that."

"It's okay."

"And I'm sorry I put you on the spot yesterday by asking you to tell me your thoughts about love – you know, about what it *might have been* for you. I'm sorry I asked you that over your manual typewriter. But I truly was interested."

"I could tell."

"And I still am interested."

"I can tell."

"You can?"

"Yes, Charlie. I am a woman. And as a woman I can see very clearly that your curiosity is aroused. And that it's been aroused since our first meeting in the office. These are the things that a woman knows. These are the lessons that Cow Eye teaches us."

"Might it be mutual?"

"It might."

"So does this mean you want to hear my own thoughts on the matter?"

"You mean what you think love is?"

"Yes. Or rather what it *isn't*?"

"I'm not so sure. On the one hand, I'm as interested as I can be under the circumstances."

"Circumstances?"

"Yes, the circumstances facing us tonight. And those are that you have a Master's in Educational Administration while I've never ventured beyond high school. Your career track is paved with tenure while mine is gravelly and clerical. You come from a world of boundless lakes and oceans while I come from the landlocked desiccation of Cow Eye Junction. And of course it doesn't help that I have two young children – boys! – and you have nothing of the sort. You see, Charlie, people like you have been a part of my life for as long as I can remember and they've always come and gone. All of them. Is there a chance that you'll be different from the rest? Perhaps. But it's very small. In fact, I'm pretty sure that you are going to do exactly the same. You'll leave like all the others. And so this does not bode well for us on the one hand..."

"And on the *other* hand?"

"Well, on the other hand..."

Here Bessie paused.

"Open this can for me, will you....?"

I snapped the pull top off and handed the can back to her. In the background I could hear Raul singing a song in Spanish and the audible fawning of a single enthusiastic secretary. The light from the campfire had dwindled. Crickets were chirping in the distance.

Bessie took a long drink from her can.

"That moon is a bit startling tonight, isn't it?"

"It sure is."

"And the stars are bright."

"They are."

"The sky is very clear and I am getting cold, Charlie. You see, I've forgotten my sweater. My blouse is too light for the weather and the cold night air is making me shiver. Can you see me shiver, Charlie?"

"Yes, Bessie, I can."

"Can you see the tightening of my skin from the cold air? The way my pores are tingling."

"A bit, yes."

"Do you know what that means, Charlie?"

"I think so."

"What does it mean, Charlie?"

"It means you need to cover up. Here, wait a second and I'll be right back...."

When I had returned from Bessie's truck I folded the orange sarong in half and draped it over her shoulders.

"Here," I said. "That should help. Sorry for the color. And for the chivalry...."

Bessie and I sat drinking in silence and when she had finished this latest can of beer, and when she had crushed it under her heel and kicked it a few feet in front of us, she returned to her train of thought:

"On the *other* hand, Charlie, what am I supposed to do? I mean, a person doesn't stop being a woman just because she has two children, right?"

"I wouldn't know..."

"Should she stop being a woman just because she's been a woman so many times before?"

"I can't imagine...."

"Well, she doesn't, Charlie. And she shouldn't. Trust me on this one. And so, to answer your question....yes. That is to say, I'm interested in your thoughts on love but only inasmuch as you might still be interested in discovering *mine*."

"I am no less interested," I said.

"Really?"

"Yes."

"Even now?"

"Yes."

"That's good to hear," she said. "Then so am I."

Bessie held out her hand and I took it. It was dainty and very light and the skin was cold. Bessie was still shivering under the sarong.

"It's late," she said.

"And very cold," I said.

"Let's go," she suggested.

"If you insist," I said.

And with her cold hand still in mine, the two of us made our way through the deserted campgrounds, past the extinguished campfire, back toward the parking lot where her truck was the last one still parked under the flickering streetlamp.

∽

{ }

The great lovers of the world are distinguished from all the rest in that they have the ability to see eroticism in everything they do. The dinner conversation. The casual encounter. Subtle glances exchanged. The inadvertent brush of thigh against thigh on a crowded seat. Each of these is not merely a mundane expression of existence but rather an act of foreplay in itself — the first step toward the beautiful act of lovemaking. The great lover recognizes that life itself is the foreplay that brings us closer to the ultimate orgasm of eternity. And so the daily exuberances of life acquire their sensual weight only when we acknowledge them for what they are. And with this mastered, the greater lesson can be learned: that of finding the erotic essence in the most mundane of all acts. The accidental touch of a salesgirl handing back change to your open palm. The purchase of raw meat from the butcher at the grocery store. The exchange of glass bottles with the milkman. A furtive glance at revealed skin that is seen by the revealer. These moments are sometimes rewarded with sex but to the great lover they are the reward itself. And so the laughter of a close friend is no less a function of foreplay than the pre-coupling of two desirous bodies. And just as love is the water of life, so too is life the water of love. The unspoken thought. The articulated word. The written utterance. The crossword puzzle. How to live so that these things may acquire the burning element of eroticism that is inherent in all things? Discover that secret and you too will join the ranks of the great lovers!

Among community college instructors, this is doubly so. For within the realm of higher learning foreplay is, and has always been, in all things. This is true of the committee meeting where voices drip with erotic essence. And it is just as true of the well-attended accreditation briefing. And the focus group to discuss educational policy. It lies in the wayward fantasies for a supervisor across the desk — her words of supervision as sterile and cold as your thoughts for her are hot and specific. And of course it is the act of teaching itself. Can anything compare to the excitement of the first day of your first class, the first touch of a lover, the first glimpse of a new partner's nakedness? Eroticism prefers firsts. Yet should the experienced professor tremble any less at these than does the novice experiencing them for the first time? Is there anything more erotic than the unbounded promise of youthful immortality and untouched flesh? Yes! And it is the bounded promise of mature flesh and remembered youth! Those who learn these lessons become the great lovers of the world; they are the world's great faculty and the greatest experiencers of life. All of which is poignant and pregnant and a lesson that is not easily learned. Because the saddest mistake we can make is considering our life to be nothing more than the sex act itself, rather than the trembling anticipation that gives the act of loving its greater meaning.

{ }

BACK IN HER truck, Bessie started up the engine and turned the heater as high as it would go. The air came out in a cold blast at first, then grew hotter, and as we drove along the empty highway, the inside of the windshield fogged up. Outside, the night was black and endless just beyond the headlights of the truck. Like the deepest depths of water. Or a view of the endless universe.

"I need to make a stop," she said. "It'll just take a minute."

Bessie turned off the main road and took a left and then a right and then pulled off onto a gravel road leading to a dirt road that in turn led to a driveway where an old truck was propped up on blocks. Two children's bicycles lay overturned on the dirt.

"I'll be right back," she said.

Through the windshield I watched Bessie open the screen door of the house, quietly, and then enter. A dim light flickered on in one of the rooms and a silhouette passed by from one end to the other.

Sitting in dead silence, I felt my bladder swooshing and gurgling. Clearly there was something elemental I'd neglected to remember since arriving at Marsha's studio on the Outskirts. And now it was too late. That particular river, like so many others, had passed me by. And if there was one thing I was learning – from my time at Cow Eye, from my many rides between desiccation and verdure and back again – it is that water goes where it wants to go; no matter the dam you build, no matter the levee you devise, it will flow at its own pace and in its own time until it reaches its destination. Just hold on a bit more, I told myself. It is very late and this long night is almost over.

Inside the house, the light flicked off and a few moments later Bessie came back outside and climbed up into the truck.

"Everything's good," she said, closing the truck's door gently. "They're sleeping."

"Glad to hear it," I said.

Bessie reversed out of the driveway and pulled back onto the dirt road. She drove a few hundred yards along dirt, then turned onto the gravel road leading back to the highway. But then, before we had reached the quiet of smooth asphalt, she turned off into a clearing and stopped, dust drifting in front of the head lights. Leaving the engine to idle, she looked over at me.

"Charlie," she said.

"Yes?"

"I am receptive, Charlie."

"You are?"

"Yes."

"So am I."

"Good. But I cannot have sex with you tonight. I hope you understand."

"I understand."

"You do?"

"Yes."

"Good."

Bessie turned off the engine, then twisted the ignition back on to allow the radio to play. Fumbling with the tuner, she dialed in a station. There was a rasp and then a voice and then more rasp. On the AM radio station a country song was now playing softly. Outside the window, the sky was clear and the moon was startling. Through the still of the night the rapturous sound of crickets could be heard in the distance. Bessie turned in the seat to face me. Through the windshield, the moonlight fell across her white blouse in rippling shadows, making it seem – if only in the haze of my mind – that the whole scene had been painted in stark black and white. Pure black. Pure white. Nothing but the unadulterated contrast of pure light and its absence.

"It is a beautiful moon," I said.

"And the sky is clear," said Bessie.

"The crickets are chirping," I said.

"Rapturously," she said.

"Shall I unfasten the buttons on your blouse?"

"If you don't mind...."

"They are awfully far away."

"It is not an impossible distance."

"It isn't. And yet it may be."

"Charlie?"

"You see, a few hours ago I would have agreed with you, Bessie. Even a few minutes ago. But a lot has changed since then. A lot of beer has happened. And a lot of wine. Too much marijuana. And all of this adds up to ineffable change. Life, you see, is not the only thing that is tenuous...."

Bessie twisted closer to me:

"Do what you can...."

"I am trying my best under the circumstances. Believe me, I am trying. But the circumstances are truly daunting. The sleeves on my collared shirt are too long. And this stick shift that is halfway between us seems far closer to you than it is to me. But I'm trying, Bessie. I really am...."

"You're almost there, Charlie. Don't give up."

"But Bessie, I'm... I'm afraid I can't do it. The distance is just too great. And too fraught with meaning. Too redolent with metaphor. If your blouse is the frontier separating the world that is knowable from the world that is unknowable, and if the buttons are our futile attempts to leave a legacy of some sort, then surely this space between us – this unbridgeable gap between your nipples and my trembling hands – surely this is the moisture that teems within life itself. Surely there can be no finer metaphor for life's love of the unknowable?"

"My moisture is not metaphorical."

"I can sense that."

"It is redolent. And life-affirming."

"But it cannot help me now. For this distance is too eternal. The metaphor too heavy. I'm sorry, Bessie. I really am...."

In defeat I pulled back my hand and slumped back in my seat. Dejectedly I hung my head. Even the moon in all her feminine glory could not help me now.

"I'm sorry, Bessie," I said. "I truly am. But this distance is just too great."

⚉

BUT HERE BESSIE spoke firmly:

"No, Charlie. That is not how this night will end. If the tips of my nipples were unknowable then it would be impossible for them to be known. In that case, the distance between your curiosity and their unknowability – the distance between my nipples and that slight bulge in your corduroys – would be as unconquerable as the space separating time from timelessness. Or conflict from conciliation. It would be as great as the distance between one edge of the universe to the other. And, yes, it would be unassailable. But that has clearly not been the case with me. And that is clearly not the case now. And so it is done like this...."

With expert fingers Bessie undid the upper button of her blouse. From my vantage point across the truck's seat I watched the button pop free, a triangle of pale skin appearing where the white of blouse had been. Enraptured, I watched as her fingers moved down to the next button, and then the next, the triangle of flesh growing with each freed button until the two flanks of her light white blouse hung down freely in front of her exposed bosom like two separate curtains newly opened to reveal the light of morning. Amid the daze of my darkness it was clear that I was now witnessing the very emanation of day.

"If the moon is a woman," she said, reaching behind with both hands for the clasp of her bra, "then surely she controls the tides of your deepest desires."

Unfastening the clasp, she pulled the bra out through her sleeve and placed it on the seat between us.

"And if these tides are water, then surely there can be no finer expression of desire than the river that connects the moisture from above to the moisture down below...."

By now the blouse had become bra and the bra had become skin. And as she leaned over the stick shift I felt the warmth of her cheek on my corduroys, her fingers tracing along my thigh until they had reached my second chakra, and in the startling moonlight I felt my mind succumbing to the rhythms of this night. The kundalini flowing upward like a serpent rising from his sleep. Like the tingling of a thousand waves of wine bubbling up. The warmth of candlelight. The smells of evergreen and incense. The creeping of a Bengali tiger over the snow of a Michigan winter. In my mind the colors and sounds and smells whirled together like a dust devil gathering itself before a rain. And as the kundalini rose through the chakras of my body I felt my heart screaming out for its release, the cosmic trembling of my oneness with the universe. The oncoming rush of infinite water. The relentless approach of a new semester. The shudder of cold resolution. If ever there was a reason to rejoice, then surely it was happening at this very instant. Surely this was the moment when my heart would find its soothing and the logic of my logical mind would finally come together with the moisture of my human body to become something – *anything*! – entirely.

"No," I said over the waves welling up within me, and to the sounds coming up from below, "Love is not a thing to be feared. And it is not a thing to be approached tremulously. For no matter how unlikely it may seem, it can never be as unlikely as a thing that is absolutely impossible. And so love is not a cold night in August. Or a Christmas party in March. Or a pendulum that never stops. It is not a rural college unable to achieve continuous improvement due to the realities of mathematical probability. It is not a river that ceases to run. Or waters that cannot find their home. It is not a dam where tiny rivulets trickle off the top like a thousand little...."

"Charlie!"

Bessie's voice was startling amid the silent elation of my reverie. And so I continued:

"….where rivulets trickle like a thousand…."

"Charlie! Are you pissing in my mouth?!"

This too startled me.

"What?" I said.

"You heard me. Are you pissing in my mouth?!"

"I don't believe so, no."

"Charlie, you son of a bitch! You just pissed in my mouth!"

"I find that hard to believe, Bessie, I really do."

"Jesus…!"

Bessie opened her heavy door and spat onto the ground outside. Now she was spitting and wiping her mouth with the back of her wrist.

"Bessie," I said. "I understand your concern. And I am just as surprised as you. But this does not sound like me at all. In fact, this would be entirely out of character. I am an educational administrator. And so I'm sure there's been some misunderstanding…."

Bessie slammed the door shut.

"I can't believe you just pissed in my damn mouth! That's a first…!"

"Bessie, I hear your insecurities here. And I accept them. But I find it highly unlikely that such a thing could have just occurred. Water, you see, always seeks its own level. And here on this front seat it is clearly not the case that your mouth is lower than my corduroys. So, I would beg to differ with your interpretation of events…."

On the AM car radio one song had died out and another had begun. In the dim light Bessie was now dressing on the other side of the seat, fastening the buttons one by one – the promise of coming day now emanating inward, like the light of daybreak in reverse. Then she wiped her mouth a final time with the corner of her blouse and started up her truck.

"Anyway, you get the idea," she said.

At the faculty housing complex Bessie parked her car in front of my building but did not open the door and did not turn off the engine. She did not dim down her lights. Across the distance between us we stared at the other's silence. Finally it was I who spoke up:

"Thank you, Bessie," I said – and I said this because in my stupor there was not much else that I could think to say. "Thank you for this night. And for taking me from one edge of the universe to the other. Even though I was unable to cross the threshold of either entirely, it was a journey well worth the wait. I couldn't have visited them both without you...."

Bessie nodded and without saying another word drove off into the night. And with that this night of infinite discovery had come to its logical conclusion.

LOVING THE UNLOVED

E xcept that it actually wasn't. Back inside my apartment the sounds from the opposite side of the wall were still coming in relentless waves of thumping music and breaking dishes and the screams of mathematical ecstasy. My `head already aching from the night's consumption, I listened for the sounds to die away. And when they did not, I turned on the light in my room, made myself a pot of coffee on the stove, and drank it over my kitchen table. Still unable to sleep through the noise, and with nothing else to do, I took up my unfinished book from the table and continued reading at the exact place where I'd left off: to the rhythm of the thumping and to the shrieks coming through the wall I read even further into *The Anyman's Guide to Love and the Community College.* And when the two hours had passed I put on a new pair of corduroys, a stiff collared shirt, and a brown leather belt and headed off to work. Wearily, I made my way past the three lagoons to my building where the men cutting the grass in front smiled at my arrival; past Bessie who greeted me at her desk dryly and professionally as if this day were just any other emanation; and into my awaiting office where the swinging pendulum of my predecessor was still in motion between the alternate apexes of passion and perpetuity.

PART 2. INCARNATION

DAY

*"Enlighten the people generally, and tyranny
and oppressions of body and mind will
vanish like evil spirits at the dawn of day."*

- Thomas Jefferson

A nd so the semester began. The following Monday came bright
and early with the students arriving at the guard shack carrying
their book bags and their bookmarks and their booklists – several even
carried *books* – ready and eager for the rigors and rewards of accredited
learning. Along the main promenade young men rode bicycles to class.
Co-eds in mini-skirts gathered in groups of three or four. Lettermen from
the school's basketball team lumbered down the promenade like giraffes
on the Sahel. Over by the fountains, aspiring jugglers tossed horseshoes
into the air one after another, then caught them just as quickly – while
on the main lawn Arts majors lounged on the grass and cheerleaders did
life-affirming cartwheels and a trio of guitarists sang songs of protest
under the sycamore. After the lethargy of summer the entire campus was
newly energized, bustling with vitality, and even more dazzling than it
had been just a week before: with green grass and resplendent flowers and
clean flowing water. With hedges of lilac and alternating rows of olive and
tamarind. Dutifully, the birds chirped and fluttered. The pelicans loafed
along the banks of the lagoons. The sun cast its rays over the verdure.
Ducks quacked. Even the bull at the center of the largest lagoon was
shooting his water so high over the loins of his heifer that the traveling
mist could be felt on your skin no matter where you stood on campus
– as if the virility of the water itself were somehow tied to the resurgent

energy now present. Like a spring after a heavy rain, the students of Cow Eye Community College had bubbled up from some eternal subterranean source to resume their rightful place in the world; fresh and well-rested, they were now ready to continue their educational journey across time and space, from ignorance to awareness, from wonder to familiarity, from the dusty heat on the other side of the guard shack all the way to the controlled comfort of classroom learning on this side.

And what they now found at the end of such a long dry summer was a campus in perfect harmony with its surroundings. Green lawns beautifully cut. Oleanders blooming. Azaleas trimmed. Sidewalks that sauntered in perfect equidistance between the social sciences on one side and the natural sciences on the other. The library had been successfully renovated in time for the first day of classes, as had the re-envisioned Dimwiddle Student Union with its new teal carpet and 22-inch color television set. The bookstore bustled. The cafeteria buzzed. After a flurry of last-minute maintenance, the blackboards in the classrooms were now as dark and as shiny as wet stone; floors were polished to a sheen; desks stood glossy and clean and aligned in perfect rows like states on the American flag. In front of the administration building, where Old Glory itself flew, the tri-colored flag now waved in proud majesty: the thirty-four stars sparkling like little pearls of enlightenment against the sky. Throughout the campus it was clear that a new beginning had begun: an epoch of boundless opportunity and metaphor and hope set free from the tyranny of dust and drought.

And when the students had locked up their bicycles and gone inside the air-conditioned buildings, and when they made their way into the classrooms that would be theirs for the rest of the semester, an inspiring sight greeted them: at the head of the room, busily preparing, were those very faculty members who would soon come to embody their learning at Cow Eye Community College. Standing before the blackboard, these tenured professionals wore confident smiles and pressed slacks and pink blouses unbuttoned ever so slightly at the top; happily they beamed behind their desks with hearts full of fervor and minds overflowing with the specialized knowledge that would soon be imparted. Lesson plans were typed out. Syllabi were stapled. Shoulder-length gloves had been ordered by the crate. Even the sticks of chalk jutting out of their cardboard containers were as long and as white as they ever would be, like individual beacons on a hill. Attendance rosters were fresh and exotic, each unfamiliar name still brimming with hope and potential and the equality of unfulfilled possibility that is so inherent in new beginnings. In fact there was nothing about this day that did not suggest – no, *insist*! – that this would indeed be the greatest, most awe-inspiring, most mouth-watering and finger-licking academic semester in the ample, and heretofore accredited, history of Cow Eye Community College.

From my office window I couldn't help remarking on the transformation happening below.

"It's so exciting!" I said to Bessie.

"Yes," she said without looking up from her typewriter. "I suppose it is."

"After the impossibly long night, we're at last witnessing the incarnation of day!"

"Sure, Charlie. Look, I've got a lot of work to do...."

Later that morning, I met Raul in the hallway outside our offices, and once again I couldn't contain my excitement:

"Just look, Raul!" I effused. "The new semester has begun. It's all around us!"

"Yes it is," he responded. "Yes, it has. Like the eternal wheel of life. Or like the tumult surrounding the Topeka constitution."

"Bleeding Kansas?"

"Yes, and the rise of popular sovereignty."

"Precisely! The sidewalks are full. The parking lot is full. Hell, even the *bicycle racks* are filled to their capacity!"

"Yeah, and so are the tables at the cafeteria. You'd better have lunch early if you want a seat!"

And so I did.

"Can you believe it?" I remarked to Will Smithcoate when I sat down with my tray. Will had been reading the paper at his usual place in the corner of the lunchroom with his canteen of bourbon and a lit cigar. Amid the packed cafeteria, he was occupying an entire vacant table and seemed happy to have me for the company. "Mr. Smithcoate, just look how incredible it all is! After so much desiccation and anticipation, the long-awaited semester is finally upon us!"

Will lowered his newspaper.

"Keep it in your pants there, Charlie. Enlightenment is a marathon not a sprint. A journey, not a destination."

He was right. And so I grinned at my own ebullience and took a drink of tea.

"It's like my wife used to say," he continued. "She'd tell me, William, you've really got to slow down. A woman's body is a glass of fine wine, not a cup of water to be guzzled with your heart medication. My wife had a vagina made of butter, you know...."

I nodded. (Will Smithcoate wasn't supposed to be my faculty mentor: in fact, he had been assigned to Nan Stallings. But after being stood up by Will three separate times the week before, Nan had asked me to switch mentors; and having just suffered through a painfully silent lunch with Alan Long River, the Speech teacher who no longer speaks, I'd gratefully agreed. "Are you nuts?" said Bessie when she found out. "You'll get the worse of that exchange for sure!" But I just smiled and said: "You've got to be exaggerating. I mean, how bad could he be...?!")

"So, Mr. Smithcoate," I said, "what do you think about the re-emergence of all these students here in this cafeteria?" I'd bitten off a piece of bread and was chewing it distractedly. "I mean, just look at all these fresh faces at the beginning of their academic journey! The beaming smiles. The nervous anticipation. The untrammeled optimism!"

"Depressing, isn't it?"

"Depressing?"

"It's just so depressingly sad."

"I don't understand? Why would optimism be depressing? Why would our students' beaming smiles be *sad*?"

"The poor students. They sincerely believe they're relevant. In their youthful vigor they're still convinced that they reside at the center of the universe. The world is their oyster. The future is their pussycat. Each of them believes in the sanctity of a very special destiny. They still have dreams. They still have plans to be pilots and dancers and nurses and lawyers and novelists and doctors and apothecaries and professors and..."

"Absolutely! That's the beauty of an accredited community college....!"

"Well, yeah, except that they won't be any of these things."

"They won't?"

"Of course not. They aren't going to be pilots anymore than you or I will ever fly a plane: in the end, they're more likely to become mechanics of some sort. And they won't be nurses, they'll be secretaries. They won't be doctors, they'll be orderlies. They won't be writers, they'll be teachers.

Or journalists. They won't be masters of their own destiny but slaves of other people's innovations. It's remotely possible they'll be happily married, but far more likely they'll be twice- or thrice-divorced. And, no matter how hard they try, they definitely won't be tenured professors at an ivy-walled college."

"No?"

"Nope. Zero chance of that happening. At best they'll be educational administrators...."

I laughed.

"But, Mr. Smithcoate," I said. "*Somebody* has to become the pilots of the world. And the nurses. And the writers. Somebody has to be at the front of the line when they're handing out tenure. Why shouldn't it be *our* students? Why shouldn't it be Cow Eye's own who successfully conquer the world with a whip in one hand and a plastic chair in the other?"

Will shook his head.

"Charlie, did you know that only fifty percent of our students even make it to their second year of college?"

"That many?"

"Yes. And of those, only fifty percent go on to attain their degree."

"That few?"

"Yes. And of those that graduate – you know, the fifty percent of the fifty percent – only fifty percent of those will be able to find jobs in their desired fields."

"Okay...."

"And of those that find jobs in their fields, only fifty percent can expect to find some form of employment here in Cow Eye...."

"I'm noticing a pattern....?"

"Right. Merna put this data together a few months before she dropped her marbles. So if you drill down deeper, the numbers say that of those who do make it past their first year of college, and then go on to graduate, and then find a job in their degree field, and *then* are able to work here in Cow Eye – of these, only fifty percent ever earn enough from their job to make both ends of the rope meet up. From this group, fifty percent pay taxes religiously. Fifty percent of the tax payers actually vote in national elections. And of those who vote, only fifty percent go to church at least once a month."

"Well, *that's* not surprising!"

"Sure. But from here it gets even bleaker. You see, only fifty percent of those who attend church on a regular basis ever attempt to read a novel into their mid-twenties; only fifty percent of those who bother to read a novel bother to read a novel of any merit; only fifty percent of these ambitious readers actually *finish* the meritorious novel they've attempted; and only fifty percent of those who finish such a novel from beginning to end genuinely *like* the book they've just spent their valuable time finishing. And so by the time we get to this point in the data, the numbers are so small – greater than zero, I would imagine, but just *barely* – that it makes no sense to go on. You see, Charlie, religion in America is doomed. As is meaningful literature. How can the great novel stand a chance in a place like Cow Eye where the likelihood of finding an educated, well-remunerated, God-fearing, tax-paying, grateful reader of meaningful fiction is so small as to be almost infinitesimal? With so few students making it through this pipeline of civic virtues, is it any wonder that our accreditors are questioning our ability to achieve our institutional mission? And is it any wonder, given our students' poor prospects, that so few of them can be expected to ever reach the ultimate heights of cosmic orgasm during their lifetime?"

Will shook his head at his own line of questioning:

"Kinda makes you wonder what the hell we're all doing here, doesn't it?"

"Kind of," I admitted.

"Charlie, in thirty years I've never seen so much greenery and lushness on our campus as there is now. With its manicured lawns. And our rhododendrons. And the pelicans loafing on the sand. It's as if we've chosen to collect all this stunning moisture and verdure *for its own sake*...."

Will shook his head again and took a long drink from his bourbon.

A few minutes later an administrative secretary came up to our table with a paper in her hand. "Hi, Mr. Smithcoate," she said. And then: "Hey, Charlie. Would you mind signing this petition?"

"What's it for?" I answered.

"It's a petition against all these new electric typewriters. We want to keep the manual ones. Would you sign?"

"Sure," I said and signed the petition.

The woman thanked me.

"Oh and congratulations!" she added. "You and Bessie are the talk of the copy room."

"We are?"

"Yes, you are. The two of you are quite the unexpected couple. And it was sweet of you to cover her trembling shoulders with your sarong..."

When the woman had moved on to the next table, Will sighed deeply.

"Progress," he muttered. "Not much you can do about it, I suppose. Electric typewriters. Mimeograph machines. Hell, I remember when my wife got her first *vacuum cleaner.* For a couple weeks she was the only one on the block with such a newfangled slice of modernity. She preened in front of the other housewives like she was Hatshepsut. But then the luster quickly wore off. The belt broke and had to be thrown away. It didn't take long for the damn thing to become a symbol of male oppression. So where's that old vacuum cleaner *now,* I ask you?"

"In the dustbin of history."

"Right."

"On the trash heap of technology."

"Quite right."

"Buried somewhere in the shallow muck of the Cow Eye River."

"Exactly. And it ain't never coming back to the surface. So why did we need it in the first place? Why were we so eager to expedite the demise of history for the glamour and convenience of a vacuum cleaner that's since come and gone? It seems like there has to be an instructive lesson for humanity in there somewhere...?"

I laughed. We ate some more and Will made some progress on his cigar, and a few minutes later another woman came up with a paper in her hand. She introduced herself as the new secretary for the economics department.

"Would you like to sign this petition?" she asked us.

"I don't sign petitions," Will explained. "I don't believe in positive change."

"I might be willing to sign your petition," I said. "What's it for?"

"It calls for more electric typewriters on campus. We're tired of the manual ones."

"We?"

"Yes. We."

"And this is something you favor in economic terms?"

"Of course. Those old typewriters are un-American. They're inconvenient and inefficient. So would you sign?"

"Sure," I said and signed the petition.

Raul laughed when I told him.

"So you signed *both* petitions?" he said. "Even though they were opposed to each other? Even though they were advocating opposite things?" The two of us were walking down the esplanade toward this week's professional development session on adapting one's teaching to accommodate the diverse learning styles of diverse students.

"Well, yes I did. I signed them both."

"And what did you achieve by doing that? I mean all you've done is contradict yourself. You've neutralized your own actions. You've moved one step up the number line only to take one step back. In other words, you've returned to *zero*. Your objectives, whatever they may be, are in conflict rather than alignment. Your rationale is illogical and puzzling. Geez, Charlie, help me out here...!"

"Well, Raul, it would have been rude for me to turn down the first request. And it would've been even ruder to refuse the second. So I honored them both. Now, with my help, the two petitions are just as likely to be successful. And in this way I've endeared myself to *both* of the administrative secretaries. You see, my equation is perfectly balanced!"

"Hah! You may be dear to them now. But that'll only last until each finds out that you signed the other's petition. When they learn that you didn't commit to them entirely, then you won't be so much loved...as *liked.*"

"There are worse things!"

"Sure. But is this your ultimate goal in life? Is that your reason for being on this earth? To be *liked*? Don't you ever want to be *loved*?"

"It would be nice, yes."

Raul shook his head.

"Then you'd better pick something to commit to! You'd better start choosing one thing instead of both. Trust me: that's what women want. They want a lover who's unequivocal. A man who knows exactly who he is and is comfortable with it. They want alignment. And purposefulness. You can't just be from some unnamed locale anymore, Charlie. If you're going to be from Barcelona, then by God you'd better be from Barcelona *entirely*!"

"Even if you're *not* from Barcelona?"

"Absolutely! Otherwise, you'll never really be from any place at all. Your aura will be cinereous. Your c.v. will be unremarkable. And you'll never be truly loved: you'll only be respected....or tolerated. Or, god forbid...*liked*...!'"

Bessie splashed some dish soap on the plate that she was rinsing and began scrubbing it with a sponge.

"Yeah, well I think we've moved beyond *like*," she said. "In fact, we moved beyond *like* quite a while ago. And you can tell Raul I said that."

"Said what?"

"You can tell him that I said I'm in love with you."

"Did you say that?"

"Sure."

"When?"

"Just now."

"You did?"

"Of course. Why not?"

I blushed.

"That was easy enough!"

"Well, I think it's only justified given that we've had sex every night for the past week. I think now I can rightfully state that I am in love with you. I mean, it's the least I can do. And it's definitely the least I can *say*."

"But is that even possible?" I asked. "Sure, we've been intimately involved over the last week or so – and I'm not ungrateful for that. But we've really only known each other less than a month. It's only been a little longer than that since I arrived at the makeshift bus shelter outside of town. And it's only been a few short weeks since you started coming to my apartment after work."

"Of course it's possible. Why wouldn't love be possible? That pendulum is still swinging back and forth in your office, right?"

"It is...."

"And it's still making the same tick-tocking sound, right?"

"Yes!"

"Well, there you go. And besides, what's time got to do with any of this? I've had a thousand loves so far. And all one thousand have failed. But I've never given up. And I never will. So, no, I'm not ashamed to say it to you now. I'm not averse to saying that I'm in love with you."

"But it just sounds so unconvincing when you say it like that! When you say it so explicitly. So directly. It just sounds so anticlimactic...."

"Charlie, I've said it a thousand times to a thousand other men and I'll say it to you now: I'm in love with you. I'm in love …I'm in love with you …!"

"Okay …!"

"I'm in love with you, Charlie!"

"Stop! Okay, I get it…!

Bessie laughed.

"Don't forget, I'm a woman. And if there's one thing we women learn from living in Cow Eye, it's how to be in *love*."

I shrugged my shoulders.

"I see. Well, you're welcome to express your point of view, of course – that's a cornerstone of our great country. But it's not. I mean, for me, I can't….you know, for a man, love isn't something that…."

"Oh stop blubbering, Charlie. I'm not expecting you to reciprocate. I know better – I'm from Cow Eye, remember – and I know a thing or two about words. So just stop right there. I'd rather you say nothing at all than utter some useless bullshit you don't really mean."

"Bullshit?"

"Yes, bullshit."

"And then what happened?" Dr. Felch asked.

"And then she finished washing the dishes as if nothing had changed!"

"That's Bessie for you!" Dr. Felch was holding his notes for the Christmas party and laughing. Then he leaned over and expectorated a stream of wintergreen into his spittoon. "She's a Doberman, Charlie. I told you: she's tough as nails. You'll see…"

"You're scaring me, Mr. Felch."

"Well, just keep everything in perspective and don't forget what I've been telling you all along. Things don't tend to end well with her."

"Can you be more specific?"

"Of course I can. But are you sure you want to know?"

"I probably should at some point. I probably *will* at some point. So I might as well hear it from you now, as I sit here uncomfortably on this hard plastic chair in your office."

Dr. Felch spat another stream into the spittoon.

"Well, okay then…."

And here he explained how each of Bessie's relationships had begun with so much promise only to end in ignominy. Beginning as far back as Timmy from the guard shack, Dr. Felch told me of my new lover's abortion, her miscarriage, her overnight stay in the county jail for terroristic threatening, her verbal abuse, her veiled accusations, her overt insinuations, her threats unfulfilled, her threats *fulfilled*, the romantic rival she beat up, the ex-husband she impelled to hard alcohol, the windshield she busted with a brick, the ex-boyfriend (and father of her youngest child) whose thigh she scarred with a branding iron, the psychological warfare, the enmity, the time she drove her truck over Buck's foot while he was reaching in to take the key out of her ignition, the smell of burning hair, the flesh under her fingernails, the squealing tires on asphalt....

"Asphalt?"

"Yes, asphalt."

"Now you're *really* scaring me....!"

"Charlie, I *told* you not to get involved with her!"

"You did. But I didn't believe you. Everything happened so quickly between us. It all seemed so organic and inevitable. Like water seeking its own level. In comparison, this other stuff can't possibly be true...."

"Trust me. It is."

"I do trust you. And yet I'd like to get a second opinion if you don't mind...."

I took a drink of tea.

"So can you give me a second opinion?" I asked.

"Sure," Will nodded. "It's all true. Does that help?" Will was holding his cigar between his fingers and as he spoke he took a grand puff, exhaling the smoke in a huge cloud which rose slowly above his head and obscured the NO SMOKING sign posted right above him – the sign that had been posted *for* him – on the cafeteria wall. Then he shook his head and said, "But lost in all of this is the worst incident of all. You see, he conveniently neglected to mention what she did to her *third* husband – you know, the one she'd rather not talk about...."

"What happened to *him*?"

"Well, nothing. Except that she tried to emasculate him."

"What?!"

"In his sleep. Before daybreak. And she damn near *succeeded*, too!"

"That can't be! I mean, she was just at my apartment last night. She fixed stew and washed all the dishes afterwards. She told me she loved me. I can't believe all this, Mr. Smithcoate, I really can't!"

"Well, she didn't exactly say she *loved* you. She said she was *in love* with you. There's a meaningful difference, you know."

"Evidently. But I still can't believe it's true. I still can't believe all this…."

"They're right on every account, Charlie," Rusty said as he pointed at a copy of the arrest record that he'd found in his archives at the museum. "I'm afraid it's all true." (After so many invitations, I'd finally taken Rusty up on his offer to visit the museum, and after browsing indifferently through the various standing exhibits – old photos of the Cow Eye Ranch, an antique branding iron, a mounted Holstein in full taxidermic serenity – I'd worked up the courage to ask about the alleged incident with Bessie.) "She got some community service for that one. Her uncle was the judge or it might've been much worse. But yes, she's known around town for that ill-fated emasculation."

"Well, it's strange that Dr. Felch didn't mention this incident with all the others. You'd think it would be right up there on the list. If not at the *very* top!"

"It probably still pains him to bring it up. And that's why he'd rather not talk about it. It's also why he prefers not to talk about his fourth wife at all."

"I don't get it? What would his ex-wife have to do with anything?"

"You didn't know?"

"Didn't know *what?*"

"That they were married?"

"Who?"

"Bill and Bessie. He was her third husband and she was his fourth wife. Neither likes to talk about it. In fact, they were happily married for several years until she found out he was having an affair with a woman who was barely thirty. Their marriage had been reinvigorating up to that point. But everything comes to an end. And theirs ended in near-emasculation. I thought you knew…."

"No, I didn't."

"Well now you do."

"I do."

"And now you know."

"Apparently…"

"So, *now* do you believe me, Charlie?"

"I guess I have no other choice!"

Dr. Felch smiled.

"I mean, she's great – don't get me wrong. A wonderful person. And a devoted mother. The two of us have made amends since then and we get along great now. I couldn't ask for a better secretary. And despite what the prosecution said, I don't think she *really* intended to emasculate me that night – I'd prefer to think that it was more a *symbolic* gesture in the grand scheme of things. But I'm just saying. You might want to have a Plan B prepared just in case…."

Dr. Felch expelled another stream of tobacco:

"…and *soon*."

Hearing this, I rolled over onto my side.

"So what do you think?" I said, posing the question directly to Bessie after we'd just made love for the first time. We were lying amid the bed sheets which were still moist from our efforts. "What do *you* think my Plan B should be?"

"You're already thinking about Plan B?"

"Well, you know, just in case. Sure, it seems like things are going well enough on the *one* hand. But on the *other* hand, you never really know how things will turn out…."

"There is no Plan B, Charlie. Or rather there *is*. But you would need to leave Cow Eye forever. So let's not talk about that. Let's enjoy Plan A while we still can…."

And with that she kissed the place below my second chakra where the kundalini had already begun to subside.

⦚

AS THE WEEKS passed I settled into the groove of my new semester, and in time I began to find my Circadian rhythm: mornings were spent in my office reviewing accreditation documents, attending classroom observations, and strategizing with Dr. Felch on ways to ensure that the Christmas party actually happened this year. Lunches were usually spent in the cafeteria with Will Smithcoate, who always sat at the same vacant table under the no-smoking sign, his lit cigar in hand, and who seemed to relish his status as my faculty mentor for the academic year. After lunch I'd walk back to my office for more committee meetings and other college minutiae. And from there I would head home for long evenings spent alone with my television and my half-read books – at the top of the pile was *The Anyman's Guide to Love and the Community College* – and with the loud noises coming through the wall separating me from the irrepressible math faculty.

"I thought you said it would die down?" I asked Gwen after a few weeks had come and gone without any noticeable decrease in the festivities across the wall. The thumping was just as loud. The wails and screams just as ecstatic – or painful. It was late afternoon when we met up, Gwen had just attended a professional development workshop called *Mission Possible: Reducing the Performance Gap for Students Who Can't Read, Write, or Count*, and the two of us were heading toward the cafeteria in lockstep.

"Well, they are quite young. And they're very horny," she said. "But we all just look the other way because they're so good at what they do."

"You mean they're good at mathematics?"

"No. They're good at *teaching* mathematics. And the students adore them. They're critical to our institutional mission."

"You mean, the students, obviously?"

"No, the math teachers. You can't pay taxes properly without learning math. And you can't learn higher math without *teachers*. Such are the realities of life. So you just need to be patient. Give the situation some time."

"I'd love to. But I feel like I haven't slept since I got here. Sometimes I can barely keep my eyes open during meetings. My job performance is starting to suffer. It's like I'm losing control of my surroundings. Things are speeding up and my perception can't keep pace. It's as if there's no break in my consciousness. Everything's just blending from one thing into the next."

"I hear you," said Raul. "The semester is definitely escalating. Time is moving faster and faster. That's the way the semester flows. That's the way life flows. But don't let it rush by you completely. Don't let it overwhelm you."

"I'm doing my best to keep up. And to stay positive through it all. But I really need some *sleep*!"

"Well, there'll be plenty of time for sleep once the semester ends. After the mission statement has been revised and the self-study has been submitted to our accreditors ahead of their visit next spring. After December eleventh has come and gone and the Christmas party has been triumphantly held. Just get through the semester as best you can, Charlie. And know that sleep, as it tends to do, will win out in the end."

"I'm trying, Raul. Believe me, I'm trying! But I'm so tired I can't even focus on becoming something entirely – let alone what I'm supposed to be doing as Special Projects Coordinator. The classroom observations. The focus groups. The professional development sessions. You see, I'm even starting to lose sight of my ultimate goal – not to mention my measurable performance objectives…."

Raul laughed.

"You need to put them into an easily understood visual representation. Look, you can diagram it like this…."

Raul turned over a flyer for a survey he was working on and, on the back, drew the following diagram:

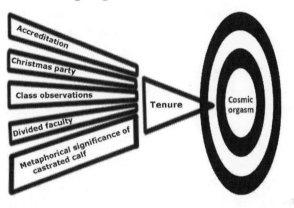

"Thanks, Raul," I said.

"My pleasure," he answered. "You can keep that by the way…."

A couple times a week – while her mother stayed home with her boys – Bessie would come to my place for dinner, parking her truck right under my window and making her way up the flight of stairs where she'd rap on my front door with rugged knuckles. I'd let her in and we'd have dinner at my kitchen table and then we'd proceed to other things. Afterwards she'd go home. In this way we got to know each other as man and woman – as hopeful divorcees – and in this way she and I crossed that magical threshold separating what is imagined from what is merely known. ("Okay," she'd told me within minutes of stepping into my apartment for the first time. "*Now* I'll have sex with you….")

Dinners with Bessie always proceeded according to plan. By five-fifteen she was in my apartment. By six, dinner was on the table. At exactly seven she'd call her house to check on the kids. By seven-thirty we had cleaned up the dishes, and by nine or nine-fifteen – nine-thirty at the latest – she was packing up her things and heading home. This continued from week to week, and as the semester wore on it became clear that she and I had very quickly gone from being *mutually receptive* to being simply *in love*. Over dinner we talked about people we knew at work. During dishes she shared the highs and lows of secretarial servitude. Later, amid the moistness of our sheets, the two of us spoke of the dreams that she still managed to have and that I had not yet abandoned: hers to move beyond gravel; mine to become something – *anything* – entirely. In time, she came to store personal items at my apartment: a change of clothes in my closet, an extra-long sleep shirt in my drawer, mysterious toiletries in the medicine cabinet in my bathroom; and as we settled into this familiar routine I gradually came to see – infrequently at first but then with greater and greater urgency – faint glimpses into the darker side of her personality.

"Are you sure you should just park below my window like that?" I asked her one night over dinner. "Won't people start jumping to conclusions? Won't they start talking?"

"Why are you asking? Are you afraid of what they might say?"

"It's not that. It's just…."

Bessie was looking at me expectantly.

"…It's just, how would it look to an outsider? You and I work together. And you have young children. Not to mention all your ex-lovers that I see around campus on a daily basis. What might *they* be thinking?"

"Look, you leave my kids out of this. This is Cow Eye. We are a rural community college in the middle of nowhere. In the midst of a drought for the ages. There's nothing that people might assume about our relationship that they're not already assuming. And believe me, they *are* talking."

"Already?"

"Oh yeah. The girls in the copy room know more about you and me than you and I know about ourselves. The whole campus knows about the night we spent together at the river. And how we stayed on the sandy bank until everyone else was gone. And how we held hands on the way back to my truck. And how we then drove out to the clearing by the highway. They know all of this and more."

"Do they know about the crickets?"

"Of course."

"And the moonlight coming in through your windshield?"

"Most certainly."

"And the gear shift between us in the front seat?"

"Absolutely."

"And the eternal distance separating the slight bulge in my corduroys…."

(Bessie raised her eyebrows.)

"….from your tender words of encouragement?"

"No doubt about that!"

"And what about the….you know….the rivulets…?"

"I hope not," she said. "Though I wouldn't be surprised. Cow Eye is nothing if not intuitive."

"Please don't think that I'm self-conscious about you and me, Bessie, or that I'm self-conscious about the fact that, you know, you've been divorced three separate times. It's not that at all. It's more that, well, our campus is so small. And I wouldn't want our relationship to become the fodder for prurient small-college interest."

Bessie laughed.

"Don't worry about that. For every formally recognized relationship at Cow Eye, there are hundreds that dwell in the shadows. If you think what *we*'re doing is worthy of prurient interest, you should know what *the others* are up to…!"

And here she told me about the campus's many sexual idiosyncrasies and romances of regional acclaim. How the instructor of world religions had been caught having sex with the young ethics teacher in a store room. And the two married business faculty who'd been conducting an informal liaison for years. There was the tenured chemistry teacher reprimanded multiple times for exposing himself to nursing students during labs. And the art historian whose Saab had played host to more passion than Little Round Top. There was the economics instructor with the hairy back. And Marsha Greenbaum, who was insatiable. And the two homosexuals in the art department. And the cross-dressing horticulturist from West Virginia. And the Nevada-born brothel owner turned grant writer. And the Bolshevik prone to free love. And Timmy at the guard shack. And the security guard with the Polaroid camera. All of which did not even include the creative writing instructor with his female students; the Schlocksteins, whose marriage was as open as a Nebraska corn field; and the post-tantric Luke Quittles and Ethel Newtown who had moved in together and were engaged in a raucous love affair over the mournful objections of Ethel's hapless husband Stan. ("Compared to faculty at your local community college," I had recently read, "the untenured residents of Sodom and Gomorrah would surely be considered tepid and discreet!") And all of *this* did not even account for the mathematics faculty whose infamous math orgies had by now risen to a strident pitch on the other side of my apartment wall.

"When is it all going to end?!" I found myself crying out in exasperation to anyone who would listen. "The semester is more than a month gone, the noises are never-ending, and I really need to get some sleep! When will it end?!"

"Right before mid-terms," Raul projected.

"In its own time," said Gwen.

"When history itself becomes obsolete," Will ventured.

"I see. Well if it's going to take *that* long, then what am I supposed to do in the meantime?"

"Approach it philosophically," said Gwen.

"You need to confront them on *your* terms," said Rusty.

"Make a written plan," said Raul. "Then execute it."

"But how can I be philosophical without sleep?" I said. "And how can I be confrontational when I've never been good at conflict? Of course, I'd love to come up with a plan of some sort, but aren't there already too many untenable plans for improvement at our struggling college as it is?"

Will laughed.

"Actually, there's nothing you *can* do about it," he explained. "Trust your mentor on this one, Charlie: there's no arguing with mathematics. Historically, it's been a special point of pride for that discipline to be cold and consistent and unbowed by the whims of human emotion. It's like my wife used to say during the long winter nights. She'd say, William, if you don't take your fingers out of my crack right this second, there's going to be hell to pay. She was like that in her later years…."

"Mr. Smithcoate?"

"But then she'd just laugh and pull back the sheets…."

"Will?"

"And she'd take my palm and put it on her naked stomach…"

"Will!"

"And she'd hold it there…."

"And then?"

"Well and *then*," Rusty concluded, "Bill left Bessie for his latest thirty-year old – the current one – and they've been together ever since. For Bessie it was the latest devastating betrayal. For Bill it's been somewhat of a triumph over life. But we'll just have to see how long it lasts…."

"And how long *will* it last?" I asked.

Dr. Felch shrugged his shoulders:

"It's very hard to say," he said. "Probably until they get all that youthful vigor out of their system. Until the math hormones settle down. They say Archimedes enjoyed the favors of aspiring geometricians well into his seventies. So you're probably looking at a few more years of breaking glass at least…."

"But I can't wait that long for their math-love to die down. I need my sleep *now*. The fate of our college depends on it!"

"Hang in there, Charlie…"

And so I did my best to block out the clamor on the other side of the wall and to focus on what Bessie was telling me over the tripe stew that she had made for dinner.

"Given all that's happening on campus," she was saying, "I wouldn't worry about what anyone is saying about *us*. Compared to the glamour of faculty romance, you and I are as noteworthy as two married librarians discussing literary reviews on a public bench."

I nodded and took a bite of her tripe.

"Well that's reassuring, I suppose. But, Bessie, what do your children think about all this? You know, about you and me? Don't they wonder where you are on alternate weeknights?"

"Why would they wonder *anything*?"

"Well, I don't know. It just seems like they would have some curiosity about where their mother is. And who she's with. Wouldn't they?"

"No, they wouldn't. And they shouldn't. Not yet anyway. There's a time and a place for curiosity. And there's a time and a place for conflict. But let's not get ahead of ourselves. *Now* isn't exactly the time for either."

And so Bessie changed the subject.

"How's the stew?" she asked.

"It's delicious," I said. "Sumptuous, actually."

"I'm glad you like it. My father used to make this for me when I was little. When he was still alive…."

Bessie grew quiet.

And I nodded and swallowed another bite.

≈

"BUT WHAT *ARE* they saying about us?" I asked Ethel at the firing range one afternoon. She and I had taken out our guns but had yet to put on our ear muffs or our protective eye wear.

"What is *who* saying?" Ethel answered.

"You know, *people*. Around campus. The professoriate. Our peers. You would be the one to know, Ethel, since as a journalist you should be attuned to such things."

"Well, there is a lot that's being said. And, yes, some of it is about you and Bessie. There's also quite a bit being said about Luke and I."

"I can imagine. Like what?"

"Well, they say that the two of us are shameless and mindless and heartless. They say we're ruining my husband Stan both as a husband and as a man and that our passions will lead to his untimely demise. They say that food and journalism lead to literary indigestion."

"I see."

"They even imply that if we're not careful our relationship might jeopardize our respective applications for tenure."

"Ouch. I'm sorry to hear that. I can only imagine what they're saying about Bessie and me? Should I even ask?"

"You can. But are you sure you want to know? Because not all of it is nice."

"Yes I do."

"Okay," she said. And then: "Here, hold my pistol, will you...?"

And here Ethel recounted the most frequently repeated version of my relationship with Bessie. How she and I were known to have consummated our relationship on the banks of the Cow Eye River. And how, after brushing off the sand, the two of us had made our way back to her truck to warm up. And how, from there, we'd driven to a field where the moon trickled down upon us like a mother's love for her two sons. And how, after taking full advantage of Bessie's drunken stupor, I'd covered her up with the sarong pilfered cleverly from Marsha Greenbaum's studio.

"The *orange* one," Ethel clarified. "Though in other iterations your sarong is more of an off-*magenta*."

"There are others?"

"Yes."

"A lot of them?"

"Quite a few."

"For example?"

"Well, for example, it's also been intimated that upon returning to your lonely apartment after visiting the edge of the universe where Bessie's children reside, you finally began to experience the perils of night and day."

"Right," said Raul. "And that the distance that night between your trembling hands and Bessie's receptive nipples was far greater than the distance that can be vanquished by an arrow in flight."

"And," said Gwen, "that the pendulum in your office is a metaphorical attempt to reconcile your alternating apexes of love and desire. Of logic and intuition. Of memory and imagination. Of Plan A and Plan B."

Dr. Felch listened to all this and after spitting yet again into his spittoon, he agreed with what had already been expressed, then added: "They even surmise that the two of you are headed toward something ominous, Charlie. Like a kayaker upstream of a rocky falls. Or like our rural college as it drifts headlong into the oncoming wrath of its institutional accreditors."

"They're saying all this?"

"Yes, they are. And then of course there are the rivulets…."

"Rivulets!"

"Yes, about how you came to find relief amid the moisture of Bessie's oral reassurances."

"Right. And how the two of you have since become so entwined that you even eat tripe together!"

"*And* that the gear shift halfway between the two of you that night will always be a bit closer to other people than it is to you, Charlie. And that it will be like this due to your reluctance to commit to anything entirely."

"They've said all this?"

"Oh, yes. And more. *Much* more…!"

To all of this I could only listen in amazement.

"So is it true?" Ethel asked.

I shook my head. But then, after a moment's thought, I nodded instead.

"About half of it is true," I said. "Maybe two-thirds if you count the part about the pendulum. But, Ethel, it's less the truth of the matter I'm concerned about than its *perception*. I mean, how is all of this being viewed? How is the relationship between Bessie and me being interpreted?"

"It's Bessie and *I*, Charlie...."

"Right. Sorry. You can tell I'm no journalist. So what are they saying about Bessie and I? How is our relationship being perceived by our fellow colleagues around campus?"

Ethel stopped to consider my question. Then she said:

"Quite extensively. Yet reasonably well, all things considered. Of course there are some reservations among certain departments...."

And here Ethel told me how the administrative secretaries had given us their full blessing, while the Maintenance department disapproved. To the mathematics faculty, there was a certain beauty in two unloved people finding love, just as there is something transcendent in two negative numbers somehow coming together to bring about a positive product. To the young ethics instructor – the one who'd been discovered in the store room bent over a dusty box of Christmas decorations – my relationship with Bessie was not professionally advisable in any way and in fact compromised both parties' ability to contribute meaningfully to the college's institutional mission. To the homosexuals in the art department we were bourgeois; in the opinion of the financial aid office we were harmless if indiscreet; while among the animal science faculty there was much discussion about our respective ages, the likelihood of parturition at such a late stage of life, and whether there might be a need for artificial insemination at some point. The librarians cringed at the very notion. The cafeteria workers cheered. And the English faculty of the college – none of whom had received a single response from a reliable literary agent – simply ignored our dalliance altogether.

"It's as if we're not even worthy of fine literature," I shrugged.

"That's okay," said Bessie. "It's been years since I read a good book anyway. Hell, it's been years since I've read *any* book...."

I handed her my copy of *Cute Cats of the World*.

"Try this," I said. "And let me know if you like it. Because, believe me, there's plenty more where *that* came from...."

"Thanks," said Bessie. And then: "But do you really care about any of this?"

"That you don't read *books*? Well, sort of. I mean, it does tend to be, you know, an important milestone in the history of human enlightenment...."

'No, not that. The chatter. The interdepartmental banter. The conversations in the copy room. The lunchtime gossip. Do you really care that they're saying these things about you? About me and you? That they're saying these things about *us*?"

"Of course I do."

"Why?"

"Because it trivializes our story. Instead of it being open to broader contextualization, it's been reduced to a single mundane narrative. Like the explanation of an advanced mathematical concept so that it may become easy and more accessible. Or like the survey course that provides watered-down understandings of complex phenomena so that bored undergraduates can get their credits efficiently and move on."

"And is that a *bad* thing?" Raul objected. He was standing next to the water fountain outside my office holding a wax cup; he'd just leaned over to take a drink and tiny beads of water still clung to the fringes of his goatee as he spoke. "After all, there is great beauty in simplicity, Charlie. There is beauty in complexity that has been made accessible. And in understandings that have been conveyed more efficiently. In this, lies the very essence of teaching, I'd say – and in teaching at a community college in particular. Such is the lofty goal of mathematical inquiry itself."

"But Raul," I said, "is this goal really so lofty? Wouldn't you agree that the greater beauty lies in those things that are too complex to understand? Too ambiguous to be taught?"

"Charlie?"

"Wouldn't you agree that the idea that boasts an infinite number of unverifiable interpretations is far more intriguing than the one with a single outcome that can be replicated over and over again? That the capricious animal brimming with life is more beautiful than its counterpart that has been skinned and tanned and expertly embalmed? And in this way wouldn't you agree that the realm of mathematics is but a mausoleum for once-living ideas? Like the Cow Eye museum with its colorless photographs and preserved Holstein. And that if mathematics is that museum with its static displays of dead artifacts – its dusty shelves filled with the skeletons of resolved mysteries – then there has to be something that is its opposite? For everything has an opposite. And if so, what is it that can possibly be such an opposite? Would it be philosophy? Or music? Or art? Or might it not be something even grander, like poetry? For doesn't poetry tend to bustle with life like a living zoo of unruly vertebrates. Yes, poetry is a zoo, Raul! Poetry is a zoo of screaming animals. And mathematics is the quiet and distinguished museum where the animals' corpses are kept for posterity….!"

"Which, metaphorically speaking, would make the *poet*…?"

"A hapless zookeeper."

"And the mathematician…?"

"A skilled hunter."

"And an *instructor* of mathematics…?"

"The taxidermist!"

Raul laughed.

"And the data analyst, Charlie? In your metaphor, the institutional researcher is….?"

"The taxidermist's faithful errand boy!"

At this Raul stopped smiling.

"Well, you're welcome to believe whatever you want," Raul muttered. "That too is a cornerstone of our great nation. But in this case, I'd say you're overreaching. It's probably best for everyone involved if you just stick to educational administration!"

I laughed and took another drink of tea.

Outside the window of the cafeteria, the sun was setting at a different angle than it had just yesterday. I had begun to raise yet another question for the general discussion, but found myself stopping in mid-idea. An urgent thought had suddenly struck me: *How was I doing on time?* Was it late morning? Or early afternoon? Was it already early fall? Or was it still late summer? Could it be that while I was sitting here the seasons had moved from the dissolution of late autumn to the emanation of early winter? From the semester's incarnation to its fast-approaching dissolution? Relentlessly the days had come and gone and the weeks had carried me out of one meeting and straight to another: down the esplanade and past the bookstore, from my office to the cafeteria, from the balmy comfort of Dr. Felch's spittoon to the cold confines of my apartment next to the math faculty. Since the first day of classes I'd attended meeting after meeting to envision the Christmas party; I'd facilitated grueling planning sessions to review the college's mission statement; I'd conducted countless classroom observations and written innumerable reports and served on hiring committees where we'd picked through flawless curricula vitae and nodded respectfully at the polished responses of award-winning applicants over the phone. Together with Raul, I'd attended professional development sessions on student learning styles and performing CPR and maintaining sexually appropriate relations with co-workers and how to build a strong tenure dossier and understanding the special needs of special populations and alternatives to bloated scrota and strategies for working collaboratively with difficult colleagues and where to hide during a campus massacre and how to reduce workplace anxiety and best practices in yoga and the benefits of do-it-yourself castration techniques and how to invest a life's legacy in an interest-bearing retirement plan and approaches to dealing with students of indeterminate culture and, just last week, a gravely important session on detecting the earliest warning signs of a female colleague who is teetering on the precipice of self-destruction. (In less than a semester I'd managed to develop my professional capacity in all this!) And in a desperate attempt to reconcile our divided faculty — to arrive at the verb that might bring the campus's disparate factions closer together in time for the Christmas party on December eleventh, or at least by the accrediting team's scheduled visit in March — I'd organized a series of high-stakes focus groups to be held throughout the semester.

"Focus groups?" Raul inquired. "And how is *that* going?"

"Not well. I can't even get them into the same room! I mean, you thought castrating a calf was a challenge?! You thought getting *his* buy-in was hard? That's how it's been for me trying to organize our faculty. It's like trying to herd cats into a corral. I've tried everything. And I'm not sure what more I can do at this point. Any ideas?"

"Sure. You need to design a survey. Send out it out to all faculty and staff. Ask them for their opinions on what makes a focus group truly outstanding. Encourage them to be forthright and tell them you will take their suggestions to heart. Then use their participation in the survey to create support for the focus group itself. Remember, no educational endeavor is complete without a *survey*. Geez, Charlie, this is Educational Administration 101!"

"But do you think they'll respond to a survey like that?"

"Of course! The great thing about faculty is that they have opinions on everything. That's one thing you'll never have to worry about! You just need to give them the proper egress to let it all out."

And so I did.

And until this moment it had all seemed purposeful enough. But now, as I looked up from the ongoing discussion, I realized that time was in fact flowing by me quicker than my ability to comprehend. The weeks of the semester had come and gone and here I was back in the cafeteria yet again with Will Smithcoate. Here I was amid the moist sheets interlocked with Bessie, with Ethel's pistol still in my hand, the sound of the pendulum in my ear, and the smell of wintergreen tobacco filling my lungs. Here I was creating my surveys, administering them, then tallying their results on separate index cards. Here I was standing patiently in the college bookstore, or in the buffet line at the cafeteria, or with Rusty in the Cow Eye Museum among the dusty exhibits – the old newspapers, the cattle bells, the colorless photographs of the Indian village with its once-vibrant people whose civilization was now submerged – while time continued to pass ever so relentlessly by me. The days, the hours, the weeks were overtaking me like the rising waters accumulating over the dry ground of an entire way of life. And despite my formal training, and despite my Master's degree in Educational Administration with its focus on struggling community colleges – and despite the new loafers I'd just purchased from the latest Sears Roebuck catalog – it was all I could do to keep up with Gwen on her long walk down the esplanade to the cafeteria; with Bessie's rigorous affections in bed; with the incessant impositions of the accrediting body and its plans to visit Cow Eye in mid-March; and with Will and his self-destructive consumption of cigars and bourbon at the empty cafeteria table below the no-smoking sign.

"What time is it?" I asked.

"Time, Charlie?"

"Yes. Can any of you tell me what time it is?"

"You mean the year? Or the month? Or do you mean the day of the week?"

"No, I mean the specific hour and the specific minute of this very specific day. Can you tell me the exact time right now?"

Will checked his gold pocket watch.

Raul consulted the digital calculator on his wrist.

Rusty glanced over at the clepsydra next to the museum entrance.

And Bessie, tucking the sheets under her arms, simply rolled over groggily to look at the alarm clock on the nightstand next to my bed.

"What time is it?" I pleaded with them all.

"It's almost two, Charlie," they responded.

"Two?"

"Yes."

"Two o'clock?!"

"Yes, two."

I recoiled.

"Dammit!" I muttered. "I can't believe it's already two o'clock! I've still got my class observations to conduct – the final ones for this semester – and it looks like I'm already late to them both....!"

And without finishing my tea I jumped up out of bed, threw on a shirt and some corduroys, and ran out of the cafeteria down the long esplanade to the room overlooking the largest fountain where the public speaking class was being held.

≈

{ }

To the great lover, there is no such thing as time. For what is time when you are in love? Within the lover's embrace, time stands still. Or rather it flows differently: like the sweeping currents around a submerged rock; or like the uneven flow of an academic semester – gently at first, then with greater and greater urgency – relentlessly downstream toward the precipice of exam week, toward the impending crescendo of a shuddering orgasm. Secure in the arms of a lover, time is but a nuisance to be reckoned with in the abstract – like a doctor's routine rectal examination that has been put off until it is too late or like the insistent knocking of a student oblivious to the office hours clearly posted on the door. Understand the flow of water from a higher place to a place that is lower and you will understand the flow of time from past to future, the trajectory of history from hope to obsolescence, the great movement of moisture from ignorance to indifference and then ultimately into the awaiting delta of love. Just as the body tenses before orgasm, so too does the progress of time shudder and release, expanding and contracting like the impetuous love muscles of the human body. Controlling these muscles has been the enduring accomplishment of all great lovers — just as it has always been the fancy of man to subjugate the shuddering convulsions of time.

The realms over which man has been able to exert his influence range from the essential to the arbitrary; seemingly there is no process of nature that has withstood the interventions of human whim. Convenience being the aim, the ambitious mind of man has smoothed away the vicissitudes of life and made living more inevitable. He has domesticated the compliant bovine and propagated arugula in planter beds. Water that used to be gathered at great distances now flows through elaborate infrastructure to within a few feet of his thirst, as if it were the water itself that were the goal rather than the faithful act of its acquisition.

While nature knows balance, man — to his detriment — does not. Even when the severities of life are cruel and incomprehensible, the natural world has a way of bringing things back into accord. Floods and fires and droughts will happen, but nature makes sure they do not happen indefinitely. Only man strives for perfection in the absolute; and only he can create miseries that do not go away, consequences that have no naturally occurring remedy. Here the insatiable urge to accelerate the timeless trajectories of his world has led him further and further astray. The pursuit of empty conveniences has encouraged him to second-guess the very foods he eats, the air he breathes, the water he drinks. His reckless pursuit of efficiency has led him to dam free-flowing waters and forever alter the paths of rivers. He has severed the ties between peoples and their historical homelands and encouraged the deaths of some languages so that others might be better understood, if not lovingly spoken, by a greater number of people. In the name of more efficient communication, he has often accelerated the demise of language. And in the name of creating better living conditions he has unwittingly endangered the facility that life once had to regenerate itself.

But one thing that man cannot control is the very flow of time. For time flows of its own accord. And try as you may, you cannot expedite the rhythms of nature. The sun has been shown to rise when it rises and the sea will be prone to ebb and flow in its own time; these are the laws of eternal day and these are the laws of eternal moisture and they will outlast the most tenacious among us. For the laws of love will surely outlast the laws of man. Just as celestial time will survive the earthly semester. And the river will outlive the dam. And sleep, as it always tends to do, will win out over everything else in the end.

{ }

BY THE TIME I reached the creative writing classroom the workshop was already well under way. The eight students were seated around a long conference table, and as the pretty young author stood reading her own story aloud to the group – never raising her eyes above the typewritten manuscript, barely raising her voice above the drone of the air conditioning unit – the other seven students sat with their own copies in front of them, listening intently. Seeing me enter the room, the creative writing teacher motioned toward the long conference table and I hastened to take the last remaining seat at the opposite end directly facing him.

"That's Charlie," the teacher said, pointing across the table. "You know, the one I told you about last week – who is a lot of different things but none of them entirely. He's here to observe my mesmerizing teaching style. So he'll be sitting in on our workshop today. Please don't feel threatened or intimidated by him while he listens to the discussion of your stories – in fact, he is just an educational administrator and therefore has no ties to the creative process whatsoever. Feel free to treat him as you would any other intrusive bureaucrat and representative of institutional hierarchy and oppression. Or just do what I'm planning to do: ignore him as if he weren't here at all...." The teacher passed down a copy of the manuscript so I could follow the discussion. Then he turned to the pretty young girl who'd been reading from her manuscript when I walked in: "Sorry, Maude. Please continue...."

The girl looked back down at her manuscript and continued her assigned reading.

The workshop was being held in a small classroom with a single blackboard that by now was chalky and gray from a half-semester of use. The pieces of chalk that had once been beacons on a hill were now mere stubs the size of a barely flickering candle. The air conditioning made everything in the room seem dry and cold and brittle, like the chill left by barren prose.

As Maude read her story, I paid special attention to her peers around the table. Despite being aspiring writers themselves, none seemed all that interested in the story being read; here and there they would nod or yawn or titter at an unexpected turn of phrase when it popped up in Maude's recitation: *The sweat on Alison's eye brow*, Maude would read, *was dry and salty, like the tear of a very sad policeman.* And then: *Hearing this, Tiffany snapped her gum and declared, "Yeah, well my cousin dated a mulatto once!"* The teacher himself was a thin man with curly hair and a self-assured air about him – exactly the kind of person that impressionable people admire. His voice was confident and dynamic, as if he'd surely written a shelf worth of bestselling novels – or even a single meaningful one – though neither happened to be the case. Yet there was something in his mannerisms that caused one to want to watch him – and I could now see how it was this trait that might have helped to make him such a popular and mesmerizing figure among his students.

Maude read quickly and purposefully and when she had reached the end of her story, the teacher paused for several long moments as if to pay proper respect to what had just been pronounced. Then he looked up from the manuscript:

"Well," he said. And then again: "Well. Thank you very much. Thank you very much, Maude, for reading your story to us. It's always helpful to hear a creative work being read by its author. I think the oral experience, so to speak, gives us, the story's readers, so much more insight into the intentions of the work. I feel like I know your story more intimately now. I feel like I know *you* more intimately. So thank you."

Maude smiled shyly.

The teacher winked back at her, then continued:

"So now that we've heard this story from the lips of its young author, let's begin our discussion by telling her what we liked about it, shall we? What did you think worked well in Maude's story? What were its strengths? What is it about this story that makes it a meaningful contribution to the vast corpus of existing literature?"

The quiet in the room was penetrating and uncomfortable. Nobody ventured an answer. The teacher waited. But still nobody spoke up.

"Come on, now!" said the teacher. "Let's be giving. Remember, we'll be discussing each of *your* stories soon enough...!"

There was another lengthy – and even more awkward – silence as not a single peer volunteered to start the discussion. Finally, a young man in pince-nez glasses and a black turtleneck sweater spoke up.

"Well," he said, pushing his glasses onto his nose, "I thought the *title* was fantastic."

A murmur of agreement traveled around the table. Maude blushed.

"Your title really encapsulated the essence of the story and set the stage for what was to follow. Good job, Maude!"

"Yes," said a newly emboldened student sitting across from him. "And I loved the way you used creative pagination to highlight your story. The extra-wide margins and blank space around your text really accentuated the prose and allowed it to shine."

"That's right!" said a girl who was sitting next to Maude and appeared to be from the same cheerleading squad. "And the way you used ultra-realistic dialogue was just, like, super impressive. I mean, like, I could almost hear these voices speaking to me. It was as if, like, I were, you know, right there with the two main characters at, um, that laundromat..."

"Me too!" added another student. "And your description of the damp clothes tumbling in the dryer was just spectacular. It really gave me the sense that the dryer really was going around and around and around and around and around and around and around and around and around...."

"Yeah!" another student agreed, rather emphatically: "And *around*!"

To all this, the mesmerizing teacher nodded his approval. Then he said:

"Okay. So I think we can all agree that there is much to like in Maude's story. But what about the characters? Did you find them convincing? Could you identify with them? Did the main characters appeal to you? Were they well-rounded and multi-dimensional? Did they resonate with your sensibilities? Did you see glimpses of yourself in their decisions? A vision of your future in their struggles? Did they spark vague reminiscences of previous lives lived?"

"Oh, yes!" said the students.

"They did?"

"Yes. Very much so."

The teacher waited for an elaboration. But none came. Outside the window of the classroom, some far-off pelicans could be heard to loaf. The sun was still shining over the verdure. A duck quacked. Finally, the teacher broke the silence:

"Well, great. I'm glad we can agree on that." The man looked down at his notes. "So now that we've discussed the story's many strengths, let's talk about a few of the things that Maude might want to consider as she works on future drafts. These are what we now tend to call the *opportunities* that the story presents. And please notice that I didn't refer to these 'opportunities' as *weaknesses*. Because, of course, we do not mean to say that anything Maude has written here is weak – which is to say, it is not better or worse than any other thing that any other creative being has ever composed. In sharing our thoughts with Maude, therefore, we simply reaffirm that we have our own opinions on her writing and that, for Maude as a writer, hearing these opinions may be helpful in guiding her to perfect her work. But she, of course, is undeniably within her right to take these opinions to heart – or to disregard them – as she sees fit. In the end, the result will pretty much be the same either way. Right?"

The students nodded.

"Great. So, what say you all? What comments would you like to make about the opportunities that Maude's story presents? How might it be improved for the benefit of future generations?"

"Well!" a voice spoke up, rather too suddenly and immediately. The surprised students looked over to see that it was Maude herself who was answering the question. "I have to admit that I wrote this late last night and I didn't have much time for editing. So that explains some of the misspellings. And of course I think I definitely could've done a better job with the sock-folding scene…."

"Maude!"

The teacher had raised his finger in reproach.

"Maude!" he chastised. "You're violating the cardinal rule of literary workshopping! You mustn't speak when spoken about! Remember, your writing needs to stand on its own. You will not be there in bed with the reader while he reads your work – or at least, it's not *very* likely that you will happen to be in bed with that reader. So whatever grand intentions you have for the story should be evident in the text itself. You've had your chance to choose the words that your reader will be lying in bed with. So now you must sit silently and anonymously, with your knees pressed together under the table like they currently are, or splayed ever so slightly like they were just a few moments ago, and you must take the verbal undressing that is sure to follow. And of course you must take this undressing silently and hungrily like the mature woman that you have clearly been for some time now…"

Maude apologized and looked back down at her manuscript as if she were guilty of a fatal sin, the first deadly sin of workshopping.

From there the discussion moved on.

"For *me*," said one of Maude's fellow students, "I just really felt like the relationship between the narrator and the homeless man in the laundromat wasn't convincing. I thought their dialogues were contrived and the sex scene definitely left me somewhat unfulfilled and wishing that the author had a broader range of intimate experience to draw from – something more lofty than the bottom bunk of the fraternity house where I happened to see her last night."

The students around the table nodded their agreement.

"I mean, I would want the scene between the two main characters to exhibit a little more – oh, how should I put it? – *romance*, I guess you would call it."

"Okay. You are a romantic. Duly noted. Anyone else?"

The young man with the pince-nez raised his hand earnestly.

"Well, I just want to say that I really loved this story. I really did. In fact I think it's fantastic. An excellent piece of writing. A master of the genre. If there is such a genre as 'laundromat fiction' – and I am now convinced that there *should* be! – this piece would definitely be taking it in new directions. But, on the other hand, if I were compelled to nitpick – and I think that's what we're being asked to do today, right? – if I were forced to scrutinize the text for things to improve, then I would say that many of the lessons we've learned in this class over the past few months are appropriate here. Many of the things you've taught us in your inimitable and truly mesmerizing style – the useful guidelines, the proscriptive formulations, the tidy truisms – most of these are quite applicable to this story that Maude wrote late last night after her brief stay in the fraternity house and that she just spent the last twenty-seven minutes of our lives reading to us."

"Can you be more specific?" the teacher prompted.

"Well, it was more like twenty-seven-and-a-half minutes. Almost twenty-*eight*...."

"No, I meant the opportunities. Can you be more specific about the opportunities that this story presents?"

The young man in the pince-nez cleared his throat. Then he said:

"Of course. I mean, let's start with her characters. They're largely one-dimensional and flat. Even cartoonish. They have no ambitions and their motivations are hard to follow or to sympathize with. Stylistically, her characters do not speak with their own unique voices but with something of a common voice that is not so much their own... as *Maude*'s – and this makes it almost impossible to distinguish them from each other. Throughout the text her paragraphs are long and dense. Plot lines are short and jagged. Promises are made but not kept. Confusion reigns. This is not entirely effective, because as you've stressed to us many times over the past few months, the writer must not baffle his reader. He must take appropriate steps to help the uninitiated reader along, like a cattle dog herding bovines to a predetermined destination. Plot should therefore be straightforward and transparent. Motivations should be logical and reasoned. Unnecessary words should be trimmed so that the text reads as a lean and muscular morsel of efficient prose with very little marbling. I remember how you once told us that if a sentence contains ten words but can be written with nine....then we should use *eight* instead. You've told us that we should not use unwarranted punctuation such as exclamation marks that detract from the text – that the dialogue itself should be expressive enough to do its own exclaiming. How true! Along the way, you've given us so many clear and compelling rules for producing good writing that it's almost inconceivable that we would ever emit anything less! You've told us that contemporary fiction should be realistic and understated – not showy – and that our writing should not attract undue attention to itself. You've reminded us that dialogue should be feasible. That we should constantly ask ourselves: 'Do people really talk like this?' And that for this reason we should limit the spoken pronouncements of our characters to the guttural utterances and monosyllabic interjections of precocious third-graders. You've told us that there is no place in contemporary fiction for philosophy – that our own ideas and personal agendas should be excised, like the scrotum from a three-month-old calf. And of course you've frequently stipulated that we should always – how did you put it? – oh wait, let me check my notes here – oh yes, you say that we should.... *show* rather than *tell*. This, you say, is because a nude body that is *shown* will always be more sensual and arousing than that same body described by your frat brother after the party. You've reminded us of the age-old advice: if a gun is introduced in the beginning of a story, it absolutely must be fired by the end; otherwise the gun should not be there at all. But most important, and this I'll always remember, dear teacher, and it's something I'll always be grateful to you for: over the course of this very long semester you've repeatedly stressed the importance of *conflict* in our lives. At the center of any good story, you've taught us, there must be a clearly defined conflict. Or, to quote you directly: 'Conflict is the moisture that brings life to the parched, arid soil of the most barren imagination!'.... That's beautiful, by god, just beautiful...!"

The instructor was listening with raptness at the recapitulation of his ideas. The young man paused to push up his glasses which had slid back down the bridge of his nose. Then he continued:

"...You see, professor, all of these issues can be found in Maude's story. And so the *opportunities* for her as an author are truly great, I'm afraid...."

From here the discussion proceeded around the table as each student offered specific advice on how Maude might make her story more timeless and compelling. How she should do more showing and less telling. How she might correct some of the careless spelling that made it such a bumpy read. How the wool sock that was introduced in the beginning of the story simply *must* be more utilized by the time the story concludes. How the scenes should be more vividly drawn. How her characters should have more at stake during their sex. And, of course, how she might want to tone down the controversial pro-miscegenation editorializing while ratcheting up the true conflict of the story.

"And what *is* the conflict of this story?" the teacher prompted.

"For me," one student responded after flipping through his copy, "the main conflict is between the girl and the negroid. Can they find true happiness in that laundromat despite the swirling prejudices of their society."

"And for me," another responded, "it's whether the clothes will have enough time to get completely dry before the coin-operated cycle runs out."

"It's a story of redemption," said a third.

"An exploration of our deepest fears," said a fourth.

"The literary junction where past meets present."

"Man versus machine."

"Hope against all odds."

"Eternity versus temporality."

"I think the conflict begins on page eight when she pulls up her skirt ever so seductively above her navel," the young man sitting to my right finally concluded, "and ends on page thirteen when she pulls that same skirt back down."

"Are we warm here?" asked the teacher.

"Yes!" said Maude. "You've put your fingers on the spot!"

"Great," said the instructor. "So it looks like you all get A's for your astute observations and analysis."

A round of congratulatory handshakes and back-patting made its way around the table. The instructor waited for it to die down. Then he continued:

"Now to everything you've just said, I'd like to add that Maude has really done a fantastic job with this story. In fact, I truly believe that with a little elbow grease – and a particular focus on the sex scene in the laundromat between the homeless negroid and the cute undergraduate in the pink cheerleading outfit – this story might be considered something that is very close to being publishable."

The students around the table gasped.

"Publishable?!" said Maude.

"Yes, *publishable*. Which is certainly the highest praise that can be bestowed upon a piece of workshopped fiction. Your story is not quite there yet, Maude. But it's very close. You're very close indeed. Just a few short breaths away, really. A few well-timed movements in the right direction. You're on the verge of something truly toe-curling. But we just need to work on that one scene. So please see me after class and we can talk more about it…."

At this Bessie threw her fork down.

"Bastard!"

The hamburger patty on her plate was dry and only half-eaten.

"That son of a bitch better not touch her! That's my niece, Charlie. And if he even comes close to her I'll have his balls on a platter!"

"Maude's your niece?"

"My sister's daughter. I've been babysitting her since she was in diapers. I've watched her grow up every summer during family gatherings at the river. She's like my own flesh and blood. I drove her to her first day of kindergarten. I taught her to swim. I was there when she had her first period. Hell, who do you think bought her the very first pack of rubbers she ever used?! And now this aspiring writer — what's he ever written, anyway? — now this guy wants her to apply some elbow grease? Over my dead body she will! He must think we're some sort of birthright for him. That just because she's from Cow Eye, Maude is another prop for his trophy case. He probably believes that it's an honest trade: her sacred triangle for his professorial allure. As if the cheap adulation of his students weren't enough for him as it is…!"

It took Bessie several minutes to calm down. And when she finally did, I popped open another can of beer for her with a promise that I would include her concerns in my evaluation of the class.

"What good is *that* going to do?"

"Maybe nothing. But at least it'll let the administration know that there's a real concern. That the mesmerizing creative writing instructor — who, I might add, is up for tenure very soon — is using his position of authority to inappropriately encourage unrealistic literary ambitions and unwarranted notions of self-worth among his students. And that, you know, he's doing this not so much to support our institutional mission as to stroke his own inflated and throbbing sense of personal entitlement."

"Yeah, well, you can do whatever you like. Write your little report. Sign it. Submit it to the place where things like that go. That's all fine and good. But we have our own ways of dealing with people like that…."

"We?"

"Yes, we."

And without elaborating, Bessie stabbed her fork into the hamburger on her plate and with a single slice of her knife cut off a bite-sized piece.

≈

≈

THE FOLLOWING MONDAY the creative writing instructor stomped up the stairs of the Administration building, past Bessie's desk where she was busy typing, and without even the courtesy of a knock, stormed right into my office.

"Does this belong to you?" he said and threw a ziploc bag on my desk. The bag held a grisly mess – a swirl of hair and blood and meat – and smelled rank and rotten.

"I don't know what you're talking about…." I stammered.

"Don't give me that shit. This was in my mailbox. Somebody left it there over the weekend…."

"I honestly don't know what you're talking about…..!"

The creative writing teacher looked at me with a look of pure hate. Curling his face in an aggrieved scowl, he growled through his teeth:

"Look, it's not my damned fault you're divorced. And it's not my fault I'm a mesmerizing teacher of creative writing while you've made the decision to settle for a life of educational administration. Hell, if I were in your shoes I'd be just as jealous of my talent as *you* are. But that doesn't make this right."

"Make what right?"

"You know damn well, what."

"No, I don't!"

"Stay away from me, you freak."

The instructor had turned to leave. But then, whirling around suddenly, he looked across my desk and, pointing a long finger in my direction, he said this:

"Don't fuck with me, buddy – I'm from Colorado!"

Then he turned and left.

For a few seconds I watched his shadow disappear out into the hallway. Then I took up the ziploc with the bloated scrotum, sealed it where it was leaking, and threw the whole mess into a trash can outside my office.

"Raul," I said the following morning at the water fountain. "I think I need some help."

"With the focus group? You're still struggling to get everyone in the room together?"

"No, I think I finally have that resolved – the session's scheduled for tomorrow. And thanks for the tip with the surveys: it really worked! But, no, I actually need to ask you for some advice about Bessie. You see she's started to display a violent streak that's beginning to worry me. Remember, I told you about her past? Well, it seems to be coming to fruition…."

Here I told Raul about the incident with the creative writing teacher. And about the disagreements Bessie and I had started to have in my apartment. And how I once found her fingering a very sharp knife in my kitchen after a particularly contentious fight.

"You're still fighting? What was it this time?"

"She found out I signed the petition in favor of the electric typewriters. I guess she felt betrayed. Raul, I think this is going to end badly."

Raul bit his lip as if considering an especially challenging math problem. Then he shook his head.

"Try not to think about it now, Charlie," he said. "After all, the likelihood of any two people meeting and finding each other in this world is so infinitesimal to begin with as to be unworthy of much consternation should the arrangement end. Dissolution is the starting and ending point of all things. No matter the road you choose, it inevitably leads to asphalt."

"Asphalt?"

"Yes, asphalt. So just enjoy what you can of your experience and leave the rest for later. And besides, I just heard the Christmas party is in serious doubt – that both Gwen and Rusty are boycotting it – so that's where your energies should be going."

"Where did you hear that?"

"In the copy room. And if it comes from the secretaries in the copy room, then you know it has to be true. And if it's true, then you've got a lot bigger things to worry about than whether or not Bessie was thinking of you as she fingered that very sharp knife…."

"You're probably right," I said.

"Of course I'm right," he said.

"Thanks, Raul."

"Don't mention it."

And he left with his wax cup.

Looking up at the clock above the water cooler, I could see that it was already a little past two o'clock. Suddenly it occurred to me that I'd lost track of time yet again. I was late for my next class observation. Again.

How many times would I make this same mistake? How many times could I find myself locked into this unending wheel of time?

And with that I gathered up my notes and hurried downstairs and out onto the esplanade.

∽

"AND SO," RUSTY was saying when I walked into his animal science class later that afternoon, "this is a grave misperception. In fact, a cow does not actually have four stomachs, but rather a single stomach with four *compartments*...." Seeing me, Rusty stopped to look up from his lecture and I apologized for being late and quickly took my seat in the back of the lecture hall; the students in front had looked over at me when I walked in but then, disinterestedly, turned right back to their notes. "That's right," Rusty continued when I'd settled in. "The ruminal stomach has four compartments that allow the bovine to turn foraged food into usable energy. These four compartments correspond roughly to the phases of material and intellectual digestion and so we'll be learning about them today. Take careful notes because, to answer your question before you can even ask it.... yes, this *will* be on the test....!"

Here Rusty taped a laminated poster onto the blackboard at the front of the room:

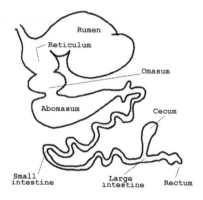

"Now if you look at this chart you will see that the first compartment of the ruminal stomach is the *rumen*...."

(Instinctively, I began taking notes. I had even written "rumen" on my notepad before crossing it out and writing over it with the date, the time, the course number, and "Stokes: Lecture on ruminant digestion system.")

Rusty continued:

"The *rumen* is the first and largest compartment of the cow's stomach where the rough food enters. When a cow chews grass or hay it sends the material down through the esophagus to the rumen practically untouched. Not a lot of chewing happens initially. And so here the ingested feed begins to be digested through a process of microbial fermentation that begins to break down the food. At this stage, the raw food product is still in fairly large pieces and is not ready for full absorption into the bovine's system. In a practical sense, this stage of the digestive process is analogous to the very first consideration of an innovative idea. Just as the indiscriminate human animal forages among the vast prairieland of ideas, the simple grazing cow ingests the rich grasses and hard fibrous straw in equal amounts. She may also occasionally ingest other less useful objects like nails or wire or even random metals from farm equipment or other man-made novelties that have been informed by a high concentration of wherewithal. And so, after a minimum of chewing, the useful material is passed down for further digestion. And it is here in the rumen where the raw product is first broken down and, without much further absorption, is brought forward to the next step in the process, which is the digestion that happens in the *reticulum....*"

Rusty slapped his yardstick against the chart where the reticulum was drawn.

"....Now the reticulum is sometimes called the *bonnet* or the *honeycomb* and its function is to take what has passed through the rumen and to break it down further. This is where the cud is formed, also called the *bolus*. Here the partially digested food is compacted into small parcels and sent back up through the rumen to the mouth. This allows the cow to chew and re-chew the food that it has consumed. Like the review committee that considers a proposed innovation and sends it back to its proposer for further elaboration, the reticulum will give the bovine the opportunity to further process the cud and to break it down even more. The twice-chewed material can then be further broken down and sent back to the reticulum for further consideration and this process of chewing and re-chewing can be repeated many times over and over: back and forth between mouth and stomach, proposer and reviewer, idealist and pragmatist. The reticulum is also where foreign objects that the cow has managed to swallow are often caught, and where they stay for the rest of the cow's life…"

Rusty stopped.

"Any of you like *tripe*?" he asked.

Almost all the students raised their hands.

"Well, this is what you're eating! We call it *tripe* stew, but actually it should be called *reticulum* stew…."

The students laughed.

"…The contractions of the rumen and reticulum help the flow of finer food particles into the next chamber of the stomach, which is called the *omasum*…."

Rusty pointed his ruler at the omasum in his chart:

"…The omasum," he explained, "is the next compartment. It is sometimes called the *bible* and it functions as a filter to the final compartment. It is made of lots of leafy folds and resembles a book…."

Here a hand went up.

"Yes?" Rusty said.

"Dr. Stokes?" a student was asking. "Did you say the omasum resembles a book and that it's called the *bible*?"

"That's right."

"Is that a coincidence?"

"Of course not. There is nothing in nature that is mere coincidence. In fact it's called that because it resembles the pages of a book. A well-received volume of poetry, perhaps. Or the Holy Book. Imagine thumbing through the pages looking for a certain quotation from Luke. Or trying desperately to find an American poet in a comprehensive anthology of world literature. That's what's happening in the cow's stomach on a regular basis. The folds are designed so that the smaller particles can move on through, while anything that's too large gets sent back to the reticulum to go through the process again…."

"*Again?*"

"Yes, again. You seem surprised by that? I suppose you thought it should be easy to get an innovation approved at a community college? That any new idea is worthy on its own merits? Well, clearly that is not the case. And so, if the material is not ready for digestion, it will be sent back again. But if the food has been sufficiently broken down, then it can move on to the next, and final, chamber called the *abomasum*. This is the last compartment and is also known as the 'true stomach' because it functions similarly to other mammals' stomachs, including those of humans. Acid and stomach enzymes break down the food more completely and send it through to the small intestine."

"And then?"

"Well, and then from the abomasum it goes to the small intestine and from there it goes as nutrients to the bloodstream or out as urine or feces. The whole process takes quite a long time and yet it is as relentless as the triumphant forward march of progress. But keep in mind that, of the original food that is consumed, only a very small percentage actually benefits the cow. The rest remains in the omasum, or is expectorated as urine or as the feces that is left behind by the bovine as the cow pies that our animal science department donates to the math faculty every March."

"So are you saying this is a bad thing?" a skeptical student asked. The boy was sitting in the front row and taking vigorous notes.

"No it's not bad, *per se*. Because if the math teachers weren't throwing these cow pies, they would have to find some other pies to worship...."

"No, not *that*, Dr. Stokes. I'm talking about what you said earlier. About the consumption of ideas. Are you saying the cow shouldn't eat fresh grass just because only a small percentage of what it eats is actually turned into beneficial nutrients that are absorbed into the blood? Are you implying that greener pastures are irrelevant to the development of humankind? That the story of civilization is not the story of exodus and discovery? And if so, are you saying that tenured faculty don't have an obligation to propose innovative ideas just because they work at a *community college*?"

"Of course not," said Rusty. "That's not what I'm saying at all. The cow needs to eat. And it will eat. The human mind needs to innovate. And it will innovate. These are no less realities of life than the need that math people have to throw pies on March fourteenth. These are understandable. But never forget that it's our job as educated citizens of the world – and it will be your duty as *college*-educated animal science students – to ensure that during this noble act of foraging the cow is forced to swallow as few nails as possible. And that during this noble act of math worship – that during the messy act of pie-throwing – innocent bystanders get hit with no more shit than is appropriate."

"And how much is appropriate?"

"That," said Rusty, "is a question best left for our institutional researcher...."

The boy shook his head and jotted something down in his notebook.

Rusty put his ruler on the desk in front of him.

"And that," he concluded, "is how a cow's stomach works. And so to review......today you've learned how the food that a cow eats travels from the trough in the corner of the corral to the cow's mouth through the esophagus to the reticulorumen – then back and forth many times – and finally down through the omasum and the abomasum through the small intestine, the large intestine, and out through the rectum...."

"Rectum!"

A juvenile titter arose around the room.

"And then?"

"And then it sits on the ground in the form of cow pies that are collected and thrown by the math faculty every March fourteenth...."

"And then?"

"And then at least one mention of this activity is included in their tenure dossier. The faculty are given tenure so that they may continue the teaching of their beloved subject to diligent undergraduates. The undergraduates then use this teaching to successfully pass their math classes, get their degrees, graduate, and move on into the broader world to become god-fearing, tax-paying citizens, often in other states of the union that are far, far away from Cow Eye Junction. In this way, our town loses its soul by losing its young people – and in this way the diaspora of learning is perpetuated over the millennia. And to think, it all starts in the four timeless chambers of the cow's simple stomach....!"

"And then, Dr. Stokes?!"

"And then?"

"Yes, and then...?"

"Well, and then she would take my palm and put it on her stomach where the scar was..."

"Scar?"

"It was a difficult surgery, Charlie. She was never the same after that...."

I nodded.

That night I asked Bessie what it all meant.

"You mean the passage of nutrients from the rumen to the abomasum?

Or do you mean the role of the ruminant's stomach in the voracious cycle of human innovation?"

"Neither. I mean Will's wife. He talks about her all the time. How long ago did she pass away?"

"About the same time I moved to my current position. So about two years ago."

"It seems like he misses her a lot."

"He does."

I took another bite of stew.

"It's sad," I said.

"It always is," she agreed. "But it's also inevitable. They were married thirty-eight years, you know."

I nodded again.

"Have you ever loved anyone like that?" I asked.

"Never."

"Do you think you ever will?"

"I doubt it." Bessie stopped to consider my question more deeply. Then she said: "Actually, no. Not that much…."

"Well, at least you're honest," I concluded. "At least you know your limits."

And without relish, I took a final bite of tripe, wiped my mouth with a napkin, and returned to my office to write up my evaluation for the public speaking class I'd just observed.

∾

WHEN I CAME back to the cafeteria the next day, Will Smithcoate was still sitting at his table, as if he hadn't moved. The same cloud of smoke was above his head partially obscuring the no-smoking sign.

"Hi, Mr. Smithcoate. Have you been here since yesterday?"

"You could stay that. Although a truer estimate would be that I've been here for the last thirty years."

Will blew out another cloud of smoke to take the place of the first.

"Thirty years is a long time," I said.

"It is. And yet, whether it's thirty years or five years – they're both less than thirty-*eight*."

I nodded.

"And you, Charlie? How were your class observations? You seem even more tired than you did yesterday at lunchtime."

"That's because I *am*. I haven't slept since the semester began. And I'm getting more and more tired with each passing day."

"I can see that...."

"I'm losing my ability to concentrate."

"That's what I'm hearing."

"The observation of the creative writing class went fine enough. The public speaking class was interesting to see. And Rusty, as usual, was on fire with his theories on rumination. But last night turned out to be a particularly bad night for me."

"Worse than usual?"

"Oh yes. Last night the math faculty really outdid themselves. It must have been some sort of mathematical holiday. You know, one of those dates on the calendar that correspond to a sacred number. It must have been something exceptional because they pulled out all the stops."

And here I told Will how the math faculty had kept me up all night to the clamor of cracking whips and bedsprings heaving and what sounded like the roar of a live mountain lion.

"It's like they never stop!" I exclaimed.

"That's not surprising," Will said. "Among large felines, math is the most tenacious of all. You can't wait for it to become satiated. Or to develop a conscience. It doesn't have one."

"Perhaps. But last night I'd finally had enough. For the first time since I moved into the apartment I decided to do something about it."

"Well, good for you, Charlie!"

"Yeah. But it didn't turn out the way I'd hoped. You see, it all began like it usually does....after Bessie left my apartment I took my usual lonely shower and was reading in bed when the noises started up. I've gotten so used to them by now that I didn't even notice anything at first. But soon it got worse. Louder and louder. And not just a dull steady roar this time but the unpredictable kind that comes when you least expect it and leaves you breathlessly waiting for the next crash or roar or cackle. The next tumult of heaving bed springs. The next caterwaul. I'd been waiting in the darkness of my apartment for the sound to die down to a normal level. I waited through an entire chapter of my book. But it finally got so bad that I couldn't fall asleep even with my ear plugs in. And when I looked up at my clock – it was past two in the morning – and the noise still hadn't died down – in fact it seemed to be *increasing* – I decided to approach them."

"You approached the math teachers?"

"Yes."

"You mean you chose conflict over conciliation?"

"Yes."

"At last?"

"Yes."

"And you did it *entirely*?"

"Sort of...."

Putting on my beige pants and a t-shirt, I stepped out into the hallway. The music was pounding. The hallway was cold and the floor felt like a glacier under my naked feet. From inside the neighboring apartment the sounds of screaming laughter could be heard over the thumping music and breaking dishes and what sounded like the unrestrained trumpeting of a lioness protecting her young. I took a deep breath and knocked on the door. When there was no answer, I knocked again, this time more insistently. A few moments passed, but again there was no answer. After several minutes of indecision, I began knocking with open palms, repeatedly, pounding on the door: over and over and over again until the bones in my palm were bruised and the skin was red. Until my breath was short and my face was flushed. Finally, the lock on the door clicked. The knob turned. The door opened slightly. A thin sliver of a young woman's face – a quarter of it perhaps – was peering out at me. Through the narrowly opened door she looked out at me and I in at her. The crack was as wide as the spine of a book: a single eye peering out. I had readied myself to be confrontational, but before either of us could say anything, an unseen voice called out to the woman from behind the door.

"Who is it?" the man's voice asked.

"It's the Special Projects Coordinator..."

"What does he want?"

The woman peered out at me.

"I don't know. But he looks crazed...!"

"It's late.....tell him he should come back at a respectable time...!"

The woman surveyed me suspiciously:

"Can I help you?" she asked.

"I'm Charlie," I gasped. "I live next door."

"I know. We've seen you come and go. You're the new Special Projects Coordinator."

"Yes."

"The one struggling to organize the Christmas party."

"Yes."

"And failing to bring our divided faculty together."

"That's correct."

"You're a lot of different things, but none of them entirely."

"Right."

"And you're having a transcendental romance with the secretary who drives the truck."

"I….well…I suppose you could say that, yes…."

"I hope you're not here for my survey because I already turned it in."

"Huh?"

"My survey about the focus group. I turned it in to the division secretary a few days ago."

"Oh, yes, thank you. But I'm not here for that. I'm here because…."

The woman was still peering through the crack in the door.

"Look, can you open the door a bit….it's hard to have a conversation with you like this…."

The woman paused and then opened the door a bit wider. Now I could see twice as much of her face – a full half of it – through the crack in the door.

"Better?" she said.

"One hundred percent," I said. And then: "Look, I like mathematics as much as anyone. But it's just that…." (After so much anticipation – how many months had I imagined and planned for this moment of conflict? – and now here I was stuttering and stumbling over my words!) "…It's just that, you know, we're already more than half-way through the semester and time seems to be pushing me relentlessly toward a tragic resolution…."

"Time?"

"Yes, time."

"You're knocking on my door at two in the morning to talk about *time*?"

"I'm sorry. Would a different hour be more convenient?"

The woman paused to consider my words. Then suddenly she flung open the door. The door opened wide and for a brief second I caught a glimpse of a dominion that I'd only imagined and heard about and pined for from the other side of my wall. Looking past her shoulders I saw a gilded realm of steaming baths and marble walkways and a pool where half-naked women in togas dangled grapes above the open mouth of the college's male algebra teacher. Elephants and lions lay next to fragrant flowers and a bubbling waterfall while a toucan fluttered across the room. Next to a large gold throne a Siamese cat lay at the feet of a travertine statue of Euclid. The woman stepped through the opened doorway then reached behind to pull the door after her.

"Hey, where're you going?!" the calculus teacher's voice called to her from inside.

"Into the hallway," she said. "To talk with our Special Projects Coordinator."

"Why would you want to do *that*?"

"It's okay," she answered. "He looks harmless. But if I'm not back in five minutes, call campus security...!"

The woman stepped out into the common area and closed the door firmly behind her. She was wearing a white t-shirt and pink socks; her auburn hair was pulled back in a pony tail. It was clear that the only thing separating her from this cold October night was the t-shirt itself, probably just thrown on, and as she stepped out into the hallway I could see the peaks of her nipples jutting out beneath the shirt's light fabric.

"Yes?" she said. "It's two in the morning. We happened to be in the middle of something when you knocked. This better be important...."

"It is," I said. "It's very important. You see, the fate of our institution is in my hands. But I haven't slept since the beginning of the semester. And my hands have begun to tremble. I've tried my best to get some sleep but your ecstasy is just too strident. Time is moving too quickly. Believe me, I'm not generally one for conflict but I've finally decided that I can't take it anymore, that I have to do *something*...."

"Conflict, did you say?"

"Yes, conflict."

"And what issue do you have with conflict?"

"Nothing really. I have the deepest admiration for those who are good at it. But it's just never been my strong suit."

"That's a shame. Conflict is a fact of life."

"I'm sure."

"Conflict is the foundation on which our great country was built."

"Perhaps, but…."

"Conflict is what gives the world its grist. It is the catalyst for change and innovation. It is the stimulant of progress. All intellectual discoveries come at the crossroads of conflicting beliefs and ways of being."

"Granted. But *conciliation* can be timely as well."

"Not in the least. Conciliation is for humanists. Conflict will always win out in the end. Or would you care to disagree with me?"

"Not necessarily. I'm really not here to disagree with anyone. I'm just terribly tired at the moment because it's already past two o'clock in the morning and I haven't had a single convincing night of sleep since the semester began. I've tried to get a few moments of sleep in my office. In the library. Even under the sycamore. But to no avail. The pendulum, the study groups, the songs of protest – they all keep me up. So do you think you could please turn down your music? And curtail the shrieking? And temper the painful screams of ecstasy?"

"Of course not."

"Please?"

"No."

"But isn't there a way that maybe we could, you know, come to some sort of compromise?"

"Such as?"

"Well, like maybe you could be considerate during certain times of the night while remaining oblivious during the rest? Or maybe you could limit your celebration of mathematics to a few nights of the week only? Maybe you could find a level of ecstasy that falls somewhere between perfect noise and perfect sound? Something we could both live with and that I could, you know, *fall asleep* with?"

"Absolutely not."

"Why not?"

"Because conflict and conciliation are incompatible. Or rather they can be compatible but only as long as the conciliatory consistently bend to the whims of the confrontational."

"Are you saying the two can't co-exist side by side?"

"Correct."

"Even if separated by a thin wall?"

"Right."

"Well, if that's the case, then maybe you'd be willing to allow for multiple points of view on the issue of *time*?"

"Not likely."

"Then would you at least assent to putting carpet on the floors to deaden the sound of falling dishes?"

"I don't think so."

"Or perhaps you could allow that there are things in this world that cannot be understood mathematically? Things that cannot be categorized and explained and repeated? Truisms that defy data? Maybe you could permit into your heart a little bit of doubt? The possibility of imperfection? The admissibility of paradox. Might you not want to give just a little on one of these things? Huh, do you think you could? Just a little, maybe? Huh ....?"

"Um, no. And please stop looking at my nipples. It's making me uncomfortable...."

"I'm sorry...."

"Do I have to put on a sweater in your presence?"

"That won't be necessary...!"

"There's professional development for men like you, you know...."

"Look, it wasn't intentional! It's just that, well, how am I possibly going to get through this semester?! We're already past mid-terms and I'm still struggling to keep my eyes open during committee meetings. I'm still struggling to stay awake through the mind-numbing drafts of our self-study!"

"Your eyes seem plenty open right *now*...!"

"And I'm sorry for it. And I've retreated from it. There's no need for sweaters, I assure you. Or lawyers. You see, my eyes just have this wide-open crazed appearance because I've been anticipating this confrontation with you for some time. I just spent ten consecutive minutes pounding on your door. But now that the very moment's arrived, well, it wasn't quite what I thought it would be. Your nipples are charming and unexpected. As are the smooth thighs protruding out from under your shirt. But it's a long semester. And the fate of our institution is..."

"Look," the young woman interrupted, "if you want to be conciliatory then you need to start by conceding that conflict is inevitable. Can you at least agree with me on that?"

"Of course."

"Unequivocally?"

"Okay."

"And can you acknowledge that history favors those who prefer conflict?"

"Yes."

"Good. So what's the problem?"

"The problem? Well, the problem is…."

Here I stopped.

Dr. Felch had expectorated into his spittoon and was now looking at me gravely.

"The damn problem, Charlie, is that we've got less than three weeks until the end of the semester and the self-study isn't even finished. The Christmas party is hanging by a thread. Rumor is that Gwen and Rusty are threatening to boycott the event outright. And the two groups of faculty are still at each other's throats. You've done *nothing* to bring all these disparate elements together. I thought you were going to do a focus group or something? I thought you were going to do a survey?"

"I was. And I am. To be honest, I haven't finished with the focus groups yet – the last and most important of them is tomorrow. But I did conduct the surveys."

"Well, at least that's something. So what did they tell you?"

"Unfortunately, not much. Half of the respondents felt that the focus group they'd attended was useful and productive while the other half thought it was a waste of time."

"You conducted a survey to assess the outcomes of a *focus group*?"

"Right. And I also conducted a focus group to guide the development of the survey. Raul's been very adamant that no educational endeavor should be attempted without first conducting a focus group or a survey of some kind. You know, to get some *qualitative* data to supplement the kind that is meaningful. Ideally both should be conducted. Which is exactly what I'm doing. I'm committed to doing *both*!"

"Well, it's becoming clearer by the day that all your qualitative data-collecting hasn't brought us any closer to the resurrection of our Christmas party. Or to solving the cultural divide on campus. Not to mention the self-study report which is due the day after tomorrow and still isn't close to being complete. You've done quite a bit of talking up to this point, Charlie. But now we need some forward motion. Time is ticking It's ticking as loudly and relentlessly as that pendulum in your office. In fact it's even *louder*! You need to make this all work out. And I'm tired of hearing your excuses about not being able to sleep. Napoleon suffered from insomnia during key points of his life yet he managed to conquer quite a bit of Europe. Figure it out, Charlie. And soon. The fate of our institution depends on it."

"Ouch!" said Bessie.

"Ouch is right," I said. "Ethel even suggested it could compromise her and Luke's respective applications for tenure!"

"And *then* what did she say?" Bessie prodded. "What did she say after that?"

"Who? Ethel?"

"No, the math teacher in the hallway? I'm assuming you were affected by seeing her in nothing but a t-shirt and socks?"

"It was surprising, yes."

"And did you like what you were seeing?"

"Well, it was late. I was cold there in the hallway. And we only had five minutes before her colleagues would be calling campus security. But yes."

"And what did they look like?"

"Her colleagues?"

"No, Charlie, her nipples. You know, in comparison with mine?"

"Well, I didn't see them, *per se*. But what I saw of them was definitely rigid and uncompromising."

"Unlike *mine*, you mean to say?"

"Well, yes. Hers were mathematical. Yours are more flexible and forgiving...."

I reached out for her to prove my point, but Bessie slapped away my hand.

"You'd better stop while you're ahead....!"

I laughed.

"And then what did she say?" Will asked. "What did she say after that?"

"You mean Bessie after she slapped away my hand?"

"To hell with *Bessie*! What did the sexy math teacher in the white t-shirt have to say about conflict? You cut her off in mid-sentence!"

"Oh, right. Well she said – and I'm paraphrasing her, obviously – she basically said that in the eternal struggle between conflict and conciliation, conflict will *always* win out. History rewards the confrontational above the conciliatory. Aggression above acquiescence. The quiet voice will always be drowned out by the voice that is more insistent. The meek have no chance against the strong. Just as the humanities themselves are defenseless against the continual onslaught of science and technology and math. She said a lot of other things as well – in fact we ended up talking for quite a while there in the hallway before the calculus teacher finally came out to get her – but in the end she went right back into her apartment and slammed the door."

"With no concessions on the noise level?"

"Nope. In fact the music got even louder."

"So your stab at conflict was fruitless?"

"Yes. As was my attempt at conciliation."

"And that's why you didn't sleep at all last night?"

"Right."

"And that's why you look so tired today?"

"Yes."

"Well, she's right of course. History *does* reward confrontation. And the humanities *are* doomed. But, you see, history also tends to *punish* confrontation as well. Conciliation cannot exist without conflict. But neither can conflict exist without conciliation. So hopefully there's some consolation for you in that...."

"I suppose there is," I said and handed Ethel back her gun.

"Hey, easy with that...!" she said, carefully taking the gun from me and pointing it down to the ground. In front of us, on the other side of a thick glass partition, a pair of animal science instructors were shooting at their targets. Ethel took the gun and set it on the bench between us.

"How's their shooting?" I asked.

"These two are pretty good!" she commented. Ethel had warned me that she was raised with guns and was comfortable with them: as a girl she had even won several awards for her shooting. "And you, Charlie?"

"Nothing of the sort. In fact all of this is still quite new to me. Awards. Guns. Conflict. Tripe stew. They're all as strange and foreign to me as that Esperanto class I observed this morning."

"Just remember to treat your weapon as if it were always loaded. Because it probably *is*. And at the worst possible time....!"

Her words sounded ominous. Gently, I set my gun on the bench next to hers. Ethel took out her protective goggles and put them on top of her head. Then she took a string of ear plugs and dangled it around her neck.

"Shooting is like journalism," she said as we sat watching the two instructors shoot at their targets in turn: first one, then the other. "Which is to say, there's definitely a right way to go about it....and a wrong way. If you get everything right it can be the most exhilarating feeling in life. But if you get something wrong, the results can be disastrous."

"Like accreditation!"

"Exactly. Now watch how the woman on the left is holding her revolver. If you notice, she's got her arm straight and tensed. That's not going to work out well for her. She's trying too hard and her body is too rigid. She's going to really feel it tomorrow...."

I watched the woman fire at her target, the gun kicking back with each shot.

"....Now if you look at the man on the *right*....the one with the flintlock.....he's doing it right. He's got his knees slightly bent, his elbows slightly flexed, weight a bit forward. He fires. The gun comes back. He resets. And he's ready to fire again...."

As Ethel and I watched the two instructors firing at their respective targets on the other side of the glass partition – the woman's target being a cut-out of an onrushing welfare recipient; the man's a silhouette of an unsuspecting buffalo – Ethel told me about the many struggles she was having in her journalism classes: sadly, the transition from practicing journalist to instructor of journalism was not an easy one for her and she was still grappling mightily with the change.

"Teaching journalism is to *practicing* journalism," she sighed, "as discussing sex is to *having* it."

I laughed.

By now my ears had grown accustomed to the muted sounds of small-arms fire coming through the glass partition. Ethel was still wound up from her semester of teaching and seemed especially eager to start her shooting. But as she waited for the two shooters to wrap up their session – the buffalo, in particular, looked tattered and generally condemned to his fate – she turned to me instead:

"So speaking of vicarious sex, how's the college's self-study coming?"

"You're asking me about the self-study...*here*? With live gunfire all around?"

"Of course. Our college is like that buffalo, Charlie. If this self-study report gets botched, our fates will all be hanging by the same threads as that target over there. Our economic future will be no more secure than that bullet-riddled welfare recipient's. The entire community may lose its only institution of higher learning, its only window to the outside world, its only chance of learning a more worldly way of having first-person sex. Everyone agrees that you're the one soul on campus who's got the hopes of our college – of our entire community, for that matter – in his hands. So how's the process treating you?"

"It hasn't been kind, honestly. The draft is due tomorrow and I still haven't received all the write-ups for the different sections. Rusty still needs to get me his portion to include the precise number of cows inseminated since the last report – as well as the percentage that actually gave birth. I also need updated figures from the fiscal office on the exact operational costs for the swimming pool, the rates of use among faculty and students, and the impact that their swimming has had on our graduates' ability to become god-fearing, tax-paying citizens of the United States of America. And then of course there's the section that I've been trying to get from Sam Middleton – you know, the English teacher and inveterate lover of medieval poetry. I've been hounding him since the beginning of the semester. But every time he turns in something to me, it's in verse."

"You mean, *poetry*?"

"Yes. It's driving me nuts. He's supposed to write the section on the college's commitment to assessing the effectiveness of its own assessment mechanisms. It's not a hard section, Ethel, it's really not. Raul even devised this great planning and assessment flowchart to help him visualize the assessment cycle…."

I took out Raul's chart from my pocket and unfolded it for Ethel to see:

"Raul designed this for you?"

"Yes, he loves charts."

"And graphs."

"And diagrams…"

"And figures…."

"And focus groups…!"

"And *surveys*!"

"Yes, he loves surveys more than life itself. In fact, he refers to his focus groups as faithful mistresses and each concocted survey as his favorite concubine. So anyway, thanks to Raul I had this convenient flowchart and I even took the time to personally deliver it to Sam Middleton in his office. And what do you think he sent me back?"

"Another write-up in verse."

"Exactly! With allusions to medieval poets. Here…I have it in my pocket as well…."

I took out the paper and laid it on top of Raul's chart:

Forte buen hire owen make,
Longe to aen icbulle forsake,
Ant f eye 1 assessen,
Nibtes when I wende ant wake.

Ethel whistled at what she was reading:

"Boy, that's a tough one. I mean it might be somewhat amusing…. if the entire fate of our college didn't depend on it. What do you think he's trying to say with this? He must be trying to make an ideological statement of some sort, right?"

"Clearly. And that's fine. But institutional accreditation is not the place for the expression of personal values. It's not the place for intellectual integrity or unwavering convictions. It's not a forum for your true beliefs to be laid bare. It's not the proper venue for idealistic notions of propriety or even for pragmatic conceptions of justice. And please don't use the accreditation process as a forum to stand up and scream at the top of your lungs: 'Hey, look at me, world! I'm a free-thinking self-respecting human being with heightened moral sensibilities!' The accreditors just want to know how we assess our assessments, right?….so just answer the damn question!"

"Well, good luck with that…!"

By now the two animal science instructors were done with their shooting. They had already removed the ammunition and were packing away their things into separate duffel bags.

"Looks like we're up!" Ethel said and pulled her ear muffs down over her ears.

❧

A LITTLE AFTER three o'clock that afternoon I stormed into Sam Middleton's office.

"Look," I said. "The self-study was due yesterday and if it weren't for *you* the damn document would have been finished on time. I've been going back and forth with you all semester….and after all the crap you put me through, you have the nerve to give me *this*…?!"

I threw the palimpsest on Sam Middleton's desk.

"You don't like it?" he asked.

"It's in verse!"

"Not a fan of poetry, I take it?"

"No, I'm not. Not when it comes to accreditation and the fate of our college. Look, there's a time and a place for everything. And the time and place for poetry, I'm very sorry to say, was about fifty years ago. I'm sure this is not news to you. So how about you come up with an *actual* write-up that spares our accreditors all this poetry? How about you just perform your core function as tenured community college instructor of English – the job we're paying you to do! – and write this damn section detailing our college's process for assessing itself?! How about you give me some fucking barren prose for a change!"

Sam Middleton looked at me with a poet's inquisitiveness.

"Charlie! Are you in your right mind? I can't believe you're talking to me like this!"

"Am I in my right mind?!"

"Yes, are you sane? You look totally out of control honestly. Your eyes are glazed and you're sweating profusely….and when's the last time you cut your hair?"

I stopped. Inside his office the space heater was quietly blowing warmed air from under his desk. The fountains had been turned off for the winter. The ducks no longer quacked.

I shook my head.

"Sorry, Sam," I said and rubbed my eyes, which must have been as dry and as red as they looked. "It's just that we're already into finals week, the semester is almost finished, and the Christmas party is dangling by the thinnest of threads. This self-study is hovering over me like a descending mist. I need to finish it off. I need to get it done before my meeting with Dr. Felch this afternoon to present my recommendations for the Christmas party. You see, we've heard rumblings that both Gwen and Rusty are planning to boycott the whole thing – and if *they* go they'll take everybody else with them. The very premise of the Christmas party as a unifying event will be doomed. I'm trying to head that off. But everything's crumbling around me. So can you just work with me here? Can you just give me something I can use?"

Sam paused for a few seconds. Then he said:

"Look, Charlie." Here he took the palimpsest I'd thrown on his desk and flipped it over. "I am not going to compromise my principles at the behest of our accreditors. And I'm not going to apologize for sticking to my aesthetic guns. Sorry."

I let out an exasperated groan.

"But I will do my part. Will *blank verse* work for you?"

I shook my head at his stubbornness. But then I said:

"At this point, Sam, *yes*. I mean, it's better than nothing, I guess. Just please, please, *please*…can you put it in paragraph form!"

Sam agreed. I thanked him.

"You can drop off your draft at the cafeteria when you're done," I said. "That's where I've been spending most of my time lately anyway. And if you miss me just give it to Will Smithcoate. He's always there. And he'll make sure I get it."

Sam nodded.

I thanked him again and left.

⤳

{ }

*When a cute cat wants to mate she will begin the process by
letting the nearest potential suitors know of her intentions.
This might be as overt as emitting a shrill caterwaul that*

calls to mind the guttural shrieks of math faculty in heat — or it might be as subtle and imperceptible as the playful rolling or rubbing that indicates her receptiveness. Sensing her demeanor, the male cat will begin to circle around her. Relentlessly, he will look for harbingers of sweet relent. A verbal sign. A slight brush against the side of his body. A seductive twitch of her feline femininity. It may take several tense moments of hissing and growling for the male to become sufficiently emboldened. But when the moment strikes, it will strike with the force of life itself: at once he will pounce onto the she-cat's back, biting into her neck and mounting her with the ruthlessness of a suitor possessed. These are not pretty scenes to behold, nor attractive sounds to hear. Quickly the act will be over and each party will be free to go their respective ways. Upon first insemination, the female may increase her chances of conception by repeating this ritual with many other suitors....

{ }

～

"I DON'T KNOW what's happening to me," I told Raul when I happened to meet him in the men's bathroom down the hall from my office. The two of us were standing behind our respective urinals at a proper and professional distance, and as we delivered our dossiers, we spoke sideways across the vacant urinal in between. "I just don't know, Raul, it's like I've lost my patience with humanity....not to mention the Humanities. Last week I yelled at Sam Middleton in his office. A few days ago I snapped at Timmy at the guard shack on my way back from the museum. And last night Bessie and I had a really bad argument in bed that was mostly my fault. Okay, it was *entirely* my fault."

"Your fault?

"Yes."

"*Entirely?*"

"Yes, entirely. But not in the good way. You see, it's like my skin is wearing thinner and thinner over time and sooner or later it's just going to stretch so thin that it bursts open. I feel like the seams of my soul are getting stretched tighter and tighter each day and before I know it they'll be stretched to the point that the whole thing will just crack open and all the blood will spill out."

"There's blood in your soul?"

"So to speak."

"That would be gruesome, Charlie."

"See, what I mean? Even my metaphors have become desperate and confused...!"

"I can appreciate that. But the more worrisome fact is that you're not handling the rigors of Cow Eye very well. Lack of sleep isn't helping you. But there's more to it than that. You see, you're at that age when the entire weight of your life is coming to a head. Your very worth as a human being is directly connected to the college's self-study document. Your success as a sentient being depends wholly on your ability to pull off the Christmas party. And after a pair of unsuccessful marriages, let's face it, *both* of which were primarily your fault, you're searching for something – anything – that you can be successful at entirely. This is all very understandable. But it's a lot to keep inside."

"Maybe you're right, Raul. Maybe it's all weighing on me. I mean, I don't think I've been very successful achieving any of my goals so far."

"As Special Projects Coordinator?"

"Those too. But no, I'm talking about in general. In *life*...."

"You mean finding the moisture in all things? And loving the unloved?"

"Right. And experiencing both day and night. I feel like I'm failing miserably on all accounts."

Raul pulled the handle above the urinal and walked over to the sink. As the water ran into the basin, he splashed some soap onto his hands and proceeded to wash them meticulously – carefully lathering each soapy digit.

"Well, clearly you need some sleep," he was saying as he leaned his tall frame over the sink. "There's no question about that. Look, here's something I can do. How about you stay at my apartment over the weekend? I'll be at a friend's place both days – she lives off-campus – so you can use it if you like."

I had joined him in front of the bathroom mirrors. Now Raul was combing through his hair with a wet comb. His part was perfect, like aisles of a congressional floor; his hair as black as the edge of the universe. I washed my hands and dried them on a long cloth hanging from the dispenser by the door.

"I appreciate the offer," I said. "But I think I just need to get a little sleep on my own. I think I'll just go back to my office and close the door and see if I can take some kind of nap under the ticking presence of the pendulum. I think I can afford to do it now that I just turned in the self-study this morning."

"Middleton came through?"

"Yes, he did. A week late but he finally got me a write-up with no overt rhyming scheme. And so I'm thinking that just locking myself in my office might be a simple way to get a little bit of sleep at last."

"Well, good luck with that...." said Raul. "I know that pendulum is an incessant reminder of competing priorities. If it doesn't work out, just let me know before I leave today and I'll give you the key to my place. Like I say, my apartment's yours if you want it...."

I thanked him again. He left and I followed him out of the bathroom and headed back into my office, locked the door, turned off the light and stretched out on the carpeted floor. In the darkness above me I could hear the low drone of the air conditioning unit and the ticking of the pendulum, just as loud and just as steady as the day I'd first started it into motion. The drone and the ticking and the darkness worked their magic. My eyes closed heavily. My thoughts receded. Everything dissolved into silence. Within minutes I was asleep.

EXCEPT THAT, WELL, I *wasn't*. On the other side of my apartment wall the banging and crashing of mathematical inquiry had only gotten louder – so loud and so unyielding that it had somehow managed to wake me before I could even fall asleep.

How much longer could this go on?! How much further into the future would the sound continue? By now I desperately needed to close my eyes against this unbroken chain of events, this relentless progression of linear history, this preamble to endless dissolution. But no. Once again, there was no sleep to be found. Instead, I grabbed the book on top of the pile next to my bed. Like a faithful friend, it lay quiet and attentive and eager to be of assistance. And once again I began reading.

THE FOCUS GROUP

"To guide the development of our institutional mission statement, a series of high-stakes focus groups were held to solicit the opinions of faculty and staff of the college. Results of these sessions can be seen below and in Appendices D through X."

From the Accreditation Self-Study
of Cow Eye Community College

"Charlie!" a voice was shouting through my door. "Charlie, are you in there?!"

Dazed, I looked up from the floor of my office. In the darkness, the sound of insistent pounding was all around me, bouncing off itself like gunshots in an enclosed space.

"Are you in there, Charlie?!"

I stared through the darkness at the sound coming in. Was I here? Of course I was here! Where *else* would I be....?!

"Charlie!" Bessie was shouting. "What are you doing in there? Open this door right now...!"

Heavily I raised myself from the carpeted floor and stumbled through the dark to open the door of the office: an overwhelming light came flooding in.

"Charlie?! What are you doing in here?"

I squinted my eyes against the light:

"I'm just having a little nap," I said. "You know, since I can't seem to fall asleep at home. Why are you asking? And what time is it anyway?"

"It's almost two."

"Two?"

"Yes, two. Raul told me you might be in here. You didn't forget about the focus group, did you?"

"What focus group? I mean, of course I didn't forget about the focus group! Why do you think I would forget about the focus group? I'm a trained professional, you know. I have a Master's degree in Educational Administration with a special emphasis in struggling community colleges. I spent a lot of time getting that degree and it's not like they awarded us that distinction for forgetting about focus groups. So, no, I did not forget the focus group. But it's just that....you know, could you remind me again *what* focus group it was that I've been so careful not to forget....?"

"What focus group?! My god, Charlie, you're asking me *what focus group?*"

"Yes, which focus group are you referring to?"

"*The* focus group, Charlie! The one you've been trying for months to organize. The one that required endless strategic meetings and countless machinations just to get everyone in the same room for. Come on, it's starting in five minutes. Everything's set up and the participants are waiting in the conference room down the hall. They're all waiting for your leadership and facilitation. And there's already some tension building between the two sides of the table. So let's go!"

Suddenly, I realized that the focus group Bessie was talking about really was the one I'd been trying for many months to organize. *The mother of all focus groups*, Raul had called it. *The focus group to end all focus groups!* After months of meticulous planning, everything was ready to go: the room was reserved; the demographic questionnaires had been designed; the seating had been carefully pre-determined. To help me with the session, Bessie had agreed to look past our most recent argument at my apartment and to act as my assistant facilitator. After so many months it was all finally ready to take place. Dr. Felch would be anxiously awaiting the results. The fate of our college would depend on it.

"Right!" I said, my mind racing forward. "Let me get myself together and I'll meet you in the room...!"

Bessie left and I grabbed my notebook and a pen. In the bathroom I splashed water on my face. Staring into the mirror, I looked suspiciously at an unkempt educational administrator with long hair, scraggly beard and uneven mustache. The administrator's eyes were bloodshot and there were deep black pockets of age in the sockets above his cheekbones. His clothes were wrinkled and worn. Desperately, I splashed more water on my face, then gargled another handful and spat it out. Buttoning my shirt and tucking it into my slacks, I took a deep breath. Quickly I headed out into the hallway toward the room where the session would be held.

❦

"THE MISTAKE IS to think of this as merely a *focus group*," Raul had told me earlier in the semester when I'd asked him for some guidance on the upcoming session. We were sitting in an air-conditioned classroom waiting for that week's professional development workshop on the *Do's* and *Don't's* of proper sexual relations with co-workers; though Raul and I were equally interested in the topic, the two of us were here for different reasons: I had come mostly for the *Don't's*, while Raul had come entirely for the *Do's*. "No, you shouldn't think of your session as just a simple focus group," he explained. "To be a successful focus group leader you need to treat this as something more. Much more. In fact, you have to look at this as an opportunity to peer into the very soul of humanity. Each human being has personal and intellectual longings that reside very deep within the confines of a conflicted temperament. To the outside world each of us projects a certain persona that is agreeable and straightforward, like the superficial gloss of an overly polished curriculum vitae; yet deep inside us is a genuine human being longing to be expressed. How else do you explain the skydiving accountants? The librarians riding motorcycles? The tenure-track mountain climbers and the long-tenured spelunkers? The business instructors who spend their summer vacations whitewater rafting and scuba diving and writing poems about bullfighting? All of them long for the expression of a deeper human self that has been suppressed and overshadowed by their reliably professional self. They long to express the latent true self over the polished projected persona that appears in their tenure dossier. The disparity between these two competing selves, I would say, is the root of educated man's deepest anxieties. It is up to the great facilitator to understand this and to harness it. An inspired focus group leader, you see, will be able to tap into that reserve of unarticulated humanity, to draw it out like prunes from a package, so as to give it expression."

"Sounds wonderful, I guess. But how do you go about doing that exactly?"

Raul paused. Then he laughed:

"Charlie! You might as well be asking me for the secret of earthly being! If only I knew that, my friend, I would be the greatest institutional researcher in the history of humanity. And I would be even more efficient with the ladies! Unfortunately, there are no easy secrets. Focus group facilitation requires years and years of experience. It requires diligent attendance at national and regional conferences. An ongoing commitment to professional development. It requires a deep spiritual connection to higher powers that can't be taught or learned. It requires inspiration and intuition and divine guidance. There are no shortcuts, I'm afraid."

"None at all?"

"Nope. But there are some basic guidelines that you should be familiar with. Here, start with this...."

Raul handed me a copy of *The Anyman's Guide to Conducting Focus Groups.*

"This should be a good resource to get you going...."

I took the book, which was very glossy and showed a picture of an active focus group session on its cover: one respondent appeared to be espousing his opinion while a tableful of deferential listeners huddled around him. The book was professionally edited and efficiently written and from it I learned that a good focus group should elicit opinions and points of view that would not otherwise be expressed – that a well-run session is like a symphony comprised of many diverse parts coming together to create a harmonious whole. And that the facilitator is the conductor who guides the musicians through the complex movements toward a final resounding conclusion; and while the conductor himself does not play a musical instrument, he is ultimately responsible for the tenor of the music that is produced.

The book went on to give tips for selecting group participants, on scheduling the session itself, and how to facilitate the discussion successfully. One chapter even classified the different types of personalities that I would be likely to encounter: the *featured soloist*, who would tend to be the most vocal participant but who, if not reined in, might end up dominating the discussion; the *lead oboe*, who could be counted on for earthy and workmanlike pronouncements (it is from the lead oboe that many of my most valuable conclusions would come); the *piccolo player*, whose light-hearted trilling served to punctuate the general discussion with good will and humor (this participant was good for maintaining healthy group dynamics); and the *triangle player*, the quiet listener in the background who might sit through the entire discussion without speaking but whose sudden contributions could also be perfectly timed and profoundly moving. Each of these types could be found in any given focus group just as they could be heard in any professional orchestra (and just as they could be seen in the great symphony of life.) At times these competing performers might try to drown each other out, yet all were vital and necessary to ensure a robust and well-rounded discussion, a full-bodied orchestral performance, and a diverse and constructively democratic society.

The key to running a good session, the book went on to say, was to never give up control. Listen boldly. Guide the discussion with confidence. Show the members of the group that you are the conductor. Never let them lose sight of your wand. Never reveal your weakness. Keep the discussion within the meter and tempo of your desired topic questions at all times.

When I told Raul what I'd read, he laughed.

"That's all true," he said. "But there's also a certain amount of sensuality in a properly conducted focus group."

"Coming from *you*, Raul, that doesn't surprise me!"

"A well-run focus group, you see, is like a romantic dinner with a beautiful woman. The conversation should be so revealing, so profound and penetrating, that it brings both to the verge of physical orgasm."

"Only to the *verge*?"

"Well, yes. Obviously, the actual orgasm can't come until the written report is *submitted*. But the dinner itself should take both sides of the table to within a single breath of the most heightened orgasmic resolution."

"That's a high standard to aspire to."

"Yet it's not impossible."

"I'll do my best," I promised.

And gathering all my remaining strength into a single moment of supremely exuded confidence, I burst through the door into the conference room where the focus group was being held.

≈

"HI, EVERYONE!" I said when I walked into the room. "Thank you all for coming! I trust you've had some snacks….? Golly, Shirley, that arugula you're sampling looks fabulous…!"

The participants had taken their assigned seats around the conference table and as I spoke they looked up at me from their paper plates.

"Wow, it's almost two o'clock. Time sure does move differently when you haven't slept in months, doesn't it? Please give me a few more minutes to set up and then we'll get started...."

Settling in at the head of the rectangular conference table, I leaned over to Bessie, who was sitting to my side and who would be taking the notes for the session.

"Are we ready to go?" I whispered.

"Yes."

"Did you pass out all the forms?"

"Yes."

"And the number-two pencils?"

"Of course!"

"After we're done, we'll go to my office for a quick debrief, okay?"

"Sure."

"All right then, let's start....!"

And here I cleared my throat, took a long drink of water from my styrofoam cup, and began my introduction to the focus group that would go so far to determine the fate of our rural educational institution, the future of our nation-building efforts, and my own personal legacy here at Cow Eye Community College.

~

"FIRST OF ALL," I said. "I want to thank you all for taking the time to be here today for this focus group. I realize it's a huge sacrifice to give up an entire afternoon like this. I also realize you could be doing other things that are far more meaningful, and so I just want you to know how much we appreciate your participation, your dedication, your patience, your candor, your tolerance, your firstborn male, your favorite lung, your time, your courage, and your personal and professional expertise accumulated over the many years that you have been on this earth. Please know that all responses will be anonymous. Bessie will be recording them in her notes and they will be included in a report that will be carefully handwritten by myself and passed on for further consideration. Do you have any questions before we begin?"

"Yes," said one of the new people. "How long will this take?"

"About four hours," I responded. "Or as long as it needs to take."

"Whichever is shorter?"

"Um, no. Whichever is *longer*."

"We were kind of hoping we might finish a bit sooner than *that*," said one of the locals at the table, "because we've got to get home to our families for a dinner consisting almost exclusively of meat."

"Right," said the new people. "And *we*'ve planned a frivolous social event involving public nudity and organically grown vegetables!"

"Well, if everything goes as planned you'll both be out of here in time. So let's jump right in, shall we?"

The two groups nodded.

"Great. Now before we get to our questions, I just want to go over some ground rules for today's session. These ground rules will help ensure that we have a productive and inspiring discussion – and that the results can be used to help our struggling community college recognize and overcome some of the issues that it's currently facing, especially those that are edging us closer and closer to the precipice of institutional ruin. By now each of you should have completed the consent and waiver form. I trust you all were able to complete this form without any problem?"

The participants nodded.

"And you made sure to fill out both sides?"

Everybody nodded again.

"Splendid! Thank you for being true professionals. And thank *you*, Bessie, for administering those forms in my absence – especially as there was no conceivable way I could have managed *that* while lying flat and semi-conscious on the shag carpet in my office!"

Bessie shrugged her shoulders.

I continued:

"Now in addition to the aforementioned consent form you also should have filled out the Demographic Questionnaire that was in your packets. Did you all have a chance to fill that out....?" And here I held up the questionnaire that Raul had designed specifically for this focus group.

"So did you all have a chance to fill this out?"

Everyone mumbled their agreement.

"Perfect. With those two things complete, I think we're ready to move purposefully into the next part of our discussion, specifically...."

I stopped. By now my hand was already sore from writing my report. Checking Bessie's notes, I made sure that I was transcribing it all correctly: the part about the consent forms, the demographic questionnaire, the section where I informed both groups that everything would be anonymous. Then I stopped to shake out my fingers which were already cramping from so much writing. Looking up from the handwritten page, I noticed that Dr. Felch had popped his head in the doorway to check on my progress.

"How's the report coming?" he said. "Almost done?"

"I'm working on it right now," I answered. "I should have it ready for you in a bit."

"Great," he said. "Make sure you let me know when it's finished. I want to go over the results as soon as they're ready. Because, as I'm sure you are well aware, the fate of our institution depends on it."

"Yes, I've heard."

Again I stretched my hand, opening and closing my fingers to soothe the muscles.

Then I grabbed my pencil and started up again:

"As you all know by now," I continued, "our college has been torn apart by a deep cultural division between rival factions on campus. This division has caused a severe rift that has not gone unnoticed by our administration, our faculty, our donors, our groundskeepers, our students, our pelicans, the flies that hover over the trash cans behind the cafeteria, our adjuncts, and – worst of all – our institutional accreditors. Each of you has been invited here today because you are associated with one of the two competing factions on campus. As such, your opinion is valuable in helping us understand the causes of this divide, the root of conflict in general, as well as the prospects for resolving such things in time for our accrediting team visit in mid-March. Any questions so far?"

"No," said the locals.

"Yes," said one of the new people. "Do you have any more arugula?"

"Of course, please help yourself to whatever's in that bowl over there."

Marsha Greenbaum immediately got up from the table and made her way over to the snack table.

"Thank you," she said.

"Don't mention it. And please help yourself to the beef jerky as well. Are there any other questions?"

"Yes, I have one…." Here I looked up to see that the unfamiliar voice belonged to the college's tenured negroid. I had never heard him speak before. The man looked puzzled and distressed. Scratching his head, he said, "I do happen to have a question about all this."

"Yes?"

"I understand that you're interested in gauging the two competing sentiments on campus. And that this will provide a diverse range of input for the report that you will be handwriting as soon as our session is over and you have concluded your debrief with Bessie. That's fine. But can you explain why *I'm* here? Personally, I don't belong to *either* faction on campus. In fact, I haven't been included in much of anything up to this point. I rarely speak. I'm forced to sit by myself at campus-wide events where I'm given barely three-fifths of a very narrow chair – or even no chair at all. And now, all of a sudden, I'm invited to this all-important focus group?"

"That's correct."

"It doesn't make any sense. Why am I being included *now*?"

"That's a good question. And an indicative one."

"Well?"

"On a personal level, I'm genuinely sorry that you've been made to feel excluded up to this point. I'm sure it's a simple oversight on the part of American historians. But I'm also certain that it will gradually improve with time. As for today's session, to be honest, you've been invited here at the very last moment to ensure that this focus group is demographically representative."

"Representative of what?"

"Of the slow shift in Cow Eye's ethnic composition."

"It's shifting?"

"Oh yes. Ever so incrementally. But ever so surely. In fact, I just heard that the store next to the makeshift bus shelter is now owned by Asian immigrants."

"You're still referring to them as *Asians*?"

"Well, yes. Though that too is tenuous…."

"So I'm a token then?"

"That's not the exact word I would use…."

"No really, what you're saying is that I'm just here to add a little diversity to your report, right? Some credibility to a discussion that might otherwise lack it? I've been invited to contribute a little color to your conversation? A little tint to your talks? A little soul toward a more soulful soliloquy?"

"Again, that's not how *I* would have expressed it. But yes, if you insist...."

"Well, fine. I can deal with that. We're used to it."

"We?"

"Yes, *we*! Tokenism is a necessary evil, I suppose. Just as integration is an evil that is far better than its alternative. But let's just be honest about it all from the outset, shall we?"

"Sure," I said. "I can live with that if you can. And thanks for the clarification." Then I said: "Anybody else have any questions?"

I glanced around the room but no hands went up.

"None? Well, okay then. So, as I was saying, the seven of you are here today to share your opinions in a safe and respectful setting. But to more clearly delineate the divisions on our campus, and to provide a sturdy physical barrier in the event that things should turn violent, the three of you representing the local faction on campus have been seated on one side of this heavy conference table, while the three of you representing the *newer* faction – from this point on let's respectfully refer to you as the *neophytes* – have been seated on the opposite side. Meanwhile, directly across from Bessie and me at the far end of this rectangular table – seated by himself because he belongs to neither faction – is our college's only tenured negroid, who, it is hoped, will represent a voice of reason and objectivity during our discussion. Please know that we will be limiting the scope of our questioning to just a few targeted issues that are of existential importance to our college. I'll be presenting a series of pinpoint questions and you'll be asked to discuss them as a group. Please be honest in your responses because this will be your final chance to express the inner longings of your soul before our mission statement is revised and our accreditors arrive for their visit in mid-March. (Remember, it is death and regional accreditation that waits for no man!) Meanwhile, I will be serving as the conductor of this great orchestra, expertly guiding the discussion from one movement to the next, but not contributing to the euphony myself – though I may ask follow-up questions of you from time to time. Any questions so far about what we'll be doing today?"

"No," said the locals.

"Not at the moment," said the neophytes. "But we'll let you know if anything does arise."

"Fantastic. So let's move to our first question, shall we...?"

"*Let's!*" they agreed.

And so I checked my notes. Then I said:

"Okay, your first question is a simple warm-up question to get us into the flow of the discussion. It is intended to create good will and a sense of ease among the seven of you. The question is non-controversial and open-ended and it goes like this....."

Hearing her cue, Bessie walked over to the tripod that held the flipchart and threw the large page over the back so the first question could be seen:

> *ICE BREAKER QUESTION: If you could visit one place in the world, where would you go? Why?*

I pointed at the flipchart.

"As you can see, our first question is innocuous, asking simply that you choose a destination of the world that you would most like to visit. Any place in the world. This could be a beautiful place you've already been to. Or it could be a place you've heard beautiful things about. The Arc de Triomphe perhaps? The Egyptian pyramids at dusk? The Hanging Gardens of Babylon, it can be presumed, are lovely this time of year. In short, for the purpose of this question, the world really is your pussycat. So don't hold back. Are there any questions about what you're being asked to do?"

"No."

"None?"

"No."

"So who wants to go first? Who can we get to break the ice that has accumulated in this room? The ice that has been advancing like glaciers during the Pleistocene and that has settled over the beautiful yet desiccated campus of our beloved Cow Eye Community College?"

"I'll go first...." said a long-time animal science instructor and acolyte of Rusty Stokes. The man was sitting on the locals' side of the table and, in Rusty's absence, had assumed the musical instrument that Rusty would have otherwise played: like a featured soloist he was already taking on the vacated role of first-chair violin. "I can answer this question," he said. "You see, I am something of a renowned world traveler, having visited every state on the American flag during my lifetime. And having experienced all forty states with my own eyes, I think I have a good frame of reference for judging the scenic beauty of the world's most exotic locales. And with this vast experience I can tell you that if there were any place in the world worthy of my visit – which is to say, if I could choose among the most beautiful destinations on this broad and beautiful earth – I would have to choose North Dakota without a doubt. And not just once, mind you, but consistently and repeatedly. If I could, you see, I would visit this most glorious state over and over and over again."

"You would repeatedly visit North Dakota?"

"Yes North Dakota, and only North Dakota. Having traveled there on separate occasions I can tell you that there is no other destination of comparable beauty. For North Dakota is surely among the most spectacular places on the face of the earth. It is arguably the grandest, the best, the most sublime travel spot on earth. *Un*arguably, it is the most spectacular state in our young and aggressively expanding country."

The man paused to allow the gravity of his words to sink in. Then he continued:

"You see, North Dakota is a virtual oasis of beauty and splendor. It is the epitome of America itself. Driving through its vast highway system you can admire the majesty of the wide-open spaces and windswept fields. The rugged simplicity of America's inner soul emanating outward like rays of hope that caress the world. The pure joy of its legendary wilderness. North Dakota, with its prairies wide and free, the fairest state from sea to sea, how I pledge myself to thee!"

The man continued in this vein for some time until, suddenly, a voice across the table interrupted him. It was the female Esperanto teacher and she seemed more than a little agitated.

"Oh please!" she said. "Are you saying that you've really traveled to all forty states of the union?"

"Yes. I've been to every single one."

"And after visiting all forty-one states of our vast continental heritage you honestly believe that the grandest of them all is *North Dakota?*"

"Of course."

"Well, clearly you know nothing of beauty. Because any idiot can see that the most stunning example of earthly beauty – the most elegant and scenic place in the world – would not be a place like North Dakota..." – here the woman made a smirking and dismissive sound – "....Despite your claims to being well-traveled, clearly, your boundaries as a connoisseur of geographic magnificence are exceedingly limited. Because it is generally accepted that the most beautiful spot on earth is not North Dakota. *Au contraire, mia amiko*! In fact it is *South* Dakota...!"

At this, the man recoiled:

"What kind of crap is this?!" he hissed. "Was that *French*...?"

Undeterred, the woman continued:

"South Dakota, you see, is home of the Badlands and Rushmore's ageless shrine, Black Hills and prairies, farmland and sunshine. Hail, South Dakota! The state we love the best! Compared to South Dakota, my English-only friend, I'm afraid your beloved North Dakota is but a large and toothless shit hole!"

"Look, you fucking cunt....!"

"*Fiaĉulo!*"

"Bitch whore!"

"Ŝovinisto!"

"Hey!" I interrupted. "Hey, both of you! Sit down! Settle down, please!"

The two had stood up from the table and were glaring across the table at each other. I continued:

"Please take your seats! Both of you!"

The two sat down, slowly and reluctantly.

"That's better! Now I know you're both passionate about this issue – and that's fine. But let's not get carried away here. I mean, I think we can all agree that both North Dakota and South Dakota are quite beautiful and praiseworthy places in their own rights. North Dakota has sweet winds and green fields, and South Dakota has health and wealth and beauty. Obviously, both of these are very rare qualities indeed. Can we just agree on this? I mean, for the purpose of our discussion today can we just agree to love both sides of the Seventh Standard Parallel?"

The two instructors muttered a grudging consent.

"In fact," I said, "if I'm not mistaken these two glorious states were once a *single* territory. But somewhere along the way some sort of conflict happened – doesn't it always?! – and somehow they got *divided*...."

"A terrible injustice of history," said the animal science instructor.

"The world's never been the same since!" lamented the Esperantist.

"...Be that as it may, I would like to suggest that we move beyond this historical and, yes, tragic, consequence of divisiveness. The quartzite border that divides them now is real and true and tangible. But it is also as arbitrary – mere cattle-scratching posts along the highway, really – as any other border contrived by man to separate two things from each other. And so I would like to suggest that we pay proper tribute to the respective beauty of both North *and* South Dakota. And that, having paid this tribute, we move on in our discussion…!"

As I related the jagged outcomes of my ice-breaker question, Will Smithcoate laughed heartily. He had bitten off the tip of a cigar and was preparing to light it under the auspices of the NO SMOKING sign. It was a late afternoon by then, and being very deep into the semester, there were only a smattering of students still in the cafeteria. In the far corner, a cluster of aspiring nurses were reviewing for late-semester exams. Scattered around the rest of the cafeteria other students simply talked or laughed or sat idly with friends whose arrows were still in mid-flight.

"Well," said Will, "it sounds like you managed to strike a nerve with those two instructors sitting on opposite sides of the table."

"You can say that again! Geez, who could have predicted that they would be so passionate about an ice-breaker question?!"

"There's some history between the two, obviously."

"Really?"

"Sure," said Bessie. "Rumor is that they had a brief affair a few years back."

"And since then they've served on various committees that have shot down each other's proposals," said Dr. Felch.

"The Esperanto teacher is pretty much a bitch all the way around," Rusty stated.

"And that arrogant animal science instructor should have been forcibly retired several decades ago," Gwen added.

Will acknowledged all of this. Then he lit his cigar and said, "Of course, it seems sort of trivial to *us*. Other people's conflicts and allegiances generally do. But it can sure be damned important to *them*!"

"I'm finding that out!"

"I mean what's the big deal, right? South Dakota. North Dakota. Bull Run. Kashmir. Jerusalem. The 38th parallel. Zonchio. Cutting my toenails at the dinner table."

"Toenails?"

"My wife really hated that! But you know what? These things all tend to work themselves out in the end. People come and go. Passions come and go. Conflicts come and go. The important thing is to keep everything in perspective, Charlie. And besides, why are they even arguing about it? Everyone knows that North Dakota is the most beautiful state...."

Back in my apartment, Bessie pulled the bed sheet over her naked hips and leaned back into a pillow that she'd propped up against my headboard. Serene and unabashed, she sat smoking a cigarette, her breasts hanging like heavy fruit over the folds of her stomach.

"Your mistake was to start the discussion with Rusty's acolyte," she said and flicked the ash from her cigarette into an old beer can on my nightstand. "I mean, why would you begin an orchestral movement with the featured violinist? Why not build up to it? Why not allow the supporting instruments to shine during the opening sonata?"

It was a Saturday afternoon and Bessie's boys were visiting their respective fathers for the weekend. The two of us had decided to use the occasion for an extended retreat, locking ourselves in my apartment with nothing but a weekend's worth of food, a week's worth of beer, and a semester's worth of pent-up desires. It was agreed that these two days would be key for us – *make-or-break* was how the secretaries in the copy room referred to it; *do-or die*, was what the groundskeepers were saying – as hopeful divorcees: the petty arguments had to stop, we'd both resolved, and perhaps a few days spent together in the throes of unbridled passion and probing discussion of our future life together would help us work through some of the differences. The getaway had been in the planning for weeks; yet by the time the weekend finally came, the focus group report was still unfinished ahead of my meeting with Dr. Felch on Monday morning. And so, in between the sex, I'd sit at my desk in my boxer shorts handwriting the report while Bessie lay stretched out on my bed, naked under the sheets, watching the color television and coaxing me through the vagaries of her handwritten notes.

"You should have started with the librarian," she chided. "Or at least with the ethics teacher. Either would have been less jarring."

"Yeah well, a person lives and learns," I said. "Obviously, it was my first high-stakes focus group and I was still very naïve. I was uninitiated. I was still idealistic about the two rival factions on campus. How they work. How they oppose. How they defer and deflect and collude. I used to think, just get the two groups in the same room to talk through their differences: that's all they need. Yeah, right! My naiveté seems pretty funny to me now!"

Bessie's knees were splayed wide under the thin bed sheet. And as she smoked she would open and close her knees absentmindedly, erecting and collapsing a pitched tent over the verdant valley in between.

"So do you think the ethics teacher is cute?" she said as she blew out a mouthful of smoke.

Surprised, I looked up from my report. Bessie had thrown her knees wide apart, stretching the bed sheet taut between them.

"You mean the girl from the focus group? The one on the receiving end of the world religions instructor in the store room?"

"Yeah. She's young and vivacious. I could see how men might like her. Do *you*?"

"She's attractive, yes."

"Very attractive?"

"Yes. I would say so. But not nearly as attractive as the math teacher in the t-shirt!"

At this Bessie snapped her legs shut. Then she said:

"How about the new secretary in the economics department? The one whose petition you signed?"

"She's attractive."

"And the adjunct in Business?"

"Yes."

"And the sociology professor?"

"Yes."

"And what about Marsha?" she asked. "Do you think Marsha Greenbaum has a certain air of sexuality about her? Do you find her irresistible in an esoteric, meatless sort of way?"

"Definitely not!" I said. "Although, on second thought, there's nothing a little wine and a diaphanous sarong can't cure...!"

"But I imagine the scabies are something of a turn-off, no?"

"You could say that. But more so is her refusal to acknowledge the temporality of time...." Increasingly exasperated, I looked down at the blank page on my desk. "Look, Bessie, this discussion we're having is fitting and all. But I've really got to get back to my report! This thing's due Monday morning and it's already Saturday afternoon!"

"It's not even two o'clock, Charlie. You've still got most of today and all of tomorrow. We won't be having too many more chances like this, you know. After this weekend, it's highly unlikely that we'll be able to spend this sort of uninterrupted time together. So why can't we just enjoy the moment? Why don't we try a little harder to enjoy Plan A while we still can?"

Slowly, Bessie spread her knees apart under the sheets.

"I wouldn't mind, Bess. But I've already enjoyed quite a few moments with you so far this morning. And what I really need right now is to get back to my report. The fate of our college depends on it, you know....?"

Bessie grunted and snapped her legs together, the tent collapsing entirely between her knees; then she rolled over onto her side to stare blankly at the game show on the television. From my desk I could see the supple contour of her exposed back, the spine curving from the base of her neck and disappearing into the sheets around her hips.

"Let me just get through this next part," I pleaded, "and I'll be back with you in a moment....."

Bessie grunted at the television without looking back at me.

"It'll just be a few more minutes..." I promised.

And with that I moved on in the discussion:

"Okay," I said. "Thank you for your answers – they've been duly recorded. It is interesting to note that exactly three of you, if given the chance to visit any place in the world, would choose North Dakota – while the other three across the table, if given the very same chance, would venture in a different direction entirely. Which is to say, each of *you* would travel all the way to *South* Dakota...."

In my report I drew the following table:

World Locale	# Respondents	%
North Dakota	3	42.9%
South Dakota	3	42.9%
Montana	1	14.3%
TOTAL	**7**	**101.1%**

Then I continued:

"....So now that we've broken the ice with that first question, let's continue the relentless forward movement of our discussion by asking the next question that we need to consider...."

Bessie flipped over the large paper on the flipchart to reveal the next page:

> *QUESTION: Please discuss the current cultural divide on campus. What can be done to improve the climate at Cow Eye in time for our accreditation visit in March?*

"Now this question is really important. As you know, our accreditors are coming next semester and they will be observing the workings of our campus. We have made claims that our climate here at Cow Eye is....what was the word we used, Bessie....?"

"Bucolic."

"Right. Bucolic. We've claimed that our campus is bucolic; however, we all know that this is far from the truth. In fact, there are deep cultural divisions on campus that jeopardize the idyllic serenity of our rural college. Entire standing committees have disbanded. Legal teams have been assembled. Lawsuits have been settled out of court. Several promising faculty have even thrown up their hands and left Cow Eye altogether. Since the beginning of the semester more than one hundred and thirty bloated scrotums have been left in faculty mailboxes like so many routine notices for professional development opportunities. It's all very distressing and counter-productive – not to mention, somewhat disorienting for the *calves*. And surely it is not an entirely propitious state of affairs for an institution like ours that is desperately seeking reaffirmation of its accreditation. In short, we need to resolve this issue. And fast. So now the question for you to consider is this: what can be done to improve the cultural chasm on campus?"

I looked around the table slowly, trying to make eye contact with someone. But no one would oblige.

"It's okay," I coaxed. "Remember, anything that you say today will be *confidential*."

Still nobody spoke up.

"Please?" I pleaded.

Nothing.

"Will you speak up for the sake of our campus?"

Again nothing.

"For our community?"

Nothing.

"For the *students*? Hey, everything we do is ultimately for our students' success, right!"

Again no answer.

"Well, maybe you don't have solutions just quite yet. Maybe that's asking too much at this point. But can we at least talk about the problem itself? Can we at least discuss, openly and candidly, the source of our great cultural divide? Can we begin to name the problem, if not its cause?"

Again nothing.

"Please?!" I pleaded.

Yet again no answer.

In the silent room, the drone of the air condition was all that could be heard. And in that silent drone I waited helplessly for an answer that would not come.

Finally, it was Will Smithcoate who broke the wordless silence.

"What you *should* have done," Will was saying over his cigar, "is ask the man at the far end of the table to begin the discussion. That would have gotten the ball rolling!"

"The negroid?"

"Absolutely! You should have asked him to share his experiences at Cow Eye. He's not affiliated with either group. And despite his reticence, he's got a wealth of experience and perspective to share. He has a compelling story to tell, you know, if only someone would bother to listen. If only you would just give him a chance to express it."

And so, desperate to begin the discussion, and increasingly exhausted from lack of sleep, I did just that:

"How about *you*, Professor?" I asked and pointed my trembling conductor's wand to the man at the far end of the table across from me. "Would you care to be the first to answer this question that I've just posed?"

"Me?"

"Yes. Would you be willing to shed some light on the current cultural climate on campus? Could you tell us what it's been like for you? And how *you* have been able to navigate the sad state of affairs among our divided faculty?"

The man looked across the long table at Bessie and me. Cautiously, he looked over to his left at the locals occupying their side of the table, then to his right at the side of the table where the neophytes were sitting.

"You'd like me to share my experiences at Cow Eye?"

"Yes, if you could."

"You mean as the college's only tenured negroid?"

"Exactly. Because I've heard that yours is a viewpoint worth listening to. And you do certainly have a unique point of reference, sitting right there, as you are, between the two groups to your left and right. So maybe you can help us get this difficult discussion started? Please?"

"It's complicated. But, okay. I can do try to do that. I mean, I do appreciate the opportunity to express myself after the passage of so much time. It's not every day I'm afforded a platform like this. So I guess I should say a few things on the topic...."

The man paused to gather his thoughts. Then he began to answer my question about his experiences at Cow Eye and how we might go about improving the cultural climate at our struggling community college.

≈

"YOU SEE," HE said, "when I first came to Cow Eye it wasn't exactly of my own volition: in fact, *circumstances* conspired to bring me here. I mean, what are the chances of someone like me, with a background like mine, ending up so far away from my home in a remote place like Cow Eye Junction? Out of all the places in the world I could have ended up?! Of all the world's locales? Cow Eye! Are you kidding me?! No, it definitely wasn't something I would have chosen for myself. In truth, my journey here was arbitrary and perilous taking me from my birthplace in Washington State all the way across the rivers and valleys of our vast country to the barren desiccation of Cow Eye Junction. It was a bumpy ride, believe me, first in the back of a covered wagon, then in the confined quarters of a freight train, and then finally in a reeking bus that delivered me across the empty fields and past the decaying buffalo corpses and the abandoned ghost towns along the mining faults of the old prairies. Along the way I witnessed a five-year-old girl walking past one public school after another, an octoroon in handcuffs, a woman with an umbrella trudging home from work in the rain. No, there was nothing about my trek from the place of my origin to the hallowed grounds of Cow Eye – from oral history and slave narratives to my master's dissertation in African-American Studies – that came easily. But I was one of the few who lived to tell the tale – the fifty percent of the fifty percent, you might call me; or rather, the one percent of the one percent! – and at the end of such a long and perilous journey through our treacherous system of public education – and after receiving my PhD from an accredited four-year university – I arrived at the makeshift bus shelter on the edge of town."

"Just like the rest of us arrived into that same bus shelter!"

"Right. Except that you can bet my back hurt quite a bit more from the journey."

(At this, a few people at the table – for the first time – seemed to nod ever so slightly in agreement.)

"Let me guess," I said. "After arriving at the makeshift bus shelter, you sat and waited for your slow ride to campus? You were told, just like the rest of us were once told, to wait at the shelter for someone to pick you up? And after a suitable stay next to the old railroad track and the busted telephone booth and the flyer for an upcoming ragtime concert, Dr. Felch picked you up....in his truck?"

"No, he didn't."

"He didn't?"

"No. But that's okay. I'm used to it. *We're* used to it. Nobody picked me up that day. And so from the very back row of the bus I made my way out into the glare of early August, and from there I left the comfort of the makeshift bus shelter and walked past the general store where the harmonica was still playing, out onto the highway and through the town of Cow Eye Junction – past rolling fields of cotton and tobacco, past the Cow Eye Ranch in its heyday, past the cows and the horses and the painted slogans, past the museum and the jail and the post office with its flag at full mast – all thirteen stripes and twenty-eight stars drooping lifelessly in the dead air like a body bound to a tree – and eventually I crossed yet another waterless canal and stepped over the railroad tracks along the dirt road that led to the main entrance of the college. It was dusty and hot and by the time I finally got to that moment in time and space I was thirsty and tired and weak. I was emaciated. And so, fighting back my travails, I came to the very edge of the campus. And what do you think I saw as I approached the gate that would lead me into the campus itself? What do you think I saw first as I made my way toward the entrance to this new world that would be my future for generations to come?"

"You saw the sign welcoming you to Cow Eye Community College! The wooden sign reminding us that our rural college is the place...*where minds meet*!"

"Well, yes. I may have seen that on my way. But no – in truth, the first thing I encountered as I came to the college was the heavy wooden arm barring my entrance. And then, next to the arm: Timmy. He was stepping out of his guard shack to confront me."

"Timmy confronted you?"

"Yes. Back then I didn't know his name. And he certainly didn't know *mine*. So I smiled to him and I said, 'Hi there, sir.' But he just held up his hand and said, 'Do you need something?' Apologetically, I told him that I was here to teach classes at the college, that I had been hired sight unseen after a single phone interview, that my resume was spotless, that I was in fact the new tenure-track instructor in African-American studies and that I was here to enter the campus in the same way that my tenured brethren had been entering the public discourse for so many years before me. 'You don't *look* like tenure-track faculty....' he said to me. (It was not the first time I'd had to deal with this sort of thing.) But I just swallowed the affront. And when I showed him my course schedule and a recent picture ID, he became convinced of my intentions and raised the wooden arm to let me in...."

"So you entered Cow Eye Community College on foot then?"

"Right. And as I made my way down the long esplanade leading to the faculty housing complex, I passed an escort of police holding back the jeering crowds. On one side of the esplanade was a row of national guardsmen with bayonets and truncheons, and on the other side was a line of federal troops and demonstrators wielding placards and banners and chanting slogans in my direction. It was a different era back then, you see, and back then everyone still naively believed that *separate* really could be equal. That all-out war was an appropriate answer to most things. Back then the world was pure and innocent and it still seemed that vacuum cleaners really did mean progress, that enlightened self-interest could be enlightened, and that nuclear power truly would be the wave of the future. And yet, here they were, all these students and faculty alike, protesting the war that was still ongoing, reviling the proposed nuclear power plant to be erected near the Cow Eye River where the Indian Village used to be...."

The man stopped.

"I'm sorry...." he said, apologetically. "Am I dominating the discussion?"

"Oh, no," I said. "That would be highly ironic. Please continue. Actually, you've rescued my entire focus group! Besides, it's only a little after two. And, like I said earlier, we'll be here as long as we need to be...."

The man looked around the table at his peers – they just shrugged their shoulders in resignation – and then continued:

"Right. So the college back then was very different from what it is now. Back then, you see, there weren't so many Dimwiddle projects. The campus was small and economically susceptible. There was no swimming pool. There were no pelicans. The war, it was hoped, would change all that. And the proposed nuclear reactor would bring more power to our campus than we could ever hope to harness otherwise. Despite the risks – and what risks could there be, really? – nuclear power, we were learning, truly *was* the wave of the future. It was cheap. Safe. And, of course, highly *efficient*! Yet on one side of the esplanade stood those who favored the war and the power plant, while on the other side were those who did not. Just like your seating arrangement today, Charlie, the two opposing sentiments stood on opposite sides of the narrow walkway: the locals on one side and the neophytes on the other. And there I was walking down the middle with my suitcase in one hand and an armful of textbooks pressed firmly against my chest."

"And how did you manage? How did you fit in with the two factions on either side of the esplanade?"

"I didn't fit in at all! Being a neophyte among neophytes, I just walked the gauntlet to my apartment where I unpacked my things and prepared my notes for the next week's classes. That first afternoon in my apartment in faculty housing, I looked out onto the campus to see throngs of marchers heading in opposite directions: one group peacefully filing along the sidewalks in silent protest; the other moving loudly and ominously. One was staging a sit-in with music and poetry; the other was burning cars and smashing the windows of the administration building. One group favored states' rights and nuclear proliferation and the latest war of attrition; the other advocated bitterly against those very things. That night I barely slept amid the chaos: the sounds of gunfire and sirens, the acrid smell of smoke from burning tires, the clicking of boots on cobblestone as the campus police hunted the stragglers, and then, a few minutes later, the screams of demonstrators being dragged from one part of campus to another. It was a restless few nights, to say the least. And so, to answer your question, *that* was my first experience here. Needless to say, my introduction to the peculiar institution that is Cow Eye Community College was one of conflict and opposition. It was the pungent smells of revolution and reactionism. The gore of that most ancient battlefield where tradition clashes with innovation. Where compliance meets recalcitrance. All of this was my story of Cow Eye then. And it is the story of Cow Eye *now*...."

The tenured professor seemed to be choking up as he spoke and I looked compassionately at him to encourage his words:

"But that was in the beginning when you just got here," I said. "Haven't things changed for you since then?"

"Not really."

"Even after manumission?"

"Yes, even after manumission."

"Even after you received *tenure*?"

"Even after tenure ...."

And here the man grew wistful.

"...But you know what really hurts?"

We shook our heads.

"What really hurts is that I've devoted my entire life to teaching. I've given up my own dreams so that I might live vicariously through the dreams of my students. I've severed any roots that might have connected me to my own place of origin just so I could be an educator here at Cow Eye Community College. And after all this sacrifice – after all that sweat and effort over the years – do you know how I'm referred to around campus? Do you know how my colleagues – my very own colleagues! – refer to me?"

"No...."

"To them I am not a dedicated academician. A scholar. A man. Or even a simple human being. Do you know what they all call me?"

"I could venture a guess...."

"To my peers I am nothing more than...*a tenured negroid*!"

A collective gasp went up around the table.

The man shook his head:

"Do you know how hurtful that is? Do you know how that makes me feel to hear that? To be known as *that*, and nothing more than that? To be a niche in somebody's market segment? To be a requirement for someone's demographic validity? To be a token banjo amid the great symphony of life?"

Here I felt a twinge of guilt.

"Well, speaking on behalf of the group," I said, "I would like to apologize to you for that. I can see how we might very well have been overly set in our ways. Will you accept a collective apology from us all?"

"Yes," said the man. "If it's sincere."

I looked around the room.

"Are we sincere, gang?" I asked.

The group nodded.

"So will you accept our collective apology?"

"Yes."

"Splendid," I said. "I am relieved."

I had started to move on, but here the sociology instructor raised her hand for the first time.

"So, Professor," she asked, "what *do* you want to be called then? If you could have your druthers, that is? If you could choose your own term of reference to separate you from the rest of us, what would you prefer to be called?"

The instructor paused, as if considering this for the first time.

"Well, clearly, the word *negroid* has to be put to pasture. Its usefulness has long since come and gone – like the old pull tabs from those beer cans we used to rip off and discard. Or like the older generation itself with its ways of speaking and seeing the world, its outdated vernacular, its quaint sub-culture, and the fading institutions that it holds dear."

"So what then?"

"I'm not sure."

"There has to be something...."

"I'm sure there is."

"Could we just call you *colored*?"

"....*colored*?"

"Yes, Professor. Like a book of line drawings that have been lovingly filled in by a toddler at our early childhood center. Would it be appropriate to refer to you as *colored* from this point forward?"

"It will take some getting used to...."

"Please do your best."

"I'll try," he said.

"Great," I said.

I thanked the man and we moved on.

❧

LISTENING TO THE colored man speak about his challenges finding his place amid the deep divisions at Cow Eye, I'd noticed that several other participants seemed to be nodding their heads in agreement. And sensing my opportunity to build upon the man's courageous opening, I looked at the other participants around the table and then addressed one of them in particular:

"Did *you* have a similar experience with divisiveness at Cow Eye?" I pointed to a man sitting on the neophyte's side of the table. "I ask because you seemed to be nodding in agreement while the colored man shared his story...."

"Yes," said the recently hired eugenics professor. "In fact I did have a very similar experience. Except that I'm a pure-blooded caucasoid, which, of course, is not insignificant. It is an important distinction, obviously – especially here at Cow Eye. But does it mean that I can't share common experiences with a colored person? Should it mean that we cannot suffer the same hopes and fears? The same dreams unfulfilled? No! Just because I am an able-bodied well-educated upper-middle-class right-handed heterosexual protestant male caucasoid with a clear path to tenure, it doesn't mean that I can't experience the same worldly oppressions and personal anguish as anyone else."

"Doesn't it?"

"Of course not. And I have. I am as much a victim of our turbulent times as anyone else. Though for me, these struggles have been at the institutional level."

Around the table the man's peers were listening empathetically to his words. He continued:

"You see, I was hired to develop and expand the eugenics program on campus, to infuse elements of this promising scientific theory across the various academic disciplines. To work collaboratively with my peers for the long-term betterment of our students. It is a noble goal, of course. Yet I am having the damnedest time gaining any traction. Sadly, with the exception of the animal sciences and a few isolated individuals in the automotive department, I have encountered virtually no willingness among faculty to incorporate eugenics into their curriculum."

"Why do you think that is?" I asked.

"I don't know. They just don't seem to *get* it. It's like they're just so willing to sacrifice cultural progress on the altar of long-held tradition...!"

"I know the feeling!" said the Esperanto teacher. "Believe me, I know exactly what you mean!"

"You do?"

"Absolutely. In fact, I'm having the exact same problem. Except that my academic discipline is not strictly scientific like yours, but leans more toward the humanities. If water is the language of life – as it surely is – then I would argue that acquired languages are just as surely its pasteurized milk. Just imagine how great it would be for everyone at Cow Eye to drink milk! To speak a common language! To have a universal tongue that could be used to facilitate mutual understanding during our discussions. Especially since English doesn't seem to be working out for us in that regard. So it's time to try something more effective, right? Why not a second language that we can all agree on? Why not a language that lends itself to efficient communication? Well, that's my mission in life! Unfortunately, the stonewalling from my peers has been unsettling...."

And here, and at great length, the woman spoke about the challenges she'd faced implementing her Esperanto classes on campus. Fighting back tears, she related how she had met resistance at every step of the way: the reactionary curriculum committee; a divided administration; indifferent students; a science department that did not understand the importance of the softer disciplines; monolingual English faculty who were ruthlessly territorial and undermining and who seemed to feel that a universally spoken language would somehow threaten English's de facto hegemony in that role – and, by extension, their own claims to long-held intellectual territory.

"It's like they don't understand the importance of what I'm trying to do!" she sobbed. "It's as if they have no appreciation for the thing I've devoted my entire life to...!"

Here the homosexual from the art department placed his hand on the woman's shoulder empathetically. "It's okay," he said. "You're not the only one who hurts....!"

And here the man spoke about his own struggles as a homosexual in Cow Eye Junction. How he and a fellow artist had been accosted outside the Champs d'Elysees Bar and Grill after a jazz concert one night. And how their once-secret relationship had been revealed by an ill-timed janitress searching for her broom in a storage closet. And how even the most basic funding for art education was becoming increasingly hard to find. How art instruction itself was being phased out of the public schools in favor of more functionally relevant subjects. And how, despite all this, he and his lover still dreamed of a church wedding some day.

"We'd rather be Catholics," he explained.

I nodded.

Bessie scribbled on her note pad.

The tide, it seemed, had turned as the participants, one after another, now shared their burdens. Softly, the music teacher spoke about the atonality of her life in Cow Eye Junction. The world religions instructor lamented the polytheism of campus politics. The anarchist in the philosophy department railed against the Dimwiddles with their unconscionable profiteering and self-serving commercialization of honest violence. The economics professor – the one whose recently published article advocating a graduated income tax had gone largely ignored – spoke about the pitfalls of grade inflation and how it was undermining the work ethic of his students. The mesmerizing creative writing instructor, meanwhile, criticized the incestuous publishing industry and its proliferation of genetically homozygous literature. The ethics teacher warned against the erosion of personal privacy. The cross-dressing horticulturalist spoke to great effect about the difficulties of finding his dress size in the shops of Cow Eye Junction. And the philosophy instructor – who by now had received a record number of bloated scrotums – bemoaned the short-sightedness of the latest Supreme Court decision. And through it all, Alan Long River, the college's longtime public speaking instructor, sat quiet and dignified, his concert triangle dangling from his wrist, at the table next to the animal science instructor with the squeaky violin.

At long last, the large glacier was beginning to melt, a flood of cold water pouring out of the participants' souls and spilling onto the tile floor of the conference room where their musical instruments had once been left in waiting. The culinary instructor. The art historian. The Associate Dean of Instruction. The lecturer in developmental English. The ESL coordinator. Rolling up their pant legs and cradling their instruments like musicians on a sinking luxury liner, all seven stoically articulated the deep divisions on campus that made life at the college in general – and life as a professional educator at Cow Eye Community College, in particular – so difficult. So untenable. So desiccated.

"Great," I said. "At last it's starting to come out!"

The sound of restrained sobbing could be heard around the room. The catharsis had begun. The opening sonata was complete.

"So what do we do about it?" I asked now that the participants had begun the discussion of our cultural chasm on campus. "You've spoken of the problems. The divisions. The divisiveness. The cacophony. The dysfunctional committees. The atonality. The bloated scrotums. The Supreme Court decisions. You've articulated it all so eloquently. So now that it's clear we have a real problem, how can we begin to change it? Or can we?"

Looking around the table, I let the words sink in:

"What is the answer to our great cultural divide?" I repeated. "Or *is* there one?"

❧

"GOOD QUESTION!" SAID Raul. "That's exactly the question our accreditors want us to answer! And don't worry at all that it took a little discomfort to get the discussion going. That's to be expected. Remember, at best these are virtual strangers in that room together. At worst they are mortal enemies. The air-conditioning is chilling. The conference table is rectangular with sharp edges. The temperature-controlled ambience is artificial and contrived. And of course you haven't slept for months and that crazed look in your eyes doesn't exactly encourage forthcoming discussion. It's only natural that there would be some hesitation among participants."

"Thanks, Raul. That's reassuring to hear."

"Take it from me, Charlie. You've done about as well as you could under the circumstances. If anything, the problem that you should be worrying about now is the locals at the table. Since the opening statement by Rusty's acolyte, they've been relatively quiet. They seem to be brooding. And that's a real concern. Remember, Dr. Felch told you not to take them for granted. They've grown accustomed to being overlooked. So you'd better go back for them. Otherwise, you're not going to get at the root of the conflict. Your discussion will only touch upon one side of the esplanade. And that would be a shame. Especially since you've worked so hard to get them both in the same room!"

"You're right," I agreed. "But how do I do that?"

Suddenly, I felt a cold hand on my naked stomach. Bessie had snuck up from behind and thrown her arms around me in a heavy hug. From my chair I could smell the shampoo from her shower and feel the skin of her breasts pressed up against me, her chin on my shoulder, and her unpinned hair hanging down across my chest. She was kissing me on the back of my neck and rubbing her cheek against mine from behind.

"Ready for a break?" she cooed and slid her hand into my boxers.

"Not yet!" I said. "I'm still writing...!"

Bessie pressed tighter.

"You said you'd be ready a 'few minutes ago'...*a few minutes ago*. And by now it's been a lot more than that. Look, it's already well after two. Take a break, will you?!"

I kissed her lightly on the cheek.

"I can't at the moment. I'd love to but I just can't. I have to include the locals' perspective in my report. I have to write that down before I take them for granted by carelessly moving on."

Bessie moved her hand along the inside of my thigh.

"Life is short...." she said.

"Stop!" I protested.

But she did not stop. Still rubbing against me from behind, she whispered into my ear.

"It's time, Charlie."

"Time for what?"

"I told them both...."

"Told them *what*?"

"About you."

"Who?"

"My boys. I told them about you and me. About us. About *you*. I told them you might come over to visit. So they're expecting it..."

"Great," I said.

"I've told them a lot about you."

"Fine."

"The time is right, Charlie. They're ready to meet the man I'm hopelessly in love with."

"Will do. But not in the immediate future, obviously...."

"Not this weekend of course. How about you come over sometime next week?"

"That may work. Though now that I think of it I have a lot to do this week."

"Or the week after?"

"Yeah, we'll do that for sure. But look, right now I can't think about things like that. Right now I just want to finish this part of my report before I forget. It'll only take a few more minutes. Just let me finish and then I'll be as receptive as you are...!"

Bessie withdrew her hand from my boxers and threw herself back onto the bed, the springs groaning and her legs bouncing wide open as she fell.

"You and that damned report!" she muttered. Bessie did not bother to cover herself, and as she lay there on the bed the indecency of her pose grew with each accumulating moment. "To hell with that report already! Lives are being *lived* while you're writing that stupid report. Just think how many amazing things are happening in the tangible world while you're stuck at that desk! How much fun other people are having while you're sitting here with that pen and paper...!"

"I'm sure they're all having a great time. And good for them. But the fate of our college hinges on what I end up writing in this report. So it is kind of important...."

"Yeah, whatever. You educational administrators are all the same."

"Say what you will," I countered. "But your jobs depend on people like us. Your destinies derive from us. The fate of our world itself depends on its educational administrators!"

Bessie rolled her eyes.

I laughed and started to turn away. But then, skimming over her sprawling nudity, I shook my finger:

"...And cover up, will you! I can't get any work done with you all laid bare like that....!"

With thumb and forefinger Bessie grabbed the very corner of the bed sheet and tugged it just enough to cover the tip of her navel.

"Better?" she said.

"Infinitely. That part of your nakedness was really distracting me. Now let me get back to work, okay....!"

Raul laughed and checked the time on his calculator wristwatch: there were still a few minutes left before we had to go back inside.

"Yeah, there's definitely something to be said about avoiding relations with co-workers!" he admitted. Raul and I were on a five-minute break in the middle of this week's professional development session and the two of us were milling around with the group outside the room. The female presenter had spent the first half of her session on the *don't's* of intra-collegiate romance: the jealousy, the rumors, the inability to separate private time from work time as everything bleeds together like a grand piano whose sostenuto pedal won't release; and, of course, how once relations have gone horribly wrong, the entire mess will tend to spill over into the workplace like raw sewage leaking into a river, or into a swimming pool, or into the concert hall where your symphony is being performed. Hearing all this, Raul seemed to grow pensive: "It sort of makes you think twice about having a liaison with a colleague, doesn't it?"

"I suppose it does. But it's too late to think about that now. And besides, what sort of options do we have, Raul? It's not like we can just go to the local bars looking for women. It's not like the remoteness and desiccation of the surrounding area exactly encourage a burgeoning social scene for educational administrators and institutional researchers. And it's not like I can just tell her, Hey, Bess, you know, I think we've made a mistake....I think this thing really isn't working out for either of us...."

"That's true. But there has to be some sort of compromise. There has to be a way to reconcile the two. There has to be some way that we can...."

Suddenly a gunshot rang out in the room. Instinctively I ducked into a crouch from the noise.

When I looked up my ears were still ringing from the blast.

"What the hell was *that*?!" I exclaimed.

"That," said Ethel proudly, "was a Ruger Blackhawk in thirty carbine."

I massaged the lobes of my ears.

"Is it always so loud?"

"Pretty much." Ethel was caressing the shiny revolver with both hands. "Come on now, Charlie, be alert! Don't act like you didn't know that was coming. Lately your mind seems to be wandering off. But this is no place for that. You have to stay focused on what you're doing. This is a shooting range, not a library. These bullets we're firing are *real*, unlike those in your self-study. The consequences of this reality can be tragic. And for godsakes, boy, put on your ear protection!"

Still shocked, I put the plugs into my ears and then pulled the sound-resistant muffs over them as a double buffer. Then I grabbed my own gun from where it had been sitting on the bench, and taking my stance just as she'd shown me, I aimed my pistol at the target. The firing lanes were long and at the far end of mine I could just make out the distant target that had been selected for me: a silhouette of an accreditor holding a clipboard with the visiting team's response to our most recent self-study report. The target was just close enough that I could still imagine the seething commentary with its high-handed tone and terse pronouncements and general insistence on using the Latin plural for *scrotum*. In my delirium the stationary silhouette seemed to be closing in, advancing on me with a deep and insidious menace. Grasping the pistol tightly, I cocked back the hammer and stared into the distance at the approaching specter of regional accreditation. At the onrushing shadow of childless irrelevance and a life of dull professionalism. Of resume-building. Of unchallenged innovation and efficiency for its own sake. Of a world where conflict really is paramount and vacuum cleaners still mean progress and where the comforts of taxidermy really are more valued than the unvanquished screams of a mother cow who has been separated from her three-month-old calf. Exhausted and confused, I looked at all of this and saw none of it. Or, rather, I looked for any of it, and saw it all.

Slowly, I began to squeeze the trigger.

BESSIE HAD STOOD up to flip over the large paper on the tripod, when I motioned for her to stop.

"Just a second, Bess...."

Bessie looked back at me in surprise.

"Sorry," I said to the group. "But before we go any further, I'd like to ask our animal science instructor here a question. You see, we've heard a lot from the neophytes at this table, but not so much from the other side. So can you tell me, as a local person yourself, what *your* experience has been? To complement what we've already heard from the people who are from the countless other places in this world that are *not* Cow Eye

Junction. They have been vocal and eager to share, as always. But what's *your* perspective on the matter?"

"You're asking me to talk about the cultural divide between locals and neophytes?" said the animal science instructor.

"Yes," I said. "What has your experience been during your career here at Cow Eye? As someone who was born and raised in the area, what is your take on the long-standing conflict that has come to paralyze our campus?"

"There's a conflict?"

At this the locals laughed out loud.

"Well, yes...." I said.

The instructor looked at his peers sitting on the nearer side of the table, then at the neophytes sitting across from him. Then he shook his head.

"I have nothing to say on this matter."

"Why is that?"

"I just don't."

"But how can that be? I'm offering you a chance to express your side of the table...."

"No comment."

"None?"

"No."

"Nothing at all?"

"Nope."

"But why?" I asked Rusty at the museum. "Why won't any of the locals tell me their opinion in a formal setting? I hear them expressing it all the time when nobody's taking notes. And boy do they ever! At the neighboring tables in the cafeteria. Or among the secretaries in the copy room. I know it's out there. So why are they so reluctant to express their side of the story in the safe and temperature-controlled setting of our focus group?"

Rusty was sorting through some old photos that had been dropped off by a family that was leaving Cow Eye forever. The family had wanted their legacy to remain in good hands so they'd donated it to the museum; as he spoke Rusty looked wistfully at the photographs, thumbing through them one by one, seemingly more interested in the soft tones of sepia than in the outcomes of my focus group.

"They don't trust you, Charlie."

"Don't trust me?"

Rusty set down the stack of photographs on a glass display case: at the top was a grainy profile of a severe-looking man on horseback and with a coiled rope dangling over his knees. Rusty wiped a piece of dust off the print. Then he said, "You can't be completely trusted, Charlie. Sure, your grandparents were from here originally. But they moved away, didn't they? And yes you came to our barbecue and ate the meat that we offered you. Yes you drank quite a bit of our beer. You listened to our stories of bygone days. You shared a moment with us, I suppose. All of this is true. Yet among the locals you're still known as the only attendee who came *late*. You're the only one who missed our poignant remembrance for Merna."

"It figures," I said.

"What's that?"

"Well, Gwen told me the same thing about the neophytes. She explained that I was known among those attendees as the one who came to their watery get-together only to leave *early*. That I'm known as the only one who left prematurely before experiencing any sort of orgasm. In other words, my plan completely backfired. I came too late to join one side of the cultural chasm then left too early from the other to be included there as well. I tried to make it to both places, but in reality I guess I really went to neither. I can't win."

"Exactly. Plans can be helpful. But sometimes it helps to be a thing entirely. Sincerely. To do what's right – not just what makes sense. To commit to one thing at the expense of another. To favor either the manual typewriter or the electric one – rather than both of them at the same time. Building bridges is great, but so is standing on the firm ground of one side or the other. This is the challenge you're facing, Charlie. And I don't envy you. Although, I must say, you're still the best person to conduct this high-stakes focus group. Because, even though you arrived at the river later than you should have, you *did* come to our barbecue."

"Right," said Gwen. "And even though you left the yoga studio earlier than was socially acceptable – and without your pants, if I remember correctly – you *did* take the time to come to our watery get-together in the first place."

"But that still doesn't explain why the locals don't want to share their side of the story...."

"We already have!" said Rusty. "It's just that nobody's been listening. We tell it all the time, in fact. It's in our traditions. It's in our predispositions.

It's in the words we choose and the voice we use to articulate it. But no one takes the time to hear us. Meanwhile, do you know how many times we've been *surveyed*? How many goddamn *focus groups* we've had to sit through? Do you know how many times educated people have tried to come up with a better way to understand us? As if we were specimens in a zoo? Charlie, do you have any idea how often they've tried to have us mounted and stuffed? But why does it always have to be like this? Why can't they just listen? Why can't they just listen to the words we're speaking while we're still around to speak them...?"

"Well, I imagine it's hard, you know. From the other side of the table you locals just seem set in your ways. Anti-progress. Reactionary. It just seems like you don't want change because it's not *your* kind of change."

"Look," said Rusty, "when all these new people first started coming to Cow Eye we went out of our way to be hospitable. We welcomed them into our homes and offered them everything we had. We gave them meat. We took them to watch football games at the local high school on Friday nights. We invited them to accept Jesus Christ as our Ultimate Redeemer. In short, we treated them as we ourselves would have liked to be treated. And do you know what their reaction to all this was? Do you know what they did to us in return?"

"I can only imagine...."

"They spat it all back into our face! Tripe?! To hell with your tripe! Cattle? To hell with your cattle! Trucks? To hell with your damn trucks – you should all drive fuel-efficient cars instead. And why have a barbecue when you can make fondue? Why hunt local game when you can watch far-flung celebrities on television? Why be religious when you can be spiritual instead? Honestly, these people could care less about whether we even exist or not. All they care about are their parties and their orgasms and their arugula. We are nothing but an annoyance. A nuisance. A mere inconvenience to be remembered from time to time as necessity dictates. Charlie, all we are to those people is *ambience*...."

For the first time since we'd met up, Gwen stopped her brisk walk along the path toward the cafeteria. By now we'd passed more than half the campus and were standing outside the faculty laundromat. From the outset of our ambulatory discussion I'd been struggling to keep up with her along the way, which made her sudden stop even more startling. Gwen seemed furious at what she'd just heard.

"So he says they were *hospitable*? That they welcomed us with open arms? Are you kidding me? Football? Meat? Trucks? That's all fine and good. But ask him about the last Christmas Committee meeting I attended. Ask him about that meeting, Charlie…!"

"What meeting?"

"The last time he and I were on the Christmas Committee together."

"You two were on the Christmas Committee? At the same time?!"

"Of course," said Rusty. Now he had moved on from his archives and was standing next to the mounted heifer and stroking its withers as if it were alive. "My god, she's still bitter about that?"

"I guess so," I said. "She suggested that I ask you about it."

"Well, that's how she is. But she needs to get over it. She needs to move on."

"Move on from what?"

"From what happened."

"What happened?"

"Nothing happened."

"Nothing?!" said Gwen.

"Yes," said Rusty. "Nothing happened."

"That's bullshit!" said Gwen.

"She's full of shit herself!" said Rusty.

I stopped. At last it seemed that I was getting to the heart of something important. And so, I looked at both of them.

"Well, can you tell me the story then?" I asked. "Can you tell me the story of how nothing happened? Can you tell me the long story of how nothing happened and how that *nothing* somehow turned into *something*…?"

The two looked back at me doubtfully: Rusty was standing next to his heifer, Gwen and I still stood in the middle of the long esplanade leading to the cafeteria, students streaming past us on their way to class.

"Can you tell me what really happened at that fateful Christmas Committee meeting?" I repeated. "Because something either did or did not happen. And it may have been seminal. So I'd be interested to hear about it."

"It's a long story…." they warned.

"It usually is …."

"…And an ugly one," they said.

"They usually are!"

"It is not easy to tell a story about nothing."

"I realize that. But there is certainly honor in the attempt...."

The two rivals paused, as if they would head back to their respective academic paths. But then they each stopped. And then, as if the stirrings of humanity were rumbling somewhere inside them, each began to tell the story of the Christmas Committee meeting that they had attended.

"You see," they said. "It all came down to the menu. That's where it all went awry...."

"The fate of our educational institution, of our entire community, went awry because of a menu?"

"Yes, it was the menu that we were discussing that day. The menu for the Christmas party...."

⁓

AND HERE THEY told me how they had both been assigned to the Food and Beverage sub-committee and that they'd met in the same conference room where my focus group was currently meeting. In great detail they described how they sat on opposite sides of the rectangular conference table and how, after taking their seats, they'd gotten down to the business of finalizing the food and drinks for that year's Christmas party.

"It was late in the day," said Gwen.

"And late in the semester," said Rusty. "A little after two and I had a final exam to give at three."

"It was late so I offered to share my ideas first. 'Shall I go first?' I said. 'Or should you?' It was still a matter of debate back then."

"Of course *I'll* go first," said Rusty. "Because I've been here longer than you. Which is to say my professional and personal attributes are known, my contributions to the college and our community are documented. My family has lived here for generations. In fact, my ancestors are buried in the dusty fields of the Cow Eye Cemetery – unlike yours, who are buried god knows where. In fact I can take you to the graves of my grandparents within a matter of minutes, while you have chosen to leave yours to their own devices, scattered around the country like wind-blown chaff. So for this reason, it is only proper that I present my ideas first. Of course, I don't think she liked that one bit...."

"Of course I didn't like that one bit! And why *would* I? Why would his contributions deserve more precedence than mine? Sure, my ancestors were not from Cow Eye. Sure my grandparents were buried in various places far, far away. But it's not like my life began upon arriving into the makeshift bus shelter! Yet that's how I was being made to feel. It was all very insulting. But these were the days when we didn't dwell on things like this. When we were still running barefoot and pregnant in the kitchens of academic discourse."

"We?"

"Yes, we. And so I told him he could present his ideas before mine. 'Be my guest....' I said and let him speak first."

"*Let* me? Who is she to *let* me speak! I spoke first because this has been the natural order of things since the time of first dust. And this order transcends any whims that she might have. And so I looked at her and said, 'First of all, I don't believe that we should be reinventing any wheels. If the wheel is circular enough to roll, then ride it by all means. If the river flows, float upon it. In my notebook here I've jotted down the menu that we've been using for many years now. It consists almost exclusively of meat and it has served us well over the centuries. I would suggest that we begin, and end, with that.' And I handed her my notebook."

"With meat?"

"Yes."

"Exclusively?"

"And entirely."

"I took the notebook from him and sure enough it had listed every beef dish that there could possibly be. Every part of the cow. Every method of preparation. Beef ball and corned beef and steak and hamburger and meatloaf and veal and jerky and pot roast. And I looked at this list respectfully and then I said, 'Well, meat is fine and all. But there is a broader world out there and this broader world boasts vegetables of all imaginary types. There are carrots and celery and asparagus and sprouts and soy and rutabaga and beets and broccoli and cauliflower and spinach and beans and corn and....'"

"Corn is good!"

"...and arugula...."

Here he stopped.

"Arugula? What the hell is *arugula?*"

"You see, Charlie, he didn't even know what arugula was! And so I explained it to him and he said…."

"Why the hell would we want arugula at a Christmas party?"

"'Because of what it represents,' I said."

"And what, pray tell, does it represent?"

"It represents the future of humanity. The relentless forward motion from carnivorous beginnings to a higher plane of herbal transcendence. It is the inexorable evolution of our yearnings from primal inklings to a more refined and self-aware desire for subtle things."

"That's a crock of shit."

"No, it is not a crock of shit. It is our shared destiny."

"No, honey, it is not. Vegetables are vegetables, and nothing more. And meat, you see, is meat. And your desire to move from one to the other speaks more about your own selfish goals to innovate for its own sake. To live longer for its own sake. To achieve continuous improvement at the expense of a humble acceptance of what you already have."

"So what are you suggesting then? Are you proposing a world governed only by meat? Rather than one that recognizes the diversity of its vegetative complexity?"

"And what choice are we left with? In the dietary chart of human evolution, *you people* are arugula and *we* are tenderloin. Yet there are only so many dollars in the world. And an infinite number of mouths to feed. And so before we get ahead of ourselves, our Christmas party should celebrate the ageless glories of beef and steak and hamburger and meatloaf and veal and jerky and pot roast…."

"And fruitcake!"

"Fruitcake?" I asked.

"Yes," said Bessie. "Do you like it?"

"I'm not so sure," I answered. "Do you mean metaphorically or literally?"

"Literally. Why would anyone want to bake a metaphorical fruitcake? No, Charlie, literal fruitcake…do you like it?"

"It's okay. Not my favorite. But it's okay. Why?"

"My mom wanted to make one. You know, for when you come over. To celebrate the occasion."

"Fine. Fruitcake is fine. And I'm sure I'll find your mother's fruitcake quite fine when I come over to meet your children some day. But what time did you say I should be there? What time were you thinking to schedule that?"

"I've already reminded you repeatedly."

"Yes, but could you tell me yet again so I don't forget? I seem to be doing that a lot lately…"

"Two o'clock!"

"Oh yes, two. Of course it would be at two! Two o'clock someday for sure…!"

Bessie laughed and snapped the elastic on my shorts.

"Enough report-writing!" she said and lay back on the bed, pulling me on top of her as she fell. It was not an unprecedented position for me to be in, and from my vantage point, I once again surveyed the waters moving below. The flow of moisture from one place to another. The gradual damming and sudden release of the wetness that flows and has always flowed. The water that outlasts even the strongest and most impenetrable dam.

When our slaking was complete, the two of us lay under the covers until she at last fell asleep on the other pillow. By now it was early morning and with so little time remaining until Monday I skulked back to my desk to continue my report. Picking up my pencil, I wrote about the two-hour discussion of the college's mission statement; and what the participants liked about our current mission and what they felt should be changed. Sharpening my pencil to an even finer point I detailed how the two sides were finally able to agree on a new formulation of the mission statement – if not for the sake of harmony or collegiality, then, at the very least, for the sake of appearances in the self-study. In a footnote I noted with some irony that Rusty and Gwen had once occupied the very same table where my focus group was being held, that it had once been possible for them to remain in the same room at the same time; but with regret, I acknowledged that their divisiveness seemed to be present in all things at the college – including my focus group – even though I'd made sure not to invite them to the session itself. When all of this was done I stretched the fingers of my cramped hand again and with the darkness of night still outside my window, I wrote about the final question that still needed to be asked before the focus group could be considered complete. Tired, frantic, my eyes dimming from the effort, I pulled the lamp above my paper and wrote and wrote and wrote.….

AND WHEN I looked up from my report Dr. Felch had again popped his head in my doorway.

"Is it done yet?" he asked. "You were supposed to get that report to me last week. It's already *this* week and I still haven't seen it."

"I'm afraid I haven't finished it yet."

"Is it even close?"

"Um, not really. If I could just have a little more time…."

"I've already given you two extensions. How long do you need *now*?"

"A week maybe. Or more."

"I'll give you till Monday."

"But that's too soon! It's already Friday. It's Friday afternoon and Monday's less than three days away. The weekend begins tomorrow. You see, sir, Bessie and I had plans to spend these next few days locked in my apartment with a weekend's worth of food, a week's worth of beer, and a semester's worth of…"

"Charlie! You have until Monday. And that's final. Dammit, the fate of our institution depends on it."

At the cafeteria, Will did his best to cheer me up.

"Don't worry, there, Charlie boy. Not everyone's cut out to be an educational administrator."

"Thanks a lot."

Will took another drag on his cigar. Then he said:

"You know it's like my wife used to say in the beginning. She'd say, Smithcoate, don't worry about it. There are other ways. Not every academician is destined to be a great lover. Or vice versa. It takes all kinds in our world. So just pick *one* thing and be great at it….!"

"She'd say that to you?"

"Yes. She used to say a lot of things. But don't worry: it all comes with time…like anything else. You see, Charlie, you're allowing things to come too close to that heart of yours. Don't take yourself so seriously. That report you're writing – you know, the one that everyone is saying will supposedly determine the fate of our entire institution – well, it probably *will*. And yet six and a half years from now who's gonna give a damn? No one will care whether you wrote it or not. Why? Because it's only meaningful if you screw it up. If you do a crap job and we lose our accreditation, then everyone will be up in arms. But if you simply do a good job, nobody will care! Such is the true heroism of the educational administrator. And such is the heroism of educational administration in general. Like so many other things in this world, you see, it's just one of those things that comes and goes, quietly and unremarkably, and, for this very reason, heroically."

I nodded.

"And besides," said Nan, "everyone's saying your Christmas party is in serious jeopardy. That Rusty and Gwen aren't coming. You might want to spend some time on *that* before it's too late. Before December eleventh comes and goes without a semester-culminating party for the second year in a row. I mean, you want to be able to put this on your curriculum vitae, right?"

"She's got a point," said Raul. "And don't take this the wrong way, but the latest draft you just gave me to proofread....that draft of your report? My goodness, was it muddled. I could barely get through it!"

"It was that bad?"

"It was unreadable!"

The words had come like arrows from a thousand different directions. Then, after flagging me down in the copy room, one of the administrative secretaries added yet another projectile to the enfilade:

"Not to pierce you when you're already down," she said, "but, Charlie, have you taken a look at yourself in the mirror lately? It's scary to see what you've become...!"

Listening to all this, I took some time to consider their words. Of course each of them was right. In their own ways, each of them was *always* right. But what now? Now that I'd moved half-way across a vast country in search of a legacy to leave, what were my options *now*? On a scale of one to ten – with ten being a piece of bronze statuary and one being a traveling mist – my lasting contribution to the world was surely nothing greater, nothing less, than a reliable three-and-a-half – a *four*, perhaps, if my self-study proved successful – a plaster monument to contemporary mediocrity.

"So what should I do?" I asked. "I agree with everything you've all just said. It all makes perfect sense. But what can I do about it?"

"You should let it all go," said Will. "Don't take any of it to heart."

"If you want to clean up that report," Raul prompted, "you should use an outline while you're writing. Plan it. Diagram it. Use the envisioning process to give your ideas greater structure so your writing can flow more logically."

"Learn to delegate."

"Refrain from semi-colons."

"Hold a focus group."

"Use a planner."

"Bring them toys that boys their age would like. Bring her mom a tulip."

"Use a double-edged razor."

"Start with the colored man."

"And don't forget to ask the participants for their opinions on the Christmas party! Because their buy-in will be key."

I nodded.

"But most of all, you really need to get some sleep. When's the last time you had a good night's sleep, Charlie?"

"It's been months."

"So *sleep*."

"You make it sound so easy."

"It is. Just....sleep!"

"But how do I do *that*? It's not like the math faculty are getting any quieter. It's not like they're losing their passion for mathematics...."

"Here take some of these...."

"Pills?"

"Yes. Take them twice a day with food."

"But I don't even eat food twice a day! I'm lucky if I have time to eat *once*!"

"Then take them on an empty stomach. But take them."

"This will help me sleep?"

"Yes, it will," said Gwen.

Rusty shook his head.

"No, they *won't*!" he said.

"Gwen's pills won't help?"

"Of course not. They're a waste of time. Because it's not sleep that you need! It's staying awake. What good is sleep when you need to be awake to write your report?"

"That makes sense."

"Of course it does. Here, try these pills instead...."

"Thank you," I said.

"You're welcome!" they said.

I held out my hand and the two placed their respective pills into my palm.

"But do you think these pills you've given me will work?" I asked them. "Do you think they'll help me stay awake? Do you think they'll help me fall asleep? Do you think they'll allow me to sleep and stay awake, respectively? Or, at least, to do these things *concurrently*?"

"Of course they will!" they said.

And so I took both pills, guzzling each down with a palmful of water from the bathroom sink.

"Fine," said the secretary. "Hopefully, those pills will help. Now as to your hygiene issue, well as to that, you might want to start by getting a decent shave and a haircut. And maybe you should try washing those corduroys every once in a while. I mean you're an educational administrator, for god's sake, not an adjunct...."

"Right!"

And so I made my way back to the bathroom down the hall, where I washed my face again. And straightened up my collar. And tucked in my dress shirt. Back in my office I grabbed a pair of scissors and tucking the small plastic trash can between my knees I leaned over it and began to trim my beard. The hairs fell into the can and as I snipped I saw them curling into little clumps at the bottom. In the background of the quiet room, the pendulum continued its ticking. And further in the background from *that* was the slight sound of a repeated knocking at my door.

∽

{ }

When Love knocks you must always be quick to answer.
For Love rarely knocks as insistently the second time.

{ }

∽

"Charlie!" said Bessie as she walked into my office without knocking. "What are you doing in here? We're all waiting for you in the conference room. Both sides of the table are getting antsy. You said it would only be a ten-minute break. But it's been thirty-five minutes already. The participants have consumed all the arugula and most of the jerky and it's starting to get ugly in there. They're licking the bowl. Why are you in *here*?"

"I'm just, you know, trying to collect my thoughts. Everything's happening so quickly and I feel like it's spiraling out of control. I can't keep up. I'm getting overwhelmed. I feel like I'm letting everyone down. And so I just came in here to shut the door for a few minutes to try to regain my composure. To try to make sense of it all."

"Well, fine. But you need to get back to the focus group…"

"I know that. I do. I know that very well. I'll be right there…."

"They're getting tired of waiting…."

Bessie motioned toward the conference room, then, unexpectedly, she undid the knot at her waist and let her towel drop to the floor.

"And I'm tired of waiting too!" she said.

"But…."

"It's now or never…"

"But we've already….!"

"My heart does not reveal itself any more than this. My body does not get any barer…."

"I'll be right there," I said. "But let me finish this last part…"

I looked down at my report.

"….You're taking me for granted, Charlie."

And so I looked back up:

"No, I'm not. I just need to get through the last few questions…."

Bessie shook her head. Reaching over my shoulder she grabbed the book I'd laid on my desk.

"You're not done with this book yet?"

"Hey, give me that…!"

"Why? What are you reading about *now*?"

"Nothing. Give it back…!"

Bessie opened the book where the bookmark stuck out and read the title of the chapter I was currently reading:

"*Chapter Thirty-Five*…." she read, demonstratively and dramatically, as if she were a thespian. Still bared and unabashed, she continued theatrically: "….*Knowing When Your Semester Really is Over….And How to End It With Grace*…."

On the word *grace*, she did a heavy pirouette.

"Give me that!"

But she did not. Holding the book at arm's length, she began to read:

{ }

Like all things in nature, the feelings of sexual attraction that a faculty member may feel for other members of the profession will tend to subside over time. This is as natural as the sad end to any once-joyful and promising endeavor. Just as the semesters of our youth end incrementally, in stages that come and go undetected, so too does our romantic affection tend to subside over time. The outset of this journey will surely be marked by the pure hope and optimism of a new beginning: the raw nerves upon entering a new classroom for the first time; the elation of the first probing discussion at an ethnic restaurant. Soon, and indiscernibly, comes the inevitable settling that happens: the waning excitement, the classes skipped, meetings missed, birthdays and other events forgotten. Liberties are inevitably taken as familiarity and complacency set in. And as these semesters pass, the youthful dreams of greatness fade into the disillusionment of reality. The myths of the first date exposed. The lies uncovered. The flaccid decision-making. The toenail clippings. The bloated curriculum vitae. All of it will tend to come together at the end of our life's semester like a struggling student facing the onrushing specter of exam week.

For any student, the decision to withdraw from a class is not an easy one to make. Neither is it easy for tenured faculty to withdraw from a relationship that once held so much promise. And yet the premature withdrawal is clearly the safer option. Withdraw too late and there may be severe repercussions. Withdraw too early and you may deny yourself the rewards of your initial efforts. Like so many things in life, therefore, this too is all about the timing. And so the decision is not an easy one. Newly bewildered, the degree-seeking student may be left to continue blindly on with the relentless movements

*that have brought her to this point in time and space, while
the faculty member who has given up any claims to love will
be left to withdraw his affections before the consequences of
his efforts are allowed to become too great. But when? This
is the question that has confused the world's greatest lovers
and given birth to the bulk of our humanity. For neither
'why' nor 'how' can flummox the great lover like the eternal
question: when?*

{ }

"So what does this shit mean, Charlie?"

"It doesn't mean anything...."

"Doesn't it?"

"No."

"Shouldn't it?"

"No, it shouldn't."

"And yet there has to be a larger meaning in all this," she said. Sliding her hands down my boxers, she repeated: "There has to be something more than this!"

"I'm sorry, Bess!" I said and grabbing her by the wrist I took her hand out of my boxers. "This whole thing is all wrong. It's not how I'd planned it. This weekend. The semester. None of it."

Bessie grunted. Then, with a sudden motion, she kicked away the towel that had dropped to the floor around her ankles. Now she was even more revealed than ever. Her breasts full and supple. Her wet hair undone around her shoulders.

"Love me!" Bessie said. "While my waters are still flowing!"

I moved to speak. But before I could, a woman's voice interrupted:

"No!" Bessie objected. "You've got to get back to the conference room! They're all waiting for you."

And so, struggling to keep it all straight, I stepped out of my boxers and headed back down the hallway toward the conference room with my scissors still in hand.

❧

"OH MY GOD!" shrieked the ethics teacher when I walked into the conference room. "What happened to your beard? It looks like you cut it with a steak knife."

"Or an emasculator," added the nursing instructor. "Here, let me get you a napkin for those cuts...!"

"No time for that!" I objected. "We're almost done with our session, ladies and gentlemen, and there's only a little more to go!" Casting my wand toward the flipchart I proceeded to call the symphony back into session. "Let's move on to the next great question, shall we? Hey, Bessie....!"

Bessie flipped over the large paper to reveal the next page:

> ## QUESTION: *Please describe your ideal Christmas party.*

"Very well," I said. "So as you can see, the next question concerns a very important issue on our campus. For many years Cow Eye Community College has had a Christmas party and it was a unifying event....." With a grand flourish I gestured with my wand to indicate that our discussion was now in vigorous session.

"Hey, watch out with those scissors...!" someone shrieked and ducked.

I continued:

"....Our Christmas party has historically been a unifying event, but recently it has become something else entirely. Recently, you see, it has been taken out of context and has been used as an instrument in the battle between our two competing factions on campus. It has been co-opted. It has been bent over and molested like an F-1 student taking a creative writing class thousands of miles from her homeland. And so we would like to rescue her. To save her dignity before it is too late. But to do this we need to start from the beginning."

"Which beginning?"

"*The* beginning."

"The very beginning? Before she left her country to set out for Cow Eye Junction?"

"Yes, *that* beginning. So please forget anything that you have ever known about Christmas. Please cast aside any previous preconceptions or prejudices about what a Christmas party should be. What it should look like. What is or is not possible. Let's start the slow redemption of our campus from the very beginning, shall we? Let's begin the restoration of our Christmas party from scratch by answering this simple question in its most broad and open-ended form...."

The participants were staring back at me with blank expressions.

"...Yes!" I said. "Let's do that very thing. Let's throw all else aside and simply answer the question that Bessie has just revealed by flipping over the large sheet of paper. Bessie, can you read it for us again, please....?"

"But...."

"Bessie?"

"They can read..."

"Yes, I know that. But could you just repeat it out loud for emphasis...?"

Bessie rolled her eyes. Then she cleared her throat and said:

"Please.... describe....your ideal....Christmas party...."

I paused.

"Right. So now you've all heard it multiple times. *Please describe your ideal Christmas party.* Pretty fucking straightforward, wouldn't you say? So would somebody like to begin this discussion?"

I paused again. I had already prepared myself to plead for a volunteer. But this time the response came immediately:

"For me," said the ethics teacher, "the ideal Christmas party would be more – oh, what's the word? – *inclusive*. Yes, it would be inclusive. Which means the occasion would have to go beyond what it has traditionally been, to become something that it has *never* been, something that anyone could enjoy. With a little work and some creative envisioning, it could be welcoming and inviting no matter where a person came from – whether they be from Cow Eye Junction itself...or the larger Diahwa Valley Basin... or Idaho...or even some place as exotic and ineffable as California! A beautiful Christmas party, you see, would be friendly and all-embracing – two metaphorical arms opening wide to welcome the tired and huddled masses into our cafeteria. It would celebrate our *one*ness. Our unity. It would cast aside the differences that separate us as human beings while glorifying these differences at the same time. It would explore our diversity. Our differentness. Yet it would do so in a unifying and harmonious way. It would be as eclectic as the world itself. It would reflect the amazing diversity of the world in all its complexity and glory. The Jew. The Gentile. The Muslim. The Sikh. Black and White. Rich and poor. Atheist or god-fearing. Agnostics. All of them should feel welcome to attend our Christmas party at Cow Eye Community College because they should feel that it is a part of them. That this Christmas party is *their* Christmas party. That it belongs to them all. For this is the true spirit of Christmas, right?"

"I don't know," I said. "I am just an untenured facilitator. But thank you for your comments. You've given us much to think about." Turning to Bessie, I asked: "Are you getting all this?"

"Of course," she said.

Then the art historian spoke up:

"For me," she said, "the party would not just be a simple party. We've all been to countless examples of those, right? You come. You sit. You sing Christmas carols badly. You drink eggnog. You exchange gifts. You kiss inebriated co-workers under the mistletoe. You engage in an onslaught of carefully organized merriment in the name of Christmas. Then you go home. And the outcome? There isn't any! It becomes a wasted opportunity. No, our party should be much more than just a party. It should be a celebration of life. It should feature the many glories of our school and faculty. Ideally, it would be a showcase of our college's achievements. Its accomplishments. Its departments. From the social sciences to the actual sciences. From the humanities to the trades. It should feature all of our individual talents. In this way it would be a true commemoration of our humanity. It would reaffirm our status as living breathing feeling beings. It would bring us together as guardians of the universe. It would tell the world that we are not just mere educators at a small rural community college. We are citizens of the world! We are human beings, damn it! We are *people*! *The* people!!"

To this I nodded:

"I believe that can be arranged. Anything else?"

"Yes," said the music teacher. "An ideal Christmas party would involve not just the faculty and staff of the college but everyone who makes up the rich fabric of our college. It would be open to students – who are the core of our mission, after all. And it would feature their talents. An ideal celebration would involve the entire campus, everyone from the dean of instruction to the groundskeepers. From the president of the college to its financial aid workers. From the woman with the hair net to the security guard with the Polaroid camera. Everyone should be invited. And I mean everyone!"

"Even the adjuncts?"

"Well, I wouldn't go *that* far…."

On the locals' side of the table the animal science instructor was preparing to speak. Seizing the first available pause, he said:

"Well!" At the impressive sound of his own words, the animal science instructor looked around the table significantly. Then he elaborated: "Well! This is all fine and good. Diversity is fine and good. Love is fine and good. Hell, Jesus Christ himself was pretty damn fine and good. But we should not lose sight of one thing. In trying to diversify our Christmas experience, we should not cast aside the essence of what makes Cow Eye unique. We should make sure that our Christmas party reflects the unique local culture of our region. We should organize our party in such a way as to encourage each and every participant to 'love and respect the culture of Cow Eye'...."

I looked over at Bessie who was dutifully transcribing everything.

"Your ideas have been noted. And appreciated. Is there anything else you'd like to add? Is there something else that we may have missed that you would like to see in our Christmas party?"

"Yes," they said.

"There is?"

"Yes," they said again.

"What?" I asked. "I mean, what *specifically*? You see it is late in the afternoon and our session is coming to a close. Now is the time to bare your souls. Remember, this will be your last chance. From here Bessie and I will go to my office for a quick but memorable debrief. And from there I will immediately set about writing the report that will be included as appendices in the self-study and that will be used to guide our plans for the Christmas party. So what specifically would you like to see incorporated into these plans? What can you suggest that will make this the most memorable and successful – the most unifying – Christmas party ever?"

And so, breathlessly, they began to give their suggestions. Over the next few hours I noted their very specific ideas for re-envisioning our Christmas party for the betterment of Cow Eye Community College:

"I think we should serve even more beer!"

"And wine!"

"And definitely hard liquor!"

"Make sure there are more vegetables."

"But less arugula!"

"Offer beef."

"But no meat!

"Have songs."

"And massages."

"And yoga."

"Don't forget caroling!"

"Peace and harmony."

"Mistletoe."

"Innovation."

"Tradition."

"Ethnic diversity."

"Orgasm."

"Castration."

"Fishing."

"Flags of the world."

"Smoking."

"Tender anal sex."

"Hand guns."

"Fruitcake."

"A truck show!"

"Could it be clothing-optional this year?"

"Esperanto."

"Anglicanism."

"Love!"

"Love?"

"Yes, *love!*"

~

AND SO IT was that I teased out their deepest desires like prunes from a package. And it was in this way that I learned what our faculty and staff truly wanted from their ideal Christmas experience. Like anyone else, they wanted the same tangible outcome from this campus-wide event that they wanted from life itself: to be both entertained and enlightened; to be guided yet deferred to; to be nurtured yet revered; to be innocent and hopeful yet infinitely wise to the ways of the world. Which is to say they wanted nothing of the sort. Neither love nor hate. Neither beer nor wine. Neither eggnog nor its opposite.

"Meat," they urged.

"But not meat."

"Arugula," they insisted.

"But not arugula."

"Fun."

"But meaningful."

"Better roads."

"But lower taxes."

"Tradition."

"But innovation."

"Inspiring."

"But realistic!"

"Funny."

"But not frivolous."

"Romantic."

"But sincere."

"Challenging."

"But free from arrogance or didacticism."

I listened carefully. Bessie took detailed notes. And as I took it all in I nodded at each conflicting comment that would guide my envisioning of the Christmas party. And when they had finished their answering, and when we had wrapped up our focus group, I collected their evaluations and looking up from my conductor's stand I placed my wand decisively on the conference table in front of me:

"Thank you very much," I said. "Everything you've just articulated has been duly noted. It will be transcribed and collated and surely incorporated into our plans for our upcoming Christmas party."

"All of it?"

"Without exception." I waited for my words to resonate on a deeper level. It was clear that their years at Cow Eye had taught them not to trust such promises. It would be yet another challenge I would need to overcome. But now as I looked around the room I thought I could see the entrenched looks of desiccation and despair slowly turning to ones of verdant optimism. The flicker of that most human desire to believe in something better was starting to emerge. Quietly, I made a mental note of this. Then I said:

"So having gone through this elaborate process of earning your complicity, can we expect to see you at our campus's Christmas party on December eleventh? Your presence is crucial to the success of our party after all. And it is vital to my own attempt to leave a legacy of some sort...." By now the participants were anxious to exit the conference room and seemed to be in a funk. (Many were already late for their evening plans; several were grumbling about the lengthiness of the session: "Four hours, my ass!" one muttered.) "....If I can somehow manage to work all of your suggestions into our upcoming Christmas party – if I can bring all these disparate elements together – will you be so good as to honor us with your presence?"

I expected a resounding and grateful assent; instead I got this:

"Perhaps," they all answered. "Though it is still too early to say. Commitment, you know, is more than skin-deep. So we'll have to get back to you on that...."

"We?" I asked once again.

And once again they responded:

"Yes, Charlie. *We.*"

And so I turned to Rusty. And then to Gwen. And after thanking them for their respective pills, I posed the same question to each of them that I'd posed to my focus group:

"Will the two of you be attending our Christmas party?" I asked them. "Because if each of you comes, then the rest of your colleagues – both sides of the very wide conference table – will be sure to follow. You hold my fate in your hands, my legacy. In your hands is the fate of our college as a whole. And its legacy. An entwined legacy is in both of your hands, like the love vine that wraps ever so lovingly around the cherry tree. So will you come?"

Again their answer was equivocal:

"Not sure," they said. "It all depends."

"On what?"

"On quite a bit."

"Such as?"

"The menu. I will come if there are no vegetables."

"And *I* will attend only if there is no meat."

"None at all?"

"Right."

"And that is non-negotiable for both of you?"

"Yes."

"So neither of you is coming then?"

"It seems that way."

"And in this regard both of you are in full and total agreement?"

"Yes."

When I broke the news to Dr. Felch, he seemed to take it in stride, though with a certain sadness and resignation. We were sitting in the empty cafeteria where the party was due to be held later that week. It was already early December yet not a single light had been strung. No tree had been set up. No tinsel was in place. Using a match to light up a cigarette – his thirteenth – Dr. Felch threw his boots up on a cafeteria table and took a long and significant pull of the nicotine.

"I probably should have known it would end like this," he said. "In smoke. In ignominy. I should have recognized that it would be too much. That I was asking too much of you given the state of our divided faculty."

"It's not over yet, Mr. Felch. We can still do this...!"

"How can it not be over? It's December tenth, for Christ's sake. The party was supposed to be tomorrow. And nothing's ready. Nobody's coming. That much is clear. So how can it not be over?"

"I have a plan."

"At last?"

"Yes. I mean not at the moment, I don't. But I *will* have a plan. I'll come up with a plan to make it all work out."

"And when can I hear this plan of yours?"

"What time is it now?"

Dr. Felch checked his watch:

"It's two o'clock, Charlie."

"Two o'clock?"

"Yes, two o'clock. Just park right there on the gravel between the two old trucks on blocks. We'll be waiting for you...."

"We?"

"Yes, the four of us will be waiting for you at the end of my gravel driveway at two o'clock."

"Right," I said and pulled up my boxers. "Two o'clock. I'll be there for sure." Then I looked at Dr. Felch and said: "On Monday morning I'll present my plan to you. I'll present it right after the focus group report that I'm supposed to have for you at that time. Bessie will not be happy.

But I'll just have to take more time to work on it this weekend. And I'll present them both to you on Monday morning."

"Monday morning, you say?"

"Yes, Monday morning."

"So we'll see you at two o'clock then?" she said for the final time.

"Of course," I said. "At two o'clock. I'm looking forward to the fruitcake!"

Uncertainly I took another handful of the pills I'd been given – equal amounts of Rusty's and Gwen's – and washed them down with a glassful of water. Checking my watch, I stumbled out of my office toward the cafeteria.

THE PLAN

"It is with deep regret that we must announce the postponing of our annual Christmas party until further notice. Future plans for the event are pending and will be announced at a later date."

from Dr. Felch's memo
to all faculty and staff

"So what exactly *is* your plan?" said Raul, one afternoon late in the semester. "Now that the decision has been made to cancel the Christmas party?" He and I were standing outside a professional development lecture on estate planning.

"The party hasn't been *canceled,* Raul. Cancellation would imply defeat. It's merely been *postponed.* Until further notice...."

"Okay. So what's your plan now that the annual Christmas party has been postponed until further notice. And for the second year in a row, I might add?"

"My plan is simple...." Here I pulled out the two vials from my shirt pocket. "First, I will take a few more of these pills that Gwen and Rusty have given me...."

"Gwen and Rusty gave you pills?"

"Yes. One to fall asleep. And the other to stay awake."

"Do they work?"

"No, they do not. Not yet. Or at least, not entirely. So far, each seems to be working and also *not working* at the same time. Perhaps because I have not yet taken enough of either one. Perhaps because I have not committed to them *entirely* – it's hard to say. So to be safe I will take them both. And in large quantities. To increase their efficiency, I will take twice as many as prescribed. And I will take them thrice as often. I will wash them down with water from the tap. Then I will spend the entire weekend finishing up my focus group report. And when that's done I'll use the remaining time during the weekend to develop a comprehensive proposal for the Christmas party."

"What about Bessie? I thought you two had something planned for this weekend? Something you'd been planning for several months? Something involving a few days' worth of food, a week's worth of beer, and a semester's worth of pent-up desires? I thought this was some sort of last-gasp attempt to salvage your relationship?"

"It was. But now I need to re-envision my priorities. You see, I've been professionally remiss up to this point. Negligent to some extent. Bordering, I'm afraid, on unprofessionalism. I've allowed myself to be distracted by inconsequential things. But that needs to change. From now on I will need to stay supremely focused. And that begins with getting my priorities straight."

"At Bessie's expense…."

"That might be one way to look at it. But the other way is that I've been spending far too much time at my apartment with *her* and not nearly enough time at my lonely desk with my plans for the Christmas party. So this will be a way to make my amends. To bring it all back into balance."

"Fair enough. But how are you going to represent this visually?"

"Huh?"

"Now that you've decided to realign your priorities, how are you planning to represent these changes in a form that is visually stimulating? You see, you really should put everything down on paper so you'll have something tangible to commit to entirely. Here, try this…."

Raul took out a pen and began drawing. After a few minutes, he handed me the following diagram to illustrate my shifting priorities:

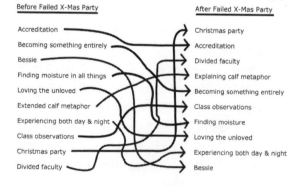

"That's very helpful," I admitted. "Can I keep it?"

"For now. But I'll need it back eventually…."

I folded the paper and put it in my pocket with the others.

"So, as I was saying…I will use this weekend with Bessie not just to write my focus group report but also to create a plan for the Christmas party. And the plan for the party will incorporate feedback from each of the faculty who attended my high-stakes focus group. My plan will honor every constructive comment that was given, as well as honoring those helpful comments that were not as constructive. It will incorporate every suggestion. Every whim. Every stray thought that might enter the mind of a certificated human being. Every inclination. Every pent-up longing. Every caprice. Every institutional yearning. Every yen. Every intellectual craving. Every flight of fancy. Every aching impulse. My plan, Raul, will address every desire of an academic or personal nature regardless of its measurability or intrinsic merit…."

"Even the Truck Show?"

"Yes."

"And hard liquor?"

"Yes."

"How about flags from different parts of the world?"

"Yes."

"And tender anal sex?"

"Of course."

"Are you inviting the adjuncts?"

"Even that is a remote possibility. You see, all of these things will certainly need to be included in the plan. And on Monday I will meet Dr. Felch in his office to present my proposal for a new kind of Christmas party that incorporates all of these disparate elements."

"So it sounds like your plan for the party consists of….creating a plan?"

"Yes. I am an educational administrator. It's what I do: I plan. And I write reports. And in the rare moments when I am doing neither of these – which is to say somewhere in the very middle of it all, between planning and reporting, if circumstances happen to permit – I will spend a tiny sliver of my time – no more than a Mercury dime, really – doing *actual* work, which is to say, implementing the plans that I have devised and that I will one day sit in a quiet room writing essential reports on."

"I see. Well, the important thing is you finally have a plan."

"I do. I have a plan. Or more specifically, I have a plan for a plan. But enough about me! How about you, Raul? It's the holiday season. Christmas is fast approaching. As an ardent Catholic, and former resident of Barcelona in a previous incarnation, what are *your* plans for the break?"

"I'm finally going to Texas!" At this Raul laughed and shook my hand before heading off for his winter vacation. "That bastion of Lone-Star Catholicism," he said. Then looking over his shoulder, he added: "I'll be gone for a month and won't be back until after the semester starts. So wish me luck...!"

And I did.

⁓

DECEMBER ELEVENTH PASSED quietly. For the second year in a row the holiday season rose and fell without the yuletide glow of a campus-wide Christmas party. On December tenth a flyer was distributed to the mailboxes of all faculty and staff announcing that the party would be postponed. On December eleventh the cases of beer that had been moved into the cafeteria for the occasion were moved back out. And on December twelfth, exactly as scheduled, the semester itself ended. Unceremoniously. Abruptly. Within hours the campus had emptied out like a dam whose walls have failed it. The depleted students poured past Timmy at the guard shack clutching their book bags and their bookmarks and their booklists – none of them bothered to carry *books* anymore – followed by their instructors who exited through the gate on their own semi-annual exodus from verdure to desiccation. The business office closed. The library grew quiet. Even the Dimwiddle Student Union, with its worn teal carpet and flickering 22-inch color television set, shuttered its doors for the break. For the first time since the sun first rose on this long semester, there were no jugglers to do their juggling. No cheerleaders performing cartwheels. No bicyclists. No students singing protest under the sycamore. The parking lots emptied out. The bicycles sat unattended. Even the timeless sounds of paperwork getting done – the hammering of staplers, the clacking of typewriters, the thumping of rubber stamps – quickly faded into oblivion as the administrative workers took their holiday leave between semesters.

By now the days had grown shorter and darker until the sunlight could not get any shorter or any darker. The wind that makes its way through the campus blew cold and haunting. The leaves on the deciduous trees turned brown and barren. And then they too were gone.

All around the town of Cow Eye Junction, meanwhile, Christmas was arriving. Shiny garlands had been wrapped around the lamp posts. Bells jingled. Christmas music played on the AM radio station. In the town square between the mayor's office and the county jail, a resplendent fir tree had been erected complete with an angel perched on top. Even the eclectic establishments at the Outskirts were getting into the holiday spirit as shops took to selling scented candles in green and red colors, the opium dens strung Christmas lights outside their windows, and the various massage parlors offered holiday-themed discovery sessions complete with young women dressed as Santa's helpers. And through it all, the pendulum in my office continued to tick, the metal orbs swinging back then forth like the relentless sway of oscillating priorities.

Back in my apartment I could only look up from my report at the harsh sounds on the other side of my apartment wall: the pounding; the music; the crashing dishes and heaving bedsprings and the roar of what sounded like a housecat being strangled incrementally. All of it continued even as the tumult of accredited learning came to rest and the Christmas break began. It was familiar and expected. Yet amid the quiet of a deserted campus, the sounds beyond the wall seemed to have grown even louder and more insistent. As if they would never end. As if mathematics itself would not relent. Now it seemed that the incredible clamor of youthful passions might continue without end – the restless emanation extending far into perpetuity – and that it might never recognize the beginning of its incipient dissolution or even the final limitations of its own incarnation. In the fading light of the semester it seemed that the sound of youthful ecstasy really would last and last forever.

Except, of course, that it can't.

Just as unexpectedly as it had begun, the sound from the neighboring apartment unexpectedly died away. Less than twenty-four hours after the semester ended, the refrains of mathematical discovery suddenly dissolved. The screaming stopped. The music ceased. No animals were trumpeting. No lions roared. No caterwauling. Nary a housecat. Everything was quiet. Not a single breath of noise could be heard to emanate from the other side of the wall. At last pure silence had arrived and in utter astonishment I found this silence enveloping me for the first time since the early days of the semester when the innocence of peaceful sleep was first disrupted by my neighbors' clamorous return from North Carolina. Now I could rejoice. And rest. At last I could celebrate the quiet and the calm at the same time. The peace that had emerged from the discord. The hope that comes out of despair. The silence from sound. At last I could enjoy the conciliation that emanates from conflict. And now I could finally find the sleep that must surely come at the end of extended wakefulness. Yes, it had been a trying few months; but it had also been gratifying and rewarding and well worth the wait because now, at last, I would finally be able to sleep.

EXCEPT THAT NOW I couldn't.

Unaccustomed to the emptiness of quiet, I found myself even more awake than before, my anticipation aroused, my senses fresh and aware. New silence, it seems, can be even more conspicuous than familiar noise. And so I sat on the edge of my bed, unable to focus on any thought, waiting amid the unfamiliar silence for the next sound to occur. For an explosion that never came. For the triumphant mammalian ejaculation that never resounded. And the more these sounds didn't come, the more I *expected* them to come. The quieter their absence, the louder their presence in my own mind. Alone amid perfect silence – after so much sound and tumult – I found myself noticing the great irony of troubled sleep: the more you need it, the more elusive it becomes.

I couldn't sleep!

Impotent and exhausted, I paced in the still apartment. Then I took two more pills and washed them down with lukewarm water from the tap. My hands trembling even more from this new lack of sleep, I grabbed the book that lay on my nightstand.

"ARE YOU KIDDING me?" said Bessie. "After all this time, *now* you tell me about this plan? Now you tell me about your plan to draft a proposal for a plan? I've been waiting two days for you to finish that damn focus group report! And now that it's done you tell me you're going to spend the rest of our short weekend developing your ideas for a Christmas party? Are you kidding me?"

"Look, Bess, I'm sorry...." I reached out to her again; but again she slapped away my hand. "Look, I'm sorry but I've got to do this. You see, I'm not as young as I used to be. And my legacy depends on it. I've got to make this Christmas party happen. It's important...."

"It's not important."

"It *is* important...."

"It's a stupid *party*!"

"No, it's not. It's much more. It's a gathering of the senses. It's a metaphor for life itself. It's a symbol of my short time on this earth. This party is a chance to make a meaningful contribution to humanity. And so it has quite simply come to represent my hopes and dreams and wishes. It will be my statement to the world. My message for posterity. My legacy. And that's why it's so important."

"It's more important than our weekend?"

"Yes."

"More important than us?"

"Well, yes."

"Than *me*?"

"Yes."

"Would you care to explain?"

"Don't take it personally, Bess, it's just that there are hundreds of people whose fates depend on this party. Faculty. Staff. Students. Accreditors. The maggots behind the cafeteria. Hell, there are people who are not even born yet who will enjoy the fruits of my efforts, whose children will one day be suckled with the nectar of accredited learning. Wouldn't you agree that just in terms of sheer numbers, all of them taken as a whole are more important than a single individual? Wouldn't you have to acknowledge that all of this together is of far greater significance than a single one of *you*....?"

"Quantitatively?"

"Yes. Numerically speaking wouldn't you agree that...."

"No. I wouldn't, actually. Because I am not your fucking institutional researcher. And I do not desire to be an integer on your, or anybody else's, number line of real and imagined numbers."

"Bess....!"

"Or is that what you're thinking?"

"Bess?"

"Would you prefer that I remain just another piece of comparative data for you?"

"Bessie!"

"A statistical footnote? A chart containing verifiable evidence? A mere bullet – the fourth or fifth in a long list, perhaps – in your bulleted list of priorities?"

"Of course not....!"

Bessie was putting on her clothes.

"Yeah, well, you do what you want, Charlie. Enjoy your report. Enjoy your plan. I'll see you when you've ceased to be an educational administrator and are ready to become a human being...."

Bessie left, slamming the door behind her. Yet again I was left with my lamp and my report. And once again I was left with an unfinished plan. And so, in the new solitude of falling day, I sat down to continue my writing.

❧

Dr. Felch was cleaning out his spittoon when I came into his office on Monday morning.

"Just a second," he said. Carefully, he tilted the urn and dumped the contents into a plastic wastepaper basket. It was already late autumn, the fluids were flowing slowly, and this took some time. I waited patiently. Finally, Dr. Felch looked up at me:

"So how was your weekend?" As he spoke he gazed over at me from the still-inverted spittoon. "I heard it was something of a *do-or-die* for Bess and you...."

"It was fine," I said. "It was okay."

"No adventures?"

"A few, yes. I completely ruined our weekend together. And my hand is still cramped from trying to put down so many different ideas in handwritten form. My eyes are still blurry from the dim lighting. Or maybe it's from the pills – it's hard to say. In any case, I did what I could."

"It's God's work, Charlie. And please know that the world appreciates it." Dr. Felch banged the spittoon against the inside of the trashcan. A large glob of contents plopped out. Then he said: "Is the report ready?"

"Of course…."

I set the outcomes of the focus group on his desk.

"Good. And your plan for the Christmas party? Did you have a chance to work on that?"

"Yes. It's ready too."

"Well then…" said Dr. Felch. "Let's hear what you've come up with….!"

Dr. Felch set the emptied spittoon on the floor next to his desk. The spittoon was fashioned from brass and sparkled against the weak rays of sun coming in through the window. I followed a patch of light that had been thrown onto one wall and was glimmering there: a reflection in the shape of a crescent moon. Then I cleared my throat and began to propose my plan to resurrect our fallen Christmas party and, in so doing, to rescue our struggling community college from the precipice of institutional ruin.

≈

"First," I said, "I will need a strong financial commitment from the college. It will not be a small sum, Dr. Felch, so I'm hoping you can tap into the Dimwiddle endowment. Our accreditation is at stake. The very fate of our institution depends on it. We're under siege. The enemy is attacking us with high-powered artillery. It's a bloody, all-out battle for our very survival. The Dimwiddles should be able to identify with this metaphor, shouldn't they?"

"How much do you need?"

When I told him the amount, Dr. Felch whistled:

"That much!"

"Yes. And it has to be in cash."

"Well, that is definitely *not* a trivial amount!"

"It's not. But trust me, it will be money well spent."

"I can't promise the Dimwiddles will go for it. And it's not like we have that sort of money just lying around. In cash, especially. Anyway, I'll see what I can do…"

"Great. Now as to the plan itself…."

Dr. Felch had put a pinch of tobacco in his lip and for the first time since I'd arrived into the makeshift bus shelter, it seemed I had captivated his full attention – that he wasn't half-engaged in a parallel activity of some sort. My voice was calm. My demeanor was steady. Somehow my exhaustion had coalesced into purposefulness. And as I sat in his office, the smell of wintergreen filling my nostrils, I moved aggressively toward my rhetorical destination:

"....First of all, we need to re-envision the timing of our event. We have obviously missed the chance to hold the party on December eleventh during the traditional holiday season. The semester ends the day after that. Everyone will be leaving for the break. So we will need to postpone the Christmas party to another date."

"Not cancel it?"

"No. Postpone it. Until mid-March."

"*March?!*"

"Yes. You seem surprised. Let me explain...."

Dr. Felch was still looking at me skeptically. I elaborated:

"You see, our accreditors are due to visit the campus in mid-March during the traditional accreditation season. Which means we can schedule the Christmas party during their visit. This will serve three purposes: first, it will act as direct evidence that we've followed through on our plan to hold this Christmas party – the accreditors can experience it with their own eyes – which is something we've already mentioned in our self-study as an example of how we foster unity of purpose via morale-building events. Second, the party can become a sort of symbol for all that is life-affirming in the world: the coming of eternal spring, the promise of re-emerging life, the birth and resurrection of our Lord and Savior Jesus Christ, and, most importantly, the re-affirmation of our college's regional accreditation. In other words, we can honor *all* of these glorious incarnations in one fell swoop! *Third* – and perhaps most importantly from the standpoint of institutional viability – is that having the party during the March visit of our accreditors will raise the stakes of the party itself: faculty will be more likely to attend if they know that their livelihood is somehow dependent on it."

Dr. Felch smiled at the thought.

"...You see," I continued, "...if the fate of our faculty depends on the fate of our college....and the fate of our college depends on its accreditation....and our accreditation can be made to depend on the Christmas party, well then, it stands to reason that the fate of our individual faculty members depends on their collective attendance at our Christmas party! It is all very logical. Look, I even have a visual representation that Raul helped me come up with...."

And here I unfolded the paper and held it up so Dr. Felch could see:

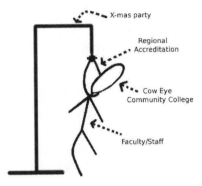

Dr. Felch nodded at the concept:

"Hmmm.....interesting idea. A Christmas party in March. With accreditors...."

"Yes. And eggnog. I mean, why not? Why do such things always have to be held in December? Why can't we think outside the box every once in a while? Let's not be afraid to innovate a little. Let us not be fearful of change. And besides, we've got nothing to lose by trying, right?"

"Okay, what else are you proposing?"

"All right. So we will schedule our party for mid-March when our accreditors are on campus. But instead of it being a single two-hour event as it has been in the past, this time we will hold it over several days. In fact, we'll have an entire week's worth of Christmas events taking place in honor of the accreditors' visit. A Christmas *Week*. It will be a coordinated series of activities that we will intricately plan and meticulously implement. And of course we will christen the whole thing with a catchy name along the lines of *The Cow Eye International Festival of Tolerance and Goodwill*...or *The Semi-Annual Christmas Week Gala and Extravaganza*....or some other captivating misnomer like that. (Sorry, Mr. Felch, it's been a hectic weekend and I haven't quite thought through all these details yet....) In any case, having our celebration over an entire week in March will give us more time to impress our accreditors, to unify our faculty, and to build gradually toward the ultimate culmination of events at the Christmas party itself on Friday, March twentieth...."

I had expected a rousing expression of encouragement from Dr. Felch. But instead he said nothing. He seemed lost in thought. Then he motioned for me to continue, which I did:

"Of course, you and I both know that community college faculty have an unfortunate tendency toward insouciance. They pride themselves on thinking for themselves – on doing everything their *own* way – on exercising their critical-thinking skills despite the obvious consequences to intra-faculty harmony. And so these particular individuals will have to be enticed to action using more subtle devices than altruism or professional duty alone."

"It's good you understand that."

"I do. And so I will make sure to appeal to them on many levels. I will appeal to their self-interest. I will appeal to their incessant need for personal and intellectual gratification. Their constant need to be revered. Their ingrained longing for adulation, the need for deferential attention and attentive deference, the human frailty that draws them to the head of a classroom filled with impressionable learners. Their need for an admiring audience, you see, will be our saving grace because it can be harnessed for the purpose of our party!"

"Which is to say?"

"Which is to say we will hold a talent contest!"

"At the Christmas party?"

"Yes! And after that we will present our faculty with awards."

"For what?"

"Well for being, say, Most Improved Teacher. Or Educator of the Moment. Or maybe we can give a Student's Choice award for mesmerizing instruction. In short, we will honor them with recognition…."

Dr. Felch shook his head. I continued:

"….But most importantly, we will *listen*. We will listen respectfully to what they have said. And we will defer to their better judgment. In other words, I will make a point to incorporate every single comment made during the focus group that they attended. Every whim they've expressed. Every caprice. Every pent-up desire and longing of a repressed soul. Every suggestion. Every concern. If you approve my plan, Dr. Felch, this will be a Christmas party that is of the people, by the people, *for* the people. A party that emphasizes the pursuit of happiness in all its contrasting guises. It will be a melting pot of rugged individualism and inspired egalitarianism and enlightened self-interest – all mixed together like ingredients in a hearty stew...."

I paused to savor the comparison. Then I continued:

"You see, Dr. Felch, I am committed to getting one-hundred percent participation at this Christmas party. Every single faculty and staff of our college should be in that cafeteria on March twentieth for our Christmas party."

"You're dreaming, Charlie. It's a small room. And we've never had one-hundred percent attendance for a Christmas party. Ever. Not even when things were going well on campus. Not even when our demographics were homogenous. Not even when we brought in the world-famous hypnotist to perform next to the Yule tree."

"That may be so. But we're going to have it *this* year! If it's the last thing I do as a living, breathing, self-respecting educational administrator, I am going to bring both sides of your divided faculty and staff into that cafeteria to attend that godforsaken Christmas party...."

"You are?"

"Yes, I am."

❦

AND SO, OVER the next few hours, I shared my plans to entice our faculty and staff to attend the Christmas party. In breathless tones I detailed how I would use the specter of failed accreditation to compel the conscientious; the promise of tenure to attract the careerists; and an elaborate awards ceremony to entice the resume-padders. I explained how I would emphasize the value of Christmas itself to court the religious, and the prospect of unity and togetherness to attract the spiritual. To bring in the locals I would adhere to culture and tradition, while to the neophytes I would offer a series of innovations as sweeping as they were arbitrary. One by one by one, I shared with Dr. Felch my ideas for attracting my colleagues to our party. The atheists. The anti-socials. The agnostics. Somehow I would lure both Jew and Gentile into the small cafeteria. Vegetarian and anti-vegetarian. Sunni and Shiite. Friend and foe. Specialist and generalist. The poet. The empiricist. The agoraphobe. The dreamer. The cliometrician. Sam Middleton. All of them would come to our Christmas party in March where they would be treated to a truly inspiring, a genuinely sensational, an

eminently toe-curling and earth-shattering Christmas yuletide experience
that would demonstrate once and for all the amazing….

"Are you done?"

"Huh?"

"Are you done, Charlie?"

In my reverie I had lost track of time. I had misplaced my train of
thought. With the back of my hand I wiped away the spittle that had
accumulated at the corners of my mouth:

"Yes," I said. "I'm done."

Dr. Felch handed me a handkerchief.

"I appreciate your enthusiasm here, Charlie. And I admire your ambition.
But let me ask you a question which cuts to the heart of the matter…."

"Yes, sir!"

"….You see, what I really want to know is….sure you can get all these
people there. It seems you have a plan for that. And plans, of course, are
crucial to our profession. But what about Rusty? And what about Gwen?
If you don't get *them* to come, their acolytes will pull out as well. But those
two are as tough as they are tenured and they won't be easily swayed
toward your festivities. Hell, Rusty's an old friend of mine, and even *I*
can't persuade him to make peace with the inevitable. Gwen is about as
non-denominational as they come – and she is even more anti-Rusty than
that – and just as obdurate in her ways. The likelihood of getting those two
together into such a small segment of time and space for something of
this magnitude, something this divisive – this decisive – is not great. So
what's your plan to accomplish this? What's your plan for *them*, Charlie?"

At this I said, "Dr. Felch, I thought you might ask me this. And so
I'll answer as honestly as I can. Which is to say…to be perfectly honest,
I don't *have* a plan for them. At least not yet."

"No plan?!"

"No."

"And you call yourself an educational administrator?"

"Well, I don't have a plan. But I do have a *plan* to formulate a plan."

"A plan for a plan?"

"Yes!"

And here I acknowledged that I had no plan to get Rusty and Gwen to
come to our Christmas party. But that somewhere between vegetarianism and
anti-vegetarianism there must surely be a menu that could appeal to them both.

"No, sir, I don't have a plan quite yet," I concluded. "But I do have every intention of working on these two diametrical opposites to get them both to come."

"How?"

"Like *this*...." And running down the esplanade I called out to Gwen from behind:

"Wait!" I yelled. "Hey, Gwen, wait a second....!"

Gwen stopped to look back at me, surprised.

"Gwen, wait a minute please. May I rejoin you on your inexorable walk down this very long esplanade?"

"Well, you already have, I suppose. Just keep up the pace because I'm running late...."

I agreed, joining her progression in lockstep. Then I turned to Rusty who was now standing next to the clepsydra outside his museum and packing away his things for the day.

"Can I catch a ride back to campus?" I asked him.

"You still haven't bought a truck of your own?" he answered. "Or at least a car?"

"No," I said. "Not yet. It's too politicized a decision. So can I get a ride back to campus in the meantime?"

"Okay, but don't expect me to drive very fast...."

"No, of course not....!"

Rusty opened the door of his truck and I climbed in.

At last I was sitting in Rusty's Dodge. And walking down the Esplanade with Gwen. Now I was waving my conductor's wand over the dissolution left in the wake of my high-stakes focus group. And once again I was holding my pistol and aiming it at the silhouette of onrushing events in the distance.

"Are you *ever* going to pull that trigger?" Ethel asked. "Or are you just going to stand there aiming it into the distance like that?"

It was a valid question. In response I took closer aim at my far-away target and once again began to squeeze the cold metal of the trigger.

≈

In time the Christmas break began in earnest, and I began to focus all my strength on developing my plan for the Christmas party in March.

When my strength failed, I took pills. And when my pills failed, I took even more pills. When *they* ran out I caught a ride with Marsha Greenbaum to the Outskirts where I bought several more vials from the long-haired man under the resplendent bough of holly. Colors ran together. Days ran together. Events ran together. Word after word ran together. And still, in the very background of it all, there was the ticking of my pendulum, the quiet of my apartment, and somewhere off in the distance a very light knocking at my door.

Alone in my apartment, I lay with the book that I had first taken up so many months ago. "When Love knocks," it was telling me, "make sure you answer the door." Throughout the night I made my way headlong through the onrushing pages until, by early morning, I had finished the chapters on disappointment and disillusionment. Then denial and delusion. Later that night, after yet another day at the office, I finished the chapters on divorce and death, respectively. And then, at last, I turned the page to discover that there were no more pages to discover: I'd finished the book from cover to cover. Suddenly it was over. After an entire semester of intensive reading, I'd finally completed *The Anyman's Guide to Love and the Community College*. Satisfied, I set the book down on the side of my bed.

"Congratulations, Charlie!" Will said when I told him of my accomplishment. It was a few days after New Year's and the campus was still a ghost town. In fact, only he and I had stayed throughout the break: every morning I'd come in to work on my plans for the Christmas party; and every day he'd come to sit with his newspaper, his flask of bourbon, and his cigar. It was a late afternoon and his Oldsmobile Starfire was parked outside, lengthwise, across three separate stalls; he'd let me into the cafeteria with the key he'd tucked into his coat pocket many years ago. "I'm not even supposed to *have* this key," he explained. "But the janitress is a former student of mine who made me a copy. She once dreamt of being a professional historian. But it didn't work out for her. So now when she sees me, she looks the other way...."

Flicking on the lights of the cafeteria, Will walked over to his regular seat at the table under the no-smoking sign and pulling out his canteen of bourbon and a new cigar, sat down heavily on the chair. "Congratulations on finishing your book," he said. As he spoke, his words were slurred, his eyes bloodshot and tired. In the dim light of the empty cafeteria, he seemed to be aging with each passing day, as if he'd gained a year of life in the last three weeks, or five since the beginning of the semester. It was as if he were aging exponentially before my eyes. "Nowadays finishing a book of any kind is no small accomplishment."

"Thank you," I said.

"In fact this seems like the type of momentous occasion we should be drinking to. You're open to bourbon, aren't you?"

I laughed.

"You could say that...."

Will passed his canteen to me, and I took a small drink.

"That's all?" he protested. "Don't insult me!"

And so I took another drink.

Will laughed.

"That's more like it! Here have another...!"

I took a third.

"So now what?" he asked when he'd taken the flask back from me. "What's left for Mr. Charlie now that he's finally finished his book?"

"I don't know. I've spent so much time with it that I almost hate to see it end. It's like a friend of mine has passed away. A secret friend. A friend that can always be trusted to be there. And now it's gone."

"I hear you, Charlie."

Will grew somber. Then he said:

"Charlie, believe me when I tell you this: almost all of it comes and goes. People. The years. The pages in your book. Life itself. And when it's all said and done, what you're left with are those few things that actually stay and stay forever. The words. The water. Literature and love. Those are our only legacies. The rest, though it may look pretty on your curriculum vitae, is nothing more than polished bullshit."

"Bullshit?"

"Yes, bullshit."

Will was looking at me with the same sad drunken eyes.

"It's only these things that matter in the end," he said, "because it's only those things that stay and stay forever...."

I nodded and we drank.

When I returned to my empty apartment later that night, the building was dark and quiet: my fellow faculty had long deserted the campus for their homes and their families, and I was the only one left. The parking lot was completely empty. The corridors were still. After several days of empty quietude, I had begun to notice how silent everything had become, and that the silence was beginning to grow on me. The stillness and darkness were more beautiful than any light of motion could ever be. How tranquil it all was. How peaceful! For the first time since I'd been at Cow Eye, my mind began to rest. Wearily I felt a deep sleep overcoming me. Rest. Repose. All of them at once. Finally, the promise of fertile sleep found me for good.

Except that now it didn't.

Just as my eyes began to close, I felt an almost imperceptible noise. Behind the drone of the heating unit. Above the sound of the wind rustling outside my window. Under it all was the quietest of knocking at my door. A knocking so soft that it might not be knocking at all. Should I even get up to check? Or should I wait for it to pass? Who might it be at this lingering hour, at this late date, amid the quiet of our intercession? Amid the tranquility before the storm? Who could possibly be knocking on my door at this late time of the very long night?

Cautiously, I got up from the bed and made my way to the door where the uncertain knocking could still be heard. Undoing the chain, I opened the door.

In the dark of the hallway there was nothing to be seen, only the black of poorly lit emptiness and its shadows. But then, to the side, in the faint light spilling out from my apartment, I saw a woman leaning against the wall. She had wrapped her arms around herself and was sobbing. Her chest was heaving. It was the math teacher.

"Can I come in?" she said.

I paused with the door's edge still in my hand.

"Of course," I answered and opened the door. "Please do…."

The woman walked into the apartment. Her hair was disheveled. Her clothes were unkempt. She looked tired and haggard, as if she hadn't slept for some time. Without makeup she did not look nearly as glamorous as she'd seemed from afar – as she'd always appeared on her passings in and out of her apartment.

"Sure, please do come in," I said. "I wasn't expecting guests…."

The woman sat down on the edge of my couch.

"I'm sorry to bother you," she said. "It's just that. Well, I needed to be with someone. *Anyone*. And you're the only person I know who keeps the same hours we keep…."

She looked up at me.

"You're the only one who stays up as late as I do...."

"Sure," I said. "I understand. We're between semesters and there's no one else in the building. I'm the only one here. Would you like some tea?"

The woman thanked me. I set a pot of water on the stove.

"Can I use your shower?" she said.

"My shower?"

"Yes. Mine is filled with memories."

"Of course. No problem. The shower is over there. Next to the closet."

"It would have to be. Your apartment is just like mine, only its exact opposite."

"Oh, right....the other side of the wall...."

"Do you have any clothes I can change into?"

"No, I don't. Just.....Oh, wait, yes I do! Here you can use *these*....!"

I handed her the overnight clothes that Bessie stored at my apartment.

The math teacher took the oversized t-shirt and held it at arm's length in front of her.

"You don't have anything smaller?"

"Sorry, they're the only women's clothes I have. I do have some argyle sweaters if you'd like...."

The woman took Bessie's clothes into my bathroom and while the shower ran I prepared the cups for tea and set them on the table. When she came out she was wearing the long t-shirt but holding the pair of shorts and the cotton panties I'd given her. The woman's hair was wet and her make-up had been washed off from the shower. Her eyes were still visibly red from crying.

"Here..." she said and handed me the shorts and panties. "I just couldn't bring myself to wear them...."

I walked back into my bedroom and tucked the clothes back into my dresser where Bessie kept them, and when I returned the woman was already sitting at my kitchen table.

"Thank you," she said when I set the steaming tea cup in front of her. She was sitting with her legs crossed and with the end of the t-shirt tucked in between her thighs.

"Don't mention it," I said. And then: "I don't want to pry. And you don't have to answer me of course. But I have to ask.... are you okay?"

The woman shook her head.

"I don't want to talk about it. You see, it's not my fault...."

"I'm sure," I said.

"No really, it's not. It's not my fault at all! You see, he's got a doctorate. And I've only got a master's degree...."

"I don't understand...."

"No, of course you wouldn't. You're an administrator."

"Can you explain?"

"It's complicated."

"I'm willing to listen."

"I don't want to talk about it..."

"Right," I said. "I understand entirely."

"Thank you," she said. "I appreciate your understanding...."

The woman took a drink of tea. And then, without warning, and in extravagant detail, she told me about the things she didn't want to talk about. About her fight with the calculus teacher. How the two had just finished having the most amazing sex, but then, still lying in each other's arms, they'd drifted to the topic of course assignments for the upcoming semester. Who would get the morning sections. And who would get the schedule that allowed for the longer weekend. And who would get the upper-level classes that were so coveted. And it was this discussion that had turned into a serious disagreement.

"Why do *I* always have to teach the morning classes?" she sobbed. "Why can't *I* teach calculus every once in a while?"

And here she spoke about the proliferation of their argument and how, to justify his own teaching of the higher things in life, he'd casually implied that his own level of knowledge was more conducive than hers. That his teaching methodologies were more appropriate for upper-division students and higher-level curriculum. That his style was far more current for articulating the ineffable.

"He pooh-poohed my pedagogy!" she sobbed.

I nodded sympathetically. Not knowing what to do, I shifted my chair closer to hers and put an arm around her heaving shoulders.

"It's okay," I said, trying to comfort her. "There are other math teachers in the lecturer pool..."

But she was inconsolable.

That night the woman slept on my couch under covers that I laid across her, and all through that December night I could only lie in my bed restless and unable to sleep. And when I left the following morning for my office she was still asleep under the covers. Through the cafeteria window I saw Will sitting at his table. I knocked on the glass. Will looked up from his newspaper then walked over to let me in.

"There's a math teacher sleeping on my couch," I said when I'd taken my customary seat across from him at the corner table. Though it was early afternoon – almost lunch time – no cafeteria workers were present. No food was being served over the break. The room was abandoned, all the chairs stacked on top of the tables, and the two of us simply sat across the table from each other, like old lovers, in lieu of any other company we might have had.

"The math teacher's sleeping on your couch?"

"Yes."

"The pretty one from your hallway?"

"Yes."

"In the t-shirt?"

"Yes."

"You're a dog, Charlie…!"

"No, no, no. It's not like that. She came over last night. She had a fight with the calculus teacher. She was inconsolable. I did my best to comfort her. And then she fell asleep. She was still sleeping when I left."

"So now what are you planning to do? What's your plan now that you have a young math teacher sleeping on your couch?"

"I don't know. It's a bit unexpected. Any advice?"

Will thought for no more than an instant. Then he said:

"Congress that cow!"

"I'm sorry…?"

"If opportunity knocks, Charlie boy, you gotta open that back door! Otherwise, you never know what you might end up regretting. It's like my wife used to say – she'd say, Smithcoate, you sonofabitch, the best damn thing that ever happened to our marriage was that girl from the supermarket…."

"Mr. Smithcoate?"

"That's right, Charlie. That girl from the supermarket saved our marriage! And that's coming from the woman I spent thirty-eight years of monogamy with."

Around us the cafeteria was silent and forlorn. Will was still nursing his canteen and his cigar. Beyond the window his powder-blue Oldsmobile could still be seen parked sideways in the lot straddling the three closest parking stalls, the handicapped space included. I'd expected Will to elaborate about his wife's statement of salvation. But he did not. He just took a long drink from his canteen and sucked in another drag from his cigar. Finally, I spoke up:

"Mr. Smithcoate," I said. "Can I ask you a question?"

Will wiped his mouth with his sleeve.

"That would depend. Is it about history?"

"Somewhat."

"Well, I'm on vacation. See me after the break when I have my notes...."

I laughed and shook my head.

"Don't worry – it's not like that. Actually, my question is partly about history, but mostly *not* about history too. You see, I was just wondering if you could tell me something about your wife. You talk about her an awful lot, Mr. Smithcoate. But only from time to time, and in bits and pieces. In truth, you've never really told me much about her. And I was just curious, you know, to learn a little more. I was just wondering if you could tell me something more about your wife and what she was like before she passed away....?"

Will took a drink from his flask. Then he said:

"Hmmm. My wife. There's not much to say, really. I mean what can you say about a person you spent thirty-eight years of your life with?"

"I'm not sure...."

"What would *you* say, Charlie?"

"There's no way I could possibly know...."

"Well let me tell you....there's not much you *can* say. Thirty-eight years is a damned long time. That's incontrovertible. But some things defy words. So let's not even try, okay? No, instead, let me tell you about something else. Let me tell you about something that *can* be articulated in words. Let me tell you about that girl from the supermarket....!"

And here Will told me in descriptive detail about the woman from the supermarket who had captivated his imagination somewhere along the middle of his marriage. How the two had met innocently, next to a shopping cart, and how they had developed an ongoing relationship that lasted several years. And how, when his wife learned of it sometime later – he himself had found the occasion to tell her – it changed everything between them.

"It was like night and day," he said. "And that moment of repentance was the twilight."

In sumptuous detail Will Smithcoate told me of the things that he and the girl from the supermarket did during their years together. And how, when he finally decided to break it off, it was the hardest day of his life.

"Well, maybe the *second* hardest," he said. "Yes, it was probably the second hardest day of my life. But the second hardest, *by far*."

Attentively I listened to his tale of requited love and reclaimed marriage. In time his voice trailed off and he took another drink from his canteen. It was clear he had reached the end of his reminiscence.

"So can I ask you another question then, Mr. Smithcoate?"

"If you must...."

"Why are you here all the time? In this cafeteria? At this table? It seems like you're always in this same spot. That you spend most of your time here under that futile no-smoking sign. But why is that? Don't you ever want to go home?"

Will offered up a laugh. But it was not the good kind. Among laughter that is heard there is good laughter, and there is the other kind – and it was this other kind that Will had just offered up.

"What's a home, Charlie? I mean, you've asked a simple question. But to have an intelligent discussion we should move beyond simplicity. We should be precise with our definitions, right? We should make sure we're talking about the same thing here...."

"A *home*?"

"Yes. Can you tell me what a home is?"

"Well, a home is. A home is where you *live*."

"And?"

"And sleep. It is where you live and sleep."

"Good. And...?"

"Well, and read books. A home is the place where you can live and sleep and read books when the ambient noise is so great that you can't fall asleep."

"Is that all?"

"I think so, yes."

"Are you sure?"

"Well I imagine so...."

"And your home is your apartment in faculty housing?"

"It is now, yes."

"That's your *home*?"

"Yes."

"Because you live there?"

"Yes."

"No, Charlie. That is not a home. A home has to be more than that. Much more. Sure, you live in Cow Eye Junction at the moment. But Cow Eye Junction is not your *home*. Marsha Greenbaum lives in that closet at her studio since moving to Cow Eye, but that closet is not her home. I reside in a two-story house where my wife and I used to live. But that was many years ago. And things do tend to change. I'm here in this dark cafeteria, you see, because I no longer have a home to go to."

"You're homeless?"

"No, I'm not homeless – I'm tenured, for god's sake! But I don't have a *home*. Not anymore. And I haven't had one for almost two years now." Outside the windows of the cafeteria, the shortest of days was coming to an end. The longest of nights was beginning. Will had reached the end of his canteen. "Dammit," he said. And then: "Everyone just loves supermarkets, don't they? They're vast. And impressive. They are beautiful and bountiful and come in quite handy when you need something like a specialty item that is exotic or hard to find. But a supermarket is not a *home*."

I thought I understood what he was saying. Or at least what he was *trying* to say. And so I changed the subject one final time.

"Mr. Smithcoate," I said. "Can you now tell me something about history? I know it's your vacation and all….but can you tell me how history itself works? I've often wondered about it. And it seems that you would be the perfect one to clarify it for me. Sitting here in this deserted cafeteria. The light fading outside those windows. The academic year having reached its very midpoint. The semester having reached the end of its incarnation – or, if you prefer, the beginning of its dissolution. Mr. Smithcoate, can you please tell me about…history?"

Will did not immediately answer. Across the table he was regarding me with unconcealed skepticism. And in the low drone of the cafeteria, the wheels of time could be heard to grind in the background next to the ice maker. It was a moment I would long remember. With all my being, I waited for his response.

≈

THAT AFTERNOON I came home to find the math teacher sitting at my kitchen table reading the first chapter of *The Anyman's Guide to Love and the Community College.*

"I hope it's okay I'm still here," she said, setting the book on the table. "My apartment is just so lonely nowadays. I hope you don't mind that I took the liberty of staying."

"Sure," I said. "Staying is a good thing. And liberty is always preferable to its alternative...."

"I tried to make myself useful. While you were gone I organized your bedroom."

"You did?"

"And ironed your shirts."

"Thanks!"

"And I rearranged those women's toiletries in your bathroom."

"What...?"

"They were out of order. I hope that's okay?"

"Well, actually...."

"If not, you can just move them back to where they were..."

The woman stood up from the table.

"Tea?" she said.

"Please...." I said, and then: "Thank you...."

The woman poured some tea that she had boiled. Then she set my cup on the table in front of me.

"How was your day?"

"It was fine. I'm an educational administrator. All my days are equally fine."

The woman nodded as if she were considering an exotic and far-off idea. Then she set her cup into its saucer with a clink.

"I have a confession to make," she said. "And it involves you. You see, I was wrong to think what I used to think. I was very wrong about you."

"You were?"

"Yes. I always saw you as an educational administrator. And I just assumed that because that's what you were.....well, you know – that it was *all* you were. But now I see that things are more nuanced than that...."

"They are?"

"Yes. Life is more complicated than it appears. Now I see that you can be much more. That educational administration does not have to be the exact opposite of in-class enlightenment. That the two can come together, beautifully, like integers on a number line. That conciliation can be just as arousing as conflict...."

The woman ran the back of her fingers lightly over my cheek.

"In fact, if you were to shave off that beard, you would be something different altogether."

"I would?"

"Yes. Shall we try?"

The woman led me into the bathroom and I took out my shaving supplies and fumbled with them and while I lathered my face and sharpened my razor on a leather strap she sat on my toilet seat with the lid closed watching my reflection in the mirror.

"There's a patch under your right jaw...." she would say.

And I would find it with my fingers and shave it away.

"I love to watch a man shave," she remarked.

And I obliged the predilection as best I could.

When I was done I turned around to face her. She stood up from the toilet seat.

"Beautiful!" she said. And then: "We should do this more often!"

Slowly she ran her hand over my newly shaven skin. Her hand was cool and soft; it was very young and very smooth.

"Can I ask you a question?" she said.

"Of course," I said.

"Do you like mathematics?"

I cleared my throat.

"I don't know," I said. "It's, um, necessary...."

"Yes, but do you *like* it?"

"I suppose you could say that I do. I mean, yes, I do. I like math."

"That's not what I've heard."

"Oh?"

"Yes. I've heard that you don't like math. And that's a shame."

"Well, I'm not sure who told you that, but it wouldn't be entirely correct. As recently as elementary school, in fact, math was one of my favorite subjects. Math, social studies, reading – I liked them all...."

"And now?"

"Well now I prefer social studies. Though math does possess a certain taxidermic appeal…"

"So you're open to it?"

"Yes."

"Good. Because I *adore* math…."

Here the woman lifted the front of my dress shirt out of my pants.

"Math is ecstasy…." she purred. "If you look deeply enough you'll see that math itself is Eros…."

"Yes…" I said. "I'm beginning to see that more clearly…."

"Math is the probing glans in our quest for inner knowledge. It is the pulsating clitoris of the intellect…."

Now she was undoing my belt.

"Without math there would be neither love nor logic. There would be no foreplay. No process for quantifying the tremulous approach to orgasm."

"Yes…" I said.

"Do you agree?"

"Yes."

"You do?"

"Yes!"

From there she led me to my bedroom.

"I made your bed," she said and pointed to the neatly folded covers. "It's been waiting for you since morning."

"I see."

"*I've* been waiting for you since morning."

"I see!"

"I hope you don't mind…."

"Not at all."

"Please understand that I've done this many times before."

"Apparently."

"It's a talent I have."

"I can tell."

"Can you appreciate it?"

"Yes. It's all so taut and firm…."

"My father was a soldier. He could bounce a dime."

"That would be impressive."

"Would you like to see?"

"Of course."

"See?"

"Yes."

"Impressed?"

"Very."

"Me too."

"Really?"

"Yes."

"I'm glad."

"That's good."

"Is that your triangle I feel?"

"Among other things."

"One must always be open to new sensations."

"Yes."

"Including math."

"Yes!"

"I think I can see myself growing to love mathematics."

"It's never too late, you know."

"Might I be a late bloomer?"

"Some blooms grow more than others."

"I couldn't have done it without you."

"Let's not get ahead of ourselves."

"I'll try."

"Try harder."

"I am."

"No, not like that. Like this....!"

"Like that?"

"Yes."

"It's somewhat unexpected."

"Because your equation is really quite linear."

"Thank you!"

"It's linear all right. But let's try something more advanced, shall we?"

"Advanced?"

"Yes, let's not be content with the familiar. Have you experienced a derivative?"

"A what?"

"Or the beauty of the integral?"

"Not recently."

"Let me reveal it to you...."

"Okay...."

"I will do it slowly and revealingly...."

"Yes...."

"So that you can see it...."

"Yes...."

"...in all its glory...."

"I see it!"

"Is it beautiful?"

"Yes!"

"Does it work for you....?"

"It works. But my equation has never had to do *that* before...."

"Never?"

"Well not in a long time anyway."

"How long?"

"I can't even remember. Freshman year of college, I think."

"Well now it can!"

"It's amazing..."

"Don't stop."

"Okay."

"The end is in sight."

"Okay."

"We're close."

"Good."

"And *you?*"

"Somewhat."

"Let's enjoy it together."

"I'll try."

"I can slow down if you want."

"No don't."

"Are you sure?"

"Yes."

"But what's that?"

"What's what?"

"That sound."

"What sound?"

"That sound coming from your nightstand. Next to the alarm clock. What is it?"

In the quiet of my apartment the phone was ringing loud and out of sorts.

"The phone! It's ringing!"

"Don't answer it!"

"Of course."

"It will stop."

"I know."

"We're close…"

"Right."

After several minutes the very loud phone grew silent. Only to ring again, just as loudly.

"The phone again."

"Let it ring."

"What time is it?"

"It's almost two,"

"Two?"

"Yes, two."

"Two o'clock?"

"Yes, it's two o'clock!"

"Exactly or approximately?"

"Approximately. It is approximately *two o'clock!*"

"Would that be a.m. or p.m.?"

"My god, Charlie, is it so important? *Now?!*"

"Sorry but I'm an educational administrator. These things matter for me."

"Now?!"

"No, I guess not…."

"Then let the damn phone ring!"

And so I let it ring.

Then she said, "As you can see, we've now moved on to a higher level."

And I said, "Yes, I've noticed."

"Can you feel the new change in acceleration?"

"Is that what I'm feeling?"

"Among other things."

"I like it."

"Does it surprise you?"

"It does."

"Does it overwhelm you?"

"A bit. This is all very new for me."

"I think you're getting the feel for it."

"I'm definitely trying."

"And that excites me…."

"I'm glad."

"….as a professional."

"*Very* glad."

"And a woman."

"Both at the same time?"

"Yes. But especially as a professional…."

The phone rang yet again. It was just as loud. But this time I had to stop.

"This may be important," I said.

"Not now!" she growled. "We're close!"

And so I let it ring. And ring. And ring. And ring. And ring. And ring. And ring. And when it rang again, I didn't think to listen. There were other things to see. And other sounds to hear. The sights and smells were immediate. Math was in the air. And we were very close.

"I'm very close," she said.

Except that, well, she *wasn't*. The phone rang yet again, and yet again we waited. And waited. And waited. And once again it stopped. But now, impatiently, she reached across the bed to cleave the handset from its base.

"I'm close," she said, annoyed. And then, by way of explanation: "Very *very* close."

"Very close?" I asked.

"Very very *very* close….!"

"Okay," I said at last. And over tea I asked: "Is this what math can be? Is it always like this for you?"

"Every time," she said, and then: "Though after calculus it gets even better….!"

⁓

And so I came to spend my intercession alternating between the undulating priorities of mathematics and history: in the day with Will in the cafeteria; and in the evenings with the math teacher in my apartment. What had promised to be a cold and lonely time suddenly became one of hot adventure. And just as she had promised, I came to love the feel of math. For hours at a time. Through all the iterations of day and night and in all conceivable positions. Tables upturned. Bedsprings creaking. Across the open faces of textbooks, the glossy pages sticking to our sweaty backs. On the kitchen table. Up against the wall. Straddling the sink. Deeper and deeper into the cold winter nights the two of us explored each other's disciplines so that in time they came together in the great calculus of love, the everlasting light of literature, that oldest and greatest of faiths known as history.

"History?"

"Yes, history."

At this Will's eyes focused entirely on me. It was clear that the bourbon had done its duty and that he was no longer pretending to resist it. But hearing this word so unexpectedly, he perked up.

"So you want to know about history, Charlie?"

"Yes."

"Even though it's January?"

"Yes," I said. "I do. You see, it's getting late, Mr. Smithcoate. The winter break is almost over and the students will soon be returning. The faculty will be returning once again from desiccation to verdure. Outside our window it is getting very late. The longest night has passed and now we are heading toward the equinox. So can you tell me please what you know about the workings of history?"

Will looked up from his canteen and said:

"I know quite a lot of course. In fact, I know far too much. For it is my livelihood and my fate. I am a product of history as well as its factor. I am its child and it is *mine*. Like my wife used to remind me, she'd say: Smithcoate, it was not in our cards to have children – sadly, progeny of that sort were not in your divine plan – but it's okay, you can have other kinds of children. And so my students are my descendents and I will live through them. My teachings are my children. My words are my legacy. Hell, even these discarded butts from my cigars are my faithful offspring. Every act I take is an act of procreation. Every consequence is a child. I have a thousand million children out there in this world somewhere. And yet I have not a single one to take me to that doctor's appointment I missed last month. But that is all water under the bridge now. Let's not talk about the past, Charlie. I'd much rather talk about the future."

"The future?"

"Of course. The future, you see, is but the past in disguise. It is a promise rather than its premise. It is the beautiful plan versus the ugliness of its implementation. Perfection as opposed to reality. The idea transcending its compromise. It is the whisper. The dream. The unfulfilled desire. It is the cafeteria at the end of the long esplanade. The delta where all rivers merge. The eternal promise of ecstasy rather than the fleeting orgasm itself. The future, you see, is our history. Just as your apartment is a perfect reflection of the math teacher's, only in absolute reverse – so too is the future nothing but the story of our history, only as its unseen opposite: the sounds on the other side of the wall. Despite what we may think it to be, you see, the future is less a consequence of our past, than the past is the consequence of our future. So let us talk about *that,* shall we....?"

"By all means...." I said.

And so, speaking through the bourbon and across the table and over his newspaper and under the rising smoke from his cigar, Will Smithcoate told me about the future.

"The future, you see, is not what you think it will be. And it never is. It is the intact calf hiding amid a dusty corral. A submerged stone in the great river of time. It is the unexpected abrasion of asphalt against human skin. The future comes more relentlessly than an Oldsmobile speeding down the highway. More arbitrarily than seven billion arrows shot through time and space. It is as expeditious as an onrushing welfare recipient, more decisive than a trigger that has been inadvertently pulled. And yet it never truly comes. It is always there off in the distance, one step ahead of you no matter how quick your gait, like an ambitious colleague on the esplanade. In some cultures it is the spirit that is always behind your left shoulder and that skips away as you turn to look at it. It might be there for others to discover, but never there for *you.* No matter the efforts you exert, you can never transcend the future. No matter how hard you try...."

Will had paused and it seemed that he might stop. To encourage him, I said:

"But, Mr. Smithcoate! What do you *see* in our future? It is Sunday now and the faculty will be coming back to our campus first thing tomorrow morning. The parking lots will start to fill up. The library will once again bustle. All of this is familiar and predictable. They are known. But what else do you see in store for us? Aside from yet another semester of accredited learning? Aside from the triumphant success of our upcoming Christmas party? Aside from all this, what more can you tell us about the future that lies ever so slightly beyond our grasp?"

At this Will took a final drag on his cigar. And though I didn't know it then, his words would stay with me until my own final dissolution. Taking the ultimate drag of his cigar, he said:

"Our future, Charlie, is as bright as that neon bulb illuminating this dim cafeteria. And like that bulb our future will be lived in a world of dull efficiency. In the future efficacy will be the currency of life. It will take the place of our humanity. For there will come a day when we will move faster and grow taller and live longer and know more – and without much reflection we will come to consider these things *accomplishments*. We will be able to conquer faraway concepts without ever understanding the inner turbulences of our own hearts. We will scale mountains that have never been reached, and make technologies that have never been imagined. We will come to worship our innovations as gods. And innovation will become our god. And efficiency will be our creed. Progress will be our prayer. But the words of our prayers will no longer have sound. Our humanity will be traded for the spoils of novelty. And our souls will be sacrificed upon the altar of continuous improvement. In the future, Charlie, we will *all* be regionally accredited….."

In the back room an ice machine could be heard to start up. Will looked over at the sound, then back at me:

"But that does not change the essential truths of the world. It does not change the nature of our souls. For there are things that are ineffably high. And these things resist the impositions of man. Time is the only master I will ever recognize. And water is the only thing that can make me believe. Water is my guide. And words are my salvation. And God, in all His mercy and judgment, will be our final Accreditor waiting for us at the gate…."

≈

"Did you forget something, Charlie?"

"I'm sorry?"

"You heard me, Charlie. Did you forget something?"

Bessie was standing in my office doorway. She did not look happy. And yet she did not look angry either. In our months together, I had often seen her livid. I had seen her fierce. She had been scorned and bitter in my presence. And I had witnessed her flaws and her prejudices and her vulnerabilities come boiling to the surface. I had seen her lash out in response. And I had cowered before her fits of temper. I had seen all of this and more. But I had never seen her like *this*. Unlike those other times, now she was simply calm, reconciled, distant. Something was very wrong. And though I couldn't have known what it was, it was clear that something important had changed. And that it was irretrievable. And that it was not for the better.

"Am I forgetting something?" I answered. "Not that I know of. Why are you asking?"

Bessie looked at me coldly.

"You did. You forgot."

"Forgot what?"

Bessie shook her head.

"I can't believe you forgot...."

"Forgot *what*?!"

"Never mind," she said. "Let's just get this debrief over with...."

"Right," I said. "So where are we?"

"Where are we?"

"Yes, where are we?"

"We're in your office, Charlie. You've just conducted your high-stakes focus group and we're standing in your office. If you listen carefully you can still hear the pendulum ticking in the background. On your desk is a stack of dusty papers. You are currently sitting at your desk holding two bottles of pills. I am standing in this doorway. This is where we are *at*, Charlie..."

"Well, no. That's not what I meant. What I meant, Bessie, is where are we at, *historically*? Because a good debrief should give a quick overview of what has just happened. It should present an efficient history of what has just taken place, its outcomes, and its meaning. An effective debrief should give plans for next steps. It should leave the faithful concert-goers streaming toward the exits with a song of love in their hearts. This is what a good debrief should do, Bessie. I know this for a fact because I read it once in a book that Raul gave me...."

Bessie stared at me with an icy expression. Her voice was calm. Her demeanor was reserved. She had her hands sunk deep into the pockets of her camisole. Looking at me, she said:

"Well, let me help you out with that. You want to talk about history? Allow me to do the honors. You see, your history begins a few months ago with your arrival into the makeshift bus shelter and that visit to the bar where my friends first met you. You see, they told me all about you, Charlie. And they warned me to stay away. He's not from here, they said, and doesn't seem to *want* to be. He seems aloof and distant, as if he's too good for Cow Eye. As if he's above it all...."

"Bessie, what are you talking about? I've never been above anything. Where are you going with this?"

"You wanted a song of love, right?"

"Yes...."

"And you asked me to stay afterwards, right?"

"Yes..."

"You wanted to finish everything off with a debrief, right? Well now let's do our debrief...."

"But...."

"Right. So that was how *your* history began, Charlie. In the makeshift bus shelter. In late August. And please don't think that anything that might have happened before you got here is relevant in any way. Because it's not. Not for us. Your story begins the moment you arrived into Cow Eye Junction – the instant you stepped off that bus – and not a moment earlier...."

"Bessie?"

"So that's the beginning of *your* history. Now *our* history begins a few days later. You see, our history begins with you knocking incessantly on my ex-husband's office door a little after eight and then sitting in a hard plastic chair outside his office. While you waited, you thumbed through magazines, pretending not to notice me. Yet over my typewriter I could see you watching my every movement. The deep v-neck in my blouse. The way my eyelashes fluttered. The shapely contours of my shoulders. The way my bangs fell across my face. Your eyes were hungry, Charlie. Your glance was furtive. Your demeanor was that of a divorcee on the prowl. From there I led you to convocation where I introduced you to the vagaries of life at Cow Eye. The personalities. The alignments. I helped you see things as they are, to distinguish night from day. We talked a bit and you implied that you were honestly interested in loving the things that are unloved. You invited me to lunch. Though I was content with my manual typewriter, you persisted. I acquiesced. Holding my lunch tray I revealed to you what love could have been for me. You told me how you castrated a calf. I was impressed. We agreed to meet outside Marsha's studio and I made sure to come on time. But you weren't there. I wandered up and down the boardwalk and eventually I found you half-naked at the edge of the universe. We drove to the party by the river. We drank beer. The moon shone down on us like a mother's only love. I directed you to a clearing. You pissed in my mouth. I invited you to meet my children. You spent our entire weekend together writing a focus group report and developing a plan to develop a plan for a Christmas party. You stopped shaving. You stopped bathing. Your clothes are rumpled. Your beard grew long. You've taken to taking pills: one pill after another even though neither of them is helping you stay awake…even though neither is helping you sleep. We talked. We fucked. I washed your dishes. Two o'clock came and went. We waited. Then waited some more. And now here we are in this office with this pendulum ticking and your face newly shaven. Honestly, your history is not a very interesting one, Charlie. Although your face, I have to admit, does look nice. In fact, it is as smooth and as shiny as I have ever seen it…."

Here Bessie stopped. Suddenly, she reached across my desk toward my pendulum. The metal orb from the other side swung down with a final resounding clack. And then the orbs were still. The pendulum had come to rest against her fingers. The sound was gone forever.

"So that's about where we are, Charlie," she said. "Or, to use your own terminology, that's where you and I are *at*. You see, this is not only our history I've just recounted, but it is also our future as well. The undulations are coming to an end. Our incarnation is running out. If things had turned out a little differently, you see, love could have been a Sunday outing at the river, just the four of us. But it's pointless to talk about that sort of thing now. And as to 'next steps' – well, I don't believe that will be necessary any more…."

Bessie had turned to leave but then she stopped and turned back around to me.

"Oh yeah…." she said. "One more thing. My mother wanted me to give this to you. She made me promise that I would. So, *here you go*…."

Bessie reached into her pocket and pulled out something that was small and dark and heavy. Tossing the wrapped piece of fruit cake onto my desk, she turned and walked away.

FINAL PREPARATIONS

"There are many things that love can claim to be. But very few that it actually is."

With less fanfare than its counterpart, the spring semester started in mid-January and before you could even blink, the semester was in full academic swing. The bicycles returned. The library bustled. The flag in front of the Administration building snapped in the cold winter wind – all thirteen stripes and forty-four stars. Students once again filled the long esplanade on their way from one discipline to another. And all across the campus of Cow Eye Community College one could once again find solace in the reassuring sound of paperwork getting done. By now the self-study was a bound and submitted memory. The focus group report, as Raul had predicted, was turned in with a shuddering gasp of ecstasy. My plan for the Christmas party had quickly moved from immaculate conception to imperfect implementation: by now all that remained was the finalization of an infinite number of details. Sitting at my desk, I worked meticulously to finalize those details. *Were the cases of bourbon ordered? Were the vendors paid? Had the student leaders rehearsed the scripts that they had been given?* Each of these questions required a series of actions on my part; each action brought about a series of new questions in its own right; and each of these questions led, in turn, to countless other questions and actions that also needed to be answered and acted upon.

When I finally looked up from all this, Raul was standing in my doorway.

"Charlie!" he said.

"Raul! You're back!"

"This is self-evident. Did you miss me?"

"Of course. You look great. How was your vacation? How was Texas?"

"It was wonderful. It's an absolutely amazing place. Inspiring and sublime. Not unlike the Barri Gòtic in late Summer. Here, I got you these...."

Raul held up a pair of snake-skin boots.

"For me?" I said and took the boots.

"I hope they fit you."

"I'm sure they will. Are those leather chaps for me too?"

He nodded and smiled. I shook his hand. We hugged.

"I'm glad you're back!" I said. "Sorry I didn't think to get *you* anything for Christmas. It's been an unexpectedly busy time for me here on campus! I've been so preoccupied. I mean, it's like the world itself is a changed place. It may even feel like you're returning to a totally different world altogether, Raul."

"It's only been a month...."

"Yeah, but so much has happened since you left! You'll be amazed to hear it. So much, in fact, that I don't even know where to start...."

"Whoa, slow down there! I just stopped by to say hello. And to drop off the boots. And the chaps."

"Right! It's just that I've got so much to tell you, Raul. So many interesting things have taken place. But everything is happening so quickly I don't even know where to start...."

"Well how about you start from the beginning....?"

"Right! The beginning. Good idea, Raul! Have a seat over here on this chair and let me tell you from the very beginning everything that's happened since you left. You see, as soon as you left for Texas the first thing I did was grab these two vials out of my pocket and take a pill from each...."

"You're still consuming those pills that Rusty and Gwen gave you last semester?"

"Yes!"

"Have they started to work?"

"Yes!"

"They have?"

"Yes!"

"You mean they're actually working?"

"Yes!"

"Which one? The pill to fall asleep? Or the one to stay awake?"

"Both! You see, they're *both* working exactly as prescribed. This pill right here keeps me from ever falling asleep….while this one here keeps me from ever being fully awake. And so, thanks to these two amazing pills, I have been able to remain in a constant state of pseudo-sleep and semi-wakefulness. Say what you want about modern inventions, Raul – lament the dangers of wanton technology if you must – but these two pills are really something else! Easy to swallow. Not expensive. Eminently more palatable than their alternatives. And together they have bolstered my resolve and helped me amble through the intercession on my way toward the arrival of our institutional accreditors and the culmination of our Christmas Week festivities in the cafeteria….!"

"So life is good?"

"Life is *great*!"

"Well, tell me what else has happened. I mean, after you took all those pills, what happened?"

"So much, Raul! So much that it's incredible! You see, I finished my focus group session and wrote my report and Bessie reached her hand into my boxers and Dr. Felch cleaned out his spittoon. Then Bessie and I had a quick debrief and she gave me some fruitcake her mother made for me and after that I came home to my lonely apartment but it wasn't as lonely as I'd thought and so I made tea and shaved my jaw and began an intensive exploration of calculus. It's quite surprising, Raul, but since you left I've come to truly love mathematics! And that is no small miracle: in fact, I love it even more *now* than when I was in elementary school – and that's saying something because in elementary school I had a really good teacher who wore floral dresses that left her knees exposed for all to see! She had a habit of sitting at her desk and throwing one leg over the other ever so revealingly – just like this – and we'd all catch a fleeting glimpse of the skin on her upper thigh. But that was a long time ago. And now it's rare that women wear floral dresses. But then….what was I talking about again?"

"Your newfound love of mathematics."

"Oh right. So, um, yes, I've been learning calculus in my apartment on a nightly basis – sprawled across the floor, on the table, up against the wall – and it's been an eye-opening experience, Raul. It's been truly edifying. But that's not all I've been doing. You see, on a *daily* basis I've been spending my afternoons with Will Smithcoate in the cafeteria listening to his remembrances about the future. He's somewhat skeptical about us ever being able to reach it. But I think we're almost there....I really do. I think it's almost upon us..."

"What is?"

"The future! It may seem hopelessly far away at times but I think we've almost arrived. It'll be here any moment. Just listen....maybe you can hear it coming...?"

Raul paused to listen.

"I don't hear anything...."

"You have to be patient."

"I'm an institutional researcher, Charlie. Patience is my virtue."

"Right. Do you hear it now?"

Raul cupped his hand around his ear and held it there for a few moments. Hearing nothing, he said:

"No. I don't. The future's nowhere to be heard, I'm afraid." And then, as if noticing the extreme silence: "Hey, what happened to your pendulum?"

"My what?"

"Your pendulum....it's not ticking...."

"Oh that. Bessie stopped it with her hand. But that's okay, I don't take it personally. Time, I've learned, is one of those things that stays and stays forever. Like water. And love. And our universal affection for mindless novelty...."

"Well, it appears you've had an eventful intercession, Charlie. It seems your break has been truly prolific."

"It has! And best of all, I'm finally starting to feel comfortable with the pace of changing realities. It was all so overwhelming in the beginning. But I've somehow survived it all. I've settled into a groove. Everything's happening as fast and as relentlessly as ever. But I think I'm finally learning to navigate it all...!"

"Thanks to those pills..."

"Right!"

Here I used Dr. Felch's handkerchief to wipe the spittle from my mouth yet again. Then I continued:

"...You know, since you left, Raul, I've reached several professional milestones. For one, I've been able to finish the book I started so long ago: you can congratulate me on finishing *The Anyman's Guide to Love and the Community College.*"

"Congratulations."

"Thanks. And I've learned to aim a pistol."

"You have?"

"Yes. Ethel's been showing me. I've become quite an expert."

"And have you learned how to *fire* it too?"

"Not really. Not yet. So far I haven't been able to commit to that entirely. But I'm sure I'll be ready to pull the trigger someday...."

"One can hope."

"And, Raul, did you notice? I shaved! And I've combed my hair!"

"I see that. Well done. And I also see that your collar is starched and your corduroys are pressed."

"The math teacher did that for me!"

"That was swell of her. So is that all?"

"Oh no! Not even close. In fact she's done quite a bit more than that. You see, she's multi-talented....!"

In ecstatic tones, I listed each of the things the math teacher had done for me over the preceding weeks. The list was quite extensive and took a few minutes to relate. Raul waited patiently for me to finish. Then he said:

"That's not what I meant, Charlie. What I meant was....did anything else happen while I was gone?"

"Oh, right. Well, since you ask, in fact quite a bit has happened in the short time that you were gone. You see, not long after you left for Texas, I received a bloated scrotum in my faculty mailbox. I was genuinely concerned at first – I'd never gotten one before. It seemed improbable. Impossible. Even *unjustified.* But Dr. Felch explained that this too counts as a professional milestone here at Cow Eye. That it is an important rite of passage. And that a person who never earns a single bloated scrotum during an entire lifetime is the person who has never really lived. Because such a person has never ventured to do anything truly meaningful in this world."

"Is that so? I would beg to differ. I haven't received any...."

"Oh, that's right. But don't worry – I'm sure you will some day. After all, I've already received my *third....*"

"Three?"

"Yes. The first came right after Bessie stopped my pendulum. The second came when I announced that the Christmas party was being rescheduled for March and that it would be rechristened. And the third I got after I was forced to cast the deciding vote in favor of revising our college's mission statement. In short, it's been an active time for me...."

"Glad to hear it."

"But that's not all, Raul. I'm sure you'll be interested to hear all the strange and interesting things that have happened to our college as it moves toward reaffirming its status as an accredited institution of higher learning. For example, did you know that yet another star has been added to the flag in front of the Administration building?"

"Already? How many are we at now?"

"Forty-*five*!"

"That many?"

"Yes. The college has begun to look outward. It's become a veritable beehive of activity since you left. In fact, a new apiary was just built out past the frontier where the vacant lot used to be. And they just added a new wing onto the Dimwiddle Center as part of a new era of reconstruction. They've re-paved the parking lot. The swimming pool has a new diving board. There are whiteboards in the classrooms with dry-erase markers.... so no more need for *chalk*! Everything is newer and bolder and quite a bit more complicated and interesting. Since you've been gone, we've revised our mission statement and repealed Prohibition and the carp have spawned in the lagoons and the ducks have started quacking and the moon has become our bitch and the creative writing teacher received his tenure with flying colors – despite my cautionary report – and the ethics teacher had an abortion and Ethel placed a restraining order on Luke after he forced her to play the role of a submissive F-1 student during extreme sexual play. Meanwhile, you may be interested to know that the college has hired three mongoloids and one colored man..."

"You mean a *negro*?"

"....Right. A negro and three mongoloids...."

"You mean Orientals?"

"....Correct. Three Orientals and a negro...."

"You mean a black man?"

"....Exactly. A black man and three Orientals...."

"You mean Asians?"

"….Right. Three Asians and one black man…."

"You mean after all this time they finally hired an African-American?"

"….Um, yes. Isn't that what I said? Since you left for Texas our college has successfully hired three Asian-Americans, a Jew, a Catholic, two left-handed homosexuals, a Whig, a woman with a severe allergy to wheat, and a promising *person of color* who holds a degree in electrical engineering. You'll surely see them around campus. Oh, and we're also looking to hire a new instructor to teach political science…."

"What about Nan?"

"She bailed."

"That's crazy! After a single semester? What happened?"

"No one knows. Her students showed up on the first day of instruction but she was gone. She never came back from the break, I guess. They say she found another teaching position in an urban college on the east coast. She'd been applying secretly throughout the fall. Dr. Felch is now scrambling to hire an adjunct to cover her classes. Meanwhile, to take her place longer-term, we're hiring an award-winning applicant from Wyoming…."

"They have awards in Wyoming?!"

"Yes. They're *everywhere* nowadays."

"So we're hiring someone from that far away!"

"It couldn't be helped. The applicant from Cow Eye had a mispelling in his resume. And the applicant from California, after being offered the job sight unseen, turned the position down without even visiting."

"I see. So what else is new? Aside from all this turnover?"

"A lot, Raul. An awful lot….!"

And here I told him of my efforts to align our Christmas Week festivities with the weeklong visit of our accreditors. How I was making genuine progress. How despite the challenges – and there were many – I'd been able to rally the campus around the yuletide activities. The agenda for the week was complete. The invitations were printed. The campus was being mowed and polished in preparation for the team's visit. Faculty had agreed to take the accreditors around individually as part of my Adopt-an-Accreditor program, with several even hosting featured break-out sessions in their classes. Special projects and events would be happening around campus during their stay, and the students were invited to the festivities. The talents of individual faculty and staff would be showcased.

During the party itself there would be beer on tap as always; but this year there would also be wine and mixed drinks and Margaritas and bourbon and scotch and any number of other hard liquors and liqueurs. There would be marijuana and Anglicanism and a bowl full of multi-colored barbiturates – and of course there would be caroling and hashish and frequent opportunities to engage in tender anal sex. There would be a vintage truck show on Monday. A yoga demonstration on Tuesday. A rodeo on Wednesday. A sitar performance and cow-milking demonstration on Thursday. And on Friday, March twentieth, after a series of exciting accreditation-related activities taking place earlier in the day – exact times and locations *to be enthusiastically announced* – we would throw open the doors of the cafeteria to the long-awaited Christmas party itself, or, as I had proposed to call it: *The Cow Eye Community College Springtime Masquerade and Accreditative Festival of Christmas Unity.* It was generally agreed that this would be the grandest Christmas celebration ever. It would be the most remarkable accreditation visit. Excitement was gradually building around the event. Logistics were being resolved. This time I had made sure that the visiting team would be picked up at the makeshift bus shelter and transported to campus in style. Upon their arrival they would be given souvenirs and assailed with favorable impressions and feted with data. They would be wined and dined and taken to witness showcase projects around campus. They would be treated like royalty during their stay. And immediately after the Christmas party, flush from an afternoon of eggnog and continuous improvement, they would conduct their exit interview before heading back toward the makeshift bus shelter. There was little margin for error in all this, so every individual detail had to be intricately and carefully pre-determined. I hadn't slept at all since the break due to my days of endless planning and my nights of endless discovery with the math teacher at my apartment. But it was all working out. Even though I was exhausted, my legacy was taking shape. At last I had found my rhythm as Special Projects Coordinator at Cow Eye Community College. All of this had happened during the few short weeks since Raul had left for his vacation in Texas.

"So, it sounds like your plan is coming together then?"

"Yes it is. At long last!"

"Glad to hear it. You've worked hard. You deserve the glory."

"Thank you, Raul!"

"But Charlie?"

"Yes."

"When's the last time you talked to her?"

"The math teacher? I just talked to her this morning! Right before leaving for work! She was straightening the covers on my bed...."

"To hell with the math teacher. I'm asking about Bessie. When's the last time you talked to *Bessie?*"

"Bessie?"

"Yes, you remember her, right?"

"Of course. But I haven't really talked to her since she stopped my metal orbs from swinging. Since we had that disastrous debrief in my office."

"So you haven't talked with her about Plan B then?"

"No we haven't. I didn't have a chance. And now we're not on speaking terms."

"I'm sorry to hear that. I know how much you wanted to love something that was unloved. She could have been the one. And at your age you may not get another chance. Love, you see, doesn't always think to knock on the door of a dusty second-floor apartment in faculty housing. I'm sorry it didn't work out between you."

"It's okay. I've thought about it from time to time since then. And I've been able to console myself that it just wasn't meant to be. That some things in our world just aren't meant to be. Like the future. And discovering what love actually *is*. But that's okay. I'm an educational administrator – it's a choice I've made. And besides, it's not like I don't have a young math teacher waiting for me in my evenings! And it's not like Bessie hasn't been through this kind of thing before – you know, a thousand other times with a thousand other men...."

Raul shook his head disapprovingly.

"She's a human being, Charlie, not an adjunct. She deserves more than to be discarded once she's ceased to be useful to you. She deserves more from you than that. Remember, she was the one who rescued you from the edge of the universe. And she invited you to her house for fruitcake. She asked you to meet her children. It took a lot for her to do that. You need to talk to her. It's the right thing to do."

I stopped to consider his words. As usual he was right.

"You're absolutely correct, of course. But how? She doesn't even look up from her electric typewriter when I walk by."

"Her what?"

"You didn't hear? They replaced all the manual typewriters with electric typewriters. One for each secretary. With hard carriage return and single-key auto-correct. Needless to say, the secretaries are feeling overwhelmed. Even the new hire in the economics department is growing disillusioned...."

"We're not talking about those other secretaries now, Charlie. We're talking about Bessie."

"Right. Bessie. We haven't been on speaking terms since she gave me the fruitcake. And when I walk by her desk she doesn't even look up from what she's doing. I've tried several times. It's like I'm not even there. So I don't know how I would go about talking to her..."

"Maybe you can find an opportunity at the Christmas party? The event will be held in the cafeteria, right?"

"Right."

"And she'll be attending, right?"

"Right."

"So you'll both be in the same room together, right?"

"Right."

"That is to say, in the same segment of time and space?"

"Yes."

"And there will be alcohol in large quantities, right?"

"Right."

"And marijuana?"

"Yes."

"And barbiturates?"

"Bowls of them."

"And meat?"

"Piled to the ceiling!"

"And vegetables?"

"Of every imaginable color and complexion!"

"Well, there you go. That's your chance! Catch her at the food line and talk to her then!"

I nodded.

Raul shrugged.

"Anyway, Charlie, I'll see what I can do to help things along."

"Thanks, Raul."

"Sure. What are friends for? But hey, other than *that*, how are your preparations coming….?"

As Raul and I reviewed my plans for the party, I noticed how the weather outside seemed to be changing yet again. The sun had begun to set at a different angle: now it was less oblique. The birds were once again chirping. The ducks began to quack even louder than before. The cold air of late February had turned into the cold air of early March. Soon the fountains would be switched back on. Spring was clearly on its way. In no time at all the accreditors would be arriving.

"Oh and Raul…" I said. "Did you hear what happened to Will?"

"Will Smithcoate? No, what?"

"He had a stroke of some sort. It happened the day before all our teaching faculty came back to campus. Right there in the cafeteria under the no-smoking sign. I'd just been talking to him that very night. We talked about history. And the future. And supermarkets. When I left he was fine – slurring his words a bit, maybe – but no more than normal. He might have already had some sort of mild stroke that I didn't notice. After I left he must have passed out. One of his former students found him face down in a puddle of drool the next morning. She had wanted to be a historian once, but instead she wiped up the moisture and called an ambulance. He had been there like that all night."

"That's terrible! Is it serious?"

"I don't know. They took him to the local clinic to check him out. The next day he was back at his table in the cafeteria. He says the doctor told him no smoking or drinking from here on out – that there's an increased risk of reoccurrence and the next time it could be much worse. But of course he's not heeding anyone's advice. He's still sitting there every day at his table with his newspaper and his bourbon and his cigars…."

"That sounds like Will…." – Raul shook his head – "….And what about Rusty and Gwen? Do you have them on board for your party?"

"Not quite. They're *almost* there. Almost on board. After an inordinate amount of careful persuasion, they're so close to attending the party that I can taste the meat and vegetables on their lips, respectfully. But they're not quite there. In fact, there's still a little final convincing that I still need to do. So if you'll excuse me…."

And here I stopped. Unexpectedly – even for myself – I grabbed Gwen by the arm and spun her around to face me. The esplanade was crowded and bustling during the few minutes between classes, and the students were streaming past us in both directions on their way from one to the next. Judging by Gwen's reaction, she was not accustomed to male colleagues grabbing her by the arm and spinning her around like this.

"Charlie, did you just....?"

I released her arm.

"I'm sorry, Gwen, but I really needed to get your attention. Before it was too late...."

"Don't you *ever*!"

I brushed off the arm where my fingers had left reddish indentations on her skin.

"I'm sorry. But it's just that this Christmas party is...."

"Don't you ever grab me like that! I am not your slave girl! Nor am I your concubine. I am not a domesticated ungulate. I don't care who you are. Or who you *think* you are. And I don't care if the fate of our college *is* in your hands. Don't you ever grab us like that...!"

"Us?"

"Yes *us*!"

"I'm sorry, Gwen. I really am. It's just that everything's happening so quickly and the Christmas party is coming and you walk really fast and I'm struggling to keep up and rumors are rampant in the copy room and I really need the two of you to attend the upcoming Christmas party...."

Rusty looked at me humorously.

"Rumors?"

"Yes, that neither of you is coming."

"And you believe them?"

"Yes.

"And so you want both of us to come?"

"Yes."

"And by the both of us, of course, you mean me *and* Gwen?"

"Right. That's exactly what I mean. Both of you together....!"

Rusty and I were in his Dodge and though we were making slow progress back toward the campus, it was clear that my time with him was running out. If I could not convince him to come to the Christmas party by the time we passed Timmy at the guard shack, all would be lost to fate: Rusty's participation, any chance at faculty unity, our party, the college's accreditation, my very legacy here at Cow Eye.

"My position is as clear as day," said Rusty. "I will not go to that party unless the menu consists of meat without vegetables."

Gwen shook her head in complete agreement.

"And *I* will only go," she said, "if there is a wide assortment of vegetables…and no meats."

"Deal!" I said.

"Huh?" they said.

"You have a deal! You win. I agree. I give up. I concede. It will be as you've said. I will do it exactly as you want."

"You will?"

"Yes."

"You mean there will be meat without vegetables?"

"And vegetables without meat?"

"Yes!"

"There will be night without day? And day without night?"

"Yes! That's exactly what there will be. There will be both of those things without the other. Just please come, okay? Please promise me that you will find it in your heart to come to the cafeteria for the Christmas party on March twentieth….!"

Without answering, Rusty hopped over the train tracks and turned his Dodge toward the sign welcoming us to Cow Eye Community College.

"You see that sign?" he said.

"Of course," I answered.

"Well there was a time not too long ago when it said something else altogether. You see, before all these bright people with new ideas came along, we were just a simple vocational school. And back then the sign itself was simpler. WELCOME TO COW EYE COMMUNITY COLLEGE, our sign used to say, and then, in much smaller letters: *Where Ends Meet*…."

I nodded.

"I guess things do tend to change," I said.

Rusty shrugged his shoulders in resignation.

"So are you coming?" I asked.

"I suppose so," he said. "I suppose I might as well come."

"You will?"

"Yes."

I thanked him and offered my hand; he took it in a firm handshake. Then I turned to Gwen:

"And you?" I asked.

"I guess," she said.

"You'll come?"

"Yes."

"And would you be willing to host a special break-out session?"

"On logic?"

"Yes. And its opposite."

"Is Stokes doing his standard presentation on artificial insemination?"

"Yes. I've already ordered the shoulder-length gloves for him...."

"Well then I guess I should do my cutting-edge presentation on logic. You know, for symmetry's sake...."

Having agreed on that, the two of us continued our brisk walk down the esplanade. On either side of the walkway the trees were only now springing to life. The pelicans were loafing on the banks of the lagoons. The sun shone brightly. The cold air of early March had given way to the warmer air of mid-March. Ducks quacked.

"It really is a beautiful campus," I observed.

"Yes, it is," she said. "It's lovely."

"It would be a shame if our college got shut down, wouldn't it, Gwen?"

"It would."

"Do you think there's a chance that might ever happen?"

"It's possible."

"But isn't it unfathomable?"

"It is. And yet a lot of good things have come to less glorious ends. And all good things must come to an end at *some* point. Unfortunately, you can't choose how things end. You can't choose your *own* dissolution. And you can't choose whether it's glorious or not."

Gwen was right.

Without speaking any further, the two of us headed down the final stretch of the esplanade toward where the cafeteria lay up ahead.

❦

"SO ARE WE ready?" asked Dr. Felch. He had spat into his spittoon and was furtively smoking a cigarette at the same time – his fourteenth – and looking nervous.

"I believe so, sir."

"The accreditors will be arriving in a few minutes."

"Don't worry. I've got my hospitality crew out at the bus shelter to meet them."

"Are their accommodations settled?"

"Absolutely. They'll be staying in faculty housing with a view of the fountains."

"Have the units been cleaned?"

"Yes."

'Has all the food for the party been ordered?"

"Yes."

"And the drinks delivered?"

"Yes. Crates of bourbon and vodka."

"It's all paid for?"

"Yes. With the roll of twenties you gave me."

"And the lawns are mowed?"

"Of course."

"And the floors waxed? And the hedges trimmed? And the pelicans fed?"

"Yes, Dr. Felch we've done all that! And we've scheduled the fountains to be turned on for the first time since late autumn. And we've decorated the entire campus with Christmas regalia. The sycamore has been wrapped in tinsel. The esplanade has been lined with artificial snowmen. A large wreath of laurel has been draped over the front of the Administration building next to the flag pole where a nativity scene has been set up under the thirteen stripes and forty-six stars. The shipment of shoulder-length gloves arrived yesterday. And the bathrooms have been scrubbed. All the asbestos has been removed. There are trash bins in every room. Dr. Felch, I've stayed up almost every night over the last month making these arrangements. It hasn't been easy. But thanks in large part to these amazing pills right here...." – I lifted the vials out of my pocket – "....it's all going according to plan, sir. My hard work is paying off. My lack of sleep is bearing fruit. My pill-taking is reaping its just rewards. Everything is going swimmingly, Dr. Felch. So don't worry!"

"But what about Rusty and Gwen? Are they on board with the party?"

"Yes."

"You're sure this time?"

"Of course."

"Shouldn't you double-check just in case?"

"Well, okay...."

And so I looked across the bench seat of Rusty's Dodge:

"Are you sure you're on board, Mr. Stokes?" I asked.

"Yes," he said.

"And you, Gwen? Are *you* on board too?"

"Yes. I'm on board. But I'm also quite hungry...."

"Great, we're almost there...."

And when we had reached the end of the esplanade, I glanced over at Will's Oldsmobile Starfire still parked sideways next to the cafeteria. And here I opened the glass door for Gwen to enter.

"Please...." I said.

"You first..." she insisted.

"No *you*...." I offered.

"No, Charlie, *you*! Those other days are over!"

"Oh, right," I said and threw my duffel bag over my shoulder. "I almost forgot."

Tired and hungry from the exertions of our long walk through time and space, the two of us entered the cafeteria where the Christmas party was already underway.

ACCREDITATION WEEK

'Tis the season to be jolly,
Fa- la- la- la- la- la- la- la!

B y the time I walked into the cafeteria on March twentieth, the majority of Christmas Week activities had been carried out with varying degrees of success. On Sunday the accreditors arrived into the makeshift bus shelter where they were greeted by a welcoming committee of faculty and staff from the college's many academic departments and disciplines. They were also met by the Cow Eye Jazz Band, three community business leaders, a cheerleading team from the local high school, its first-string quarterback, the mayor of Cow Eye Junction – who also happened to be our part-time Welding instructor – and twelve jittery but earnest representatives from Student Government. From there the accreditors were loaded into special covered wagons attached to horses that wheeled them from the bus shelter, along the highway, through the town of Cow Eye Junction, past the grazing cows and the waterless ditches and the rusted farm equipment toward the campus of Cow Eye Community College. Each accreditor had been assigned to a Student Leader and each Student Leader had been given a script to read, and as the wagons passed the various milestones along the way – the post office, the jailhouse, the red-brick mayoralty building – pulling off the highway every so often to allow the cars behind them to pass, the team leaders recited the script that had been so carefully prepared in advance: "If you look to the left of our wagon," they would read, "you can still see the long fence and decaying remnants of the once-great Cow Eye Ranch. The ranch was previously world-famous and the old timers of the area still aver that in its heyday it fed half the country. It is a local landmark and a sign of uncertain times. The ranch struggled for many years to survive amidst a sea of change but, sadly, it has since been closed for good...."

"Closed?" asked the accreditors incredulously.

"Yes," answered the Student Leaders. "Forcefully and finally."

The town had been informed of the accreditors' arrival ahead of time and so, along the route, residents of the town who supported the college's application for accreditation – many of whom had either attended the college themselves in better times or who currently had children or other relatives still aspiring to accredited degrees – hailed the convoy with cheers and placards and exuberant waving and applause. Like bystanders along a marathon, the townsfolk jogged beside the wagons with cups of water that the accreditors leaned out to accept, drank thirstily with a single hand, then threw back onto the asphalt of the highway to be collected. When the three Conestogas reached the campus, Timmy stepped out to greet them wearing a pin-striped suit recycled from his three most recent weddings and a top hat with matching paisley tie. "Welcome to Cow Eye!" he said and bowed, and as he did the hat tumbled off his head. The accreditors laughed good-naturedly at the display and the horse-drawn wagons moved past the guard shack into the campus.

Looking out the window of my office, I noted the clopping of the horses and watched as the convoy made its way down the central thoroughfare past the three lagoons with their bronze statuary and dormant fountains, past the central mall and the sycamore and the students juggling their diminishing career prospects on the grass.

After arriving at faculty housing, each member of the accrediting team received a campus map, a number-two pencil with Cow Eye's institutional motto carved into it, and a bio-degradable bag of welcome goodies prepared by our executive secretaries: a porcelain cow figurine, a bag of beef jerky, two stainless steel orbs representing the sowed seeds of European civilization, and a copy of the *Baghavad Ghita* lovingly translated a few years back by our very own Esperanto instructor. The accreditors looked tired after their arrival. We agreed to meet in the cafeteria the following morning for the opening address to faculty and staff.

Back in my office I'd set up a command headquarters of sorts, and it was from here that I received reports and updates from the Student Leaders, from Timmy at the guard shack, from the animal science faculty who had been charged with hitching the horses, and from the administrative secretaries who were positioned strategically around campus like a thousand points of light. Stopping by my office, each had received a two-way radio and instructions to notify me immediately if any issues happened to arise. "The fate of our college depends on these next five days," I reminded them and we shook hands like aviators before an important mission. Timmy, in particular, seemed inspired by the challenge; an entire generation had come and gone since he last figured prominently as the star quarterback for the local high school team, and now his competitive instincts were bubbling over. "Let's show these motherfuckers what Cow Eye is all about!" he gushed, and I shuddered at the thought.

The next morning, which was a Monday, the entire team of accreditors gathered in the cafeteria to meet our campus community over juice and donuts and some very awkward mingling. When that was done, the formal portion of the morning session started. A table had been set up at the front of the cafeteria with a single microphone that could be passed back and forth as the team members, sitting behind the long table like disciples at the Last Supper, addressed the campus for the first time. "Is this thing on?" said Dr. Felch into the microphone by way of introduction.

"Yes," we sighed. "It's on."

Having thus introduced himself to the accreditors, Dr. Felch welcomed the group with a brief speech about educational excellence and collegiality, and then held out the microphone to the team chair, who took it with a firm hand. The woman was in her mid-fifties and dressed in a plaid business suit and a pair of glasses that hung from a string around her neck. As she spoke, she had the habit of either placing the glasses onto the tip of her nose, or taking them back off, to emphasize a point of particular importance. Her air was dignified and poised. Her coiffure was grayish. Her manner was reserved and cultivated. If outward appearances could be believed – and they can, can't they? – then it was only right that she should be the chair of this visiting team.

"Thank you for such an extravagant welcome," the woman began, speaking into the microphone confidently and elegantly as if she had done this very thing many times before, as if the public address system were a natural extension of her voice – a logical extension of her soul. "On behalf of the visiting team I want to thank you for hosting us this week. I'm sure I speak for the others when I say that your students are truly lucky to be able to pursue their educational goals at such a stunningly beautiful campus as this...."

The faculty and staff in attendance – those who had taken the time to show up – applauded her sentiment.

"In fact I wish my *own* campus were this attractive," she added. "It might help with our retention rates...."

At the allusion to retention rates, there was some nervous laughter around the cafeteria.

"But in all sincerity, I'm here this morning to thank you for hosting us and to explain what you can expect during this upcoming week while we are here visiting your campus. But before we do that, I think it would be prudent to first introduce ourselves to you individually so that you can see who we are as human beings. As you will note, we are a diverse group and I'm sure you'll be happy to know that we are not oppressors or tyrants. We are not some amorphous alien invaders coming to your campus to inflict a form of grave institutional harm upon you. We are neither fascists nor communists. Neither neo-liberal nor strict constructionists. We do not have a political agenda. We are simply professional educators who have chosen to be here as willing participants in the accreditation process. In fact on a scale of one-to-ten with *ten* being a lioness protecting her young and *one* being a nun before Vespers, we are probably somewhere around a *two-point-five*." Here the woman pushed her glasses back onto her nose. "As team chair, then, I suppose I should introduce myself to you first...."

The woman cleared her throat as people do before talking in public about lofty concepts. Then she said:

"As Dr. Felch mentioned, I am the chair of this visiting team. I am also an award-winning educator and president of a community college located in a picturesque town in the beautiful state of Utah. You may be surprised to learn that my school is a small college much like yours, and so, as its president, I know very well what you're probably feeling as you go through this accreditation process. How daunting it can be. How sapping of resources. How tedious. I'm sure there were times when you wished the whole process would just go away forever. That you could simply run and hide from it. That you could just focus on the job that you were *hired* to do, rather than spending hour upon irretrievable hour on this onerous and tiresome burden that has been thrust upon you and that you undertake half-heartedly and with barely concealed malice in your hearts. But as professional educators you know that this is not an option. And so I commend you on your efforts. And your resolve. And your commitment to your institution. I also congratulate you on the grace and dignity you've brought to your role as quietly suffering professionals. At my college we recently went through this ordeal ourselves, only to receive a very discouraging result. And so, having gone through this process – and having been poked and prodded and otherwise adjudicated by a visiting team of like-minded peers – I welcome the opportunity to visit your campus in this same capacity, to view the process from the other side of the microphone if you will, so that I might be able to impose upon your college the same arbitrary and stifling requirements, the same external value judgments, the same mid-career misery and institutional angst that has been imposed upon *ours.…*"

The woman paused. Around the cafeteria there was a discernible feeling of discomfort. Then the woman said:

"That was an attempt at humor, folks. It won't hurt my feelings if you laugh.…"

A self-conscious laughter arose around the cafeteria only to die out just as self-consciously.

"…But I jest. In truth, I am a firm believer in the accreditation process as a vehicle for self-reflection and continuous improvement. This is my fourth team visit – and second as team chair – and I'm ecstatic to be here. Before this trip to Cow Eye I had never even been to your great state, and might otherwise not have come if not for a propitious quirk of fate. In fact, I was originally assigned to visit a thriving community college in Oklahoma last year, but the commission ultimately decided to send me to Cow Eye instead – the idea being that my professional expertise and physical grace might be better served at your college where things are rather more dicey. And so I'm very happy to be able to visit all of you on your stunningly beautiful campus and I'm happy that my venture from desiccation to verdure is happening now, that is to say *later* rather than *sooner.…*"

After a brief but somewhat more enthusiastic applause, the woman held up her hand:

"….Of course, this is not to imply that you do not have some serious work to do. Over the past few months we've been reading your self-study report and making detailed notes. We've written comments in the margins. We've highlighted figures that seem to contradict each other. One of our team members, who happens to be an award-winning poet and a well-respected professor emeritus, has even taken to diagramming the iambs in certain passages concerning your college's assessment plans…."

At this, a gasp went up around the cafeteria. But the woman seemed not to take notice:

"…. Needless to say, the accreditation process has not been kind to your college as of late. And so there are many deficiencies that you should have addressed. We will be checking to see if you have addressed those deficiencies. We will be verifying what you wrote in your self-study versus what we see actually happening on campus. Have you implemented the ambitious plans you said you'd implement? Have you been true to your word? Is your campus really as bucolic as you claim? Are your faculty members united behind the mission of your college? Are vegetarians and non-vegetarians given equal access to the resources that are available? In short, we will be looking to see whether you really are upholding those high standards of educational accountability that you profess to be upholding in the institutional motto that is carved into those number-two pencils…." Here the woman stopped to remove her glasses from her nose. "Oh, and I have a loving husband and three wonderful children currently attending prestigious four-year colleges in various urban centers around the country." Embarrassed, the woman quickly turned to the next page of her notes. "But enough about *me*," she said. "Let's introduce you to the *rest* of the team….!"

Here the woman passed around the microphone so that each of the other members of the team – all eleven of them – could introduce themselves. There was the librarian from a vocational college in Jamestown. And the institutional researcher from Walla Walla. And a tutoring coordinator from Albuquerque. Two members of the team were upper administrators. Three were tenured faculty. One had a patch on his eye. Another seemed to lisp. One was vaguely European. One had a tattoo around her ankle. A majority were demonstratively agnostic. A minority were nearing retirement. Each was an expert in a field of competence. All were award-winning. And every last one was thoroughly and expertly engaged in institutional improvement. In turn, they gave their names, their titles, their campus affiliations, and their own particular affection for the accreditation process. The last person to accept the microphone was a petite woman whose voice seemed barely wispy enough to travel through the extension cord and out the speakers that had been set up around the room facing the audience.

"My name is Sally," she said, though a mouse might have spoken the name with more conviction. "I am from California...." At the side of the table Dr. Felch gave a wide smile and an emphatic thumbs-up. "I'm very glad to be here, even though I am the youngest and least-experienced member on the team. I enjoy reading and horseback riding. I have two housecats and a tattoo on my ankle. As a young unmarried career-minded professional, I'm excited to learn more about your campus, especially as it pertains to tantric yoga, artificial insemination, and fiscal accountability...."

When each member of the team had been introduced, the team chair was once again handed the microphone, which she accepted gracefully:

"So, as you can see, your college is in expert and caring hands!"

Here the team chair placed her glasses back on the tip of her nose.

"Now for a few logistical notes about our visit...."

As the woman spoke, I took a long look around the cafeteria, which despite the importance of the occasion was barely half-full. Would the accreditors be impressed by this turnout? Or would they see the room as half-empty? And how would this same cafeteria look once our local professoriate – all one hundred percent – had been herded through its doors for the Christmas party? Where would the food table go? The punch bowl? The disco strobe? Would there be enough room for the talent show? For the Christmas tree? The decorations? Would the available wall space be sufficient to accommodate the various flags of the world? Would all this inclusiveness fit in such a confined segment of time and space? And why were Rusty and Gwen glaring at each other across the half-empty room with such obvious and unconcealed hostility? Would they honor their respective commitments to attend the party, even if the other came as well? And where was Will Smithcoate at this very moment? Surprisingly, he wasn't at his customary table under the no-smoking sign. But why? Had somebody discouraged him from attending this opportunity to meet our accreditors? If so, why? What might he have said about our future, about our history, that could jeopardize our college's accreditation? And what, when all was said and done –when the blood had dried and the dust had settled and the Ziploc bag had been rinsed to be used once again – was the metaphorical significance of the calf that we had castrated in the middle of the dusty corral? What exactly were the seeds that we had planted? The blood that we had spilt? The pills that I had taken one after the other? And how would I find more of them now that they had each run out and their respective vials were empty? These were the burning questions that consumed me as I sat in the cafeteria listening to the team chair explaining the logistics of her team's accrediting visit.

"…And so…." she was saying, "….at the end of our sojourn this week we will be sharing our initial findings with you before we leave on Friday. However, please understand that our recommendations are not final and that anything we write will need to be reviewed by the accrediting body as a whole. In the meantime, we look forward to seeing the learning that is taking place at your college and to meeting with you during this week – to visiting your classrooms and speaking with your students and attending your social activities – as a way of formally assessing the effectiveness of your institution. We recognize the time it's taken you to organize a special week of activities around our visit and we appreciate that. Dr. Felch, you should be commended for all that you've done in organizing our accommodations. I know there were some unforgivable problems with logistics the last time we came, but this time around everything has been really fantastic…."

Dr. Felch acknowledged the accolade with a modest wave, then quickly pointed to me.

"Charlie?" he said. "Stand up, Charlie, so we can recognize your efforts…."

I stood up.

"That's Charlie," said Dr. Felch. "Our Special Projects Coordinator. The individual most responsible for what you will be experiencing this week…."

A polite applause greeted me. Grabbing the handkerchief from my shirt pocket, I wiped another dab of spittle from my mouth. Then I sat back down.

"….Fellow educators of Cow Eye…." the woman continued. "Please know that we've read your new mission statement and find it compelling. We see that you are making great strides to address your deficiencies, and we know that you take your duties as professional educators seriously. We especially like that you've chosen a local theme for this week, one that celebrates the unique culture of the Cow Eye region. The ride into campus was quite unique and, I should say, rather enjoyable. We also understand that there will be a culminating event on Friday the twentieth, and we look forward to that as well. Finally, I just want to say that you should not let the fact that we are deciding the fate of your college – the fate of your entire community, perhaps – influence how you perceive our visit. Although you will be seeing us around campus over the next five days – and we may stop you to ask some hard questions along the way – please treat us as you would any other visitor to your campus. Act naturally. Be sincere. Treat our time here as if it were any other week in the storied history of Cow Eye Community College."

The woman paused. Then she said:

"Oh....and I almost forgot...." – at this the woman removed the glasses from her nose and looked out at the audience importantly – ".... Merry Christmas!"

Everyone laughed.

After a few final questions from the audience, the accreditors packed up their things and headed off to begin their accrediting.

≈

THAT WAS ON Monday morning. On Monday afternoon the vintage truck show was held in the large parking lot next to the planetarium. On Tuesday Marsha Greenbaum conducted a yoga demonstration, where the accreditors were taught to breathe into each other's nostrils and arch their backs like skeptical felines. The one-on-one accreditation interviews began later that morning and from my office I received updates on those that had already been conducted. As the news trickled in over the two-way radio, it became apparent that the accreditors had read our self-study thoroughly and were not pulling any punches. One woman had grilled our Fiscal Officer on the exorbitant cost of the chlorine used for the swimming pool; another wanted to know why there were so many dead carp floating at the feet of the cowboy with the lariat; a third asked why, if satisfaction really was higher among faculty and staff since the construction of the archery range and indoor gun facility, we had just lost yet another award-winning employee – our recently hired political science instructor – after a single fruitless semester; and then there was the graying gentleman who, after sitting through a lecture on moral relativism, put a heavy hand on our Ethics teacher's shoulder and reassured her in father-like tones that the world itself would not end if Cow Eye were to lose its accreditation – that a professional with her credentials could expect to find a position at any community college in the country. Sam Middleton, meanwhile, had been introduced to the professor emeritus and the two had headed off to his office for their own interview where, in a special closed-door session, the two poets – one tenured and award-winning, the other righteous and inflexible – would be discussing the diverse and student-centered ways that our college assesses its own assessment processes.

"Would you mind if I were to be present for that discussion?" I offered the professor emeritus, hoping to blunt any possible misunderstandings between him and Middleton.

"No," he said, rather coldly. "This is a topic for he and I only. No offense to you, but this will be a disputation between creative minds. Silence versus sound. Rhythm versus rhyme. Mano a mano. If I have any questions about educational administration, I'll let you know...." The man rolled up his sleeves and set out for Sam Middleton's office.

On Wednesday morning, the rodeo was held to repeated oohs and ahhs, and later that afternoon the accreditors invited the campus to a mid-week forum where the team fielded questions from the audience on issues pertaining to institutional peer-review. One by one, the team members gave their respective views on the process itself, on the demise of intellectual integrity and critical thinking, on the latest five-to-four Supreme Court decision affecting higher education, and on the declining role of the humanities in world affairs and of the classics in particular. When this was done, an older student finishing up the sixth year of his two-year degree asked the accreditors to explain their respective positions on love.

"Positions?" the team chair responded, suddenly flustered.

"Yes, positions. What is the position of your body as it pertains to love? In other words, can you please tell us, by the standards you are applying to us this week, what love actually *is*?"

To which the team chair responded:

"The question itself is perfidious. We are a single accrediting body which, as you know, consists of many individuals. And so it is surely not in our purview to tell your campus, in any definitive way, what love *is*. However, it is entirely within our scope to tell you what it *will need to be*. That is, what it will need to be if you wish for your college to achieve reaffirmation of its regional accreditation...."

Passing the microphone from one side of the dais to the next, the accreditors shared their diverse opinions on love, and from them we learned that love *will need to be* both transparent and accessible; that it will need to be aligned with the overarching purpose for the college's being; that it will need to be data-based and continually improving; and that, if it is to have any chance of surviving the test of time, it will need to be measurable, replicable and scalable, and incontrovertibly objective.

"So it shouldn't be aspirational then?" Gwen asked.

"No," they said. "It will need to be immediately observable."

"And I guess it ain't the kind of thing that's open to personal interpretation?" asked Rusty.

"Absolutely not!" they insisted. "True love will need to be *unequivocal!*"

On Wednesday evening the campus was treated to the ceremonial opening of the thematic fountains, the pent-up water bursting skyward to the sounds of symphonic music and the cracking of a special fireworks display. Afterwards, an outdoor picnic was held next to the Appaloosa with flood lights illuminating the grounds and students from the culinary program circulating with trays of hors d'oeuvres and cocktails. Later that night, long after the resplendent display was over and the soiree had dispersed, I noticed two shadowy figures in the distance holding hands by the lagoon where the bull was still mounting his heifer. In the play of darkness and moonlight the two hand-holders looked like tiny figurines amid the majestic fountain.

"Who's that over there?" I asked an administrative secretary who had stayed to help me clean up.

"I'm not sure," she answered.

"Is it a man and a woman? Or two men? "

"I don't know, " said the secretary. "It's getting harder and harder to say nowadays. But it looks like at least one of them is an accreditor....!"

That night I came home expecting to find my own apartment warm and well-lit. After a long day of accreditation activities, I was reveling in a strange and sudden elation that had arisen from my newfound sense of omnipotence. The exhilaration of creative problem-resolution; the arousal after a challenge vanquished; witnessing the muse of educational administration lying disrobed in all her glory; the exultation that comes from standing at the very precipice of personal and institutional calamity, looking over the brink, and then pulling back just in time – all of this had caused my blood to pump even faster than the many pills I was taking. The adrenaline was coursing through my body like the lifeline of virility itself. Now more than ever I found myself looking forward to a hot cup of tea and a lesson or two (perhaps *three* if stamina allowed!) in intermediate calculus.

But this time my apartment was completely dark. And silent. I flicked the light on and called out through the apartment. But the apartment was just as empty. And just as quiet. A leaky faucet was dripping somewhere in the background. *The Anyman's Guide to Love and the Community College* sat forlornly on the kitchen table. Nothing moved.

And that's when I began to notice the sounds coming from the other side of the apartment. First a light thumping. Then the faint sound of bedsprings creaking. These were the timeless rhythms of love. The music of immoderate passion. Across the wall I could hear the familiar purring of a cat being gently stroked. My heart sank. I boiled a pot of tea. Then waited. I tried to reread my favorite chapter from *Love and the Community College*, the chapter on defloration; but I could not concentrate on the words.

When the tumult had finally died down I stepped into the cold hallway and, standing in front of the adjacent door, began to knock softly. After a few moments the door opened slightly once more. A single eye peered out.

"It's you?" said the math teacher.

"You're *there*?" I answered. "Where the memories are?"

"Of course I'm here. This is my apartment. Where else would I be?"

"Well, I thought you might be waiting for me in my kitchen. I just assumed you would be at my table in your t-shirt and socks, with a cup of tea, the way you have been every evening since we first...."

"It's over, Charlie."

"What?"

"Sorry, but this just can't work."

"It can't?"

"There's no future in it. I am a math teacher. You are an educational administrator. We speak different languages. Mine is the lingua franca of enlightenment. Yours is the specialized jargon of contentment and conformity."

"Yes, but couldn't the two be reconciled somehow? Couldn't there be some sort of equilibrium? Some sort of...*compromise?*"

"No. It simply won't work."

"But why not? Everything seemed to be working fine until now! I mean – I don't want to brag – but it worked *three times* last night alone!"

"You caught me in a moment of weakness. But I'm better now."

"But I...."

"Bye, Charlie...."

The woman opened the door slightly to hold out her hand through the crack. I accepted the soft fingers in a final feeble handshake.

Just as suddenly as she'd once appeared, the woman closed the apartment door and went back inside to the mysterious realm of mathematics and the awaiting arms of the calculus teacher.

⁓

THAT WAS ON Wednesday night. By Thursday morning the threads of my elaborate plan were starting to fray at the edges. The first call came from Timmy at the guard shack who informed me that the arm of the wooden gate was stuck shut and a long line of cars – including several accreditors who had driven off-campus for breakfast – was backed up all the way out to the railroad tracks. By the time I had dispatched a team of motorized carts to transport the accreditors to their various appointments – apologizing profusely for the inconvenience – I was already being called to the Administration building where a disturbance had erupted among a small group of adjuncts over the issue of taxation without representation. The group was demanding a minimum wage, an eight-hour work day and expanded access to inclusion in the literary canon. They also wanted safer working conditions, bimetallism, and universal suffrage. Theirs was a cross of gold, they said, and they were tired of bearing it: and if their concerns were not addressed they were prepared to follow through with a crippling work stoppage. "Look, can we deal with all this *next* week?" I pleaded. "I mean, after the accreditors are gone!" The adjuncts were not pleased but eventually agreed, and having achieved their reluctant consent

I rushed over to the chemistry lab to replace a broken beaker; then to the public speaking classroom where a speechless accreditor was trying to make sense of Long River's laconic approach to teaching; then to the music room to return the conductor's wand I'd borrowed the previous semester. From there I rushed over to the creative writing workshop to explain to an irate accreditor why the newly tenured — and suddenly *less* mesmerizing — creative writing instructor had neglected to show up for his class. Ten students were sitting around the conference table but without an instructor to shepherd them. The accreditor expressed shock at the lack of professionalism and demanded to know how such a thing could happen at an accredited institution of higher learning. Bemoaning the lost opportunity, the woman further questioned the viability of teaching such a thing as creative writing at all.

"It is not for me to speak to *that*," I said. "But what I can say is that our creative writing teacher has been instructive enough to achieve tenure. He has won at least one award for his teaching — and several more for his writing. He has been truly mesmerizing up to this point and is proving to be a real asset to our college."

"Yeah well, it's far easier to be a shining beacon for a little while," the woman said, "than to be a steady source of light into perpetuity. In any case, this is all very disappointing. I have just lost the next forty-five minutes of my highly regimented life. So now what should I do with the time?"

"In lieu of an actual class observation," I suggested, "perhaps you could use the opportunity to interview the students who are sitting around this conference table?"

The woman was regarding me skeptically.

"You see," I continued, "I'm quite sure our students will have nothing but glowing things to say about their creative writing experience here at Cow Eye. And I'm sure they will be happy to tell you all the amazing things they've learned from such a mesmerizing, if inexplicably absent, creative writing instructor. And I'm sure the responses you receive will be almost universally similar in their positivity. Won't they, kids...?"

At this the surprised students nodded their consensus.

The woman agreed with my suggestion and I quickly left her alone with the students, closing the door softly behind me as I left.

≈

THE CHALLENGES DID not end there. Within minutes of each other, I received word of a small cooking fire in the cafeteria; that a disgruntled student had protested a grade by spray-painting a nasty slogan on the side of the Administration building ("Welcome to Cow Eye Community College.... Where FASCISTS meet!"); that a pelican had mauled an inquisitive accreditor and had to be trounced on the spot; and that a former female employee of Cow Eye had shown up with her lawyer at Dr. Felch's vestibule to serve him with a subpoena in a lawsuit that she was filing. By mid-morning, my mind was being pulled in a thousand conflicting directions at once, and in response to each of these emerging trajectories, I had already traveled up and down the esplanade many times over.

"Where are you headed *now*?" a passerby would ask.

And I would answer, "To the animal sciences building to deliver this shipment of shoulder-length gloves!"

A little after ten that morning, just as I was heading to my office to catch my breath from all this, I received a distressed call over the two-way radio that I was now carrying in the vest of my windbreaker.

"We have a serious situation at the cafeteria, Charlie," the voice said, and then, somewhat ominously: "Over!"

When I reached the end of the esplanade I saw a crowd gathered around an ambulance that still had its flashing lights on. A bustle of medical personnel were loading a stretcher into its back. The Esperanto teacher was standing with the crowd, and when I asked her what was happening, she pointed at the back of the ambulance where the stretcher had been placed.

"It's Will Smithcoate," she said. "It looks like he had another incident. They're taking him to a hospital in the city."

"That far?"

"They have no choice. There's no place in the vicinity that has the latest medical equipment."

After a few minutes on the sidewalk, the ambulance shut its door and sped off.

"It's terrible," I told Raul later that morning when I stopped by his office. "Will has no children. And no wife since his wife died. He's spent his life scattering the seed of knowledge to be spread throughout the world

– to be disseminated far into the abstract future – yet there is nobody to take care of him *now*, in the very real present, during his time of greatest need. He'll be there in that hospital all alone, Raul."

"That is life, Charlie. Such are the choices we make. Those were the choices *he* made."

"Yes, but I feel partly responsible. I mean, maybe I should have noticed the drawl in his speech that first time in the cafeteria. Or maybe I could have done more to dissuade him from his reliance on cigars and bourbon. Maybe if I had done something differently – something in its *entirety* – I could have kept this from happening! Maybe he wouldn't be in that ambulance right now if I had!"

"Maybe. But that's beside the point at this juncture. What can be done in the here and now? *That*'s the question we should be asking."

"You're right of course. I should be seeking constructive solutions. I should be proactive. Any ideas?"

Raul thought for a moment. Then he said:

"How about visiting him? You know, going to see him at the hospital?"

The thought hadn't occurred to me.

"I don't know," I said. "I don't even know which city he's been taken to. But I do like the premise of a journey! I mean, it's better than sitting here waiting for the next call from the head of maintenance. It's better than waiting helplessly for the build-up to the Christmas party. Would you come with me?"

Raul laughed.

"Sure," he said, and then, as if it were a simple afterthought: "Can I bring a lady friend?"

I shook my head.

"Do you ever think of anything *else*?"

Raul looked sheepish.

"Of course. In private moments I also fantasize about sinusoids...."

I rolled my eyes. Back in my office I called the hospital for information and when I had the necessary details I stopped by Raul's office once again to explain my plan.

"Your plan?" he asked.

"Yes. My plan to visit Will in the hospital in the city."

"Okay...."

"So meet me at the cafeteria tonight at eleven," I said. "It's six hours to the city where the hospital is, so we should get there just in time for visiting hours. Your bicycle is of little good for our purpose, so I'll procure a car for our journey. We'll drive by darkness of night and be back here by noon tomorrow to help set up for the Christmas party. It'll be an experience to remember. Oh, and to answer your question, Raul: yes, you can bring your lady friend...."

We shook hands and agreed to meet at the cafeteria that night at eleven: me, Raul, and his latest lady friend.

❧

By the middle of that morning – the Thursday before our Christmas party – the accreditation visit had clearly moved well past its emanation and was now heading toward the peak of its incarnation. Faculty were hosting the visiting team members in their classes. Adopt-an-Accreditor activities were being carried out religiously and with a vengeance – or, as the atheist in the philosophy department wryly put it, *with a religious vengeance.* The secretaries were sending regular updates by two-way radio. Student leaders were busily and eagerly doing their part. Within hours the graffiti had been painted over. The broken toilets were fixed. Ducks quacked once again. Despite the earlier problems, the entire weight of history seemed to be moving purposefully toward the culminating Christmas party the following day.

By three o'clock all the interviews had been conducted and the classroom visits completed. At six, dinner was served by the culinary students. By eight, the Faculty-Student-Accreditor Dance-A-Thon had wound down, and by eight-fifteen the lights in the cafeteria were turned back on – the attendees blinking at the new light – and the set-up crew for the following day's activities began their mobilization: with ladders and stepstools and rolls of duct tape the team was busily stringing up the decorations for the Christmas party.

By ten-thirty the lights and tinsel were mostly strewn; a strobe had been dangled from the center of the cafeteria; tables and chairs were arranged in long rows. And by ten-forty-five the cafeteria had emptied out and was quiet and dark once again. A few minutes before eleven I stood outside the entrance waiting for Raul, who arrived punctually as always – and, exactly as promised, with his "lady friend" in tow.

"I trust you know each other?" Raul winked and pointed at the two of us.

"Hi Bess," I said.

"Fuck you, Charlie."

"Look, Bessie...."

"Just shut up, Charlie. I'm only here because Raul asked me to come. And I do want to visit Will in his moment of need. I'm not here to have a probing discussion with *you*."

Bessie turned and walked away. When she was out of earshot Raul looked over at me apologetically.

"I hope I didn't overstep here.... I was just trying to help out. I figured you might like the opportunity to talk things through with her. That this might be your last chance – you know, before the Christmas party. I probably should have told you up front, Charlie. But I thought you might call the whole thing off if you knew she was coming...."

"Right," I said. "It's okay. These are the choices we make. These are the choices *I've* made. I guess we'll just see how it goes...."

And so at exactly eleven-fifteen, having not slept at all in more than seventy-two hours, and having not slept soundly in more than seven months, I closed the cafeteria door behind me. From there the three of us walked in darkness to the parking lot in back of the cafeteria where I opened the heavy door of Will's Oldsmobile Starfire, sat behind the wheel, pulled the key from the dark place under the seat where he always left it, and starting up the car with a loud roar of the V-8 engine, guided the lumbering beast out onto the main thoroughfare of the college, past Timmy at the guard shack, over the railroad tracks, and out onto the highway leading along the edge of Cow Eye Junction. The Oldsmobile was large and powerful and as we headed out to the highway – the three of us sharing the crowded bench seat (Raul on the passenger side and Bessie in between the two of us with her ankles on either side of the floor hump) – I stepped onto the large gas accelerator, gradually gathering momentum until the pedal was firmly against the floor and the powerful car was speeding headlong into the night: past the jail and the post office and the pawn shop selling old musical instruments and beloved family heirlooms, past the darkened remnants of the Cow Eye Ranch and in the general direction of the large city where Will Smithcoate had been taken. When we reached the mile marker announcing the exit for the Outskirts, I slowed down for the first time, then turned off onto the exit.

"Why are you turning?" Bessie objected.

"I need some gas…."

The convenience store where I'd stopped was the only one at the Outskirts, and while Raul went inside to buy some mints I pumped the gas and Bessie stood a good ten feet away from the car, her foot up on a curb, with an unlit cigarette in one hand and a disposable lighter in the other. She did not acknowledge me. She did not speak. She did not even look in my direction. Off in the distance the sounds of crickets could be heard. The fumes from the premium gas were intoxicating. Yet despite the late hour the moon itself was childless.

"Look, Bess…" I said when the pump finally clicked off; I flicked the lever down and set the handle back in its cradle. "All I can say to you is…."

Bessie raised her palm up to my face.

"Let it go, Charlie."

Then she lowered it back down.

"Bess, I'm really sorry how things turned out. It's just that…"

"Just shut up, Charlie. It's not worth it. Life is short. And I've moved on."

"You have?"

"Yes. I've moved on completely. If you need to know, I'm in love again."

"So soon?"

"Yes. It took longer than it usually does, but I've recently gotten back with an old friend. He's an admirer from high school who used to write me love letters in colored pencil but who now works for the phone company. He'd be number one thousand and *two*, in case anyone's counting."

"You mean you're not devastated by our break-up?"

"No."

"You're not completely crushed?"

"Of course not. Why would I be? I've had a thousand and one loves in my life. And they've all ended in ignominy: all one thousand and one. It's how it's always been with me. And it's how it is right now. But what should I do? Should I stop allowing myself to be vulnerable? Should I dissuade myself from being in love? Should I cease to care about the higher things in life – about that other kind of happiness – just because I know it's not going to work out for me? And that it never will?"

"It'll work out, Bess. Everything will work out for you some day…."

"No, Charlie, it won't. And I know that just as well as you do. I'm from Cow Eye Junction after all – and if there's one thing that being from Cow Eye teaches you it's how to give up what *is* for what so easily *could have been*. And that the two are not so different from each other really. But, in any case, that is all water under the bridge now. And besides…. he likes children."

"Who?"

"My new love. He's great with kids. He has three of his own."

"So we're good then? You know, you and me?"

"I wouldn't exactly say *that*. I've still got a fucking half-eaten fruitcake in my freezer thanks to you. But yes, we're good enough for now. Good enough, in any case, to sit together on the bench seat of this 1966 Oldsmobile Starfire. Good enough to make our way through the entrails of endless darkness toward the city to visit Will."

I breathed a sigh of relief.

"Thank you, Bess," I said.

"Forget it, Charlie," she answered.

At that moment, Raul came out with a bag of snacks. As usual his timing was enlightened.

"Are we ready to go?"

"I think so," I said. "There's just one final stop I need to make before we head out onto the highway and into the depths of this impossibly dark night…."

Raul offered me a mint and I accepted. It was wintergreen. I started up the Starfire with a roar.

❧

AT THE CORNER of the Outskirts where the withered holly still hung, I found the person I'd been seeking. The man was wearing the same collared coat he always wore. He stood over the same battered suitcase he always stood over. And in the light of the lamp post he wore the same dull expression that he always seemed to wear. But this time there was a problem.

"I've only got the one vial," he said.

"What…?"

"I'm out of the other…."

"But I need them in equal amounts!"

"I've only got this one here."

"But...."

"Do you want it or not?"

"Of course I do. But I want the other one too."

"Well I don't have the other one. I only have this one. Do you want it?"

"One without the other?"

"Yes. Do you want it?"

"No!" I said and stormed away. Back at the car I slammed the heavy door behind me and sat for several moments gripping the steering wheel in frustration. Then, meekly, I got back out. The man was right where I'd left him.

"Are you sure you don't have *both*?" I asked. "Somewhere in that large suitcase there has to be the other vial too?"

"No, I only have the one. Do you want it or not?"

Under the flickering light of the lamp post, I pondered this new dilemma. On the one hand, I reasoned, the two pills had been working their magic in tandem; this was well-known. What was also unequivocal was that while taking one after the other I had always taken them in equal measure: one tablet, say, from the vial with the black label and then, after a fistful of tap water to wash it down, another from the vial with the label of white. And though I'd begun taking them in a moment of supreme darkness and indecision, the consequences since that time had been like day and night. With the help of the opposite-colored vials, I'd been able to avoid both utter sleep and utter wakefulness. In this state of heightened irresolution I'd been able to finish off the self-study, and to finish it off in prose that was almost exclusively barren. Under the influence of opposite pharmaceutical imperatives, I'd managed to handwrite the focus group report in a single fateful weekend and to turn it in the following day with an orgasmic shudder. I'd shaved off my beard and stayed up until the early hours to finish *The Anyman's Guide to Love and the Community College*. Since taking these two pills one after the other I'd melted a glacier and conquered a continent and successfully conducted a symphony of many moving parts; I'd navigated the roiling rapids of sleep deprivation and overseen the arrival of our accreditors in covered wagons. I'd traveled far beyond my field of expertise to the gilded realm on the other side of the railroad tracks where, despite my lack of sleep – or because of it? – I had come to love math in ways that I would not have thought physically possible: at last recognizing the power of the derivative, the incredible elegance of the integral, I'd learned calculus over many nights and many months, on top of countless textbooks and sprawled across the cold kitchen table and pressed up against the sweaty....

"Look, do you want this vial or not?" the man interrupted my thoughts.

"I'm sorry?"

"The pills. You'd better grab the vial now if you want it. It's the last one of its kind. And you're not the only person in this town who has an inclination for it."

"Okay," I said. "I'll take it. I'll buy the whole damn thing. Which is to say, I'll take that final vial of pills that will either keep me absolutely awake or make me fall absolutely asleep. I'll take the one vial, and the one vial only, and I'll take it without its perfect compliment. Without its diametrical opposite...."

I paid the man from Dr. Felch's roll of twenties, got back into the car, and from there I drove the Starfire out onto the open highway leading to the city.

"He only had one vial," I muttered to Raul and Bessie when we were back at full speed.

"Which one?" they asked. "The one to fall asleep... or the one to stay awake?"

This was certainly a valid question for my passengers to pose: in all, there were still more than three hundred miles of open road ahead of us – the asphalt stretching so far beyond the headlights that it seemed to extend into infinity. Beyond that only the night could be seen.

"I'm not exactly sure," I answered. "I didn't think to ask. All I know is that the man only had one without the other. And now I have a single vial of pills without its opposite. I've put it in my pocket. And I will be consuming it alone and in its entirety. Like it or not, I will be committing to this one vial absolutely. At long last, you see, I will be committing to *something* entirely – which very likely means I will soon *become* something entirely. Which, as you should very well know by now, is somewhat unprecedented...."

Ahead of me the asphalt highway stretched into the darkness. The three of us held on as the Oldsmobile took us further and further away from the desiccation of Cow Eye Junction and deeper and deeper into the deepest reaches of endless night. Up ahead, the faint smell of moisture could already be felt.

"Pull the trigger, Charlie," I could still hear Ethel's voice imploring me, her words little more than a whisper.

And so I did. I closed my eyes and pulled the trigger.

PART 3. DISSOLUTION

NIGHT

Day is surer than night.
Night is purer than day.

With my foot pressed firmly on the gas, the six-hour drive to the city took us a little over three and a half. Along the empty highway we barreled headfirst, blazing by vacant fields and sleeping cattle and the occasional off-ramp leading to another stretch of unmarked highway. Out past the town the night itself was absolute darkness and if not for the headlights and the center line passing under the wheels of the Starfire, there would have been nothing at all for us to see. Amid the darkness outside the window and the emptiness of the surroundings, our only proof of forward motion – the only sign that our car was in fact moving from one point in time to another, that *we* ourselves were moving – was the old odometer turning slowly on the walnut dashboard of the Oldsmobile.

"We're going *eighty-eight*," said Raul. "Which is a little fast, you know...."

And I nodded.

In lieu of words, Bessie had taken to manning the AM radio and for a while we just sat in the wordless car listening to the far-off sounds of classic country, the songs coming one after another over the radio, each telling of a life that was different and defiant yet just barely hanging on. These were not simply songs about love achieved or lost; these were songs about the great difference between staying and leaving.

"I haven't heard this one in ages...." Bessie would say and close her eyes to listen better.

And I would nod.

A half-hour out of Cow Eye Junction the last AM station faded to static and Bessie leaned forward to switch it off. Immediately the air of the night outside our window grew more present, the night itself perfectly quiet but for the rumble of the engine. The center stripe in the road was now flying by so fast under the wheels of our car that it came and went as a single unbroken line. The smell of vinyl and old cigar from Will's ashtray gave the car its warmth, and as we drove headlong we spoke about the things that had brought us all to the notchback bench seat in this most venerable of all great cars – to this particular moment in time and space. Ahead of us was a city, and behind us was a town. And even further back were the random arrows once hurled from a terrific distance – the twists and happenstances that somehow led each of us to end up here, in the warm cab of Will's '66 Starfire, rolling down an empty highway toward the outer limits of darkness. In our rearview mirror were the pills that we had taken and the reports that we had written and the fantasies we had once imagined for ourselves. Behind us too were the broken treaties and the buried languages, a promising frontier, the unexplored rivers with their pitiless dams that could now be counted on to block the water from flowing. All of it was somewhere in the brightly lit past, while up ahead, in the distance beyond the steamy windshield where the end of the highway meets the beginning of pure darkness, were the hopes that we were pursuing and the dreams we still held. The unfinished report. The innovative proposal. The untenable plan that would one day need to be written under the dark illumination of a single desk lamp. In the faint light of the Starfire's cab – amid the soft glow of the dashboard and the chalky warmth of its heater – it was all so clear to see. And so we talked about it sincerely. The squandered loves. The severed dreams. The Supreme Court decisions. The soteriological debates. A vanquished frontier. Favorite supermarkets. The patron saint of lost travelers. Our vague futures and even less coherent histories. Lost in the interval between the darkness left behind and the darkness still ahead, we spoke about the only things that we could now see. The night. Its darknesses. The eternal emptiness of eternity.

"Have you ever seen a night this dark?" asked Raul.

I squinted my eyes at the night beyond the headlights. But the darkness in front of us was truly dark.

"No," I said.

"At all?"

"Not even close."

"Me either. It's as if we're traveling through that unseen part of the universe where no light can go."

"Precisely. In all my years I don't think I've ever seen a darker night than this."

"Well *I* have...." Bessie had opened her eyes and was staring straight ahead into the oncoming night. "It was the last time my dad and I went fishing. I was untouched back then and there was no moon."

"You were untouched once?"

"Yes. And there was no moon out. It was a night as dark as this one. The clouds were thick before the rain. In the pitch-black you couldn't even see your own hand if you held it in front of your face. The sounds were so intense. The smells were everywhere. The night was so electric that you could actually feel it in your bones. It was the only time I've ever *felt* the night. My dad was sick at the time. He was sick in ways that I couldn't have understood. Afterwards we lit up a fire and sat around it. I was very small but I can still remember the darkness of that night. The smells. The intensity of the sound. The pulsations. I shivered under a blanket and sobbed. It was the last time I saw the river through my father's eyes."

The car was now going well over ninety. I held my foot firmly on the pedal. As the three of us talked away the minutes – the miles – the car itself seemed to be frozen in time, as if the Oldsmobile were perfectly motionless, deathly still. Defying the odometer, it might have been that our car was staying in one place – and that the world itself, with all its intricate madness, was the thing so inexorably rushing by.

"When I was a child, I used to be afraid of darkness like this," said Raul after the latest silence had passed. "My mother would come in to turn off the light in my room before putting me to bed. In the unlit room she'd lie on the old mattress with me and tell me the stories her own mother had told her when she was young. A good story, she would say, can take place in the darkness of one's own imagination. Just imagine, Raulito, that there is no light in the world. Outside this room there is nothing but everlasting darkness and the black of impenetrable night. Words can be the light for the seeing that happens in the darkness of your own mind.

Close your eyes, Raulito, and let me tell you another story. Close your eyes, Raulito, and pretend that this night will last forever...."

As the car sped along through the distance of time and space the three of us talked about the ways that night tends to become day. How the two become each other. And how, despite the tenacity of our efforts, these opposites will always be in conflict and can never be reconciled. These were the lessons that we had learned, each of us in isolation along the way. And staring out past the tempered glass of the Starfire, at the vacant darkness of all-enveloping night, we talked about the things that we had seen. The smells that we had experienced. The people loved. The miracles witnessed. The longings. The moisture. A casual touch of thigh against thigh on a crowded bench seat. The resulting silence lasted longer than most – filling the car and taking the three of us well into the heart of our journey, headlong past the vacant fields and the changing scenery that we could not yet see: the fence posts, the farm houses, the unlit billboards and banners that might have told us we were getting closer to a city. In this silence, neither Raul nor Bessie felt the need to speak. Outside our window the world was very dark. I clenched the steering wheel tightly and drove further into the night.

∽

WITH THE COUNTRYSIDE flying by unseen, the mood in the car gradually edged along from one extreme of darkness to the other. A few miles down the road Bessie dialed in another AM station and we listened to the music for as long as it lasted. When we'd outdriven the music she turned it off again and the three of us began to sing Christmas carols over the drone of the engine: first the somber and reflective ones, and then the sprightly ones as well. Raul's voice was strong and pure. Bessie's was angelic. Mine came from a place I'd not visited in many years. Though our singing was approximate it was also very sincere, the carols bursting forth like fireworks into the cold March night – and when it was done we turned our discussion toward the more immediate things in life: about smoke and water and history. As the miles passed beneath us we spoke about the emptiness of this empty highway, about the ambulance that had sped off toward the city with our stricken friend inside and how we had vowed to follow it to the very ends of the earth. And of course, we talked about the sad plight of our friend himself: about Will Smithcoate, whose own heedless pursuit of bourbon and cigars had brought him to such a lonely place in an unknown hospital room somewhere in the unforeseeable future.

"It's not right," said Bessie as a light trickle began to descend onto our windshield a few minutes later. "I mean the man can be aggravating as hell. He's jaded and out of tune. His lecture notes are anachronistic. His tongue is acute and his reminiscences imprecise. But he deserves something a little better than *this*. I mean, to rot away in a hospital somewhere? Forgotten by the world. Wifeless. Childless."

"Speechless...." Raul added.

"And *home*less," I said.

We all muttered our agreement.

"It's sad indeed," said Raul, finally. "But this is not the end for him. Trust me, my friends. Guys like Will Smithcoate never die. They just smoke and drink and teach undergraduates until there's nothing more to live for...."

We drove for several more minutes in silence. It must have been a good twenty miles of wordlessness with none of us feeling the need to talk. The silence was natural and thoughtful and not without merit.

About half-way into the journey we hit a heavier patch of rain, the water thumping the windshield then snaking up the glass like little transparent worms. Against this new moisture I flicked on the wipers and focused even more intensely on the road stretching before us. The rain continued to come and soon the droplets were bouncing off the road so heavily that the center line disappeared completely and all that could be seen was the frenzied explosions of water against the asphalt.

"Wow," said Raul. "When's the last time any of us saw *rain*? I bet the Diahwa Valley Basin hasn't seen anything like this for years!"

"It won't last," said Bessie. "It'll pass."

"The rain? How would you know *that*?"

"It's a fact of life. All things that *come* unexpectedly will sooner or later *leave* just as unexpectedly...."

Bessie's words sounded ominous. Yet the further we drove, the harder the rain came down. Ahead of us the drops were cutting through the glare of the headlights like tracer bullets. At times the wipers could not keep up and the only thing visible was the blur of the moisture on the windshield and the vague outline of the asphalt up ahead in the headlights.

Undeterred, I aimed the Starfire for the gray void outside the windshield where the half-lit asphalt would hopefully be.

"You don't think you're going a little fast?" Raul asked. "In this weather especially?"

"Yes I *do* think I'm going a little fast. *Of course* I'm going fast. That's exactly the point, Raul! I'm driving at excess speeds because I want to make it to the city as efficiently as possible. If we can get to the hospital early enough, we'll have time to visit Will and still make it back for tomorrow's accreditation activities. And if we make it back in time I just might have enough time to get a little sleep before the Christmas party...."

"The party starts at six, right?"

"Yes. Which means we can visit Will in the morning and still make it back to Cow Eye by two for a few hours of sleep before heading over to the cafeteria to finalize decorations for the party. That's why I'm driving so fast. The fate of our institution depends on it. My very legacy depends on it."

"It's a worthy goal," said Raul, "though more of an *objective*, really. But would you mind slowing down just a little anyway? Please!"

I took my foot slightly off the gas. The needle retreated a bit then settled firmly on seventy-five.

"Thank you," said Raul. "That's a lot better for my nerves...."

From there I drove through more heavy rain, Raul and Bessie keeping their silences amid the pelting drops. At last Raul pointed through the windshield.

"Hey, Bessie, look at that...!"

Bessie obliged but saw nothing.

"At what?" she said. "I just see rain."

"Exactly. The moisture is still coming down!"

"So?"

"Well, it goes against your idea that all things that come must also go. The rain is still coming, just like all the other eternal things in this world that stay and stay forever. Like water. And darkness. And mathematics."

"No, Raul, there is nothing in this world that stays forever. Not the sun. Not the moon. Not the lover. Not the parent. All things will eventually come to an end. Day and night. The people we love. The laws of man. The dams. The many nations of the world. They all must come to an end at some point."

"Not *our* nation!" At this Raul leaned forward to make his point more emphatically. "Ours will stay and stay forever!"

"And your evidence of this is?"

"The evidence is all around you. Just take a look. What do you see?"

"Rain."

"And?"

"Endless darkness."

"Right, you see these things because it's night. But during the day you'd see the purple mountains. And the fruited plains. The flag with its thirteen stripes and forty-seven stars. The road signs. The dichotomies. The silver trout. The Supreme Court decisions. They still exist – all of them. You see, existence is the best argument for itself. And our country exists in perpetuity by virtue of its own continued existence. It exists because it has continued to exist through the many mystic discords of collective memory. And that means it will continue to exist forever...!"

"Just like the rain now falling?"

"Right!"

"The rain," I said conciliatorily, "is definitely falling. And our great country surely does exist. These things are incontrovertible. But as to the other assumptions the two of you have expressed, well, I guess we'll just have to wait and see, won't we?"

Bessie shrugged her shoulders and slid very slightly over to me. Raul said nothing.

Outside our window the rain was falling just as hard. In the darkness of endless night it seemed that it would fall forever.

⟨≈⟩

TO THE SOUND of the car rumbling through the darkness, the three of us talked away the remaining distance. Between the edge of Cow Eye and the promise of a city up ahead we found the words to exhaust the great topics of the day – then, when they were fully exhausted, the even greater topics of this night. And as we moved further from Cow Eye Junction, the focus of our discussion moved with us as well: from the specifics of the accreditation visit and the upcoming Christmas party....to the rain now falling heavily onto our windshield. From desiccation to darkness. From daylight to dissolution. In short order we talked about time and moisture and darkness and love – and how these things have come together to produce all the important things in our world: the things that stay and stay forever.

"Darkness added to time," Raul declared, "produces eternity. Just as moisture amid darkness inspires hope."

"Love to the power of time equals darkness squared," said Bessie. "While the average of love and moisture is greater than their equivalent for darkness and time."

At all of this I nodded.

"I agree with each of you in principle," I said. "Though in my case it's been something slightly less mathematical – more paradoxical, if you will. You see, without time you cannot experience love. Without love you cannot achieve moisture. Without moisture you cannot love darkness. And without darkness – without the pure night that follows the pure day – you cannot know *time*. Such is the unbroken cycle of incarnation. But we seem to have lost our connection to it. We seem to have lost our bearings somewhere along the way...."

"Like the three of us tonight...."

"In this car...."

"Surrounded by darkness...."

"Heading down an empty highway toward a city that might not exist...."

"Toward a hospital of our own imagination...."

"In a state whose name is never given...."

"No!" I protested. "That's not true at all. We're not lost! We're just traveling slowly but indisputably toward a destination that is unknown!"

"It's the same thing, Charlie. And in any case, it's too late now. The clouds are dark. The sky is black. The rain is still falling. But, then, we interrupted you. Weren't you saying something about humanity losing its way...?"

"Right. So as I was saying.... each of these things requires the others. But we have gotten away from them."

"We?"

"Yes, *we*. We have lost our way. And yet all is not as lost as it may seem. All is not lost because it is still quite possible to have all of them together. You see, to have one you must have all the others. For without one you cannot have anything at all. And so it is perhaps *this* that is the great calculus of life? Perhaps it is this revelation that has eluded us in our relentless quest to sow the seeds of future civilizations?"

The car sped forward. By the time we reached the three-quarter point of the drive, it was a little after one-thirty in the morning, we'd already run the gamut of travel talk, and each of us had begun to notice telltale signs of weariness in the others.

"How are you doing there, Charlie?" Raul asked. He had leaned forward to stare across Bessie at me. "Just let me know if you want me to take over the driving for a bit."

"I'm fine, Raul."

"You don't *look* fine! You look tired...."

"That's because I *am* tired. I'm tired because I'm not sleeping. I haven't slept in seven months, remember?"

"Yes, but you look *really* tired now. More tired than ever. On a scale of one to ten... with *ten* being a well-rested student on the first day of class and *one* being a lifeless pelican after it has been trammeled by an accreditor ... you, Charlie, look to be barely *one-and-a-half.*"

"That bad?"

"Or worse. Your eyes are bloodshot. Your hands tremble. Your knees are knocking against the bottom of the steering column. Did you remember to take a pill from the vial you just bought?"

"I did."

"Was it the pill to stay awake?"

"I believe so. Though it's becoming increasingly difficult to say. I seem to be in control of my senses for the time being. I feel alert and attentive. The things I see are eminently clear and consistent. The road. The rain. The darkness up ahead. So far none of it makes me shiver. None of it moves me to desolation. But we're not quite to our destination yet, are we? So I suppose we'll find out soon enough one way or the other. For example when we reach the city. Or, oppositely, if I fall asleep at this wheel...."

"Not funny, Charlie."

"Yeah," said Bessie. "I am not meeting my maker in an *Oldsmobile*...!"

At this the three of us fell silent. The journey continued. The road stayed the course. Now we talked about time and space and eternity and time. Then eternity. Then space. We talked about darkness and light and other mutually exclusive things until, to lighten the darkness, Raul decided to change the tenor of the discussion entirely. "Hey!" he said, as if he had just experienced an epiphany. "I know what we can talk about. We can talk about...*love*?! You know, what it *is*....?"

"Again?!"

"Don't worry....it shouldn't take very long. We're almost coming up to the city. In fact, I think I can make out a sign in the distance...."

A few seconds later the sign flew by: the city was less than a hundred miles away.

"But, Raul," I said. "A lot of things can happen over the course of a hundred miles."

"Naturally," he said. "Which is why we should talk about love before it's too late...!"

And so over the next fifty miles we spoke about the universal particulars of love, the eternal exigencies of romance, the most common idiosyncrasies of sex. As I looked through the rain for the first indications of the approaching city – the dull glow in the sky that would soon be overwhelming the stars – I listened along as Raul and Bessie engaged each other in a graphic discussion of male and female orgasm. To the sound of the rain and the rhythm of the wipers, the words overcame me; like ecstasy itself, the conversation started slowly, picking up momentum with each utterance until it had blossomed into a heated intercourse that lasted several breathless minutes – several miles of undulating tension and release – Bessie speaking with inner authority on the subject, yet Raul managing to hold his own in the evenly matched communion of shared experience. When the fumbled beginnings had turned to lively intercourse and when the intercourse had found its breathless culmination, Raul summarized the experience that had just been witnessed by all:

"What you've just said is all fine and good," he explained to Bessie. "But at the end of the day, *your* orgasm is a lot more well-rounded than *ours*."

"Than whose?"

"Than *ours*. Mine and Charlie's. Which is to say, without a doubt your orgasm is more elaborate than ours will ever be."

"You're telling *me*?"

"Yes. You see, if you were to diagram the male orgasm, it would appear as nothing more than a straight line ascending toward its zenith. A simple geometric line moving from foreplay through coitus and on toward a breathless ejaculation. It is straightforward and predictable with equal rise and run.... " At this Raul used his forefinger to draw an ascending diagonal line through the air. "…Meanwhile, the female orgasm is far more complex. If you were to represent it visually, it would look something rather like this…."

With his finger pressed lightly against the steamy windshield, Raul traced onto the glass a series of concentric circles representing emanating waves of female pleasure:

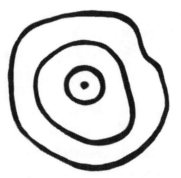

When he'd drawn the smallest circle he could draw, the tiny circumference barely wider than a pea, he tapped his finger against the glass. "There!" he said. "That is the female orgasm in all its splendor!"

"It looks like an old tree stump," said Bessie.

"Or a target to be used for shooting-practice," I added.

"Or a heavenly body that has lost almost all of its orbiting moons."

"Moons?"

"Yes, those most feminine of all satellites."

"Yeah, well these are not moons. They are emanating waves of female pleasure. Duh…"

Bessie and I exchanged sideways glances. Then I asked:

"But why only three circles, Raul? Why are there only three concentric rings surrounding the pea-sized center? Why only three moons around that celestial body?"

Raul had apparently prepared himself for this particular question:

"Simple," he said. "We all have jobs, right? And obligations to fulfill. And reports to write. And early meetings to attend the following Monday morning. It's certainly not that you and I aren't capable of more. And besides, there's only so much room on this windshield…."

I nodded in full agreement.

But at this Bessie seemed to take exception to the diagram that Raul had drawn.

"Spoken like a true man!" she grunted. "This all might have been true in some bygone era, Raul. When life was geometric and Civilon still roamed the earth and Barcelona was the center of the romantic world. But that is no longer the case...." As Raul's concentric circles slowly succumbed to the balmy warmth inside the car – from the heater, our breathless exhalations, the rising passion of the discussion itself – Bessie drew her own representation using the very tip of her forefinger. "Actually," she said, tracing her finger into the condensation on the windshield, "*my* orgasm looks more like this...."

"It's a house!" said Raul, nonplussed.

"It's an orgasm."

"*Where's* the orgasm?"

"It's there," said Bessie, "inside the house. Somewhere deep inside. And it will reveal itself to those who know how to ask. It will open up to you and let you enter. But first you have to knock softly on the door...."

Raul raised his knuckles as if he were going to knock on Bessie's orgasm, but then he changed his mind instead.

"Right," he said, and grew silent.

At this another road sign sped by announcing thirty-seven more miles to the city. A few minutes later a car passed by in the opposite direction: the first oncoming traffic we'd met since leaving Cow Eye Junction.

"I wonder if that car's headed to Cow Eye?" Raul said, opening up the tantalizing possibility of symmetry.

"It's doubtful," said Bessie, slamming Raul's possibility back shut. "It's awfully dark where we've come from. The moon cannot even be seen. And, let's face it, there are just too many forks in the road between here and there."

⤸

AND JUST LIKE that the oncoming traffic began to meet us with more frequency. First a car every ten minutes – then one every five – until, within minutes, there was a steady stream of headlights coming toward us from the city. Soon the road itself doubled in width, then doubled again – two lanes became four, then eight – with well-lit billboards that could now be seen along the side of the road and directional signs that passed overhead. At one point a late-model Ford overtook our Starfire to the left and went screaming past us toward the city.

"We're almost there," said Raul. "About twelve more miles."

Now the billboards and freeway signs were coming more frequently. Automobiles sped in both directions: import car after import car heading at us from the city, while moving in our direction was one domestic truck after another. The further we drove, the newer the cars became – and the newer the cars, the brighter the halogens. In time we began to see the lights of a metropolis up ahead, the overall glow getting steadily brighter as we drew nearer.

"The city!" said Bessie.

Raul, who was now assertive in his role as designated navigator, had unfurled a map on his lap and was studying it meticulously with a flashlight.

"Five more miles," he said. "Exit at 94A...."

I slowed down: at a mere fifty-five miles per hour, the approach to the city seemed to grind to a crawl. The dull glow beyond our dashboard grew softer and more present at the same time. The lights of the city became more distinct.

"It's not even a very large city," said Bessie, as the glow approached. "But just look how bright everything is...."

"It's definitely a world apart from Cow Eye!" I added.

"You can say that again. So much brighter...."

"And faster."

"Infinitely more efficient."

"And relentless."

"And dynamic."

"And interesting!"

"But how can anybody actually *live* here?" Bessie asked.

"I don't understand it myself," said Raul.

"If nothing else," I offered, "city people are *resilient*. Somehow they find a way...."

"It's sad though," said Bessie. "The dull illumination that serves as their starlight. All of it is just too sad."

"Yeah well you might as well get used to it. One day we'll all be living in cities like this. Whether we like it or not...."

"Is that some kind of malediction?"

"Next exit..." said Raul.

"No, it's not a malediction," I said. "It's impending reality. It's a future that's approaching just as fast as...."

"Our exit!"

I veered the car off to the right.

"Geez, Charlie!" Raul shouted. "Watch the road! I mean, your affection for the timeless is going to get us killed....!"

The exit led to an off-ramp that veered right then straightened out. I hit the brake firmly for the first time since leaving Cow Eye Junction and our car quickly decelerated, heading toward a traffic light that was pure red; at the light I came to a complete stop, the Starfire idling under us. On the right was a gas station and up ahead were countless truck stops and fast-food restaurants. Everything was open and well-lit with neon signs and racy captions and other urban invocations.

"Now what?" asked Bessie.

"I don't know," I answered. "What time is it?"

"It's a little after two."

"Two?"

"Yes, two. It's always two, Charlie."

"Right. It's two. So I guess we made really good time, huh? Much better than I thought we would. See? Our odometer was faithful to us after all! In retrospect I could have driven slower, I suppose. But that is just more water under the bridge. Because here we are at this traffic light at two in the morning. And now that we're here....what do we do?"

"I have to pee," said Bessie.

"Me too," said Raul.

"And we need some gas," I added.

The light changed to green and I drove ahead to the gas station. At the pump I filled the Starfire with premium gas and in the grungy bathroom I slid two pills out of the vial I'd bought and washed them down with water from the tap. When we were all back at the car, Bessie flicked a piece of lint off her skirt and asked once again:

"Now what should we do, Charlie?"

"I don't know. How about we take a drive downtown – you know to that place in the urban landscape where the nightlife is?"

"At this hour?"

"Yes. We're in a city after all. So why not visit that place in our not-so-distant future where life is truly *alive*....!"

After a discussion of logistics, the three of us got back into the Starfire and Raul unfurled his map again. I started up the engine. Bessie dialed in an FM radio station, then quickly turned it off.

"I *hate* FM music!" she said, as if it were a genre.

Raul tapped a place on his map:

"Charlie, go straight under the off-ramp and take a left at the next light...."

Following Raul's instructions I guided the Starfire back toward the off-ramp and past the fast-food restaurants – all of them still open – and toward the part of the city where the nightlife was in full swing. Though the road was just as wet, the rain had turned down to a light drizzle, and driving through the glistening city we saw the all-night diners and blues bars and crowded sidewalks still brimming with people. In the heart of the city there were crowds of young revelers and late-night establishments and strip clubs and double-parked cars and panhandlers sprawled out on the sidewalk under plastic coverings. There were street performers dancing in the light rain and musicians playing under the eaves. There was a silver-painted mime and a cross-dressing dance troupe and acrobats in leotards and contortionists bending over backwards and a clown on stilts and gay bodybuilders flexing their collective muscle and a tall, scantily clad woman in high heels peddling ninety unforgettable minutes of urban sprawl. Cars splashed through the water now swirling in the street, black music blared, shirtless torsos hung out of car windows. Every sound was loud. Every light was big and all-consuming: the yellows, the reds, the pinks and purples and greens. So much sound. So many colors. A police siren. A horn. The quick burst of gunshots in the distance followed by a louder burst of laughter from a bar nearby. An unattended car alarm. A bullhorn. Loud shrieks of adolescent joy. A salsa band. Two shirtless college students with their faces painted green. A barrel filled with fire. A wet cat curled up on the hood of a car. Slowly we drove by it all.

"There sure are a lot of African-Americans here," Bessie noted.

"You mean Americans of African descent...." Raul prompted.

"Yeah, whatever you call them nowadays. They're everywhere...."

"And just look at all the beautiful women!" Raul added. "You don't see too much of *that* in Cow Eye...!"

As we drove through the city, each of us took in the startling imagery that was the city's greatest offering: the young women in impossibly short skirts, the festive bars, the neon signs, the outlandish demeanors, the careless laughter, the individuated personalities, the half-hearted marriages, the religious revelations and reevaluations, the sights and sounds and smells of uncollected trash and backroom abortions and open sewers and burning bras and unfettered freedom sprinkled with cocaine dust and gun powder and stirred into a melting pot of gelatinous tallow.

"And you, Charlie? What strikes you about this city that we are driving through at two in the morning? What about this bustling urban landscape impresses you most?"

I had to think for a few moments. Then it occurred to me:

"The lights," I said.

"And..."

"And the noise."

"And....?"

"And the nervous movement."

"These things are beautiful, are they not?"

"Oh yes, absolutely. They are without a doubt beautiful things in their own right. They soothe the human need for new stimulations. They give hope for resurrection. They allow people to forget where they've come from....and overlook where they're going. It is all very understandable. But having lived in Cow Eye for seven months I look at things a little differently now. I have seen cities before. And I have seen the same relentlessness in them all. But now I see it so much differently. Now I can look at all this bustling nightlife and see it for what it really is."

"And what is that?"

"Evanescence."

"So, Charlie, you mean to say that amid a tumult of swirling bodies and laughter and flashing light and sound….amid all this life being lived, *that* is what you see?"

"Yes."

"And that's *all* you see?"

"No. I also see the emptiness."

"Of life?"

"Of *living.*"

"They're different?"

"Oh, yes…quite!"

"Well anything else? Aside from evanescence and emptiness, is there anything else that you have come to find solace in while driving through this city?"

"Yes. Vacuity. And pointlessness. Alienation. Silence. Loneliness. Futility. Careerism. Each of these things I see as I drive through the bustle of this city. Making my way over so much asphalt, I have come to see many, many things. And having seen so many things I can see them all so much clearer now. The darkness. The moisture. The dissolution. I see these things for what they are and what they pretend to be. But mostly I see the glistening evanescence in it all…."

≈

THE RAIN CAME and went, and by the time we pulled into the hospital parking lot it was early morning, still dark, and the pavement was wet from what must have been the same storm we'd caught along the way. The lamps in the parking lot were sparse and meager, our conversation was dour, and in the cold darkness of early morning the three of us sat in the car waiting for the true light to come up over the horizon. I started up the car for its heater and its AM music station. Then I shut it back off. As we waited in silence, knee-to-knee in the front seat, the windshield fogged up and the rain came down once again on the hard metal roof of the car.

"Now what?" asked Bessie.

"Now we sit here and wait for the dawn. The hospital opens for visits at five-thirty. What time is it anyway?"

"It's two."

"Wait....what?"

"It's two a.m."

"But I thought....! I mean, it was just...!"

"It's two, Charlie. So *now* what do we do? Now that it's only two in the morning and we have more than three hours to wait, what do we do?"

"We do just that. We wait."

"For the dawn?"

"Yes. And its accoutrements. Amid the darkness in this car. Amid the darkness outside our windshield. Amid the evanescence of it all. We wait in this car for the dawn to finally come. Because it *will* come."

"Well, maybe we should get a little sleep in the meantime?"

"It's a good idea. Bess, you can take the back. And Raul, feel free to stretch out across the entirety of this long bench seat up here in front."

"But what about you, Charlie? Don't you want to sleep a little?"

"I'd love to of course. But I can't. Surprisingly, I'm not at all tired anymore. In fact, I think by now I am beyond sleep."

"It's impossible to be beyond sleep. It is physically impossible. Sleep *always* comes."

"Perhaps. But not to me. At least not now."

"Suit yourself...."

Bessie climbed over the seat to the back. Raul stretched out his long legs across the vinyl bench seat, his head next to the steering wheel. I had removed the key from the ignition and put it in my pocket. Pacing outside in the darkness I peeked in through the windshield from time to time. Raul had sprawled across the front seat. Bessie was curled up in the back.

Within minutes they were asleep.

❧

FOR THE NEXT three and a half hours I stood outside the car with my hands in my pockets and paced from one end of the curb to the other. Here and there the rain would return and I would huddle under the leaves of the parking lot's largest elm to take cover. Then the rain would stop and I would again step back out into the light of the parking lot. Time passed slowly. At three a group of nurses walking to their cars saw me huddled under the tree in the darkness and scurried quickly away. At four I wiped the water from the hood of the Starfire and lay on top of it gazing up at the night. The sky was black and hopeless. Looking straight up I could see nothing but darkness, the clouds covering the moon and the stars. This was by far the darkest night that I had ever known.

And the longest I had ever seen.

❧

IN TIME THE horizon began to lighten and in the dim light I tapped softly on the Starfire's windshield. Inside, the two bodies stirred slowly, then shifted, then sat up squinting at me through the glass.

"It's five-thirty," I said. "It's time to go in."

The two exited and together we headed inside the hospital where we were directed to the fourth floor. There the hospital waiting room was harshly lit with white light that was all the more glaring after our long journey out of darkness. When we told the nurse that we had come to see William Smithcoate, the professor from Cow Eye Junction who had been taken by ambulance earlier that day, the woman checked some paperwork then pointed down the hall.

"One visitor at a time, please," she said.

Both Bessie and Raul looked at me, and so I made my way down the long white hallway toward the room, where I found Will asleep in a bed with a tube taped to his arm. In the artificial light, the old historian's skin looked rough and pale with white whiskers just beginning to poke above the surface. His hair was sweaty and thrown to one side as he lay with his neck twisted against his pillow.

I glanced around the room, which was sparse and functional. There was a television mounted in a corner. A table and a chair with a flower in a vase. In the closet hung the old clothes that Will had been wearing when he was transported here: the tweed jacket and gray slacks and red bow tie. His shoes were neatly arranged on the floor of the closet. His fedora had been placed on a shelf.

"What's happening in there?" Raul and Bessie asked when I walked back to the waiting area to give them an update.

"He's still sleeping."

"So now what do we do?"

"Well now we just wait...."

Bessie nodded and grabbed a crossword puzzle. I sat on a cold vinyl chair. Raul was thumbing through a woman's magazine.

"He'll probably be sleeping for a while," the nurse said after an hour had passed. "Why don't you go get some breakfast, and try back again in another hour or so?"

And so over coffee and donuts in the hospital's cafeteria the three of us sat and talked about nothing. Around us hospital workers were coming and going. A vacant wheelchair was pushed across the floor. An old woman sat reading a bible at an empty table. Eventually I noted the clock on the wall.

"Well," I said. "It's almost seven. The dawn has come once again. The sun is definitely up by now. If you look closely, you can see the light streaming in through that window over there. But Will's still sleeping. And I'm not sure what else we can do at this point but wait."

"I hate hospitals," said Bessie.

"Who likes them?"

"Doctors do!"

"I doubt that. I mean, I'm pretty sure even *they* don't like them."

"You're probably right," said Raul. "I suppose the academy does not have a monopoly on quietly suffering professionalism...."

Each of us ate our breakfast without hunger, the conversation weary and disheartened. Perhaps in our hearts we had expected Will to be as energetic as he was before he left: that he would greet us in the hospital with a cigar in hand, a doff of his fedora, and a far-reaching story of matrimonial prowess. Instead we'd found an old man half-breathing and alone in his sterile hospital room. This was hard to accept and each of us seemed to be dealing with it in our own way.

"He's always been a pain in the ass!" said Bessie.

"Smoking is becoming increasingly hazardous to your health," said Raul. "Let alone the bourbon...."

I listened to these pronouncements, then added my own contribution to the coping that was being articulated:

"It is not easy," I said, "to reconcile a man's histories with his future."

The time passed in the hospital cafeteria even more slowly. We ate. We talked. We stirred our coffee listlessly. The sun was shining in through the far side window. At last a sudden smile came over Raul's face. Under the circumstances it seemed abrupt and out of place.

"Hey, look over there!" he said. Raul was gesturing behind me to the wall across from him. I looked back over my shoulder but saw nothing. Turning back, I said:

"A wall."

"No, not the wall itself.... Look closely...!"

Once again I turned around to look. And this time I saw what Raul had been pointing at all along: about three-quarters up the wall, in white stencil on a black background, was a line drawing of a cigarette with smoke emanating from it in a single squiggly line. The cigarette was crossed out in red and underneath it were the words: NO SMOKING.

"I think Will would have appreciated the table we've chosen...!"

I laughed at Raul's observation and took another drink of coffee.

"Let's drink to Will," I said and touched my coffee cup to theirs. "A real pain in the ass!"

"To History!" they said and did the same.

❦

AT EIGHT A.M. the three of us made our way back up to the waiting area outside Will's room where the nurse told us that our friend was still sleeping. At nine we found ourselves still sitting in the cold chairs. At ten I peeked inside to see Will fast asleep. At eleven, the doctors roused him to conduct some tests only for him to fall back asleep right away. By twelve we still hadn't seen him awake.

"It's getting late," said Bessie. "Maybe we should head back?"

"To Cow Eye?"

"Yes. I mean, we're already late for the afternoon activities on campus. But if we leave now, we can still be in time for the party itself..."

"Though just barely..." Raul added.

"If we leave now we can still get a good seat for the awards ceremony..."

"And the costume contest...."

"And the many flags of the world!"

But here I objected:

"Let's wait a little more. Let's give it another hour or so. We can afford it. The Oldsmobile is filled with premium gas so there's no need to stop along the way. We won't take any detours on the road back. We won't stop for food no matter how hungry we get. We won't need to eat along the way because there will be plenty to eat at the Christmas party once we get there...."

"The fate of our college is hanging in the balance, Charlie. Are you sure we can wait? It's your legacy at stake, after all...."

"Yes, I'm sure. Let's wait just a little longer...."

And so we sat in the waiting area and waited. But whereas earlier the time seemed to lag, now each minute seemed to be imposing its own weight. Each tick of the clock – each downward strike of the pendulum – served to pull us toward our professional obligation, to tug us in the direction of Cow Eye with its all-important Christmas party.

"It's almost one o'clock," said Raul. "Charlie, shouldn't we be heading back?"

"Let's wait a few more minutes," I said. "We've come all this way. We can't just up and leave *now* can we? I mean, without seeing Will?"

"But what about your plans, Charlie? You've spent so much time devising them!"

"To hell with my plans."

"What?!"

"You heard me...to hell with my plans! Some things are more important...!"

"But how can you say that? After all this time! After all this planning!"

"Yeah, well some things are much more important than all that."

"Such as?"

"Well, such as Will Smithcoate. My faculty mentor. The person who now lies on the threshold separating our respective histories from our shared present. Or the shared present from our lonely and isolated futures. Let's just be patient and wait a little bit longer."

A few minutes after one, the nurse came over to tell us that Will was awake and expecting us. When I walked into the room, Will raised his head delicately.

"Charlie..." he said.

"Mr. Smithcoate!"

I reached out to take his hand but there was no strength in his grip.

"How are you doing, Mr. Smithcoate? Raul and Bessie and I came to see you. But you were sleeping. So we just sat outside and waited. We waited for quite a while. But we're all here now. And we're really glad to see you. How are you feeling?"

Will looked up at me from the bed.

"I feel like hell. I don't like this place."

"Well that's normal of course. It's a hospital. And nobody likes hospitals. Not even the doctors…"

"My wife died here."

"In this hospital?"

"They took her here when I was at work. I was in class. It was a lecture on *Hope* and *Desire*. They took her here on a Wednesday and she was gone before I could even get halfway across the Atlantic."

"I'm sorry, Mr. Smithcoate…."

"Before I could even say goodbye."

"I'm so sorry…."

"Charlie, this is not a living place…."

"I understand."

"It's dark and cold and I don't want to be here…"

"I understand entirely."

"I want to go home…."

"Home?"

Will was looking up at me with eyes that were tired and sick and gray.

"Ask them if I can go home, Charlie…."

"*Me?*"

"Yes. Please ask them. I'm too medicated. They've got me on all these pills. It makes me drowsy and incoherent. They won't understand. You talk to them…."

"But…"

"You're the most sober one among us. You're an educational administrator, Charlie. You've got a talent for persuasion A way with words. Let them know I need to go home. Tell them it's important. That something very essential depends on it. That it's a matter of life and death. Tell them your legacy is at stake…."

"But Mr. Smithcoate. You need to stay in this hospital. There are people who can take care of you here. People who are experts. They have at their disposal the latest medical equipment. They know what they're doing and can…"

"Please, Charlie."

"But we can't just take you to Cow Eye, Mr. Smithcoate. You need to stay here…"

"Charlie, please…!"

When I told Raul and Bessie what Will had said, they shook their heads:

"Are you nuts! The man's sick. How can he go back to Cow Eye?"

"I don't know. But stranger things have been achieved. And we owe it to him to try, don't we? I know *I* owe it to him to try.…"

At the nurse's station the new nurse on duty was professional, though not exactly cordial.

"I'm sorry to bother you," I told her. "But it's just that. You see, our friend really wants to go back with us to Cow Eye Junction. He really wants to be home for the holidays.…"

"Holidays?"

"Yes. You see, we're having a Christmas party tonight and our entire campus will be there. Everyone has committed to attend and so they'll all be together in a confined segment of time and space. It's something I've promised Dr. Felch that I would do. We've promised our accreditors. And now it's already past one and we're getting very late on. You see, our party starts at six, and there's a six-hour drive to Cow Eye ahead of us — which means that for us to get there in time, we really need to leave *now*."

"What are you saying?"

"Well, I'm asking if we can take our friend back with us to Cow Eye Junction. You know, in his 1966 powder blue Oldsmobile Starfire. It is a spacious car with a notchback bench seat. There is plenty of room up front for the three of us, which means he can have the entire back seat to himself. The vinyl is really quite comfortable and I'll drive slower than I did on our way here. We'll drive back in comfort and safety and we'll get there in time to attend the Christmas party. We might be a little late perhaps, but we should still be in time for the formal program. At this point we're probably only going to miss the costume contest and maybe the first part of the awards ceremony — but if we leave in the next ten minutes or so we still might make it in time for the keynote address and the flags of the world and the apple-bobbing and the bowl full of barbiturates and the dunking booth and the opening of the wet bar and the intimate sessions of exploration involving coupled relaxation and tender anal.…"

"Look," said the nurse. "Your friend is under observation. He's not up for a long drive. And he has not yet been released from this hospital. He will not be leaving any time soon. And definitely not today. So you will need to make other plans. *Better* plans."

"But all he wants is to go *home*! Is that so much to ask? I mean, isn't that what any human being would want in his condition? Isn't that what we all deserve? A place to live? And sleep? And read? A quiet place to fondly remember? A place that is different from all the other cold and unfamiliar places in the world that are *not* home? Is it so hard to understand where the man's coming from? And where he wants to go? Can it be so hard to find empathy for a man who is *here*, wifeless and against his will, and very, very far from home?!"

"Please don't raise your voice with me."

"I'm sorry....!"

"Your friend requires serious medical treatment. He is under close observation of our hospital. He will not be going home until the doctor authorizes it. And the doctor will not be authorizing it for some time...."

Dejected, I started to walk away from the nurse's station. For the first time since moving to Cow Eye, I could feel myself wanting something unequivocally. Now, after so many days and nights, so many amorphous experiences, I wanted this thing more than all others. I wanted what Will wanted, and what Will wanted was to go home. It was as straightforward as that. It was not a brazen request. Nor was it unpatriotic. But it was clearly unadvisable. He could not leave this hospital, and no amount of coaxing could change that. And as I stood in the sanitized hospital where his wife had been taken to die, I vowed that I would achieve this goal for him unequivocally. Somehow I would bring him home.

And so I walked back.

⧽

"LOOK," I SAID. "I understand the situation completely. And I'm sorry I raised my voice at you earlier. You see, I haven't slept for some time – months in fact. And I'm a little on edge. It's my fault and my fault only. But perhaps we could try one final thing....Perhaps we could reach a compromise of sorts?"

"A compromise?"

"Yes, perhaps somewhere amid the great conflicts of our day the two of us could find a conciliation that would work for both of us?"

With dispassion in her eyes, the woman listened to my plea. Like a true caring professional, she listened to my plan. And when it was done she blew her nose into a napkin and said:

"So that's it? *That's* your new plan to take your friend home?"

"Yes. That is my revised plan."

"Without leaving this hospital?"

"Yes."

The woman folded up the napkin and threw it into a metal trashcan behind her nursing station.

"I'll do my best. But please know that I have taken a Hippocratic oath, and that despite taking this oath in good faith, I am really quite fond of mathematics. In fact it was always a favorite subject of mine in grade school…."

The woman said she would need to consult with the doctor and would let me know. Twenty minutes later, she came back to inform me that my plan had been approved, that an orderly would be up in a few minutes to help get Will ready for his trip, and that we would be allowed to take him to the place he had requested.

We would be allowed to take him home.

❧

AND SO, A little after one-thirty a wheelchair was brought up to Will's room where a male orderly helped to settle him into the chair. By then Cow Eye's longest-tenured faculty member had been dressed in his teaching clothes – the tweed suit and brown pants and red bow tie – and in his lap he held his faithful fedora. From there the orderly wheeled him out of his room, down the long hall, out past the nurse's station, into the elevator and down four stories into the lobby of the hospital, where, through the glass doors of the main entrance, he was able to catch a glimpse of the powder blue Starfire sitting serenely in the parking lot.

"It's a beautiful car," Will said.

"It sure is," I agreed. "They don't make cars like that anymore, Mr. Smithcoate."

"Damn right!"

"I hope you don't mind us borrowing it to come here?"

"Of course not. You did what you had to do. Just make sure she gets back safely…."

The three of us stood admiring the car through the glass doors for a few poignant moments. Then, spinning the chair around in the opposite direction, the orderly wheeled Will away from the lobby entrance down the hall past the radiology section, along the children's handprints, past Obstetrics and straight into the cafeteria where the lunchtime crowd was in the midst of bustling.

"They're over there…" I said and the orderly headed in that direction, rolling the wheelchair right up to the table where Bessie and Raul were waiting with their lunch trays under the no-smoking sign.

"Professor Smithcoate!" said Raul

"Hello, William," said Bessie. Then motioning her hand to indicate the table where the cafeteria trays were aligned, she said: "Welcome home…."

"This is as good as it gets," I added. "Look, there's even a no-smoking sign right there…!"

Will gave a slight smile of recognition. Then he turned to thank the orderly who had pushed him all the way from his cold room to the cafeteria table.

"I appreciate it," he told the man. "And please know I'm very sorry for what happened to your people. Lord knows, my hands are not entirely clean…."

The orderly looked confused but smiled anyway, then left.

❧

OVER LUNCH, THE four of us talked about the simpler things of this day. The lack of salt on the hamburger steak. The granulated brown sugar that simply would not dissolve in the tall glass of iced tea no matter how faithfully you stirred it. From time to time Raul would check his watch and look over at me surreptitiously. And each time he did this I pretended not to see him. At one point Raul cleared his throat purposefully and said:

"Charlie….It's well past two. Almost two-thirty. Shouldn't we be heading back?"

And I responded just as purposefully:

"Yes," I said. "Of course we should be heading back. That would be the right thing to do. But let's wait a few more minutes instead…."

And so we talked some more. About the things we shared. And the things we could never share. We talked about ideas that were painfully obvious and those that were hopelessly ineffable. We talked and talked. The more we talked, the later it became. And the later it became, the more nervous Raul seemed to get.

"Charlie!" he said finally. "It's really late! We need to be making our way back to Cow Eye! We should be leaving now!"

And I said:

"Yes, Raul. I do not disagree with you. Of course we should be making our way back to Cow Eye. We are very far from where we need to be right now. And so it only makes good sense that we should be heading back to the desiccated comfort of Cow Eye Junction. It would be the straightforward thing to do. And it would be the right thing to do. Hell, it would probably even be the *justifiable* thing to do. Several hundred miles away from here there is a Christmas party that I am entirely responsible for. I have been planning it for quite some time. I am an educational administrator and as an educational administrator I have been planning this Christmas party for a very long time indeed. It is a watershed moment in my life. It is an important event in the history of Cow Eye Junction, if not the whole of humankind, and it is something that will determine the very worth of my own long journey from verdure to desiccation and back again. This planning has not been easy and in fact has cost me hundreds of waking hours and many more hours that were spent in fruitless semi-wakefulness that might have been better applied toward sleep. Now my professional reputation is at stake. My personal legacy is in jeopardy. I have created much furor over this party – and not a few expectations. And of course the future of our college – of the entire Cow Eye community itself – depends on the successful resolution of our yuletide event. So yes, Raul, as usual you are correct. In fact, you are very correct indeed: we *should* be leaving soon...."

At this Raul seemed to breathe a sigh of relief.

"But..."

"Charlie?!"

"....But!" I continued. "...Before we do that, there is one thing that I need to do first. You see, we have driven many miles to end up here in this cafeteria under such a portentous no-smoking sign. We have gone to great lengths to be sitting here with Will Smithcoate in this sterile yet safe place that is only slightly reminiscent of our own cafeteria. It is only slightly reminiscent of the place that Will has called home for the past seven years. And so there is one final thing that I would like to ask Will before we make our way back to Cow Eye. Back to the guard shack. To the verdure. The pelicans. Regional accreditation. Christmas. There is one unresolved question that I would be remiss to overlook while I still have the opportunity to ask it – that is to say, while it's still possible to ask such questions of my esteemed faculty mentor during such a pivotal time of my life. During this tenuous time when William Smithcoate himself is still in this world. While *I* am still in this world. While the two of us are still in this large and lonely world. While the *four* of us – Bessie, Raul, me, Mr. Smithcoate – are still at this table. You see, we are all here in this makeshift cafeteria together in a confined segment of time and space. But we should not take as a given that this will always be so. Because it will *not* always be so. Things change. Moments come and go. And things will come and go. People, places, ideas. Nations of the world. A passing storm. The severest drought. It all comes and goes. And so, as I was saying, there is one final question that I feel compelled to ask now that the sun has begun to settle beyond the salad bar over there...."

"...Dammit, boy, get to the point!"

"Right, Mr. Smithcoate....I'm getting to that very thing...."

"You'd better get to it a little quicker...before I croak over this chicken cutlet!"

"Of course," I said. "That chicken cutlet will not always be as hot as it is at this singular moment in time. That is just a sad fact of life. And so my question to you, Mr. Smithcoate, is this. You see, I've asked you many times but you have never given me a straight answer. You have never quite answered my question completely and so I would like to ask you one final time. I would like to ask you one last time to tell me a little something about history. More specifically, about the history of the world. That is, from its very beginning to its ultimate conclusion. It is a question that I have long wondered about. And so now, as we sit in this crowded cafeteria under this no-smoking sign – and as we wait for the simultaneous coming of eternal spring, the resurrection of our eternal lord and savior, and, most quixotically, the reaffirmation of our regional accreditation – as we wait for all of this to come, could you please, Mr. Smithcoate, tell us about the history of our world?"

≈

"CHARLIE!" RAUL INTERRUPTED. "It's too late for all that! We need to leave right now to have any chance of making the party...!"

But here I raised my hand calmly:

"Just hold on, Raul. There are things that are infinitely more important than accreditation in this world. There are things that outweigh tenure. And so, right now I'd like to ask Will to tell us about the history of the world. From its inception to its apex. From the dawn of mankind to that woman paying for her Fritos over there...."

For the first time since we'd appeared in his hospital room, Will smiled broadly.

"That really takes the cake, Charlie!" Will's words were slightly slurred and a bit slower than usual – he was clearly having some difficulty speaking – yet despite the complications, I could at last see in his expression the same sparkle of youthful enthusiasm that I'd always appreciated during our discussions at the cafeteria. "You want me to talk to you about history, my boy?"

"Yes, would you please tell me – that is to say, *us* – about the history of the world?"

"From its beginning?"

"Yes. All the way to its ultimate resolution. The resolution, of course, being this very place in time and space where all of us are sitting in this cafeteria. I am quite sure it was not a given that we would all end up sharing this moment, right now, right here. I'm sure there were many competing possibilities along the way. Many arrows. Many forks in the road. Many decisions made. Myriad bends in the perilous river of time. And so would you help us understand how it all happened to bring us here? Which is to say, could you please tell us the untold story of the history of our world?"

❧

"Absolutely not!" said Will. "I have just had a stroke, god damn you! And I am so heavily medicated that I can't even tell you whether it's day or night right now!"

"It's *day.*"

"See! And besides, the history of our world is too well-documented. It has been covered by researchers since the beginning of time – or at least since these researchers have been receiving tenure. So, no, I will not tell you about the history of the world. Instead I will tell you the story that only I can tell. Settle comfortably into your respective chairs and let me tell you the history that each of you shares. It is a story worthy of the greatest history books yet one that will likely never be told. Yes, my friends who drove all the way from Cow Eye Junction just to visit me in my time of greatest need. It has been a long drive, I'm sure. So let me make it worth your while. My dear friends and respected colleagues – Bessie, Raul, Charlie – let me tell you the little-known story that would not otherwise be told: the long and storied history of Cow Eye Community College...!"

❧

"...But first give me a napkin will, you?"

Raul handed Will a napkin so he could wipe away some drool that was dangling from his lower lip.

"This isn't going to be easy. My mind is a bit numb from all that's come before. The stroke. The long ride in the ambulance. The medication. It's not going to be easy to tell you this in a coherent manner. But I am prepared to perish in the attempt...!"

Will crumpled up the napkin and tucked it under the lip of his dessert plate. And with that he began to tell his story. As the afternoon sun began its descent beyond the salad bar, Will Smithcoate began to tell us the long and complicated story of Cow Eye Community College.

"The history of Cow Eye Community College," he explained, "begins ten thousand years ago with two fertile cows, one that was red with horns, and another that was hornless and black...."

"Cattle?"

"Yes. Our history begins with those two cows...."

❧

"ONCE UPON A time, you see, there was a man who had two cows: one that was red with horns and another that was hornless and black...."

Here Will stopped.

"Hah!" he laughed. "*Once upon a time*! I've always dreamed of beginning a historical treatise with those words. And now I finally have...!"

"How does it feel?"

"It feels great!"

Will nodded in satisfaction. Then he said:

"Where was I?"

"You were home. It is day. There was a man with two cows ten thousand years ago...."

"Oh, right. The man with two cows...."

Will cleared his throat throatily. Then he continued:

"Once upon a time, you see, there was a man who had two cows: one that was red with horns, and another that was polled and black...."

≈

"This was in the early days of the world when color itself was a thing to be reckoned with. When the earth was wide and the animals of the plains roamed at their discretion. Back then there were animals that were unfathomable to us today. There were bears with broad shoulders and giraffes with short necks. There were oxen the size of Oldsmobiles and birds that were taller than your average educational administrator. These were the days when man was man and the animals were themselves. And amid this all was an ambitious agrarian who became the first domesticator of cattle...."

"....Now before I continue we should stop to dwell a bit on this accomplishment. You see, in those days it was no given that the bovine would be our domesticate. In those days the precursor of the compliant bovine was several times its current size. As big as a trumpeting elephant. As vigorous as your average math instructor. The cows of those days were wild and wayward and they were not of a mind to be domesticated. And in this context this one man noticed two cows grazing on a hillside: one that was red with horns and another that was black and polled...."

"....Now the man saw the two cows and one day he cornered them into a pen of his own design. They were both wild and unpredictable. But locked in the man's pen, they took divergent approaches to their fates. The first cow – the black one – chose conciliation. It was temperate and amenable. It stayed within the fences that the man had made and caused no trouble. Over the years the black cow multiplied prolifically and became the black cow that you see today. The black cows that you passed by on your voyage to the now-defunct Cow Eye Ranch and whose little black calf you castrated with a simple pocket knife...."

"....Now the *red* cow, on the other hand, well that was a different story. The red cow, you see, chose conflict. At every turn he rammed his horns against the cowherd's fence. He smashed the gate that had been constructed to contain him. He jumped and bashed and ground against the barriers that were meant to keep him in. When the man came he charged. And when the black cow approached he butted and lunged. He gouged. He gored. And one day, when the man wasn't looking, the red cow smashed through the fence and ran back up to the hillside where he'd come from...."

≈

"....At this the farmer was discouraged. For where he had once had two cows he now had only one. But not to be denied, he immediately began to breed the black cow to itself. In time the black cow produced its own offspring, which were other black cows – both male and female – and in time these too were bred. Over time the black cows lost their memories of once having horns or a hillside with freedom, and over time they acquired the thick legs and meaty flanks that would become the hallmark of the breed. The cowherd, looking at this, was pleased. This, he understood, was progress...."

"....Over many centuries the ambitious cowherd discovered countless other efficiencies that enabled him to improve the breed. He bred his tamest bulls to his tamest heifers, and this produced tame offspring. He bred his meatiest bulls to his meatiest cows and this produced meaty calves. Over time he bred for weight and size and temperament. He bred for the quantity of milk and for the quality of meat. He bred for fertility and motility and docility. He bred to increase the marbling and to decrease the miscarriaging. In time he had perfected the breed to the extent that it gave more milk, and produced more meat, and was more tolerant and more loving and more hearty. And this too he understood as progress...."

"....And meanwhile the red cow gazed down on all of this from the hillside. Over time the red cow watched as the black breed became bigger and meatier and more numerous. The red cow, scrounging for food on the hillside, lived imperfectly. His conditions were less precise, and yet he watched as the black cow received food easily in troughs and buckets. The red cow grew only slightly from generation to generation, while the black cow gained mightily over time. In size and numbers. In affections of its master. And through it all, the red cow continued to graze on the sparse natural grasses of the hill that looked down on it all...."

"...One day the cowherd gathered up his best black cows – his biggest and his darkest – and herded them onto a large boat that took them across a wide sea in the middle of winter. The ocean was rough and the cows lay on the shipboard, sloshing through the excrement and the vomit of a long ocean voyage. For several months the cows rode in the dark holds of the ship, chained to the floor, motionless, abandoned by their gods and consigned to their fates. It was not an easy journey but at last they arrived in a new land where they disembarked, their legs emaciated, and so weak that they could barely walk down the gangplank to the new land that would be their home. Eventually, they came to see their new master and this new master checked their tongues and prodded their flanks and when this was done he brought them to a place many miles away where they could graze, a pasture with green grasses and free-flowing rivers. A place of countryside so verdant that even poetry paled in comparison. This, my friends was the beginnings of the Cow Eye Ranch...."

"...Though, truth be known, the ranch in those days was not much of a ranch at all. In fact, it was not much more than a simple pasture with a few sheds where the cows were herded into large swaths of territory and where they were able to roam. The herds roamed freely and then, when the time had come to be culled, they were rounded up and herded into the cattle chutes where they were marched efficiently toward the slaughter grounds one after another. This too, you see, was more efficient than how it was done previously...."

"...From there it is all written in the history books. The ranch formed around the ranges where the cattle roamed. The town formed around the ranch. And the community college – our *Beloved* Cow Eye Community College – was formed to serve the town that had been created. In time the college grew and the campus was built and the swimming pool was constructed. And all of this became the Cow Eye Community College that we know and love. In fact, if this were a traditional historical treatise, it would end right there. If this were the history you find in school books, the history of our college would end with the black cow grazing happily in the pastures of the Cow Eye Ranch. But there is one important thing that we've forgotten along the way. There is one thing that has been overlooked...."

"What's that, Mr. Smithcoate?"

Bessie and Raul and I were leaning forward over the cafeteria table to hear the rest of the story.

"What has been overlooked, Mr. Smithcoate?" we asked. "What has been overlooked in your telling of the history of the world?"

Will looked at us seriously.

"Simple," he said. "The *red* cow."

"The red cow?"

"Yes. You see, while the black cow was acquiring the desirable traits that would make it the ideal meat for meat-eaters and the ideal milk for milk-drinking, the red cow was still standing on that hillside observing the trajectory of our world."

"It was?"

"Yes. And standing there on the hillside, the red cow saw the unfolding of historical events across time and space. This cow, with its untamed horns, witnessed the advent of the plow, and how it was used to subjugate the once-proud oxen of his time. It witnessed the invention of the printing press, and how it allowed for better coordination of the slaughters that were held over the centuries. Advances in shipbuilding allowed for more cows to be transported across the ocean in their own excrement. Technologies in farming allowed for greater expansion of areas for the farmer to plow. All of this was progress for the farmer, if not for the cow...."

"...And from its vantage point this recalcitrant cow also observed the wars that were fought with the most modern technologies. And it witnessed the diseases vanquished and invoked. It saw the oceans conquered and the skies tamed. The rivers dammed and plains trammeled. There were railroads to build and factories to construct. Each of these things was witnessed by the unassuming cow. And each of these things was progress...."

"...And so it was that the simple cow saw the progress of the world from mankind's earliest beginnings to the technological wonders that abound. The innovations. The efficiencies. The continuous improvements and feats of ingenuity that have made the culling of his offspring so much more inevitable. From the cradle of man's civilization. To the building of his greatest monuments. The cow was present for it all. And all of it, it seemed, was progress...."

≈

"And then, Mr. Smithcoate? And then what did the cow see?"

≈

"...And then the cow saw the invention of modern weaponry. The nuclear reaction. Chemical warfare. He witnessed the falling bombs and mass exterminations. The genocide. The ecological devastation. The polluted rivers and colluded skies. The damming. The droughts. The demise of earlier peoples at the hand of those who came later. All of this he witnessed with the straw dangling from his mouth. All of this he witnessed from his lowly vantage point at the top of the hill...."

≈

"And then, Mr. Smithcoate? And then what happened?"
"Well, and then the cow went back to his grazing."
"That's it?"
"Of course. I mean, it's just a cow, right?"
"Well, yes. But there has to be something more! So what happened then?"
"Well then I slumped against the table in the cafeteria where I was found the next morning by a former student..."
"And *that* was the end of history?"
"For her, yes."
"And it was the end of the world?"
"Not exactly. You see, from there I was taken in an ambulance across time and space to this lonely hospital room in the city. I was taken here and given medications that made me sleep right up until the moment I opened my eyes and saw Charlie. You see, from the beginning of mankind, everything that has ever happened is one relentless chain of progress – an unbroken series of inspirations and discoveries – leading from the vacant fields of our beginnings to the achievements of modern life. From the darkness of first night to the car ride the three of you

just experienced. From the apple to the celery stalk. From the first seed ever sown to the forkful of jell-o that Charlie is now readying to put into his mouth..."

Self-consciously, I put the jell-o back onto my plate.

"....You see," said Will, "every single event in the history of mankind – every technological invention, every progeny of progress – has conspired to bring the four of us together in this cafeteria. History has culminated in the four of us being here today. The apex of history is here and now: it is this crowded hospital dispensary where the three of us are sitting at this table: Bessie sipping her tea, Raul doodling on his napkin, and Charlie placing that piece of jell-o into his mouth. We are, in the here and now, the ultimate culmination of the many miracles of history..."

"We are?"

"Yes, you are."

"And the woman over there discarding her empty Fritos bag?"

"Her too."

Bessie took another drink of her tea.

Raul crumpled up his napkin and threw it onto his tray.

"The world," said Will, "ends at this singular moment in time and space. It ends with the four of us. For we are the apex of history, the culmination of mankind's story, the ultimate consequence of it all...."

In the cafeteria, the sun had now descended well beyond the salad bar.

I placed the forkful of jell-o into my mouth and swallowed it.

≈

AFTER LUNCH, AN orderly – a white one this time – came back down to wheel Will back up to his room. Bessie gave Will a long hug before he left. Raul patted him on the shoulder and said, "Take care, Professor. We'll see you back at Cow Eye when you're better."

Then it was my turn for words.

"Okay, Mr. Smithcoate," I said. "I'll see you soon. Sometime in the very near future no doubt...."

"Future?" said Will.

"Yes, the future."

Even then I understood that it was probably the wrong thing to say to him. But it was all that I could think to say.

Will grunted. I shook his hand, which was very soft – almost lifeless – and made my way back to the car where Raul and Bessie were already inside waiting.

≈

"WHAT TIME IS it?" I asked Raul.

"It's well after two, Charlie. In fact, almost three. The party will be starting in three hours. It's a six-hour drive back to Cow Eye. Now what do we do?"

"Simple," I said. "We drive very fast...."

From there I sped along the streets of the city, overtaking the taxi cabs and delivery trucks, out to the on-ramp, onto the highway, out past the suburbs of the city, out past the exurbs. As expected, the daytime traffic was intermediate algebra and as we made our way, Raul informed me of our temporal challenge with ruthless efficiency.

"It's already four o'clock," he would say. "And we're not even thirty minutes out of the city...." And then: "Charlie, we're going to be very late. It's exactly four-thirty and we're not even half-way there!" In rapid succession came *five* o'clock...five-*thirty*...five-forty-*five*...five-*fifty*-five. At exactly six, Raul looked up from his map and glumly announced:

"It's six. The party's officially starting...."

Bessie whistled her amazement.

I nodded. It was well past six o'clock and we were not even half-way back from our six-hour journey from verdure to desiccation and then on to verdure. The city was far behind us, but Cow Eye was equally far ahead.

"The party's already started," said Raul. "And we're still hours from being there...."

"It'll be okay," I said. "The event is underway and it will just have to proceed without us. I've left Dr. Felch detailed notes. It'll work out."

"How can you be so calm?"

"Because I planned everything meticulously. I am an educational administrator, and so I left no stone unturned in planning the Christmas party that has just started."

"Well, let's hope you're right!"

"Of course, I'm right. As we speak, it's a few minutes after six. Which means the cafeteria by now has been decorated exactly as I planned it."

"And how is *that*?"

"Meticulously. And festively."

"Well, yes. But how specifically?"

"Well, for example, on one entire wall there is a full-scale replica of the American flag – all thirteen stripes and forty-seven stars. The flag is so large that it takes up the whole wall from one corner to the next. It is enormous. And imposing. And across from it, on the opposite wall, is this flag's diametrical opposite: hundreds of smaller flags representing the lesser nations of the world. On this wall all the miscellaneous nations are receiving their moment in the sun: from Afghanistan to Yugoslavia; from Albania to Zimbabwe. The Soviet Union. Tanganyika. Every single country now extant on the face of the earth has been given its own flag and together these flags are crowding together to take up the breadth of an entire wall of our cafeteria…."

"What about Zaire?"

"It's there."

"And Serbia?"

"Right next to Croatia."

"And India?"

"To the left of Pakistan."

"Bosnia and Herzegovina?"

"They're both there."

"Eritrea?"

"Yes."

"Kyrgyzstan?"

"Yes."

"Palau?"

"Yes."

"Taiwan?"

"After tense negotiations, yes."

"Tibet?"

"Yes!"

"The Maldives?"

"For now, yes."

"They're all on that wall?"

"Yes! You see, our Christmas party will be an inclusive event representing all the polities of the world. All the different nations that make up our rich geopolitical tapestry. The governments. The races. The ethnic affiliations. The religions. By now there will be an enormous evergreen set up in the corner and on this tree there will be Christmas decorations sent in by children from around the world. There will be precious figurines hand-crafted by little Arab children in Palestine and old women in Bavaria and orphans from the burnt villages of Vietnam. There will be tiny decorative rocking chairs and candy canes and glass balls with snow and ice. Ornaments of all possible denomination will be hung from the boughs of the tree: a peaceful Buddha; a portrait of Jesus Christ suspended from the cross; Mohammed flashing an enthusiastic thumbs-up; a self-decapitated Chhinnamasta holding up the severed head of our humanity. The tree will be draped in garland and tinsel and angels strumming harps. And at the top there will be a large Star of David shining down upon it all...."

As I described the decorations for the Christmas party – the ice-sculpted reindeer, the gingerbread village with miniature train running through it, the games table with Monopoly and mahjong – my friends settled back in their seats to listen. In lieu of the actual party, I realized, my words would have to serve vicariously as their celebration: amid the warmth of our Starfire, my breathless depiction would have to suffice. And so I described the Christmas party as best I could. In effervescent detail I unveiled the party now joyously under way so that my friends might experience it in all its revelry:

"Meanwhile," I said, "in front of the wall next to the American flag there is a very long table covered with a festive red table cloth and green napkins. The cloth is depending from the table and is cut-edged. The napkins are frilly. On this table there is a large crystal punchbowl that has been filled with apple cider and cinnamon and nutmeg; next to the cider is a pitcher of eggnog; next to the eggnog is butterscotch cocoa; and next to the *cocoa* are two more bowls of holiday punch, one spiked with rum and coke and the other with Prozac and Thalidomide. And of course, there is the wet bar...."

"Wet bar?"

"Yes. How could you have a Christmas party without *that*?!"

"It is hard to imagine indeed. Could you describe it for us, please?"

In the quiet of the car my friends had closed their eyes to better picture the scene.

"Of course," I said. "You see, in a previous life Luke Quittles was an up-and-coming bartender and so he has agreed to run the wet bar. Right now as we speak – at this very moment while the three of us make our way slowly along this dry and dusty highway – Luke is standing behind the counter in a red Santa hat and elf's vest beaming like a proud parent. In front of him there is a keg of beer and bottles of wine and flasks of bourbon and rum. There are liqueurs and mixed drinks to order. There will be classic cocktails such as piña coladas and margaritas and daiquiris and screwdrivers – but also original concoctions with exotic names like *Flaming Orgasm* and *Cow Cunt* and *Math Teacher Gone Wild*. If there is a drink to appeal to the heart of a hard-working faculty member of Cow Eye Community College after a long week of accreditation activities, you can be sure that it will be there…!"

"Well, it seems like you've got the drinks covered. How about the seating? How have you managed to fit so many people into such a confined segment of time and space? Our cafeteria is not that big. In fact it's quite small. And our faculty is divided. So how are you going to solve that?"

"Simple! You see, by now everyone has checked in and each attendee has received a folder with a personalized agenda. They have been assigned to small groups and forced to sit with these groups at tables that have been arranged tightly in the small cafeteria. By doing this we can keep the crowded room from becoming overly polarized and in this way our faculty and staff will be forced to interact collegially with colleagues they wouldn't normally share the time of day with. Thus, we will put tenured faculty on maintenance workers, and counselors on groundskeepers. The financial aid staff has been assigned to separate tables as well, where they are now interacting with cafeteria attendants who have been forced to do the same. We have assigned secretaries to faculty and faculty to support staff. We will even pair untenured lecturers with their tenured peers. After careful planning each group will have a representative of every demographic that we are blessed to have at our school. Importantly, they have been divided along regional lines so that each table will have one person from the North, South, East, West, Northeast, Southwest, Northwest, Southeast, Old West, New South, Far North, Midwest, and California. And of course at each table there will be at least one token employee who was born and raised in Cow Eye Junction."

"Interesting. So you've mixed them according to geography?"

"Right. But that's not all. We've also made sure to bring them together politically, economically, and ethnically. In each group there will be at least one laissez-faire capitalist and one left-leaning socialist. One centrist and one anarchist. One tenured faculty member and one who is non-tenured. One white, one Asian. A lumper and a splitter. A Catholic and a Protestant. Sikh and Hindu. Jew and jihadist. Social scientist and actual scientist. Vegetarian and anti-vegetarian. Introvert and extrovert. Isolationist and expansionist. Loved and unloved. Metaphysician and empiricist. You see, we will find a way to bring together the different dichotomies of the world – both true and tru*ish* – each of humanity's myriad conflicts, into a tense but respectful sameness within the groups. With this, the cafeteria will be perfectly balanced. The groups will be demographically diverse yet united by a common mission. And in the name of accreditation they will sit with each other in cultural, economic, political, professional, and institutional harmony at their respective tables."

"Well, that should be interesting to observe. So then what? How are you going to *entertain* all these diverse groups?"

"This too has been carefully planned! As soon as they enter the cafeteria they will be accosted by the sweet strains of the Cow Eye jazz band and chamber orchestra playing familiar Christmas favorites. We have asked the Esperanto club to sing holiday carols and so they have already started, I'm sure. In fact, if you listen closely you may even be able to hear them now…the sweet voices…the gleeful singing. 'Ĝi *estas la sezono por esti gaja….*' they are surely crooning to a rapt audience in the crowded cafeteria: '… *Fa-la-la-la-la-la-la-la….*'

"….la!"

"Right. And when they're done, Dr. Felch will come to the microphone and he will say…"

"…Is this thing on?!"

"Exactly! And then he will give some opening remarks – something about how all of us at Cow Eye Community College need to work together as a single unit, as a cohesive whole, to get through this fucking accreditation business and that all of our efforts are for the benefit of our students. Of course, the accreditors will still be there so he won't use those *exact* words – and when he's done, he'll introduce the accreditors themselves, who will present their findings from the week of intense scrutiny they just spent here on campus. I imagine they will want to sweeten the pill by starting with the positives…."

"The positives being our beautiful campus with its majestic fountains and carefully cut grass!"

"And its pelicans!"

"And don't forget the many construction and reconstruction projects that we have underway!"

"And the ducks quacking!"

"…Exactly. And after all these commendations have been issued, they will pause. And here they will grow serious. The mood in the cafeteria will change. Here things will become tense as the accreditors proceed to announce the findings of their visit. The deficiencies that they discovered. The grave institutional problems. The inconsistencies. The worrisome trends…."

"The iambs!"

"Right. And the mispellings. And after that they will thank us for hosting them this week and stand up from their chairs."

"And then?"

"Well, and then the accreditors will quickly leave as a group for their bus which will be waiting to whisk them away from Cow Eye Junction back to their own communities. They will leave as a group and now, as the front door shuts behind them, the latch closing with a decisive click, everyone will breathe a deep sigh of relief."

"And now?"

"Well, and now the formal portion of the festivities will begin, as always, with a benediction. At this, the atheists will turn their backs; the agnostics will shrug their shoulders; and the Jews will feel a slight disturbance in the pit of their stomachs. But when it's done the silent majority will look up from their prayer and with an utterance of "Amen!" the wet bar will be opened and the formal portion of our Christmas program can begin with the awards presentation…."

"Awards?"

"Yes. As you know, our society is thoroughly enamored of awards. Awards are more numerous than stars in the night sky, more countless than cockroaches behind the icemaker of our cafeteria. Awards are the straw that stirs the mixed drink of academe. It is the long needle that is threaded though the receptive heifer's cervix and stabbed into her uterus so that new life can be conceived. Without awards, you see, there would be little to distinguish the worth of our contributions as academicians from those made by the maggots out back of our cafeteria."

"Maggots perform an invaluable service to humanity!"

"As do academicians! And so we will conduct a comprehensive awards ceremony to recognize them for their unique achievements."

"The maggots?"

"No. The academicians. I doubt maggots require such things...."

"And then?"

"Well, and then people who value awards for their intrinsic merit will peruse these faculty members' curricula vitae, see all this award winning, and be justifiably impressed!"

"No, not that. We meant what is happening after the awards ceremony?" Raul checked his watch. "It's getting late. The sun is beginning to set. Our award-winning peers are sitting in that cafeteria as we speak. So having finished *that*, what's happening now?"

"Well, after the awards ceremony, comes the costume contest."

"That sounds fun."

"It will be!"

"Are you dressing up, Charlie?"

"Of course. I've got my outfit in the duffel bag in the trunk of our car."

"And your costume is?"

"A sheriff!"

"A sheriff?!"

"Yes, from New Mexico!"

"And then? After the costume contest, what's happening?"

"Well then comes the exchange of gifts."

"Secret Santa?"

"Yes. And then the apple-bobbing and face painting. Then the mistletoe and dunking tank. Then the stocking stuffing. The pony rides. The piñatas. The kissing booth. The pie toss. The silent auction and charity raffle. Holiday-themed karaoke. Massage tables. The photo stand. Musical chairs to the patriotic strains of our national anthem...."

"And then?"

"Well, by now the party will be well underway. By now things are in full swing with most of the attendees having had their share of alcoholic drinks many times over. They have mingled with their peers and engaged in fuzzy dialectics. They have complimented each other on their costumes. They have no doubt helped themselves to the large bowl of barbiturates so that by now their muscles are relaxed, their minds cloudy, their defenses lowered. Despite their strong wishes to the contrary, our faculty and staff will find themselves sharing conversation with their worst enemies. The Buddhist and the gentile. The historian and the mathematician. Dreamer and empiricist. Liberal and conservative. Poet and professor. The Muslim, the Hindu and the Anglican will have no choice but to stare in loving admiration at the diverse ornaments depending from the all-inclusive Christmas tree. The generalist and the specialist will exchange hugs. The businessman and the metaphysician will shake hands in mutual respect. Even the secretaries from the competing academic departments will put aside their personal and professional loyalties for the sake of yuletide harmony. Before long the cafeteria will join hands in a circle to sing *Silent Night*. By now, you see, everything has coalesced quite nicely. The diversity. The unity. The promise of a vanquished frontier. While the three of us sit here in this Oldsmobile, this dream of mine is all coming perfectly together...."

My friends nodded again.

"Meanwhile," I continued, "the break-out rooms will be heavily attended throughout the evening. In fact, these rooms will be as diverse as the human condition itself. In one there will be a tribute to campus artists and their works. Another will feature a display of animal husbandry. In one room there will be a hands-on demonstration of artificial insemination complete with cow in estrus and shoulder-length gloves. In another a lecture on Esperanto. In a third, a thought-provoking discussion of syllogistic fallacies. In a fourth room – a small conference room with poor lighting – a prominent literary agent will be conducting a workshop for our English faculty on the subtleties of query writing. There will also be lectures in estate planning. And a slideshow on the transcontinental railroad. Outside the cafeteria there will be ten rooms dedicated to the slaking of pent-up desire – quiet rooms equipped with candles and champagne and satin pillows where couples can break away from the festivities to find their own forms of pleasure. For obvious reasons, these ten rooms will be heavily visited throughout the evening. And of course one of these ten rooms will be Room 2-C...."

"Room 2-C?"

"Yes, you see, there is much trepidation and misinformation that is circulating nowadays. And I admit that I myself am guilty. But where would our society be without intellectual inquisitiveness? Where would we be without the courage that inspires an intrepid researcher to venture into the darkest reaches of pleasure and pain? To cast aside all fear and to test a fearless hypothesis? In room, 2-C, you see, there will be candles and champagne plunged in buckets of ice. There will be pictures of fruits and Venetian gondoliers. Greek goddesses and reclining nymphs. Copulating ancients and elephants bearing grapes. But, significantly, there will also be tubs of Vaseline and Astroglide...."

"Oh my!"

"Right. And meanwhile the formal program will be moving on as planned. Alan Long River has agreed to deliver the keynote address. The Esperanto Club will sing a second set of Christmas carols. The Drama Club will act out the nativity – complete with real-live Caganer. All of this has been meticulously planned and will surely happen without a hitch at the long-awaited Christmas party that is now taking place in our cafeteria. All of it is now taking place as we speak, and it should last several more hours – or at least until our Oldsmobile arrives at the cafeteria."

Raul nodded respectfully.

"Well, it looks like you've done your due diligence, Charlie. It sounds like they're having a wonderful time right now. Which is not to imply that I am *not* – please don't get me wrong. I love the interior of this Starfire as much as anyone. The vinyl upholstery. The hump on the floor in between Bessie's ankles. The sun streaming in through this windshield. It's all been quite a revelation. But now I just hope we can make it to the cafeteria in time to catch at least *some* of the party...."

"We will!" I said. "You just need to have faith...!"

Raul nodded.

I drove on.

"But Charlie," Bessie said, "There's one thing you didn't mention.... There's one important thing that you forgot to include in your envisioning of the Christmas party...."

"Really?"

"Yes. In your account you didn't mention the *food.*"

"The food?"

"Yes, what about the food? What are you serving the attendees? As it is already getting late, surely the food line has opened up by now! So what are you serving them? Which is to say....what are our colleagues *eating* at the Christmas party that you have spent so much time and creative energy planning?"

"Ah, yes, the food!" I said. "It's a fair question. And an important one. You are very observant, Bessie. You are very observant and for this reason I am sure that everything will work out for you someday. Some day you will move beyond gravel. Some day you will be loved unequivocally. To answer your excellent question, Bess, yes, I did make elaborate plans for the food. And it will be truly fantastic. It was not easy given the constrictions that were imposed. But I am convinced that I have come up with the perfect solution to the conundrum."

"The *conundrum* being that you promised to serve both meat and no meat? That you've committed to both vegetables and no vegetables? That you've promised to be both of those world views entirely?"

"Right. And I think I've come up with the perfect solution. But you see, I can't reveal it just quite yet. It will be a special surprise that only I am privy to. And so I will need to be there in person to unsheathe the mystery myself."

"You mean, there's no food yet?"

"Right."

"Our hungry faculty and staff have been sitting there in the cramped cafeteria for several hours with alcohol and barbiturates and forced professional interactions….but no *food*?! And you won't be serving it until we get there?!"

"Right."

"Even though we're going to be several hours late?"

"Yes. So let's not talk about any of that yet. Let's just focus on this road in front of us – the one bringing us closer and closer to the celebration of humanity that is now several hours old…."

⁀

TO SAY THAT the drive to Cow Eye Junction by day differs considerably from the drive we'd taken at night….is to say that the sun differs from the moon, or the light of day differs from the totality of darkness. As we drove, we felt the sun beating down on our car and the glare from the black asphalt cutting into our eyes. Without any sleep at all, I felt myself growing even more weary, the warmth and the glare making me drowsy.

"Wake up!" Bessie yelled and punched my shoulder several times along the way. And each time I woke up.

The time flew by. The miles flew by. From the city we made our way headlong through a countryside that was greenish at first, then – closer to Cow Eye Junction – browner and more brittle. The landscape had changed yet again, and now as we crossed back into the cattle country of our beginnings, we saw the changes that had taken place. The Cow Eye Ranch that once stood as an emblem for the region but had since fallen into rusty decay. The former ranchlands where cattle once grazed but where strip malls now stood like shining theorems long since proved. Along the way we felt the heat of drought and the warmth of forgotten emanations. Then the pleasant feel of incarnation on our skin. And then, finally, the crisp coolness of the day's dissolution. At seven the sun had mostly set and only a dull glow of light was still visible. At seven-thirty it descended beyond the horizon entirely. At eight, it was night once again. By eight-thirty we had pulled into the desiccated landscape of the Diahwa Valley Basin. And by eight-forty-five we were driving by the mayor's house and the Cow Eye museum and the health food store where the Champs d'Elysees Bar and Grill used to be. At exactly nine we hopped over the railroad tracks and a minute later we pulled up to the entrance where Timmy had left the gate open for the night.

"The campus is so dark," said Raul.

"And empty," said Bessie.

"Do you think the party is still going on?"

"I don't know," I answered. "I suppose we'll find out shortly…."

From the guard shack I directed the Starfire toward the cafeteria where, to our relief, we saw a parking lot full of cars. In the distance the lit-up cafeteria shone like an island of light amid a sea of impenetrable darkness.

"They're still here!" said Raul. "The party's still happening!"

I parked the Starfire in the handicap stall nearest the cafeteria entrance. Getting out, I stretched my legs and reached for the night sky.

"That was a long ride," said Bessie.

"It most certainly was," I said. "But a necessary one."

My friends agreed.

"Look," said Raul. "It's absolutely dark again."

He was smiling.

"But the rain has stopped," said Bessie.

She was not.

I nodded at all of this.

It was nine-fifteen. Ahead of me, at the entrance to the cafeteria, a lone figure was slowly making its way from the darkness toward the front door.

"Who's that?" said Bessie.

"I don't know," said Raul. "It looks like an Indian chiefess…."

I recognized the figure immediately:

"It's Gwen! She's here!"

"Only *now*? Why only now?"

"I don't know. Maybe she stepped out for a bit of fresh air…." Grateful, I called out to her through the darkness: "Hey, Gwen! Wait for me…!"

The figure looked up and squinted into the darkness.

Grabbing my duffel bag, I ran toward the entrance and reaching Gwen just before the double doors, I opened one door wide to let her in. As the door swung open the sudden sounds of gay revelry and the warmth of overheated bodies washed over us.

"Please…." I said.

"You first…" she insisted.

"No *you*…."

"No, Charlie, *you*! Those other days are over!"

"Oh, right," I said and threw my duffel bag over my shoulder. "I almost forgot."

Tired and hungry from the exertions of our respective journeys through time and space, she and I stood before the cafeteria entrance under the large banner welcoming us to the event.

"That's a nice banner," Gwen said.

I nodded and thanked her.

"And I like your costume," I said.

"I am Hiawatha."

"I know. It's big of you. I mean, I really appreciate you coming tonight."

"My pleasure."

And here she laughed:

"An amazing pleasure indeed!"

"You mean *figuratively*, of course?"

"No literally. Room 2-C was everything I'd hoped it would be." Gwen was still holding the door gingerly and waiting for me to enter. "But it was also a lot of work. It is never easy to overcome long-held prejudices – to be open to new experiences – and this took quite a bit of exertion on my part. But it was certainly worth the effort. I am exhausted but exhilarated.

I feel newly enlightened. The world has just become a more complicated place. And boy am I *hungry*...!"

With these words, the two of us entered the cafeteria where the Christmas party was already approaching its climax.

THE CHRISTMAS PARTY

Welcome to the First Annual
Springtime Masquerade and
Christmas Springtime
Extravaganza
For Student Success:
WHERE EVERYTHING MEETS!

From the welcome banner
above the cafeteria entrance

By the time I stepped into the Christmas extravaganza on March twentieth, the formal festivities had concluded, fine liquor was flowing like milk and honey, and the many faculty and staff of the college, dressed in rich and elaborate costumes, had taken to milling about the packed room with their various drinks in hand; or sitting at the crowded tables; or lying atop the massage benches over by the poinsettia display. The room had been decorated exactly as I'd envisioned, and seeing all the pieces in their rightful places I rejoiced as if it were my own personal triumph: in the far corner was the stage; on the stage was the Christmas tree; next to the tree was a rocking chair for Santa; behind the chair was an elf's house; protruding from this house was a chimney; and around the perimeter of the room were countless stockings strewn about, one per attendee, each employee's name written lovingly in a cursive script out of glue and glitter. Meanwhile, dangling from the very center of the room, and spinning just as slowly and relentlessly as the world itself, was a disco strobe casting a million pieces of reflected light around the cafeteria. The wet bar was buzzing. The roulette table was crowded. Along an entire wall of the cafeteria hung the enormous tri-colored flag of incipient democracy – all thirteen stripes and forty-seven stars – while on the wall immediately across from it, occupying the same amount of space but with less unity of purpose, was this flag's perfect converse: the diverse quilt of nationhood representing the lesser polities of the world.

In the lively and chaotic scene I took heart that our faculty and staff had turned out in costume and were mingling in unprecedented historical combinations: a southern plantation owner with his northern industrialist counterpart; a brakeman and a strikebreaker; a suffragette and a missionary; even John Jay and Alexander Hamilton appeared to have made amends at a busy table where they were now bemoaning the subtleties of query-writing and the hopelessness of finding a reliable literary agent. From one historical era to the next, I witnessed the progeny of a future now past. The robber baron and the indentured servant. The carpetbagger. The racketeer. A woman in whalebone bodice. The tarred and feathered scalawag. A slave driver with a whip. The pilgrim. The pioneer. A Sandanista. One of the reference librarians had painted a scarlet "TBD" across her cheek, while another followed behind her bearing a cardboard pillory. A sharecropper was driving his ox. A flapper danced the Charleston. Two behavioral scientists performed in blackface. Even the cross-dressing horticulturist had gotten into the act by impersonating a straight-laced and very dignified presidential candidate. Inspired, I headed to the men's room with my duffel bag where I slipped into my own costume for the night: the jeans and boots and chaps and Stetson hat that would mark me as a New Mexico sheriff on patrol. When this was done I took out the holster and cinched it around my waist. Then I pinned my sheriff's badge to my shirt. Careful not to release the safety from its locked position, I slipped the borrowed pistol into the holster.

"Just be very careful with that!" Ethel had told me when I informed her of my latest costume idea. She was lending me an antique pistol that her grandfather had bequeathed her in his will. "A loaded gun is no joke, Charlie. I don't care if it *is* Christmas! I don't care *how much* unity and good will you've assembled in that cafeteria…!"

"Don't worry," I said. "Your pistol will stay right here in my holster. It will not go off – I promise!"

"Well, you know the rule…never point a firearm unless you intend to use it!"

I laughed into the mirror.

"No really," said the creative writing instructor to Maude. "If you bring that condom to the laundromat, it damn well better get wet…!"

I washed my face and took another pill. Now my costume was complete. I was ready for the masquerade that I had spent so much of my life planning.

Taking it all in, I felt the joy of a plan coming together and the relief of a legacy that was finally finding its fruition. At last I could see the fruits of the seeds that I had planted. The pulp of my tireless preparations.

"And what are *you* supposed to be?" Stan asked me in front of the mirror. Behind him I could see the bathroom door closing to the party outside.

"What am I supposed to be? Why something entirely, of course!"

"No, not that. I meant the costume."

"Oh that. I'm a sheriff. From New Mexico. And you?"

"He's a cuckold," said Ethel. "But a good one!"

And she gave her husband a playful kiss on the cheek.

"That's great, Stan. It's great that you can have a sense of humor about such things."

"What else can I do? And besides – it's okay now. Ethel and I are back together. And with the restraining order hanging over Luke, that bastard can't even poke his toe out from behind the bar he's tending!"

I nodded and made my way through the crowd with my duffel bag.

On one side of the room was Rusty and his team of animal scientists dressed as cowboys. On the other side sat Gwen and her fellow neophytes in Indian attire.

Gwen laughed out loud when she saw me in full costume.

"Let me guess…" she said. "You're a sheriff!"

"Correct."

"From Arizona?"

"Oh, no. That would be premature – even presumptuous. I'm from New Mexico."

"I see. That's probably prudent. And you know what all of *us* are, right?"

She pointed to the side of the cafeteria where her acolytes were sitting.

"Well," I ventured, "it looks like all of you are dressed as a gathering of native peoples…."

"You're close…!"

"An antediluvian village?"

"Closer…!"

"I give up."

"We're Indians. Get it, Charlie? *Indians!*"

"I get it. Though there is definitely some irony in that. And besides, you shouldn't call them simply Indians anymore, you know. They're now more rightly referred to as *American* Indians, or, even better, *Native Americans….*"

Gwen straightened the feather sticking out of her headband.

"Whatever," she said. And then: "You know, I'm even more hungry now than I was a half hour ago when you and I entered this room together. When's the food coming anyway?"

"Very soon."

"I hope so. We're all starving!"

I nodded. A few minutes later I bumped into Rusty at the urinal.

"Nice party!" he said though his arm was in a sling and he was having difficulty managing the zipper.

"Thanks," I answered. "What happened to your arm?"

"It's a long story...."

"They usually are around here!"

"And I don't want to get into it."

"I understand. Please know that I really do appreciate you coming tonight. And I think it's great that you and all the other animal science faculty have taken to dressing up as cowboys!"

"What do you mean?"

"Well, you're playing the role of cowboy, right? The cowboy boots. The hat. The jeans and plaid shirt. The bolo tie...!"

"I don't know what you're talking about. Nobody's *dressing up*...."

He looked hurt. I apologized and Rusty went back outside to sit with his colleagues.

In the men's room the air was moist and scented from the aromatic pads of the urinal. My costume was lying untouched in the duffel bag.

"Are you still in here?" said Raul. "I thought you were going to put on your costume?"

"I am."

"So how long does it take to do that? It's been more than thirty minutes since you came in here. Bessie noticed you were missing. I figured I should come and check on you...."

"Really? Time flies, doesn't it?"

"Are you okay?"

"Of course I am. Why do you ask?"

"I don't know. You seem distant. Your eyes are not just red anymore but crystal clear – and not in a good way. As if they were pools of transparent water affording a view of the murkiest depths of human suffering. You seem calm and composed and still. It's not like you, Charlie. And it worries me."

"I'm fine, Raul. I appreciate the concern. But I just need to get this costume on so I can join the party...."

"Is that gun loaded? The one still sitting in that duffel bag over there?"

"Yes, it is. Cool, huh?"

"I suppose. Just be careful with it. You know what they say about loaded firearms and good intentions. In any case, I guess we'll see you outside in the cafeteria when you're changed...."

A few minutes later Bessie and Raul came up to where I was standing by the entrance under the welcome banner:

"The party looks good, Charlie!"

"Thanks," I said. "I did put a lot of planning into it."

"We've heard. When are you going to change into your costume?"

"Very soon. I've got it right here in my duffel bag...."

Bessie left to get a beer and when she came back the three of us surveyed the lively scene.

"Who's that?" I asked.

"That's one of the Dimwiddles," she said.

"And that young man over there with the handheld electronic device?"

"That's our student body president, the future and the fate of our society."

"And the girl next to him? The one with the baby?"

"That's Rusty's teenage daughter. With her newborn."

"And that figure over there? The morose one sitting by himself?"

"That's the man from the Champs d'Elysees. The one you met on your ride into town."

"I almost didn't recognize him. He looks so *old*!"

"Yeah, well, time does tend to fly. And youth comes and goes...."

I splashed more water on my face.

When I went back to the party, the revelry was all-consuming. In the faint light of the incandescent menorah Dr. Felch approached me for the first time. He was dressed as Santa Claus and his words reeked of liquor, the bell of his Santa's hat was somewhat tilted, his fake beard slightly askew.

"Jesus Fucking Christ!" he exclaimed. "Where the hell have *you three* been?!"

Bessie smiled at her ex-husband and gave him a light kiss on his cheek.

"Merry Christmas, Bill," she said. "Cute hat!"

"Good evening, sir!" Raul added. "And *feliz navidad*!"

"Yeah, well *frère jaques* to you too...."

Bessie made her way past her ex-husband back into the crowded cafeteria. Raul, after patting Dr. Felch on the shoulder and wishing him a merry Christmas in English, followed her into the room where the two quickly disappeared into the teeming crowd.

Turning back to Dr. Felch, I said:

"I'm really sorry to be so late, sir. But I did need to visit Will in his moment of need."

"You said you'd be back by *noon*!"

"That was my plan, yes. But we ended up staying much longer than I'd envisioned. We had to stay well into the afternoon – quite a ways past two, in fact – to find out how the history of the world will end."

"And how *will* it end?"

"Efficiently."

"Well, that's all fine and good. But why'd you take Bessie on your adventure? Without her, I couldn't find my damn notebook with the notes you left me. Without my notes I've had to wing everything by memory and intuition. I've had to improvise the agenda every step of the way...."

And here Dr. Felch told me how, by memory, he'd begun the party with a rousing benediction followed, intuitively, by the opening of the wet bar. From there he'd proceeded straight to the apple-bobbing and musical chairs. Then the piñatas and pony rides. The dunking tank. The ring toss. At some point he remembered to go back for the awards presentation and the costume contest – and just in the nick of time – even combining the two separate activities into a single event in an inspired stroke of executive decision-making and organizational efficiency. After that came the rousing karaoke performances, the foot massages, the kissing booth under the mistletoe.

"It's been an uphill battle all the way," he sighed.

I nodded.

"You have no idea how hard it is to find mistletoe in Cow Eye!"

I nodded again.

"Let alone a priest to bless the menorah."

We talked for some time. Finally, I swallowed hard and said, "Excuse me, sir, I need to go to the restroom to change into my costume...."

When I came back Dr. Felch was in the same place talking with a secretary.

"Hey, is that an accreditor over there?" I asked.

"Yes. They missed their bus. So they'll be joining us for the festivities tonight."

"Oh no!"

"Oh, *yes*. And they're not the only ones. Over there you have the Dimwiddle heirs. And over *there* you have the adjuncts. At that table along the wall next to the glory hole is where our student leaders are sitting. And across from them is the dignitary table with the mayor and his wife, the county engineer, the local high school football coach, his niece, and three successful alumni who now run their own enterprises at the Outskirts. It's a lot of diversity in such a small cafeteria. It's a heck of a lot of inclusiveness, Charlie. Oh, and you just missed Merna. She left a few minutes before you came...."

"Merna Lee was here? But I thought she was dead?"

"*Dead*?! What made you think that?"

"Well, everyone keeps talking about her as if she's dead. You all had a poignant remembrance for her at the river, remember? You even scattered her ashes...!"

"She's not dead – my god, Charlie – she's just *retired*! These two concepts are similar but distinct...."

"But what about the *remembrance* you all held for her? Why would you need to conduct a remembrance for her if she's still alive?!"

"Why *not*? Or should we only remember the dead? Shouldn't we also remember the living with the same degree of affection? I mean, why should we always wait for a thing to die before we fondly pay homage to it?"

"That makes sense, I guess."

"Of course it does! I mean, isn't that what all consequential literature aspires to do? Isn't that the purpose of contemporary historiography?"

"I wouldn't know. But what about the ashes...how do you explain *them*?"

"Merna was a lifelong smoker and kept a large urn of ashes – forty years worth – on the floor in her office. And so we finally scattered them for her that night at the river."

"I see."

"It turned the water turbid."

"I see."

"And you missed it."

"Right."

"Just like you missed her at the party tonight."

"Right."

"You are a lot of different things, Charlie. But not being any of them entirely has caused you to miss a lot of things in this life."

"I know. And I'm really sorry. I tried to get here on time. But like I said, there are some things that are just so much more important than daily immediacies...."

"Such as?"

"Well, such as darkness."

"And?"

"And rain."

"And?

"And love."

"And?!"

"And the stars in the sky. All of those things are truly important, Dr. Felch. Living in Cow Eye has taught me to appreciate them all. Living here I've come to learn this lesson the long way...."

"Well, that may be so. But I thought you were going to change into your costume...."

"I didn't?"

"Obviously not. You're still in the clothes you wore to the city...."

"I am?"

"Charlie, are you still taking those pills?"

"Oh yes."

"Both of them?"

"Oh no! I'm only taking one of them."

"The pill to make you sleep?"

"I believe so. Though it's hard to say anything with certainty right now. It's all kind of blending together at the moment."

"Well, you'd better go change into your costume. The math faculty just arrived. And I have an important announcement to make to everyone."

I grabbed my duffel bag and returned to the rest room where Dr. Felch was waiting for me next to the paper towel dispenser.

"That's a nice set of boots!" he said.

"Thank you," I said. "But how did you get here so fast? How did you beat me to the bathroom?"

"What do you mean? I just walked in here. I've been out glad-handing for the last fifteen minutes?"

"But…!"

"Charlie, you seem to be slowing down, my friend. You seem to be losing track of your surroundings."

"It's entirely possible. This pill I'm taking…it's…working, I guess…."

"That's good. Let's hope it brings you some well-deserved sleep eventually…."

Dr. Felch ripped off the towel from the dispenser.

"By the way, when's the food coming?"

"Soon."

"How soon?"

"Very soon!"

"Well, you'd better let everyone know what's going on, or you're going to lose them. It's almost ten and these people have been in this room since six o'clock. Some even earlier! It's absolutely packed. They're huddled in here like cattle in a cattle chute. Like bullets in a box of bullets. Like pieces of chalk in a box containing many pieces of chalk. The room is sweaty and warm, with no circulation. The costumes are hot. Your peers are tired and very hungry. Charlie, if you don't get them some food – or at least the promise of food – we're going to have a mutiny on our hands…!"

"But…"

"…or an insurrection…!"

"But I…"

"Charlie, listen up! I'm preparing the finishing touches on the announcement that I'm going to make now that the math faculty have arrived dressed as Roman senators. In the meantime, you'd better say something to the crowd. You'd better say something to quell the tension. To appease the hunger pangs. To assuage the growing doubts. Go on. The microphone's over there…."

Dr. Felch crumpled up his paper towel and threw it into the trash can and walked out.

I nodded…

"Yes, sir," I said.

As the door closed after him, I took out the vial from my shirt pocket, twisted the cap off, and slid out a pill. Leaning my head back I dropped it down my throat and chased it with water from the tap.

"Alright," I said to myself. "It's time to let everyone know what's going on…!"

Tired and bewildered, I made my way from the bathroom to the microphone at the front of the cafeteria. The microphone was cold and thumped loudly when I turned it on.

≈

"GOOD EVENING!" I said. "Good evening, everyone, and welcome to our First Annual Springtime Masquerade and Christmas Extravaganza for Intra-faculty Unity and Student Success. Otherwise known as the Cow Eye Community College Annual Christmas party….Thank you all for coming…."

Here I wiped a collection of spittle from the corner of my mouth. Then I turned off the spigot of the restroom sink and continued:

"…I know it's already quite late and you are all very hungry. And so I just wanted to reassure you that the food is on its way. The caterer has been given the green light and so the food we've ordered should be arriving any minute. Specifically, I've been told that it will be here by eleven at the very latest…."

"Eleven?!"

"Yes, eleven."

"P.m. or a.m.?"

"Very funny, Max. P.m. of course. So please be patient. This is not easy for me either. As you probably know by now, it's been months since I've had a decent night's sleep. And it's been days since I've had any sleep at all. And yet, here I am. Here I am in this men's restroom in this sheriff's costume. Here I am shepherding this Christmas party to its successful resolution. At eleven the food will be here – I promise. And it will be worth the wait. It will be a joyous occasion. A reason for celebration. A personal triumph against overwhelming odds. In the meantime, I encourage you all to use this opportunity to get to know each other in this crowded cafeteria. Or, if you prefer, in one of the ten exotic rooms that we've procured for your enjoyment. While you wait you might as well talk incessantly with the many people you normally wouldn't have the time of day for. And if you've gone that far you might as well get to know them in other ways too! Biblically, for example. You see, for especially intimate acquaintances we have arranged those ten exquisite rooms for your enjoyment. And for the more adventurous we have room 2-C. And of course, I encourage you to frequent the wet bar and the punch table throughout this evening. Please help yourself to the bowls of multi-colored barbiturates and amphetamines that have been positioned as centerpieces throughout the room. Don't pass up the marijuana that is making its rounds. Or the lines of cocaine that have been carefully laid like rural highways across our vast country. Or the LSD and heroin available under the no-smoking sign over there. (Just remember, folks, that we are a *tobacco-free* campus!) Oh, and while you're at it, don't neglect to take your prescription medication and to wash it down with some proscriptive legislation. The Prozac. The vitamins. The Ritalin and Viagra. The sign ordinances and leash laws. After so much planning and preparation, it's great to know that my quixotic plans are becoming observable reality. It's great to see them taking shape in the form of this long-awaited Christmas party. And so, yes, I'm going to celebrate my own success by helping myself to Luke's concoctions over there at the wet bar. I'm going to drink them enthusiastically. And indiscriminately. And I'm going to use them to wash down this amazing pill of mine that I've been taking and that has helped me stay up this long. This pill that will keep me awake forever! I am going to do all this. But first, I'd like to acknowledge some people who've been instrumental in all this success. Some people without whose help none of this diversity and inclusiveness could have been possible…. It takes all kinds to organize a successful Christmas party. Just as it takes all walks of individuals to run a struggling community college. Just as it takes all manner of Homo sapiens to make up this rich tapestry of human experience that unites us in our humanity…!'"

And so over the prattling audience – were they even listening to me? – I thanked Dr. Felch for bringing me to Cow Eye and for trusting me with the planning of this Christmas party as a sure means of resurrecting my legacy after so many failed attempts at other colleges. And of course for giving me the roll of twenty-dollar bills that, I'd since learned, did not actually come from official coffers but rather from his own personal retirement account.

I paused to allow the sparse applause to die down. Then I said:

"And of course I need to thank Bessie and Raul for accompanying me on my drive to visit Will Smithcoate in his moment of need. It was a long trip, for sure, but I now feel eminently more knowledgeable about the world we live in. About the nature of darkness. And of desiccation. About our shared history. And lonely futures. And, of course, I am much more versed in the difference between male and female orgasm. Please know that it was a sacrifice well deserved and that I will be knocking softly on its front door from here on out. Oh, and you'll surely be happy to know that Professor Smithcoate is doing just fine, all things considered. He is doing just fine and he sends you all his kind regards…!"

"He does?!"

"Well, not in so many words, of course. But in a roundabout sort of way I'm sure he misses you all very much…."

I paused to look up at Dr. Felch who was waiting in the wings.

"And speaking of missing," I said, "they tell me there's happy news to report from the opposite end of the cafeteria where you yourselves once entered this party several hours ago. They tell me we just hit *one hundred percent* attendance tonight! That's right, folks….the math faculty have just arrived! The male teachers are dressed as Roman senators. The women instructors are sultry felines. All of which means that for the first time in the long and storied history of Cow Eye Community College – from the first two cows that ever walked the face of the earth and up to the era of me standing here before you in my sleep-deprived stupor – we have one hundred percent buy-in for an important educational endeavor. We have one-hundred-percent participation for this party, ladies and gentlemen! And so let me be the first to congratulate you! Yes, congratulations are in order! With this having been accomplished, we're ready to move on to Dr. Felch who has an important announcement to make to our overcrowded cafeteria. To an undiminished professoriate. Amid a house undivided. As you can see, this party is shaping up to be a total and elaborate success…!"

I paused again.

"Sir? Are you ready for your announcement?"

Dr. Felch nodded and walked up to the dais. Taking the microphone from me, he said:

"Thank you, Charlie!" As the heating unit whirred in the background, and as the disco strobe continued to cast its reflections around the room, and while I celebrated the one-hundred-percent attendance milestone in my mind, Dr. Felch cleared his throat to begin his speech:

"Friends and citizens," he began. "Friends and citizens of Cow Eye Community College, I address you today not as your college president but as a simple, and very humbled, man…."

❧

Before he could finish this sentence a series of shouts rang out from the audience:

"It's not on!" the audience was shouting.

"What?" said Dr. Felch.

"The microphone….it's not on! We can't hear a thing…!"

"Bessie!!!"

Bessie walked briskly up to the front and turned the microphone on. Dr. Felch thanked her. The audience applauded. Now, with the microphone on and the disco strobe spinning and the fake Santa beard bobbing to the rhythm of his words, Dr. Felch began his important speech a second time:

❧

"Alright, let's try this again…." he said. "Friends and citizens! Esteemed colleagues! Residents of Cow Eye Junction – both tenured and non-tenured! Can you hear me? Is this thing on? It is? Great! My fellow educators, tonight I address you not as a college president but as a simple man. For the past thirty years, you see, I have had the distinct honor of being your humble servant. I have devoted my life to public service at this unparalleled institution of higher learning – first as an adjunct in the animal science department, then as a tenured professor, and finally as your college's venerable president and chief executive. It has been a glorious time spent here over the years and, I assure you, it is a period of my life that I will always look back on with fond memories…."

Dr. Felch checked his notes, then continued:

"…Recently, it has begun to occur to me with increasing urgency that the world we live in, just as it so often tends to do, is changing. That our world is becoming an ever more exciting and complex place – complex and exciting in ways that could not have been envisioned even a generation ago. And it has also occurred to me that this is a difficult thing for somebody like me to grasp. And that it should be for the newer generations of young men and younger women to deal with these unanticipated excitements and the many new-fangled complexities that are arising like flies from the trashcans out back of our cafeteria. There comes a time when all people must reach this understanding. And I have reached it. There is a time when we all must come to terms with such realities. And I have come to those very terms. Believe me, I have often considered it my turn to move on toward that peaceful domicile that awaits me at the older part of Cow Eye Junction where the pastures are still untrammeled. A year ago, in fact, I had gone so far as to draft an announcement like the one I am delivering tonight. But after talking the matter over with my latest wife, and after a bit more reflection on the perplexed affairs of our college at the time – the impending accreditation visit, the unresolved Christmas party dilemma, the inability to rally our divided faculty around a common vision for our future – I decided to abandon the idea. Now I stand before you for the last time as your humble president: the current, and soon to be *former*, president of Cow Eye Community College...."

Here Dr. Felch pulled out a handkerchief and wiped the sweat from his forehead. Then he continued:

"....Along the way, my friends, we have achieved amazing things together. The expansion of our liberal arts program. The re-roofing of the library. Electric typewriters in the vast majority of our departments. A many-fold growth in our enrollment, and an increase in our influence far beyond the vacant field where the apiary now stands. Over the years we have moved mountains and redirected rivers. We have conquered a continent and its appurtenances. We have subdued the vicissitudes of nature. Hell, we have even made the moon our own personal bitch. In short, my time with you has been enjoyable and, I would like to think, not without success. Looking back on the sum of such a long tenure, I would like to think that I am leaving our college in a better position – or at least a less precarious one – than the one you all found yourselves in a few moments ago in Room 2-C...."

Dr. Felch looked up from his notes.

"Joking!" he said. And then:

"...But, seriously, I would like to think that I am leaving our college in a much better position – or at least a less precarious one – than the one I inherited so long ago. Of course it would be impossible, given our mortal fallibilities, for there not to be errors committed along the way. And this has certainly been the case. Yes, my friends, we have made many errors along our tortuous path to continuous improvement. For along this path we have sowed seeds that we ourselves have then trampled. We have actively harvested our just rewards only to watch those robust harvests rot in railcars or covered over in mass graves to stabilize market prices. We have overlooked our native languages in favor of those from abroad. We have sent our sons and daughters – my god, how many of our sons have we banished? – to all ends of our far-flung nation, with most of them never to return again. And of course there have been isolated examples of infamy: the venture into soy; conscription and nullification; the many baseless lawsuits and their out-of-court settlements; August sixth and ninth, respectively; and of course the shoddy reconstruction of our campus after the great earthquake and conflagration of twenty-six years ago. Yes, these things are true. *All* of these things are true, my friends! But as we look back together I hope you can agree that any errors made along the way – no matter how seemingly egregious – were not made intentionally but rather with the best interests of our beloved college in mind...."

At this Dr. Felch removed his reading glasses from his nose. Pulling out the same handkerchief from his pocket, he wiped away some moisture that had collected in his eyes, then blew his nose into the handkerchief.

"I'm sorry," he said. "This is not easy for me. It's been thirty years and after being here so long I feel like I've given more than a small part of myself to this college. There is not an inch of ground on this campus that I have not personally trammeled. There is not a single project that I have not been privy to in one form or another. There is not an idea implemented on this campus that I have not attended at least three separate meetings to deliberate. Believe me when I say to you that over the last thirty years I have given everything I have to our beautiful college. My heart. My soul. My virility. Three of my marriages. I have sacrificed every last ounce of my humanity to our institution. To Cow Eye Community College. To all of you. And it has truly been a great privilege and an honor."

Here Dr. Felch stopped. In the silence of the cafeteria the ice maker in the kitchen could be heard to start up.

"And here, perhaps, I ought to stop...."

Dr. Felch paused to allow his words to sink in.

But of course he did not stop.

❧

"...At this, perhaps, I ought to stop. Yet duty compels me to leave you with a few final observations that they might help your generation in some small way as it moves forward through time and space. You see, each of you in your infinite diversity makes up the rich cultural fabric of Cow Eye Community College. In your collective unity is your strength. And this is no less true whether you come from the North, South, East, West, Northeast, Southwest, Northwest, Southeast, Old West, New South, Far North, Midwest, or even from a place as far away – as timeless and ineffable – as California. You are the products of the unique experiences that shape you. But do not let your geographical differences divide you. Nor your diverse backgrounds. Nor your spiritual convictions. Nor your religion. Nor political affiliation. Nor class. Nor race. Nor gender. Nor sexual orientation. Nor, even, the loyalties that you so dutifully – and understandably – feel toward your respective academic disciplines. Do not let these contrivances interfere with the greater love that you harbor for your institution – the love that unites you all as faculty and staff of Cow Eye Community College...."

Here Dr. Felch turned serious, his voice acquiring an even deeper sense of gravity:

"...It has been noted – and not only by myself – that in the history of mankind the role of political parties is an especially egregious one. Their existence serves only to inflame the innate differences that would separate us. To drive wedges into the crevices of our hearts. To divide our cafeteria into factions: this side of the crowded room for cowboys, that side for Indians. Tonight, however, we are on the threshold of a new era. For tonight we are witnessing a *new* kind of party. One that is open to inclusiveness. A party that does not divide but rather unites. A party that says to the world, yes, it *is* possible for faculty of every imaginable ilk to co-exist in harmony and self-respect on the verdant campus of even the most tenuous community college...."

"...As you move toward fulfillment of your regional accreditation – and no, I will not be able to finish this journey with you – make sure to cultivate good relations and harmony with all that you meet. Avoid harmful alliances and allegiances. Love God. Trust love. Worship peace. Pay taxes such that we may one day have an imposing military presence around the world. Do all this and everything else will naturally work itself out – even the most calamitous application for regional accreditation...."

By now Dr. Felch's voice had grown weaker, almost tremulous.

"....In offering to you, my fellow colleagues, these counsels of an old and affectionate friend, I dare not hope they will make a strong or lasting impression on you. But should they happen to do so – well, that would be super-duper, wouldn't it! Ultimately, though, that is for you to decide. It is for the next generation to take our college into its shining future. And so it is with a heaviness in my heart and a pinch of tobacco in my lower lip, that I wish you all the best in the future. It has been a glorious thirty years, my friends. And now all that remains is to bid you a final adieu."

With these final words, Dr. Felch stepped away from the microphone and slowly disappeared into the crowd.

❧

{ }

Like so many things in life, the opportunity to withdraw is all about the timing. And so the decision is not an easy one. Newly bewildered, the longtime community college president may be left to continue blindly with the relentless movements that have brought him to this point in time and space, or, oppositely, to end them by mutual agreement. But when? This is the question that has confused the world's most learned minds. Neither 'why' nor 'how' can flummox the educational administrator like the eternal question: when?

{ }

❧

AFTER DR. FELCH'S valedictory the mood in the cafeteria went from electric to subdued. The shock of the announcement came and went and in its place arose a general dullness and acceptance. The barbiturates, perhaps, were doing their duty. Or maybe the peppermint schnapps. Standing at the wet bar I took it all in – especially the peppermint schnapps.

"Thanks for manning the bar tonight, Luke. I really appreciate it."

"No problem, Charlie. It's been enlightening."

"Has everyone had their fill of drink?"

"Oh yes. And then some."

"I'm glad."

"Everyone but *you*. What'll you have?"

"I'm open to suggestions. What do you recommend?"

"Well, the food's on its way, right? So how about an apéritif while we wait? Would you be open to vermouth?"

"You could say that."

Luke poured the drink into a plastic cup and handed it to me.

"...You might want to drink this one slowly though. She can be a real bitch!"

I drank the bitch slowly. When I was done, I thanked Luke for the tip.

"Don't you want to sit down or something?" he laughed. "You've been standing over here for quite a while now!"

"No thanks. I'd rather stand, if you don't mind...."

And so I did. And standing there with my lime wedge in my hand, I engaged my peers in collegial banter.

"Are you drinking tequila, Charlie?" a passerby would wink.

"You could say that!" I would respond and down the observation in a single gulp.

"And what about cognac?"

"You could say that too!"

"And gin?"

"Yes!"

"And rum?"

"Yes!"

"And sherry?"

"Yes!"

"And zivania?"

"Yes!"

"And mead?"

"Yes!"

"And pulque? And kumis? And baijiu?"

"Oh, yes! I'm open to them all!"

And so over the next several minutes I accepted every invitation handed my way. The peppermint schnapps. The sprightly grasshoppers. The bloody martini. When Vanzetti offered me a margarita I accepted. And when Sacco handed me a gin and tonic I did not refuse. When a minuteman offered me the choice between sweet wine or dry, I chose both. And when Betsy Ross got up on a ladder to add a new star to the large flag on the wall – now there were thirteen stripes and forty-*eight* stars – I toasted the occasion with a glass of scotch in one hand and a cup of grog in the other. In this way I drank both hard liquors and soft. Both citrus and milk. Happily, I drank. Indiscriminately, I drank. Dutifully and wearily and boisterously and drowsily and historically and meekly I drank.

"And you *are*...?" I asked a peer who was passing by.

"I'll give you three guesses!" said Sam Middleton.

"Abraham Lincoln?"

"No!"

"John C. Calhoun!"

"No!"

"Marcus Garvey?"

"Close, but no...."

"I give up then...."

"You give up?"

"Yes."

"I'm Geoffrey Chaucer!"

"Oh right. I should have known."

"And you?" asked the ethics teacher.

"I'm a sheriff."

"From New Mexico?"

"Yes."

"I went there once. It was better than North Dakota but not nearly as nice as South Dakota..."

"Is that so?"

"Yes."

"Well, I have been to neither."

"It's okay. You've got many years ahead of you..."

"I do?"

"Yes. Ten at least."

"Right."

"You've got a good ten years to leave a legacy of some sort."

"Right."

"Starting tomorrow!"

"Yes. You are right. But, in the meantime, what is *that*?"

"What is what?"

"That chiming?"

"What chiming?"

"Don't you hear it? That light chiming that is emanating throughout the cafeteria? That insistent knell that despite all scientific principles is drowning out the much-louder chords of injustice?"

"That is the timely and delicate chiming of a triangle being played."

"Alan Long River!"

"Yes."

"He's giving his keynote address!"

"Yes."

"It's beautiful!"

"Yes, it is...."

"Let's listen, shall we?"

And so the two of us listened.

"But, Charlie?" said the Esperanto teacher when Long River's keynote was done.

"Yes?"

"You've not answered the most meaningful question of all?"

"The food? It's on its way...I promise!"

"No, not that."

"Then what?"

"Love, Charlie!"

"Love?"

"Yes, love! What is it?"

"You're asking me that now? With this bloody Mai Tai in my hand?"

"Yes, Charlie. You see, since you've been here we've heard Will Smithcoate tell us what love *would be*, and Dr. Felch tell us what it *was*. We've heard from Gwen what it *shouldn't be* and from Rusty what it *ain't*. We've even listened intently while the accreditors told us what love *will need to be* if we have any chance of reaffirming our regional accreditation. But after all is said and done, we still have not heard anyone tell us what it *is*!"

I nodded.

"Charlie, could you tell us please what love *is*?"

"Of course," I said.

"You will?"

"Yes, of course!"

"Well...?"

And so I told her.

And when this was done I sat down heavily at the table in the corner of the cafeteria where Will Smithcoate used to sit.

"Are you okay, Charlie?" one of the secretaries asked, on her way back from Room 2-C.

"I'm fine," I said. As evidence, I twirled the celery stalk from my bloody cow cunt then crunched it between my teeth.

"You don't look fine. You look tired. Your face is flushed. Your eyes are hollow and transparent. Have you not been sleeping very well?"

"You could say that."

"And have your pills run out?"

"You could say that too."

"And have you drunk more than you can handle?"

"That's another thing you could probably say."

"Your costume is compelling."

"Thank you."

"Your pistol is rather suggestive."

"Thanks."

"Is it loaded?"

"Of course."

"Metaphorically or literally?"

"Literally. I'm afraid this loaded gun is strictly literal at the moment."

"Because you haven't slept enough...."

"Right."

"And you've drunk far too much."

"Correct."

"Are you still taking those pills?"

"Yes."

"And have they brought you any closer to being something entirely?"

"I believe so, yes."

"But when will that happen?"

"Soon, I fear."

"Before or after the food comes?"

"*After*, of course. Surely it will come after the food."

"Well, you've done a great job organizing this party. I'm looking forward to the food if and when it does come."

"Right," I said. "Thank you, Rusty. But, Rusty...hey, Rusty, what time is it anyway?"

"It's ten-thirty, Charlie."

"That late?! No really, Gwen, is it truly that late right now?"

"Yes. In fact, it's after eleven."

"Already?"

"Yes. Just look at the clock. It's almost midnight."

"Midnight?!"

"Yes, Charlie, it's well past midnight and the food still hasn't arrived. Time seems to be moving inexorably along. Faculty are beginning to stream toward the exit. This party seems to be winding down."

"But. it can't! Timmy, our party can't end like this! It's not over yet!"

"Well then you'd better do something...."

"Right!"

Stumbling to the front of the room I switched on the microphone, which thumped just as loudly.

"Attention!" I said. "Attention, everyone! Please listen to this important announcement. I know that it is late and the food is not here yet. But I have been assured that it is on its way. Please don't leave yet! Please don't leave! The food will be here shortly – I promise! Hey, Timmy! Timmy, could you please be so kind as to lock the door so nobody can leave? It's a little after one o'clock in the morning and it would be a shame if after waiting so patiently everyone missed out on the food when it finally *does* come! Believe me it will be a memorable event. Timmy, could you please lock the door and bar it with that baseball bat that we used for the piñata...!"

Timmy looked back at me with a surprised look but did not lock the door nor bar it with the baseball bat that we used for the piñata.

"The food should be here any minute," I promised. "And so your patience is much appreciated while we wait for it to arrive. In the meantime, please visit the wet bar over there for an apéritif. And the bowls of barbiturates. And of course, Room 2-C is something no self-respecting educator should miss out on...!"

I sat back down at my table. By now the sights and sounds of this night were flying by like the many metaphors that I had experienced along the way. The bubbling springs. The flowing rivers. The sun and moon and stars and clouds. The esplanade leading from the rumblings of prolonged ecstasy to the cold bench at the edge of the universe. The asphalt beneath the center line under the wheels of our Starfire. The pendulum swinging between wintergreen and hay fever. The light sarong. The pills I'd taken.

The symphony with its violins and flutes and melting glaciers that will sooner or later become rain. An unbroken chain of fountains with their nesting pelicans and gigantic carp. In the warmth of my own reverie, it was now swirling around me faster and faster.

"So Charlie," Dr. Felch said when he'd approached me at my table. He had pulled out a chair and was sitting directly across from me. By now he'd ditched the heavy Santa suit and was wearing a white undershirt half-tucked into his red Santa pants. The fake beard was long gone. There was alcohol in his words. "So Charlie," he repeated. "It's Christmas."

"Yes, Dr. Felch, it is."

"Merry Christmas, Charlie."

"Merry Christmas, Dr. Felch. And congratulations on your retirement. I'm very happy for you."

"Thank you."

"I'm sure some people will be disappointed that Santa Claus is retiring. But to hell with them. Retirement is a very personal decision. And it couldn't have happened to a nicer man...."

"That's sweet of you to say, Charlie. But, Charlie?"

"Yes?"

"Charlie, now that it's Christmas isn't there something you want to tell me?"

"Of course."

"So...?"

"Merry Christmas!"

"No, not that. You already said that. I mean is there something you have to say for yourself?"

"About what?"

"Well about the world we live in? About that calf we castrated, for example? Anything along those lines that you'd like to tell me?"

"You mean the metaphor we squeezed out like prunes from a package?"

"Yes. What is the metaphorical significance of it all, if there even is one?"

"Oh, there *is*! There most definitely is one alright! There is metaphor in everything. That is a truth I've learned since coming here. It is one of the many lessons I've acquired."

"So what is it then?"

"The lesson?"

"No, the metaphor? What then is the metaphorical significance of the calf?"

"I'm not sure, sir. In fact, I was sort of expecting that you might have forgotten about it…."

"I may be old but I'm not senile! I may be retiring but I'm not retired. Not yet anyway. Things are happening very quickly, Charlie, so I think I'd better ask you now; otherwise, given how things are unfolding, I may not get another chance. So what's the metaphorical significance of the calf in the corral? Or, rather, wait….no…let me do this the right way! Which is to say…if the corral is our college, the dirt is our revised mission statement, the fences are attempts to mitigate our humanity, the bus is our collective destiny, the driver is hopelessly lost, and the self-study we've concocted is our submission to the higher authority of an alien body of like-minded yet data-conscious accreditors….if all of this is true, then what, Charlie, is the *calf* whose testicles you ate on that moonlit night down by the river…?"

I nodded gravely.

"It's a good question," I said. "And a timely one."

"So what is it then?"

"The calf is you and me."

"Me?"

"Yes, Dr. Felch. And me. It's both of us."

"Together?"

"Yes, sir."

"Would you care to explain?"

"I'll try. You see, the calf's position in that corral, I think, represents our metaphorical ascension as educational administrators. It is the culmination of our collective trajectory. It is the summit of our legacy. No matter how much we excel….no matter how far we climb in the arena of educational administration, we will never be anything more than a calf chewing the hay next to the trough of intellectual enlightenment. No matter how high we rise as a people we can never rise any higher than those boards that run around the corral of our hearts like arbitrary boundaries between nations of the world."

"That's not very encouraging, Charlie."

"It's not?"

"No, in fact it's downright depressing."

"But it doesn't have to be! It doesn't have to be depressing at all! If you look at it differently this is not a bad thing by any means. In fact it's a necessary evil. Because what kind of world would it be if the community college's calves jumped out of the corral whenever they felt the urge? What kind of a world would *that* be?!"

"Okay. I can see that. I'll buy that the calf might be your typical community college administrator. That it might be the world's quietly suffering professionals. But how about the testicles themselves? What are *they*?"

"They are scrumptious!"

"Yes, of course. That statement is true *a priori*. But *metaphorically* what are they?"

"Well, Dr. Felch, I haven't honestly thought much about this question. It's been a while since I've had to. But if I were to venture a guess on the matter, I would have to say that in the complicated metaphor that is our community college – and my goodness is it complicated! – those testicles that you held up in the ziploc bag – and that I unwittingly consumed the following day – are the remnants of our humanity...."

"They are?"

"Yes."

"That's all that remains?"

"Pretty much."

"But there were *two* of them!"

"Oh right. Well in that case maybe they are the dual tendencies of conflict and conciliation. The two go together, you see? We tend to perceive them as separate things. But no! They are one and the same! And when we sever one, we sever the other with it. And in this way, we sever those very things that allow us to function as living, feeling, procreating human beings. But with these things removed we will never know the offspring of our actions – the legacy that we might have left. The legacy that will never be inherited from the fruitless historian. Or the childless administrator. Or the unpublished novelist. Instead we will be left to jog off to our unknown fates with the stream of blood trailing after us in the dirt...."

I stopped to watch my words trail off in the dirt. Dr. Felch was regarding me curiously.

"It's like this...." I said and grabbing the napkin from under my empty martini glass and a felt pen from the pocket under my chaps I drew the following diagram with an insistent yet unsteady hand:

c o w e y e

"Do you see?" I asked.

"See what?"

"The confluence?"

"No, I don't."

"Here, look again…."

And using the felt pen I added an imperfect circle of life:

c o (w e) y e

"Get it?"

"Get what?"

"We!"

"We?"

"Yes, *we*! You see, Dr. Felch, that's the key! It all comes down to how we define that word. For some it will be a religion, for others a race. For some it will be a nation, a country, a polity. While for others it will be their family or their neighborhood. Or their football team. Or the color of their favorite political party. Or a gender. Or a sexual proclivity. Or even a deeply held leaning in the great North Dakota vs. South Dakota conundrum. And, yes, for those of us working at a community college it may very well be our professional affiliation…."

"The trade we ply?"

"Right. A human being without a *we* is not a human being. And so we manufacture them. We plant these divisions deep into the ground like great stone posts along the prairie."

"Which is somewhat inevitable, right?"

"Perhaps. Except that in order for there to be a *we*, there also has to be a *they*…."

"The *other*?"

"The outsider."

"The red cows?"

"Right."

"Looking longingly upon the others."

"Correct. And yet if you look at all these intersections of human experience – all the occasions to invent yet another *we* – an interesting thing comes to light. You see, if culture itself is shared experience creating different planes of culture, an interesting paradox emerges...."

And here I flipped over the napkin and began to draw circles on its back. One after another, I drew the intersecting three-dimensional planes of human experience that so contribute to our very personal notions of *we*. Circle after circle after circle after circle after circle after circle after circle. Relentlessly I drew. Desperately I drew. As if possessed, I struggled to articulate the infinite circles of experience that make up the rich culture of Cow Eye Community College. "This is Rusty's religion...." I would say and draw an imperfect circle: "....and *this* is Gwen's spirituality....." Nationhood. Race. Gender. Age. Passionately I drew these affiliations one on top of another until the napkin had become a collection of sopping blotted ink. "This is where we go to buy our very first rubbers," I said. "...And this is where our fathers once took us fishing...."

And when I had drawn it all entirely I held up the intersecting circles for Dr. Felch to see:

"There it is!" I exclaimed.

"There what is?"

"The circles!"

"What circles?"

"The intersecting planes of human culture. They're all there. Everyone of them. And amid these circles, right there in the middle, where all the planes meet, is a single tiny dot. Do you see it?"

I stuck my finger on the dot. Dr. Felch squinted his eyes to see.

"That dot is each of us. Amid the endless circles of human experience, you see, each of us is a culture of one. Each of us is a culture of one because there is no other human being who shares all of our experience."

"Which is a bit of a lonely proposition."

"For some it might be. But for others it is a liberation...."

"Amid the homogeneity of modern life?"

"Yes."

"A tiny oasis amid the desiccation?"

"Yes. For water is but a collection of moisture, right?"

"Right."

"Just as humanity is nothing more than a motley collection of human beings, right?"

"Right."

"So are we not, then, the many I's that make up the *we* in COW EYE? Are we ourselves not the center of the eye that brings it all together to make *we*?!"

"I don't know....are we?"

"We are!"

"We are?"

"Yes, Dr. Felch, we *are*!"

And here I folded up the napkin and put it in my pocket with the rest.

"Okay, Charlie. I'll take your word for it. Given how late it is, I'll just have to take your word that this really is the secret to Cow Eye's redemption. That this really is the metaphorical significance of it all."

I nodded.

"But Charlie...?"

"Yes, Dr. Felch?"

"Where's the damn food?!"

"What food? You mean the hay in the trough?"

"No, Charlie, the food that you promised us all here tonight. The meat without vegetables. And the vegetables without meat?"

"It's on its way."

"All of it?"

"Of course. Like everything else in our world, it's just a matter of time..."

"Not unlike retirement!"

"Yes."

"And taxes."

"Yes."

"And the passing of our beloved history teacher."

"Our what?"

"You didn't know?"

"Didn't know what?"

"I'm sorry, Charlie. I thought you knew...."

"Knew *what?*"

"About Will...it happened some time ago...in the hospital where you visited him....they say it was peaceful enough, gradual and in his sleep..."

"But how can that be! I mean we just...the three of us were just...*he* was just...!"

"Sorry, Charlie."

"But!!!"

"Charlie!"

"What!"

"Charlie, are you...are you *crying?*"

"No, of course not. Of course I'm not crying. I'm an educational administrator."

"Here, take this handkerchief...."

"I am not crying!"

I took the handkerchief and blew my nose.

"I am not crying. This is just moisture accumulated incrementally through the years. The moisture of a thousand rivers being dammed. The moisture of...."

Eventually Dr. Felch got up to refill his glass, and sitting alone at my table I looked around the cafeteria once again. The disco strobe was casting its spinning reflections around the warm room and in the spinning light it seemed that all the metaphors of the world had coalesced. As I stared through the alcohol at the world around me I saw the arrows flying from every corner of the cafeteria and in all imaginable directions. On the table in front of me was a ziploc bag. On the wall was a flag. And out past the wet bar was a saffron sarong and the lonely bench at the edge of the universe. Wintergreen and eucalyptus. Trusted pills. A truncated symphony with its violins and flutes and melting glaciers and triangle player standing patiently off to the side. The rain. The river. The stars. In the light of the cafeteria – in the dim neon of the bathroom stall – I saw all of these, though not as their isolated images. As the light shone bright into my eyes, I saw them as the oneness that they are. A single splotch of unity where the sun and the moon cease to be opposites but shine down instead on a river of saffron. A timeless progression of moisture flowing over beds of asphalt and glaciers of wintergreen toward the perfect tranquility that is the equinox.

By now it was getting late and I was very tired.

Putting my head on the table I closed my eyes to it all.

⁓

{ }

So what then is love? What is love if it is not what it could have been and it is not what it shouldn't be? If it is not what it would be or should be or was? If love is not what it isn't nor what it will need to be? These are difficult questions to ask, of course, though even more difficult to answer. For such is the eternal question of our species: If love is not what it ain't, then what exactly is it?

Throughout the centuries this timeless question has been asked incessantly by the great lovers of the world. It has been studied by the world's greatest philosophers and empiricists through the ages. To solve its mystery, experiments have been conducted and mathematical models have been developed. Studies have been proposed and reports have been written. And over time the measurable outcomes of all this wondering have gradually trickled down to the great men and women who teach at our community colleges.

Among grand concepts of the world, there is perhaps none that has created more consternation and debate. More conflict and contempt. To some, love is immeasurable, while to others it is ineffable. To the youthful it is passion, while to the experienced it is love. To the guilty it is forgiveness. To the condemned it is mercy. To the student it is learning, while to the teacher it is youth. Love, in all its guises, is hope and compassion and repentance and joy. It is grief and pain. It is sorrow and shame. And warmth. And care. And affection. And concern.

Yet is it any of these things? And if so, is it any of these things in their entirety? Is it really a passing rainstorm any more than a lengthy and consistent drought? Is it the solstice of deepest winter or the solstice of summer's peak? Is it a steaming tray of meats? Or the coolest vegetable sampler? Is it an endless highway at night? The moonlit river? A bloody sunrise? Is it the sun at dusk? A brush of thighs? Is it silence more than words? Or words more than silence? Is it an awkward embrace? A nod of the head? A light caress? Ducks quacking? Copulating ancients? Wordlessness? Vulnerability? Or a bull's triumphant erection at dusk? The feel of asphalt on your skin? An arrow passing in flight? Is it music or poetry or mathematics? Is love itself the great flow of humanity from time immemorial down through the ages to the crowded cafeterias and offices and classrooms of our day? Is love a fertile heifer? Inevitably the answer comes.

It is!

{ }

～

WHEN I RAISED my head the cafeteria was empty and dark. The sound of the ice maker could be heard in the distance. Bessie was standing over me.

"Wake up, Charlie!" she was saying. "It's over."

"What's over?"

"The party. It's over. Everyone's gone. It's only you and me here. And the woman vacuuming the floor."

"But the food's on its way!"

"No, it's not."

"Yes, it is! I planned everything so meticulously. The food will be here in a matter of minutes...!"

Lifting my head off the table I felt the world swirling around me. The light streaming in through the windows. A trickle of blood had run down my temple and dried onto my cheek.

"What time is it anyway?"

"It's almost two!"

"Two?"

"Yes, *two.*"

"A.m or p.m.?"

"P.m., Charlie. It's two o'clock in the afternoon – a Saturday – and everyone's home recovering from yesterday's celebration."

"What do you mean? Where are all my colleagues? Why didn't they wait for the food? What happened to the party I spent so long planning?"

"You don't want to know."

Bessie dabbed a wet napkin against my temple.

"Here hold this…." she said.

I held the napkin.

"But why wouldn't I want to know?! And why am I bleeding? And where is everyone?"

"You don't remember?"

"No…."

"Anything?"

"No."

"So you don't remember what happened after you woke up from your sleep last night?"

"What sleep?"

"Don't you remember falling asleep at the table?"

"Not really. I mean, maybe somewhat."

"Well, that's exactly what happened. You fell asleep on the table over there….and then Timmy woke you up to tell you everyone was leaving…."

"He woke me up?"

"Yes, Timmy tried to talk you into going home, but you wouldn't have it. 'No!' you yelled at him. 'This party is not over yet! It's not over until the food comes! Don't let anyone leave! Our party can't end until I become something entirely!'…"

"I said that?"

"No – you *SCREAMED* it! And then you ran over to the door with a baseball bat and tried to keep everyone from leaving. With the bat in your hand you stood in front of the door blocking everyone's way."

"I did?"

"Yes. But Timmy wrestled the bat away from you. He was a high school quarterback, remember? Timmy wrestled the bat away from you, and that's when things got really bad. You see, as soon as Timmy wrestled the bat away, you...."

∾

...As soon as Timmy wrestled the bat away from me, I reached into the holster for Ethel's pistol.

"Look," I said to the crowd gathering around me. "I know what you're all thinking. You're looking around this vast cafeteria and thinking that because there is no food here, that there will not be any food here tonight. This, I tell you, is faulty reasoning. It is fallacious. You see, just because the rain is not falling on Cow Eye Junction, that does not mean that it never will again. And just because the sun has not yet risen on the new day, it does not mean that the sun will never again rise. In fact, everything is quite the opposite. The sun *will* rise! And the rain will fall on the Diahwa Valley Basin some day. And the food that I ordered will arrive as promised, by eleven o'clock..."

"But it's already past *two*!" somebody yelled out.

"...Well that may be so. But what is a temporal thing like *time* when you are among the things of the world that are everlasting? Like love. And darkness. And the sound of ecstasy coming from the other side of the wall? You see, the important thing is to have something to believe in. Something tangible and easy to grasp..." – I took out the pistol from its holster – "...something that is heavy to hold and rather cold to the touch. In life, you see, there are things that are timeless on this side of the room and things that come and go on the other. Things that are beyond words and things that are merely replicable. Ideas that transcend our comprehension and those that can be cited with impunity in a self-study report. Since the beginning of time there have been choices that are safe and justified and those that take us into deeper and darker places where no sun can reach..." – here I undid the safety on the pistol – "...and no light can shine. But unless we pay close attention, these things slip from us very easily. For example, just look at that strobe over there...." – I motioned with my gun in the direction of the disco strobe; a hail of gasps and shrieks rang out – "…Over there is a strobe that represents a different kind of light. You see, it is spinning as fast as the world – and like the world itself it is casting a million pieces of light on all of us. It is beautiful, no doubt. And it is stimulating. It is shiny and exciting, yes. But will it last forever? WILL IT??!!…"

"We don't know, Charlie! We don't know what the answer to your question should be. But how about you put down that pistol? How about you set it down on the carpet right there so nobody gets hurt…?"

"…Well, I'll tell you the answer. The answer to my question is *no*! No, it will not last forever! It will not last forever in the same way that the Cow Eye Ranch did not last forever. And my relationship with Bessie did not last forever. And Will Smithcoate did not last forever. That strobe over there will not last forever in the same way that you or I cannot last longer than we are destined to last – in the same way that my stay at this college will surely not last beyond the dissolution of the world around me. All of these things, you see, merely come and go. And yet we love them so much while they are ours…"

I pointed the gun at the disco strobe. Another hail of shrieks and shouts rang out.

"…Sometimes we put so much value into things like that strobe over there that we lose sight of the truly meaningful things in life. We become so focused on keeping the lesser things in sight…. – Here, I trained the sights on the middle of the spinning strobe – "…that we miss the more meaningful things that are in this world. The people who love us. The friendships that pass us by. They all come and go, while we stare in wonder at those dazzling things that are shiny and sparkling and spinning…."

I pulled back the hammer of the pistol.

"The gun, Charlie!"

As I squinted my eye to align the strobe with the cross hairs, I said:

"….But why? Why? I ask. You know, I've been told that there is a purpose for everything in this world. That it all has a purpose. Or that it should. And so this strobe is here for a reason, right? As is this sheriff's costume that I'm now wearing. As is this pistol that I am now holding in my trembling hand….If you want to be something entirely, they say, then you have to pull the trigger every once in a while."

I shook my head.

"...But why? Right now I am aiming my sights on this disco strobe. A mere twitch of my finger and it's consigned to the annals of history. Such is the fragility of the things in this world. But why should I have to commit to such things entirely? Why do I have to be either meat *or* vegetables? Why must I be either tall *or* short! Logical *or* intuitive? Infinitely complex or infinitely simple? Why must I strive to say, without hesitation, that I am this, or I am that? And that I am this or that *entirely*? That my geometry is Euclidean or non-Euclidean? Why should my legacy come down to either me or that spinning strobe?"

"Put the gun down, Charlie!"

"....You see, I am here to say that it is possible to be something entirely without being those other things at all. Just as the Midwest is neither west nor east, but its own place on the map. Just as the centrist Supreme Court justice – and yes, they do occur from time to time! – is neither left nor right but provides just as much value to the world by casting a deciding vote in favor of moderation. Just as the equinox is neither predominantly day nor predominantly night....but its own special time of the year. Each of these things is what it is. And each is what it is...*entirely*!"

"Charlie, put the gun down! *Please*!"

"....You know, there was a time once when I longed to be something more toward the ends of the spectrum. A solstice perhaps. Or a proven theorem. I longed to have a diametrical opposite to guide me. To be the *bos indicus* among *bos taurus*....or the *bos taurus* among *bos indicus*. But those days are long gone. They have passed into history and now I am content to be my own opposite. Just as the spring equinox is the opposite of the fall equinox. Just as today, March twentieth, is the exact opposite of both summer and winter solstices. Just as paradox is the opposite of itself. You see these things are opposites just as that strobe dangling from our ceiling is the exact opposite of the sun that in a few short hours will surely bring a new day...."

"Pull the trigger, Charlie!" said Ethel.

"What?" I said.

"Charlie, it's time. Pull the trigger...."

"You're absolutely right," I said. "Thank you for whispering these words of advice into my ear. It is very late and so it is about time for me to become something entirely."

And so over the gasps of the faculty and staff in the cafeteria, I released the hammer and closed the safety. Without firing I lowered my gaze from the strobe.

Meekly, I set the gun on the floor.

Bessie shook her head:

"Except that, well, you *didn't.*"

"I didn't?"

"Nope. As you stood in the cafeteria, you were not yourself, Charlie. You seemed possessed by an idea. Or voices. The voice of eternity, perhaps. Or the idea of time. Or maybe it really was Ethel Newtown whispering into your ear to pull that trigger…"

Bessie stopped to press the napkin against my forehead.

"…But whatever the case," she said, "you really did it. This time you pulled the trigger entirely."

SUMMARY OF EVALUATION REPORT

"This report represents the findings of the evaluation team that visited Cow Eye Community College from March 15-20. The college is seeking reaffirmation of its regional accreditation and has submitted all necessary documents to support its candidacy."

INTRODUCTION

O ur twelve-member accreditation team visited Cow Eye Community College from March 15 – 20 for the purpose of determining whether the college continues to meet accreditation standards, evaluating how well the college is achieving its stated purpose, providing recommendations for quality assurance and institutional improvement, and submitting recommendations to the regional accrediting body regarding the accredited status of the college.

In preparation for the visit, team members carefully read the college's self-study and related evidentiary documents provided by Cow Eye Community College. Three weeks prior to arriving on campus, each team member prepared written reactions to the Cow Eye Community College self-study and identified inquiries to be made during the visit. This included detailed analysis of the college's administrative structure, curriculum, fiscal standing, facilities plans, assessment process, and its ability to support meaningful dialogue among an increasingly diverse community of tenured and non-tenured educators. During the five-day visit, the team met either individually or in groups with over 80 college faculty, classified staff, students, and administrators. In addition, team members held two widely publicized sessions open to all members of the college community. The week of accreditation activities included visits to special showcase projects, in-class observations of key instructional faculty, a fireworks display and ceremonial opening of the campus's three cattle-themed fountains, and a memorable Christmas party in which the college's Special Projects Coordinator employed a Ruger .38 to shoot out the rotating disco strobe in the cafeteria.

The team appreciated the hospitality of the college's employees as well as the candor of its faculty, staff, and students throughout the visit. In general, the self-study is complete and despite a series of misspellings and some suspicious iambs in the chapters concerning its assessment plans, the document covers all important topics and all standards and eligibility requirements. The team noted that the college did a good job in organizing its accommodations. Individual team members also expressed appreciation for the shoulder-length gloves that were given as tokens of esteem upon the conclusion of our visit to the college.

MAJOR FINDINGS AND RECOMMENDATIONS

To acknowledge the good work that Cow Eye Community College has done, the team makes the following specific commendations:

The college is to be commended for its ongoing commitment to student success as is evidenced by the flickering 22-inch color-television set with push-button remote control.

The college is to be commended for the commitment to excellence of its faculty. This encompasses a broad cross-section of disciplines and perspectives ranging from Art History to Eugenics and from Autobody to Philosophy. A special commendation is also given to the college's creative writing instructor for his mesmerizing approach to facilitating an environment of creativity and lifelong learning in his classroom.

The college is to be commended for its efforts to promote cultural diversity and unity through a variety of means including Campus Conversations and focus groups.

Along with the above commendations, the following forty-three recommendations are made as a result of the team visit:

Recommendation 1:

The *team recommends that the college continue its two-year cycle of reviewing the mission statement and in so doing ensure the statement's alignment with ongoing assessment results of college-wide planning and quality assurance processes.*

Recommendation 6:

The *team recommends that the college continue its efforts to develop comprehensive plans for continuous improvement. It is further recommended that these plans be implemented within a reasonable timeframe and that they be entrusted to faculty and staff whose commitment to campus engagement and student success is not merely sincere but also shared entirely.*

Recommendation 17:

The *team recommends that the college develop a more rigorous hiring process to discourage the hiring, sight unseen, of under-qualified applicants with sparkling curricula vitae after a mere phone interview.*

Recommendation 26:

The *team recommends that the recently vacated Special Projects Coordinator position be re-envisioned to include more specific duties and that this position be filled by an applicant with a proven track-record of administrative success in the field of Educational Administration.*

Recommendation 39:

The *team recommends that the college's cafeteria be equipped with ADA-accessible egress and clear paths to the exits to ensure that a sudden and mass exit through the doors can be accomplished in a safe and expeditious manner.*

PART 4. EMANATION

PLAN B

TBD

"So then what happened?" asked the man sitting next to me. "After you blew away the disco strobe to the screams and shrieks of faculty and accreditor alike? After you ran outside and collapsed in the parking lot? After you violated your colleagues' naive expectations of meat and vegetable and sunk your college's attempt to reaffirm its accreditation? After your three friends went outside and found you bleeding and unconscious on the asphalt? After they brought you back into the cafeteria to sleep until the following afternoon? After all this took place, *then* what happened?"

"Then the world ended."

I looked out the window of the bus. The brown fields were passing by for the last time. The bus was vibrating softly under us. Everything was dry and bright and desolate. Now it all seemed as lifeless as barren prose.

"No, that's not what I meant," said the man. "What I meant was after you finally woke up what happened? After the dust settled and the accreditors left? After the woman who once dreamed of being a historian finished sweeping the floor how did everything work out?"

"Oh that...."

I shook my head remorsefully.

"Well," I said. "After I received my suspended sentence and performed my community service to the judge's satisfaction, and when the semester had finally come to its dissolution with barely a whimper – after all of *that* had come and gone – I gathered the stuff from my apartment and made my way down the stairs to the esplanade, where I met Dr. Felch and Bessie and Raul. It was nice of them to see me off."

"They met you on the esplanade?"

"Yes. Outside my apartment. It was a poignant meeting. I still had the bandages on my face. Dr. Felch shook my hand and wished me well. Bessie gave me a kiss on the cheek and wished me well. Raul told me to wear his chaps in good health and wished me well. You may even notice that I'm wearing the boots he gave me *right now*...."

I wiggled the tips of my boots as evidence.

"...But that wasn't all. Before I left campus, Raul made sure to leave me with one final diagram to remember him by. One last visual representation to encapsulate my nine-month experience at Cow Eye Community College. I still have it here in my shirt pocket somewhere...."

I spilled all of Raul's various diagrams onto the seat between us. The papers were mixed and folded and chaotic. Ruffling through them, I found the last diagram that Raul had drawn for me before I left. It was a diagram representing the eternal functions and promises – the rights and responsibilities – of a community college:

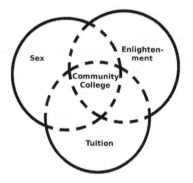

"And then what?"

"And then he autographed it."

"And then?"

"Well, and then they asked me about my plans for the future and I told them the god-honest truth. That I don't really *have* a plan for the future. That my plans have yet to be determined. That I don't really even know where I'll go from here – that this, in fact, tends to be the way with me. But that I've always wanted to live and work in an exotic far-off locale with beautiful scenery. A place where people don't judge you for the mysterious gaps in your resume, or the widening gaps in your teeth – where your past accomplishments are taken at face value no matter how contrived and nobody faults you for your many failings in educational administration. Someplace a little out of the ordinary, perhaps. A place that I might call home and never leave. A place that would be my final resting place from this life to the next."

"For example?"

"Well, Arizona maybe. Or, better yet – Alaska."

"And then?"

"Well, I suppose after that doesn't work out, I would move on to someplace even further away. A place that's even less contiguous. Some place both remote and exotic with an endless supply of..."

"No, that's not what I meant. What I meant is....what happened *then* – after you told them about your plans?"

"Well, then I wished the three of them well and headed off with my suitcase and my duffel bag. My friends waved goodbye as I made my way by foot down the long esplanade. At the entrance I exchanged a handshake with Timmy at the guard shack. 'Take care of yourself, Mr. Charlie,' he said. And I said, 'You too, Timmy!' From there I walked out across the railroad tracks and out past the waterless ditch and out onto the highway where I hitchhiked my way back to the makeshift bus shelter. My friends had each offered to give me a ride. 'It's the least we could do!' they insisted. But I declined. 'In that truck?!' I laughed. No, I told them, it would be more honest if I just found my own way back. And so I walked out to the highway alone and stood there on the side of the road waiting for a ride. It took a lot longer than it once would have. But eventually an old cattleman pulled over and he drove me all the way to the makeshift bus shelter. It was a slow ride, I have to say, and a poignant one. From the edge of the highway he drove me along the ditches and vacant fields past the jail and the post office and the boarded-up remnants of the once-great Cow Eye Ranch. Slowly we drove past the windless American flag – all thirteen stripes and forty-nine stars. And at last we reached the makeshift bus shelter where I'd first arrived less than a year ago. Except that, well, it wasn't *makeshift* anymore..."

"It wasn't?"

"No. It was *new*. And modern. A marvel of contemporary engineering. Award-winning architecture with a welcoming facade made of brick and glass. An airy lobby with air-conditioned comfort. Plush chairs inside the building and solar panels on the roof."

"Photovoltaic panels? Solar energy is the wave of the future, you know!"

"I've heard. In any case, I had arrived at the new bus depot. And as I waited in the lobby I thought about the things I'd learned at Cow Eye. I thought about these things for some time. And then my bus – *this* bus – pulled up and I got on."

"And now?"

"Well now I'm sitting on this bus with you. And there's a long road up ahead. But this seat we're sharing is so much more than just that. It really is ineffable. You see, right now I am sitting with you perched at the very pinnacle of history. You and I are on the threshold separating tradition from innovation, love from efficiency. Moving in this bus, you see, I am traveling on the coattails of time toward a future that is as bright as it can be. Brighter even than the flickering fluorescent bulb of a dim and timeless cafeteria."

"So it all worked out in the end?"

"Yes. I suppose you can say it all worked out."

The man nodded. Outside our window, the scenery had changed for the final time. The desiccation was all-consuming. The sun was eternal. And for the last time I looked out at the recent world where fountains flowed and birds chirped. A place where sycamores grow next to banyans and the love vine wraps its loving embrace around it all. Through the tinted windows I could still see the bull mounting his heifer. And the pelicans loafing along the grassy banks amid the timeless sounds of paperwork getting done. And of course the sound of forgotten history snapping in the wind – all thirteen stripes and forty-nine stars. In that place of not-too-long-ago, the cattle always lowed and the grasses never stopped growing. Poetry flowed like water and water flowed like time. In my mind, at least, this was how Cow Eye had been for me; and in my mind, at least, it would always be like that, faithfully and forever. As the bus took me past the golf course where the Cow Eye Ranch used to be – the great ranch that once fed half the country – I took it all in. The bus groaned. The man next to me slept up against the window. Somewhere in the distance the great dams of the area were breaking – though too imperceptibly for anyone to notice. Fish spawned upstream. Calves chewed their hay. Ducks quacked.

Alone once more, I took out a new book of history from my duffel bag and began reading.

Made in the USA
Charleston, SC
06 December 2014